The Fortress

Walter Herries swore he would destroy everyone in Fell House. Judith Paris knew that she alone could prevent him . . .

This compelling novel traces the widely differing fortunes of the Herries family through fifty momentous years – from the summer fair at Keswick to the coronation of Queen Victoria, from a family Christmas at Uldale to the splendours of the Great Exhibition . . .

At times it is dark, jagged and violent – at others glowing with excitement, passion and the fullness of life amid the unchanging countryside which all the Herries so worshipped.

'One of the great literary triumphs of our time' DAILY TELEGRAPH

Hugh Walpole

The Fortress

Pan Books
in association with Macmillan London

First published 1932 by Macmillan & Company Ltd
This edition published 1971 by Pan Books Ltd,
Cavaye Place, London SW10 9PG,
in association with Macmillan London Ltd
3rd printing 1977
This book is copyright in all countries which
are signatories to the Berne Convention
ISBN 0 330 02642 9
Printed and bound in Great Britain by
Cox & Wyman Ltd, London, Reading and Fakenham

For my friends
Gertrude and Muirhead Bone

Thy gentlest dreams, thy frailest,
Even those that were
Born and lost in a heart-beat,
Shall meet thee there.
They are become immortal
In shining air.

The unattainable beauty,
The thought of which was pain,
That flickered in eyes and on lips
And vanished again;
That fugitive beauty
Thou shalt attain.

Those lights innumerable
That led thee on and on,
The masque of time ended,
Shall glow into one.
They shall be with thee for ever,
Thy travel done.

A.E.

Contents

Part One

MADAME

Part Two

ADAM AND MARGARET

Part Three

CUMBERLAND CHASE

Part Four

MOTHER AND SON

The Herries Family in the *The Fortress*

Judith Paris, *daughter of Rogue Herries*
Adam Paris, *her son, m.* Margaret Kraft
Vanessa, *Adam's daughter*
Sir William Herries, *son of David Herries*
Christabel, *his first wife*
Walter, *their son, m.* Agnes Bailey
Valerie, *Sir William's second wife*
Ellis, *their son*
Uhland, *Walter's son*
Elizabeth, *Walter's daughter, m.* John Herries
Francis Herries, *son of David Herries*
Jennifer, *his wife*
John, *m.* Elizabeth Herries ⎫
Dorothy, *m.* Arthur Bellairs   ⎬ *their children*
Benjamin, *John's son*
Timothy Bellairs
Veronica Bellairs, *m.* Robert Forster ⎫
Amabel Bellairs   ⎬ *Dorothy's children*
Jane Bellairs   ⎭
Sir James Herries, *son of Sir Pomfret Herries, m.* Beatrice Ferry
The Ven Rodney Herries, *his brother, m.* Rebecca Fox
William ⎫
Dora   ⎬ *Rodney's children*
Garth Herries, *grandson of Pelham Herries*
Sylvia, *his wife*
Amery, *his brother*
Maria, Lady Rockage
Carey Bligh, 3rd Lord Rockage, *her son*
Cecily, *his wife*
Roger, *m.* Janet Vane ⎫
Alice   ⎬ *their children*
Phyllis, *Rockage's sister, m.* Stephen Newmark
Horace Newmark ⎫
Mary Newmark   ⎪
Phyllis Newmark ⎪
Katherine Newmark ⎬ *Phyllis' children*
Stephen Newmark ⎪
Emily Newmark   ⎪
Barnabas Newmark ⎭
Montague Cards, *son of Morgan Cards*
Bradley Cards, *son of Robert Cards*
Fred Ormerod, *related by marriage to Montague Cards*

Part One

Madame

THE SHADOW AGAINST THE SKY

'ALL IS WELL,' Judith said quietly, coming forward and stroking the red apples of the sofa. 'I shall not leave you, Jennifer. It is better I remain.'

As her hand mechanically stroked those same rosy apples, so friendly and familiar, she reflected.

Yes, this simple sentence declared the crisis of her whole existence. Nothing ever again could matter to her so deeply as this decision. With it she had cut away half her life, and perhaps the better half. She was not by nature a dramatic woman; moreover, she had but lately returned from the funeral of the best friend she had, and she was forty-seven years of age in this month of January 1822. So – for women then thought forty-seven a vast age – she should be past drama. Quietly she sat down on the sofa, leaned forward, looking into the fire. Jennifer Herries was speaking with eager excitement, but Judith did not hear her. Jennifer was fifty-two and should also be past drama but, although a lazy woman, she liked sensation when it did not put herself to discomfort.

Judith at that moment heard and saw nothing but the past, the past that she was irrevocably forsaking. Strange how the same patterns were for ever returning! Her father had been a rogue and a vagabond, a rebel against all the order and material discipline of the proper Herries. In his early years he had married Convention and of her had had a son, late in life he had married a gipsy and of her had had a daughter in his old age, when he was over seventy. David at one end of his life, Judith at the other.

In their histories again the pattern had been repeated. David of his marriage had had two sons: Will the money-maker, Francis the dreamer. Will prospered even now in the City; Francis was a failure, dead of his own hand.

And with their children again the pattern was repeated. For Will's son Walter was triumphant near by in his house at Westaways, and Francis' widow, Jennifer, and Francis' children, John and Dorothy, remained, undefended, here at Uldale.

It was here that she, Judith, came into the pattern. Daughter of two vagabonds, mother of an illegitimate boy, she should be vagrant. Half of her – the finer, truer, more happy and fortunate half – (she nodded at the fire in confirmation) was so. But the other half was proper, managing, material, straight-seeing Herries. She threw her wild half into the blaze (her hand flickered towards the fire). It was gone. She remained to fight for Jennifer, Jennifer's children, John and Dorothy, and, maybe who knows? . . . her own boy Adam.

To fight whom? Here Jennifer's voice broke through:

'. . . That will be most agreeable. I have always said that the Yellow Room needs but a trifle altering and it will make . . . but Francis would never see it. And with a new wallpaper . . . We must certainly have a new wallpaper . . .'

To fight Walter Herries, and all that were his. As 'Rogue' Herries in his tumble-down house in Borrowdale had fought all the world, as Francis his grandson had tried to fight the world and failed, so now would she fight Walter, flamboyant, triumphing Walter, made of Will and his money-bags, sworn to extinguish Jennifer and her children and all that were in Fell House, Uldale.

It had been the wish of her whole life to flee from all the Herries and live in the hills as her mother had lived before her, but Walter Herries had challenged her and she had taken up the challenge.

'. . . Not that it should be difficult,' Jennifer was saying, 'to find another girl to work with Doris. Girls will come willingly enough now that you are going to remain, Judith, dear . . .'

Walter and his two children, Uhland and Elizabeth, with all the money in the world, against Jennifer and *her* children, undefended and helpless, Judith and her Adam, fatherless and by law without a name . . .

Jennifer was going on: 'And Walter will not *dare,* now that you are remaining, Judith . . . You are the only one of us all of whom he is afraid . . . He will not *dare* . . .'

Would he not, so large and confident and powerful? Had he not said that he would snuff them out – Jennifer, John, Dorothy – raze Fell House to the ground? And what had *she*, small, elderly, alone, with no one in the world belonging to her save Adam, to oppose to that strength?

Nevertheless, she looked across to Jennifer triumphantly.

'We will give Walter something to think about,' she said.

'And you can go to Watendlath when you wish,' Jennifer said.

'Oh no. Watendlath is over for me. Watendlath is ended, a closed valley.'

'But how foolish, Judith. It is only a mile or two.'

'It is the other end of the world.'

She did not tell anyone how that night, with Adam asleep beside her, she cried. She lay awake for half the night, hearing the owl hoot, a mouse scuttle, and seeing a slow, lonely moon trace with her silver finger a question mark across the floor.

Her thoughts were wild, incoherent, most mingled. At one moment she was fiercely rebellious. She sat up, staring about her. No, she would not remain! She would tell Jennifer in the morning that she revoked her decision. She allowed her fancy then to play with the lovely sequence of events if she went. Tom Ritson should arrive in his cart. She and Adam would be packed into it, and, after tearful farewells, they would be off, down the hill with one last backward wave at the bottle-green windows of the Uldale shop and the slow friendly shoulder of the moor, along the road to Bassenthwaite, beside the Lake, Keswick, then up the hill again, above Lodore, and then— Oh, happiness! Oh, joy! The little valley closing them in, the long green field, the tumbling Punchbowl, the two farms, her own, John Green House, and the Ritsons'; below the farm the round scoop of the Tarn, black or silver or blue, the amphitheatre of the hills, the sheep nosing at the turf, the cattle moving in the byre, and best of all, Charlie Watson, straight as an arrow in spite of his years, riding towards her over the stones ... the fresh sweet air, tang of soil and bracken, glitter of stones, sweep of the changing sky ... she had to catch the sheets between her hands.

That life was for ever surrendered. Then, at once, her other practical self came running in. She was mistress of Fell House now. They would all do anything that she told them. Jennifer was her slave. She had seen, at the Ireby funeral, what the neighbours and villagers thought of her. Yes, in spite of her illegitimate son. Many things would have to be done. Had she strength enough? It was the convention that a woman over forty was an 'old thing' without savour. It was true that she had been aware, for some time past, of the troubles, melancholies, miasmas peculiar to her time of life, but she had refused to surrender to them. She felt within her a wonderful vitality and energy, as though she were at the beginning of life rather than more than half through the course of it. Just as in earlier days her love for her husband Georges had filled her with fire and splendour, so now her love for her son Adam glorified her. She was such a woman.

Yes, many things needed to be done. Walter Herries thought that Fell House was at an end, did he? She would show him. Jennifer had money. They could purchase the piece of land towards Ireby ... four more cows, two more horses. The dairy must be enlarged. They were lucky in their servants. Bennett was devoted, would do anything for her. Jack was a good boy. Mrs Quinney was honest and hard-working, although she had a tongue when she was put out. Martha Hodgson was a good God-fearing cook, who never grumbled so long as she was not interfered with, and Doris would do well if they had a child in from the village to help her.

They must entertain more than they had done. John and Dorothy were growing now. John was fourteen and Dorothy thirteen. It was right that they should take their proper place in the County ... She must find a tutor for John and Adam. Someone who would have no dealings with Walter. There was Roger Rackstraw in Keswick, a friend of Miss Pennyfeather's. He had a broken nose and looked altogether like a prize-fighter, but he had been for two years tutor to the Osmaston children and had done well there. She would see about that in the morning. She would lose no time. And, maybe, she might, after all, shortly pay a visit to Watendlath, stay with the Ritsons for a week, ride over to Watson's farm ... No, no ... Better leave that alone until she was settled here, settled deep, deep down so that she could never pull herself up again.

Then once more desolation caught her. She lay back on her pillow sobbing. She could not help it. She had given up all that she loved best in the world, all save Adam. And for what? She had been considering Walter Herries as too serious a figure? What was he after all but a big, blundering bully? What could he have done to Jennifer and the children? John would soon be able to protect his mother ... But no. John was soft, sensitive, gentle. She remembered how years ago Mrs Ponder, a servant in the house, had thrown his pet rabbit out of the window. She had thought then that he would have died of misery. And yet he had courage. Only a few days before, when the rioters had set fire to the stables, he had sat with his mother through all the noise and confusion, reading to her, trying to comfort her . . . He had courage, but he was no match for his Cousin Walter. She, and she alone . . . At that she fell, at last, asleep.

It was natural that the world of Judith's son, young Adam, should be very different in shape, colour and contents from his mother's.

He was now in his seventh year and as strong as a young colt. He was, most certainly, not handsome. Even his mother could not think so. His hair was black and straight without a suspicion of a wave in it, his nose snub, his mouth large, his legs and arms too long for his body as yet. Nevertheless, he gave promise of both height and breadth. His grey eyes held both humour and caution, and he was brown with health. He was clumsy in his movements – indeed he was to move all his life short-sightedly, and this not because he was short-sighted but because he was absent-minded.

Were his interest thoroughly caught, absent-minded was the last thing that he was, but he was often thinking of the unexpected instead of the customary.

It seemed that his character would be warm and loyal, but he was sparing of words. He hated to show feeling or express it. He was independent, always venturing off on his own, busy on his own purposes. Whether he liked or disliked anyone he never said, but he had a very especial connexion with his mother and would, on a sudden, leave what he was doing and search for her because he thought that she needed him.

When he did this his intuition was always right. He was quite fearless and could be very pugnacious, but he would attack someone without warning and often when he had been smiling but a moment earlier. He was inquisitive, would ask questions and remember carefully the answers given him, although he would not always believe their truth. On the whole, his independence, his loyalty, his taciturnity and his courage were at present his strongest characteristics. He walked very much by himself.

His horizon was larger than that of many boys of his age, for his first years had been spent in France and after that he had lived like a young peasant in the Watendlath valley. His friends had been farmers like Charlie Watson and the Ritsons, farmers' wives like Alice Perry, farmers' boys like the young Perrys.

Then on coming to Fell House he had known the first attachment of his life (he was never to know very many). His mother was part of himself and he of his mother, so that did not figure as an attachment, but at the moment that he saw John Herries he adored him.

John, Jennifer's boy, who was eight years older than Adam, was fair, slender, handsome and an aristocrat. He walked with his head up, as though he were made to rule the earth. But he was too gentle and unselfish to wish to rule anyone, and it soon happened that the young black ruffian Adam did all the commanding. John was impetuous until checked, then was hurt and silent. He had a very occasional stammer that added to his shyness. He had most beautiful natural manners and was over-aware of the feelings of others. He loved to be liked, hated to be disapproved of, while Adam did not care whether anyone liked him or no. Nevertheless, Adam responded deeply to affection, although he said nothing that showed this. He forgot neither kindness nor injury, but John was always eager to heal a quarrel; John was wretched in an atmosphere of unfriendliness. Adam enjoyed a fight if he felt that the cause was a worthy one.

John's sister, Dorothy, was fair, plump and amiable. She was a type that was always recurring in the Herries families. She had some of her mother's laziness, but took a livelier interest in the outside world than her mother did.

Adam's world seemed sufficiently filled with these figures – his mother, Jennifer whom he called his aunt although she was not, John, Dorothy, Mrs Quinney the housekeeper, Mrs Hodgson the cook, Bennett the coachman, Jack the stable-boy, Doris, two dairy-maids. Until now there had also been Mr Winch the tutor, but Mr Winch was gone for ever.

Geographically his world held first the house, the garden, the stables, then the moors that fell to the very edge of the garden, Skiddaw and Blencathra under whose shadows all the life of the house passed, and beyond them Keswick, and beyond that the world of Watendlath becoming speedily to him now a dream world, a sort of fairy kingdom where all the glories and wonders of life were enclosed.

However, he had then (and he was always to have) the great gift of accepting what he was given and making the best of it. It is true that did he feel he was being given something that he ought not to be given, he would fight relentlessly to change it. He had, for instance, felt that he was *not* given Mr Winch, and he had fought Mr Winch most gallantly. It seemed only in the proper nature of things that Mr Winch should be removed.

His attitude to John changed as time passed. He did not love him less, but when he found that he could make John and Dorothy do as he wished he had his way with them. Although he was only six he knew very well on every occasion what it was that he wanted to do. The only trouble was that others did not always want to do likewise.

Like a stone flung into a pool so the fearful adventure of the rioters had broken into the settled pattern of Adam's life. That had been one of his proudest moments when his mother had told him to go into Aunt Jennifer's room and wait there until 'the men who were throwing stones at the windows' had gone away. He had known that there was more in his mother's mind than she expressed in words. She had in fact said to him: 'I shall have occupation enough. I trust *you* to guard all that I have no time for.' A strange scene that was in Aunt Jennifer's bedroom with all the familiar things, the high bed with the crimson curtains, and Aunt Jennifer's lovely black hair in a lace cap, her silver shoes and a green turban with a feather in it lying on the floor, Dorothy sitting virtuously on a chair pretending that she listened to John who was reading from Goldsmith's *History of England* (Adam did not, of course, know what the book was), John with his gentle voice reading on and on, never taking his eyes from the book – all this so quiet and ordinary, while the reflection from the flames of the burning stables played like living figures on the wallpaper, and the muffled echoes of shouts and cries came from below. He would never forget the white tenseness of John's face, the little exclamations of Aunt Jennifer: 'Oh dear! Oh dear!' 'Listen to that!' 'We shall all be murdered!' 'Children, we shall all be murdered!', the ridiculous aspect of the leather cushions that had been pushed up against the windows, the way in which everything in the room jumped and sank and jumped again in accordance with the fiery hands that stroked the walls. He himself sat on a low chair near the bed and had no doubt but that he was there on guard over them all. He was prepared that at any moment Aunt Jennifer should jump out of bed and run as she was into the passage and down the stairs. It was privately his opinion that she showed great cowardice to remain there while his mother and Bennett and Mrs Quinney were defending the house, but he had a patronizing, forgiving affection for Aunt Jennifer, as though she were a pony gone at the knees, or a dog that wouldn't fight other dogs, or a doll whose stomach oozed sawdust.

It was all that he himself could do to sit there thus quietly, but his mother had given him that piece of work and so without question there he was!

The worst moment of all was when Aunt Jennifer suddenly cried (just as John was reading about the Princes who were murdered in the Tower): 'Oh, it is me that they are after! I know it is! ... They have always hated me! They will burn the house over us! ... We mustn't remain here, children ... We must fly or we shall have the house burnt over our heads!'

Although Adam was too young to be aware of it, it was perhaps the serious regard that the three children bestowed upon her that forced her to lie back again upon her pillow, to close her eyes and await, as best she might, the outcome.

Indeed the affair was soon at an end. Quiet fell in a moment. The shadows and tremblings of the flames' reflections continued to play upon the walls of the room. John opened the door and listened. Below there were shufflings of feet, whispers, someone was weeping. They waited ... At last Judith herself came, and Adam learnt that Uncle Reuben was dead.

The news was the first real crisis in young Adam's life, the first occasion on which he had been close to a death that was real and actual to him. In France the old Curé of the village had died when paying them a call, but Adam had been too young to understand. In Watendlath a cow had died and one of Charlie Watson's horses. But Uncle Reuben had been his friend. He had spent whole days with him in the hills and, although he had been fat and puffed as he climbed a hill, he had been able to talk to hundreds of people at the same time and had known stories about Abraham, the Lord Jesus, the Giant of Poland, King Arthur's Round Table and scores of others. He had never bothered Adam with making him do things he did not want to do, as Charlie Watson sometimes did, and he carried gingerbread and lollipops in the pocket of his gown.

Now Uncle Reuben was dead, shot with a gun that had been fired by one of the wicked men who wanted to burn the house down. As the consciousness of this absolute fact, positive, not in any circumstances to be changed, sank into Adam's mind, something affected him for ever. He was, his whole life afterwards, to remember the moment when his mother, breaking off from some story that she was telling him, drew him towards her and said to him that now they were to remain at Fell House, not go to Watendlath as she had promised, and they were to remain to fight ... To fight whom? ... Was it Uncle Walter?

He suggested Uncle Walter because he himself wanted to fight him. Once in the hills when he had been bathing, Uncle Walter had ridden past on a white horse and tried to strike him with his whip. He had not forgotten that. He would never forget. So it seemed to him quite natural that he and his mother should fight Uncle Walter. And now when his mother said that they would remain here and not go to Watendlath he connected that with Uncle Reuben's death and concluded at once that it was Uncle Walter who had shot him. That being so, he, Adam, would one day shoot Uncle Walter. The sequence of ideas was quite natural and inevitable. He said nothing. He asked no questions. But he did one thing. He had a black doll, a black doll with a red coat and brass buttons. He hung the doll from a nail on the wall and threw marbles at it. Within a week he could hit the doll from a great distance. The doll's face that had been made of painted clay was no longer a face.

Then on an afternoon late in February, John and Adam had a curious adventure. Adventures were for ever happening to Adam, whether watching a carriageful of ladies tumbled into the ditch on the Carlisle Road, seeing a drunken old man fall off the top of the Kendal coach, looking at the gipsies who came and pitched with their caravans painted orange and blue on the moor above the house until they were ordered away (they had brown babies, two monkeys and a basketful of snakes; a woman in a crimson kerchief with silver coins through her ears invited Adam to join them: had it not been for his mother he would have done so). Adventures for him were perpetual, but this one had for him a new quality, terrifying had he allowed himself to be terrified.

It had been a strange day. In the forenoon there had been showers of rain that had filled the road with puddles of silver. Then Skiddaw about two of the afternoon took a step or two and came face to face with the house, dragging a stream of clouds over his shoulder with him. He had a way of doing this: a shrug of shoulders, a quiver of his sides and there he was staring in at the parlour window. The air was fresh with a sniff of spring (although spring would not be with them for a month or two). Adam walked out as far as the stream in the hollow below the Tarn; the water glided and leapt. The moss was wet on the gleaming stones above the brown water; the Fell rose straight from the hollow and was thronged with little moorland streams, for there had been heavy rains. He thought that he saw an eagle and he looked up and up into the sky that was whitish blue and

empty until the clouds that clung on to Skiddaw's shoulders. All
these little things belonged to the adventure. As he entered the
house again Skiddaw receded and the clouds turned rose; the
road beyond the garden wall was very hard and white. He could
hear a young owl hooting. He climbed the stairs to find two large
marbles, one crystal white, one purple, that he liked to carry in
his pocket. Then slid down the banisters to the parlour. He knew
that his mother and Aunt Jennifer were paying a visit. They had
gone in the carriage with Bennett.

In the doorway of the parlour he found John and saw at once
that he was shaking with some event. He pulled Adam by the arm
into the room, which was lit only with the dusk of the falling day
and the sharp jumping flames from the fire.

He spoke in a whisper.

'Adam! . . . Cousin Walter has been here!'

Adam looked to the window.

'No,' said John, 'he has gone.'

'He came into the house?'

The two boys whispered like conspirators.

'No. Not so far as the house. He was on a white horse. He got
down and stood at the gate. Then he opened it and stood in the
garden. He stayed looking at the house without moving, for a
long while. Then he went out and rode away. I saw him through
the window.'

Adam drew a deep breath and clutched the two marbles in his
pocket.

'Did he look angry?' he asked at length.

'I could not see his face. Everything was so still. I thought he
would knock at the door, but when he was inside the gate he
never moved. He stood there looking. I thought he could see me
through the window and I hid behind the curtain.'

Adam went to the window and peered out. The glow in the sky
was bright and shredded now with little yellow clouds like gos-
lings.

'He is gone,' he said, his nose pressed against the cold pane.

'Yes – but a moment back. He rode slowly up the hill. Oh,
Adam, why did he come?'

'To spy on us.' Adam nodded his head. 'I shall go after
him.'

'Oh, Adam, will you?'

'Yes, why not? Perhaps he has a gun and is waiting to shoot
someone.'

John must go too if Adam went, but he felt an overwhelming fear, sprung from years of his mother's dread. Adam was too angry just then to be frightened. When he was angry he was possessed with rage; there was no room for any other emotion. When he had been a baby his anger had sometimes almost choked him because it boiled inside him and he could not shout nor cry. He took John by the hand, and together, as quietly as might be, they stole out of the house, closing the big heavy door gingerly behind them. The owl hooted at them as they hurried on to the road.

Outside the gate Adam halted. Something in the whiteness of the road pulled him up. But he knew what it was. A week ago he had been walking up the hill and had come upon a fat and distended frog. This frog was croaking in a despairing manner; around its neck were folded the thin spiry legs of two smaller frogs who clung thus, motionless, without sound. From the mouth of the large distended frog protruded a tip of tongue scarlet red.

Adam came the next day and found that the swollen frog was dead (the red tongue still protruding), but the two live frogs were still there, their legs interlaced, while another frog, small and green, squatted near by on guard and to see that justice had been done.

Adam was too young to feel spiritual disgust: his original instinct had been one of interest and curiosity, but now the scene around him was ghostly with evening mist, and out of the mist sprang the sharp white road; by the side of the road was a yellow-bellied frog with a tongue like blood and around him croaked a chorus of green frogs. The moor was filled with green frogs. He stood staring intently in front of him.

'What is it?' whispered John. 'He will be gone in an instant.' They stood very close together and listened. All was still. The lights of the little village were coming out; Fell House was a black mass against the mist.

It was perhaps the cold that drove them forward. They walked on the turf at the side of the road so that they should make no noise. They turned from the road and began to climb the moor, stumbling over the unevenness of the turf. Suddenly John caught Adam's arm: 'Keep down ... He's there!'

Just in front of them a shelf of turf rose above a cutting. To the right of them, very close to them, three sheep, aware of them, held together, their sides panting. But quite clearly the boys could see the figure on the hill. He seemed gigantic in that light, his white horse colossal. The mist, into whose vapours the moon would soon pour her light, made a ghostly background to that motionless horseman, great of bulk, in a black overcoat with a high black collar. His thighs, his riding-boots, were jet against the whiteness of his horse's flanks. Neither he nor his horse moved. The sheep too seemed to be carved against the moor, and the two boys, kneeling behind the rising of turf, their hearts thumping as it seemed to them into their throats, waited to see what he would do.

He did nothing. He stayed there looking down on to Fell House. Then, as darkness fell, he turned his horse's head and rode away.

AT WESTAWAYS

WESTAWAYS was a very different place from Fell House, Uldale.

Fell House would have always, whatever were done to it, the atmosphere of the farm from which it had sprung. David Herries, John's grandfather, had in his time made certain enlargements. He was greatly proud – and so was Sarah his wife – of his dairies, the garden with its fine lawn and Gothic temple, the parlour and the best bedroom, but both David and Sarah had been simple people, nor, since their marriage, had they travelled far afield. Sarah, for a brief while, had been bitten with the London fashion, fostered by Horace Walpole, *The Castle of Otranto*, Mrs Radcliffe and the rest, for pseudo-medievalism, suits of armour, stained-glass windows and plaster gargoyles, but she was not by nature romantic and the craze had soon passed. Fell House, nestling its warm cheek against the breast of the moor, was an improved farmhouse and no more.

Utterly different from its very inception was Westaways. In the early years of the eighteenth century old Pomfret Herries, brother of 'Rogue' Herries, and so uncle to David, young John's grandfather, had had it built, not because he wanted a beautiful house but because he wished to go one better than his neighbours. However, it *was* a beautiful house because he chose for architect old John Westaway, saturnine and melancholy hermit, one of the finest architects then alive, trained in Italy, the friend of Van-brugh and Chesterman, famous through all the north of England not only for his skill but also for his eccentricities and savage temper.

Old Pomfret had to pay for his ambitions and grumbled at the cost for years after, but he had, in the end, a lovely house. It is true that the only room in it of any value to himself was his own apartment thronged with guns and fishing-rods. He was proud, nevertheless, for people came from miles to see the house.

It was situated between Crosthwaite Church and the town of Keswick. At that time the gardens ran down to the fringe of the Lake. The virtues of the house were its beautiful tiles of rosy red, the delicate wrought-ironwork across its front, the sash windows – at that time a great rarity – the pillared hall, and especially the saloon, whose decorations were designed and executed by John Westaway himself. The subject of the design was Paris awarding the apple, and the three goddesses were painted with extreme vigour.

After old Pomfret's death the house passed out of the family for a while, but Will, David Herries' money-making son, bought it back again and thought to live in it. However, London, and especially the City, held him too strongly. He found the country both dull and fruitless. His son Walter reigned in Westaways in his stead.

Walter, who had little taste but great energy and a readiness to take the advice of others (for his own profit), enlarged and im-proved Westaways. For a number of years workmen were always about the place. He added a wing towards Crosthwaite, doubled the stables, extended the gardens and had a grand conservatory. He also put fine things inside the house; he had a famous piece of tapestry that showed Diana hunting, some excellent sculpture, and a Van Dyck and a small but most valuable Titian. There was also over the door of the saloon a painting of the Watteau school in deep rich colours of some French king dining with his ladies – a picture all purples, oranges and crimson that the Keswick citi-zens thought the finest thing they had ever seen. Only old Miss Pennyfeather laughed at it and called it 'stuff', and Mr Southey, after dining with Walter, was said never even to have noticed it.

Walter Herries himself cared for none of these things for themselves, but only in so far as they represented strength and power.

At this time he was thirty years of age and his children, Uhland and Elizabeth, who were twins, were seven; they were born in the same year as young Adam and were a few months older than he.

Walter was large in girth and limb, but could not at this period be called stout. He was in appearance a survival of the days of the Regency, now swiftly slipping into limbo. He seemed already something of an anachronism with his coats of purple and red, his high thick stock with its jewelled pin, his capacity for eating and drinking, his roaring laugh, his passion for sport. But he was not really such an anachronism as he seemed. In politics, when he bothered to speak of them, he appeared as reactionary Tory as Wellington or old Lord Eldon, but in reality he stood closer to Huskisson and Canning. The fact was that he learnt much from his father, who, one of the astutest men in the City, had his eye more firmly fixed on the past. Walter, caring for nothing but his personal power and the aggrandizement of his family, loving only in all the world his crippled little son, building his edifice in part for himself but in the main for Uhland's future, considered that future very much more deeply than anyone supposed. He suffered from the fact that no one in his immediate surroundings was of any use to him in these things. He reigned in a passionate loneliness and perhaps in that had more in common with his great-grandfather, old 'Rogue' Herries, than he would ever have dreamed possible. His wife Agnes he held to be an imbecile, and she was truly as terrified of him as all timid wives are supposed to be of tyrannous, loud-voiced husbands.

On a certain fine September morning of this year, 1822, a long-legged, supercilious individual named Posset (William Posset, son of William Posset, coachman at Levons Hall) brought into Walter Herries' dressing-room a large tin bath. The floor of this dressing-room drooped in its centre into a hollow and in the floor of this hollow was a small iron grating. Over the hollow the bath was inserted. A pinch-faced youth in a uniform of dark red and brass buttons then arrived with two vast pitchers so large as almost to conceal him. With an air of extreme relief and under the cold eye of the lengthy Posset, young Albert emptied the pitchers into the bath. Posset then with delicate tread stepped into the next room, pulled back the curtains and approached the four-poster. Walter, his mouth wide open, his chest bare, his nightshirt pulled down over one shoulder, was snoring loudly. Posset, with a gravity worthy of a tax-collector, shook the bare arm. Walter woke, gave one glance at Posset, sprang from his bed, tugged his nightshirt over his head, rushed in to the next room and plunged into the bath. Young Albert, accustomed to the fierce eruption of water, always at this point retired to the farthest corner of the room, where he stood, towels over his arm, admiring, with an amazement that custom never seemed to lessen, that great body, that splutter of exclamations, grunts and oaths, and that sudden magnificent figure of a man withdrawn from the water, suffering the lusty (but always reverent) towelling of Posset – and water dripping everywhere, running in little streams and eddies into the hollow and away safely through the iron grating. Albert always informed those less privileged that there was no sight in the world quite so fine as his master as he plunged into his bath – no lion in a show, no tiger in Indian jungle, could have the energy and vigour of his master at this moment. It was Albert's top moment of his day – a pity that it came so early; every event was a decline from it.

Walter had long ago insisted that any visitor in the house – his mother, his wife, very definitely included – must, unless a doctor forbade them, be present at the family breakfast table. It was the beginning of his patriarchal day. Only thirty years of age, he already felt himself founder of the whole of the Herries stock, and nothing pleased him better than to have Herries collected from all over the country and seated at his table.

This was not at present easy, for Keswick was tucked away in the North and travelling was difficult. Nevertheless, this was not a bad halting-place on the way to Scotland, and the number of Herries 'bagged' for Walter's dining-table in the last five years was remarkable.

Walter liked further to collect Herries who were oddities and to encourage them in their idiosyncrasies – granted, of course, that these idiosyncrasies did not inconvenience himself. Here he was instigated by the old motive of the King and his Court Jester. Walter might be said to have a great sense of fun, if no very strong sense of humour. He liked, for example, to indulge old Monty Cards in his femininities (Monty painted his cheeks and powdered his nose), in his little meannesses and his nervous terrors. He enjoyed the company of old Maria Rockage (for whom he had a real liking) that he might shock her Méthodist principles. He even was childish enough to play on his wife's terrors by laying a book on a door that it should fall on her when entering a room. He was not at all above practical jokes and horseplay. They were part of his 'Regency' manner.

He had just now as his guests, Phyllis, Maria Rockage's daughter, her husband, Stephen Newmark, and three of her children – Horace aged three, Mary aged two, and Phyllis only one. She was anticipating a fourth. They were all very healthy children and Mr Newmark looked upon them as just rewards tendered to him by a grateful Deity.

For Stephen Newmark, tall, long-nosed, sanctimonious, was a perpetual joy to Walter. He took life seriously. He enjoyed Family Prayers. Walter, therefore, indulged his fancy and insisted that all of them, Agnes his wife, his mother (who was staying just then with him), his own two children, and all the household should be present on the stroke of eight and offer up, under the leadership of Mr Newmark, thanks to the Creator for the dangers of a night safely past and the glories of another day vouchsafed. It puzzled Mr Newmark a little that Walter should be so truly determined on Family Prayers. This determination did not altogether 'go' with his cock-fighting, horse racing, cardplaying, but Newmark had long ago decided (and confided to Phyllis) that his Cousin Walter was 'a strange fish'. In that conclusion he was perfectly correct.

On this morning, however, Walter had a small matter of business to discharge before breakfast. Rosy, scented, his stock starched until it glittered, his pantaloons of dark purple hiding his magnificent legs, 'rings on his fingers and bells on his toes', he descended, like Jove from Olympus, to the study where he transacted his affairs.

Here his agent, Peach, was waiting for him. Peach was a short, stocky, beetle-browed little man who had been in the service, for most of his days, of the Duke of Wrexe. He came, therefore, from the South and hated the North *and* the Northerners with a dreadful passion. He would not have stayed here a day had it not been for the odd power that Walter Herries exercised over him. He could not be said to *love* his master – he was not known to love any human being; he was not deferential, showed no servitude, disputed his master's wishes hotly and was grudging in thanks for benefits, but he seemed to have found in Walter Herries a man who had stung, reluctantly, his admiration – the only man in the world it might be. He appreciated Herries' dominating roughness, coarseness, liking for horseplay, and then something more – outside and beyond these.

In any case he made a wonderful servant and was hated cordially throughout the countryside.

He was standing now, his legs, that were slightly bowed, apart, his hand gripping the shoulder of a slim fair-haired boy who, his hands tied behind him, his eyes wide open with fear and apprehension, stayed there, his heart beating like a terrified rabbit's.

'This is the boy,' Peach said.

'Yes,' said Walter, looking at him.

The boy's eyes drooped. In his heart was the terror of death. He knew that he could be hanged for what he had done.

'I discovered him,' Peach went on, 'last evening. He had a small wheelbarrow and was placing in it some logs from the pile outside the further stables.'

'What did he say?' Walter asked.

'He said nothing. At least not then. Later when he was shut into the cellar for the night he admitted that he was hungry and had a mother who was hungry and a small brother who was hungry.' Peach gave a click in his throat, a favourite noise of his, and it resembled a key turning in a door. 'They all say they're hungry now.'

'What's your name?' asked Walter.

'Henry Burgess.'

'Well, Henry Burgess . . . You know what the Keswick Justices will say?'

The boy was understood to mutter that he didn't care.

'You don't care? Well, all the better. It's a hanging matter, you know.'

'I gave him food and drink,' Peach remarked reluctantly. 'He wouldn't have held up else.' Then he added: 'His mother's been waiting outside all night'.

There was an interruption. The door opened and Uhland came in. It was his habit to find his father here before breakfast. For a boy of seven he was tall and very spare and his face was grave and sadly lined for a child. One leg was longer than the other and he walked aided by a little ebony cane. When he saw that there was company he stopped at the door. It was characteristic of him that he stood there looking at them solemnly and said nothing.

'Well, what's your defence?' asked Walter.

The boy was understood to say they were all hungry.

'All hungry, were you? That's not much of an excuse. Couldn't you work?'

No work to be found. Hard times. Had been working for a hostler. Turned away for fighting another boy who insulted his mother.

'Young ruffian,' said Walter complacently. He stood, his chest thrust out, his thumbs in his armholes. Then he nodded to Uhland, who came limping forward. Walter put his arm round his son and held him close to him.

'Uhland, this boy has been stealing my wood. He says he did it because he was hungry. If he goes before the Justices it will be a hanging matter. Shall I send him or no?'

Uhland stared at the boy, who suddenly raised his eyes, glaring at them all.

'He doesn't *look* hungry,' he said quietly.

'No, upon my word he doesn't,' said Walter with boisterous good humour. 'That's good for a child, Peach, is it not? He does not look hungry. You are right, Uhland, my boy.' He laughed, throwing back his handsome curly head. 'Well, what shall we do with him?'

'Let him go, Papa,' said Uhland. His voice was cold, but he looked at the boy with interest. 'We have plenty of wood.'

'Yes, but we shall not have,' said Walter, 'if all the young vagabonds— Very well, let him go, Peach. He shall have the dogs on him if he comes this way again.'

Without a word Peach, pushing the boy in front of him, took him from the room.

Walter laughed, yawned, stretched his great arms.

'Well, my boy, how are you?'

'Very well, Papa, thank you.'

'Slept? No headache?'

'No, Papa, thank you.'

'Will you come with me into Keswick this morning?'

'Yes, Papa.'

There was a pause; then Uhland said:

'Elizabeth wishes to come.'

'She can go with Miss Kipe.'

'Yes, Papa.'

A roar like a wild beast's cry for his food filled the room. It was the ceremonial gong – a gong brought from India, purchased by Will and given by him to his son, a superb gong of beaten brass and carved with the figures of Indian deities.

So they went to breakfast, Uhland's small bony hand in his father's large one.

They were all assembled in the bright, high room whose wide windows looked out on to the garden with the splashing fountain, the Lake and the hills beyond. Stephen Newmark was there, standing behind a reading-desk; Phyllis his wife; two of her children; Elizabeth with her governess, Miss Kipe; Christabel Herries, Walter's mother; Agnes, Walter's wife; Montague Cards and the whole household – Posset, young Albert, the cook, the maids and the little kitchen-help.

Walter took his place beside his wife and instantly they all knelt. A long row of upturned boots met the interested gaze of two robins on the window sill. After a while, with creaking of knees, rustling of aprons, they all rose and sat down while Mr Newmark read a selection from the New Testament. The sun flooded the room. A large fat tortoiseshell cat came stealthily down the garden path, its green eyes fixed on the robins. On the bright road beyond the house the Burgess family began to trudge in silence towards Carlisle. Walter put out his hand and laid it on Uhland's shoulder. The cook, who was fat and had trouble with her heart, began to breathe heavily, Posset caught the eye of the prettiest of the maids and instantly looked away again. Little Elizabeth, looking out, saw the cat and the birds. Her eyes widened with apprehension.

'Let us Pray,' said Mr Newmark, and down on their knees they all went again.

'May the blessing of the Lord rest upon us all this day,' said Mr Newmark. There was a pause, then a rustle, a knee-cracking, a boot-scraping, and they were all on their feet again.

The domestics were in line – Mrs Rains the cook, Posset, the maids, Albert, the little kitchen-maid who had a round rosy face and a neat waist – all in their proper order.

'Fresh country girls you succeed in getting, Walter,' said New-mark after they were gone, his mind meditatively on the kitchen-maid.

'Anybody wanting the barouche this fine morning?' said Walter genially. He was in an excellent temper, which fact the three ladies perceived and brightened accordingly. Christabel Herries, Walter's mother, was fifty years of age and thin to emaciation. She wore gowns of black silk with a purple Indian shawl thrown about her narrow shoulders. She moved with timidity, as though she were ever expecting a rude word. She adored her son but feared him. She had been, all through her married life, under the domination of Herries men. Her husband had never treated her with unkindness, but the City had swallowed him, leaving Christabel alone on shores of domesticy so barren that she occupied half her London evenings talking to

herself in a large drawing-room all yellow silk and mirrors. Will
her husband, had hoped to make her a social success. But after a
disastrous Ball that they gave in the summer of '96, a Ball that
had ended with a scene between Christabel and Jennifer, then a
radiant young beauty, Will, with a shrug of his shoulders, had
reconciled himself to her disabilities. He very quickly saw that the
thing for him to do was to make the money so that his son Walter
might carry on the family glory.

Walter had always been kind to his mother, but for family
rather than personal reasons. He thought her 'a poor fish', but
then he had no opinion of women unless they were handsome.
Christabel was, however, the mother of Walter Herries; she must
therefore be honoured by the outside world. And he saw that it
was so.

Agnes, as the wife of Walter Herries and the mother of his
children, should also have secured honourable treatment had the
thing been at all possible. But in this Walter saw that the world
was not to blame, for a more miserable woebegone sickly female
was not, he was assured, to be found in the civilized globe. When
he married her she had been something of the type of that new
rosy-cheeked kitchen-maid (whom he had noticed, and saw also
that Newmark had noticed). She had been merry at first with a
certain rather kittenish charm. But she was 'cold'. Marital relations had terrified her from the first. Their marriage night had
been a horror, and after the birth of the twins they had occupied
separate bedrooms. Then she had had one sickness after another
now did not choose to trouble to talk; 'sulky', Walter told himself. She pretended to be fond of the children but, he was happy
to say, Uhland had already as much scorn of her as his father
had.

He felt (and with justice surely) that Fate had dealt unfairly in
giving so magnificent a man so wretched a partner. He was fair
to her, he gave her everything that she needed; all that he asked
of her was that she should keep out of his way and not interfere
with his plans for Uhland. With Elizabeth she should do as she
pleased.

Phyllis Newmark was tall, of a charming pink and white complexion, and had a laughing eye.

Her father, Lord Rockage, in his place, Grosset in Wiltshire,
had given her love and kisses combined with general disorder,
poverty and Methodism. On these mixed virtues she had thriven.
She was kindly, cheerful, intelligent and quite uneducated. She

was born to be a mother, and a mother she was most assuredly
proving. She did not mind how many children she had. She
adored them all. Newmark, having helped to provide her with
three, must receive her grateful thanks. She gave him her obedi-
ence, laughed at his foibles and understood him better than
anyone else in the world. She too had noticed his glance at the
kitchen-maid although at the same time she was murmuring
(with real devotion) the Lord's Prayer and observing a pimple on
the neck of little Horace and wondering whether Walter would
allow them the barouche that morning or force them into the
post-chaise or order them to walk. She knew, however, exactly
how to deal with the kitchen-maid, the pimple and the walk (if
that were compulsory). Nothing could defeat her; she inherited
from both her parents courage, honesty and an insatiable zest for
life.

Soon they were all around the breakfast-table and set to with
an eagerness that spoke well for their digestions. Rounds of beef;
pies; fish, broiled and fried; eggs, baked, fried, boiled; hams,
tongues, jams, marmalades, buns, scones – everything was there,
and tankards of ale, tea, coffee . . . Agnes Herries alone pretended
to eat but did not.

'Yes, you may have the barouche,' Walter observed, 'and
Phyllis shall have the barouche box if she chooses – I know that it
gives her the greatest gratification both to see and be seen.' Then,
having paused sufficiently to catch all their attention, he
added:

'But first I have a visitor.'

'A visitor?'

'Yes. At ten o'clock precisely a lady is to come and see me.'

'A lady?'

'A friend of you all – Mrs Judith Paris.'

He allowed his words to sink in. And indeed they caused a stir.
Both Christabel and Phyllis Newmark had the deepest affection
for Judith. To Phyllis she had been a familiar friend since her
babyhood, for Judith had once lived at Grosset, and to Christabel
she was perhaps the only woman in the world who had never
failed her, the one human being who did not patronize her, cared
for her as she was, knew with tenderness and perception the
barrenness of her life.

Yet Christabel had only seen her once in seven years. Only
once since the night when Judith had dined at Westaways, the
night of the news of Napoleon's escape from Elba. After that

Judith had fled to Paris, borne her illegitimate son there. Since her return to Uldale there had been war between the two houses. Whenever Christabel came up from London to stay with her son she hoped that there would be some chance meeting, in a lane, in a street. She had not dared herself to prepare a meeting.

'Oh, Judith!' Phyllis cried joyfully. 'I had been intending to ask ...'

'She is coming,' Walter said, greatly amused at the disappointment that his womenkind would suffer, 'solely on a business matter. The visit is only to myself.'

Then Christabel showed courage.

'Walter, you should invite Judith to dinner. Bygones are bygones. You should most certainly invite her to dinner.'

'And Jennifer?' asked Walter, laughing.

Christabel's pale cheek flushed. No, she could never forgive Jennifer. That old quarrel, twenty-six years old, could never be forgotten. It had too many consequences. It had split the family; it had been the close of Christabel's social life. She had never had the courage to give a real party again. And then Jennifer had behaved scandalously. She had been another man's mistress under her husband's nose. That poor Francis had shot himself in London was all Jennifer's fault. No, Jennifer was another matter.

'Well, then,' said Walter, observing his mother's silence. 'You see, ma'am. And you cannot have Judith here without Jennifer. Judith rules that house. She has become, I hear, a perfect Turk ... Well, well, it may not be for long.'

He added these last words in a half-murmur to himself. With a final pull at his tankard of beer, wiping his mouth, with a bow to the ladies, he got up, walked for a moment to the window and stood there, looking out, then left the room.

As soon as he was gone the children broke out into little pipings and chirrupings. The two Newmark children (who should have been in the nursery, but their father wished them to take their part, even thus early, in the morning ceremony) rolled decorously on the floor at their mother's feet. You felt that already their infant eyes were cautiously on their father. Uhland sat without moving, one leg over the other, an attitude protective of his deformity. Elizabeth, shyly crossed the room. She was a beautiful child, most delicate in colour and build. She had none of the high bones of the Herries tribe. She did not seem like a Herries until suddenly with a lift of her head you saw pride and resolve, two of the finer Herries characteristics. Her mother took her hand and they stayed quietly together, remote, in a world of their own, without speaking ...

Judith was shown into the little parlour next the saloon. It had not been long since she had had a talk with Walter there – last Christmas-time it had been. Now, as she sat on the red morocco chair waiting for him, she thought of that, and how there had been a bowl of Christmas roses. A petal had fallen lazily, wistfully to the carpet. Their talk then had been almost friendly. She had gone with him afterwards to the nursery to see the children, and she had been touched by his protective love for his son.

But now all was changed. In the interval between that meeting and this she had had proof enough of the serious danger that this big laughing man offered to her and to hers.

She was here to defend her own, and a wave of hot fierce pride beat into her cheeks as she sat there, a small unobtrusive woman in a black bonnet, her hands in a black muff, waiting for him to come in. It was he who had written to her, a short polite note asking her whether she could give him a few moments on an important matter. She would not have come, but she also had something of her own to say. She would see that she said it.

When he came in she got up and bowed, but did not offer her hand.

'Well, Cousin Walter,' she said grimly. 'What do you wish to see me about?'

His own tone changed when he saw her attitude. He had intended to be friendly, jolly, a mood that he preferred, for he liked himself in that role. But he was like a child if anyone affronted him. It might be, too, that Judith was the only person in the world of whom he had some fear. Still, his ground was sure and he began confidently enough.

'Forgive my asking you to take this trouble, Cousin Judith. You will agree, however, that I should be deceiving myself if I fancied that my presence would be welcome at Uldale.'

'Nevertheless,' she answered, 'you have paid us already at least one visit this year.'

'Indeed?'

'Last February I believe it was. You did us the honour to ride over and even to inspect our garden.'

He was confused. He had not thought that she knew of it.

'Well – it happened that I rode that way ... But come, Cousin

Judith. I am certain that we have neither of us time to waste . . .'
Then he added, a little awkwardly: 'I am sorry that you are
already determined that our talk shall be unfriendly.' (What was
there, he asked himself, about the little plain woman in the
homely bonnet that made him feel like a scolded schoolboy? She
had, in the last six months, acquired the devil of a manner – as
though she were already Queen of Cumberland. Well, he would
show her that she was not.)

She regarded him sternly.

'Cousin Walter, I was in this same room Christmas last. We
had a conversation that was not altogether unfriendly. Since then
facts have come to my knowledge. I know that it was through
you that Francis Herries left home and put an end to his life in
London. I know that it was because you bribed and suborned
that the riot occurred at Fell House – the riot that ended in the
undeserved death of the best friend I had in the world – Reuben
Sunwood. And since then,' – she spoke without emotion and
without removing her eyes from his face – 'since I have been in
charge of things at Fell House, your hand has been everywhere.
Those fields towards Ireby that we intended to purchase – you
paid an absurd price for them, although you could not need the
ground. You bribed the cattle-man whom we had last March
from Mungrisdale to poison our cows. Within the last month
you have attempted to bribe Mr Rackstraw, who has been with us
all this year as tutor, to spy upon us as Mr Winch did before him.
Mr Rackstraw has been gentleman enough to show us loyalty.
After these things – and I have no doubt that there are many
more with which your conscience can charge you – it is perhaps a
little without meaning to speak of friendliness between us.'

Walter did not move, did not shift his great bulk, did not turn
his eyes away. He admired her. By God, he admired her! There
was someone here worth fighting.

'Very well, then,' he said at last. 'We know at least where we
stand, you and I. I will not, however, admit responsibility either
for Francis' weakness or Sunwood's rashness. Francis would not
have shot himself had he been another sort of man. It was his
whole life condemned him, not I. As to the riot, no one regretted
more than myself its most serious consequences. And what evidence have you that I was concerned in that matter?'

'The evidence of Mr Winch,' Judith answered.

'Faugh! A wretched little time-server who cheated me quite as
steadily as he cheated yourself, Judith. As to other more recent

matters, well – do you recollect our last conversation in this room?'

'Perfectly.'

'Then you will remember the challenge I laid down. I told you – what I trust you sincerely believe – that I had no animosity whatever towards yourself. I told you also that for reasons both private and public I was resolved that Jennifer and her children should vacate Fell House, and that if I could not see to it by fair means that they went, then I would see to it by unfair. I was honest in that. I gave you warning.'

'And on what ground,' Judith cried indignantly, 'had you the right? Fell House is Jennifer's place. It is where her husband was born and his children after him.'

'My father also was born there,' said Walter quietly. 'As you may have observed, Judith, I have a great sense of family. It is perhaps the greatest quality in me. Jennifer with her rotten public history offends my sense of family. There is also an old quarrel between her and my mother that possibly you have not forgotten. In any case, I made you a fair offer then. I make you a fair offer now. Let Jennifer and her children leave Fell House and go to live in the South – and the matter is for ever ended.'

'We are only beating the old ground,' answered Judith impatiently. 'There is nothing to be said on that score. We defy you now, Cousin Walter, as we defied you then. There is only now this difference – that they have me to fight for them, and life has made me a determined woman, not easily moved.'

'No,' he answered quickly. 'I am aware that you are not. We are alike at least in that. But you know that my quarrel is neither with you nor your boy. Indeed, it has never been. That is one matter on which I wish to speak to you.'

He hesitated, then went on:

'It seems that my boy, Uhland, has met your boy Adam on several occasions.'

'Yes, I know it.'

'They are only babies, but Uhland is old for his age. He has taken an unaccountable liking for your Adam.' He paused, laughed, continued: 'Forgive me for that word "unaccountable". But for children as young as they are—' He broke off.

She felt herself, against her will, touched. When Walter mentioned his son a different character seemed to speak from his eyes, his mouth, his very hands. He was young and proud when he spoke of his son. Some better light shone through his coarse texture. But she did not want to be touched.

'You must know,' she said impatiently, 'that it was through no wish of mine that they met. It was in the woods beyond Portinscale – pure accident.'

'Oh, I know, I know ... I was not charging you with any intention. But my boy speaks of him, wishes to see him—'

'Yes,' Judith answered, 'that is a mischance that we must correct.'

'A mischance?'

'Yes. It would be good for neither of them, things being as they are, that they should be better acquainted.'

Walter choked back some reply that he was about to make. His control was remarkable.

'I had hoped,' he said steadily, 'that you would allow the children occasionally to meet. We elders may have our divisions. There is no reason—'

She broke in, jumping impetuously to her feet:

'No reason! No reason! There is *this* reason, Cousin Walter – that you are our enemy. You have killed Francis Herries, you would rob his children of the very roof over their heads. Only a moment ago you threatened me. And yet you wish that my son and your son—'

She stopped, sat down quietly, smoothing her skirt.

'I have still some of my old temper remaining although I am near fifty ... In fact, I may tell you, Cousin Walter, that I was never in better health in my life. Aye,' she nodded her bonnet, 'that is what I had come to say. You may think me an old woman, but I am young enough yet to keep my son from your influence and, pray God, I ever will be.'

He was angry; she had touched him. His hand fingered the jewelled pin in his stock. But his voice was level as he answered: 'Very well, then. You are confident, Cousin Judith. I am an impatient man by blood, but in this case I can school myself to waiting.

'Now hear my offer. It was to make it that I asked you to visit me. Last week I purchased the land at High Ireby. It was my intention, unless we come to some agreement together, to build a house there.'

High Ireby? At once she grasped the implication. The High Ireby land was on the hills above Uldale. It was at some distance, but nevertheless it overlooked Fell House. Walter there in some big place of his planning, with his fields, his cattle, his servants

. . . In spite of herself she showed some agitation.

'That would be done,' she said at length slowly, 'to spite us.'

'It would be done,' he answered, smiling (for he saw that she grasped the consequences), 'because I admire the view. It would not be perhaps altogether happy for Jennifer and her children to have me so neighbourly.' He looked at her closely. She gave him back look for look. 'But,' he went on, 'you have not heard my proposition. This house here is now too small for for me, but there are other sites that I could choose, other than High Ireby. Then it is one of two things. Either Jennifer sells me Fell House – I will give her a good price for it – and removes herself South. And in that case I would make you the offer of it. You should be my tenant at a most moderate rental. Or I build on High Ireby. There is no necessity for an immediate decision. I only wished that you should know what I had in mind.'

Judith saw then his plan; that this should hang over them night and day. If Walter built a house at High Ireby, it would kill Jennifer. And John? His nature being as it was, he could not endure it. Nor would it stop at Walter's living there. He would be able, in a thousand ways, to molest them at Fell House, to spy upon them, to break their privacy . . . Yes, it was a clever notion.

'At any time, Cousin Judith,' he said, moving towards the door, 'that Jennifer is ready for me to have Fell House at a good price—'

She got up, putting her hands in her muff.

'You are clever, Walter,' she said. 'I grant you that. You are clever.'

'I am flattered,' he said, bowing. 'I must be clever to fight so brilliant an adversary.'

'Stuff!' she answered, tossing her head. 'None of your fine manners. Time's wasted by them.'

Outside the door she turned.

'You are a strange man. So much trouble to persecute two weak women.'

'One weak woman,' he corrected her.

At the top of the stairs he said: 'You understand my offer?'

'Oh yes, I understand.'

'Well, good day.'

'Good day to you, Walter.'

As she climbed into the chaise she was surprised to find herself trembling. Her desire at that moment was to hasten home and find them safe. Then to gather them all into her arms – Jennifer, John, Dorothy and Adam.

But all she said aloud for the benefit of Bennett's broad back was, once again, 'Stuff!'

ADAM'S WORLD

IT might be claimed that in spite of all that happened to him afterwards, the most important years of Adam Herries' life were from 1822 to 1826, from the age of seven to the comparative maturity of eleven.

It was true that the French years and the Watendlath years were important, but it was Mr Rackstraw who really woke him into active conscious life, and Mr Rackstraw didn't come to Uldale until after the riot at the beginning of 1822.

The five years that followed had for Adam three outstandingly influential personalities – his mother, Mr Rackstraw and John. Looking back, in later years, he sometimes fancied that everything that he did afterwards, all the things that brought him into trouble, all the things that gave him happiness, sprang in reality from those three people. At least, it is true that afterwards one person only was to influence him so deeply, and for two others only was he to care with such strong endurance as he did for his mother and for John Herries. But it was his character that was, in the main, to settle the result of events for him, as it does with all of us. What he was he was partly born, partly formed by people and events, partly fashioned by his own free will.

During those five years he lived, as all small boys do, a kind of under-water life with his own particular anemones, sea-horses, coloured weeds and stones for his absorbed attention. Of the traffic of the waters above his head he knew nothing; it mattered to him not at all, of course, that Mr Canning, staying with John Gladstone in his Liverpool home, watched a small boy called William Ewart playing on the lawn, or that there was a skirmish at Missolonghi, or that taxation grew ever higher and higher, that men and women cursed the machines that were taking the bread from their mouths, that the word 'Reform' was becoming an ever-louder battle-cry on men's lips . . .

He was always to have a great capacity for choosing at once the things that would, he thought, be useful to him and rejecting all the rest. From the very first he went his own way, and this independence was the beginning of all his trouble with his mother.

On the first occasion when he went off for a whole day without warning, indeed without word to anyone, he was on his return in the evening, tired, dirty and triumphant, beaten, and by his mother. She could not but remember, as she watched him adjusting his small trousers, the occasion so long ago when David Herries had beaten herself, hating it more than she did. The memory made her catch Adam to her breast and cover his face with kisses, an act of sentimentality that was to be, on the occasions of these punishments, her last. For she saw that he thought poorly of her for relenting, and for a day or two despised her a little.

She fought her first serious battle with him over this affair. He would neither tell her where he had been nor would he promise her not to do it again. For an awful week it seemed to her that her whole relationship with him was broken to pieces, until she discovered that she was now more intimate with him than ever before. For, when she said that she no longer wished to hear where he had been, he told her everything. He had been in the woods beyond Ireby, had had food with a farmer, had stroked a wild dog that everyone else feared, had found birds' eggs and fought a boy about tying a cat to a log and throwing stones at it. He told her everything and then tried to convey to her that he would always do so, but that he must have his freedom. He was to be always very inarticulate, and when now he found that she did not understand what he wanted, he simply fell into a complete and unyielding silence.

She explained to him that if he really loved her he could not give her anxiety and unhappiness by disappearing without telling anyone first. He wanted to say that if he told anyone he would be prevented from going and that therefore it was plain that no one must be told, but this was too deeply complicated for him, so he said nothing. Then she, the least sentimental of women, descended, in her distress, to the desperate expedient of asking him whether he loved her or no, and he, who loved her with all his being, disliked so profoundly to speak about his feelings that he said nothing at all. He, being seven, was not, of course, aware of his reasons for these things. He simply knew that he was hungry, that his posterior was sore where his mother had struck him, that he hated to be questioned, that he had had a grand day, and that he would go off again in a similar manner as soon as opportunity offered itself.

Judith was a sensible woman and she had an especial talent for understanding other people. This was not 'other people' but her own flesh and blood, and, just as forty years ago she had climbed out of the window and ridden away to Uncle Tom Gauntry at Stone Ends, so now her son Adam must also be free.

She did the wisest thing – she left the whole matter to Mr Rackstraw. This was, in fact, very remarkable on her part, for at this time in England the great parental movement for the proper discipline and benefit of the children was just beginning to achieve force and power. All the children of England were learning to say 'Sir' and 'Ma'am' to their parents, never to speak before they were spoken to, and to ask questions in the manner of Little Henry – but Judith was never like other people, and their ways would never be hers.

Mr Rackstraw had from the first a strong influence over Adam. He was a man made up of very striking opposites. In appearance he was a little, wiry fellow with a face like a slumbering coal, red, dusky and shadowed ash-colour. He had a broken nose and sparse sandy hair. No beauty, but with clear bright eyes and a lively mouth. He wore always rough country clothes, his legs were a little bowed, and did he wear a straw in his mouth would have been the perfect hostler. Nevertheless, he was beyond mistake or question a gentleman. His rather sharp voice that would crack in moments of excitement, his eyes, the way that he carried his head, and the fine aristocratic shape of his hands told you that. He was, in fact, of a very good family, the Rackstraws of Rackstraw Manor in Rutlandshire, and his elder brother was Sir Wilfred Rackstraw, 14 Mount Street, London, and some minor official in the Foreign Office. He told you these things if you asked him, said the Rackstraws were poorer than mice, and that he had also a brother a smuggling trader on the Whitehaven coast. Whether this last were so no one ever knew. But he certainly had some very odd friends and some very mixed tastes. There was not a farmer, hostler, stableman, huntsman, poacher in the district he didn't know. But he was on social terms too with the County families – the Osmastons, the Derricks, the Tennants. He was an intimate friend of old Miss Pennyfeather, and they cracked jokes continually: he often took a dish of tea with Mr Southey and, they said, knew as much about his library as he did himself. There was not a cock fight, a football match, a boxing match that he did not attend, and yet he gave himself nobly to the two boys, John and Adam. His passion was for Homer, and Adam owed that at least – that the *Iliad* and the *Odyssey* were to be ever friendly companions to him because of Roger Rackstraw. He had a pretty sense too of the virtues of Virgil, Horace, Thucydides and the Greek dramatists, and could make them live under his fingers. He had a poor opinion of contemporary English Letters, although he said a good word for the *Waverley* romances and told everyone that there was a young poet, John Keats, who would be remembered. For Mr Wordsworth he had more praise than was locally considered reasonable, but when alone with a friend confessed that he thought Southey's poetry 'fustian'.

However, his great and abiding passion was for this country in which he lived, and it was here that he and Adam had their great meeting-place. He was not a local bumpkin, of course, and his principal charm for Jennifer was that he seemed to have ever at his fingers' ends all the London gossip. He was always very courteous and tender to Jennifer, as though he felt that she needed protection and guarding. It might be too that she appealed to him, for, over fifty though she was, she was yet beautiful in a sort of tumbling-to-pieces, letting-herself-go fashion, and he would say, to the end of his days, that he never anywhere else saw dark hair and fair complexion to match Jennifer Herries'.

He would sit in the parlour and tell her things, how Brougham after the Queen's death, defending his not going with the body to Brunswick, had said: 'It was well known through the whole of the business he had never been much for the Queen' (and a dirty tyke Brougham was, said Mr Rackstraw); how Castlereagh's suicide was because of a pernicious blackmail that he had suffered under, how the King now is become an awful bore and talks about nothing but his old age, how Lady Holland persecuted her guests with her odious cats that were for ever scratching and clawing, how the King was seen somewhere walking with his arm round Canning's neck, how scarcely anyone went now to Lady Jersey's parties, and that the gambling saloon in St James' Street was the most splendid ever known and that young William Lennox and others were certainly being ruined there ...

These were Jennifer's happiest hours, when lazily sitting before the fire, warming her beautiful hands, she could, without

moving, transport herself into a world where indeed she did not
wish herself to be, but about whose movements she was never
weary of hearing.

Nevertheless, it was to Adam and Judith that Rackstraw was
closest. He seemed to understand Judith exactly, submitted to
her domination but treated her with a sort of quizzical honesty
that she found delightful.

It was Adam, perhaps, whom he really loved, although he
never showed him much liking, treated him often with roughness, lost his temper with him completely (and then he would
shout and swear like a trooper) and ordered him about when he
wished as though the boy were his slave. He understood, however, the child's passion for independence, and it was he who
persuaded Judith to buy him his pony, Benjamin, and never,
after one of the boy's disappearances, did he reproach or punish
him. It was the rule, as Adam well understood, that if he went off
alone he must be always back again by nightfall. He made, himself, many expeditions with the boy. These were the grandest
occasions of Adam's life. Rackstraw taught him to see the
country rightly. It was a country, he said, of *clouds* and *stones*.
Stone walls, grey clouds, stone-coloured seagulls on dark fields
like fragments of white stone, streaks of snow in winter thin cloth
of stone, and above these stony crags pinnacles of stone, needles
of stone, piercing a stony sky. He learnt to see a small imprisoned
valley, wind-swept, as a living thing subject to growth and decay
like himself. Through this vale twisted the mountain torrent,
fighting with stones, letting its life be dominated by these piling
stones that heaped themselves one on another, that fell in showers
down the hillside, that at length perhaps choke the life of the
stream and form a stony pathway that leads at last to new shapes
of grass and moss and fern. The clouds feeding the streams, the
streams fighting the stones, life moving ceaselessly from form to
form, from pattern to pattern.

He learnt that it was impossible to live in this country, loving
it, without having always in his heart the colour and shape of
clouds. When, later, the drive of his life carried him to the South,
he brought the clouds with him: he was never again to be rid of
them. He knew all their patterns, forms and vagaries. He knew
the clouds that flew in flags and pinions of flame and smoke over
the brow of the hill, driven forward as though by gigantic
bellows, he knew the moth-coloured clouds that with soft per-
sistence gathered like great boneless birds around the peak of a

hill, he knew the clouds of rose and silver that lay in little companies against a sky of jade in winter above sun-drenched snow, he knew the fierce arrogant clouds of jet and indigo that leapt upon a pale sky and swallowed it, he knew the gay troops of cloud that danced and quivered around the sun, he knew the shining clouds that the moon, orange-ringed, gathered round her on a frosty night when the hoar glittered on the grass and the only sound under the black trees was the chatter of the running streams. The clouds were of themselves reason enough why this country was first for him in the world.

But Rackstraw taught him also detail and reality. He learnt to know ash and oak, birch and thorn, holly and hazel. He knew about the cutting of the coppice woods for firewood and for 'spills' and how it was 'coaled', and what was a 'stander' and what a 'yarding', and from what woods houses of 'crucks' were made, and what 'dotard' oaks were. He learnt to know every variety of rain, from the stampede when it comes down like animals rushing a thicket to the murmur and whisper of a hesitating shower. He knew how sudden gusts would come as though someone threw a bucket of water at you, and again how it would be as though you walked down a staircase of rain, catching your breath for a pause, slowing up on the step's very edge while the water trickled under you.

During those five years he went on many rides with Rackstraw, and sometimes they would be away two nights, sometimes three, and once and again a whole week, he on Benjamin, and Rackstraw on his bony ugly horse Satan. He remembered all that he saw. He had in his heart and brain for evermore the Brathay, set in its circumference of meadowland, the view like a crumpled handkerchief from Pike o' Stickle, the cold, haunting loneliness of Black Sail, the glassy perfection of Small Water, the fall of screes from Melbreak, the sudden flight of birds so that the sky seemed darkened at Ravenglass, the long stretch of shore pale and lucent towards Whitehaven, the evil cleft of Simon Nick whose ghost seemed ever to be watching from the thin darkness, the great view from Yewdale to the Old Man, the Roman Fort on Hard Knott, the grand silence of Waswater where the Screes, the proudest of all the hills, plunge scornfully into unknown depths – these and hundreds more were to be his companions for ever.

He knew the dalesmen, their wives, sons, daughters, dogs, horses and cows; he knew the Herdwick sheep as though he were one of them. He knew the birds, the golden eagles, soon to be gone for ever, the osprey, the dull heavy kite, the redshanks and larks, the fishing cormorant. He felt like his own the flight of the peregrine, the black-and-white wheat-ear, and the mocking little cry of the sandpiper as it flitted in front of him along the Lake's edge. The kingfisher and the moorhen spoke to him, one of rushing water, the other of pools so still that the reflection of a cloud on their surface was like a whisper.

And all the singers – the willow-wren, the chiff-chaff, the blackcap, the whitethroat, the tree-pipit – he mocked and imitated and whistled to.

From all this life there came three lives – one, the life of the outer country; two, the life of his home, the building of Fell House, the village and the moor; three, the personal life with the human beings around him; and from all the events that occurred to him during those five years three were of particular importance. One, the affair at Watendlath, was the matter of a moment – and it was thus.

In all these five years he went over only on three occasions to Watendlath. This abstention was proof of itself of his love for his mother; it was because of her that he did not go more often, for he loved Watendlath more than any other place on earth. Judith never once told him that she did not wish him to go, but he knew from the first that it made her unhappy. Why, he wondered, would she herself never go? She cared for Charlie Watson and the Ritsons and the Perrys. Once, looking out of window and he standing at her side, after some trouble that she had had with Mrs Quinney, she burst out: 'Why am I tied here? I am missing my whole life!' and he knew that she was thinking of Watendlath. She never mentioned the place. Once or twice Charlie Watson rode over to Uldale, but his visits were very brief. He seemed constrained, and even to Adam he was sharp and curt.

It was on the third occasion – a week after Adam's ninth birthday – that the strange thing happened. It was early autumn, the hills were on fire with colour above the grey stone, the dead bracken flamed, and the Tarn, rocked by a little wind, was scattered with tiny feathery waves. Adam and Mr Rackstraw had ridden over and stayed the night with the Ritsons. Charlie Watson never appeared, although the Ritsons said that they had told him that Adam was coming. So it was an unsatisfactory visit, for without Watson Watendlath was only half alive. Moreover, even the Ritsons seemed to be not quite so friendly as they had been. Adam, who was quick for a little boy, fancied that they

were offended because his mother had not been to see them, and
in arms as he always was if he thought that his mother was
attacked, he attempted some sort of defence, but only made
things the worse, for Alice Perry smiled and said she knew that
Mrs Paris was busy, she had heard that she had much to do: they
all called her 'Madame' now, she had heard, a kind of foreign
way of calling a person, and, of course, were she busy they could
not expect her to come all the way to Watendlath, and so on, and
so on. Everyone began to speak of other things.

This made Adam angry and he went down, a rather desolate
little figure, in the late afternoon to the Tarn alone. The wind
had died; mists were rising. The sky that had been cloudless all
day was frosty white, and the amber of the hills was fading into
dun. Behind him sheep moved, like a concrete part of the dusk,
up the slope. He was cold, lonely and disturbed by a sense of
having betrayed his mother in coming here. He wanted to go
home: he would rather not stay the night in the farm. The Perry
boys, although they had known him since he was a baby, were
stiff with him. And where was Charlie Watson? Why had he not
ridden over? He wanted to go home.

Standing there, looking at the Tarn, he had the sense for the
first time (it was to return to him very often) of being outside
himself. He could see every movement that he made and he felt
that, if that boy threw himself into the Tarn and disappeared,
Adam Paris would still be there, nor would he feel any loss. It
went so far that he pinched his arm to see whether he were real.
Then he threw stones into the Tarn. The noise of the splash
echoed in his ears, but even that was unreal – as though someone
else, far from himself and having no relation to himself, had
thrown the stones.

It was then that directly in front of him, rising from the Tarn,
he saw a figure on a white horse. While he looked the figure grew
clearer – a man in odd clothes, a black hat, and under the hat a
wig. He wore a long, heavy, purple riding-coat, and down one
spare thin cheek ran a deep scar. This man was quite clear to him
in every detail to the silver buttons on his coat. He was not
looking at Adam but away, gravely, up into the hills. Neither
horse nor rider made any movement. They were like coloured
shapes painted on the mist. Then they vanished. That was his
grandfather, who had lived, years ago, below the hills at Rosthwaite. He had talked of him to his mother so often and had asked
so many questions about him that he knew exactly how he would

look, and in later days he might realize that it was his own imagination, at that moment of loneliness and longing for his
mother, that had conjured up the figure.

But now he was only a small boy who believed in ghosts and
pixies, warlocks and witches. So for once in his life he took to his
heels and ran and ran until he arrived breathless in the warm and
lighted kitchen.

He never told anyone of what he thought he had seen, but that
night in bed, listening to the snores of Mr Rackstraw, he was
comforted as though he had made a new friend.

The second affair concerned John, and this was one of the most
dreadful half-hours of Adam's life, dreadful because he was not
at this time old enough to meet the emotion that he encountered.
When mature things break in upon childhood a picture is
broken, a view destroyed; the picture and view never quite
return.

Adam was nearly ten when this thing happened, and John
seventeen and a half.

Their friendship had by now grown so close that they were
more than brothers. They had the intimacy with that edge of
strangeness and interest belonging to a friendship that has no
blood relationship.

John had caught and held Adam in the only way that he could
catch and hold him – by demanding his protection. He did not
consciously demand it: this had grown out of Adam's fearless-
ness and John's sensitiveness. John was handsome beyond all
ordinary standards; he was the best-looking young fellow, it was
generally admitted, in the County. He was tall, slender, fair, with
a straight carriage and an air of such breeding that when he
moved both men and women unconsciously watched him, feeling
perhaps that he was of a different strain from the rest of mankind.

When he came into a place he walked haughtily and seemed
proud, his head erect, his mouth sternly set, but at once, when he
was in contact with another human being, his smile shone out,
lighting up his face. His proud carriage sprang from an intolerable shyness that he could never overcome. It was agony to him
to meet new people or anyone of whose kindliness he was not
sure. At any unfriendliness he flung on instantly an armour of
reserve. With the men and women about the place he was in
perfect relations; they all loved him and would do anything for

him. His beauty seemed to them something rare and wonderful, and when they knew him also to be so gentle and kind they served him without further question. Nevertheless, he was no commander of men; any tale of distress touched him, however false it might be. He believed what he was told, and when he was deceived thought that it was some wrong in himself that had caused the deceit.

It was here that Adam, whom even when he was so young a child he trusted and loved as he trusted and loved none other, protected him. Adam was uncouth and rough beside him. He did not grow more handsome as he grew older. The darkness of his hair, the brown of his face and body, made him seem someone foreign and apart. He wore always the roughest country clothes. He spoke, when he did speak, with a slight Cumberland 'burr', he was often silent when he ought to speak and would look at people with a sort of frown as though he were summing them up. His worst fault was exactly the opposite of John's, namely, that he suspected everyone until he had proved his case.

It became plain to him soon that John was his charge. In spite of the difference of their ages he was already wiser about the world than John and, because he was not sensitive and because hostility only made him hostile in return and because he was afraid of no one, he was a good bodyguard.

Only one thing at this time came between the two of them. A chance meeting brought them into contact with Uhland, Walter's son. Adam had long ago decided that Walter Herries was his enemy and the enemy of all those whom he loved. He was not aware, during these years, of the developing battle between Walter Herries and his mother, but he did know that everything round Westaways was enemy country.

The queer thing was that Uhland, who was Adam's age, never missed an occasion of an encounter with Adam if one were possible. They met but seldom, in the Keswick street, once and again at the Hunt, at a sheep trial, at a running-match: once when Adam was fishing by himself beyond Crosthwaite Church, Uhland, unattended, came limping through the field. He stood looking at Adam, apparently afraid to speak. Adam would have had nothing to do with him, but the boy was lame, his face was pale, he seemed so sickly that it was a wonder he could move at all. So he spoke, and Uhland came and sat beside him. What followed was most uncomfortable, for Uhland sat there, staring out of large protruding eyes, and said nothing.

At last he felt in his jacket and offered Adam a top, a large one coloured green and crimson. Adam did not wish to take it, but Uhland clambered to his feet and went limping away across the field without another word ...

Now John had from the very first the strangest fear of Uhland. There was something about his deformity and sickliness that affected him as though the boy had a disease that he could convey to others. He saw him on the rarest occasions, but he was often conscious of him, would, in the middle of the night, think of that leg longer than the other, those protruding eyes, the little body that seemed to be bent by a head too big for it.

Once he burst out passionately to Adam and wished him to promise never to speak to Uhland again.

'But I don't speak to him,' said Adam, astonished.

'You meet him. He talked to you in Keswick a fortnight back.'

'He has a horse,' said Adam irrelevantly. 'It is called Caesar. It's coal black with a white star on its forehead.'

'I tell you,' John repeated, 'you are not to talk with him.'

'Why not?' asked Adam.

John could not say. The boy and his father hated them, would do them any harm ...

But Adam fell into one of his silences. John would not speak to him for days.

Then came this terrible distressing thing.

It came like a door banging on to a silent room. It was in the early summer. Adam had been riding, had shut Benjamin into his box, stroked his nose and talked some nonsense to him, then very happy, whistling out of tune, had wandered into the house. He had a room to himself now, one that he had chosen, an attic with a slanting roof and a fine view over the moor to the slopes of Skiddaw. He and Skiddaw were now on speaking terms, and there was nothing about Skiddaw that Adam didn't know – or so he thought.

He had but just sat down upon his bed and was thinking of the coach that had passed him with a fine tantivy and a grand cloud of dust from the horses' hoofs, thinking perhaps that he would like to see the world a bit, when the door opened and John came in. He stood without moving. He had been paying some visit and was dressed very smartly in a claret-coloured coat, the hips and chest padded, a white frill, his dark chestnut trousers strapped under his boots. Adam remembered then that, urged by Judith,

John had been to call on some people with a house on the border of Bassenthwaite Lake. They were called Sanderson and were new arrivals in the neighbourhood.

He stood there, his face pale, his lips quivering. He crossed to the bed, sat down by Adam, then to Adam's horror burst out crying, his head in his hands.

Adam put his arm around him and sat there, not knowing what to do or say. He had never seen John cry before, and that a man should shed tears seemed to him an awful thing.

'What is it? ... What's the matter, John?' he said at last, his voice a funny broken bass from his emotion. For a long while John, crying desperately, made no answer.

Adam stared out of the window at Skiddaw and watched birds flying slowly, dreamily, across the faint glassy sky.

'This is what it is ...' John caught Adam's hand. 'My mother—' He hesitated, then the words poured out of him. 'I had visited the Sandersons. Young Robert Sanderson was there. He is a friend of Cousin Walter's, and I could not abide him from the first. He was affronted by something I had said in the house about the Catholics in Ireland, that the Catholic laws were monstrous and that we should have shame for our treatment of Ireland ... He answered hotly, and when I left came out with me to my horse. He sneered at something I said. You know how it is – I hate a quarrel. I answered him gently, and then he said something about the fine man Cousin Walter was, and that by what he had heard Fell House here should be his. That was too much for me and I called Cousin Walter what he is – a damnable blackguard. Then Sanderson told me ... he said ... he said it was common knowledge that because my mother had been a man's mistress here and because my father had found them together, therefore my father had killed himself in London. Because my father had been a coward and allowed that man to come to this house, to sleep here ... he knew of it. The whole world knew ... I struck Sanderson in the face – and I rode away.'

Telling his story had calmed him. He caught his breath. His face now was as white as a peeled stick, his body trembled, but he wept no longer.

'Everyone knows – has known for years. Only I didn't know ...'

They were quiet for a long time. Adam's hand tightened on John's. He could not bear to feel John's body tremble. He longed to do anything for him, to rush out and trample on Sanderson, to burn Uncle Walter's house down, to ... Oh! He knew not what! But he could neither do anything nor say anything. He was not ignorant, young though he was. He knew – in a child's way – about men and women, without feeling that all those things, the making of love, the birth of children, were real in a real world. But he understood that this was a disgraceful and terrible thing. Nevertheless his own active feelings were those of rage against Sanderson and a passionate instinct to defend John.

He said at last in a husky voice:

'I expect he's a liar. They are all liars, friends of Uncle Walter's.'

'No – it's true ... I have known for a long while that mother was afraid, afraid of everything, of Cousin Walter and people in Keswick – and that my father had shot himself in London, but this ...'

Then he added, still shivering as though with an intense cold:

'I must fight Sanderson.'

'Yes, you must kill him, Adam answered eagerly. Here was something that he could do. 'Mr Rackstraw shall help us.'

'Cousin Walter put him on to this. I know he did. Everything we do, everywhere we go, Walter Herries is at our back. Oh, God, if I could do him an injury for all he's done to us! And now I know. I know why he has so much power over us, why my mother fears him as she does ... My father was a coward, my mother ...'

He stopped.

'Adam, you must speak of this to no one. We will settle Sanderson's affair ourselves. But that everyone should know, that they have known for years ...'

Adam said, nodding his head:

'If it's pistols, John, you can kill him. Mr Rackstraw says you're the best shot with a pistol for your age in Cumberland. We'll practise in the barn. We'll go now ...'

But nothing came of it then. They learnt that young Sanderson had gone South. He never answered John's letter, and later, joining his regiment, went abroad. The consequences were not so easily settled. After that summer afternoon nothing was the same again.

Adam's third affair concerned his mother.

As those years passed, Judith dominated Fell House and its neighbourhood ever more completely.

When Adam was eleven, in 1826, Judith was nearly fifty-two. Now fifty-two was considered in those days a great age for a woman. There were old women like Mrs Tennant of Ireby who were old women, sat in a chair and had the air of prophetesses. There were old women like Mrs Summerson in Keswick who played cards night and day but were nevertheless old women. There were old women like Mrs Clare of Portinscale who rode to hounds, cursed and swore, drank and gambled, chaffed with the stable-boys, but were still old women. Judith Paris was unique. After settling in command at Fell House she seemed with every month to grow younger. Her body, taut, neat, active, appeared not to know fatigue. Her hair, once so lovely an auburn, was now grey, her face, always pale in colour (and she would use no paint as most of the older women did), knew no wrinkle. She rode a horse like a commander. She was austere and direct when about her business, but she could behave suddenly like a girl. She went to dances, card-parties, hunts, balls in Keswick. She was known everywhere as 'Madame,' famous for her kindness, her sharp and direct speech, her common sense. She had not changed in her impulsiveness, her attention to business, her loyalty, her childish pleasure in little things. Only those who knew her well were aware that something she had had was now, to all appearance, gone. It might be dead, it might be hidden. Miss Pennyfeather in Keswick knew, Jennifer unperceptively was aware ... Jennifer said that Judith was no longer romantic.

Another thing that everyone knew about her was that she was 'mad' about her boy. Of course the boy was illegitimate, although everyone could name his father, but his illegitimacy and the fact that Judith herself was the daughter of old 'Rogue' Herries (now a legend: they said that his ghost 'walked' in Borrowdale) and a gipsy, made the mother and son something apart. 'Madame' was becoming a legend like her father. Every kind of tale was told of her. When she came into a room people stared and whispered. But they invited her, they admired her; she was a 'character' and did the neighbourhood a sort of credit.

We are in part what our friends and neighbours make us and, unconsciously, Judith began at this time to respond to the demand for her to be 'queer'. Her dress was a little extravagant. Her skirts were very full in the Dutch fashion. She liked gay colours and was often seen in a shawl of red cashmere. She had hats of fine straw worn over a lace cap – far too young for another of her age, but in some way not ridiculous for her. Her turbans of figured gauze at an evening party were magnificent.

She already carried the cane of white ivory that was, later, to be so famous. People in Keswick said, 'Madame is coming,' and gathered at shop doors and windows to look.

She ruled everyone in Fell House save her son Adam. It was at the beginning of his twelfth year that she put her power over him to the test and failed. This occasion was one of the great crises that marked his boyhood.

No one knew with what passionate emotion she loved this child. Everything else that was dear to her she had surrendered – save her love of power and her love of son. As he grew her feeling for him developed into a mingling of love, admiration and exasperation. She had always wished for him to be independent and apart from other boys. His father, poor Warren, had had but too little character. Adam seemed to have no resemblance at all to his father; he was his mother and then himself as well. He reminded her continually of what she had been as a child, and it was a curious irony that she should so often feel the same bewilderment and irritation in dealing with him felt long ago by David and Sarah Herries about herself. She learnt, very soon in their relationship, that he hated any kind of demonstration. Did he love her or did he not? She knew that he did, and with all his heart, but any expression of affection silenced and removed him. But he *must* obey her. When she had surrendered her domination of his movements (no one knew what this cost her) she consoled herself with the right to order him in all other ways.

The exercise of power grows with what it feeds on. People succumbed to her so easily that she came to expect it as her right. Adam always obeyed her when he felt that her demand was just. She had one thing more to learn – that, if he thought her unjust, he was quite beyond her power.

The incident had minute beginnings. One fine morning she had driven with Adam in the chaise to Keswick. Mr Carrick the haberdasher came on to the pavement to receive her orders, and after he was gone, before she could move forward, tiresome old Major Bellenden must limp forward and, his wide-brimmed hat gallantly in hand (although the day was cold), commence one of his interminable conversations. Major Bellenden, who lived alone on the road to Threlkeld, was a purple-faced old bachelor, tyrannized over by a peevish manservant. He had served abroad, knew the East, had had an amusing adventure or two, but all these were swallowed up by the fact that he had been actually present at the famous performance on February 13th, 1820, at

the Paris Opera of *Le Carnaval de Venise* when the Duc de Berry
had been assassinated. Nay, more, he had by a lucky chance left
the Opera for a moment and returned at the very instant when
Louvel planted his dagger 'up to the hilt', had heard the Duke
cry 'What a ruffian!' and then 'I have been murdered!' Later, he
had listened to the screams of pain that came from the poor Duke
as Dupuytren probed the wound, had seen Decazes enter to
examine the murderer, and best of all had even been witness of
Louis XVIII himself as, tossed about between the banisters of the
stairs and the wall, they had tried to push his chair that he might
get to the Duke. He told over and over again how the Duke,
dying, raised himself and said: 'Forgive me, dear Uncle, forgive
me'; and Louis answered: 'There is no hurry, dear Nephew. We
will talk later about this.' And then how, at the very last,
when the Duchess was filling the room with her lamentations, the
Duke said: 'My dearest, control yourself for the sake of our
child,' and so gave France the first news that there would be an
heir to the Bourbons . . .

So often had the Major told this very long story with all the
details of it exactly repeated, that the Duc de Berry's as-
sassination seemed to many persons to have occurred in Keswick.
However, 'The Old Bore and his Murder' was the general summary of Major Bellenden.

It chanced that on this very morning the Major mentioned his
Duke. Some remark of Judith's about the weather reminded him.
'It was weather like this . . . that horrid affair of the Duc de
Berry, of which I expect I have told you . . .', and looking up
caught young Adam smiling at him in a very irritating manner.
Adam had heard his mother in her lighter moments, imitating
the Major: 'I had my foot on the stair . . . Louvel must have
brushed my arm . . .' and giving then the very half-choked, half-
important guffaw that was the Major's.

Adam smiled, and the Major saw him smiling. His mother also
saw him. The Major was deeply hurt and went limping away.

During the drive homewards Judith scolded him, speaking of
reverence to age, of impertinence and other kindred matters.

'But, Mama, you yourself laughed . . .'

'Not to his face. That is bad manners.'

'I am sorry, Mama. Look, there is Mr Southey with—'

'Now listen, Adam. You are to listen. You must apologize to
the Major.'

Adam sat grimly silent. Of all things in the world he hated

most to apologize. The matter might on an ordinary day have stopped there, but Judith had been irritated by a number of small things, by the failure of Miss Pritchett, the little dressmaker whom she patronized, to have a dress ready; by Mrs Quinney's cold; by the customary sluggishness of Jennifer.

So she pursued it.

'Promise me, then, that you will apologize.'

Adam said nothing. He sat there, his mouth pursed in an exasperating manner.

'Promise me that you will apologize.'

At last he murmured:

'It is unfair, Mama. You yourself laugh at him.'

'That is different. He was not present.'

Then again, as the chaise drew slowly up the hill to the village:

'Say that you will apologize.'

No answer.

'Well, then, I must punish you.'

Adam was enclosed in his attic for the rest of the day without food.

In the evening Judith came in to him, her head held high, her heart aching with love. She had been quite wretched all the afternoon. She had realized with a pain that was deeper than any emotion felt by her for many days that without Adam there was nothing. All this business of defying Walter, of managing the house, the servants, Jennifer, of corresponding with various Herries all over the country, of visiting and dining and being sociable – it was all nothing, nothing at all without Adam. She had loved her husband, she loved Adam. There was nothing else. And with a sudden shudder, as though a hateful wrinkled hag in a bonnet had bowed to her in the glass, she saw her old age, of which until now she had scarcely thought – her old age, empty, ugly and cruel.

She came into his room and found him standing looking out of the window, just as, centuries ago, she had stood at her window when David was to beat her. He did not turn. She put her hand on his shoulder. She was, not by much, taller than he, but when he turned her heart leapt, for he was so lovely to her, so utterly her own, so proud and so strong, just as she would have him be.

But he was relentless – and he was utterly beyond her reach. She said something. She asked him to come downstairs. No, he would not come down. Did he not see that he was wrong, that he had hurt the feelings of an old man, that it was proper to offer an apology when one had shown bad manners?

'I did not show bad manners,' Adam said, not looking at her.

She did not know it, but he himself was terrified – terrified at this resentment that he felt to her, his rebellion as though he were fighting for something very serious and important. He had never felt like this to her before. He almost hated her.

'Well, then, you will see it later on. You will see that I am right. Come down now and we will not speak of it.'

But it could not be settled in that way. His dreadful silence which he himself hated dominated him. She put her arm around his neck.

'Come, Adam.'

He dragged himself away from her and went back to the window, looking out. That infuriated her and she surrendered to one of her old tempests of passion. She stormed and stamped her feet. He was ungrateful, hard, unloving, disobedient. She had done everything for him, and thus he repaid her. Well, he should see. She was not to be insulted by a child. He should be beaten. Maybe that would teach him . . .

'Beat me,' he said, turning round upon her.

They looked at one another, each with hatred. The look was so terrible, so new, so far from anything that either of them had thought possible, that in another moment they would have been in one another's arms.

But she did nothing, said nothing, and after a moment left the room.

When she had gone he sat, swinging his legs, the unhappiest boy in the United Kingdom.

THE SUMMER FAIR

THE scarlet cloak of Oberon cast hastily on the daisied sward of the meadow, the laughter of the fairies as they fled towards the wood, the young men as they waited by the church gate, straining forward, listening for the word to go, the strange orange turban of Miss Pennyfeather, the breaking lights of violet and crimson as the fireworks burst above the Lake, the clown standing on his head in the market-place, his calves brown as berries against the sunlight, the line of chaises, barouches, waggons, the gauze and linen of the coloured dresses shining as the ladies leant forward from their carriages to watch the runners pass, the roseate haze on Skiddaw as the reflection of the setting sun threw great lines of colour across the crowded meadow, the peal of the bells from Crosthwaite Church, the gipsies with gaudy rings, crimson kerchiefs, white teeth flashing as they told fortunes in their encampment below the wood, Titania tearing her frail petticoat as she climbed the cart to ride through the town, the riot of men and women after dusk under the stars when a kind of madness seized the place, sunlight, bells, babel of voices, scents of flowers, neighing of horses, the plashing of oars upon the water, the stars and the flare of torches – for days and months and years the smoking shadow of this life was to hang about Keswick.

It was in August of 1827 that the famous Summer Fair came, blazed, vanished. For years afterwards it was remembered; for years now it has been as though it never was. And yet the town had known nothing like it before unless it were the famous Chinese Fair of nearly a century earlier. There is no record of it. Search contemporary journals and you will find nothing. For it came, it went, as many of the finest things in life come and go, by accident; it is only a background to the history of certain private lives; a handkerchief was dropped, a horse stumbled, a word was spoken. In a week the meadow was itself again, the waters of the Lake were calm, the gipsies were in Carlisle, the booths were piled boards, the bell-ringers were practising for another ceremony, the Strolling Players were drinking in a Kendal inn.

Nevertheless, there was never anything like it again. Chance, Mrs Bonaventure, sunshine, the accidental passing of the gipsies and the Players, stars and a full moon made this thing.

Mrs Bonaventure had come to Keswick six months before. She was a large stout lady with a red face, a roaring voice, and a wealthy husband almost as large as herself. They were a jolly pair, vulgar, if you like, with their loud voices and carelessness of social divisions, but it was known that she was the daughter of a Lancashire baronet, so, as Mrs Osmaston said, 'You can be sure she can speak quietly when she wishes,' and they were generous, crazy for parties and picnics and dances, and thought there was no place in the world like Keswick . . .

It was she who first had the notion of a Fête. It was in some way to be connected with the hand-loom weaving, and in some way with the birth of a baby boy to her sister who lived in Rutlandshire, and in some way with the Duke of Wellington, and in some way with a prize that Mr Bonaventure was giving for a race for young men under twenty-five, a race from Crosthwaite Church to the Druids' Circle.

In any case, there must be a Fête.

There should be booths along Main Street with gingerbread and apples and toffee. There should be dancing in the moonlight. There should be no nasty sports like bull-baiting or cock-fighting. There should be decorated boats on the Lake, and fireworks. She did not know that some Strolling Players chanced to be performing in Penrith. She did not know about the gipsies. All these delights were added unto her.

Suppose that old Herries, remembering as he must that Chinese Fair, when in an eating booth he had sold his lady for a few pieces of silver, were present, perched cross-legged on a chimney, standing upright against a tree top, what would he think of it all? A hundred years gone (but time is of course nothing to him now), and yet here was his daughter, like a little general, marshalling her family forces, and here his great-grandson Walter commanding *his* battalions, and behind them, around them, all the lively consequences, male and female, of that wild turbulent life by which *he* had once been surrounded! Yes, wild and turbulent that Chinese Fair had been, civilized and gentle *this* Fair must seem to him – but the same battle was joined now as then, and so will be, for ever and ever, change the background as you may, for ever and ever, amen!

As his long sardonic person wanders now skywards, now mingling unseen with the crowd, now peering sardonically from behind the chimneypot, he watches that same daughter with tenderness maybe, and young John and Adam and Elizabeth with concern, and great-grandson Walter with humorous sarcasm, watches and grimly smiles and vanishes into a star, wondering why they should all be so serious over a matter so brief and trivial.

For the rest, how are they, in reminiscence, to break that confusing fantastic day into some sort of shape and order: morning, afternoon, evening and the moonlight night? – or, better than that, they divide it by event – the boats on the Lake, the race through the town, the *Midsummer Night's Dream*, the dancing on the meadow – four cantos of a happy poem.

THE BOATS ON THE LAKE

By eight of the morning the booths were lining Main Street, the
children were dancing like mad things down the road, the sun
was blazing (for they had all the luck that day) and boats were
putting out from the Islands, from Manesty, from Lodore, from
Grange. By ten o'clock the carriages were rolling up, from Penrith and Ullswater and Newlands and Bassenthwaite, from
Carlisle even, from Grasmere and Rydal, from Shap
and Hawkshead. Very early in the morning for some of them the
horses must have been led from their stables and the coaches
loaded. Many came in pillion-riding as for hundreds of years
they had done, while the grander farmers were proud in the
'shandy-carts'. Keswick, although Crosthwaite Church had not
yet begun its peal, was ringing with bells, for teams of pack-
horses, used for the carrying of pieces from the hand-loom weaving, came jingling in. Many of the women who were spreading
their apples, nuts, cakes and bottles of herb beer on the trestles
had been many a time to Hell Gill Bridge for the Brough Hill
Fair, and with that same jingling of bells came the scents and
sounds from Shaw Paddock and Aisgill and the old Thrang
Bridge in Mallerstang.

But it was down by the Lake that the day was to begin. The
sun lay on the water like a caressing hand, and the hills, from
Walla Crag, from the Borrowdale peaks, from Cat Bells and
Robinson, reflected their colour and proud forms as though they
had another life beneath their glassy waters.

Mrs Bonaventure, attended by husband and friends, was soon
seated like a queen on the commanding perch of Friar's Crag.
She loved fine colours. She wore a hat as broad nearly as her
shoulders, and from it waved four large ostrich feathers. Her
dress, magnificently full, was a brilliant orange.

Very soon the borders of the Lake were thronged with figures,
and the water whispered with the soft splash of oars. Across the
meadows and trees suddenly broke out the bells from Crosthwaite, and from the landing-stage the blast of the Town Band. A
gun was fired from the Island. The Fête was begun.

It was just before midday, when every eye was straining to see
the first boat round the corner of the Island, that the party from
Westaways arrived. Walter himself drove his coach from the
house to the end of the Lake Road, and as his four horses galloped up Main Street everyone cheered and the little boys turned

cartwheels and the pigeons flew in exulting circles above their heads.

Walter was elegant indeed as he flourished his whip decorated with coloured streamers, his many-caped riding-coat of green high above his thick neck, his chest thrust out, his head up as though to say: 'You may claim this or that for your glory today, but here is the true centre of the affair!' He had in the coach with him his wife, his children and his relations. It was a piece of fortune that these relations were present to witness his splendour, for it was only chance that the young sons of Durward Herries were passing through from Edinburgh and that James Herries (at length, after many years of weary waiting, succeeding to his old father's baronetcy) had come over from York.

But there they were: the two boys with two Oxford under-graduate friends from a house near Carlisle, and Sir James Herries, Bart., puffed out with solemn pride and complacent satisfaction. Agnes was there too, and also Uhland and Elizabeth.

After leaving the coach they walked, a cluster of splendour, to the Lake's edge.

No one could be more genial with all the world than Walter when things went as they ought to. He had left his riding-coat in Posset's care, for the day would be hot, and now at the age of thirty-five his great frame was beginning to yield at last to the stoutness that it had so long resisted. His high hat with the broad brim, rough in texture, was a dark wine-colour; his claret-coloured coat, the tails sewn on separately that it might fit his sides the better, followed the lines of his body exactly. His neck-cloth was shaped at the sides and stiffened with pig's bristles, rising to a kind of arch at the cheeks, and at its centre was the accustomed jewelled pin. He wore two waistcoats, one of dark purple, the other dark grey; his trousers, tight at the knees, widening downwards, were fawn. This must have been a warm costume for the middle of summer, but the stuff was all of a light material, and it was only at the neck as the day advanced that he was uncomfortable – which may possibly have accounted for his excitement at the end of the day: by such slender threads do human actions hang!

With his clothes, his bulk, his carriage, his merry arrogance, his vitality and *bonhomie*, he was by far the most remarkable figure on that day. Men said afterwards that to them this appeared the turning-point of his life – his last public appearance before the beginning of the Fortress!

He stationed himself with his wife, children and friends – a kind of resplendent patriarch – on a little green mound whence he could watch, above the vulgar crowd, the procession of the boats.

Scarcely, however, had the first two boats rounded the corner of the Island before the party from Fell House arrived – 'Madame', Mrs Jennifer Herries, Adam, John and Dorothy, with Mr Rackstraw in the background.

They had come almost to the water-edge before they realized that Walter Herries and his company were stationed above them. The people of Keswick could not be ignorant of the family warfare, had indeed for many years now been aware of it. The most fantastic stories were abroad: that Walter Herries had put poisoned wine in the Fell House cellar, that he had hired ruffians from Whitehaven to kidnap young John, that 'Madame' herself in the dead of night had climbed in at a Westaways window armed with a carving-knife – no tale was too absurd. Even though the procession of boats had begun, everyone watched to see what 'Madame' would do. 'But 'Madame', after a moment's glance, did nothing at all. Her Leghorn hat, trimmed with dahlias and ears of corn, her muslin dress of lilac, should have seemed ridiculous in a woman of her years. But she was not ridiculous, rather wonderfully imposing, her little figure neat and strong, her hand resting on her ivory cane, her head raised as though she ruled the world. Jennifer Herries, in a white muslin, towered above her, but was less impressive. Everyone said how handsome John Herries was, that Dorothy Herries had a fresh complexion, and that Madame's boy looked very French – the same comments were always made.

If Walter had noticed Judith, he gave no sign of it. So there they all were to watch the procession. Round the bend came the boats, the first four with twelve oars apiece. They were all decorated with flowers, and in three of the boats girls in white sang to the accompaniment of harps. The oarsmen were in white with crimson sashes at the waist. The sixth boat was a barge, and in it seated on a throne was the Guardian of the Lake. He was a stout old gentleman (Mr Barleycorn the hosier, in fact) with neck bare, garlanded, his fat legs bare to above the knees, and he carried a trident, thereby causing many of the spectators to suppose him Neptune.

In the boat that followed him was enthroned the Queen of the Lake with attendant maidens. This, as everyone knew, was Mrs

Armstrong who kept the sweet-shop just below Greta Hall. She was a commanding woman, full-breasted, and even on quite ordinary occasions, when selling a stick of liquorice to a small boy, stiff with dignity. It was because of her dignity that she had been chosen for this office.

In the boats that followed some licence of costume had been permitted: there were sailors, pirates, clowns, village maidens and Columbines. At the last there were small children carrying bouquets of flowers and watching with uneasy glances lest at any moment they should be precipitated into the water.

Oh, but it was a *grand* procession. The sun gave them his glory, the mountains wished them well, the church bells rang and the Town Band blared, the voices sang, and through it all the plash, plash of the oars gave rhythm and movement to the pattern of flowers and water and shadowed reflection.

They swept in a great circle, then drew up in line before the shore. The Guardian of the Lake rose a little unsteadily in his throne and delivered an address, not a single word of which could be heard by anyone. Then planks were thrown from boat to boat, and the goddess (Mrs Armstrong), 'every movement a symphony,' walked most majestically if uncertainly to the land, followed by her maidens, then by the little children, and last by the shouting rabble of sailors, clowns and Columbines.

Everyone now was shouting, everyone was singing; everyone rushed in unison together up to the field behind, where Mrs Bonaventure was to receive the King and Queen.

'Very pretty,' said Judith. 'Very pretty indeed.'

'Very handsome,' said Walter Herries, coming from his green mound. He took off his wine-coloured hat and bowed.

'Good day, Walter,' said Judith, looking him steadily in the face.

He smiled and seemed a boy of eighteen.

'I hope you are well,' he said.

'Never felt better,' answered Judith.

'We have a fine day.'

'An excellent day.'

Sir James bowed. Judith inclined her head.

Walter's party moved on.

Young Garth Herries asked a question.

'That, my boy,' answered Walter, 'is a relation of yours – and the most remarkable woman in England.'

THE RACE THROUGH THE TOWN

As everyone knows, the men and women of the North Country have never believed in the display of their emotions unless there is good ground for it. They prefer to wait and see what is really occurring before they venture an opinion. When they say a thing they mean it, but they mean a great many things that they never say.

The more extraordinary, then, was the outburst of singing and joy as the flowery boats circled the shore. It was a spontaneous cry as though some especial genial deity were abroad that day who, wishing for a song and laughter, saw that it was so. (In parenthesis: there had been up to this midday very little drinking. That came after.)

Adam found himself with his mother, Dorothy and John perched on a mound outside the churchyard wall, waiting with a great crowd of other spectators for the race to begin. He was, if he had cared to think of it, possibly the happiest boy in England that day. This was what he loved – the sun, the crowds, his own familiar country, every kind of sport and, as instinctively he knew, his mother as happy as he was.

In spite of the difference in their ages, mother and son were just now children together. This too was what Judith loved. She had a child's passion for small things, she adored to see other people happy. Adam's hand was in hers, and she had enjoyed her moment's challenge with Walter. There was no sign anywhere of the Westaways party, and she was quite certainly just then monarch of all she surveyed. Because she was so small of stature she stood once and again on tiptoe so that she might miss nothing. Nearly everyone around her knew who she was, and if anyone didn't he was certain to inquire; you couldn't catch a glimpse of her and not be conscious of her personality. But they were all proud of her, although they didn't quite know why. Farmers and their wives, townsmen and statesmen and better-class smiled, nodded, said it was a fine day, and she smiled and nodded back at all of them.

Adam, as was customary with him, said little but noticed everything. Dorothy stayed close beside her mother. At that time young ladies stayed as close to their mothers as though they were glued to them lest something evil should occur to them. John, very handsome in his plum-coloured coat, was apart, as he so often seemed to be. He was enjoying himself, but quietly and with that slight nervous social tremor that never quite left him when he went abroad. He did not know that within half an hour the greatest event of his life was to occur.

Across the road were lined the runners, twelve of them. They wore thin shirts open at the neck and short drawers. They were young, strong, tanned most of them by their outdoor labour. The two favourites were John Graham of Threlkeld, a tall, stringy young man with a head shaped like a hammer; and Will Leathwaite of Grange, who was short, thick and simple-eyed like a baby. Two of the men, Tom Trimble from St John's in the Vale and Harry Pender of Keswick, were famous runners but were older than the others. Trimble was a giant and as broad as he was tall. His legs and arms were hairy and his chest hirsute beneath his shirt. Good nature beamed from him and he looked round him smiling on everyone, although his brow was wrinkled with his serious purpose. He towered above the others. Pender was thin and cadaverous. He was an ill-tempered man and hated to be beaten. Mrs Pender in the hedge near at hand waited with anxiety, for she knew that were he defeated he would be none too pleasant a companion that evening. Trimble's mother, an old rosy-faced woman with a basket on her arm, kept calling out to her son to encourage him, and he would look across the road and smile at her and shout: 'Aye, mother, I'll do my best'.

Old Major Bellenden had been appointed starter, and very self-important he was. At the stroke of the half-hour from Crosthwaite Church clock he would shout 'One. Two. Three,' wave the handkerchief, and off they would go.

Adam's hopes were resting on Will Leathwaite, the thick simple-faced young man. He knew Will a little, for Will's father was a friend of Bennett the coachman, and Will would on occasion ride over from Grange or drive with a calf or farm produce. Will was Adam's kind of a man because he spoke little, was good-natured and afraid of nothing.

Then, just as all eyes were staring at the clock – it wanted but two minutes to the half-hour – up the road came Walter and his friends. They were hastening along, laughing and talking, making a great deal of display. Walter strode in front; his wife, children and the two young men followed. Room was made for them behind the Major, who began hurriedly explaining to Walter Herries a number of things, very important things, involved in his official business.

And it was then that something happened to John. He saw, as

though for the first time, Elizabeth, Walter's young daughter.

It was not, of course, for the first time. He had seen her on several other occasions, but he had never spoken to her, and never considered her at all. Now her loveliness rose at him from the crowd, the cries, the fields and road as Venus rises (constantly, we may believe) from the sea.

Elizabeth Herries was at this time only twelve, but she was tall for her years. Her fair colouring, her air of shyness, her slim erect body, above all her quietness, enchanted John. But he could give no reasons for that sudden thundering of his heart, that queer sense of being urged by some force around him, the very air about him, to run forward, to touch her hand ... He had seen her before and she had meant nothing to him. He could not understand it. It was an enchantment, a magical turning of flowers and hedge, dusty road and churchyard wall into shining glass, feathered clouds and raining gold. To run, to touch her hand, to speak ...

Then, as though he had wheeled upwards on a rising sphere from sunlit underworlds, he caught his own state again, heard the voices, saw the lilac stuff of Aunt Judith's dress. Walter Herries' daughter! He raised his head and stared at the sun.

The clock struck, the handkerchief was waved, they were off! And Adam was off too. A moment before he had been holding his mother's hand, as docile a boy as you could find. She thought that she had him for the rest of the day. But he was gone before he knew that he was going. As the white figures flashed like birds towards the town, he, driven by an impulse entirely irresistible, was after them. His mother, his amiable placidity, were lost as though they had never been. Others were running too; there were shouts and cries, and then suddenly he was aware of a known voice and there was Farmer Leathwaite, father of Will, trotting on his black horse beside him.

'Hup! Hup!' Farmer Leathwaite cried, and a moment later had Adam in his arms, then held tightly in front of him. That was a glorious ride! Leathwaite had completely lost his Cumbrian caution. As the horse trotted on, from Leathwaite's big stomach into the very pit of Adam's back come continual cries, adjurations, shouts and cheers: 'That's it, Will, my lad! Keep goin'! Keep goin'! Not so fast through t'town ... Gently, gently, my boy. You'll beat 'em! You'll beat lot of 'em ... Keep joggin' ... That's the fancy! Go to it, my lad! Fine lad! Fine lad! Gently, gently! ...'

And Adam was caught by the same fever, crying in a cracked

voice: 'Go it, Will! Keep going, Will! Hurray! ... You're winning! ...'

But the gallant horse was also stirred by the splendour of the
event and, do what the farmer would, refused to be stayed, so
before they knew it they had galloped up Main Street, horses
and shops, booths, women, dogs and shouting boys all left
behind.

'Woh! Wey! Wey! Woh!' cried Leathwaite, trying to look back
and see how his son was faring, but the mare with her ears pricked
back was racing all the other mares in the world, and before they
knew it they were out of the town and climbing the hill.

With shouts and curses the horse was at last pulled up. Small
groups were gathered about the path. Leathwaite mopped his
brow with a large yellow handkerchief.

'Do you think Will is going to win?' asked Adam breathlessly.

'Can't say ...' Leathwaite panted. 'He's in grand condition
, .. Hope so ... Hope so ... They'll be coming shortly ...'

It was very quiet here. After the dust, heat, shouts and cries it
was as though a heavy door had closed on the world. The trees
were darkly thick above their heads, the hills like blue clouds
beyond the town.

'How's he doing?' someone called from the waiting group.

'A' reet ... a' reet,' Leathwaite shouted back.

'I think he'll win, don't you?' Adam said.

Oh, but he *had* to win! The whole of the world's happiness
depended upon it. Then, after what had seemed an infinity of
time, the white figures appeared, two in front neck and neck,
then three, then at a considerable distance four or five. They were
going more slowly now; the hill was telling on them, and they
had the hardest task yet before them.

The first two were Trimble and a lad called Sawston.
Trimble's big body was almost done. The sweat poured down his
face, his breast was half bare, and on his face there was a set
mechanical smile. But Will was in the next three and running
strong ... With him were John Graham and Pender. Leathwaite
rose on his horse and waving his arms roared encouragement.
Adam shouted too.

'Go on, Will ... Go on, Will ... You'll win! You'll win!'

He was one with Will then. He and Will were running
together. He was inside Will, knew all his thoughts, his determination, his measuring of the hill beside him, his calculation of
his strength, knew the maddening irritation of Trimble's great

back in front of him, the temptation to make the spurt before it was time.

Now the horse went with them, and up the hill Adam and father and son charged together.

Trimble was giving way. Young Sawston passed him. Graham and Will drew level with him. Now Graham and Sawston were neck and neck. Here began the real steepness of the hill. The sun blazed down, the trees had drawn back as though refusing shelter.

'Now, Will, my lad! Now!' shouted his father.

'Now, Will, Now!' screamed Adam.

Sawston, Graham and Will were together. Graham, his head more than ever like a hammer, was running well. He was fresh as a skylark and breasted the hill as though he loved it. Sawston seemed on a sudden to lose heart; he looked back, missed his stride. Will passed him. At the hill-top where the path ran level to the Circle, Graham and Will were ahead.

Then, thrust on, it may be, by his father's fierce energy, Will Leathwaite made his spurt. He was ahead; Graham caught him. Graham was ahead. Will was level.

The Circle, calm, dignified, gazed indifferently out to Helvellyn and Scawfell and the Gavel. Will threw up his head; he seemed to catch all that country into his heart and, fiercely, like a swimmer fronting a terrific wave, flung himself across the string, the winner by a head.

Adam tumbled off the horse. Leathwaite, shouting his joy, caught Adam's small hand and wrung it as though he had never seen him before.

THE 'MIDSUMMER NIGHT'S DREAM'

The play was to begin at four o'clock. A platform had been erected on the rising shoulder of the fields where now St John's spire raises its finger for the friendly communion of the clustering hills. Up the slope climbed the meadows, striding to woods and sky. To the left the town, below them the Lake now richly dark under this sun with a sheen like the gloss on a blackberry; on benches raised roughly in four tiers sat the Quality. Beneath them and on either side of them crowded the citizens of England, for, although at this very moment of four o'clock of a fine afternoon in August 1827, all the Keswickians might be said to have been hovering before landing in a new world – a world of light, grime, noise, motion and confusion – yet the decencies were to be observed for a long time yet. Man still doffed his cap to Master, heads of families *were* heads of families, a mile was a mile when you had to walk it, and amusements were still simple enough and rare enough to be amusements. The little town, above whose roofs there hung a violet haze, shared in the happiness of its inhabitants as even to this day it yet does. From the days when the monks of Fountains were permitted a mill-dam on the Greta, through the stages of a weekly market in the thirteenth century over the old bridge at Portinscale, past the dark slumbering church of Crosthwaite, from the thirty citizens of Keswick in 1303, it had had its strong identity and kept it. Spirit and body were from the first lusty and self-confident. St Herbert saw to the first, the weekly market saw to the second. Through the wars of Scots and English, when Threlkeld and Millbeck must be fortified, when beacons flamed on Skiddaw, through the German invasion in Elizabeth's time until in middle seventeenth century the last smelting-house fell into ruin, comforted by the bleating of its sheep, the lowing of its cattle, resisting the constant rising of the waters that threatened to overwhelm it, Keswick stayed compact, pastoral and proud.

Then came Mr Gray riding in his post-chaise, then came the poets, and the world outside discovered it. Nevertheless, neither then nor now has that outside world even scratched the lustre of its peculiar beauty. Now it was not minerals that the invaders demanded, but scenery, so scenery Keswick would give them. Let them come and take it, for they could not diminish by a leaf, a flower or a swollen silver stream the soul of the place itself. At first wool, then shoes, then pencils, then Conventions – Keswick with an agreeable smile was generous, and could afford to be, because its soul was, and must be, intact.

But it liked best its own affairs, the fun that it had made itself for its own people, and so today it was especially happy and its chimneys purred with pleasure. There was an air of casual enjoyment about everything, and most especially about the play of Mr Shakespeare's. You would not perhaps have recognized it for Mr Shakespeare's play if you had seen it, for that was the time when actors did what they pleased to the plays that had the honour to offer them performances, and to none more than to Mr Shakespeare's.

These Players were here entirely by chance. They had been in the town from Penrith for several days, so that Mr William Greene – the chief of them – a gentleman as round as Falstaff and as jolly too, was by now almost a friend, and there was his wife, Mrs Greene, a tall lady with a deep bass voice, and his daughter Isabella, but these were known as friends always ready for a drink and none too certain about the paying for their charges.

Rain would have ruined everything, but rain for once was far, far away. It seemed, as you looked out across the purple Lake to that stainless sky, that it would never rain again.

The Quality, sitting most contently on the hard boards (for the Quality was easily pleased if there was any kind of fun toward), shared in the general cheer. Among the Keswickians there was considerable anxiety (although a happy anxiety), for a number of the Keswick children had been called in to be fairies, and no one knew how they would behave or what they would do – the children least of all – for there had been but one rehearsal, when the confusion had been so great that the final orders simply were 'to keep their eye on Titania and Oberon and follow them around'.

While they waited, the superior people held distinguished conversation together. There was not a great deal of room. Walter was pressed against James Herries, and his stout knees pushed into the thin backs of Misses Mary and Grace Pendexter, two maiden ladies who were ready to enjoy anything at any time and at any sacrifice. Evening after evening they would be out in their pattens, their old servant lighting them with a lantern, to play cards with Miss Pennyfeather or Major Bellenden, and now to have the handsome knees of the master of Westaways pressing their bones was a joy indeed. It happened, so close were they all together, that Westaways and Fell House were at last neighbours. It was as though the whole day had been working for this end, and, indeed, important consequences were to come of it. For John was near to Elizabeth Herries. When he saw how close he was to her, none of his customary shyness or caution could restrain him. In her primrose gown, sitting beside her mother, not speaking but her lips a little parted at her enjoyment of the scene, she seemed to him like a lovely bird from some Paradisal forest. It was arranged for him by some especial destiny that he should be near her. He knew that her mother, Mrs Herries, was a gentle lady who would wish him no harm. Her father, laughing and slapping his knee, was at a distance. Only one thing prevented him – Uhland, her brother, who sat staring in front of him, his brow wrinkled, his eyes like little stones, one knee – as always –

crooked over the other. As always, John was affected by a sort of cold nausea at his proximity, but today this new emotion of joy and happiness, as though like a great explorer, from the deck of his ship, over the trackless waste, he had seen the gold sands gleaming, was too strong for him to be checked.

If he moved a little from where he was sitting he would almost touch her. He rose up, stood back as though not to prevent the others' view, then raising his hat said:

'Good afternoon, Mrs Herries.'

She must have been greatly astonished that he should speak to her, but she, poor lady, bore no animosity to anyone in the world and was delighted at kindliness, so she smiled timidly and said:

'Good afternoon.' ('What a splendidly handsome boy,' she thought.)

John's eyes (he could not help himself) were fastened on Elizabeth, but he said:

'Yes, ma'am. We are fortunate in the weather.'

'It is indeed a splendid day,' Mrs Herries replied to him.

Then, boldly, he spoke to Elizabeth.

'I trust you can see well where you are sitting,' he said.

She looked up at him, and to her also he appeared as something new and wonderful. He was standing in the sunlight, very erect and tall, the sun shining on his hair. She wondered why she had never noticed before how beautiful he was. Although she was frightened of her father and had been forced all her life into the background, she was not nervous. She smiled.

'I can see most excellently, thank you.'

At her smile he could have gone on his knees and worshipped her.

'You will tell me if I am in your view,' he said, bowing. Then, just as he was moving away, he realized that two eyes were looking at him with a malignant force that seemed impossible for so small a boy. Elizabeth's brother's ... Something cold struck his heart.

The play had begun. From the first it was invalidated by the fact that Mr Greene, who was playing Bottom, wished to be in the forefront throughout, and that his wife, who was Titania, had the same desire.

So Theseus and his Court were soon bustled off the scene and the pairs of lovers were permitted to love and bicker only in brief moments while Bottom found his breath. Titania (very fine in shining ermine with a helmet – a perfect conception of Britannia) was meanwhile hovering with her attendant elves ('There's Lucy,' cried Mrs Bucket, 'her with the daisies.' 'That's our Liz – standing on one foot,' cried Mrs Ellis) near the platform and suddenly pushed forward and began, in her deep voice, to shout her lines.

'First, good Peter Quince, say what the play treats on,' shouted Mr Greene.

'What, jealous Oberon! Fairies, skip hence. I have forsworn his bed and company,' cried Mrs Greene.

For a moment it seemed that there would be trouble, but Bottom had his way, and Titania retired to sit on the grass near by and throw daisies at the children, for in spite of her size and voice she was a merry and kindly woman.

When, however, the time for the fairies was really come, they had their triumph. For one thing Oberon was a splendid young man, with a handsome red cloak and a noble pair of legs. Then the children, loving the sunshine and the freedom, exalted by the presence of parents and relations, behaved as fairies should, dancing everywhere, joining hands and singing, tumbling head over heels, running races, plucking at Oberon's cloak. The gaiety that had been in the air all day possessed the company and the audience together.

When Bottom became an ass and laid his great form on Titania's big lap everyone roared with applause, and the fairies pinched his legs, and Titania took off her helmet because it was so hot. There were fairies everywhere. When Theseus and his Court returned the sun was lower in the sky and long shadows lay across the grass. Some of the fairies, tired out, were sleeping, but behind Bottom and his companions, as they played their Play, the children danced and sang, Titania, carrying a baby in her arms, walked with half a dozen infants at her skirts (she had by now flung away most of her armour), and Bottom and Peter Quince, Theseus and Helena romped to the fiddle of an old man of the company who worked at his music in an ecstasy of enjoyment.

Puck came forward to speak his Epilogue and a sudden silence fell:

> If we shadows have offended,
> Think but this (and all is mended)
> That you have but slumber'd here
> While these visions did appear.

And this weak and idle theme,
No more yielding but a dream ...

The cheers and shouts echoed from Main Street to Cat Bells.
The gipsies under the wood heard it; an old man, driving his cart
home to Watendlath, heard it and in a piping voice began to
sing ...

THE DANCING ON THE MEADOW

The moon rose, triumphantly full, made of light and crystal,
lucent in a sky fiery with stars. The evening was so warm that
everyone brought food in baskets, in napkins and bags, and sat
about on the meadow waiting for the Town Band.

Judith, Jennifer and the children had planned to stay and see
the dancing and the fireworks, but now Jennifer wished to go
home. They had all been resting at Miss Pennyfeather's and had
started towards the Lake to see the fireworks when Jennifer
caught Judith's arm.

'I think I will go home, Judith.'

They were standing under the trees. Adam, John and Dorothy
had gone on to the margin of the Lake that they might watch the
trembling path of the moon on the water, and the boats like dark
fragments of cloud that floated into the light and out again.

'But why, Jennifer?' Judith asked. 'Are you unwell?'

'No,' said Jennifer. 'I have a foreboding.'

'A foreboding? Of what?'

'I cannot say ... Perhaps it is being so near to that wicked man
all day – the murderer of my husband.'

'Nonsense, Jennifer. You must not have these fancies, you
must not. Come. The fireworks will shortly commence.'

'No. I prefer to go home.'

'But we cannot find Bennett ... And I have no notion where
Mr Rackstraw has gone. Jennifer, dear ... Here is a seat. Rest
here for a moment.'

The two women sat down together. Judith took Jennifer's
hand, but the gaiety and happiness that had accompanied her all
day were gone. Once (what years ago it seemed!) in Paris she
had been with her friend Emma Furze, watching the dancing,
and suddenly, without warning, Warren Forster, the father of
Adam, who was shortly then to be born, appeared in front of her.
She remembered now the sharp sense that she had had of Fate
stepping up through the dark trees beside her. She had the same
sense now.

'What is it, Jennifer? ... It has been a most beautiful day. Everyone has been happy.'

'I cannot help it, Judith. I am growing an old woman now, but whenever I see that man I am afraid. He has been close to me all day – and the nearer he comes to me the greater terror I feel. And I am sure that one day he will build a house in Uldale and he will look into our windows. He will kill me; yes, he will kill me just as he murdered Francis. And then he will kill John and Dorothy.'

Judith started. Could Jennifer know of Walter's threat to build on High Ireby? She herself had never spoken of it, but someone else might have done. Walter had held his hand now for a long while; of late he had let them be except that there was a story of John's that he had looked out of window one night and seen Walter on his horse, motionless, staring at the house. But that may have been dream or fantasy. John had all the imagination of his father.

'No, no, Jennifer ... Listen – you must not think about Walter. He has forgotten us. He has not been near us for years. Really he has not. And I am looking after you. While I am there no harm can come to you.'

Judith felt as though she had a large overgrown child beside her. Jennifer was as usual untidy, her turban was a little askew. Her fine dress of white muslin that went wonderfully with her dark hair trailed at the skirt: her cashmere shawl was torn in one place. Through how many differing stages of relation she had been with Jennifer, Judith thought! From that first vision of her at Christabel's Ball in their youth when Jennifer, in her Medici dress, had been the loveliest creature in the world, through jealousy and anger, almost to hatred (she recalled vividly still that day at tea at Mrs Southey's), to this complete, kindly, but a little scornful domination!

'Come, Jennifer ... Do not go home ... It will make the children unhappy. They are having such a wonderful day. There will be the fireworks and then the dancing. It is so warm a night!'

Jennifer laid a trembling hand on Judith's.

'Judith, I know something dreadful will occur.'

'Nonsense. Nonsense ... Now this truly is nonsense. We must not spoil the children's amusement.' ('And my own amusement as well,' thought Judith. 'I have never enjoyed a day so much.')

But she had made this one appeal to Jennifer that must be successful. Selfish, apprehensive, sluggish though she was, she wished the children to be happy, and especially John, whom she adored.

So they went, arm-in-arm, to the Lakeside.

The fireworks were a great success, and when they had watched them they walked slowly up the hill to the meadow. Adam went with Judith. They were of a size now. Adam was as tall as his mother.

'Are you happy, Adam?'

'Yes, Mama.' He gave her arm a little squeeze. 'I *am* glad Will won the race.'

'Yes, so am I – but you should have told me that you were going . . . I had no notion where you were.'

'Yes, Mama . . . Can we go and see the gipsies?'

'Yes, if you stay beside me.'

When they came to the field the theatre was cleared away, and where the audience had sat the Town Band was. The great moon shone down on them all like a kindly benevolent hostess who had arranged the festivity and saw that it was good.

Young John had but one thought. His eyes roamed the scene. But poor John! He moved as we move in a nightmare seeking some person or place, but baffled at every moment by figures, mists and sudden catastrophes. The moonlight was now bright enough, the space wide enough for an army of young lovers, but fate played with him, catching him now here, now there, as though it were warning him that it would be better for him to ride home, find his bed and hide there. First he encountered one of the Miss Pendexters, who at once drew him into a babble of chatter: '. . . Well, now, that's a true saying about an ill wind, for only a moment ago I was asking your mother how you were finding it all. "John's enjoying himself, you may be sure," I said to her, "for this is just a night . . ." Oh, there's Major Bellenden. I was going to ask him . . . and a perfect little house my sister and I have moved into. We insist that you come to see us. Perfect situation, near the road so that there's always something passing, and dear Crosthwaite Church only half a mile . . . Yes, I was telling your mother – how lovely she is in the white muslin, to be sure – I was telling your mother that it will be no trouble of an evening to find our way to Miss Pennyfeather's for a game, for on a dark night Maria with a lantern is all we need, and often enough we can make up a table for ourselves. For our friends are so obliging – so very good . . .'

Escaping from this he ran into a confusion of happy life. So dry was the night that everyone sat on the grass, watching the dancing and exchanging all the gossip. The town, the countryside, all was represented. The music of the band came gently through the air.

And more turbulent every moment was the evening becoming, for there were rough fellows from Cockermouth and Whitehaven, there were the gipsies, and bottles were passing from hand to hand. The dancing was growing wilder. Stout wives picked up their skirts and romped. Old grandfathers with a 'tee-hee-hee' pinched the arms of young girls, babies cried, dogs barked, but the woods made a dark frontier, the sky a star-fretted canopy, the mountains kept guard.

Through this whirling, noisy scene John found his way, looking into every face, thinking that maybe her mother had taken her home, praying that that might not be.

Then, mounting the hill towards the gipsy encampment, he saw the whole party. They had found some trestle seats – Walter, James and the young men were exceedingly gay; Mrs Walter Herries and Elizabeth were a little apart, quietly watching. John waited, taking in with all his soul Elizabeth as she stood, a dark cloak now over her shoulders; the rest of the world, the dancers, the lighted fires, the stars that sparkled above the heavy wood, vanished. She was alone and in her silence and quiet a saint in a chapel secret and remote for his own single worship. He stayed there a long while. In his twenty years he had known no feeling like this, nothing that made him both so proud and so humble, so resolute and so brave, but so timid also with a shy foreboding.

She was a child, eight years younger than himself; she was the daughter of his greatest enemy. He was conscious then of Walter, who was being very merry and noisy, so that you could hear his laughter above all the rest. He was aware too of Uhland, who sat like a little ghost beside his father.

Without knowing it, he had moved nearer and then nearer again. On any other occasion nothing could have compelled him to approach those figures who stood to him for everything in life that he hated and feared the most.

He had come up behind them, and then, as though she had known, Elizabeth turned round to look at the downward slope of the hill and the light on the water. They were all absorbed in the dancing, and the two, as though in a trance, came together.

They had exchanged only two sentences of convention in all

their lives, but it seemed to her quite natural that he should say, looking at her but coming no closer:

'I have been searching for you everywhere.'

'Oh!' she said with a little cry of warning, looking back.

'Yes, I know . . . But I must see you again. I must, I must.'

'One day – yes . . . I would like it—'

'Where?' He came nearer until he almost touched her.

She shook her head.

'We must not—'

'Listen,' he said quickly. 'I will write. Our coachman will find a way to give it you—'

She stared at him as though she must see him so intensely that she would remember afterwards all his features. She nodded as though they had made a compact, then slowly she turned back.

No one can say what he would have done then, of what madness he might not have been capable, had he not seen, with a dismay that thrust him in an instant from one world into another, his mother, Judith and Dorothy approaching.

To his horror he saw that they, quite unconsciously, were walking directly into the Westaways group. He would have thought that for some mad reason they were doing this deliberately, had it not been that they were so plainly unaware. For Judith was laughing, pointing with her stick to some dancers, and Dorothy was teasing Adam as though she were trying to make him dance. He did dance a few steps, looking in the moonlight like a little animal, with his long arms and short body. They all laughed. John heard Judith say: 'Here is a fine place. We can see well from here.' He would have started forward to warn them, but it was too late.

In another moment Judith had almost stumbled on the bench where Walter was sitting.

John came forward as though to protect his mother. Walter Herries stood up. It was plain that he had been drinking heavily, for he lurched a little on his great legs as he stood.

Jennifer was transfixed with terror. In all the years since her husband's death she had never until now been face to face with him.

Walter took off his hat.

'Good evening, ladies! How agreeable a surprise! Not unexpected too. Will you not join us?'

Jennifer caught at Judith's arm.

'Oh, come, Judith. Come away!'

But Walter was delighted. Such scenes he fancied. The young Durward Herries boys, who saw something strange was abroad, stared, their laughter checked.

'Well, Jennifer,' Walter said. 'It is a long time since we met. It was my mother you knew, I think. I hope that you cherish no ill-will, though, for I assure you that I do not.'

'Thank you, Walter,' Judith broke in. 'This is too public for your wit. Jennifer, we will turn back—'

But he strode forward so that he almost touched Jennifer's arm. He made no sign that anyone existed for him but Jennifer, who shrank back against Judith.

'No, no. Why so unfriendly? We must be friends, we must indeed. For we are to be neighbours. Very near neighbours indeed. You didn't know? But, of course . . . At High Ireby. I am to start building in a month or so.'

'You cannot—' Jennifer answered. 'That would be terrible. I could not—'

'Why, yes,' said Walter. He took a step nearer. Then John, seized with a wild fury, struck him in the chest. Walter tottered, for he was not at all steady, almost fell. There were cries, exclamations. Little Uhland had rushed forward, hitting at John's legs.

It was, in fact, a most ludicrous, lamentable scene, for the other young Herries men, themselves rather drunk, came forward (not very aware of what they would do). Judith lifted her stick, Agnes Herries caught Walter's arm . . .

Then in a moment the publicity of it hit them all. They stood transfixed in a frozen group. Two gipsies approached and one of them, a young woman with an orange kerchief and a cage of little green birds said: 'Lady . . . Pretty lady . . . The birds will tell your fortune . . . Happy luck, lady.'

Walter steadied himself.

'Here,' he said, 'you can tell my fortune, my girl, and give me a fine one.'

With great dignity, very slowly, Judith and Jennifer, their children following them, turned down the hill.

THE BEGINNING OF THE FORTRESS

WALTER HERRIES had told Jennifer that the building of his house on High Ireby was at once to begin. It was not, however, until the month of March 1830 that the foundations were first laid – and it happened that Jennifer was there to see.

Jennifer never recovered from that shock of the encounter with Walter on the night of the Summer Fair. It was the climax to a series of events that stretched back to that old Ball of her youth, and possibly, behind that again, to her earliest nursery escape from reality. She did not know now – she had not an analytic mind – what had happened to her or indeed why anything had ever happened to her at all. She was an old woman – this year saw her sixtieth birthday – but for all her years she felt herself to be still a young girl most unjustly treated by everyone.

In the early days – they seemed to her to be as recent as last evening – she had never had justice. Her beauty had brought her nothing: everything had been always just awry. She would have been the Duchess of Wrexe and a great woman of the world had not the Duke been so unpleasant a young man and the position of great lady so tedious and wearisome. She would have been a quiet beauty in the country had not Francis, her husband, been a weakling. She would have been a splendid Mistress had not her lover been a clod. She would have been a triumphant Mother had her children loved her. She would be now mistress of her house had not Judith taken selfishly everything out of her hands. Always injustice, everywhere injustice. No one saw what she was and no one cared.

The sluggish slackness in her that had ruined her life she did not perceive, for we never catch the causes of our fate, so clear to everyone around us. She might even now have been a fine tragic figure had she had the intelligence to look noble, the energy to tidy her hair, the wisdom to have reticence.

She had never had dignity or wisdom; she had been always the slave of trifles, small jealousies, degrading idleness, lazy avoidances of trouble.

But the terror of Walter struck into her character as a snake strikes. She was poisoned in all her being. The infection spread slowly, but from the moment that Judith consented to stay and took the house into her hands, Jennifer was lost. She had now nothing to do but brood over Walter. She cowered beneath his shadow, unable to move, waiting the awful moment.

As his shadow grew ever more terrible the figures immediately around her became themselves shadows. John had once been her darling, Judith's Adam a pleasure, the servants agreeable, her daughter Dorothy 'a good girl', Judith herself, although a tyrant, exceedingly useful and a safeguard.

After her scene with Walter all these were as unsubstantial to her as figures on a tapestry. She might have been still a fine woman; she had yet all her height, her hair (once so lovely) was white with, if she had cared, a fine lustre in its silver. But she was untidy, careless, a slattern. Any old clothes did for her, her hair escaped its pins, she would tap-tap in loose slippers, an old shawl over her shoulders, from room to room. Only her eyes were good, and the blaze in them, their intensity, belied all the rest of her, so that they were like a bright fire in a lumber-room. She would begin sentences and not finish them, eat food greedily and suddenly abandon it, pet John and Adam eagerly and then look at them as though she did not know them. The servants disregarded her; they took their orders from Madame.

Judith knew that terror was of an especial danger to anyone of even part Herries blood. She had seen, in all her active varied life, that the history of the Herries, as of so many British families, was that of a building impregnable, as its builders thought, to the attacks of all outside forces. But the outside forces are strong and immortal. Nothing tempts their malicious humour so thoroughly as the complacency of the builders. Here they twist a chimney, there a window rattles, now the wind sweeps wildly up the ordered garden, the iron-sheathed door shudders, a picture falls, the carpet rises on the floor.

Jennifer's parents had been typical Herries, good, complacent, satisfied, laughing at imagination. Jennifer, so lovely, their pride, their joy, must be safe if any Herries was. Who would dare to touch her? So, in their love for her, they took from her all her defences. Now, when a vision of another world more real than the Herries one might have saved her, she had no vision. And Judith could not help her.

From the moment of Walter's threat, for two years and a half, she waited. But life does not allow you to wait. No one knew what the matter with her was and, more tragically, no one cared.

Her children had loved her, but Dorothy was all for comfort and found her uncomfortable, while John, after he knew of the reasons for his father's suicide, shrank, against all his will and wish, from contact. Moreover, he had now something so absorbing in his life that his mother was dim to him, as he was to her.

Judith could have loved her because she pitied her and pity, with Judith, was maternal; but daily contact with Jennifer's laziness, carelessness, selfishness, turned pity into impatience, and when Judith was impatient she was at her worst.

So Jennifer was alone with her terror.

As the time advanced, that terror took strange forms. High Ireby became a place of extraordinary fascination for her. It was several miles from Uldale and uphill for most of the way, but day after day she walked through the fields, climbed the slope and then stood, under the trees, gazing at the lovely scene – the walls of a ruined cottage, a small wood of whispering trees, remnants of a garden patch, and the long slope of the melancholy fields with the village and house of Uldale tucked into the hollow.

To the right were the sprawling slopes of Blencathra and Skiddaw. They lay against the sky like the careless limbs of a giant sleeper under an enormous coverlet tossed into casual shapes. She knew here all weathers, all seasons. She would stand against the ruined wall, under the trees, a tall, motionless old woman in a tawdry hat, clutching her shawl, staring in front of her. She became a familiar figure to the inhabitants of the village near by. It was not strange that she should soon have a reputation for madness, but she was not mad in the least. She would stand there, or sit on a tumbled stone, and reflect, in a lazy way, on her misfortune – not on any very definite misfortune but on the general way in which she was ill-treated and neglected. Sometimes she would determine that on her return to Uldale that day she would tell them all what she thought of them – Judith, John, Dorothy, even Mr Rackstraw – but she never did. Partly it was too much trouble, partly when she was once again in the comfortable parlour at Uldale drinking tea before the fire or, in the summer, sitting under the tree on the lawn in the sunshine, she was cosy like a cat and smiled, lazily, on everyone.

She had too, all this time, marvellous health. Nothing ailed her.

She had perhaps the idea, as she stood in the little wood, day after day, that thus she was defying Walter. During all these two years she never saw him in the flesh. He became the more monstrous because she did not see him.

Then one day at last the thing happened. That March there was a late fall of snow. During the first week of that month a blizzard blew across the North, adding discomfort to all the hardships that the poor people were, at that time, already suffering. Waters were frozen, the sun, when it broke through, turned the snow-ridges into shining marble, the crows were spots of ink on the virgin fields.

She had had a cold for a week, and Judith had kept her in bed, but as soon as she was up she strode across the fields again, her shawl flapping behind her, climbed the hill and walked into a multitude of men.

Trees were falling. It seemed that on every side of her the trees were tumbling. The walls of the ruined cottage were no more. Men walked measuring the ground. A fire was lit on the snow and illuminated the broken whiteness of the scene that stretched back into the farther shadows of the wood.

As she stood back in the road hidden by two huge horses from whose nostrils steam struck the air, a tree fell with a great crash and a groan that seemed to come from her own heart. Men shouted joyfully, and some boys, muffled against the cold, danced round the fire.

She stepped into the middle of the road and several of them saw her. Two gentlemen on horseback, attended by little Peach, Walter's agent, were watching the proceedings: one of them was the architect, Mr Humphrey Carstairs from London, the other, young Julius Hopper, a clever lad working in old Mr Bonner's office in Keswick. Old Mr Bonner was the oldest, stupidest and laziest architect in the North of England, and no one despised him quite so deeply as did young Julius. Young Julius was slim and dark and exceedingly handsome in his high-collared dark green overcoat; Carstairs was squat, thick, his head almost hidden in the curves of his plum-coloured capes. He bent low in his saddle; he suffered severely from rheumatism.

He turned and saw the strange woman in the old-fashioned hat, drawn to her full height in the middle of the snowy road. He stared, then turned to young Julius. 'Who's the old body in the shawl?' he asked.

Young Julius stared also. He knew who she was: his first thought was that this would be amusing for Walter Herries if he rode over that afternoon. His second was of alarm. She looked crazy; he knew, of course, of the feud. She might have a pistol under that shawl of hers. He was a warm young man, fond of life, very ambitious. He had no desire to die as yet. Another tree fell; men were dragging branches across the snow that blew in little smoky spirals of silver into the air. The flames of the fire leaped, and an old man sitting by it, with a great red comforter round his neck and yellow mittens, began to play on a fiddle. The mittens made his fingers clumsy, but the men liked the music and worked with a better will.

'She's a Mrs Herries from Uldale yonder,' young Julius whispered. 'She's a sort of cousin of Walter Herries.' Then he added: 'I'll go speak to her.'

With what he felt to be exceptional bravery (for it was possible enough that she concealed a pistol) he dragged his horse's head round and rode towards her. She never moved, but stood there in the road, staring at the men, the fallen trees, the old man in the bright red comforter. Young Julius raised his hat.

'Good afternoon, Mrs Herries.' Then he said, smiling: 'Very wintry for March, ma'am.'

He wasn't sure that she saw him. He moved his horse a little to the right.

Then she said: 'What is going on here?'

He was able now to see her eyes, the pallor of her face, something dignified in her isolation. He spoke with the greatest politeness as he answered:

'Why, ma'am, Mr Walter Herries of Westaways is to build a house here.'

'Indeed?' She nodded her head. 'A house of some size?'

'Oh, yes. It is to be a very fine place indeed – gardens and a fountain, magnificent stables. A lonely spot, though, to have chosen. Mr Carstairs there from London is the architect.'

'What is your name?'

She looked at him directly and there was something in her eyes that touched him very truly.

'My name, ma'am, is Hopper – Julius Hopper. I am assistant to Mr Bonner, the architect in Keswick. I know your son, Jack Herries, well. We are very good friends.'

'Ah, yes, my son.' Her eyes went back to the fire that seemed to have a great fascination for her. The thin, reedy, uncertain squeak of the fiddle came whining through the sharp air.

'And how long will it be in the building?'

'A considerable while, ma'am. Mr Herries wishes everything to be of the best.'

'Ah ... He wishes everything to be of the best ...'

'Yes, ma'am. And these are not easy times. Although so many are without employment, it is not easy to get good workmen and wages are high. As soon as we have Reform things will be better.'

'You believe in Reform?'

'I do indeed, ma'am. We shall have Revolution else, like the French.'

'You are wrong.' She spoke with slow consideration, as though she beat every word upon the ground. 'Reform itself is Revolution. The country will be ruined. The country is in any case ruined.'

'I hope not indeed.'

'Ah, you are young . . .'

She moved away from him up the road. His horse stepped beside her. He would never forget that odd, tall, black figure with the crazy hat, moving against the snow. He thought after that it had been a kind of omen, but he was a sane practical young man who did not believe in omens, although out of habit he avoided walking under a ladder.

She came so far and then saw Peach. Mr Carstairs had come down from his horse and now he and Peach were studying a plan. Jennifer scarcely knew Peach, and yet his short bow-legged figure was in some way familiar to her. She looked up at Julius, and he, not knowing what to say, remarked:

'The snowdrops are doing bravely in spite of the snow.' There was a great patch of them under the trees. Some of them were already trodden down and, as he looked, two men, carrying a log, tramped upon the patch.

'Oh, the snowdrops!' She put her hand on his knee, leaning up to him. 'Tell Walter Herries what he is destroying.'

She turned and walked swiftly down the road, catching her shawl more closely about her. The three men turned to watch her.

Meanwhile at Uldale, as it happened on that same afternoon, Judith assisted by Dorothy Herries was entertaining four lady callers – old Miss Pennyfeather, Mrs Leyland of The Ridge, Bassenthwaite, and her two daughters Nancy and Bella.

Miss Pennyfeather had been driven over by Judith, who had been taking luncheon with her in Keswick; the Leylands had come over from Bassenthwaite in their barouche. All the ladies were very pleasantly animated: the three elders, their heads together, near the fire, and the girls laughing and chattering by the window.

For the Leyland girls this was an adventure. Dorothy Herries, blooming with health and good temper, was two years older than Nancy and Bella, who were twins and were wanting to be married, for they were already twenty years of age and soon it would be too late. They were nice simple girls who had never been to London and only visited the theatre in Newcastle and were eager for gossip and adventure. They were pale, flaxen, tall and slim, and dressed alike. They wore dresses of poplin, colour violette de Parme, with heart-shaped bodices, and the corsages long and tight at the waist. They had hats of rice straw with very wide brims, trimmed with anemones. Each thought the other looked bewitching, for they were generous and warm-hearted by nature.

They had never been to Uldale before on a visit, and this was a great adventure. 'Madame' was a 'character' through the whole countryside, and it was wonderful to be entertained in her parlour. Or was it Mrs Herries' parlour? People said that she was mad and walked about the country singing songs to herself – mad, poor thing, because her husband had discovered her with her lover and he had killed himself. Very shocking, but *how* romantic! And then her son John was so handsome, the best-looking young man in the North, a little sad and pensive as a good-looking young man ought to be. (For they adored *Thaddeus of Warsaw* and Mrs Cuthbertson's *Santo Sebastiano* and Mrs Meeke's *Midnight Weddings*.) Dorothy on the other hand – whom they loved at sight – was not melancholy at all and laughed all the while.

Then there was 'Madame's' boy whom they did hope they'd get a sight of. He was, of course, illegitimate, which made him so interesting, although everyone knew who the father had been. He *should* have been romantic and melancholy, but people said that he was ugly and silent and kept to himself. Nevertheless, it would be *adorable* to see him!

While they laughed and chattered by the window they tried to keep an ear open for the company by the fire. For Miss Pennyfeather did say such *shocking* things and their mother (Mrs Leyland was stout and jolly) had told them that on no account were they to listen to Miss Pennyfeather's wickedness, so they were naturally all ears.

But the ladies seemed to be talking of nothing but Reform, Lord John Russell, and of Brougham's attack on Lady Jersey in

The Times, and how bitter she was against Reform, and so on, and so on – dull stuff!

Then Dorothy let it out that next month 'Madame' and her son were to go to London to stay with some relations. *That* was exciting! To go to London! To see the great Simpson at Vauxhall, to visit the New Zoological Gardens in Regent's Park, to attend a Masquerade in the Argyll Rooms, to catch a glimpse of the Duke, and best of all the Theatre, the Surrey, the Royalty, or Sadler's Wells.

They knew all about it; it was as though they had been in London all their lives. They looked across to the fire and that little upright dominating woman in her crimson dress with the huge sleeves; they stared (as unobtrusively as politeness insisted) at her small pale face, her neat grey hair, her ivory cane, and watched her bright eyes, her smile, the tapping of her small foot on the carpet. People said that she was the daughter of a gipsy and that her father, although of the finest family, had been a rogue and vagabond. And here she was, with her illegitimate boy, behaving as though she were Queen of England. Ah! *What* a romantic afternoon they were having!

It was made yet more splendid by the entrance of John Herries. Both girls, at sight of him, had the same thought. What a *lover* he would make! But there was something that told them at once that he was not for them. He came over to them and made himself very charming. His voice was soft and gentle. Yes, he *was* melancholy, although he teased his sister and chaffed them about their beaux at a recent Ball in Keswick. But they felt that his mind was elsewhere.

What a *hero* of a novel he would make! He was too gentle to be truly Byronic, but he would suit *The False Step* exactly! How beautifully he went and paid his devoir to their mother, with what ease! And yet he was in no way effeminate, quite unlike that horrid William d'Arcy of Threlkeld, or, on the other hand, that oaf, young Osmaston.

Well, it was time for them to be going. Darkness would soon swallow the pale saffron twilight. Already the candles were lit in the room. Mrs Leyland rose to make her adieux when the door opened and the strangest figure stood in the doorway.

Jennifer stood there, her hat a little askew, her long thin fingers clutching her shawl. She could see but indistinctly. The candlelight blinded her, coming in as she did from the dark snow-shine road. But she saw Judith.

'Judith! Judith! He has begun to build!'

The cry, shrill, poignant, broke the comfortable cosiness of the room into fragments. Jennifer had awaked at last.

'Judith! They are trampling on the snowdrops ... The trees are falling!'

She stumbled forward, her hat ever more askew as she moved, and Judith, coming to her, caught her hand.

'Wait, Jennifer. There are guests here ...'

Mrs Leyland, good and kind woman as she was, did the right thing. She chattered:

'Well, I'm sure ... How do you do, Mrs Herries? A cold afternoon to be out in. You must be weary, and a cup of tea will be the very thing. And now we must be going. So very dark, although William is a most careful driver. We brought him from Newcastle with us. He was always careful from a boy. Might William be summoned, Mrs Herries? Thank you. Most kind. Come, girls. William will have the horses in an instant. He is always so prompt. It has been truly most delightful. I'm sure ...'

But Jennifer was not to be silenced by any chatter. She saw only one thing, one terrible thing, before her eyes – and she must declare it. Judith had seated her on the sofa, had pulled the bell-rope, was pouring a cup of hot tea. Dorothy had come round to her mother. The girls stood in the window, not knowing quite what they should do but enthralled by what they saw and heard. John had gone to hasten Mrs Leyland's horses.

'Yes, he has begun at last, Judith. All his men are there, measuring the ground, and it is to be a huge place with a fountain and fine stabling. All the trees are falling, and they have lit a fire in the snow.'

'It is Walter Herries,' Judith explained *sotto voce*. 'He has been threatening for a long while that he would build on High Ireby that he may overlook us – and now it seems that he has done it.'

'Well,' cried old Miss Pennyfeather. 'Let him, and much good may it do him! I cannot endure Walter and I don't care who hears me. Fat overgrown bully! Let him build with his limping child and puny wife! Don't you worry, Judith. 'Tis all stuff and nonsense! He can't harm you and he knows it!'

'Yes, indeed,' said Mrs Leyland, gazing anxiously at the door for news of her horses. 'I should think so indeed. So he's to be our neighbour at Ireby, is he? A pretty neighbour, and so Mr

Leyland will prove to him if he comes bothering our way. Come, girls – William must have brought the horses round.'

But Jennifer looked at them all with startled, staring eyes. 'He will not be content until he has destroyed us. I knew it from the first. All his windows will look down on us. We must leave Uldale. I always said that he would have his way!'

Judith was sitting beside her. She had one of her hands in hers.

'Jennifer, Jennifer ... You must not be so distressed. Cousin Walter will do us no harm. How can he? What if he does build a house at Ireby? That can do us no harm. Come, come, Jennifer ...'

How soft and gentle her voice was, thought the girls, and how crazy Mrs Herries looked, poor woman, with her hat on one side!

Mrs Leyland beamed comfortably on them. 'I am sure Ireby is no place for a house, no place at all. I cannot think why he should choose such a spot, and Westaways good enough for anyone, I should have thought. I always said he was a strange man, and Mr Leyland, who is downright if any man is, remarked to me only a week back that he was growing far too stout for his health. If he could but give some of his size to his wife, poor woman ...'

John appeared in the doorway.

'Come, girls. Here's Mr Herries to say that William has the horses round. Has he not, Mr Herries? That's excellent. William is always so prompt. Good day to you. Good day. Good day. *Most* delightful. Never enjoyed anything more. Come, girls. *Too* kind of you, Mrs Herries. It's time we were moving on, with the snow and everything ... You must all come over to Bassenthwaite at the nearest opportunity. Oh, I insist. I take no refusal. So very good of you, Mrs Herries—'

When the Leylands were out of the room a silence fell. Jennifer drank her tea. Then she rose.

'There is no peace for us any more here,' she said. 'You may laugh, Judith, but it is so. He will destroy us all.' Then, staring at Miss Pennyfeather as though she were seeing her for the first time, she added: 'They were trampling on the snowdrops. It is to be a tremendous place with rows of windows. I think I will go to my room.'

She walked out.

Judith sighed.

'If that isn't unfortunate! Poor Jennifer! And the Leylands will talk for weeks!' Then taking Miss Pennyfeather's arm she added: 'Janet, come up with me. You are the most sensible woman I know. Talk to her. I'm of no service when she's like this.'

So Dorothy and John were left alone. Dorothy saw at once that her brother was greatly disturbed; he stood there, fingering his high stock and looking, as she remembered her father had sometimes looked, as though he were going to be sick. At such a time she could not help him. She was good about sensible practical things like a broken leg, a bloody head, a cold in the chest, but when John was in a mood she was uncomfortable as though he were improper. Although she was the soul of good nature and almost always in a good temper, she resented the states into which her mother and brother sometimes tumbled.

John said at last:

'Nothing can help mother. Now that she has this in her head.'

'I'll see about some linden tea,' Dorothy said. 'It has soothed her many a time.' And relieved at an opportunity of escape, she bustled out.

She had been gone but a moment when Adam came in. Adam was now fourteen and a half. He had filled out in the last two years and was deep of chest, thick across the shoulders. His black hair was always untidy; a lock hung now over his forehead. He was ruddy with health, with the brown colour that made so many who didn't know him think him a foreigner, but he was English enough all the same, with the broad brow, snub nose, large mouth, square body, short sturdy legs, bright eyes like his mother's. He was English, too, in his reticence and hatred of demonstration. This affected him now, for he saw at once that John was worried and would need his help. John liked demonstrations: there were times when he wanted Adam to show him that he loved him, and although Adam did love him more than any human thing save his mother, he hated to show it. Oh! how he hated it!

He was in rough country things and his high boots were muddy, for he had been out with Rackstraw, Bennett and the dogs rabbiting and had had a glorious afternoon. When he saw that John's distress was so real he thought to himself, 'Let John do what he likes to me if it helps him.' With a backward glance he threw reluctantly behind him all the happiness of the afternoon, the crisp air, the scent of the snow, the yelping of the dogs, the sunlight breaking in silver across the slow fields.

'Adam, Mother has been to High Ireby. Walter Herries has begun to build.'

'I knew it,' Adam said quickly. 'Bennett told me.'

'Mother is very unhappy. She came in while the Leylands were here and spoke as though she were crazy. This will *send* her crazy! If I could do something! How I hate him! He comes nearer and nearer with his sneer and his crooked son and—' He broke off.

'Pooh!' said Adam, cracking his whip against his boot as grown men did. 'It's fun, John – fine fun! Why should you care? And your mother will be better now that it's happened. It has been the waiting for it . . .'

'I am afraid of nothing else,' John went on. 'Nothing but this. I'm no coward. You know that I'm not. But Cousin Walter, since the days when we were small . . . Do you remember that evening when he rode up to the house and we watched him? And now that I'm managing the estate it brings me closer to him. Oh, Adam, I wish that you and Aunt Judith were not going to London—'

'It's grand!' Adam cried, throwing out his chest. 'There'll be the coach and the lights, chimneys smoking and everyone shouting, and mother says we shall go to a theatre—'

'Adam,' John broke in. 'There's something else. I must tell you. I have been intending so for three months past, but no one knows. It makes everything so difficult—' He broke off and began to pace the room. Adam, his legs straddling, waited. 'It's this. You're to tell no one, Adam.'

'No one,' repeated Adam, and meant it.

'It's Elizabeth – Walter's daughter. We are in love. We have been so for more than two years. It began the night of the Summer Fair.'

'What!'

'Yes, yes . . . Why should it not be? There is no one so lovely, so good, so lovely—'

'But she is a child, a little girl—'

'She is your own age, Adam. In two years she will be seventeen—'

'Elizabeth! *His* daughter!'

'Yes, yes . . . I know all that you can say. I have said it all to myself again and again. But it happened at sight, and now it is for ever. Nothing can change it.'

Love – love of girls and women – as yet seemed to Adam an absurdly inexplicable business, a waste of time, a ludicrous sentimentality. And now this, for a child who was a baby, the daughter of their greatest enemy whom they had sworn always to hate, the sister of the loathsome, deformed Uhland ... An impulse to despise John rose in his heart and was at once loyally driven down again.

'Oh, John!'

'Do not pity me. Do not laugh. We love one another for ever, and so soon as she is old enough we shall marry.'

'No, no, you must not!' Adam caught his arm. 'Uncle Walter's daughter! ... I shall never speak to you again if you do!'

'Well, then, don't! I don't care!'

'But, John, how *can* you? For two years? And you've been meeting?'

'Sometimes. But not often. We write.'

Adam turned, with a gesture of disgust as though he would leave the room, but John gripped his shoulder.

'Adam, you must listen. You *must*. You are the only friend I have. The only one. I love you more than anyone in the world save Elizabeth. Again and again we have sworn that nothing should separate us—'

'Yes, but this—'

'No; you are young. You don't understand—'

'I'm not young.' Adam broke away. 'If you wish to love a girl you can, but not *his* daughter.'

'But don't you see? I could not help it. As I breathe so I love her. You will yourself one day—'

John's eyes caught Adam's and held him. There was an expression in them that struck to the very depths of Adam's loyalty and devotion. He knew then that he could never desert John, never, whatever the crisis.

He muttered something, looking away.

'Mind – it is our secret.'

Adam nodded his head, then said gruffly:

'I must go to the stables. Caesar has a sore leg. Coming?'

JUDITH AND ADAM IN LONDON

THEY – Judith and Adam – had spent the most glorious night at the George, Stamford, in the very room, so the landlord himself informed them, occupied by his Sacred Majesty, King Charles the First, when he slept there on his way from Newark to Huntingdon on the night of August 23rd, 1645. This Judith, in ordinary circumstances, would never have believed (although the room was splendid with oak beams and a huge four-poster and a small closet off it where Adam slept and snored), but the fact was that she was so greatly excited by her journey and by the expectation of London (where she had not been for so long a time) and by the temporary escape from Uldale, that she behaved like a child of ten and was ready to believe anything. One of the drawers remarked to another of the drawers that he'd never yet seen an old lady like it. They had had to wait for their adventure for it was not until the second week in October that they left Uldale.

Adam was quite as deeply excited as his mother and expressed his emotions in sudden fiery little sentences, like shots from a gun, that seemed to have little or no relation to one another.

Everything was glorious, the long ride in the coach the day before (Adam had insisted on sitting outside, although it was terribly cold and there was a place for him inside), the sound of the horn, the spanking pace of the horses, the incidental humours of the road and, most especially, the powers and personality of Mr Joe Dorset, the Coachman, with whom Adam was utterly and entirely in love.

Then had come the falling dusk, the lights of the town, the bustling courtyard of the George, the wonderful dinner when, like a gentleman, Adam had drunk his mother's health in marvellous claret, sitting up in his chair so straight that he nearly broke his back in two (he and his mother so grand at a table all to themselves, while the old gentleman with three chins and two daughters entertained the table in the middle of the room with his anecdotes of Tom Hennessey and his shooting adventures in Scotland), and then the great bedroom in which King Charles had slept, and his mother going upstairs to it in such stately fashion, the landlord himself in front with two candles, that you would have thought her Royalty.

But all this was nothing at all to the glory of the next day when they started in a pale golden dawn, frost in the air, and the roans stamping their hoofs to be off. Adam, wrapped in a hundred coats, had the glory of sitting beside the great Joe with the old three-chinned gentleman on his other side.

He could observe everything and listen to everything too. He saw the gold fade from the sky and give place to one of the loveliest mornings of the year. The fields were yet frosted, the road was hard; only once had they to travel through water, which gave Joe (who had a voice like a gurgling water-pipe) occasion to describe what had happened once to the Stamford Regent when going through St Neot's, fifty-six miles out of London – how the Ouse had overflowed its banks there, and although an extra pair of leaders were put on, ridden by a horse-keeper, yet the water was up to the axle-trees and even, for a while, the Regent was afloat, to the dreadful peril of some ladies inside it. And that led the stout gentleman to talk of Tom Hennessey's famous whip, which, as everyone knows, was a crooked one so that it could tickle the lagging wheelers in a fashion no other whip could achieve. And that led Joe to show what he could do with *his* whip, and a stout lady behind them *begged* him to be careful and not to hurt the horses, which Adam thought the funniest thing he'd ever heard. (But then women *were* peculiar, all of them, even his mother.)

There came a glorious moment, later in the morning, when Joe actually entertained Adam himself in conversation.

'And what might *your* age be, young gentleman?'

'Fifteen.'

'Fifteen! Deary me! Think of that now! . . . Learnt to fight yet?'

'A little.' (Adam was modest. Rackstraw had taught him well.)

'Going to see a Fight in London?'

'I hope so.'

'Next week, come Friday, there's the Nottingham Pet and John Willis at Islington. That'll be something.' Then, after a pause, 'Going to school in London?'

'No; just for a visit.'

'Ever been to London afore?'

'No, never.'

'Ah! That's a treat for a young lad. That's a treat, that is. All the same the country's better. Live in the North?'

'Yes, in Cumberland.'

'Ever seen the Crusher?'

'No. I'm afraid I haven't.'

'Never seen the Crusher – and live in Cumberland? Why, think of that now! I remember his fight in Newcastle when he smashed Foxy Rundle in twenty rounds – in '23 I think it was.'

But here the old gentleman broke in; he hadn't seen the fight

himself but he had heard ... and here the coach had to be
stopped for a lady with enough baggage for a journey to China,
who didn't like this, and wouldn't have that, until Joe's temper
was as purple as the capes of his riding-coat. And then – somewhere early in the afternoon – the foretaste of London began to
creep upon Adam. London! London at last! How faint suddenly
were Uldale, Skiddaw, the village shop with the green bottle
window ... Dorothy and the way she'd take the jars of preserve
out of the cupboard and examine them one by one with a seriousness ... old Bennett and the way he'd pinch his leg ... even John
standing there, looking at Adam, telling him that horrid hateful
news, that he loved Walter's daughter ... all figures as dim now
as the faded pinks and blues on the Chinese screen in his
mother's bedroom! London!

Already they were at the Peacock at Islington, and the hostler
was shouting, doors were slamming, old Joe Dorset taking up
parcels, answering silly questions from nervous ladies, drinking
out of a jug, examining the horses, reassuring a nervous old
gentleman wrapped in a vast white muffler – and then, in another
moment – Tantivy! Tantivy! Tantivy! – they were off again.

'Are you comfortable, dear?' his mother had asked him, poking
her head out of the window. 'Not too cold?'

'He's all right, ma'am,' Joe Dorset had answered, 'as right as a
'edge'og''; and Adam had been proud all down his spine. Certainly he was all right. What a pity his mother hadn't come
outside! She would have enjoyed it. Now, after Islington, lights
flared on the country road, for the dusk is creeping up and out of
it suddenly loom drovers and a herd of cattle. Then Smithfield
and Cow Lane, then up Holborn Hill. But these places were, of
course, nothing to Adam. What did he see? In detail very little,
for mist is everywhere, noise is everywhere – through the mist
lights and flares, a blazing window, a crooked chimney, a barrow
alive with flame. And the noises – hackney cabriolets, drays,
waggons, wheelbarrows, shouting boys, bawling men, screaming
women, ringing bells – and through it all, above it all, beyond it
all, his heart beating like an African drum!

He was never one to show his excitement. He sat now in absolute silence, his hands tightly clenched together under his coat,
his mouth firmly closed, but his eyes staring, staring as though
they would pierce this foggy, noisy mystery through to the other
side.

Tantivy! Tantivy! Tantivy! He felt now Joe's pride that he

was bringing his coach in on time. How they dashed over the cobbles, how the roans tossed their heads, how through the murk and gloom one could dimly feel figures sliding, horses slipping, voices shouting to be out of the way. Then, one more blast and into a courtyard of light and splendour the Stamford Regent dashes. The George and Blue Boar, Holborn: London's heart is touched at last.

He discovered then, quite to his own surprise, that he was extremely sleepy; he discovered, too, for the first time in his young life, what every traveller discovers, that once at a destination and the life that only a moment earlier had been pulsating with fire and energy is collapsed at your feet like a spent balloon.

Even Joe Dorset was fading. Not that he wouldn't be pleased to meet Joe again somewhere, but his figure was shrunk and his voice sounded miles away.

No, his mother was once again the centre of his world. She dominated the place, sending hostlers here and stable-boys there, collecting their luggage, standing over it, ordering a hackney cabriolet, and all as quietly but as imperiously as though London were at her feet and knew it.

'Now, Adam,' she commanded. 'In you get!' And in he did get, into the mustiest, smelliest, darkest interior that his enterprising life had yet known. Mice, straw, newspapers, stale beer and damp cloth all seemed to have gone to the making of that hackney cab. There was indeed straw on the floor of it and old newspaper squeezed into the hinge of one of the windows. The driver was a little man with a pinched white nose and no eyebrows. He seemed to be terrified of Judith, for when she said, 'Number Nine, Cadogan Place,' he almost bowed to the ground.

They were crushed together inside the cab, for they were piled round with parcels and small boxes. Judith put her arm around him, and so they bumped and jumped and swayed and sank as though on a tempestuous sea. Houses rose and fell beyond the misty windows, horses loomed gigantic, figures sprang up before them and vanished again, and in Adam's nostrils was that smell with which he would associate London all his life long – straw, ale, and the faint scent of violets that stole from his mother's clothes.

They had arrived. The cab had stopped with a jerk, the door creaked open, and a little boy with a large broom was there on the pavement, his hand out, begging.

When Judith had given the little boy a shilling (which astonished him very much and led the driver of the cabriolet to wet his
lips in anticipation) the big solemn door (supported by black
marble pillars) was slowly opened and a very thin footman with
powdered hair and an ornamental waistcoat stood there staring at
them. It seemed from his expression that he could not believe
that anyone should be arriving in a hackney cab at that particular
moment, but Judith walked straight past him as though she were
the Queen of Egypt, and then, remembering that the driver had
not yet been paid, hurried down again, directed the bringing-in
of the luggage, smiled at the footman, said her name in a very
determined manner, and entered the house a second time, on this
occasion followed closely by Adam.

The hall was so extremely dark and a lamp by the staircase so
exceedingly dim that a white bust of a gentleman with a lot of
hair and naked shoulders, and a large picture of Moses addressing the Children of Israel, were the only things for a long while
visible.

'Madame Paris,' said Judith again. 'We are expected.'

The footman disappeared and returned to say, 'This way,
Madame,' disregarding Adam altogether. He, however, was determined not to be left alone in that darkness, and setting his face
into its ugliest scowl (his manner when he was 'against the
world') stumped along behind her. They were shown into a very
large drawing room that seemed to Adam, accustomed to the
bright colour of Uldale, the most funereal he had ever seen.
There were two large white marble pillars at one end, dark brown
curtains across the windows, a huge portrait of a gentleman with
a white stock and an immense watch-chain over the white marble
mantelpiece, a long bookcase buried in glass, and a marble pedestal with a simpering bust of a lady's head on it between the
windows.

All this he quickly observed, and then he noticed the people
present. (He had ample time for this because no one spoke to him
during the first five minutes.) Mr Newmark he knew already, his
high stock, his large nose, his long legs. He seemed more
dignified than was possible for a flesh-and-blood human being to
be. Mrs Newmark he knew too. He liked her. He noticed that she
had grown very stout. There was an elderly gentleman in a
brown wig, an elderly lady in a vast hat, and a very pretty young
lady in a most bewitching poke-bonnet of the lightest blue. So,
standing near the door, rubbing one leg against the other, he
watched the greetings.

'Judith! ... Judith!' Phyllis Newmark ran forward, kissed her again and again, dragged her to the fire. There was nothing false or affected about Phyllis.

'Oh, you are here! You have arrived! After all that *dreadful* journey! You must be frozen indeed. Frozen. Simply frozen. We have been expecting you these ages, have we not, Stephen?'

Mr Newmark, unbending in a slow solemn process from the crown of his head to the middle of his extremely thin waist, greeted them with the manner of one of England's Ambassadors receiving a deputation from a foreign tribe. He hoped that the journey had not been too positively inclement. Judith, her eyes twinkling, assured him that it had not.

'And this is Mr Pomeroy.'

The gentleman in the brown wig kissed her hand.

'And Mrs Pomeroy.'

'And this is Sylvia – Sylvia Herries, Garth's wife. You know Durward's son.'

The eyes of the young lady in the poke-bonnet – eyes alive with merriment and impudence – and the eyes of Judith – also, although so much older, alive with merriment – met, and in that instant the two of them, the girl of twenty and the woman of fifty-six, were friends for life. Judith seldom made a mistake. She had not made one now.

'Is not that perfect that you are here at last? Is it not wonderful, Mrs Pomeroy? All the way from Cumberland. Oh, I must embrace you once more. I am so *very* glad to see you. Stephen, is it not excellent that they have arrived safe and sound?'

'And there is my Adam,' said Judith, turning round. She knew that it must mean some real sacrifice of his principles that Stephen should receive a little bastard into the very heart of his sanctified family. It had been Phyllis' doing, of course. Nevertheless, it was good of him. She would not forget it. Adam came forward. Although there was always something clumsy in his movements, Judith had taught him good manners. He bowed and said: 'How are you, sir?' 'How are you, ma'am?' 'Very well, I thank you, ma'am.'

What the next step might have been no one could tell, for there came, suddenly, a portentous and dramatic knocking on the door – in fact, two knocks, most solemnly delivered, with a proper interval between.

'Come in!' cried Mr Newmark.

The door slowly opened and a procession entered. First, a tall, severe woman in black silk, then in order, it seemed, of ages, all

the Newmark children. When Judith had last seen them at
Westaways there had been but three; now there were seven if
you included (as indeed you must) an infant who, in the arms of
a stout, bonneted nurse, brought up the rear. The procession
assembled itself at the door and waited.

'Good evening, Miss Trindle,' said Mr Newmark in his deep
bell-like tones.

'Good evening, sir. Good evening, ma'am.'

'Come, children,' said Mr Newmark. 'You may bid us goodnight.'

Then they all advanced – Horace, aged eleven, first, then
Mary, aged ten, Phyllis nine, Katherine seven, Stephen five,
Emily four and the infant Barnabas of almost no age at all.

The Ceremony was magnificent.

Horace was a thin, pale-faced boy, large spectacles covering
wide-open, anxious eyes. He advanced timidly to his father, gave
an absurd little bow. 'Goodnight, Papa.'

Mr Newmark bent down and in a dignified but kindly fashion
kissed his cheek. Horace then went round and bowed to the
others. 'Goodnight, sir.' 'I wish you a goodnight, ma'am.' He
came to Judith, who caught him up and kissed him on both
cheeks, disarranging his spectacles. He looked at her quickly,
then carefully straightened his glasses. He paused before Adam
and gave him a comical twinkling look, as much as to say: 'This
is all very absurd. Don't think I'm taken in by it.' His mother
hugged him in a quite human manner.

The others followed. Mary was stout and plain. Phyllis slender
and pretty. Katherine stolid. Stephen nervous of his father.
Emily yawning. Barnabas from the arms of the nurse gazed at his
father as though he had never seen anything so droll in his life.
They were all marshalled at the door and, together, standing in a
row, made a simultaneous bow.

'And now,' said Phyllis (she was blushing a little), 'let us come
upstairs and I will show you and Adam your apartments. Mrs
Pomeroy, pray, forgive. We shall speedily return.'

Their rooms that night were of an icy chill, but English men
and women were hardened – not for them the soft and effete
comforts of more degenerate nations. Nevertheless, both Judith
and Adam slept like the dead, bathed next morning in round tin
baths brought in elaborately by a heavily breathing, muscle-
straining maidservant. They were both in time for Family
Prayers, held in the long, cold dining room. Beyond the windows

as Mr Newmark read (as it seemed to Judith) almost the whole of
the first Epistle to the Corinthians, a yellow fog wriggled and
bridled up and down the Square.

But it was afterwards, over empty eggcups, vast cold hams and
two terrific coffee-pots that Judith heard a most interesting dis-
course from Stephen Newmark. As Judith sat there listening she
decided that she liked him better, far better, than she could ever
have supposed that she would. He was at his best, serious, informed and exceedingly interesting. As he propelled his long, thin
body up and down the breakfast-room, speaking in his deep,
measured voice, he was like some prophet of old proclaiming woe
to all the world. And yet he was not unduly sensational, did not,
she was convinced, go further than the facts warranted. Being an
intelligent, active-minded woman, she had, even in the confines
of Cumberland, realized the critical time through which England was passing – and not only England but all the civilized
world. The Revolution in France that very summer had been
sufficient to point a packet of morals. The riot at Uldale ending
in poor Reuben Sunwood's death had driven home all the local
lessons. She had felt, for years past, what every other thinking
man and woman had felt, that one cry, one lifted rifle, one more
revelation of the filth, degradation, misery in which half England
was living, might precipitate here a Revolution worse than any
France had ever known. But Newmark dealt with facts, and facts
only. Huskisson's death on September 15th, at the opening of the
Liverpool and Manchester Railway, seemed to him a sort of
omen. He returned to it again and again: such a fine man, one of
the few men of intelligence in the country, such a foolish accident! These Railways – you were at the mercy of these horrible
engines. One day it would be all engines. Human beings would be
crushed by them. Will Herries had been there, had been standing
quite close to Mr Huskisson at the time. He would tell her all
about it.

'I don't suppose that I shall be seeing Will,' said Judith
grimly.

'No?' said Stephen, surprised. 'You will find him now a man
of very great importance.'

'I don't doubt,' said Judith.

After that the general lawlessness, the riots at Otmoor in Ox-
fordshire, followed by the calling out of the military at Oxford,
Captain Swing and his rick-burning, the hanging of three men
by the High Sheriff in Somersetshire, an execution witnessed by

fifteen thousand people, the stirring up of the people everywhere by Cobbett and Carlyle, outrages in Kent and Wilts, in Bucks and Surrey, followed always by summary executions.

Then to London – dirt and starvation and wretchedness cheek by jowl with a luxury, extravagance and heartlessness that had never been witnessed before in any living man's memory. Materialism, immorality of the grossest, an utter scoffing disregard of religion.

'They say,' Stephen burst out, 'that all this is still the effect of the wars. But, good God, this is 1830 – Waterloo was in '15!'

He passed on, growing ever more agitated beneath his cold and pedantic exterior, to the King, the Court and the burning question of Reform. The King was an old fool. They had hoped, in the summer when George, unregretted by anyone alive, had at last seen fit to die, that this honest, worthy old man who succeeded him would save his country. But this honest, worthy old man was nothing but a fool, nay, a maniac. Everyone had been pleased at first by his easy, simple manners. He was crazy from the first, wouldn't have his own servants in mourning, but had ordered Mrs Fitzherbert to put hers into black, put on his plain clothes and went wandering into the streets where he was followed all the way up St James's by a mob until a woman, outside White's, pushed her way through and kissed him; had a party at Buckingham House and dismissed the people by saying: 'Time you were off. Come along to bed, my Queen.'

'Well, you know, Judith, it isn't amusing. No, indeed, it is not. In such times to have such a crazy old monarch. A bad effect on anybody.'

And for the rest where was a man we could trust? The Duke, Peel, Lord John Brougham – all mad about this Reform one way or another. What's the Cabinet to do? It spends all its time sitting to concoct proclamations offering rewards for the discovery of rioters, rick-burners. That's not the way a country ought to be governed.

Stephen's agitation was truly genuine. You could not listen to him and not respect him. You could not listen to him and not think of that little procession of the night before nor see that it was in his mind that all of them from Horace to young Barnabas might have their throats cut by the mob any of these days. And meanwhile, the candles guttered within, outside the yellow fog went sliding and whispering among the tall black houses. Judith, in spite of herself, shivered. The room was so desperately cold.

'We have forgotten God!' cried Stephen, 'and God will punish us.'

But then he cheered up a little, and, pouring himself out a cup of what must have been very chilly coffee, lifted his voice a tone and began to talk about 'Our Family'.

It amused Judith greatly to discover that he considered himself completely a Herries and his children Herries too. They were the nephews and nieces of Lord Rockage and cousins to all the Herries tribe and that was enough for him. Whoever the Newmarks were or had ever been they were now altogether behind the curtain. She saw that it was his idea that the Herries were going to save the country, if not in the foreground of affairs, why, then, very active in the background.

But Will Herries *was* in the foreground; it was expected that he would be a baronet any day. And there was Carey Rockage a peer, James Herries ('stupid pompous Ass *he* is') a baronet, Sylvia Herries, Garth's wife, 'one of the loveliest, wittiest girls in town,' Walter adding field to field in the North, Jennifer's boy (as he had heard) one of the handsomest young fellows in England, and she, Judith, herself—

'And I, Stephen?' asked Judith, laughing.

'Well, anyone with half an eye—'

In short, she became aware that she had, in a very few hours, made a strong impression upon Stephen. It was idle to pretend that she was not pleased. All her old love of power came surging up within her. She began already to realize that this visit to London was going to rouse in her another crisis, a crisis not unsimilar to the one that had driven her to abandon Watendlath. She had been too long up there buried in the country. Here were the Herries going up, up, up. Here was she, even though she *was* fifty-six (and she didn't feel a day more than thirty), with all these conquests ready to her hand. A sudden violent distaste attacked her – a distaste of Jennifer with her crazy imaginings, the stout bullying form of Walter, the littleness and gossip of Keswick, the long slow curve of the Uldale hills—

'We are becoming every day more powerful as a family,' proclaimed Stephen. 'Will is intimate with Peel. He is throwing himself into these new Railways. He grows richer every hour. Carey's boy, Roger, is only nineteen but shows excellent political ambitions. My own boy Horace—' He broke off as though this were too personal. Then added: 'These are the times for people like ourselves. The best class in England, the soundest, the most solid. Money, brains, beauty – and a proper fear of God.'

He broke off and finished his cup of coffee. Strange, she thought, considering him, how although he was not a Herries he was proclaiming himself so curiously a cousin to Will, Walter, the Venerable Archdeacon Rodney, Jennifer's father and the others. All the qualities that her own father had so sadly lacked, and Francis and Reuben and now, she feared, young John. And she herself – she was a combination of the two opposites, the only one in the family who was so, which was exactly why she could, if she liked, dominate the lot of them!

'Stephen!' she cried. 'I shall enjoy my time in London!'

From the moment of that breakfast-hour she never ceased to realize that this visit was a crisis for her and for her Adam as well. Adam himself had indeed the most glorious time. It was as though Stephen relaxed his pomposity and Phyllis her house-wifely burdens under the influence of their visitors. The children – Horace, Mary, Phyllis – had never known such a time. Either with their mother or with the grim Miss Trindle they discovered all the glories of the Town for Adam's benefit. They went to Miss Linwood's Exhibition of Needlework Pictures, and saw the Malediction of Cain and Jeptha's Vow, to Barford's Panorama where were wonderful displays of foreign scenes. One of the most marvellous of all things was the Panorama of London at the Colosseum in Regent's Park, where, raised in a lift (the wonder of the Town), you saw the Conservatories, Swiss Cottage, Alpine Scenery. In St Martin's Lane was the pavilion of the gigantic whale which was found dead off the coast of Belgium on November 3rd, 1827. This skeleton was ninety-five feet long and eighteen broad, and for another shilling you might sit 'in the belly of the whale'. This both Horace and Adam were permitted to do. But better still were the Zoological Gardens in Regent's Park (only opened in 1828 and therefore still a sensation) and (best, oh, far best of all for Adam and Horace) 'Weeks' Mechanical Exhibition' in Tichborne Street, where you might see an automaton tarantula spider made of steel which moved its claws and horns, an animated white mouse formed of oriental pearls that ran about a table 'feeding at pleasure', a caterpillar of enamelled gold and brilliants feeding on the foliage of a golden tree, and an old woman who, at a call, came forth from her cottage, walked about supported by crutches 'while the joints in her arms and legs are all in apparently natural motion'.

For Judith, too, her progress about London during that first week was one thrilling adventure. All her earlier doings there rushed up to her as though they had occurred but yesterday, a strange haphazard married life with Georges, money one day, none the next, the visit to the 'Elephant' when the coach had overturned, the famous Ball, the awful moment in the Square when Georges told her that he must flee for his life – that other world, a London so different from this, so ancient, gone like a dream with its colours, its fans and powder and elegance, and Georges, dear, dear Georges, so feckless, so venturesome, so unreliable, beside her now at every step, his hand through her arm in the old persuasive way, forcing her to agree to something weak or hopeless or mad.

Georges, Georges . . . And here she was an old lady of fifty-six with a boy of fifteen who ought to have been Georges' son but wasn't, in this Town that Mr Nash had covered with whitewash, where poverty of the most hideous mingled with riches of the most extravagant, where the very pavement seemed to threaten, at any moment, an earthquake.

At the beginning of the second week she encountered Will.

She was sitting before a small, smoky, cold fire in the marble-pillared drawing room, her feet on the fender, plucking up her energy to go up to her icy bedroom and dress for dinner, when the footman opened the door, murmured something and withdrew. She looked round to see Will standing there. The same old Will, only grander. He carried his years well. He did not look sixty nor anything like it. Sixty! And it was only yesterday that, a boy on a horse outside Stone Ends, he had listened to a child, Judith, declaring firmly that she would not return to Uldale, no, not if she died for it! He did not look sixty and he did not look as though he could conceivably be Walter's father. He was dressed most handsomely in black. His coat was so waisted that it gave him an almost feminine appearance, but he was not feminine. Oh, dear me, no!

If he was startled at seeing Judith, he gave no sign of it. Her pale face was yet paler. She looked at him with all the distant haughtiness that she could command, but in her heart she wished that she did not instantly once again feel like a child in pantalettes.

'Why, Judith!' he said. He came forward and gravely shook her hand. 'I thought that I should see you. I heard that you were in Town.' Then he added, smiling a little: 'It has been unkind of you not to pay Christabel a visit.'

She did not answer that but said:

'Phyllis has not yet returned. Won't you sit down?'

He did – with great care and dignity.

'Well – how are you, Judith?'

'In excellent health, thank you, Will.'

'I am glad to hear it. And your boy?'

'Also in excellent health.'

'Good.'

There was a pause.

'And how are all at Uldale?'

'Admirable, thank you.'

'Good. I hear that John is a fine boy. You yourself, Judith, look younger than ever.'

She said nothing to that, but wished for the millionth time that God had made her taller. Then he went on – his voice was now exceedingly measured and assured as though he were always accustomed to speaking to people of the utmost importance:

'I am glad that Phyllis has not yet returned. It gives us a moment for speaking together, Judith. You are fifty-six' (how characteristic of him to remember her age!) 'I am sixty. Is it not rather childish of us to continue this feud?'

'I am continuing no feud,' she answered. 'You had better ask Walter about feuds.'

'Ah, Walter!' he sighed. 'Walter is very headstrong. I admit that that has been in part my fault – my fault and his mother's. But he would have his own way from earliest childhood. And are you not imagining things, my dear Judith? You also, if I may say so, have always had plenty of character.'

'Imagining!' she broke out. 'Imagining!' Then, controlling herself, she went on: 'You know, perhaps, that he is building on a hill above Uldale simply that he may overlook us and interfere with us in every possible way.'

'He told me that he was to build,' Will said quietly. 'I advised him against it.'

'He murdered Francis,' she said, 'and he is frightening Jennifer into her grave.' She saw then that she touched him. At the mention of Francis a faint flush coloured his sallow cheeks.

'Francis,' he said at last. 'Poor Francis! He was his own enemy.'

'He need not have been,' she answered hotly. 'It was because of Walter's spies that Francis learnt of Jennifer's infidelity.'

But he was not to be stirred.

'Is not this all rather old history, Judith, my dear? There are

two strains in our family – let us face it – and they are never at
peace together. I was never at one with Francis myself. We
sought different things out of the world. What he sought for was
perhaps harder to obtain than what I sought for. He never found
it, and in his disappointment— No, no, my dear. You cannot lay
all that upon Walter. You know the world too well. You are
altogether too wise.'

She considered that. There was something in what he said.
Then she began in another more friendly, more impetuous
tone.

'Will – cannot you persuade Walter to cease this building?
Cannot you persuade him to leave Jennifer and her children in
quiet? Then we will be friends. I shall be only too happy.'

He looked at her with a strange, almost human, smile.

'Persuade Walter? My dear, he has gone far beyond *my* persuading. I have no influence over him whatever. He would even
rather that his mother and I did not come to Westaways.' He
waited a moment and then continued: 'You know, Judith, I have
all my life been pursuing money – money and power. I have got
both. I do not regret it. But in that pursuit one loses other things.
I have lost human relationships. I have no time for them. As I
say, I do not regret it. But it is so.'

She felt herself being drawn closer to him than she had ever
been before.

He went on: 'Once, years ago, when we were children – do you
remember? – we were watching fireworks on the Lake, you,
Francis, Reuben Sunwood and I. We all said what we would do
with our lives. I have fulfilled almost exactly those early ambitions. I would not, however, say that I am a happy man. But
who is happy? I have my moments. That is, I suppose, as much
as one may ask.'

She heard the opening of the outer door and then the comfortable friendly tone of Phyllis's voice, so hurriedly she said:

'Will, I have no unfriendliness to yourself or Christabel – none
whatever – but I will fight like a tiger to keep Jennifer and her
children safe. I may be an aged tiger and not a very large one,
but I can still be fierce. I am Walter's enemy so long as he is
Jennifer's and John's and Dorothy's, so now you know.'

Will looked at her gravely and opened his mouth as though he
would speak, but Phyllis' entry in a bustle of welcome prevented
him. There was some chatter, and Will got up to depart. It was
only then that he said to them with great solemnity:

'My reason for calling – I should have told you before – I thought that you would like to know. His Majesty has graciously offered me a Baronetcy which I shall accept.'

Yes, indeed, the Herries were going up, and Judith shared now in all the drama of family life to the full. It took her only a fortnight to be considered the most impressive figure among them all.

The Family Letters of this time are filled with references to her:

> Madame Paris has been the Family Sensation this week. Your father is laid up with the gout but he *permitted* me (you know what he is) to dine at Lady Rosbey's. Our cousin, Judith (*is* she a cousin?) arrived with the Newmarks and in *five minutes* had the whole room laughing. She must be *any age* and wears the most outrageous colours. Nevertheless, she was sprightly as a kitten and without losing her dignity an instant. She was as up in everything as though she'd never moved out of Belgravia and kept us all vastly amused with her Paris adventures in '15 where it appears that she . . .

And another:

> Judith Paris is the rage. I must confess that I find her charming for she is kindly as well as intelligent, enjoys everything as though she were born yesterday (she's fifty if a day!), and is no *snob* like dear William and others of our relations. She has with her an illegitimate boy (they say he is Warren Forster's son. You remember Warren – a little *peaked* man with a nervous habit of snapping his fingers) and takes him about with a great deal of pride. It is a thousand pities that she should be buried in the North for we sadly need her *esprit* and intelligence . . .

And a third:

> We dined last night at the Bulwers in Hertford Street. That amusing young man, whom you enjoyed so greatly at Barnet last year, was there, Mr Disraeli. Rosina Bulwer was a sight! Plastered with jewels and painted to the eyes, while Bulwer himself glittered all over! There were plenty of the Family as you may suppose and of all people the solemn Newmark and his fat dowdy Phyllis. However, the excuse for their coming was our cousin Judith from Cumberland. I had heard of her

often enough and was all eagerness to behold her. Well she is a little short pale-faced thing with grey hair and had a dress of brocaded pink gauze (of all things for a woman over fifty!). She carried an ivory cane and should have been altogether absurd. But she was not! Disraeli was enchanted with her and Rosina talked to her an immense deal and even Miss Landon admitted her 'ton'. I can tell you how she does it. By being perfectly natural, having plenty of humour and common sense. I never saw anyone enjoy herself so completely . . .

Indeed she did. She went everywhere, did everything, and knew, for the moment, no weariness. Sylvia Herries was her principal companion. That girl, with her eagerness, sense of adventure and gaiety that had at its heart some undefined melancholy, was designed for her affections. Then suddenly Judith woke. That 'unhappiness' was everywhere, hidden by a superficial eagerness that had no stability.

She saw that she was in a society where nothing was real, where no one believed in anything at all, where everyone feared what the morrow would bring. The 'Silver Fork' novels of fashionable life, just then beginning to be so popular, were symptomatic of the falsehood and sham, while cruel and malicious sheets like the *Age* and the *John Bull* of Theodore Hook showed where the rottenness was hidden.

Prolonged war had killed sincerity, every kind of faith, social behaviour. The world of London that she, for a moment, invaded was dominated by a new aristocracy of wealth, an aristocracy without tradition, without breeding, an aristocracy that in its aggressive uneasiness suffered itself to be blackmailed by the vilest panders and the most worthless adventurers. Most of the great houses in London were occupied by 'new men' who hurried to learn manners that could never truly be theirs and sought with drink, gambling, orgies and ostentation, to give a semblance of splendour and security. The roads to prominence lay through scandal, back-biting and jealousy. Sport, jewels, wild expenditure covered meanness and vice. All was fake; for a woman to be virtuous proclaimed her dowdy. Men lived by their wits and climbed relentlessly over the backs of their dearest friends.

Such was the fashionable world of which Judith had a glimpse. But it was in just such a world that the opportunities of such a family as the Herries – sober, careful, traditional – lay.

The Herries in London were separated into three parts – the

business Herries, Will at their head, James the baronet following rather clumsily, and Amery Herries, Sylvia's brother-in-law, very able and sharp, a possible successor when Will was in his dotage. There were secondly the religious Herries, headed by Stephen Newmark, who, as Judith soon perceived, when he was not sensible, was *very* tiresome indeed. Stephen had his pet clergyman – Mr Aubrey Grant of St Anne's, Pimlico – a gentleman very often at Stephen's table, a stout effeminate, purring gentleman, adored by the ladies and detested by Judith. There was also in the Newmark household the Methodist tradition of the Rockage family in which Phyllis had been brought up. Maria Rockage was still alive, a kindly rheumatic old Dowager in the place in Wiltshire. She was for ever sending the Newmark family pamphlets – 'The Miner's Lament', 'The Royal Road to Hell', 'The Shopman's Vision' – interspersed with delightful, gay and very human epistles. She lamented grievously that she could not come up to London to see Judith, who had once lived with her for nearly ten years and whom she adored. Many of Mr Aubrey Grant's congregation came to Cadogan Place – old Mr and Mrs Pomeroy were very prominent – and quite awful Judith found them all. The scent on Mr Grant's handkerchief alone was enough to send her out of the room when he was there.

The third division was the social one. Into this, at times, the other two divisions penetrated, but Will and Christabel, Newmark and Phyllis, various Newmark cousins, did not truly belong.

Sylvia Herries, young though she was, was mistress here. She knew the London social, literary, Bohemian world completely. She laughingly declared that all the adventurers in London came to her tiny house in Brook Street. Indeed she did not care who came. She kept open house. Neither she nor Garth – now a very elegant, charming young man – seemed to have much money. They were for ever in desperate straits. Will – who was in these days more generous than of old – must have helped them again and again. They reminded Judith constantly of herself and Georges in those old, mad, adventurous days. That was perhaps why she came to care for them more than any other of the Herries relations, and why she made her alliance with them. Sylvia was her own kind – audacious, reckless, pleasure-loving, but also serious, practical and wise about other people.

It soon became obvious that Stephen disliked her constant

visits to the little house in Brook Street, a little house that was all
light colours, jingling pianos, poodle dogs and noise. There were
authors like the Bulwers, Letitia Landon, Theodore Hook, young
Ainsworth, of whom he could not possibly approve. There were
dancers, opera singers, racing men and ladies of extremely doubt-
ful reputation. Judith had, alas, no more of those fine serious
conversations with which on the first morning she had been
honoured. It seemed to him really lamentable that a woman of
her years should care for such a world. He had been right, as he
constantly told Phyllis in the sacredness of their huge four-
poster, in wondering whether anyone so brazen about her bastard
child was a suitable guest for them, and poor Phyllis, who loved
Judith with all her heart, tried to keep the peace. But what
Phyllis really did not understand was that Judith should be so
deeply horrified at the present state of the London world and yet
enjoy the parties in Brook Street so greatly. She seemed like two
different women in one.

Then the climax arrived. On an afternoon of the third week of
Judith's stay, Sylvia Herries was alone with Judith in the Newmark drawing-room. Sylvia was looking most bewitching with
her ringlets, rose-coloured tulle, a waist so small as to be almost
invisible, and a printed satin scarf. She danced about the room
like a fairy, she bowed with mock ceremony to the pedestal and
the lady's head thereon, she imitated Stephen, whom she found
entirely ridiculous. Judith also was seized with a devil. She
valsed with Sylvia round and round the room. The 'valse'
was still new enough to be divine. They danced ever more madly.
They danced into a small table that held a large preposterous
vase of the brightest green. It tumbled with a crash to the ground,
and, of course, at that precise moment Stephen entered with old
Mr Pomeroy.

There was nothing to be said, nothing to be done. There the
vase was in a thousand pieces. There were the two ladies – one of
them old enough to be the other's mother – hot, dishevelled, and
Judith had, a moment before, lost one of her shoes. Stephen gave
one of his grim sacrificial smiles, Sylvia departed with a private
moue of amusement for Judith's benefit (seen, however, by
Stephen). Judith did her best to become, quickly again, an elderly
dignified lady.

'Oh, it is of no importance, no importance at all,' said Stephen,
bending stiffly to pick up some pieces. 'An old family heirloom –
but still – no matter, no matter.'

But he never forgave Judith that broken vase. An ivory fan, a green vase: these are the things of which family histories are made. It was quite clear – Stephen now made it plainly apparent – that it was time that the visit of Judith and Adam came to an end.

'Come and stay with us, darling,' said Sylvia. 'For as long as you please.'

'No,' said Judith. 'Cumberland is my proper place.'

And it *was*. She would not, she knew, be happy in the little house in Brook Street. *That* was not her home, any more than was Stephen's. Her holiday (and oh! how she had enjoyed it!) was at an end.

So she looked round her to collect herself and her things, and found Adam. Not that she at all had forgotten him. It had been wonderful to see him against this new background and with new people. She found that he was enterprising, reserved and extra-ordinarily generous. She had known all these things about him since the beginning of time, but they wore a fresh dress in this fresh world. His generosity was surely astonishing, for he had very little money unless his London relations gave him some. In any case he was always buying things for the little Newmarks, for his mother, for Phyllis. To Sylvia, whom he worshipped, he gave nothing. All the little Newmarks loved him, even the spectacled Horace, who was not lavish with his affections. Mary and her sister Phyllis would be demonstrative, but he shrank from their demonstrations with horror. He allowed no one any physical approach. He produced a toy, a doll, a horse, a rattle for the baby, flowers or whatever, and he said 'Here!' or 'That's for you, ma'am'. He looked at you sternly while he presented it, for-bidding you to thank him. Then he escaped. He escaped very often, went off on his own affairs. He was, in fact, very happy during this visit.

The visit came to a close, both for Judith and Adam, with an adventure that it was not likely that they would forget. It was the recurrent adventure of Judith's life: once, in London, a boy hanging; twice, in Paris, an elephant escaping; and now, the third time.

On the evening of Monday the eighth of November, Amery Herries took Judith, Adam and his sister-in-law Sylvia to the Adelphi Theatre to witness a performance of *The Heart of London*, or *A Sharper's Progress*, by William Thomas Mon-crieff. This was a glorious play, and although not intended for the young did Adam no kind of harm.

The play over, they stepped from one melodrama into another.

The Strand, lit with the flares of burning stakes carried head-high, and in the distance towards Covent Garden by an over-turned cart that had been set alight, showed a wild fantasy of faces, a mob that now was stagnant like a dead pond and then broken as though by a whipping wind, all this driven by a roar that had nothing human in it save an occasional woman's scream.

The citizens of London, excited by Mr Hunt at a meeting at the Rotunda in Blackfriars Road, were making their way to the West End that they might assist the cause of Reform. As soon as the shouts were heard the doors of the Adelphi were closed, but Amery's party had slipped out five minutes earlier, to secure a hackney coach. The doors were closed behind them; before they could consider their position they were swung forward into the street. Judith, Adam's arm through hers, saw neither Amery nor Sylvia again that night.

It was as though Judith and Adam fell into a jungle of under-growth. Above them bodies towered and whether they wished it or no they were carried forward to the cries of 'Down with the Police!' 'Reform!' 'No Peel!' 'No Wellington!'

Down there in the undergrowth they conversed:

'Never mind, Mother: I'm here,' said Adam.

'Now, don't you let go!' Judith said crossly. This was imper-tinence, to treat her and her son in this fashion. A light swung to the sky, and stars escaping, a golden net scattered among the chimney-pots. Then the sky was darkened, and a large face at-tached to a stout body in moleskins was rosy in the glare of a burning stake stinking of tar.

'No Wellington! Down with Wellington!' roared the mole-skins most good-naturedly. He stank of gin, and his hand, roughened with honest toil, stroked Judith's cheek.

At that touch fear, that she had known so seldom in her life, caught her and pressed against her. A bear tortured, a boy hanged, Adam's father clinging to her while the horses' hoofs pranced in the air, these once again encompassed her.

'Reform! Reform!' shrieked a woman, her hair about her face and a basket on her arm. Judith looked at Adam and saw that he was quite unafraid and greatly enjoying everything.

'Adam, in a moment there should be a turning to the river. Watch for it!'

But the impetuous movement ceased. Staring around her she saw that their progress had been far more rapid than she had supposed, for they were in Downing Street and had halted in front of Lord Bathurst's residence. She knew the house well, for Garth Herries had taken her to a reception there. By squirming her body through a funny jumble of legs, chests, arms and hands she found a corner for Adam and herself against some railings, and was able to observe from there how a gentleman, his face crimson with rage, came out on to the balcony. He was armed with a brace of pistols and, shouting in a voice thick with anger, told them that if they committed any illegal act he would fire. Groans, yells, shouts of 'Go it! Go it!' answered him, whereupon another gentleman arrived on the balcony and took the pistols from him. Then everyone cheered and seemed suddenly radiant with good spirits.

At that same moment Judith perceived that Adam was gone. She became at once a frenzied woman. Any self-control that she had ever learnt, any caution or reserve, was lost. She screamed like a madwoman, 'Adam! Adam!', tried to move and found that she could not, beat on some stout manly chest: 'Let me go! Let me go! Let me through! Can't you see? My boy ... Adam! Adam!'

But it happened that a strong body of the new police had just arrived from Scotland Yard that they might form themselves into a line at the end of King Street to prevent the mob from proceeding to the House of Commons. At once a great shout went up: 'The Peelers!' 'The Peelers!' 'Down with the Peelers!'. As though the ground were agitated with earthquake, the crowd rocked forward and back, seeming to rise in places like a bulging floor about to crack. A line of wavering flame ran against the walls of the houses where men with lighted wood were ranging themselves in a line of defence. But Judith saw and heard nothing. Adam was lost, Adam might be crushed underfoot, she would never see Adam again; and at that frantic thought all the world that had seemed so important, social, political, religious – yes, and all the Herries, all Uldale, all her individual life and desires, blew like scraps of burnt paper into the air. Her shawl was torn from her, her wide-puffed sleeves rent. She beat on some face with her hands, she tore some cheek with her nails. 'Let me go! Let me go! Can't you see? My boy's gone!'

But no one saw and no one cared. A general fight was toward. Inspector Lincoln of the E Division had arrived with seventy men. The tri-coloured flag that had 'Reform' painted on it – the banner of the riot – was captured by the Peelers. There was a rush to recapture it. A man, bare-breasted, his shirt hanging in ribbons from his back, black-haired, brawny, his chest tattooed with a ship in violet and green, hung above the mob like a sign. He had in his hand a hatchet. Judith, seeing him with a strange and memorable distinctness, beheld him, as it seemed to her, trample on her boy. The crowd rose and fell; she was swept off her feet and would, it may be, have ended all her adventures there and then for ever had not some man caught her to him so that she was soaked, as it were, in his sweat and ale and dripping clothes, her head against his beard, his hand upon her breast. A fine thing for an old lady of fifty-six! But it saved her. Crushed, with her face in his rough hair, seeing nothing, frantic for Adam, she heard around her the strange sough and sigh of a mob suddenly terrified, resolved to run, the wind beating from under their feet, as though it would raise them to the sky. 'Reform!' 'Reform!' 'Reform!' 'The Peelers!' 'The Peelers!'

And then sudden quiet, a child crying, a whistle sharply blown, and she herself, her cheek bleeding, was half sitting, half crumpled on the pavement. But she was up in a moment. She could run now; there was nothing to stop her. As though God had crooked His little finger, there was no one there. Some man leant against the railings moaning and nursing his head, a beaver hat lay in the roadway, a burning faggot sent up a twist of smoke, and the silence was like a miracle. A yard away there was Adam, crying 'They're on the run! They're on the run! Mother, look, look!'

He had never been more than a yard away, then. She was furious with him and, her hair about her face, did what she had never done before – slapped his face.

'You careless boy! You careless boy!'

But he was enchanted. It was the best adventure of his life so far. His mouth was bleeding, his coat and trousers torn, but he laughed and laughed as though he'd never have done.

Then she hugged and kissed him.

'I thought you were killed,' she said. She felt an old, old woman, an ache in every bone and her head like a turnip. Very characteristically, she recovered her dignity.

'Now we'll find a hackney coach,' she said.

The watchman was calling up from the street below two o'clock

of the morning before Adam came in to wish her goodnight. She
was sitting up, a very old lady indeed she felt, propped up with
pillows and telling her different aches to mind their business and
behave. There was a bruise on her forehead, one knee was lamen-
tably swollen, but there was no real harm done ... only she was
very old of a sudden. Nine hundred and ninety.

'Come here and kiss me,' she said.

Adam was in his nightdress, and, with a purple lump the size
of a lemon over one eye, looked no beauty.

He laughed and sat on the bed, her arm around him. She made
him put on her furred dressing-gown and furred slippers, for the
room was viciously cold. There was a warming-pan inside the
bed now, and she made him slide his feet inside against hers.

So he slipped into the circle of her arm, lay there with his
black hair in his eyes, too eagerly excited to sleep yet. The panic
of her fear that she had lost him was still with her. She had never
loved him with such passionate intensity and she had never felt
so old. Her brain formed odd confused pictures for her, nothing
tangible, nothing consecutive. In the big stone fireplace a baby
fire leapt as though it were trying its first steps in life so that it
might really be a fine grown-up fire one day. An impenetrably
black picture of a forest, a lonely tower, and some horsemen
swayed a little on its cord, blown by all the draughts of heaven,
some of whom whistled through the wallpaper like lonely spirits
trying to keep their courage up. Three candles guttered on the
table beside the four-poster with the green hangings; a mirror
topped with heavy gilt feathers reflected the light. And under
and above all this was the dreadful cold, a cold worse than
Arctic, for it was damp. Soon Adam was lying inside the bed
folded in his mother's arms as he had not been since he was a tiny
boy at Watendlath.

Without words they reached a loving intimate security that
daylight and Adam's dislike of manifestation had hindered at
Uldale. It had always been there, but for long now she had not
had his heart beating, as it were, inside her very body.

Idly she watched the pictures come and go: Stephen saying
'And now let us pray'; Sylvia Herries imitating some ballet-
dancer at the Opera; young Mr Harrison Ainsworth (so handsome but wearing too many rings and his curls too heavy with
Macassar oil) telling her about his recent Italian journey, and
how he had found a rouge-pot at Pompeii; gossip about Ball
Hughes and the Bulwers and Lady Blessington and Holland

House – and then, over all this nonsense, the figure of the man with the ship of violet on his chest, raising his hatchet . . .

She held Adam closely to her, kissed him, stroked his forehead. He did not resist nor move away as he would normally have done, but sleepily murmured: 'Down with the Peelers!' 'Down with Wellington!' 'Down with the Peelers!'

'Hush, dear. Don't think of the horrid thing. I wonder how Amery and Sylvia are! Dear me! how incredibly selfish! I have never thought of them until this instant!'

Then the dancing pictures vanished. She saw something else and with extraordinary clearness. She raised herself on her pillows. Adam tickled her foot with his.

'Adam, wake up! There is something that I must say!'

He took her hand in his.

'Adam – you will shortly be a grown man and I shall be an old woman. I had not thought of it until this moment. How dreadful to be old! And I shall not be a nice old woman. I shall want my way. I made the mistake of my whole life when I stayed at Uldale. We should have gone to Watendlath. I have become Herries and made you Herries and shall wish you to be more and more Herries. Adam, promise me that, however I wish it, you will keep your independence. You are not to be Herries. You are illegitimate anyway, and your father was so little Herries as not to matter. I shall want to keep you later. You will be all I shall have. But you are not to permit me. Do you hear? However much I love you . . . Dear me, dear me, what a nasty old woman I am going to be!'

Then, as there was no response, she said again:

'You are not to allow me to swallow you, do you understand? Fight me, if need be. In another ten years I shall be completely Herries, from head to toe. How horrible! Adam, do you hear me.'

'What, Mama?'

'You are to keep your independence. I love you too much for it to be good for either of us.'

'And when the Peelers were coming . . .' he murmured.

The vision passed. She saw nothing, but gathered him closer into her arms, and he slept, holding her hand tightly in his, while she gazed out into the room and watched the little fire surrender its life, and the candles blow unsteadily in the wind.

WESTAWAYS: FATHER AND SON

IT was not true to say that Walter Herries was without imagination. He could see very vividly things that were not actually in front of him, only they must, those things, if they were
going to act on him powerfully, *spring* from facts. Then, his
imagination once started, he could be obsessed, obsessed by his
own grandeur, by his sense of power, by the thought that he was
a Herries, and, above all, by the knowledge that he was Uhland's
father.

At this very time that Judith was in London breaking vases,
meeting Mr Disraeli, and scratching the cheeks of rioters, Walter
was taking his son Uhland day after day up the hill to Ireby to
watch the Fortress growing. Uhland was now fifteen years of age,
and the Fortress was half its way to heaven.

It must be remembered that it was not yet called the Fortress –
that name came to it later – but already it was beginning to be
grim of aspect. Mr Carstairs, bothered by rheumatism and this
cursed Northern climate, was not in the best of tempers. And he
was beginning to dislike Walter Herries extremely. He had never
been bullied before, being a man of some personality and temper.
Walter Herries often spoke to him as he would to his groom, and
Carstairs would have given the job up long ago were it not that he
was aware that the Herries were now important people in
London and a useful connexion, that Walter threw money about,
and (this the most important with Carstairs, who was, finally, a
man of feeling) that Walter could show, at times, an extraordinary and even pathetic charm.

He wanted the place to look like a castle. It was to have battlements and towers, towers from whose summit a flag could fly.
That was the moment of Romanticism, of the Waverley Novels,
of *Weltschmerz,* of *Pelham* and (a little late) *Childe Harold* and
Werther. There was no *Weltschmerz* in Walter, but he would
have his battlements and a flag flying. So the place was going up,
grim and grey and forbidding. Its half-grown walls could already
be seen from all the country round.

Nearly every day Walter and Uhland rode up there, Walter on
a big white horse, Uhland on a small black pony. As you watched
them together (as Carstairs watched them) you might sometimes

think their positions reversed, that Uhland was the father and Walter the son. There *was*, Carstairs decided again and again, something most truly pathetic in their relationship, for Walter dearly loved his son. It was the one true, selfless, generous instinct in him. Selfless? That perhaps not, for an intense family pride was at the root of it. But pride? Pride in that queer, misshapen, white-faced ancient child, whose sharp countenance was always grave, whose voice was so cold and detached, whose chilly eyes watched you so solemnly, with so deep and questioning a gaze. Only once had Carstairs seen the boy moved by some human emotion, and that was when, by a chance, having met young Adam in Keswick and had a chat with him, he had said something about him to Walter. Young Uhland had been listening; colour had crept into his cheeks, light into his eye. Walter had made a scornful gesture, and it seemed that Uhland was going to say something in protest. He checked himself.

It was, thought Carstairs, an interesting thing to see that stout, red-faced man with his bright waistcoats, his pins and his rings, his confidence and his pride, surrender to that colourless child in his black suit, so silent, so neat and so watchful. Yes, watchful! That was what Uhland was, watchful and waiting. Meanwhile his sister Elizabeth, the prettiest child, Carstairs thought, that he had ever seen, never shared her father's company. It was as though he had no daughter.

That was a month of chills and mists, of sudden winds and gleaming suns. One afternoon when the sun ran in and out of the clouds like a jester, Walter and Uhland rode up to Ireby.

'Father,' said Uhland, 'why are you building this house?'

Why was he building this house? What a question! Nevertheless, this was the first occasion on which Uhland had shown any interest in the affair. Day after day they had ridden up there, and Walter, in a flood of talk, had shown his son how this would be there, and that here, that the ballroom would be so long, and the dining-room catch the sun at such a time, that he should have a room to himself, in one of the towers if he liked, so that he could look over the whole country, over to Keswick, over to Scotland . . .

And Uhland had watched him gravely and plucked at his upper lip in a way that he had, but said no word.

'Why am I building this house?' Walter explained. 'For you, my son, and for the glory of the family, so that when you marry, my son . . .'

'I shall never marry,' said Uhland.

'Ah, you think that now, Uhland, but the time will come when you will see a lady so beautiful . . .'

But Uhland shook his head.

'I don't care about women,' he said.

But, of course, he must marry. Did he not wish to carry on the family?

He looked at his father sardonically. There were plenty of people to do that – all the lot at Uldale, all his relations in London.

Walter felt a chill at his heart. Of course, Uhland must have sons, and they must have sons, and sons and sons!

'Look, Father – there is Mrs Herries!'

She was there again then, standing on the edge of the rough bare field, her tall black figure framed by the rough bare hills. A sensation of disgust caught him. He had not seen her for several weeks and thought that she had at last wearied of this crazy, imbecile watching. For crazy and imbecile she was! At first he had been rather pleased at the sight of her. He was having his revenge, although a revenge for what he by now would have found it rather difficult to say. Jennifer and her children had shrunk to rather poor game, although he hated the boy for his health and good looks, while his own son . . .

'Why does she come here, Father, day after day?' Uhland asked.

'She's mad,' Walter answered brusquely.

'But how mad? I thought mad people screamed and broke things.'

'She shall scream well enough before I have finished with her.' He felt vindictive today and would like to hurt someone. And yet he was not by nature cruel. If things only went well with him he could be as jolly and generous as anyone. But what was all this, what his treasures in Westaways, his position in the County, this new place of his, if Uhland were not to take pleasure in them? His big body throbbed sometimes with a savage desire to take his boy and squeeze him into some sort of life of response and activity. Here was he doing so much, striving so hard, and for what kind of return? He turned back on his horse and, seeing that dark figure against the skyline, thought for a moment of what it would be to have, indeed, John Herries for a son. He hated that young Herries. Yes, he would drive them all to perdition before he'd done.

He drew his horse closer to Uhland's pony and, speaking very gently, he asked him:

'Will you not care, Uhland, to have a son to succeed to all this when you are gone?'

'No, Father. Why should I?'

Walter sighed. 'If you cannot see that, I cannot make you.'

Uhland, after a pause, said quietly:

'I should be glad to have a brother like Adam Paris.'

'Adam Paris?' Walter, in his impatience, made his horse rear. 'That boy! Why do you think of him so much? He cares nothing for you.'

'I like him – just as I hate John Herries.' He looked about him, then asked: 'Father, when you have built this, will John Herries hate it?'

'Yes, my boy, he will.'

'Ah – then I am glad you are building it, Father.'

'Why do you hate young Herries so much? You scarcely see him.'

Uhland considered it.

'Why do people hate one another, Father?'

'Because of something they have done, some injury or harm they have done.'

'Well – that's the reason then.'

'But young Herries has never harmed you.'

'No. But I will harm *him*.'

An incomprehensible boy! But Walter had never been clever at analysing other people and, in any case, his clear view of his son would be fogged by his blinding absorbing love for him. He did not know it, but he would never have cared for a strong healthy son as he loved this weakling.

They arrived at the place. A great bustle was toward, men moving with barrows and carts, climbing ladders, shouting, hammering, cutting stone, filing and sawing. The house, half raised, lifted blind eyes to the sky. It was built of Cumberland stone, beautiful in its dim blues and greens and greys with here a soft blush of rose, there a strand of gold, but the effect of the whole was nevertheless grim and cold. It promised to be strong; nothing, it seemed, would conquer it.

Walter climbed over into the interior and Uhland stood and watched him. Within, on that misty day, everything was in a half-light. The men, accustomed to his presence, went about their work. Through a gap where a window would be, Walter

could see the sharp fall of the hill. There, in the cup of the
ground, would be Uldale. He savoured in his nostrils, for a
moment, the especial blend of rough soil, sharpened with the
grey-stone of some solitary farm blending with the bare outline
of the rising hills beyond, cold and bleak but strong and deeply
true – that meeting of strength and austerity and richness that is
Cumberland's gift to those who love her. He loved her as an
animal loves its home. But today he was restless and dissatisfied.
He climbed his way out again, and after a word or two to the
foreman, rode down the hill. He went a little ahead and Uhland,
watching, as he always did, for everything, saw something very
strange. His father had turned the corner by the little wood into
the road that ran from Uldale to Bassenthwaite. Out of the wood
came two people: Walter was already gathered into the dusk, but
they saw Uhland, and he saw them before they turned back into
the wood again.

They were his sister Elizabeth and John Herries.

He rode on after his father.

Uhland's room at Westaways was as bare as a monastic cell. The
walls held no pictures; the only furniture was a bed, two chairs, a
bookcase, a washstand and a cupboard.

There was, however, more in this room than this stiff furniture. There were the animals.

Uhland, since a very small child, had shown a strong interest
in any animal wounded, hurt or deformed. A very pretty little
picture might be elaborated of a pale-faced, limping little boy
sorry for hurt animals because he was himself hurt. But you
could not think of sentiment in connexion with Uhland – it froze
at his touch.

Nevertheless, in this lonely world through which we pass, each
of us shadowed from the other, who knows or can truly discern
the instincts of the human mind? It was enough, in the case of
Uhland, that in a cold, undemonstrative fashion he cared for any
damaged animal that came his way. The animals, on their side,
appeared to recognize him as one of themselves. They never
showed him that especial attention given by animals to
human beings who are kind to them; sometimes, we may suspect,
with a sense of conventional duty. They showed Uhland just as
much feeling as they would to another animal. They did not
trust him any more than they would trust one another. Yes, he
was one of themselves.

At this particular time, there was in his bedroom a bright parrot with pink feathers, in a gilt cage. His claw was bandaged. Uhland had bought him of a sailor in Keswick. There was a dog, mostly spaniel, in a basket. It wore, with an air of comic but patient protest, a large yellow silk handkerchief over one eye. Uhland had found it dying in a ditch near Threlkeld, minus an eye, after suffering torture at the hands of some farm-children. In another basket was a wild cat, minus a leg, that had been caught in a trap on Cat Bells. This animal, black, with fierce burning eyes, spent most of its time gathered on its haunches and spitting, but it allowed Uhland to do what he wished with it.

In vain had Walter protested that it was unwholesome to keep animals in the room where you slept. Uhland briefly stated that he would see to it that they were clean, that he would trust no one but himself to look after them. Walter submitted. If they made the boy happy there they must remain. And Uhland saw to it that they *were* clean. The room was spotless, with an odd, dried, mummified scent of the cloistered cell about it. Its only sign of life was the sudden chattering of the parrot, who would gibber unintelligibly to himself and rattle the bars of his gilt cage.

Today, coming in from his ride, Uhland squatted down on the floor and examined the dog's eye. Very skilfully, and with fingers that were strangely delicate, he undid the yellow silk handkerchief, washed the angry red eye-socket, put some ointment on a long tear above the right temple. The dog, a black spaniel with a touch of sheepdog, waited calmly while this was done. When it was over he lay down in his basket and licked his paws. Uhland gave him some water, then squatted down beside him, staring in front of him. There was a lamp on the chest of drawers near him that gave an ivory patina to his pale cheek. The black cat crouched in his basket and watched him with fiery eyes.

When he thought, he thought not like a little boy but like a man for whom all illusions are over. He had never had any illusions. He saw the things in front of him with cold clarity. He was only a small boy, but he knew an intensity of controlled feeling that was quite mature. He knew shame because he was not as other boys, haughty pride because he was the son of his father. His father was rich, powerful, had servants, horses, lands. He would have respected and cared for his father more deeply had his father cared for him less and showed less that he cared. The only two human beings who entered at all at this time into his emotions were Adam and John Herries. He loved the one and hated the other. He hated John Herries because he had been brought up from a baby to do so, because John was handsome and strong, but chiefly because he was gentle and submissive. Anyone who was submissive roused in him, child though he was, something wild and savage. To be submissive when you were strong enough to be otherwise, to bend your neck like a woman when you were hearty enough to be a proper man! It was as though someone preferred to be lame when he need not! He caught a sense perhaps also of John's dislike and fear of himself. He *knew* that John Herries was afraid of him, child though he was, and the contempt he felt for fear was closely allied to hatred.

For these same reasons he had always loved and admired Adam Paris. That stout, rough, untidy brown body with its independence, freedom, absence of all sentiment, caught and held for ever his admiration. Adam Paris did not care whether he, Uhland Herries, lived or died, and so Uhland loved him.

As he squatted there on the floor his thoughts were dark. He had guessed for a long while that his sister Elizabeth had some secret. They had nothing at all in common, he and his sister. She was afraid of him, and he thought her pretty but uninteresting. But now – she and John Herries! Uhland knew as yet nothing about the love of men and women, although the gossip of stable-boys and farm-hands had long ago told him all that there was to learn about the physical facts of conception and generation. The thing did not interest him. In any case Elizabeth was only a child as he himself was. But that John Herries should be on any kind of terms with a member of his family, roused, slowly, steadily, all his coldest anger. He looked like a little old brooding man as he sat there on the hard floor in the light of the lamp.

On the very next afternoon, as it happened, Uhland encountered John Herries.

Riding out on his pony (he was always happy when riding because his deformity was not apparent) he met John Herries walking alone on the road beyond Portinscale. John was strolling along, thinking deeply, his hands behind his back. As he walked his lips moved. He was very handsome in the dark-blue coat, fawn pantaloons, a brown beaver hat. Uhland pulled up the pony.

'Excuse me, sir,' he said in his queer grave child's voice.

John looked up and at once was seized with the chill of apprehension and discomfort that always attacked him whenever this boy was near him. He had been thinking of charming things – of the faint pallor of the dried bracken against the hill, of the fact that soon Aunt Judith and Adam would be back from London, of a party that they had had at Uldale for his sister when they had practised archery on the lawn – yes, and of Elizabeth whom he loved with all his soul, and for whom he was waiting until she should be old enough for marriage. And then – this hobgoblin! To be afraid of a small boy on a fat pony! But he was afraid.

Uhland did not get down from his pony. He simply said in his clear chill voice:

'If I see you with my sister again, you shall be beaten by my father's servants.'

John replied contemptuously:

'How is it you are out, young Uhland, without your governess?'

But Uhland went on:

'I mean it. I saw you both at Ireby.'

John stood there looking at him. He was determined to conquer this causeless apprehension. Gentle and courteous though he was, he had a manly spirit; it was true, perhaps, that this child was the only creature of the world of whom he was afraid. He might even if he looked at him long enough pity him for his pale face, his meagre body that could not keep itself straight even on a pony. But he looked – and dropped his eyes. He was rooted there as one is in a nightmare.

'Now look here, young man,' he said lightly, 'you keep to your own business, which is firing paper bullets out of pop-guns, I should think. This is a fine day; I'm walking for my health, you're riding for yours. We go opposite ways.'

'Then you leave my sister alone,' Uhland repeated. 'Your family and my family hate one another, and I'm glad they do. When I'm a man I'll do you a hurt if I can.'

'When you're a man—' John laughed. 'That's a long way. Good afternoon.'

He passed on, but he knew in his heart that it was all he could do to prevent himself from running.

Meanwhile Uhland rode up the hill a little way and then back to Westaways. He would have a word or two to say to Elizabeth. He found her in her room sewing 'or some such nonsense'. He limped in, sat on a corner of the sofa near to her, crossed his legs and looked at her. He recognized, of course, that she was a beautiful girl; he had all the Herries quality of perceiving things as they were, and he saw her fairness and delicacy, so that every colour from the pale shadowed gold of her hair to the warm pallor of her neck and arms was in perfect harmony; he saw all this, her fragility and strength, the gentleness of her eyes, the humour of her mouth. He admired her as a valuable family possession, and the thought that young Herries should be familiar with her revolted him – but revolted him in his own quiet child's way. Nevertheless, there is no one more determined than a child when he *has* an obsession.

'I saw you and John Herries at Ireby,' he remarked.

They were twins, but to Elizabeth he had never seemed like a relation at all. They had never done anything together, never cared for the same things nor thought the same thoughts. Elizabeth had many faults but they were not Uhland's. Her worst fault just now perhaps was her almost sulky reserve. This was the result of her father's ignoring of her. That had eaten deeply into her. She would let either her father or Uhland torture her to the last point of endurance and not utter a cry. She loved John Herries, but he was a man and she was only a child. She met him secretly, wrote to him and the rest chiefly because she knew what her father and Uhland thought of him. It was therefore not probable that Uhland would get anything from her now.

'Yes?' she said, continuing her sewing.

'You are never to speak to him again,' Uhland went on.

'Who said so?'

'I say so.'

'Indeed?' She looked at him, smiling. Then she bit off her thread. 'I shall speak to exactly whom I please.'

'You shall not. If you do I shall tell your father.'

'Tell him, then.'

'He'll beat you.'

She smiled again. 'You don't think I care for that ... Uhland, what a baby you are!'

That stung him, but he showed no signs. He nursed his knee in his hands, leaning forward and looking at her.

'Those people at Uldale are our enemies,' he said. 'They will have to leave there and go somewhere else when father's house is finished.'

'Yes?' she said.

'Father will send you away to school if he knows,' he went on.

'I shall be glad to go away,' she answered. 'I am always asking him to send me to school.'

'Well,' said Uhland, getting up, 'if I see John Herries talking
to you again I shall shoot him.'

'Then you'll be hung,' she said, smiling.

'Perhaps it's Herries that will be hung,' he answered. Then he
limped away.

But he had no intention whatever of saying anything to his
father. He liked to keep his secrets.

Walter on his side was driven, after that little talk with his son
on Ireby, by a strange restlessness. What had the child meant
about never marrying? He *was*, of course, a child. He knew
nothing of women or marriage . . . but the thin echo of that small
cold voice, like the whistle of wind through the wallpaper, frightened Walter. The boy was growing. He had now his own
thoughts and plans. Walter ought to know what these were. He
discovered with angry resentment that he knew almost nothing
about his son. The resentment may be said to have been directed
against the Deity, Who was not at that moment paying all the
attention to Walter Herries' affairs that He should do.

So Walter went in to say goodnight to his son. He was sitting
up in bed, propped against his pillows, reading, by the light of a
candle, a book. A dark cloth was over the parrot's cage, the dog
was curled up asleep, the cat sat blinking at the candle.

Uhland was reading *Ivanhoe*.

'What a silly book, Papa!' he said. 'I am certain that people
never talked like that.'

Walter placed his great bulk on the bed and put his arm round
his son. Under Uhland's nightdress there was a sharp rigid spine-
bone that seemed to protest against the caressing warmth of
Walter's hand.

'Why, not, my boy?' said Walter, who had never read *Ivanhoe*.
'Sir Walter Scott is a very great man.'

'Have you ever read a book called *Frankenstein*, Papa?'

'No, my boy.'

'That's better than this stuff. Frankenstein creates a Monster
and cannot escape it. There is too much fine writing, however.'

Walter sighed. Although this room was so clean yet you were
oppressively conscious of the animals in it. Their very silence was
alarming. He drew Uhland closer to him and felt the hard casing
of ribs on that bony little body. He kissed him. Uhland resigned
himself. He knew so well, oh, so very, very well what this was,
this having his face pushed into the thick hot vast territory of his
father's waistcoat with its hard brass buttons. Beneath his thin

cheek his father's heart pounded like an imprisoned thumping fist. If his hand slid down to the hard warm expanse of his father's thigh it was as though he touched hot steel. Moreover, he detested sentiment.

'Uhland,' said Walter, 'I was hearing this evening that they are ordering fresh troops into Carlisle. There is fear of riots over all this Reform.'

'Yes, Papa.'

'Do you understand about Reform?'

'Oh yes, Papa.' Uhland allowed his hand to be held and imprisoned in his father's. 'Parliament has chosen its members from the wrong places – little places have many representatives and big places have few. The people are not at all represented.'

('Good God!' thought Walter. 'Who *is* this son of mine?')

'Yes, Uhland,' he went on, rather heavily. 'The people want to throw us out, my boy. They want the country to belong to *them*. They're tired of seeing us have the best of everything, and I don't blame 'em. All the same it would never do if they had their way. Think what England would be like if the working-man did what he liked with it. Imagine if you had Posset in power in London instead of – well, instead of the Duke of Wellington, for example.'

Uhland agreed that it would be ridiculous. But, he added, interested:

'You see, Papa, there would be five Possets, not one Posset.'

Walter asked him to explain.

'Well, in Keswick there are hundreds of men think they're as good as Posset. But if it's you or the Duke of Wellington they *know* they're not so good, so while you or the Duke of Wellington rule there's only one of you, but if Posset were to rule all the others would want to as well.'

'Well,' said Walter after a pause, 'remember you're a Herries and belong to the finest family in England.'

'Are we the finest family in England?'

'Most certainly we are.'

'Then they are fine at Uldale too?'

'Yes,' he answered, laughing, 'so long as they go somewhere else to live.'

Then Uhland asked a strange question.

'Papa – is it part of you what your great-grandfather was?'

'What *do* you mean?'

'Well – your great-grandfather was a wicked man and married

a gipsy, who was Adam Paris' grandmother. Are you and Adam and I partly like we are because of what your great-grandfather did?'

'I can't say ... I suppose so ... Something.'

'But we are so different.'

'Now you go to sleep, Uhland ... Do you love your old father?'

'Yes, Papa.'

'You are all he has, you know. All he has in the world.'

'Yes, Papa.'

'He would do anything for you.'

'Yes, Papa.'

The dog began to move restlessly in his sleep, and he snapped his teeth at the flies of his dreams.

'I am sorry that you like to keep these animals in your room, Uhland. It is not good for your health.'

Uhland threw *Ivanhoe* on to the floor; then he turned over to sleep.

'Goodnight, Papa.'

'Goodnight, my boy.'

There was a pathos in the manner of Walter's exit: the heavy man, brilliant in his claret-coloured coat and rich brown pantaloons fitting tightly to his thighs, elaborately stepping softly on his toes that he might not disturb his son. He had blown out the candle. At the door he turned back to look. He could see nothing, and the only sound in the room was the dog in his dreams snapping at flies.

ENTRY OF THE FORTRESS

HE stood on the black edge of the rock and stretched his arms. He could have shouted with joy, for today was the great day of his life.

Near him, around him, subservient to him were many of the Family. There were present his father, Sir William Herries, Bart; his son Uhland; Sir James Herries, Bart, and the Venerable Rodney Herries, his brother, Archdeacon of Polchester in Glebeshire; Carey, Lord Rockage, and his wife Cecily and their son Roger; Stephen Newmark and his wife Phyllis; Garth Herries, his wife Sylvia, and Amery his brother; and, after these, more distant cousins, cousins by marriage or anything you like, Cards and Garlands and Golds and Ildens and Titchleys – only nobody from Uldale.

It was April 2nd, 1832, and his house on Ireby was triumphantly open.

It was six in the morning of the happiest day of Walter's life. The day, which was to end with a grand dinner and a magnificent ball to which the whole County had been invited, had begun with a run with the Blencathra Pack, and now here they were on the flanks of Helvellyn, so that the sun and the hills, the whole world as God had made it, might see the mighty glories of the Herries family and Walter Herries in particular.

Walter was as happy as a child. It was not conceit that he felt; he had no small vanities because of what he had done. Everything was inevitable. Because he was English and Herries and Walter, therefore he was King of the North. No force of heaven or earth could have helped it. No especial credit to himself that it was so.

Everything was well. God had seen to it that the weather should be right. There had been early in March a very heavy fall of snow, then towards the end of the month ten days of the loveliest possible weather, when the sun had burnt through a warm rosy mist, the crocuses had flowered in the Keswick gardens, the lambs gambolled in the meadows, the waters of Derwentwater, Bassenthwaite and Thirlmere shone with a blue as deep as any Italian lake, then colder again with a further snowfall on the tops, and now, in this early-morning misty air, a blue cloudless sky spread like a field of young violets above their heads.

As his eye covered the scene he saw that all the members of his party were there. Those staying with him were of course present, save only his mother and his wife, too delicate, poor women, for such an expedition. But the others whom he had lodged in Keswick and Bassenthwaite, in Braithwaite and Portinscale, were there also, not one of them was missing. It was a grand assemblage, headed by the great John Peel himself, whose tall bony figure, clad in his grey rough garment that descended almost to his knees, could be seen on a green knoll not far away.

Yes, it was a marvellous day: weather, scent and all would be right. The morning was as still as though it held its breath for very rapture. The hills in the distance were softly coloured in every shade from the faintest mauve to that dark indigo that has the bloom of the richest plums. On the rough ground below him he could see the huntsman's scarlet coat (the huntsman alone was permitted the scarlet), and near him the hounds, little white dots, rose and fell like shining pebbles.

His heart was moved, so that there were tears in his eyes as he caught a faint note of music. Then the music swells, running like a living human voice through the still air. Somewhere hounds have struck a 'drag'. The white pebbles draw together and all move upwards towards him.

A tall gaunt shepherd at his side in his excitement catches his arm and cries: 'Sista ... Sista ... Yonder, yonder he goes!'

Then scream and scream again bursts the silence, echoing back from valley and hill. The world that had been so still is broken with movement and shouting and the stir of action. It is good. Oh yes, it is very good indeed to be alive!

Walter had with him his father, Rodney the Archdeacon, Garth Herries and Sylvia his wife, but he was at that moment conscious of none of them. The hounds, in a kind of jolly frenzy, were answering to the holloa, and he too now had to answer, for he began to pound upwards, plunging into the boggy places, knocking his stout legs against stones and boulders. The leaders have struck the line, the hounds rush past Walter as though driven by a wild windy flurry; the music of the horn, of the cries, sweet and lovely, is all about him. He is himself crying 'Holloa! Holloa! Away! Away!'

Then the hounds were hidden by a breast of the hill and he paused, puffing a bit, blowing a trifle – for he was a big man and this ground was no light stuff to cover.

Unfortunately he found that he had Rodney the Archdeacon at his side, even clinging to his arm and blowing down his neck.

'Whoof! Whoof! Walter! Deary me! Deary me! ... Most exhausting! So early in the morning too! Whoof ... Now tell me, pray, my dear Walter, in this ridiculous hunting of yours there were some quite small dogs with the huntsman ...'

'Terriers! Terriers, my dear Rodney.'

'Really! Really! Is that so? Indeed!'

'Yes, yes. We'd never get a fox out of his hole without them—'

'Indeed! ... Do you think we shall see a fox?'

'We did see one just now. Down below us. There they are! There they are! Out on the brow. Come on, Rodney! Stir your hams. Now we're off!'

He went pounding off and fell headlong into a lake of mist. He was quite suddenly alone. No sound. No cry. The mist eddied and whirled.

He stayed where he was and was conscious of a foreboding, as though some whispering figure had crept close to his side. Why was he, who a moment ago had been so happy and confident, now helpless? A hand had been laid on his shoulder that he should stop to hear some judgement. He looked about him, but he was blind and, it seemed, deaf as well. How unforeseen a country this was, always, when you least expected it, coming up to assert its power over you. He did not put it like that, but he was like a little boy, blundering unexpectedly into the dark. The mist clung to him like thin lawn, then moved from him and faced him in a wall of blankness, then eddied like smoke, creeping along the ground, then pressed in upon him again filling his mouth and nose. He stared, dumbfounded, as though he expected to hear a voice . . .

It broke: a gap was there no bigger than a hand; a crag leapt into air, shaped like a face, black as jet. The ground, brown and then faintly green, came sliding from space, and then, in a second of time, swimming in a wall of bright and airy colour, the whole landscape was back again; the voices were there, calling, shouting. Only a little above him was the huntsman's red coat and the hounds in a broken sequence of white and brown and grey silhouetted against the blue of the morning sky. He wiped his face. 'Dammit!' he thought. 'It don't do to be alone here,' then laughed and ran like a schoolboy again up the slope.

All the world was alive and so fresh and bright that he could shout for joy. There is the sharp call of a raven; near him to the left on the slopes of the Fell are the small bodies of the Herdwick sheep – and there, just in front of him, can it really be, is the fox himself!

He is running with a slouching, slinking movement, first straight then with a jerk upwards again, stopping for an instant by some borran where he might hide, thinking better of it, round the crag, seen for an instant, running to higher ground, then vanishing.

The sight of that fox fired Walter as though he had himself created him. He began to pound upwards again. The hills rose with him, leading him on. They were bathed now in crystalline light, purer than the purest glass, alive with their own vibrant force, stronger than any human life and far more confident of their eternity. And then another miracle! For, reaching a higher slope, he was above the mist that lay below him in a sea of white shifting cloud while he himself trod on a firm sparkling floor of brilliant snow. The snow carpeted the ground for a space, glittering with points of fire, then the rock broke from it, hard and black, only to surrender to higher fields of brightness.

He crossed the snow as though on wings, the sun and the air lifting him, rounded a boulder and had the whole pack in view. Now a dreadful fear possessed him that he would be too late for the kill. He saw Garth and Sylvia swinging along not far from him and he waved his arms crying, 'Come on! Come on! Holloa! Holloa!'

Sylvia waved back to him and, great though the excitement of the moment was, his natural instinct about women, hot and strong in him, murmured: 'That's the loveliest female . . .'

His heart hammered as he leaped a low stone wall and found himself on bracken and in the thick of the mob. They had shut the fox away from an earth near by; you could just see him tracking for the rocks. But the hounds have edged him lower and lower.

'Aye,' said a little purple-faced man to Walter. 'What he's after is that borran yonder. The terriers'll have to be after him from below. That's what he likes.'

The little purple-faced man was trembling with excitement. He smelt oddly of bracken and snuff; he was a stranger to Walter, who felt a sort of indignation that he *should* be a stranger. Everyone today was a kind of dependant of the Herries family. No one should exist who was not. The little purple-faced man began frantically to run, and Walter ran with him. The fox had gone to earth, into a borran where he was 'head on' to his adversaries.

This was a big dog-fox and worth the fighting. The excitement now was terrific: the ground seemed to quiver with it. The air shuddered with shouts and cries and the snap-snapping of the hounds. The terriers were mad to get at him; one small animal, crazy with young pride and ambition, had struggled its way far into the borran. Suddenly it emerged, looking foolish. All the terriers stopped marking, and the hounds began to rush madly round the borran, yelping, yowling, bellowing. The huntsman and the whipper-in were cursing and swearing, and John Peel himself, with his funny, ill-fitting long coat, could be heard muttering his own particular Cumberland oaths. And this was where none of the Herries were of any use at all. They hung on to the fringe of the outside world – Will and Walter, Rodney and James, Garth and Amery – all of no importance. They might just as well be dead.

For the fox had slipped away underground and bolted. He was already at a considerable distance. The fear now was that he would find a borran so deep that it would be impossible to get at him or they would lose a terrier or two there. But no! He is out again, and the hounds have steered him away from the rocks. The hounds move now as though they have absolute command of the game and are certain of the end of it. The fox is out; he is tracing a thin trod through the bracken. The hounds, running from scent to view, are hard upon him. A moment later, Mischief or Satan or Hamilton has him by the throat; he vanishes beneath a flurry of white and brown and swinging tails. Walter drew a deep sigh; he stood, his legs planted wide, his chest out, burning satisfaction in his eyes. That had been a great hour, and now he must recover his dignity and gather his family about him again.

Rodney was at his elbow, but he did not want Rodney nor that fat idiot James his brother. He despised them both, because when he was short with them (as he often was) they took it like lambs. He moved among the Herries cousins – those of them stout enough of wind and strong enough of limb to achieve the 'kill' – with an air of fine and genial patronage. He felt like a king and thought it quite natural that they should feel that he was one. But the members of the family who really attracted him were Garth, Amery, and Sylvia. Amery, slender, stern-faced, grave, was the coming 'money' man of them all, already an important figure in the City, and Garth was jolly, careless and handsome: young though he was, he could drink anyone under the table and was ready for any escapade or devilry. But Sylvia! Her eyes shining, her cheeks rosy with health and excitement, framed by the hills and the glassy blue of the morning sky, she was the loveliest thing he had ever seen. She was ready, he was sure, for any gay adventure. Harmless, of course; but tonight when the splendid house was shining with light and colour, a laugh, a smile, a pressure of the hand . . .

He moved towards them. Then he remembered Uhland. How could he have forgotten him? The whole day was to be Uhland's! This day had no meaning unless it were all for Uhland. He turned back and began to search for his son on the faint green shadows of the lower slopes . . .

*   *   *

Two Titchley cousins – old maids from Carlisle and so entirely
unimportant that nobody ever learnt their names from the beginning to the end of the affair – sat on the corner of an almost
concealed sofa in the ballroom and considered the sight presented to them. One was stout and one was thin; as no one ever
learnt their names that is as far as the historian can go. They were
dressed in the fashions of 1820, with high waists, drapery of silk
netting over their busts, their ball-dresses short, with padded *rou-
leaux* at the bottom. One was in rose and the other in mignonette-
green. Their first cousin, an eminent doctor in Carlisle, had
brought them and, having brought them, completely forgot them.
However, they did not care; they had rooms in Keswick but were
determined not to return to them until the festivities were entirely
concluded. They were in a state of ecstatic and almost drunken
excitement and pleasure. A footman brought them ices and orangeade. No one else spoke to them the night long.

It was the loveliest sight they had ever beheld. They were at
first inclined to be shocked by the naked goddesses displayed in
the famous tapestries, they thought some of the costumes 'bare in
the extreme', they discovered a young man, quite drunk, behind
one of the gold curtains in a corner near to them, but soon as the
air grew more heated, the noise of the band in the gallery more
strident, they threw away convention and, their mouths a little
open, sipping their ices, surrendered to their ecstasy.

Above their turbans of figured gauze, above the high ceiling
painted with the stars of heaven and naked cherubs hanging garlands, climbed one of the two towers of the Fortress. In the high-
est room of the tower (which by his own choice was Uhland's
room) a monkey with one eye and a face of the deepest melancholy scratched his chest; a small terrier with a broken leg
whined, paused to listen, whined again; the parrot, under its
green baize covering, its head on its shoulder, slept a deep, philo-
sophic sleep. The moonlight soaked the room in a pale green light
and, very faintly, the sound of the fiddles, the bassoon and the
drums whispered in the air.

In the gardens everything was still and cold. Everything was
new – the stone walls, the steps, the fountain whose waters
flashed under the moon, the naked beds where the flowers would
soon be so splendid. The trees beyond the garden walls were old;
here daffodils were in bud, and the snowdrops dying. An owl
cried; the music, muffled but determined, drowned its cries.
Then from the heart of the trees a little wind rose and went
whistling and lamenting about the garden-beds and the paths as

though looking for its familiar friends who were gone. Beyond the
high road the landscape, falling to the valley, spreading to the
smoky hills, was soaked in moonlight and lay there as still as a
pattern on glass. A man from Ireby village walking out to meet
his sweetheart stayed for a moment in the road to listen to the
music, to stare at the blaze of lighted windows, then some sudden
apprehension – as though he feared that his girl would not be
there to meet him – hurried him on.

Around and about the lighted ballroom many of the rooms
were yet empty; some of them had ladders and pots of paint and
buckets. Here a chair lay on its face, there pictures were piled
against the wall; in one room workmen had left cheese and a
hunk of bread.

The ballroom blazed with colour like the page of an illuminated missal. Agnes Herries sat with Christabel, Walter's mother
on a little sofa, and everyone came and talked to them. Agnes was
feeling dreadfully ill; at her heart was a pain like a hand clutching and unclutching. She did not know what to say to Walter's
mother, with whom she had never been familiar. She could not
say that she liked this new house, for she hated it; nor that she
was sorry to have left Westaways, for she had hated that too; nor
that she was glad that Walter was happy, because she was not
glad. The sight of so many people whom she did not know,
whom she feared, made her sick. She knew that her little shrivelled body looked absurd in its gaudy ball-dress with the huge
sleeves like epaulettes. She knew that everyone despised her. Her
only happiness was to catch a glimpse once and again of her
lovely daughter Elizabeth, who in her dress of silver silk was, in
her mother's eyes, beautiful beyond compare. Once her son
Uhland, resting on an ebony cane that he now carried, came and
spoke to her. When he was gone Christabel said: 'What a clever
face Uhland has!'

'Yes, he is very clever.'

'I have never,' continued Christabel, who was longing for her
bed, 'seen so many of the family together in one room – never
since a Ball I once gave in London.'

She was no longer distressed by the memory of that eventful
Ball. It seemed to her now, on looking back, to have been a very
successful affair. She sought anxiously for Will, her husband.
Ah! there he was, talking to Amery Herries, a clever young man.
They would be talking about money, always Will's favourite
topic. Perhaps soon she might slip away to bed. Why, she won-

ered sleepily, had her son chosen so poor a specimen as Agnes
or his wife? But her wonderings were never very active. She had
ong ago learnt that it was wiser not to wonder about anything
ery deeply.

The band broke into one of the newest valses. The floor swam
vith colour, green and white, purple and rose. Laughter, music,
he movement of so many happy persons filled the air with a
,olden haze; the owl's cry could not penetrate the thick walls of
:umberland stone.

t was nearly midnight. At Uldale, John, Dorothy, Adam had all
;one to bed, but Judith sat in Jennifer's room looking after Jen-
iifer. Looking after Jennifer! An exasperating thing to do! Jen-
iifer had been ill for weeks, but they had had to set a guard about
ier door to keep her in bed. She was there now, propped up with
iillows, her eyes shining like fireflies. Her face was as white as
lough. Even in her bed she looked dishevelled, her heavy breasts
xposed, her nightdress torn above her right elbow, her lace
iightcap tilted over one ear. She wanted to get up.

'You can't!' said Judith.

Judith was in a violently bad temper. All day she had ordered
he maids about as though they were dirt, rapping with her stick
in the floor. It had been all that she could do not to box Dor-
•thy's ears. They had all been on edge that day. Was it because of
he Ball at Ireby? Were they, in spite of themselves, conscious of
t? In any case, you did not know of what the children were
hinking. John had been melancholy for a while now, and Adam
- Adam was silently fighting her desires. Adam wanted to get
iway and she knew it. She was determined to prevent it.

Meanwhile Jennifer was very ill. She had caught a chill walk-
ng in the country lanes in a thin dress with black satin shoes and
iilk mittens. Her heart also was bad. Her legs were swollen. She
vas deaf in one ear.

'You are keeping me in bed against my will. I insist on getting
ip.' She looked across the sheets with hatred at the neat, pale-
:aced woman in the red morocco chair. She listened. The house
was as still as a bottomless well.

She poured out a torrent of mild, lazy abuse:

'Yes, you keep me here and think it very fine. You have grown
into a bully, Judith. That's what you are. Everyone knows it.
You are impossible with everyone ... impossible ... Why the
maids stay in the house I don't know. I insist that I get up.'

'Don't be foolish, Jennifer. It's past midnight. You must go to sleep. I will give you your drops.'

'I don't wish for my drops. They are poisoning me. I expect that Walter has bribed the doctor to put poison in them.'

'Don't be foolish. You know that he has done nothing of the kind.'

'Oh, this woman!' thought Judith.

Jennifer slowly raised herself on her hands, climbed out of the clothes and sat on the edge of the bed, her swollen legs hanging heavily.

'So Walter has opened his house. All the countryside save ourselves is dancing there tonight. The next thing he will build a house just outside our garden.' She looked up with lazy maliciousness. 'You may say what you like; he has poisoned all our life here. John is not the same, you are not the same, Adam is not the same.'

Judith said nothing. Jennifer went on:

'You love Adam more than anyone in the world, do you not?'

'Yes, of course I do. Jennifer, get back into bed. You will catch your death—'

'Well, he is going to leave you. I can tell. I know. He will soon be seventeen and is not of such a character as to remain in a country place—'

A sharp pain, like the touch of a knife, struck Judith's heart, but she got up and, very gently, went to the bed. She patted Jennifer on the shoulder as though she were a child and urged her back into bed again. Quite placidly Jennifer obeyed.

'Oh, dear! I have such a pain in my chest! How they will be dancing now on Ireby! Everyone from Keswick will be there!' She sighed, a deep childish sigh. 'How still this house is! Only the clocks . . . Judith, what do you think life is for?'

'What is it *for*?' Judith was listening. It was, of course, only her imagination, but it seemed to her that she could hear very faintly drums and fiddles and a dim bassoon. One did fancy that one heard things in a quiet house at night.

'Yes. Why are we born? Why do we live? Why do you love Adam so intensely when it is all for nothing?'

'It is not for nothing.'

'Oh, but of course it is. He will grow up and marry and forget you just as I forgot my own mother and father. I should never have left them. I should never have come North. I should never have married Francis. My children don't care for me. No one cares for me. You are all waiting for me to die.'

'Nonsense, Jennifer.'

'No, but it is not nonsense. I cannot understand it, all the bother and the worry. People are born and they die, and other people are born and it is all for nothing.'

'It is not for nothing,' Judith repeated. 'It is that we may have some experience, that we may learn—'

'Yes, but learn what? I am sure that I have never learnt anything except to be disappointed and to be afraid of Walter.'

Judith, who was half asleep, struggled to comfort Jennifer.

'You have learnt more than you know, my dear. There is something immortal in us that must grow, and it grows with experience.'

But did it? Did she mean what she said? Her love for Adam was immortal. Her love for Georges was so – it would never die. There was something to *fight* in life, something strong and glorious ...

She covered a yawn with her hand. 'Now, Jennifer, you must sleep.'

Jennifer lay back in the bed. 'I have such a pain near my heart. My throat is sore. I can see Walter come dancing down the hill when I am buried. And then he will finish John and Dorothy as he has finished me.'

There was something so truly pathetic in her voice; she was like a small child who is suffering she does not know why. Judith bent over the bed and smoothed her pillow. Jennifer caught her hand.

'You are good to me, Judith, although I know that you wish that I were dead.'

'Of course I don't wish that you were dead.'

'Oh yes, you do. You have never forgiven me for preventing you from living in Watendlath. Had you lived in Watendlath you would not have wanted everything your own way so.'

This was so true that Judith felt as though it were her own voice that was speaking. But she showed no signs: she stroked Jennifer's hair.

'Judith, do you not hear something?'

'Hear what?'

'Music – violins and a drum.'

'No – of course not.'

'Oh, but I do. Go to the window and pull back the curtain.'

She went. She looked out.

'What do you see?'

'I see nothing. Only the trees and the moonlight.' But that was not true. Quite clearly she could see in the far distance Walter's house on Ireby. The windows shone like little stars.

'Can you not see the house?'

'Yes; very dimly.'

'Ah ... Judith, Judith!' It was a cry. 'He will kill John as he is killing me! I can see him. I can hear him. He is coming!'

She hastened back to the bed.

Jennifer was very ill and the perspiration glistened on her forehead. Her hand was at her heart.

'Oh, I am in such pain! Such terrible pain!'

'Quiet, dear. It will soon pass. I will fetch the drops—'

'Don't leave me ... Oh! Oh! I am going to die! The room is dark ... Judith, where are you?'

'Sir Roger' was over; some of the older people were departing, Miss Pennyfeather among others. She greeted Walter with dignity and thanked him for a very enjoyable evening. Indeed, she had had one, and Mrs McCormick was to drive her back in her barouche. Mrs Walter Herries had gone to bed; Miss Elizabeth, standing beside her father, did the honours.

The old lady, who was feeling roguish, whispered in his ear:

'You have a most beautiful daughter.'

And then, to be more roguish yet, whispered:

'But I miss Judith Paris. She is a great friend of mine, you know.'

He agreed to both these propositions as perhaps he would have agreed to anything tonight in his happiness and triumph. But he was surprised at the loveliness of Elizabeth. He did not feel that he was her father any more strongly than he had ever done, but she *was* beautiful. And he would have been delighted had Judith been there. He bore her no grudge. A little later Sylvia Herries found herself beside Elizabeth and spoke to her.

'Are you enjoying yourself, Elizabeth?'

The girl smiled shyly. She thought Sylvia Herries the loveliest woman she had ever seen. She had heard that she was a beauty in London and had a Salon attended by famous men, and yet she looked little older than herself.

'Oh yes,' she said.

'Do you like the new house?'

She did not say that she hated it, that she was miserable there, that she was afraid lest her mother should die and leave her defenceless, but her colour rose in her cheeks and she answered:

'I am not perhaps accustomed . . . Later on perhaps.'

The oddest feeling rose in Sylvia's breast. This child seemed to rebuke her by her innocence and inexperience. Suddenly she hated all her London life, with Rosina Bulwer storming angrily at her overdressed husband, and young Mr Ainsworth such a coxcomb, the tables after a party scattered with cards and over-turned glasses and the grease from candles.

She looked at Elizabeth with great affection. 'Be happy while you may. You are so young and so beautiful.'

At that moment up came Walter, a little drunk. He took her away. They were dancing the valse again. He asked her to dance. He was not a bad performer for so big a man, but why had he not even looked at his daughter? His breath smelt of wine, his heavy body was pressed close to hers.

'This is a triumph for you, Cousin Walter,' she said. 'I have never seen so many of our relations before.'

His arm tightened about her slender waist.

'I'll tell you a thing,' he said. 'I have been looking forward to this day all my life.'

'The house is magnificent,' she said. But she did not think so. She found it cold and bleak. There was too much grey stone about it, and the towers and sham battlements were hideous. It was like a fortress.

But he did not pay attention. He whispered in her ear:

'I'll tell you another thing. I think that I am in love with you.'

This was no new thing to her. Men were for ever whispering it in her ear; moreover, with his physical vitality, size and strength there was something attractive . . . also tonight he was like a boy in his happiness. So she did not answer him, but said instead:

'The hunting this morning was the grandest adventure. I never enjoyed anything so much in my life.'

His hand rested on her arm; truly he danced well for so big a man.

'Yes, was it not? Glorious weather. And, do you know, this is a strange country. I took a step and was blinded by mist with sun all about me. For a moment I was lost.'

'Yes? Indeed?' She had not heard him. She saw that her

husband was watching them. She fancied that he did not care for Walter, although he had not said so.

The valse was ended, and he led her away to an alcove near the window where they were hidden by curtains, hidden from everyone save the two Titchley cousins, whose eyes were more active than ever.

She sat down, and he stood leaning over her chair, his hand very near her lovely neck. To make conversation she said:

'Is it not comic, Cousin Walter, to see so many Herries together? What do you think of us as a family?'

'What do I think? ... Well, well ... Sylvia, how lovely you are! I am sure that I have never seen anyone so lovely.'

'I hate our family when it is together in big numbers. We are all hard and material and self-seeking. When one of us is not he is gored to death by the others, like a sick animal in a herd.'

'Sylvia, would you make an objection if I kissed you? Only a cousinly kiss, you know.'

'I should certainly object most strongly. I am married, you know.'

'So am I,' he murmured laughing, and, bending forward, kissed the back of her neck.

Her husband, Garth, had seen them dancing. Sylvia was right; he did not like Walter; he wished that they had not come. He was vaguely unhappy, a rare experience for his lively, careless temperament, and, turning, found that Elizabeth, near to him at that moment, was being left with many bows by her partner, a fat, pursy little man.

'This is a grand sight,' he said. 'Who was your elderly partner, Elizabeth?'

'A doctor from Keswick.'

'Are you very happy? You should be.'

Some restraint that she had been fighting all the evening broke down. She liked Garth; he was gay and young and kind.

'No, Garth, I am not.' She held her head high, but he saw that her eyes were bright with tears. They were away by themselves, and he wanted to put his arm round her and protect her.

'Why not?' he asked her.

'Oh, this house – do you like it? It is hard and cold. And my mother is ill. And – and—'

'You are in love?' he asked her quickly.

'Yes, I am,' she said softly. 'I have been ever since I was a child.'

She was only a child now, he thought.

'Well – is there no hope of marrying?'

'None. A year ago we agreed that we would not meet any more. It is quite, quite hopeless. But I love him the same and so I always shall.'

'That is something,' he answered gravely. 'Fidelity. That is very rare, and the best way to maintain it is never to meet. Propinquity, my dear, kills love.'

'Why!' said Elizabeth, her eyes open and startled. 'Do you not love your wife?'

'I can be jealous of her. I am proud of her. I wish to be near her. Is that an answer to your question?'

'Oh!' whispered Elizabeth, staring at him and longing for John Herries with such a desperate ache that she thought that everyone must see it. 'Would you bring me some orangeade, cousin? I am thirsty.'

The band struck up a quadrille. They moved to their places. It was the climax of all the splendour and pageantry of the evening.

'Oh, did you see—?' said one of the Titchleys to the other.

Walter, his countenance shining with wine, health, exercise, success, love and triumph, led Cecily Rockage to her place in the dance.

There was a moment's pause. Then the band struck up again and all the coloured figures moved, softly, gracefully, about the shining floor.

At Uldale, Judith, her arms about Jennifer, gazed around her desperately for help. But no help could be forthcoming, for with a sigh Jennifer bent her head and, falling forward, died against Judith's breast.

Part Two

Adam and Margaret

THE BATTLE

ADAM, on the morning of his twenty-second birthday, rode alone to Manesty Woods.

At breakfast, there had been the customary festivities. His mother had given him a riding-whip mounted in silver, John had given him Captain Marryat's *Mr Midshipman Easy*, Dorothy had sent some silk handkerchiefs, and Rackstraw the *French Revolution* of Thomas Carlyle. They had all been very kind. Especially had the love shown him by his mother moved and affected him. He had ridden over alone to Manesty that he might think, that he might resolve his strong determination into unchangeable fact.

He intended, before another twenty-four hours were past, to tell his mother that he must leave Uldale and seek his fortune in the world. It was a fierce resolve, one towards which it seemed to him that his whole life had been tending. It needed some girding of the loins! The scene with his mother would be terrific!

In the quiet autumn weather he rode through Portinscale, up the hill towards Braithwaite, then turned to the left, followed the leaf-strewn paths until the woods closed about him and, tying his horse to a tree, plunged down to the Lake's very edge.

There was breeze enough to run a slight murmuring ripple to his feet: for the rest the silence was complete. Opposite him Skiddaw rose like a dividing flower in purple shadow to a shadowed sky. Shadow veiled the Lake. Fields, hills and houses were dim.

He sat there, his hands pressed on his broad knees, and thought things out. Yes, there would be a devil of a row! His mother, as she now was, was not easy to oppose – and yet, if only because he loved her, he must oppose her. He was twenty-two today and, as he saw it, he had wasted five years of his life. For a young man five years seem an immense time. Ever since, at the age of fifteen, he had visited London with his mother he had resolved to leave Uldale, and yet here he was – seven years later, and he was still there!

It was not that he was not resolute enough! As he sat there with his mouth set and his thick broad shoulders squared, he was the very image of resolution, and yet his mother had been too much for him!

He had begun, he remembered, five years back, when Walter Herries had given his first Ball at Ireby and Aunt Jennifer had died, his Grand Rebellion. He had said, his legs apart and his hands in his pockets, that he was going. And his mother had answered him: 'Well – go!'

But she had not intended for a moment that he should go. She had used Roger Rackstraw and John to assist her. Adam was greatly attached to Rackstraw in spite of his drinking, his wenching and his gambling. Rackstraw had taught him everything that he knew – how to ride, how to fight, how to read. It was from Rackstraw that he had got more than from any other the love of this country that he so deeply worshipped. Stones and clouds! Clouds and stones! He looked up at the small vaporous clouds browsing like sheep on the fields of misty sky above him. The long white stone upon which he was sitting, the boulders that lay about him, these were his intimate companions because Rackstraw had introduced him to them. Yes, he owed Rackstraw a great deal, and it was Rackstraw who had persuaded him that he must remain, for a while at least, to help John with the property, the farm at Uldale, the land towards Skiddaw, the business affairs in Keswick. Well, he had remained. He loved John Herries very dearly; there were things that he could do that John could not. He was more easily friends with the farmers and the labourers and the Keswick people. There was something in John, some reserve and shyness, that kept him apart; he inherited that from his father. But everyone liked Adam and trusted him, which was something in these days of rick-burnings in the country and starvation in the towns.

Then, two years ago, he had tried again.

'I am wasting my life here, Mother. I want to go to London.'

This time she did not say 'Go!' She had looked at him as though she would burst into a torrent of rage. She was by then over sixty; her hair was white, but her small body was as taut and erect as ever. Nevertheless, she was not quite as strong as she had been. She sat down more frequently, would take his arm when they walked in the garden. It was not so easy as it had been the first time. Nevertheless, she had not said 'No'. Dorothy had but just become engaged to a Mr Bellairs of Ryelands, near Seascale. An excellent match. Bellairs was Dorothy's age, would succeed to a fine estate, was a good, solid sound-bottomed Englishman with

no nonsense about him. So Adam must wait until Dorothy was
married. Dorothy *did* marry in June of 1836 and had gone to
Ryelands to live. Well, then, Judith was all alone now with John.
Of course, Adam must stay. Not that Judith minded in the least
being the only woman in the house. She adored it. She had
always had an affection for Dorothy, but of late the girl had
grown into a very common-sensible house-keeping woman and
had had ideas of the way that Fell House should be managed.
She had married, Adam was of the private opinion, in the very
nick of time.

So then it had gone on, and Adam could just see his mother
nodding her little head to herself, her mouth curved in a triumphant smile. 'Now I've got him for ever! I shall marry John
off, and then the two of us will be alone here together.' (Adam
knew that she would never marry John off. There had ever been
only one woman for him. There would never be another.)

But there was more in it than this. There was Walter Herries at
Ireby.

Adam was extremely practical and saw things as they were. He
was not, as John was, frightened by unsubstantial fears. But he
could not deny that part of his resolve to run away to London
was founded on Walter and the house at Ireby.

After Jennifer Herries' death they – Judith, Adam, John and
Dorothy – had decided altogether to disregard dear Cousin
Walter and his big, ugly grey house. And so in a kind of way they
had. They never mentioned Walter except to joke about him, his
growing corpulency, his absurd airs and the rest. When Agnes
his wife died, Judith attended the funeral, and Walter spoke to
her in a very friendly manner.

Nevertheless, what Jennifer had prophesied was partly true.
The Fortress (as everyone in the countryside now called the
place) came ever nearer to Uldale. One reason of this was that Mr
Peach, Walter's agent, seemed to be on terms with all of the
Uldale dependants. Even old Bennett was seen chatting with
him. Mr Rackstraw drank and betted with him, and one night
was deposited, dead drunk, at Fell House gates with an ironic
note in Peach's handwriting.

Then Adam knew that John was always thinking of Elizabeth.
He did not, Adam believed, meet her any more nor correspond
with her, but John was certain that she was unhappy, in especial
since her mother's death, and the thought tortured him.

Then there was the matter of Uhland Herries, his liking for

Adam, his hatred of John. For a while he was continually meeting Adam, in the roads, in Keswick, by the Lake; until at last Adam told him that he did not wish to speak to him nor have anything to do with him, that his father was the enemy of all of them at Uldale, and that, so long as it lasted, there could be no intercourse between them. Uhland just stared at him out of his strange grey eyes, nodded, and rode away. But John had the fantastic, unreal notion that Uhland was always following him, waiting for him round corners and so on, would one day do him a hurt.

Finally, Adam believed it to be true that his mother was slowly more and more conscious of Walter. When little things went wrong she attributed it to Walter, just as Jennifer used to do. Adam caught her sometimes standing in the garden, staring over at the Fortress. Of course, she was becoming an old lady now, and fancies would have more power over her than they used to do.

For Adam there was a growing atmosphere in the Uldale house that seemed to him sickly and false. He must escape from it.

There was, however, much more behind his resolve than this. He was determined to do something fine in the world.

Although his reticence hindered him from declaring his thoughts to anyone, he was filled with idealism and love for his fellow human beings. On this day, as he sat there, looking over the shadowy Lake, he felt perhaps some of the sentiment that was stirring in England just then. There was a new young Queen on the throne; all the debauchery, mismanagement, selfishness of those fat old men who had pretended to govern England had passed away. With this child who already in a few months had shown strength and honesty of purpose and purity of mind there was a new hope in the land. Adam had pictures in his mind, as all Englishmen had just then, of that girlish figure on horseback in the Park, or advancing with perfect dignity and command to meet her Ministers, so that all the old men who had known that other régime, the Duke and Peel and Melbourne, were ready to kneel down and worship her. Melbourne was already her slave. Might it not mean that a New Age of Knight-Errantry and the Brotherhood of Man was to begin?

If so, Adam meant to have his share in it. He was very young, had had little experience of the world, but it seemed to him then – as it was to seem to him all his life through – that a very little was needed to make the earth a glorious place where everyone loved his fellow-man and worked, unselfishly, for the general good of mankind.

There was nothing selfish in his desires as he sat there that morning. He never thought of himself at all. His heart swelled in him as he formed pictures of life as it ought to be, as surely it would be in time to come. It seemed to him that it would be a fine thing if himself and others of a like mind were to band together and work all with a common will for the good of the world. He was proud of his family, although he himself was illegitimate, but he was not proud of individual members of the family. Something was always taking them in the wrong direction. Even he perceived, in spite of his intense loyalty, that something had happened to his mother. It might be that she had, as she once told him, made the wrong decision when she had stayed at Uldale instead of going to live at Watendlath. Then there were Francis and Jennifer, John's father and mother, Walter and Uhland, Will and Garth and Sylvia in London. He did not feel himself better than any of them – there was never anyone with less conceit – but it seemed that in life one was for ever being tempted to take a wrong step: a quick decision and one was moving down the wrong road, never again to be in the right one.

He felt life to be good; it could not hold such beauty as he saw before him that morning and not be good. Yet so many things were wrong with it – so much poverty, suffering of women and children, dirt and shame and crime. Surely, if one worked hard enough, and if enough people in the world cared for justice and equality, everything would swing round – not to perfection, perhaps, but to something in unison with this beauty, this sense of God active and moving in men's hearts?

In any case, he meant to see what he could do; so he must go out into the world, fight his way, find others of like mind with himself. He got up, stretched his arms, felt an infinite strength and hope in him. He hated this struggle with his mother. But, if he was resolute, it would be sharp, brief, soon over, and then she would see how right he was. He smiled as he looked about him and untethered his horse. How lovely and perfect this place was! Perhaps one day he would return and have a cottage here, with the hills above him, and the Lake at his feet. Nothing the world could hold would be so good as that would be! He rode home.

But alas! How noble and ideal are we at one moment; how peevish and unkind the next! Adam stopped in Portinscale for a

bottle of stout and some cold beef. There was nothing better than
to sit in the window of the Inn, drinking the stout and eating the
beef while the grey stillness of field and Lake bound with the
hedges of the cottage gardens spread like a fan before him, to sit
there and think of the world opening, of the great deeds to be
performed therein, of the fights to be fought, the weak to be
protected, the books, maybe, to be written! He had no thought
that he was a genius, but Keats (whose *Lamia* and *St Agnes' Eve*
Rackstraw had introduced to him) had not thought himself one,
and Mr Carlyle had been a peasant, and there was the author of
Sketches by Boz . . .

So he rode slowly home through the mist and the yellow
leaves, dreaming of what was coming. What immediately came to
him was the Reverend Mr Bland, the new curate at Cockermouth, who had had a London curacy and bore a letter from
Stephen Newmark. A stout wife was with him and a stout
daughter. The visitors had been asked whether they would take
port or sherry, and the glasses, biscuits and decanters were laid
out on the table. The candles shone (gas was not yet introduced
into Fell House), a table near by was ready with the round, lac-
quered Pope Joan board and the mother-o'-pearl counters, for
Judith adored Pope Joan. And she sat there like a queen in a
beautiful shawl with long fringes and her snow-white hair in
long ringlets, enjoying herself tremendously.

The Reverend Mr Bland stayed an eternity. He had endless
things to say about his new church, how the Psalms were read
'too quick,' and the red cloth on the reading-desk was faded to a
dirty brown, and how at St Mary's in Islington . . . No, they
would never be gone, for Farmer Wilson had driven them over
and had gone on to some farms about some business of his own
and . . . Oh! there was Farmer Wilson at last, and soon the Bland
family was lifted into his cart, and the dusk closed down upon
their rumbling.

He followed her up to her room, watched her shake her curls,
change her shawl, do a little *pas seul* up and down her floor in
imitation of Mr Bland's mincing steps, laugh and sing a note or
two from 'Speed on, my mules, for Leila *waits* for me,' which
was one of the popular ballads of the day. It was very difficult for
him to attack her at such a moment, and yet he could not wait.
Although so thickly and sturdily built he was nervous as a young
girl when he confronted his mother. The memory of that first
awful quarrel following his laugh at old Bellenden in Keswick
never left him; there was, too, something dismaying in her swift

transition from mood to mood. Then she was sixty-three, and, let her pretend as she might, was not as strong as she had once been. And then – hardest of all – he loved her better than anyone alive.

So he burst out at once that he might get it over quickly.

'Mother – I'm going to London. I've been thinking it over. I'm going to earn my living like other men. I must, I must . . .'

Like other men! She stopped in her invocation of 'Leila', stood there in the middle of the floor and laughed at him. Like other men! To her he was still an infant, or at most a small boy who stole jam from the cupboard and bought bull's-eyes at the shop in the village. And yet he was not! She looked and saw him standing there, stolid and square, in his man's blue coat with the velvet collar and the strapped pantaloons, a lock of his black hair falling over his forehead, whiskers sprouting on his cheeks, his grave eyes confronting her without flinching. No, he was not a child any longer. This was what Jennifer had foretold. She reached out for her ivory cane that was leaning against the four-poster.

'Not on your birthday, Adam,' she said, and moved towards the door.

But he did not budge. He felt his knees shake, but now that he had begun he would go through with it.

'Yes, Mother, I must.' He cleared his throat. 'Listen, Mother, dear. I'm twenty-two today.'

'And what has that to do with it?'

'Everything. I am a man and should do a man's work.'

'You have a man's work here.'

'No, I have not. You know quite well that for all I do here I might be shut up in a cupboard. John and Rackstraw can manage everything.'

'That is not true. John is too dreamy, and Rackstraw drinks in the village.' She felt that her legs were trembling, so with great dignity she walked to the chair near the fireplace and sat down.

The devil of it was that words never came easily to him! He could think clearly enough, but when it came to words! . . . He stood nearer to her.

'Mother, pray listen. I am not being rebellious or wicked. You know how . . . how . . . devotedly I love you—'

'So devotedly that you want to break my heart,' she said.

(Something sarcastic in her said: 'Break my heart! My dear, what stuff!')

He began to be angry, which was a help to him. When he was angry his lower lip jutted out, a sign that she knew very well.

'This is a resolve,' he said. 'Nothing shall turn me from it.'

'Well – if it is a resolve – what will you live upon?'

'I have fifty pounds I've saved, thirty I got for those sheep at Threlkeld, twenty Uncle Will sent me . . .'

'Fifty! Thirty! . . . Nonsense! . . . That will last you a month or so. And then what?'

'I shall find work.'

'Yes, but what will you do? What will you do?' She stamped her cane on the floor. 'You've been trained to nothing.'

'I can find work,' he said doggedly. (He thought of saying: 'Whose fault is it that I've not been trained?' but fortunately kept it back.) 'I'm ready to do anything.'

'And starve in a gutter,' she answered contemptuously. Then her voice softened. 'Now, Adam, this is folly. You *have* work here, your proper work. John loves you. I am sure he would not know what to do without you. You are necessary to all of us here.'

As she softened so did he.

'We can soon test whether I'm necessary or no,' he said, laughing. 'I will go to London for three months, and you shall see how well you do. Why, mother, in a week you will have forgotten all about me!'

She saw then that he meant to go. She bent her head for a moment. She wanted to deal with this quietly, but she had less control of herself now than the other day. Something leapt up within her, crying, 'I want to get out!' and out it came, disclosing itself as a nasty piece of temper that took herself by surprise quite as much as anyone else. She had always had a hasty temper, but now it was as though she had her own and someone else's as well.

She was determined on two things: not to let him go and not to be angry. So she got up and walked to the door; as she passed him she laid her hand for a moment on his shoulder, smiled at him and said:

'Now you must not be naughty, Adam. Some time – later on – you shall go to London. Perhaps I shall come with you,' and left the room. There for once her tactics were altogether wrong. Those words, as it happened, were all that were needed to stiffen him. She was still treating him like a child; she *would* not see that he was a grown man. That just showed how hopeless everything would be if he stayed.

But he must go at once. He could not endure that this relationship with his mother should continue. She would beat him down

if she had time; her ruthlessness had all the old history of their
lives together to harden it.

Very soon, in fact, the battle was renewed. Next day at breakfast alone with John, drinking beer and gobbling beef pie, he told
him his decision.

'John, I've got to go.'

'Got to go?' asked John.

'Yes, to London. I'm wasting my time here. You know that as
well as I do. I've got to be of some use in the world.'

'Well, aren't you being of use here?'

'No, nothing to matter. You see, John, there's a dreadful lot of
injustice everywhere. Look at these women in the factories and
the children in the mines. Look how people are starving. Why,
they say in Whitehaven—'

'Yes, I know. But couldn't you improve things and stay here as
well? And is it your business? I mean—'

'You think I'm a bit of a prig,' said Adam. 'But I don't want to
consider myself at all. I may be a prig or not. I don't care—' He
broke off, laughing. 'Yes, I do care. I don't want to be a prig. But
I find it so difficult to say what I mean. What I *mean* is that I
think that a number of men are feeling that they want to help to
make England a grand place – without all this injustice and
division between the rich and the poor. And I want to stand with
them.'

'And you're on the side of the poor?' asked John.

'Of course I am. I haven't much myself, I'm illegitimate, I'm
nobody. Who should be on the side of the poor if I'm not? But I
don't want to preach, you know. There's none of the parson in
me. I only want that they should have more to eat and better
homes, that young children shouldn't go down the mines and be
in the dark all day—'

'I daresay they like it – being in the mines, I mean.'

'Like it! How can they like it? Would *you* like it?'

'No, but I'm not accustomed to it.'

Adam had been unusually eloquent, so now he was quiet again
although he had not, even now, said what was really in his heart.
John got up, came round to him and put his arm around him.

'I expect you're right,' he said. 'Only what it will be here
without you—'

'You need not disturb yourself,' said a sharp voice in the
doorway. 'Adam is *not* going to London.'

They both looked up, and there was 'Madame' in the doorway,

shaking on her cane with anger. 'No, I will not have it,' she said, her voice quivering. 'You get this notion out of your head, Adam, once and for all. Your duty is here. There's been enough of this nonsense.' And she went.

The two looked at one another.

'By Caesar!' said John, 'I never knew she was there.'

Adam said in a low voice: 'It's no good. She can't stop me. But it's awful fighting her.'

'Yes,' said John. 'No one likes it. That's why she always has her way.'

Meanwhile Judith went about her household duties, and the maids had a dreadful morning of it. She felt as though she were fighting for her very life. If Adam left her, what remained? Oh yes, of course she was fond of Uldale – but to be alone here with John, the stupid neighbours, Walter on the hill . . . All the morning she was closer to weeping than she had been for years. This would not have happened had she done what she should have done – gone to live in Watendlath with Adam. He would have become a farmer and she would have lived with him.

She went up to her room. She stared out at Skiddaw, veiled now by dirty, swollen clouds. What was she to do? How was she to influence him? Behind her anger and indignation was admiration of his obstinacy. She would have behaved once just as he was behaving.

But she beat these thoughts back. No weakening on her part. If she softened she was lost.

So that at dinner in the afternoon she was severe, aloof, the grand lady, the Empress. And Adam, unfortunately, because of his knowledge that he had that forenoon ridden into Keswick and drawn his money from the bank, was not at his best.

If she knew that! But she did not know it. In her heart she was quaking, but as the meal proceeded she became reassured again. She addressed most of her remarks to Mr Rackstraw, who, with his dry, red face and weatherbeaten figure, seemed to promise her that nothing here at least could change. Adam sat there, eating and drinking as though this day were like any other day. So it must be! She had been agitated by absurd alarms.

Once she said: 'The Hunt Ball in Carlisle is to be the twenty-third of October. You and John, Adam, can have a bed at the Witherings'. They will be going for sure.'

No one said anything.

'I have been hearing,' said Rackstraw, 'about this new postal scheme. All our letters to cost us but a penny wherever we send them. We live in modern times.'

She discussed the postal scheme and Lord de Ros' gambling scandal. His manner of cheating at cards had been to have a coughing fit under the table. And there had been the massacre in New Zealand – one hundred and twenty people murdered – but really so far away that one could not visualize it. She was *almost* reassured; as she moved in a manner a little more stately than usual from the room she gave Adam a quick look and thought that she had never before found him so exasperating and never loved him so dearly.

Adam told Rackstraw that same afternoon that he was going. They were in the stables and it was growing dark. A storm of rain was blowing up, and the light in the lantern that Rackstraw carried flickered.

Rackstraw nodded his head.

'I knew you would,' he said.

'I must. I can't help myself,' said Adam.

'No, of course you cannot.'

'Care for my mother, Roger. This will hit her for the moment, but she'll see it's right later.'

'Yes, she will,' said Rackstraw. 'She's a damnably sensible woman, your mother.'

He shook Adam's hand as though he were going that moment.

'Good luck to you.' He fumbled in his deep pocket, pulled out a little book and gave it to him. 'It's the *Iliad*. Grandest book in the world. I always carry it with me. Think of me sometimes.'

'But I'm not going now—' began Adam. Then stopped. He knew suddenly that he was.

By suppertime he had made his plans. He would leave the next day, drive one way or another to Manchester, then take the new railway. The very thought of this railway made his heart beat. Yes, he would certainly be seeing the world.

After supper he went out to the stables, wearing his riding-coat and hat because the storm was so fierce. As soon as he was indoors he heard his mother's voice calling him from upstairs. He went up, his spirits heavy with foreboding. She was sitting in her bedroom by the fire, wrapped in two fine cashmere shawls and looking a very amiable and kindly old lady.

'That's well, Adam,' she said, smiling. 'Come and talk to your old mother.'

No, she was not an old lady. She was as young as Eternity and vigorous. So, in order that he might be entirely honest, he stood by the door.

'I've been vexed all day by your nonsense,' she said. 'Very foolish. Now sit beside me and I'll tell you what I've arranged. You want more to do, my son. That's the trouble. Well, I've thought of that farm at Crossways. I think, with a tightening or two, it can be purchased—'

'No, Mother,' he said. 'It's no use. I'm as resolved as last night. I must go and at once. Tomorrow.'

'And why tomorrow precisely?' she asked him, her voice trembling.

'I cannot wait and have this trouble with you. I cannot endure it. Anyone else—'

She got up. 'Never mind me,' she said. 'Don't be a hypocrite, Adam.'

'I'm no hypocrite,' he answered fiercely. 'I'm your son.'

'You are not my son if you go,' she answered as fiercely as he. 'If you go I disown you.'

'Now this is nonsense,' he fought back. 'Have you no ambition for me? If I'd been another I should have gone to school and then to some business—'

She came nearer to him.

'So you reproach me?'

'No, I do not reproach you. I cannot understand that you who have so much strength of mind can never have had any ambition for me. You—'

She came close to him.

'Take care, Adam, or I'll teach you!'

She was shaking, and that touched him so deeply that his voice grew tender.

'Mother, listen. You *must* listen. You remember that once when we were in London at the Newmarks', after the riot, I was in bed with you. You told me then that if ever you threatened my liberty I was to defy you. You said that this would happen. You urged me then—'

But she had not listened to a single word. She caught hold of him and began to shake him so furiously that she drove him back against the door.

'Take off that hat and coat.'

He was now as angry as she. Anyone looking at them would have seen well enough that they were mother and son.

'No, I will not.'

'Take off that hat and coat.' Her small body had in it an extraordinary vigour.

'No.' He put out his hand to prevent her doing herself a hurt. 'You cannot use me like this. You shall not.'

'Oh, will I not?' Her words came in little passionate sobs. 'When I was a girl – we whipped our – disobedient sons—'

He tore himself away from her.

'Well, then,' she panted, 'if it is so – you shall remain here – and consider it.'

She went out, pulling the door behind her with a bang that echoed all over the house. He heard the key turn in the lock.

'By God! She's locked me in!' he heard a voice that did not seem like his own exclaim aloud. He sat down on the bed, and the room sank back into silence like a pool after a stone has splashed it. He heard the rain beating on the window. He was more angry than he had ever been in his life, and he did not care whether his mother broke her heart or whether, indeed, the whole world blew up. He looked at the window, went over to it, stared out.

Here anyhow was a way out. He could walk to Penrith, get the morning coach ... Thank heaven, he had his money.

He climbed over the sill, felt the rain sweep against his cheek, fumbling, found the water-pipe. It was the same water-pipe that his mother, escaping years ago, had used.

THE CHARTISTS

IT was while watching the return of the Procession from Westminster – the Procession on June 27th, 1838, of the Coronation of Her Gracious Majesty Queen Victoria – that the life of Adam Paris was changed. He had exactly thirty shillings in the world. After arriving in London he had found a job reading to an old blind gentleman in Bayswater, things like Pope's *Homer* and Scott's *Lady of the Lake*. The old gentleman had died, and Adam had found, after some weeks of starving, another job with Fisher and Taylor, publishers of infidel writers like Paine. For a time all was well, then Fisher took a dislike to him and dismissed him. After that he sank to starvation. He had a room in a lodging-house off the Strand, 'Wheeler's'. No one was ever to know how lonely he was and how desperately homesick he was during those months. He wrote to his mother once a month, giving an address, but had no reply. He wrote to no one else; he was too proud. He was sick and hungry for the smell of dry bracken and the tune of running water, for the small bodies of his Herdwick sheep and the little white farms . . . And, by the day of the Procession, he was so hungry that he could think of nothing but food. He scarcely saw the Procession. Afterwards he had a picture of coloured fragments – horses tossing their heads, grand splashes of crimson caught and lost again, pennons waving, spurs and bridles jingling and glittering, cries and shouts: 'Here he is! . . . That's the Duke! . . . That's Marshal Soult! . . . Who's that little man? . . .' soldiers and again soldiers, backs erect, heads up behind the tossing manes of their chargers, a blare of music, a moment of deafening brass and thunder dying to a distant melody, and the air still save for the clatter of hooves; then a vague roar like a wind in the air, louder and louder, more and more personal, then 'She's here! That's her! . . . Oh, how young she looks!' – and, with an odd beating of the heart and mist at the eyes, for a moment his hunger forgotten, he caught the face and figure, tiny in the great gold coach, of a girl so young and unprotected that there was something deeply appealing in the risks that she was taking. Why, she was no more than a baby! She was bowing to them. She smiled. She was gone. 'She's but a child,' Adam murmured, turning away – then thought that, for the first time in his life, he was going to faint. The street and the people were spinning up to him. He lurched sideways and was held in the arms of a tall, broad-shouldered, smiling fellow in a plain, brown beaver hat and a black coat.

'What's up, friend?'

'I'm hungry,' said Adam simply. So the tall man in the brown beaver hat took him home. This man was called Caesar Kraft and he lived with his daughter Margaret in three rooms off the Seven Dials. Kraft and Adam knew, within an hour of their first meeting, that they had that deep emotional affection for one another that men, often the manliest and strongest, sometimes experience. There was a little room on the other side of the passage from the Krafts that Adam hired. The Krafts were Chartists, and within twenty-four hours Adam was a Chartist too. By the spring of 1839, indeed, Adam was a more thorough and convinced Chartist than Caesar Kraft himself.

On the morning following his first night with them he had had a long and critical conversation with Kraft. He knew afterwards that this conversation was one of the turning-points of his life. It came at a time when he was exactly ready for it – growing from boy into man, ignorant of the world, lonely and longing for affection. As a child he had loved John Herries, but with that exception, and of course his devotion to his mother, which was part of himself, he had revealed his heart to no one. Now he opened it to Kraft, for Kraft, too, needed a friend. Adam made no mistake here. Caesar Kraft was the noblest, purest, most selfless human being he was ever to know.

Their alliance formed, the rest followed.

'Do you think you can write?' Kraft asked him.

'I have no idea,' Adam answered.

'Remain here for a week and study some of these.'

Kraft put in front of him a mass of documents, pamphlets, letters, appeals, protests, from every part of the country. It was a very remarkable collection, and Adam devoured the whole of it.

This is no place to go in detail into that documentary evidence. It can be found in many volumes easy of access, but some things are worth recording because of the effect that they had upon Adam's life and outlook.

He knew that children in the mines, descending a shaft six hundred feet deep, went along a subterranean road three miles in length, and that at the 'workings' on either side of them the hewers were employed in a state of complete nudity because of the great heat. The child, sometimes not more than six years of age, was employed there to keep the doors or 'traps' shut against the flow of inflammable air. Here, then, the child would sit in the dark all day opening and shutting those doors. At first he was given a candle, but after a while when he was accustomed to the dark the candle was taken away.

Later the child would be promoted to be a drawer or 'thrutcher' and then, clad only in a pair of trousers, a belt round the waist, a chain attached to the belt at one end and the truck at the other, the chain passing between his legs, often on all-fours because of the lowness of the gallery, he would, hour after hour, act his part as beast of burden. The 'thrutchers' would push the truck along with their heads and, although they were protected with a cap, were soon bald. The women 'thrutchers' wore nothing but a pair of short trousers.

He learnt that a hedger in the country would receive seven-pence a day for six days of the week to find him clothes, food and lodging. He learnt that the soldiers in barracks had for urinal wooden tubs, and in those same tubs they must afterwards wash.

He learnt that in the Navy the sailors lived entirely on salt beef, salt pork and maggoty biscuit, and that they would bet with one another as to which piece of biscuit would, unaided, crawl across a table faster than another. He learnt that a labourer lived almost entirely on tea (often made of crusts or twigs) and potatoes. For months together he would not taste meat. A young man had been asked how he lived on half a crown a week. He replied that he did not live on it. 'I poach,' he said, 'for it is better to be hanged than to starve to death.'

Children did not go home to dinner because there was none. A man, working in a factory, told this story: 'Up at five in the morning to get to the factory, work till eight, half an hour for breakfast, work till noon, dinner an hour, then work till four, half an hour for tea, then work till nine. The master's strap, six feet long, was kept at his right hand, two cuts at a stroke, and every day some of it.'

The injuries of the bread-tax were beginning to be poignantly felt. Bread was made from barley-meal. Families lived for days on swede turnips, roasted, baked and boiled. A man had a wife and six children to keep when flour was twelve shillings a bushel. To have a red herring, to be shared by several, was a great treat. If a father obtained a penny white loaf, his children would trudge miles to meet him that they might see it the sooner. A man would, in his hunger, eat the pig-pease and horse-beans that he was threshing. The children would steal the cabbage-stalks and swedes from the fields. Some families would go early out and eat the snails. Bread was soon to be at one-and-sixpence the loaf.

So it was in factory, mine and field, in small village and large town.

Adam's nature, the more that it was so restrained, was deeply stirred by suffering, but hitherto the suffering that he had known had belonged to separate incidents and individual persons. Now it seemed to him that the whole country was spread with a cloud. It was hard to believe that there was anyone who was aware and yet would do nothing about it. But it was so; not only were there thousands who did not stir a finger, but he soon came to realize that everyone who had any power in the country was against any change. This girl who was Queen – he heard of nothing but her rides in the Park with Melbourne, that she danced in her Palace until two of the morning, that at her dinner parties the plates were of gold and the cutlery of silver.

It was good for him that he fell under the influence of such people as the Krafts or he might have become a violent agitator like Henry Lunt, Kraft's friend. But Caesar and Margaret had spent their lives among these questions. Their natures were sweet and tolerant although they were as determined in the Cause as any fanatic, and it may be said that they saved Adam at this time.

One thing, however, did happen to him, and that was a suspicion of his own family. He thought of Walter and Uhland at Ireby, of Sylvia and her gay parties, of Will and his money, of James and his greedy stomach, of the Newmarks and (as it appeared to him now) their hypocrisy, of the Rockages and their snobbery, even – in his new bitterness – of Dorothy and John. Uldale with its farm, its ordered garden and orchard, its stables with the fat horses, the lawn gleaming so smoothly under the morning sun – how could they suffer it all so easily when men, their stomachs empty, bled from the master's strap, when children of six years old sat naked hour after hour, day after day, in the dark, when women and children went into the fields and grubbed for cabbage-stalks, when in the streets outside his window the stench was so terrible that you fainted under it and fever was in every house?

He began to have an obsession about the Herries. He saw them with their horse-faces bending forward with malicious pleasure to watch the sufferings of the crawling figures beneath them, Walter guzzling, Will seated on his money-bags, Sylvia with her poodle dancing across the shining floor of her boudoir. He thanked God that he was illegitimate. He was another Herries rebel – the bull that 'Rogue' Herries saw baited, Reuben's bear and the boy hanged of his mother's youth, the falling Bastille with which Francis killed his father – these were unknown to Adam, but he was forging a new link in that strong chain of protest.

And then in the middle of this he received a letter from his mother, the first that he had had since he had left Uldale.

MY DEAR ADAM – You have been very good in writing to me with such regularity. Do not think that I have not appreciated your letters but I was *determined* that I would not *weakly* submit to your self-will and *obstinacy*. Nevertheless, for a long time now I have known that you were right to do as you did and I was too *obstinate* myself to confess to my mistake. You have doubtless heard from Mr Rackstraw who tells me that he has written to you and you have all the *news* but now that I have broken the *ice* I must further tell you that I am *longing* to see you again and that there is no day since your departure that I have not been of the same *mind*. I am growing an old woman now, Adam. I am sixty-five years of age although I must say I am extremely *vigorous* and save for a stiffness in my right arm which only comes out in damp weather I am in excellent health. All are well here. John has bought two more cows. We have been very *gay* these last weeks and Dorothy with her boy and little girl has been staying this fortnight with us. Veronica (a most *foolish* name in my opinion) is a very *engaging* baby and Timothy a good child when *managed*. Dorothy has much common-sense but is anxious to have the command, even here at Uldale, which of course, as you can suppose, I do not *allow*. John is not so cheerful as I would wish. He had an encounter with Peach, Walter's man, last week up at Bogshaw and they came I fancy to some hot words. I have of course seen nothing of the people at Ireby but I hear that Walter refuses to have Elizabeth's name mentioned since her disappearance, of which of course you've heard. Poor child! No one seems to *care* what has happened to her. It would not have been so if Agnes were still living.

I will not write more now because you are a *disobedient* son and do not deserve a long letter but I am nevertheless (*longing* to see you soon) – Your loving mother,

JUDITH PARIS.

Adam's first impulse after reading this letter was to go at once North, by coach, railway, or any other means that offered. This was no new impulse. Scarcely a day of the last six months that he had not known it, but he had always driven it back as a weakness that he must not feel. But now with the letter in his hands his love for his mother was for a while overwhelming. Behind the words he saw her pride, her obstinacy, her sweetness, her humour, her gaiety, her tenderness. It was as though she were with him in the room. He realized, once again, that they were part of one another, bone of bone and flesh of flesh. But for that very reason he would not leave the work to which he had set his hand. If he returned to her even for a day her influence over him would be so strong that she might persuade him to remain with her. He *must* be himself, develop his own life, create his own pattern. In the end that is what she would wish him to do.

So he sat down and wrote her the most loving letter he had ever penned and then turned to his work again.

They had soon discovered that he could write. He was, in fact, just what they needed, for he was honest, indignant and accurate. His youth gave his words freshness and his sincerity prevented any fustian or melodrama.

The fanatics – one of the wildest was this man called Henry Lunt – complained that he was not strong enough. They soon discovered that he was of no use at all as a speaker. He had no power over words, and the sight of an audience was appalling to him.

He went on one occasion with a number of delegates from London to Manchester and they put him on the platform. It was one of the most horrible experiences of his life. He stood there, his brown healthy cheeks pale, fumbling his hair with his hand, moving his thick legs as though he would kick the place down. He stammered, stopped, stammered again, strung some sentences together and sat down, a lamentable failure.

When he came back to London he told Margaret about it.

'I felt as though they stripped my clothes off my back.'

'Yes,' she said, 'they say it was the worst speech ever made in Manchester.'

'They'll never ask me to do it again – that's one good thing.'

'But you can write about the bread-tax and the shilling loaf and the fever here in Seven Dials,' she answered, 'better than anyone we've had since Tom Colman.'

She was standing near to him, and he put out his hand, resting it on her shoulder. She did not move away.

'Margaret, how old are you?' he asked her.

'Let me see. I was born in February 1820. This is March 1839. I am nineteen.'

'You are not like a girl,' he said, his hand holding her arm more strongly. 'You are a woman.'

'I have been a woman ever since mother died. That night when she went and father was in my arms I thought he would die too. I never knew two people love one another as he and mother did. I grew up that night.'

'It was a happy thing for me that afternoon when Caesar spoke to me.'

'It was a happy thing for us too,' she answered.

That night in bed he knew that he loved Margaret. He had loved her, he perceived, since the first moment that he saw her. She was the first woman he had ever cared for, and this excitement and tenderness was quite new to him. He lay there thinking of her, of her unselfishness, honesty and integrity. But he realized that he knew nothing about her feeling for himself. She was as quiet as he was; he had never seen her show any interest in men, but they were not very much together. She was out at her dressmaking all day and was often kept to very late hours. She might have a lover somewhere. There might be another side to her, a side that she never showed at home. He was extremely ignorant about women. Although he was approaching twenty-four years of age he had never kissed any woman save his mother, Jennifer and Dorothy. With the exception of his mother his deepest feelings of affection and loyalty had been roused by men – John, Rackstraw, Caesar Kraft. So this feeling for Margaret was something quite new, and that night, as he lay awake, listening to the drunken shouts in the street below, it grew and grew until he felt that he had Margaret in his arms. That seemed to him the happiest wonder, something that awed him with its mingling of worship and desire; lost in this new experience he fell asleep.

He was as cautious and careful in this as in everything else. His shyness made him shrink from any rebuff. He had nothing to offer her, no position, no prospects. And here for the first time his illegitimacy troubled him. Kraft perhaps would not want his daughter to marry a bastard. He was proud of his family, talked of his German grandfather as though he had been the grandest man in Germany. But when that seed of love is sown in a nature like Adam's nothing can hinder it.

But this new desire made life difficult for him. He was pulled in two quite opposite directions: his love for Margaret as the days went by filled itself increasingly with light and colour like a glass ball that becomes with every hour more radiant. But his discontent with the sickness and starvation all round him was something fierce and hostile, dark, jagged like lightning.

He remembered that once at home when he was on his favourite place at the bottom of Cat Bells, in Manesty, by the Lake a wind had come up, the sky had been darkened with hot saffron-edged clouds. All in a moment the breeze had lifted, and the Lake that had been placidly blue was edged with little frothy white waves. The whole expanse of water was mulberry-coloured and the islands were black-green, the tint of leaves turned backwards by the wind. Behind this angry scene Skiddaw and Blencathra and the fields below them rose drenched in light and sun – a wall of sun flashing and sparkling. As the Lake was dyed ever deeper and deeper with its mulberry stain and the little waves jumped with tongues of a dead white, the wall of light seemed to exult in its own glory: it shouted its strength aloud. Then, as a shutter closes, a hand swept wiping out all colour. Hills and lake together were dun.

He had never forgotten this scene. He had thought of it often in his first homesick days in London; now his experience seemed to be thus mixed – an exulting wall of light, a tossing discontented floor of stain. For the first time he was touching forces very much stronger and deeper than himself.

Then one of the great evenings of his life came. He went with Caesar Kraft and Margaret to a Chartist meeting in Seven Dials. Lunt and another, Philip Pider, were with them. Lunt was worked up to more than his customary indignation because a family living in the cellar of his building had been sick of the fever: two of them, an old man and a child, had died, and their bodies had been left there in the cellar two days and a night before anyone attended them. Adam noticed that behind his indignation was a kind of fierce joy because he had been given some more evidence to use in his damning account against all authority. He described with angry gusto the filthy state of that cellar, the pools of moisture, the loathsome stench, the rats.

He was this night like an animal himself, his strong dark hairy body moving like an animal's, his words, growls, mutters, little snatches of ferocity. The surroundings that evening were strange and fantastic. There had been a thick yellow fog all day, but now it had thinned, hanging in discontented wisps about the streets and buildings. The lamps in the street were damp and mildewed with moisture; the shops were for the most part closed, but some were yet open and you could see, in the candlelight, figures like shapes in the fire cross-legged over a boot or shoe, arms raised to fetch down some garment, a butcher standing with blood on his apron above slabs of red meat and dark amber-coloured entrails. Everyone moved through the wispy fog as though in secret, and there was that faint scent of sulphur in the air that a thick London fog leaves behind it.

For Adam that walk to the hall where the meeting was to be held was one of his most blissful moments. Margaret's hand was through his arm; he could feel the soft swell of her breast against his sleeve, she was so close to him. She spoke in a voice that was quiet and happy. He knew that she was happy, he could feel it in every word that she spoke. Once and again he could catch under her bonnet the gleam of her eyes, the shadow of her cheek above her dark green shawl. He was terribly anxious not to cheat himself (all this experience was so new to him), but he began to believe that his company must have something to do with her happiness – and then quite suddenly she told him that it was so.

'You know, Adam, since you came to us father and I have been happier than we used to be.'

His heart hammered with delight. He thought that she must feel its beatings against her arm. And as always when he was deeply moved, he could say nothing.

'Um—' he muttered.

'Are you not glad?'

'Of course, I am glad – if it's true, Margaret.'

'But, of course, it's true. Why should I say it if it was not? Father was often very lonely before you came. He can be passionate in his affections, and I think he loves you more than he ever loved anyone except mother.'

'And yourself?'

'Oh, myself – I am always there, you know. He has become accustomed to me.'

He plucked up his courage, although his tongue was dry in his throat.

'And some day you will marry, Margaret?'

'Yes,' she answered quietly. 'I hope so – some day.'

'Perhaps there is someone – already—'

'Oh, I don't know,' she answered, laughing. 'There is Mr Hooper – a friend of Madame's at the shop . . .'

'Oh, is there?' he said, his heart dropping to a dreadful deadness.

'I think he likes me,' she went on quietly. 'He wears two waistcoats and I am certain he has a corset. He speaks like this: "Oh, Miss Kraft . . . I'm sure . . . most exquisite . . . Pray, turn that I may see the back. I'm quite in raptures!" ' She imitated him and burst out laughing. 'I like him, but I fear father would not. But he has a fine little villa in Islington, and he sings to his own accompaniment on the pianoforte.'

He supposed that she was teasing him, but he could not be sure. Now they had arrived at the hall, and the other world of fire and tumult drove down upon them.

The hall was a large one, and when they entered they found it packed with people. The air was thick with the warm smell of human bodies, the odour from the oil lamps; figures were indistinct – here a face, there an arm, a body flung forward – everywhere an almost ecstatic excitement and attention. Kraft, Lunt and Pider went to sit on the platform, Adam and Margaret were pressed into the wall near the door. Adam had been to many meetings by now, but thought that he had never seen such eye-strained faces, men and women and some children, one baby held aloft and waving its chubby fists in the air.

It had just begun when they entered. The Chairman, a round tubby man with thick grey side-whiskers, was speaking. The atmosphere was at present quiet and controlled. He said something about the conditions of the time, the oppression of the authorities, the iniquities of the Bread Tax, the Six Points of the new Charter. He sat down, and a long thin fellow with a straggly beard got up. He had a rather weak, piping voice and no very impressive manner: he began quietly, so there were voices from the hall; 'Speak up! We can't hear!' and a rough growl from someone: 'Sit down, damn ye, if yer can't talk.'

That last seemed to rouse him, for he raised his rather pale, watery eyes and stared down into the hall: 'If you listen you'll 'ear all right,' he said at last. 'I ain't 'ad food in my belly for the last six months, what yer can call food.' They listened. He had control over them. He had come, he said, to tell them what it was like now to work on the land. 'We're slaves to the farmer's body, slaves like they were in the old Roman times. For ten years I served Farmer Wellin in my county – aye, you don't know 'is name likely, but one name does as well as another. Then one fine day he tells me he ain't no more work for me nor my two boys – so then I goes here, I goes there. No work. Then I goes to Manchester, starves there a bit, comes 'ome again, put in the Union, turned out after a day or two, lays abed a bit, gets a day's work, then on board-day goes to them again, gets a day's work, starves a bit, lays abed a bit, goes searching for work again, eats stuff they've given the pigs because I'm that 'ungry. My boys, as good lads as ever you see, 'anging around gets into bad ways, one of 'em roots up a turnip or two and gets gaoled. 'Is mother breaks 'er 'eart and dies of weakness. That's why I'm not speaking so 'earty, begging your pardon, friends.

'I say a poor man's a slave. He can't leave his own parish – for why? – because in a foreign parish they've plenty of their own to give work to. And what are our masters doing? They're wasting of the land, that's what I say they're doing. Give me an acre of land and I'll live well and decent on it *and* give my boys a proper life. I was out of work last spring from Christmas to barley-sowing. I goes to the farmer and asks for a scrap of land to grow potatoes on. "Oh no, you don't," says he. "Give you potatoes and you'll want straw and a pig and I don't know what all. And one day, maybe, I'll be wanting you to work for myself," he says. "Oh yes," he says, "prices be so low I must lower your wages," he says, but when prices goes up does he raise the wages again? Not if he knows of it. What I say is, if the loaf's cheap we're ruined, but if the loaf's dear we're starved. For myself I'm ready enough to die, but my boys . . .'

His piping voice suddenly stopped. He wiped his eyes with the back of his hand. Then he went on:

'The farmers say they can't live without they make four rents — one for stock, one for rent, one for labour, one for theirselves. Times is bad and they can't make their four rents. Well, does the landlord as does nothing give up his rent? Of course not. Then corn falls two pound a load and worse — farmer's forty shilling out o' pocket on every load of wheat — eight shilling on every acre of his land on a four-course shift. Where's that to come from? He can't stint the landlord so he stints the labourer. Tell the landlord, friends, what you think of him and do justice to your fellow-men.'

He stopped, his voice ending in a funny little whistle, and he sat down, his legs almost giving way beneath him. The majority of the men and women in the hall had for the most part never seen a green field in their lives — the facts and figures meant nothing to them — but the sincerity and urgency of his starved and feeble body stirred and moved them. You could feel it run through the hall like a message. There was a murmur, a restlessness, voices cried out. They were all brothers together, in field and factory, street and mine. Adam could see the faces around him change from a vague listening absorption to a personal human activity. A little man like a terrier leaped to his feet. He was plainly a practised orator. He brought the personal case of the labourer into the more general cause of them all. A woman broke out from the centre of the hall:

'They would part me from my children!' she cried in a shrill, agonized wail. 'How did I leave them this morning? Crying for their breakfasts. I've had no bread to give them for the last month and more. I've no bread. I've no fire. How can I have with one shilling and sixpence a hundred for coals? If I snatch a bit of wood from a hedge they'll gaol me. It's the women and children you should be thinking on! Oh, if I was a man I know what I'd be doing! I know what I'd be doing!'

Another woman, on that, cried out, waving an arm hysterically: 'Ax the Queen. Go and ax the Queen to come and see for herself. She's got a heart same as us . . .' And a man near her roared out: 'Why, the Queen – she's all locked up. They've got the dragoons guarding her. Do you think the Queen wants to be frightened with the like of we? She's got Melbourne, she has. What is it to him or her if poor labourers suffer and our women are stripped naked in the mines and bread's one-and-sixpence the loaf? Ax the Queen! Aye, go and ax her and see what her soldiers do to you!'

A confused babel of voices broke out. You could feel that the temperature of men's blood was rising as though with every word they moved closer together and closer and closer, so that at last they seemed to be one man, a man with eyes red and burning, a mouth hard set, cheeks hollow with hunger – a man with his hand clenched to strike.

Someone leaped up and cried shrilly: 'Let us take what is ours! Let us take what is ours! Let us take what is ours!'

Anything might have happened then. Adam, not knowing that he did it, put his arm around Margaret and drew her nearer to protect her; they were pressed back against the wall. No one thought of his or her neighbour; a stout woman in an orange shawl had her hand, without knowing it, on Adam's arm, and in a kind of strangled sob was saying over and over: 'Aye – it's the People's right – it's the People's right – it's the People's right . . .'

Adam knew that in another moment there would be that strong, swaying movement beneath their feet as though the floor were stirring under them, and that then all would be swept together in some mob-hysteria beyond control.

But it did not come. Instead the rotund little Chairman in some way made himself heard. He said that Mr Kraft would speak to them and, as Caesar rose to his feet, quiet came over everyone again. How proud Adam was of him at that moment! His square shoulders were set like those of a man carrying a banner; his eyes spoke to some distance far beyond the hall and its occupants; his voice, rich, warm, sincere, had no arrogance in it and no self-seeking.

'I do not believe in disorder,' he said. 'Neither now nor at any time. I know that our cause is just, but I find it so just that it must have victory – but victory by law and not by riot. Patience—'

At the word 'Patience' someone shouted out: 'We have been patient long enough!'

Caesar went on: 'We have not been patient long enough. We can never be patient long enough so long as we are moving. And we *are* moving! We have our Six Points of our Charter, and they are so right and so just that all the world will yield to them. We are working for a prize greater and more lasting than our immediate troubles. We are working for our children and our children's children. What do we gain by fire and murder? We place ourselves in the same case as our oppressors. We must believe in justice, for there *is* justice in the world. Men may be unjust, but behind them moves something stronger, finer and wiser than man.'

He went on then to tell them what the heads of the movement were doing, showed them their plans in detail, and was so comprehensive, clear and wise that soon the hall was as quiet as a vestry, and you could hear the rumble of the carts on the cobbles outside. All then might have moved peacefully to its close, but as soon as Kraft, to a hubbub of applause and clapping of hands, had sat down, Lunt sprang to his feet. He stood swaying on his short, strong legs, his body a little forward, his dark face with its shock of black hair alive with indignation and an almost mad impetuosity.

'I am Caesar Kraft's friend!' he called out. 'I *have* been and shall be! But I say that his advice to you is the advice of a dreamer! Wait, he says! Patience, he says! Yes, we are patient, and meanwhile what happens! Our old men and children, our wives and daughters, die in cellars swimming in filth, as I have seen two dead today; our women starve naked in the fields grubbing roots that pigs would refuse. Our men are beaten by their masters until their backs drop blood. We starve. We starve. Half the men in this room are starving now! And the Government says – let them starve! The less work for us, the Government says. Let them eat one another, the Government says, if they're hungry. Let them lie closer to one another if they're cold! Why should they interfere between slave and slave?'

He began to pace the platform, his face turned to them, his body shaking with his vehemence.

'Why do we give opium to our little children? So that they may forget their hunger! We entreat the Government to have mercy on us, we send it petitions, we show it our naked backs and our fever-dying comrades. "Oh yes," they say, and send us an answer: "Sorry to say that it is altogether out of the power of Her Majesty ..." Her Majesty! And she feeding off gold plate and riding in the Park of a morning! What does she know or care? Patience, Caesar Kraft tells you, but *I* tell you that we have had enough of patience, that they won't listen although we call, that they laugh at our tears. The Towns must win the Charter for England – men and women like yourselves – and not by patience, not by sitting down and waiting while we starve, but by rising and showing our power, by driving fear into their souls, by putting those same dragoons out of the way that we may meet the Queen face to face and say to her: "Here are your people! You haven't seen them before, but take a good look at them – see their backs how they bleed, how their stomachs are empty, their children crying for food—"'

He was interrupted by a roar of voices. 'Aye! Aye! ... We'll go now. We'll go to the Queen ... We've been patient enough! To the Palace! To the Palace!'

Like a wind through trees the roomful swayed, then broke. Men shouted, women called. The din was fearful, threatening, with that note in it that no individual man can recognize as his own and, after catastrophe, denies as his own.

They broke and rushed to the doors, Adam holding Margaret, who, however, was almost as strong as he.

The noisy, shouting mob tumbled into the street to be met with a fog as thick as a wall of suet. It was comic, that sudden dropping of voices, that check on the rush and impulse as though they had all found themselves on the edge of a precipice with the sea booming below them. The street was quiet and chill; the fog blew through the air in thick, yellow folds, laying its clammy touch on every mouth. Figures shot up out of the dark, some of them with flares, flamed and vanished. The crowd from the hall passed like smoke into smoke.

Adam laughed. He put his hand through her arm and they walked forward.

'Well – that is the end of *that* rioting. We must go forward, trust our luck. We will reach a clearer patch soon.' The fog was the one thing in all the world that could give him courage to speak, for they were close together, but in darkness.

So, when they had gone only a little way, he said outright:

'Margaret, I love you. Will you marry me?'

'Yes,' she said.

He stopped where he was, put his arms round her and kissed her. She did not move so he did not either. They seemed in a trance, protected by the fog, her lips on his, his arms tightly round her. At last when, very slowly, they moved on again he said:

'I must tell you, Margaret, that I have no money, no home, nothing.'

'Yes,' she said. 'Your home is with us.'

'And I have a mother whom I love more dearly than anyone but you.'

She held his hand more tightly.

'I have no father, as you know. I have no family. I am illegitimate.'

She laughed.

'You belong all the more to me for that,' she said.

Then a long while afterwards, when the fog in front of them was clearing, she said, sighing:

'Oh, I did hope, Adam, that you loved me, for I loved you from the first moment.'

HISTORY OF ELIZABETH

ADAM would have been greatly surprised had he realized that not far from where he was standing that June day in 1838 Uhland and Elizabeth had also witnessed the return of the Procession from Westminster Abbey. Will had invited them to London for the Coronation and they had accepted his invitation.

'Do you wish to go?' Walter had asked them. He also had been invited, but an affair upon which he was just then engaged (a highly exciting amorous affair with a lady who lived near Cockermouth) prevented his acceptance. Moreover, he did not wish to go; he found, if he were honest, his father a dull dog and his mother a quite unspeakable bore. Yet in his own way he loved them, wrote to his mother every month and sent his father presents of game.

When Elizabeth heard of the invitation she waited breathlessly to know whether she would be allowed to accept it. It was upon just such an invitation that she had been counting, for she was determined to escape from her father, from Ireby, from her brother, and, if possible, never return.

She was now a beautiful girl, twenty-three years of age. Her mother had died in the autumn of 1835, and since then she had not known one moment's happiness.

When, so long ago, she and John had agreed to separate and not to see one another again she had been but a child. She had forced the separation upon John because she had been certain that marriage with her would be for him a disaster. She was perhaps wrong there. Had they at that time run away and married, the whole course of their lives might have been altered to happiness, but how could he run away when he was responsible for everything at Uldale? Since then his sister had married Bellairs, but now there was something stronger than any practical reason that drove Elizabeth.

She believed – and had more reason for her belief than anyone outside the house at Ireby could know – that Uhland would kill John if she married him. Wherever they went Uhland would find them out. She had a terror of her father and brother that went far beyond actual day-by-day fact.

Uhland's hatred of John became fanatical after he learnt that Elizabeth cared for him. It became so fanatical that he did nothing about it, as though he knew that he had only to bide his time, as though he knew that there was no need for him to do anything yet because John at Uldale was well aware of it; it was as though he could see inside John's heart and feel the fear and apprehension growing there. It was as though he felt that if he did *yet* anything positive in word or deed it would hinder the full flavour of his act when the real time for it arrived.

There the two of them were, Uhland at Ireby and John at Uldale, very near together, and, like a spell in witchcraft, the power of the one over the other, although they never met, always increased.

And in the same way, on the other side of the account, Elizabeth's love for John never lessened, but increased.

She went about, saw many people in the County, made friends, led outwardly a quiet normal life; she tried with all her force (and she had much strength of character) to kill her love for John. She seldom saw him in public, for people, knowing well the old feud, took care that the two households did not meet. Sometimes in the Keswick street, at a hunt, at a public ball, they would catch sight of one another and turn away. John, on his side, thought that he was only waiting until Elizabeth was old enough. He knew that she was beautiful and rich and should make a fine marriage. If she married him, when her father and brother hated him so, it meant exile for her and, perhaps, disgrace. But when she was of age she had only to make him a sign and he would act. Nevertheless, although he was no coward in any other way, the thought of Uhland made him sick. Often when he was busy about the house or the farm or riding or paying a visit some dreaminess would overtake him, it would seem to him as though with one step, by unlocking some door he would pass into another world infinitely more beautiful than this one. He had dreamt once as a child of a marvellous white horse plunging through an icy tarn and climbing, his mane flowing, the steep mountainside. He had never forgotten the dream although it had never returned. If he could ride that horse he would spring forward into regions of splendour and eternal life! But again and again when such images came to him, asleep at night, walking the fells, sitting half awake by the fire, he seemed to hear a step behind him and would start up, expecting to see the cold malicious face of Uhland watching him.

So there they were, the three of them, in this summer of 1838. Again and again afterwards Elizabeth would look back to this time at Ireby and ask herself whether she did anything that fostered later events. But she could not see that she was responsible. She held on during that time to the principles, first that her father's neglect of her and his scandalous behaviour should not touch her, secondly that Uhland's taunts should not touch her, thirdly that her love of John should not touch her. It was the last of the three that at length drove her to flight. She *could* not, she *could* not be so near to him and not see him. Her father's behaviour she was by now accustomed to; Uhland's taunts she could endure, but they were ingenious. He would test her suddenly, unexpectedly. He would say: 'I hear young Herries has made a fool of himself over that farm ...' 'They are saying that John Herries has put a girl at Jocelyn's by Troutbeck in the family way. He can't leave farm girls alone. He has a low taste,' or 'They say that Herries goes to Cockermouth and gambles night after night – gambling all the estate away, poor fool ... Hard on old Madame.' All lies of course! Walter Herries would chuckle and shake his shoulders (he was growing immense now

although still handsome in a florid three-chin fashion). But
Elizabeth would not stir. She had all the Herries pride. She
would look at Uhland and smile very faintly, and he would look
gravely back at her. There would be at that moment a strange
subconscious alliance between them.

But by the summer of this year, 1838, she had reached the
limit of all her endurance. How she hated the Fortress no words
of hers could express. Even to the outside unprejudiced person it
was not a happy house as Westaways had been. Westaways had
been created by an artist, and it was a thousand pities that in the
autumn of 1836 it was pulled down by the purchasers of the
land; they had a plan for building an Almshouse there but this
never came to anything. All the eighteenth-century colour and
glitter, all the ambitions of Pomfret and Jannice, the childish
hopes of Raiseley and Judith and Anabel, the early ambitions of
Walter – all gone at the flourish of a hand, a little cloud of dust
rising slowly over the tumbling brick! And the Fortress was not
built by an artist! It was intended to stand for Herries independence, strength and superiority. Good English material
power. Most certainly it looked strong enough with its battlements and towers, its broad high rooms, its walls and garden-
paths and fountain. But it was never gay, never light-hearted,
never alive! Even Walter felt this. He entertained there lavishly,
had dinners and hunting-parties, dances and drinking-bouts
and, after Agnes' death, made it open house for all the squires of
the County. But it refused to come alive! Half the rooms 'died on
him', do what he would. He complained that there was not
sufficient feminine society in it. Elizabeth entertained and she
was a lovely hostess, quiet, dignified, kindly. Everyone liked her,
but everyone said that the place was sad. They whispered that
Walter beat her when he was in a drunken temper. He did not
beat her: he never ill-treated her: he gave her everything that she
asked. He simply did not consider her. A Mrs Fergus, a genial
stout widow, was housekeeper there during these years. She was
common, voluble, gossipy, a good manager. She liked Elizabeth
and tried to win her trust. But she did not. She confided to
everybody that something was the matter in that house. It was as
though a ghost were in every room in spite of the drinking-
parties and dinners.

It may have been that Uhland was the ghost. He had certainly
grown into a very severe, silent young man. Friendship with
Adam might have saved Uhland at this time. He showed from a

conversation that he had with Elizabeth in London that he was as lonely as she. Adam was certainly the only human being in the world to whom he would have disclosed himself. There was no doubt but that during those years from 1832 to 1838 he was as unhappy as Elizabeth was. It may be that at the end of it all he despised and hated himself quite as much as he despised and hated John Herries. No one will ever know.

Walter meanwhile, being really a foolish soul with very little understanding of other human beings, continued to persuade himself that Uhland adored him, adored the Fortress, adored the fine fortune that Walter preserved for him (already not quite so fine as it had once been: the Fortress like a heavy dull grey monster swallowed greedily all that was offered it). His love for Uhland was pathetic. He was like a big lumbering elephant cherishing a morose young wolf.

And that was how things were when Elizabeth and Uhland went to London.

When they arrived, late one evening, in Hill Street, where was Will's present town house, Uhland was in a monstrous temper because of the bad time that they had had in the coach. They had booked for the inside, of course, but there had been an asthmatic gentleman with a cough so tiresome, and an old lady with so many small packages that she was for ever undoing to see whether the contents were safe, that Uhland had sought the roof. There were not many passengers, and with extra money he had secured the box-seat, and there wrapped in the leather-covered rug might have been fairly comfortable, but then a storm had come on and the rain had driven down his neck, his overcoat was soaked, and the coachman was for ever thrusting his rein-elbow into his (Uhland's) ribs. The day following had not been much better, for the food at the inns was atrocious, and the manners of everyone appalling. Why had they not tried the new railway? It was so erratic. You never knew where it began and where it left off. Worst of all, their hackney cab, when at last they got into it, collided with a dray, and they were in perilous chance of immediate death.

So they arrived at Hill Street and discovered that a grand party was in progress. A tall gorgeously dressed footman hurried them up the stairs as though they were very criminal indeed. Everywhere were flowers; there was the distant music of a band and the crackle of many voices. Elizabeth had not been in her large cold room five minutes before a maid knocked, came in, and asked her whether she should unpack for her.

'Her ladyship is unfortunately most unwell. She has been confined to her bed for several weeks. She hopes to see you, Miss, in the morning.'

Was she supposed to come down to the party, Elizabeth wondered. Would she get anything to eat? She was inordinately hungry. The maid, who looked a nice girl, Elizabeth thought, was on her knees unpacking.

'Would you tell me your name?' Elizabeth asked.

'Ellen,' said the girl.

Elizabeth shivered. *How* hungry she was! And then, miracle of miracles, the door burst open, and in came Sylvia Herries looking radiant and lovely in pink tulle and carrying a tray!

'Oh, my dearest Elizabeth!'

'Dear Sylvia!'

'But of course I knew that you would be *starving*, and Frederick is bringing a warming-pan. You can place it under those cushions and sit on it. How are you feeling, my sweetest Elizabeth? But of course you must be *dead*! But how lovely you are looking! A little thin ... Was the journey quite, quite dreadful? Ah, here is Frederick! There, Frederick – place it beneath those cushions ... Oh, dear little Elizabeth! I am *ravished* to see you, and Cousin Will is giving the grandest party. Mr Macaulay is here and Lady Brownlow and Lady Euston and the Bishop of Oxford and *ever* so many more, and James' wife is doing the honours. You never saw anything so amazingly odd. She's wearing a turban like a pastry-cook's shop! But there's no one so lovely as you are, so you must hurry, my dearest, and eat this chicken and drink this champagne and wear your *loveliest* costume ... Now sit on the warming-pan, dearest, *quite* still for five minutes. That will warm the under part of you in any case. There's the most enravishing band and I've danced five waltzes already ...'

So Elizabeth sat on the warming-pan and then with the assistance of Ellen and Sylvia put on her dress of white organdie with a rose at her girdle, which, although it *had* been made by little Miss Trent in Keswick, suited her exactly.

When she came into the big room, blazing with lights, swimming in music, a kind of exultation seized her. How wonderful to have escaped from that cold, grey Fortress with the heavy grey clouds hanging over it, the stern dark landscape hemming it in, to this scene of splendour and magnificence! Ah! If only John were here! But one day he would be! They would be here together! She deserved some life and some fun, surely.

Will came up to her and was very kind. He was of course stiff and pompous a little, but he meant well and this was a big occasion for him. He led her up to Lady Euston who, in satin, a green turban and splendid diamonds, was the most terrifying lady she had ever seen.

'Well, my dear, and so you have come for the Coronation?'

'Yes, ma'am.'

'Let us trust that Providence will favour us with good weather. It is very cold for the summer.'

'Yes, indeed, ma'am.'

'This is your first visit to London?'

'Yes, ma'am.'

'Your cousin must bring you to Almack's, and you must visit the Opera. How do you do, Sir Henry? I hear that Mr Croker has written the most offensive article about Soult in the *Quarterly* ...'

Soon she was dancing, once with Garth, once with Amery, once with Roger, Carey Rockage's son. Then with a gentleman whose dress-coat was so extremely waisted that she was afraid lest he should break in two at any moment. He wanted, very solemnly, to tell her about the Park: 'Until recently the Park has been most sombre and I assure you most unsafe for *anyone* after nightfall. However, lamps with gas have now been introduced and throw a noontide splendour. They combine in fact ornament with utility, and vice has been banished from her wonted haunts ...' She supposed that he had something to do with the Parks, he seemed so very serious about it.

Then Garth introduced her to a stout rather plethoric young man, a Mr Temple, she understood. She had not waltzed with him once around the room before she realized that he was greatly charmed with her. He told her so; he led her away to a corner behind a mass of begonias and, breathing hard to recover his wind, said in a sort of wondering whisper that she was, upon his life, the most lovely girl that he had ever seen. He begged her, he implored her, not to take offence. The admission had been, to his own amazement, compelled upon him. She could not take offence. There was nothing offensive about him; he was like a baby in his tight clothes, with a large diamond in his shirt and his hair excessively pomaded. She wanted to laugh and, when he left her for a moment to bring her some champagne, she did laugh. She could not help it. She was happy. She was free. She would never go back to Ireby again, and John would come to her.

'You have made a conquest, my dear cousin,' said Garth, a little later.

'A conquest?' she asked.

'Edward Temple. He is the richest young man in London.'

In the course of the next week or so Elizabeth discovered a number of curious and amusing things. Poor Christabel was, alas, too ill to see her. She sent her loving messages and hoped that she was enjoying herself. Elizabeth was chaperoned either by Sylvia or by James' wife, Lady Herries, poor Beatrice. She was known as 'poor Beatrice' because she said such silly things, wore such hideous clothes, and tumbled into such foolish blunders, but like many who are pitied by their fellows she was a great deal happier than those who pitied her. She was good-natured, most indiscreet, and admired Elizabeth's beauty with a sincerity that was touching.

Will lived with much splendour. When they went to a ball or a theatre or Vauxhall of an evening they were carried in a fine painted 'chariot' with Frederick, the footman, in silk stockings, plush breeches and hair-powder, standing behind; the Herries family arms were on the panels. But the house in Hill Street could not be said to be comfortable. That there were often unpleasant 'whiffs' from the drains meant nothing. People even preferred that the drains should 'smell' occasionally because then they could tell which way the wind was blowing and whether 'there would likely be rain'. The furniture was fine, heavy and impressive, but the passages and rooms were dreadfully chill, and there was an air of mortality everywhere save when there was a party. Elizabeth had some very dreary days and evenings. Will was in the City all day, Uhland out and about on his own affairs, as men, lucky creatures, were able to be, but unless Sylvia or Lady Herries came for her she was sadly alone. All the Herries were good and kind to her, but she soon perceived that they were, nearly all of them, living above their means, reaching up to the new grand position that Will's money and Sylvia's social successes had brought to them. It said much for Will's dignity and tact that, having made his position by business, he and his should be admitted to Almack's and allowed the honours of Holland

House. But the Herries were a very old family, and the Rockages had most certainly not made their money in business – having exactly no money at all. Roger, Carey's boy, and his wife Janet had a house in Mayfair during the Season and ordered little dinners from the caterer (and *what* scrapes they went through in order to pay the caterer no one knew but themselves); then as soon as the Season was over they disappeared, with their only child Carey, into two very shabby rooms in Pimlico, and Janet did the cooking. The life of Sylvia and Garth, too, was one long and exciting piratical adventure – a very thrilling volume of hairbreadth peril and escape it would make. Garth spent much of his time at Crockford's, which was not on the face of it a very foolish thing to do, for the subscription was but ten guineas a year, and in the gambling-rooms there was served a splendid supper free, with excellent wine for all Mr Crockford's guests. Behind this were, of course, for many a man ruin and despair. But Garth was not a fool; he had some of his brother Amery's astuteness, and he knew his world.

Elizabeth, however, was not like Judith. She could not throw herself into whatever fun was going forward. She was quiet, reserved and shy. All she wanted of life was that she should be allowed to live quietly in a corner with John somewhere and never be disturbed by anyone again.

She sat of an evening in the great drawing room or in her bedroom, a book on her lap, and meditated her escape. For escape she must. She knew that Uhland had some plan; she felt as though with every hour he was the more closely driving her to some purpose of his own.

There came an evening at Vauxhall when she began to realize what his plan for her was. She went with Sylvia, Garth, Uhland and Phyllis Newmark. It was all very splendid. There were the 'twenty thousand lamps' shining against the soft velvety sky of a July evening, Ducrow and his horses, the famous bandstand round which, if you were an unattached gentleman out for the evening, you might swirl with the loveliest, if not the most virtuous, ladies of the town, the fireworks and the vocal concerts.

For a while she enjoyed herself, listening to Sylvia's chatter, liking the general gaiety and abandon; nevertheless, she wondered, as she always did on these occasions, why she could not throw herself into things as the others did. They must find her dreadfully stupid, she thought, and, in fact, Garth that same evening confided to Sylvia behind the bed-curtains that he thought that little cousin of theirs mighty handsome, by Jove, but she seemed to be feared of her life lest someone should kiss her or chuck her under the chin; and Sylvia was forced to confess with a sigh that she didn't come out as she'd hoped. She was more at home, she suspected, in the country.

Well, later young Mr Temple joined them and, after that, poor Elizabeth's evening was a ruin. Everyone beamed upon Mr Temple, and soon he was seated with Elizabeth as his especial charge, feeding her with chicken and ham. He had a great deal to say to her, admired her gown and told of his place in Surrey where he had horses, dogs and a piano. He said he was prodigiously fond of music and the Italian opera. Very tenderly he helped her to a 'sliced cobweb' – the famous Vauxhall ham. His favourite expression, the phrase of the moment, was, when he saw anything amusing: 'What a bit of gig!'

Soon his absorption of the famous Vauxhall punch led him to closer intimacies. He pressed her hand and wished to take her up one of the shaded walks. From this Sylvia saved her, but she observed with terror that Uhland watched these proceedings with approval.

She did not sleep that night in her huge bed. What was she to do? She felt utterly defenceless. She had not a friend in the world. Strangely, she thought of Judith and Adam. What it would have been to her just then to have seen that little old lady with her sharp nose and kind bright eyes entering at the door, or Adam with his strong, ugly, honest face standing beside her! But they seemed far away, and John farther. She had no one to whom she might turn. Beatrice Herries was too foolish and indiscreet, Sylvia too flighty, Christabel too unwell. Of Will she was afraid, Garth she did not trust. She was inexperienced in the world's ways, and London seemed now like a great web in whose sticky threads she was entangled.

Then one evening Uhland came to her room. She had but just lit the candles. Bulwer's *Last Days of Pompeii* was in her hand, but her mind was with John, running as it so often did over those earlier days when they had written and met . . . He was like her, she thought, shy, not caring for the world, uneasy with others. Why could they not be together in some place where no one else could come? Uhland sat near her and was kinder to her, at first, than he had ever been. He wore black; his thin sharp features had in them a shadow of suffering. She knew that he was often in pain, and that feeling of some companionship between them, something that lay deep, deep down below all this strife and antagonism, stirred in her. They *could* be friends if only . . .

He told her about some of the things that he had been doing. He seemed to be as out of everything as she.

'I hate London. I do not belong here. They laugh at us as country cousins.'

'Oh no,' she protested. 'They are so very kind.'

'Kind! Do you know what they say of us? They find us most desperately dull, sister, and that's a fact. I hate drinking. I won't play at cards. They swagger – Lord, how they swagger! And then to be up all night and for nothing – women, drink, gambling – gambling, women, drinking. Why, Ireby were better!'

He looked at her, one of those quiet speculative looks that always made her afraid.

'I am different from everyone!' he burst out. 'They mock my lameness!'

'Oh no,' she said gently. 'They don't think of it. Why, Sylvia said—'

'Yes. Sylvia said – Sylvia said—' he answered contemptuously. 'Dear Sylvia had better take care or she'll have the bailiffs in that pretty house of hers and Garth will be in the Marshalsea . . . No,' he went on more quietly. 'It is my own fault; I am no company for anyone here, not even for myself. There's a devil in me that won't let me alone. We Herries are a poor lot unless we take what's in front of our noses. We were not made to be exceptional. Not that I'm exceptional, you know, except in my temper. I despise their smugness. What do they know of what it is to have a needle stab your leg every other minute, and to be something that every woman pities? . . . No matter though. I shall show them all one day . . .'

She did not dare to show pity. She knew how deeply he resented it. But she said:

'We should go somewhere together, Uhland, the two of us. We could go to the Colosseum or the Panorama. I should adore to see the Panorama.'

But he did not answer her. He sat there brooding, looking down, nursing his leg. There was something, she thought, twisted, wizened about him, his thin small body bent, throwing strange humped shadows on the wall in the candlelight.

He looked up.

'You are secure at least, Elizabeth.'

'Secure?' she asked him.

'Yes. Temple is crazy about you. He will be proposing for you one of these days.'

'Oh no,' she whispered.

'Oh yes,' he answered. 'It is a fine match. There couldn't be a better. He's something of a fool, of course. But that's his age. He'll improve. I never knew a man more deeply in love.'

She said nothing. He went on:

'He is fabulously wealthy. He has his house in Belgravia and a place in Surrey. Only an old mother to care for. He doesn't play at cards and is afraid of loose women. You can do what you will with him.'

'That, Uhland, you can dismiss altogether from your mind. I should not marry him if there were no other man in the world.'

He looked at her.

'Still thinking of your friend in Cumberland?' he asked her.

'No . . . But I would never marry Mr Temple.'

He got up and walked, limping, about the room.

'Never is a long story. It would be a fine thing. Our father would think so.'

She smiled.

'There I am my own mistress.'

'Not entirely,' he said quietly. 'I think you had better consider Temple.'

'And why?'

He stood by the door, his pale eyes gravely regarding her.

'Dear sister, consider what a fine husband Temple would make. Consider it. Be wise,' and left her.

She was afraid after that and despised herself for being so. What was there about Uhland that made everyone who knew him apprehensive? Even the stable-boys at Ireby dropped their voices when he was approaching, and she knew that people in Keswick called him 'Little Mischief', although no one accused him of any actual cruelties. On the contrary, that habit of kindness to injured animals was still with him. He would be in a rage if he saw a horse ill-used or a dog tied by the tail. And yet it was not as though he cared for animals!

No, what they all felt about him was the potentiality of an outburst. Society is built up on the convention that we all *intend* to behave. That is the bargain we make the one with the other. Then, if there is one who hasn't made the bargain! . . .

In any case, Elizabeth felt some ring closing round her. She was perhaps at that time young for her age. She had been always

with her mother, had known no other girls intimately. But this
was a situation in which other girls than herself might have been
frightened, for she knew that her father would regard this match
as a heaven-sent chance. He had always wanted to be rid of her.
Like so many men who are for ever making love to women he
despised them heartily and wanted them for one thing only. He
preferred greatly men's company, and the only chance that a
woman had with him as friend was for her to have something of
the downright and fearless about her as Judith had. Now
Elizabeth had nothing of the downright about her whatever. She
was proud and brave, but it was a pride that was too real to
reveal itself and a courage that was too real for cheap display.

It was a misfortune for her that Christabel was so ill, but she
did have one strange little conversation with her grandfather
which was to have important after-consequences for her.

Sir William Herries was now sixty-eight years of age and as
straight as a flag-pole. His hair was grizzled and he was very thin
of body with a sharp nose, high Herries cheek-bones, and a
severe, rather chilly eye that came from considering sums, ad-
ditions, subtractions, multiplications for sixty-five years. It was
at the age of three, his father David used long ago to declare, that
he had added his first sum, accurately, and without assistance.
He was dressed immaculately, always in black with none of those
gaudy waistcoats, diamonds, pins and gold chains that orna-
mented the bodies of the Disraelis, the Bulwers and the Ains-
worths of the day. But he was a splendid sight as you saw him
step out of the carriage that had brought him up from the City,
in the high hat, high stock, coat fitting perfectly at the slender
waist, and tightly strapped trousers. A fine sight as, inside the
cold hall with a marble statue of a goddess, handsomely robed,
holding aloft a lamp, he gives his hat, gloves and cane to Frederick, passes his hand for a moment over his grey locks, pinches his
side-whiskers, and walks slowly, slowly up the broad staircase.

'How is Lady Herries?' he asks Warren, the fat butler. 'Has
Doctor Salter paid his visit?'

'Doctor Salter has been, Sir William. Her ladyship is much the
same.'

'Ah . . . Ah. Ha! . . . Thank you, Warren.'

So one late afternoon, he came into the drawing room, orna-
mented as was the earlier drawing room in the earlier smaller
house with oil-paintings of David his father and Sarah his

mother, and a huge marble clock that had Virtue seated in a toga on the top of it, window hangings of a very grave mustard colour, a table or two scattered with 'Beauty Books' and 'Keepsakes', the poems of Felicia Hemans and a book of engravings of Greece and Italy – all this as chill and as damp as a mausoleum, all this bringing pride and comfort to his soul.

Today he moved about, putting a 'Keepsake' straight on a table, arranging the hanging of one of the curtains, looking out for a moment into the summer evening that was coquetting with Hill Street. Then only was it that he discovered Elizabeth seated on a sofa.

'My dear!' he exclaimed. 'I never saw you!'

'Good evening, Grandfather.'

He was weary, he was lonely, he had a pain in his side. He sat down beside her. He had never been blind to feminine beauty although he *had* married Christabel. His daughter, Alice, who had died of a chill in 1812, had been as plain as her mother. He was proud and pleased that his grand-daughter should be so beautiful. Elizabeth's beauty lay in the perfection of her delicacy, the rosy bloom of her colouring; her shoulders and arms, revealed by the low cut of her cream-coloured dress, had the soft firmness of a child's unawareness. Her hands, exquisitely shaped, were both gentle and strong. She had the fairness of a rose scarcely daring to open.

'I am afraid, my dear,' he said, 'that I have not seen so much of you during this visit as I should have wished. I am growing an old man, but I have never, all my life, learnt how to delegate business to others. If I do not see to it myself it's done wrong. I trust that you have been happy.'

'Oh yes, Grandpapa.'

'That's good. And Uhland?'

'I think he has been very happy.'

She longed to burst out: 'I am not happy at all! They want to marry me to a young man I detest. You must prevent them.' But she did not dare. She knew him so little, and she looked so very imposing with his legs spread out in front of him and his long, thin hands with the tapering fingers laid on his bony knees.

'It is a misfortune that your grandmother has been so unwell.'

'I hope she is getting better,' Elizabeth said gently.

'No, my dear, I fear not. Doctor Salter is doing all he can, but, as he constantly says, she will not make a sufficient effort. A great pity! A great pity! Your grandmother is a wonderful woman, my dear, but she has never had quite the courage needed for a life like ours. After all, she is a woman.'

'Yes, Grandpapa.'

'And what have you been doing with yourself, my dear?'

Elizabeth told him some of the things that she had been doing.

He nodded, rubbed his hands together, rose.

'Very good. Very good. I trust your grandmother will soon be sufficiently well for you to see her. It is delightful for us to have you here.'

But as he went out of the room and climbed the stairs he was vaguely uncomfortable. Was she happy? She appeared lonely. That brother of hers was a queer fish. Very queer. But then he was crippled, poor child. Odd for Walter, big and healthy as he was, to have a crippled son. What a beautiful girl! It did one good ... But he was vaguely uneasy, and the uneasiness remained.

Two days later Mr Temple came and proposed, and after that events followed swiftly. He came with Sylvia Herries and they drank tea together in the mustard-coloured drawing room. Sylvia said that she must go and ask Mrs Arnold, the housekeeper, about some silks that she wished to match. No sooner was she out of the room than Mr Temple fell on his knees. It was a proposal in the conventional fashion!

'Dearest Miss Herries! Oh, if I may only call you Elizabeth! From the first moment I saw you I have been in a dream. You are the only woman in the whole world for me. All that I have is yours ...' and so on and so on.

Elizabeth also behaved in the traditional manner.

'Pray, Mr Temple, rise from the floor.'

He caught her hand. He kissed it.

'I shall have to call for someone if you persist in this ridiculous—'

'Adorable Elizabeth! Most heavenly—'

He climbed on to the sofa beside her and tried to kiss her cheek.

'Please, Mr Temple.' Then she broke into sheer disgust. 'Oh, go away! No, I do not love you. I can never love you. I do not even care for you. No, not even with friendly feelings. This is absurd. This is too absurd—'

She freed herself and stood with her hand on the bell-rope.

He was amazed. He could not believe his ears. This was the first proposal of his life, for he had always believed that himself and his riches were irresistible and that when the time did come for him to honour anybody there could be but one possible result.

He was deeply chagrined. Even a tear rolled on to his fat little cheek.

'Oh, dammit!' he cried, and went indignantly from the room.

Next morning Uhland came to her in her room. His look of cold, resolved anger terrified her; she felt as though he had imprisoned her and would do what he pleased. The sense of power that he spread about him was extraordinary.

'Elizabeth – what is this I hear? Temple has proposed and you have refused him.'

'Yes.'

'You silly little fool! You are to write to him immediately and say that you have reconsidered it.'

She shook her head.

'But I say Yes. It is the very thing for you. Father will wish it. All of us.'

'No, Uhland. I don't love him. I dislike him extremely.'

'Love? What is love? It is because you have still some sentimental longing for that young prig in Cumberland.'

'You know,' she answered, 'that that was over long ago.'

'I know nothing of the kind. If you will not accept Temple I shall charge your refusal to John Herries – and I shall know what to do—'

'You can't harm him!' she answered fiercely, all her dread of him gone. 'You can't touch him and you know it. But threats can't serve you. Nor your bullying. I should never marry Mr Temple if you starved me!'

'You *shall* marry him,' he answered.

He came up to her and put his cold, damp hand on her bare shoulder. 'I know what is good for you and I will see to it.'

He looked at her and left the room.

After that she had only one thought – flight. She had already for weeks been contemplating it. She had plenty of spirit, and the thought that at last she would escape from Ireby, from this house, from her father, from all these Herries relations gave her wings. That afternoon she searched *The Times* and at last found what she wanted. A Mrs Bohun Winstanley of 21A Sloane Street had an agency for 'Governesses, Companions, Situations for Genteel Persons'. Ellen, the maid, was her next resource. She had, in these weeks, won Ellen's devoted affections, not difficult considering her beauty, charm and gentleness. It seemed too that Ellen hated her place here, hated Mrs Arnold, the housekeeper, and was only waiting an opportunity to give her notice. Elizabeth told Ellen everything, even her love for John, and Ellen's eyes grew moist with sentiment as she drank in the details of such a romance. Ellen was sworn to secrecy. On the following day, having packed Elizabeth's box, she was to take a hackney-cab and meet Elizabeth outside St Clement Danes Church at midday. To this Ellen swore: she also protested that the most horrible tortures man (Ellen's natural enemy) could devise would not tempt her to betrayal. Elizabeth kissed her.

Early the next morning, wearing her quietest bonnet, she slipped out of the house into Hill Street. It was a fine morning and she walked out of her way to Charing Cross, taking her time lest Mrs Bohun Winstanley should not yet be at work. No one interfered with her. A cheap dandy with a sham diamond pin and a double-breasted waistcoat ogled her, a policeman in a blue swallow-tailed coat and white trousers glanced at her with some curiosity, but for the most part everyone was busy about his or her own business. There was a great deal of noise with the bell of the crier, the horn of the omnibus, the Italian boy and his hurdy-gurdy, and the shops with their small-paned bow-windows were opening, somewhere church bells were ringing. Everywhere everything was entrancing, for at last, at last, she was free!

When she thought the time was come she mounted inside an omnibus and at length was put down at the top of Sloane Street. Soon Number 21A was found, a dingy door, a still dingier stair-case. One flight up, in faded green letters, was Mrs Bohun Winstanley's name. Entering she found a room, grimy and disordered, with a shabby canary moulting in a shabby cage by the very dirty window, and a lady in a bonnet and mittens seated at a table strewn with papers. Standing in front of the empty grate was another lady, wearing a very gay bonnet covered with flowers, and a bright emerald-green shawl. This lady was tall, thin, and plainly in the worst of tempers. The lady at the table was small, and, at the moment, alarmed. A dewdrop trembled at the end of her nose, her mittens quivered with a life of their own, and she murmured again and again: 'Oh dear! Oh dear! But it is so *early* . . . so early, Mrs Golightly . . .'

'Early! Early!' cried the other lady, while all the flowers trembled in her bonnet in sympathy. 'Don't speak to me of "early", Mrs Winstanley. A promise is a promise!'

'But her little girl has the croup.'

'And what of *my* little girls, Mrs Winstanley? What of *my* little girls? Here have they been these three weeks, and Mr Golightly in Bath and returning tomorrow—'

It was then that both ladies together noticed Elizabeth.

'Well?' said Mrs Winstanley.

'I beg your pardon, I am sure,' said Elizabeth. 'I can wait outside—'

'But what *is* it?' said Mrs Winstanley, plainly near to tears.

'I read your advertisement in *The Times*,' said Elizabeth. 'I am looking for a place as governess or companion—'

Both ladies stared at Elizabeth. They had obviously never seen anyone so beautiful before.

'Sit down, pray,' Mrs Winstanley said at last (and it was clear that she saw, in Elizabeth, the ship of rescue). 'Now, Mrs Golightly, this is a young lady of whom I intended to have spoken yesterday—'

Mrs Golightly stared and stared.

'You are looking for a place?' she said at last.

'Yes, ma'am.'

'What is your name?'

'Mary Temple.' (Oh, how absurd! She had taken Mr Temple's name after all!)

'How old are you?'

'Twenty-three, ma'am.'

'What experience have you had?'

'I think,' broke in Mrs Winstanley, 'that you will find that she has had excellent experience.'

'Has she?' said Mrs Golightly doubtfully. 'She looks very superior, I must say.' Then she added: 'And your references?'

'I will speak for her references,' said Mrs Winstanley quickly.

'Ours is a very agreeable family,' Mrs Golightly said in a kind of dream. 'My two little girls are angelic – less than no trouble at all . . . When could you come?' she asked abruptly.

'This afternoon,' said Elizabeth.

'Very odd. Very odd, indeed. Have you French, Arithmetic, the Pianoforte, Dancing, Deportment? . . .'

'I think you will find that Miss Temple has everything that

you require,' Mrs Winstanley quickly inserted.

'Indeed!' Mrs Golightly still stared in a kind of dream. 'Very distinguished!' she murmured. 'You are familiar with the Poets?'

'I beg your pardon?' Elizabeth said.

'Shakespeare, Milton, Lord Byron, Mrs Hemans—'

'Oh yes,' said Elizabeth, 'I think so.'

'You *think* so,' said Mrs Golightly. 'Don't you *know?*'

'She is especially familiar with the Poets,' said Mrs Winstanley, speaking very gently and nodding her head.

Mrs Golightly stared and stared.

'You can come this evening?' she said at last.

'Yes, ma'am.'

'Of course,' Mrs Golightly said, turning to Mrs Winstanley, 'she may be a thief in collusion with all the thieves of the Metropolis. Pray, don't think me rude,' she went on, turning to Elizabeth again, 'but it is so very odd. I know nothing whatever about you. With whom were you last?'

'I am sure that you will find everything perfectly correct,' said Mrs Winstanley.

Mrs Golightly stared a little more.

'Well, I don't know, I'm sure. If Mr Golightly had any liking for young ladies the idea would be absurd, but as he has never given one a thought, being far too closely occupied by his beetles and butterflies . . .' She nodded her head. 'Very well, then. This evening. Mrs Winstanley will explain the terms,' and without another word she left the room, banging the little door behind her.

'And now,' said Mrs Winstanley gently, and blowing her nose, 'pray, tell me, my dear, who you are.'

THE GOVERNESS

ELIZABETH read her letter over again. In a few minutes she must go to Mrs Golightly's boudoir, where she must read for an hour while the moths buzzed about the lamp, the silly clock ticked, and the words of the novel in her hand moved in a mist of confusion before her heavy eyes. For she was very weary, as indeed she was always weary at this hour in the evening. Clarissa and Francesca were happily asleep in bed, lost in slumber, although safe neither from suffocation (for their bedroom would be hermetically sealed) nor from bugs. The little house in Islington crawled with animals, bugs and beetles and cockroaches (Alice the kitchen-maid, who slept in the kitchen, spent most of her day killing them: she was too tired at night to care), while spiders hung in every corner and dust lay on tables, sills and shelves as thick as the sand of the desert. In the meantime Mrs Golightly, surrounded with emerald-green curtains, ottomans and 'Keepsakes', sat in her evening yellow silk, her ringlets bound by her 'arcade' (a wonderful arrangement of wires twined with rosebuds, lace and ribbon), waiting for Elizabeth to continue her reading of *Agnes Serle* by Miss Ellen Pickering.

This was Elizabeth's letter:

4 PRAED STREET, ISLINGTON,
March 4th, 1839

BELOVED JOHN – I cannot, try as I may, refrain any longer from writing to you. The thought of your anxiety for me (for I do not I think flatter myself that you must be anxious) has been a motive ever more constant with me. But this I could have resisted were it not that your dear image, for so many many years now the dearest to me in all the word, refuses to leave to me the proper control of my feelings.

I know only too well, dearest John, that I am breaking all the vows that I have made and upon which I was myself formerly the most insistent. I am aware that all the reasons that kept us apart must keep us apart still: indeed their influence must be stronger with us than before since the irrevocable nature of my own desperate deed! How desperate it must seem to my own family you will realize from the fact that neither my father nor brother have made the slightest effort to find me out. I will admit to you that it is the increasing sense of my own loneliness that compels me to write to you. I had hoped that, cut off from all family ties, I might learn to forget you, but, dear John, true love is not so easily set aside and however dearly I have loved you in the past I must confess that it is only in these last weeks that I have realized to the full how deep and constant that love must be.

Perhaps it is shameful of me to make this confession to you, but shameful or not it must be made, for without some word from you I truly think that I shall die. I have not formerly been weak. I am weak now and must detest my weakness even while I yield to it.

I would not wish you to think that I am unhappy with Mrs Golightly, the lady in whose house I live and to whose little girls I am governess. She is not indeed at all unkind, only rather foolish and unable to keep her house clean or manage it with any efficiency. The two little girls are good and patient, poor little things, although entirely neglected. Mrs Golightly reads novels, recites poetry, has evening parties and attends concerts in Hanover Square, while Mr Golightly, who is fat and ab-sentminded but also kindly, collects moths and butterflies, which takes him very often into the country. Meanwhile the house is a ruin, the cooks come and go every week and only poor Alice, the kitchen-maid, is faithful and does all the work of the place.

Dear John, I think I have grown into a woman in these last months and see life more sanely than I did. I had, I do not doubt, an exaggerated picture of my father and my brother and although I know they do not love me and have never loved me, they are neither so hard nor so unkind as I at one time thought them. But do not think me cowardly, dear John, in thus writing to you. I am not thinking of changing my life but only that you should sometimes write me a letter and give me the opportunity to write to you. You understand, do you not, that NO ONE is to know of where I am nor of what I am doing. No one save yourself. It is to be a secret from everyone, but I love you so much that I think I shall be insane if I do not hear from you. Later on perhaps you will come to London and we shall meet again. Only to think of such a meeting sends me crazy with joy and happiness. But I know that you will answer this letter and that is all the happiness I wish for at this present time. Your most loving

ELIZABETH

She folded it up and sealed it.

'I am very wicked,' she thought. 'I have never done anything so really wrong as this before. But I don't care.' She further thought that she had been stupid not to have done this long ago. Her months with Mrs Golightly had made her begin to wonder whether she had not paid altogether too much attention to the decencies. She did not realize that it was the escape from the

Cumberland house that had changed her, the fact that she was emerging from the influence both of her father and brother, who until now had dominated her whole life.

She put on her bonnet and shawl, opened the door, listened, ran downstairs, down the front steps, then along the lamp-lit street to the post office. She hesitated a moment before dropping the letter in. Was it right? No, it wasn't right. Nevertheless, in it went. She stared defiantly about the street, but there was only one hackney-cab crawling along and an Italian organ-grinder with a shivering monkey in a crimson coat. She dropped a sixpence into the little monkey's cup as a sort of oblation. The monkey looked at her with eyes so old and so sad that she could not resist a little shudder. It was as though the monkey said: 'We are all cold. All lost. All doomed. There's nothing to be done about it . . .'

On the other hand, Alice, with a large smut across her nose, was looking up from the bottom of the area steps. She had a large broom in her hand which she waved in a cheerful fashion as much as to say: 'We're friends, we are. I know what you've been doing and wish you all the luck.' The thin strains of the barrel-organ echoed down the empty street as though they, too, wished her good fortune.

She ran quietly up the stairs, took off bonnet and shawl, brushed her ringlets and, with *Agnes Serle* in hand, marched down to the boudoir.

'Aren't you a little late, my love?' asked Mrs Golightly, who was reclining at ease with her velvet slippers toasting at the fire. The pug, Levilla, was on her lap, choking as usual.

'Yes, I think I am, a little,' said Elizabeth gently, and, opening her book, began to read.

She had remarked to herself again and again in these months how completely now she was separated from the Herries world. It was as though they lived, all of them, in another continent. Mrs Golightly did on occasion read out from the newspaper some social item, and once she remarked with a great deal of unction that she saw that Sir William Herries had been doing this or that. 'Let me see,' she went on. 'He is a cousin, I fancy, of Lady Rockage, and there is that lovely Mrs Garth Herries whose name you see everywhere. They are all the same family, I imagine.'

But Mrs Golightly and all her friends spoke of Gore House or Almack's as one speaks of Paradise. But with no envy. She had her world and was perfectly content with it, but the division between her world and that other one was quite complete. Mrs Golightly was a generous, unenvious person altogether. She thought her husband, children, friends and home all quite perfect. It was the fashion, moreover, for herself and her friends to be romantic about everything, and this same Romance gave them every kind of satisfaction. They liked their literature, their painting, their music, their religion to be romantic. They felt deeply and sincerely for all Oppressed Peoples. Mrs Golightly was for ever attending meetings for the poor Poles, for the Negro (whom they went so far as to call their brother), for the unhappy Greek and the neglected Hottentot. That her house was in a mess and that the slums, factories and mines quite close to home needed attention – these things were never discussed because they were *not* romantic.

Mrs Golightly enjoyed entertaining her friends in the evening (a little music on the pianoforte, a little 'dance' in the very small drawing room), she enjoyed a walk with Mr Golightly when he was at home, a visit to the theatre or a concert – but perhaps more than anything else she enjoyed sitting with her toes in front of the fire of an evening and listening to Elizabeth's reading of a novel. That original inquiry at the Agency about the Poets had been genuine enough, but when it came actually to *reading* – well, the novel was the thing! Elizabeth had a beautiful, quiet, cultivated voice, as Mrs Golightly told all her friends. It was a pleasure indeed to listen to her. So Elizabeth read, night after night, from the works of Bulwer, Ainsworth, that delightful new writer Charles Dickens, Theodore Hook, Mrs Gore, Miss Austen ('a *little* dull, my love – not enough Event') and even some of the old 'Minerva Press' romances – *Mandroni, Rinaldo Rinaldini* and *The Beggar Girl and her Benefactors*, the last in seven volumes.

Meanwhile the two little girls went on as best they might. It would not be true to say that Mrs Golightly did not love her children. She loved them very dearly. But they, too, must be romantic. She dressed them in very bright colours, showed them to her friends with pride and left Elizabeth to do the rest. They became deeply attached to Elizabeth. They never had seen anyone so lovely and, in fact, would never see anyone so lovely again. Although she dressed in the quietest way, never raised her voice and never lost her temper, they obeyed her and told her everything. Alone with her they chattered and chattered, asking her innumerable questions. She taught them what she could with the aid of Butter's *Exercises on the Globes*, Lindley Murray's

English Grammar and Goldsmith's *Poems for Young Ladies,* but she had never had very much education herself and was appalled at her own ignorance.

Although a strong offshoot of the City ran past Sadler's Wells through the High Street, Islington was nevertheless a little country town of its own, filled with trees and gardens. The Golightlys had their carriage and drove into Town on necessary occasions, but, socially, their world was their own world and they gave little thought to any other. Elizabeth's arrival here was a sensation and, during the first weeks, the bachelors, handsome young men, and gay old married ones attempted every kind of flirtation. They found her, however, so unapproachable that she achieved the reputation of an Islington mystery. It was soon asserted that she was the child of a noble lord who had attempted to marry her to a villain, that she was the child-bride of an aged marquis who violently ill-treated her, that she was heiress to a vast property and had fled from unwelcome suitors.

She was too kind and gentle to be disliked by them; she gave herself no airs; she listened to their stories and was grieved for their misfortunes. Mrs Golightly did her utmost to discover her secret, and even Mr Golightly would look up from his butterflies, smile in a mysterious manner, nod his head and say: 'We expect you to be carried off from us in a gilt chariot any day, my dear.'

Mrs Golightly's methods were more subtle. On one of the reading evenings she would break out with:

'You mentioned, did you not, my love, that your brother was in the Army?'

'Oh no,' Elizabeth would reply. 'I have no relations in the Army.'

'Indeed! Well, fancy that! It must have been the Navy you said.'

'Nor in the Navy,' Elizabeth would reply, smiling.

Or Mrs Golightly would look at her with great tenderness, remarking:

'That must have been a sweetly pretty Ball at Lady Carrington's yesterday evening. Young Lady Hermione Blossom was looking her loveliest, I understand . . . You doubtless know her, Mary, my love.'

'No,' Elizabeth would murmur. 'I have never seen her.'

'Ah, so you say!' Mrs Golightly would reply, looking very arch. 'We know what we know.'

The children were pressed into service, but they, poor dears, were so simple and innocent that they had no wiles.

'Oh, Miss Temple,' Francesca would say. 'Mama says that everyone knows that you are not Miss Temple really, and that you will be leaving us very shortly.'

'I have no intention of leaving you, Francesca.'

'Mama says that you have fled from persecuting parents.'

'Does she, Francesca? I have not fled from anyone.'

And Clarissa, who loved Elizabeth with passion, would hold her hand as though it were a pump-handle and exclaim: 'I am certain that you are a Princess in disguise, dear Miss Temple, and I *do* love you so!'

'There are no real Princesses,' Elizabeth would answer. 'Only in fairytales.'

She managed for a while well enough. They were kind to her, and it was not their fault that she knew with every week more and more unbearable loneliness and longing. Then came the egregious and appalling Mr Roberts. Mr Frederick Roberts was a stout, cheerful, noisy young man who was the practical joker of the group. He was absent during the first part of Elizabeth's sojourn, in Scotland. Everyone spoke of him with rapture.

'Wait, my love, until Mr Fred Roberts returns!' Mrs Golightly cried. 'Islington is not the same without Mr Roberts. Mr Roberts has the life of a thousand. He is the wittiest young man in London.'

Elizabeth awaited his arrival with some eagerness. He could do everything – play the pianoforte, sing a song, shoot birds, hunt the fox, dance like an angel and join anyone for any length of time at Commerce, Vingt-et-Un or Speculation. He could imitate Webster or Buckstone or Fanny Kemble as though they were in the room with you. He was the soul of good nature, and all the young ladies in Islington wanted to marry him.

When he did arrive Elizabeth found him truly terrible. He was fat, coarse, common, self-satisfied, exceedingly conceited and as noisy as the fireworks at Vauxhall. But, worst of all, he must for ever be playing practical jokes. Practical jokes were 'the thing' in Islington; everyone loved them, but no practical-joker anywhere was as inexhaustible in his energies, as fertile in his resources as Fred Roberts.

He marked down Elizabeth at once as his future bride. He proposed to her on the second evening after meeting her and, when she indignantly refused him, roared with laughter and would have slapped her on the back had she not eluded him. His 'jokes' were endless. You never knew when you were safe from him. One of his most famous was the occasion when at supper at Mrs Preedy's he poured melted butter into all the gentlemen's pockets. He loved to tie two doors together, ring both bells and watch the result round a corner. On one most laughable occasion he arrived at the Livingstone-Jones' with a tray of medicated sweets so that everyone was ill. He came to a Masquerade with mice in his pocket, let them loose and returned in another costume to enjoy the results. When Mrs Bonnington lost her husband he appeared by her bedside as the ghost of her departed (she was ill after this for weeks). Mrs Green had a stout and elderly butler into whose shoes he fastened tin-tacks so that poor James, putting them on unsuspectingly, fell down a flight of stairs and was nearly killed. How Frederick laughed when he heard of it! And the odd thing was that everyone liked him for these games! They thought him the funniest, jolliest fellow and declared that any girl who 'caught' him would be lucky indeed!

He had never, it seemed, been 'seriously inclined', although he was 'something good' in the City and could marry whenever he wished. Now he *was* 'caught', and it was Elizabeth who had 'caught' him.

Poor Elizabeth! Mr Temple had been nothing to this!

It was, however, her terror of Mr Roberts that drove her to write to John. It seemed that there was no safety for her anywhere – if not one, then another. She even discovered herself thinking of the Fortress as a place of security.

If she left the Golightlys and went elsewhere it would be the same – danger everywhere.

A few days after posting her letter a worse thing than Mr Roberts occurred – Mr Golightly fell in love with her. She had never thought of him save that he was kindly and that he passed a dazzled, bewildered existence in a maze of coloured insects. He had means of his own that he had inherited from his father, a wealthy merchant who had dealt in candles or something of the kind. He had never been known to look at a woman save Mrs Golightly, at whom, moreover, he, on the whole, looked as little as might be. His fidelity to his butterflies was absolute.

There came then an evening. Mrs Golightly went to join her two friends, Miss Sanders and Mrs Witsun, at the house of their mutual friend, Mrs Peters, for a game of Commerce. The girls had gone to bed, and Elizabeth sat in her room pretending to read and thinking of John. She thought now of John every moment of the day. How was her letter faring? How soon might there be a reply? And, surrounding John, encompassing and enveloping him, was the country of her home, the silver river through the flat Portinscale fields, Main Street in Keswick with Miss Hazlitt's bow-window and the coach standing . . .

A knock on the door. Enter Mr Golightly. She was so deeply amazed that she could not speak. There he stood with his round stomach in a flowered waistcoat, his coat-tails spreading fan-wise over his fat thighs, buckles on his shoes and spectacles on the end of his nose.

He closed the door firmly.

'This is an opportunity,' she heard him say to himself. He came forward and without another word fell immediately on his knees in front of her. His spectacles jerked to the ground and he gazed up at her with blue eyes, childlike and innocent, eyes dimmed because they had seen the world for so long behind glasses, eyes that had gazed for years upon butterflies. She tried to rise, but he put his fat hand on her knee and burst out at once:

'Miss Temple – Mary, I am well aware that this is disgraceful. I am proud that it is. I have wished for years to do something disgraceful. I doubt whether anything could be more disgraceful than this. I am old enough to be your father, but I love you passionately. I may say that I have never loved anyone passionately before. And when I say passionately I mean passionately.'

'But, Mr Golightly – this is shameful—'

'I know that it is shameful. I have been struggling against it for several weeks. At least I have been struggling against *not* struggling against it.'

She did manage to rise.

'But this is abominable. In Mrs Golightly's absence—'

'Oh, damnation take Mrs Golightly!' he burst out, clasping her skirts and holding her firmly. 'What do you think it is to sleep year after year with Mrs Golightly in a four-poster? What do you think it is to wake early in the morning and see Mrs Golightly beside you? Were it not for my butterflies I should have gone mad long ago. And you, loveliest of virgins, what do you know of four-posters? Do you realize what a four-poster *might* be? Even I, old as I am, could . . .'

But that was enough. She tore herself from his clinging hands and went, even as she had done in Hill Street, to the bell-rope.

'One word more, Mr Golightly, and I summon Alice.'

He rose to his feet. He was trembling and there were beads of perspiration on his nose. Without his spectacles he seemed oddly undressed.

'Yes,' he murmured. 'I must appear revolting to you. It is natural that I should. It is my fate that I must appear revolting to everyone save Mrs Golightly.'

He bent down and picked up his spectacles. She thought that he was near to tears.

'Forgive me,' he said. 'I could not help myself and I am glad that I could not. I am still a man, not a mummy. Oh! how beautiful you are!'

And he went, wiping his spectacles in a large orange handkerchief, from the room.

After this there was nothing for it but flight. Mr Golightly *and* Mr Roberts! And if Mrs Golightly discovered ... But she did not want to go before she had had her letter from John. *One* letter from him and she would be better prepared to face the world again. Days went by. The beetles crawled in the kitchen. *Agnes Serle* came to her conclusion and was immediately followed by *Adelaide or the Countercharm*, the odious Mr Roberts proposed to her three times, on every occasion with peals of laughter – and still there was no letter from John.

Then came the party. This was the grandest party that Mrs Golightly had yet given in Islington – dancing, music, Commerce and Speculation, everything that the heart could desire. The whole house was 'cleared' for the event. The dining room was not far from the drawing room. In the drawing room there would be music and then dancing. Mr Fortescue would play on the violin, Mrs Porter's two daughters would sing duets, Mr Fred Roberts would give his Imitations and comic songs. It was also confidently expected that Mr Roberts had some special 'joke', a secret from everyone but himself.

The supper came from the caterer's, who also provided two long, thin men with immense side-whiskers to serve as waiters. Poor Alice was driven from one pillar to another post all day and all night, while Mrs Thackeray, the at-the-moment cook (she had given notice and was to leave directly *after* the party), for a brief while permitted herself to be amiable because, like every other servant in the world, she enjoyed a party.

When the guests were all assembled the sight was very impressive. The house was swollen with the guests. They were in the hall, on the stairs, hanging out of window, flooding dining room and drawing room. The gentlemen, many of them with long and wavy hair, had high black stocks enriched with massive pins; the white shirt-cuffs were neatly turned over the wrists, dress-coats buttoned, trousers tight with straps and pumps. The ladies either wore curls neatly arranged on each side, or their hair dropped in a loop down the cheek and behind the ear, and then fastened in some kind of band with ribbons at the back of the head. Pink was the favourite colour, pink with plenty of lace and artificial flowers. The older ladies were magnificent in turbans, and some of the younger wore across the forehead a band of velvet or silk decorated with a gold buckle, or something in pearls and diamonds. Miss Sanders, who was sixty if a day, had a black ribbon across her brow, the ribbon containing in the middle a steel buckle.

Every lady, of course, wore cleaned kid gloves, and the turpentine that had gone to the cleaning of them gave off a pungent and powerful odour. Quadrilles were still danced and even the Country Dance lingered, but the Valse was the true enchantment, although in Islington it was still considered rather advanced and daring, and always everyone was afraid to be the first to commence. Once and again the dancing was stopped for a little music, and Miss Merryweather sang in her piercing soprano or the Misses Porter gave one of their delightful duets. At first everyone was as polite as polite could be. The gentlemen stood by themselves and the ladies by *themselves*, but soon the punch-bowl had been mixed – a lovely mixture of rum, brandy, Curaçao, lemon, hot water, sugar, grated nutmeg, cloves and cinnamon. There was also rum-shrub. And above all, for the gentlemen, Bishop. Bishop was a kind of punch made of port wine instead of rum, and exceedingly potent it was. It was the Bishop, possibly, that accounted in the end for Elizabeth's terror and distress.

Very soon everyone became very jolly, and of course the jolliest of them all was Fred Roberts. Before the evening had exhausted an hour of its splendour he had fastened three girls into a cupboard, let off a squib under Miss Merryweather's skirts (and her shriek was of a more violent soprano than any betrayed by her singing!), piled three plates on the lintel of the door so that they crashed on to the head of one of the long, thin waiters; but his great feat was that he had brought a live grass-snake in his pocket, and this he sent crawling over fair arms and necks until ladies stood on chairs and one Miss Porter fainted (or was it, as some said, that she had enjoyed the rum-shrub?).

He was the greatest success. Everyone voted that they had never seen him in so splendid a humour, and he *was* in fine form, for he had a bet with six of his Islington cronies that before the evening was over he would be able to announce to all the world that the beautiful Miss Temple had consented to be his bride.

During the earlier hours, however, he left Elizabeth to others, although his merry eye was always upon her. At first things were not so terrible. She sat with Mrs Devizes, a lady who was vastly proud of her house, 'twice the size of this, my dear'. And must describe with perfect happiness her mahogany table and curtains of crimson rep, her gilt fleur-de-lis wallpaper and the way that she preserved her gooseberries and currants.

How Elizabeth prayed that she might be left alone with her, for she was tranquil and calm, and, as her words flowed on, it seemed that life somewhere must be secure – an enclosed world under a glass bell, mahogany, crimson rep and gooseberries.

But she was not allowed to stay where she was. For, in the first place, Mrs Golightly was so happy at the social success of her party that she was talking about Elizabeth to everyone, how she was certain that she was the daughter of a Duke, how good she was and beautiful she was, and how indebted she was to Mrs Golightly, who 'treated her just like one of her own daughters'. So naturally the young men came up and besought her to dance with them, and then, while valsing, paid her fatuous compliments and fought with one another over the honour of claiming her. Everyone began to be greatly excited, the ladies as well. Games were proposed, Forfeits, and Blind Man's Buff and Catch-in-a-Corner.

Elizabeth slipped out of the room only to find Mr Golightly, the worse for Bishop, standing in a corner near the window, staring quite desperately in front of him.

He caught her arm and drew her to the window.

'You must not tremble,' he assured her. 'You are safe with me. Indeed, indeed you are. I only wish you to be the first to know that I am leaving Mrs Golightly.'

'Oh no, no!' she cried, deeply distressed.

'I am determined, quite, quite determined. Before you came into my life I was asleep. But now I am awake and I know that my existence with Mrs Golightly is a sham!'

Oh, those poor little girls, she thought. And Mrs Golightly,

who is so happy and confident. If only she could have taken him
away and talked to him, for she liked him in spite of his absurd-
ities. But she did not dare to go apart with him, and here they
were besieged on all sides – people were running up and down
stairs. It was quite pandemonium.

'You will feel quite differently tomorrow,' she assured him.

'Oh no, I shall not. You have changed my life. You have—'

But worse followed, for Mr Roberts appeared, carrying a glass
of punch, his red face shining with happiness, his eyes fixed
upon her as though she were already his bride.

Paying no attention to Mr Golightly, he caught Elizabeth's
hand, dragged her with him into the room where everyone was
valsing madly, and began to swing her round, dropping his glass
on to the floor. She thought it better not to resist lest worse
should befall.

'We are designed for one another!' he cried. 'It is Fate! I am
rich, you are beautiful! Let me tell them all that you will have
me! I have been waiting all my life for this moment! I am the
happiest of men!. . .' Then, before them all, suddenly, ceasing
to dance, he caught her in his stout arms and kissed her.

She broke from him, ran among the dancers, found her way to
the door and, on the verge of tears, half tumbled down the stairs
into the hall. At the moment there was no one there, but the
house-door was open, Alice was on the step, and beside her someone was standing. Alice came in.

'It is for you, miss. A gentleman asking for you—'

She went forward, trying to calm her agitation. Before her,
visible enough in the pale, smoky lamp of the little hall, was
John.

She was in his arms; *his* arms were round her.

'Oh, John – John – John,' was all she could hysterically cry.
She was sobbing on his shoulder.

'My love . . . my adored one . . . my only, only love!'

Alice was in an ecstasy. She was practical as well.

'Oh, miss, come into the Master's room. There's no one there.
Only the coats and hats.'

Into Mr Golightly's room they went, and there, among the
butterflies and beetles, John told her that he had come as swiftly
as he could and for one purpose only. At the first possible
moment they would be married.

'Married, John?'

'Yes, married, my love. We have been too ridiculous. We have been wasting our lives.'

(Uhland? Her father? Oh, no matter. Let come what might!)

'Oh, John – I have longed for you so!'

'And I for you! When I received your letter . . .'

Mrs Golightly was in the doorway, behind her Miss Porter and others.

'Mary! Why, my love . . .'

Elizabeth, holding John's hand, and looking more beautiful than ever in her life before, said:

'Mrs Golightly – allow me to introduce you – Mr John Herries. The gentleman to whom I am to be married. He has come all the way from Cumberland—'

It was the supreme, the loveliest moment of her life.

FAMILY LETTERS

6 ACACIA ROAD, MARYLEBONE, LONDON,
April 20th, 1839

MY DEAR FATHER – Yesterday morning John and I were married at St Mary's Church, Phillamont Street, Marylebone.

I am afraid that this may make you angry and I am sorry indeed that it should do so, but as you have made no inquiry after my whereabouts I am hardened in the belief that nothing that may happen to me can give you very great concern. I am sorry indeed for this, but from my very earliest years you have shown me that you would have preferred never to have had a daughter. I find it very difficult in these unhappy circumstances to appeal to your forgiveness because indeed I do not feel that there has been anything on my part very blameworthy. I studied to love you, but you wished for the love neither of my dear mother nor myself. You are not responsible, dear father, for that. If you could not love us you could not, but neither am I responsible for wishing to make some kind of life for myself where I could be happy.

Perhaps now that I am away from you I may not cause you so much aggravation and one day you may wish to see me again. I know how greatly you have always disliked the family at Uldale but they on their part have, I am sure, felt nothing but friendliness and it is the great hope of John and myself that our marriage may heal the division between the two families. John has some means of his own and we shall be in no need of assistance from anyone. Our cousins, Garth and Sylvia, are most kind, and Carey has invited me into the country. I have written to grandfather acquainting him with our marriage. I am afraid that grandmother is no better.

With every respect, dear father. I am, Your loving daughter,
ELIZABETH

John Herries to Judith Paris
6 ACACIA ROAD, MARYLEBONE, LONDON,
April 22nd, 1839

MY DEAR AUNT JUDITH – Elizabeth and I were married on April 19th at twelve noon at St Mary's Church, Phillamont Street, Marylebone.

Dear Aunt Judith, are you very angry with me? I did wrong perhaps to leave you so suddenly with that brief letter of farewell, but I am enclosing (by her own wish) Elizabeth's letter to me that she wrote from London. Now read that and I am assured that with all your tenderness and love of others you will not be able to wish my actions other than they were. Indeed I could not help myself and arrived, as it turned out, only just in time, for my beloved Elizabeth was in the very act of escaping from an Islington ruffian when I stepped in at the door. Can you imagine it? She had been a Governess, having run away from her grandfather's, to two little girls of a lady with the astounding name of Golightly! They were kind to her, I fancy, although I cannot force very much out of her. She was never communicative about herself as you know.

But you do *not* know, dear Aunt Judith! You know one another so slightly that it will be one of my happiest pleasures to make you better acquainted! Seriously you have been so long more than a mother to me (more than my own mother ever was to me I fear) that you will, I know, rejoice in my happiness. I have not, I think, ever been truly happy before. I have been always apprehensive, fearing disasters that have never arrived. In the strangest way that house at Ireby and the inhabitants in it have hung over me like a doom. You have perceived this and thought me often faint-hearted and absurd, I know – yet these things are of the spirit and I have much of my poor father's lack of self-confidence. A Herries without conceit of himself is worse off than any other man in the world, I think! If you but knew how often I have urged myself forward to some act that I feared simply because I feared it! It seems to me now fantastic that I should have so dreaded Uhland's crooked body and the coarseness of his father – but now I have rescued Elizabeth from them, and myself as well! Do you know how, for so many years, he neglected and despised her and how patiently she bore that neglect? The end of the story is not yet. I will make myself so famous that they shall crawl on their knees to me before all is done! Now is not that an unworthy sentiment?

Elizabeth has but now entered and the kettle is on the fire and the toasting-fork ready! Our happiness is surely greater than that of any other two in the world! And yet how many lovers are there in this city at this same moment swearing the same thing. But we are such old lovers and have waited so long – longer, far longer than there was any need! How clearly I see that now!

My only unhappiness is that I have left you alone at Uldale – Dorothy, Adam, myself, all gone! And yet I am not sure that you will not be happier without us – all of us save Adam of course! I shall be seeing him tomorrow I trust. He is all Chartist now, I suppose, but he cannot think ill of me, for Elizabeth and myself are as poor as church mice and happy to be so. Sylvia came to see us last evening. She was exceedingly kind and says that Garth will soon find work for me. There will be my share of the Uldale money, but I would prefer that you send me nothing – until I ask for it.

Elizabeth is at my side. She sends her love. As she sits beside me I wonder what I have done to deserve this fortune. I have done nothing. I have been a poor feckless creature all my life but now, please God, there shall come something very different out of me. Our love for one another is beyond utterance. Dear Aunt Judith, wish us well and write to tell us that you are not angry. Your loving

JOHN

Judith Paris to Adam Paris

ULDALE,
February 8th, 1840

MY DEAREST SON – Your letter received last evening. I am *sorry* indeed that you should imagine that I am not *pleased* with your marriage. I am pleased with anything that gives you *happiness* but I am an old woman with only one passion left me and that is for my *son*. If you fancy that there is any mother in the world who gives her son willingly to *another woman* then you betray only once again that ignorance of my sex which, I fear, has been always your portion and will be so to the end.

You say that I need not fear that I shall lose you. *No, indeed, I cannot lose you*, for you are a part of myself, more perhaps than you will ever realize. You will return to me. You will bring her with you, but she can never have that part of you that is mine. You can tell her so if you wish. I am prepared to love her for as we grow old *the more one can love the better for one's health*. I have no *patience* with old women who complain of being *left*. I have always been standing on my own legs and intend to continue so. I like the name Margaret. She sounds sensible. I enclose with this my present to her. This silver box was left me by my brother who had it from a pedlar when he was a boy, and the silver chain was my grandmother's. I always intended them for your wife. Bring her soon to see me. I am quite alone here at the present although Dorothy and the children shall pay me a visit very shortly.

Bellairs is not in good health. It is his *stomach*. I am for ever telling him that he overeats but he answers that I am fanatical about food and eat like a *sparrow*. Certainly all our neighbours eat and drink far too much and I attribute my own astonishing good health to my careful feeding. Why should we behave like swine at a trough? I remember when I was a young woman in London that Georges had *incredible* stories of the amount that his friends consumed and I can remember Christabel and Jennifer in their youth guzzling like *pigs*. Well, they are all dead and here am I feeling twenty. How I run on, but I enjoy talking to my son who is now a Chartist and a husband and I don't know what! Only yesterday he was pulling cows' tails in the orchard.

John and Elizabeth were at poor Christabel's funeral. Will was a very dignified figure they say. But Sylvia writes to say that a young Mrs Morgan, widow of an Army captain, is already setting her cap at him. Is not that revolting? He is seventy this year if I am not mistaken, and she not a day over thirty! And what comedy if our fat five-chinned purple-faced Walter has a baby brother, a new uncle for our pretty Uhland! Since John left here we have had no great trouble with Ireby.

Uhland spoke to me in Keswick some days back and asked most politely after you. He has eyes like Cumberland stone and his lame leg is as lively as a spiteful old woman. I think Walter has no spite against myself but would do any hurt that he could to John and Dorothy. He and Uhland have already stories circulated in Keswick about John, and John himself seems apprehensive for in his last letter to me he says that he fancied that he saw Uhland looking at him out of a hackney coach. It may be that he was right, for Uhland has been twice to London.

All is well at Uldale. Rackstraw manages to a *marvel*. He is now at war with Peach, Walter's man. They detest one another and so carry on this ridiculous feud a stage further. We have built a new Barn in the upper field. Flossie the mare is too old for the carriage and has been put in the Paddock. I told you I think that Dorothy is coming shortly for a visit. You know me well enough to understand me when I say that I do not mind at all that I am in *sole* command here. I seem to know so very much better than anyone else the way things *ought* to be done. And I was sixty-five years of age last November! – Your most loving

MOTHER

John Herries to Adam Paris

6 ACACIA ROAD, MARYLEBONE,
October 25th, 1840

MY DEAR ADAM – The fact that you and Margaret (to whom give every loving message from Elizabeth and myself) are at Uldale encourages me to write a long letter, some of which I would wish for them all to see. Other parts of it I shall mark *Private* and they are for your ears alone.

Well, first to my great piece of personal news. The writer of this Epistle has pleasure in informing you, dear Adam, that he has been now for two days personal and private Secretary to Sir Edward Mitcham, Bart, MP for Great Cottenham. What say you to that and to whose services think you I owe it? To whom but to Grandfather Will! This is, you will all at Uldale allow, a most remarkable feat and three in the eye to my dear father-in-law and four in the nose to my beloved brother-in-law. What they will say to this villainous backsliding on old Will's part I have infinite delight in imagining. It seems that I owe this as I owe every other happiness in life to my beloved Elizabeth, for it appears that a long while back when she was staying with him he was moved by her loveliness and by her loneliness, coming in one evening and seeing her all by herself and sufficiently dejected. So he has had it in his mind for some time to do something for us and this is what he has done.

Old Mitcham is a stout claret-coloured old boy who lives in Bryanston Square with a fat wife and two plain daughters. He is amiable enough so long as he is flattered and is saved from an extravagant personal vanity by his adoration of Palmerston. Palmerston can do no wrong in his eyes and already I am myself beginning to see with a similar vision and watch the affairs in Syria as though my life depended upon it. They say that it is the Syrian business that has killed Lord Holland and that his dying word was: 'Mehemet Ali will kill me'.

I do not know that I have any Parliamentary ambitions myself. Elizabeth says that I would make a good orator, but she has a certain prejudice and I am altogether too nervous and shy to thrust myself into public notice. Meanwhile old Lady Mitcham is quite in love with Elizabeth as indeed is all the world. Sylvia says that she has come out amazingly and is another creature from when she was staying with grandfather. As well she may be, for she was at that time a lonely and deserted creature.

You have heard, I suppose, the gossip about grandfather. It is certain that this Mrs Morgan is for ever in Hill Street. She is a lively, gay, light-headed little woman, all bright colours, tinkling laughter and sharp acquisitiveness. She already touches everything in the house as though she owned it. I imagine myself that grandfather would not be averse to a child in his old age, for it is my private belief that he has suffered a long and bitter disappointment over Walter, who pays him less and less regard. I suggest that grandfather sees in Mrs Morgan a possible instrument rather than a personal pleasure.

Private. I have marked this Private because I should be ashamed were anyone but yourself to see it. But you have known me from babyhood, dear Adam, and loved me as long, I think. Listen then, brother and friend. Elizabeth and I love one another more dearly with every hour that passes. Our intimacy, our trust, our devotion is perfect. And yet there *is* one thing of which we will not speak to one another. We have both a fear, an unreasonable, foolish, crazy fear of Uhland. That she has it I know well. She speaks of him in her sleep and always in terror. By the way that she so deliberately avoids his name I know that she thinks of him. She fancies that because I married her he will do me some hurt and still more now that grandfather has volunteered this last kindness. Living with him so long has bred in her a fear of him that is beyond reason and is the stronger for its vagueness. And I must confess to you, dear Adam, that all my old terror of him persists. How often you have chided me for that! How foolish to your logical and consistent mind are such fears, but I have this from my father, who had it, perhaps, from *his* grandfather – that I live partly in a world of shadows. For a Herries that is fatal and there are times when I feel caught – held in a trap – and for no cause, no reason. How you must despise me. But no, you love me and are the most faithful and unswerving friend. Otherwise I would not have the courage to tell you. But there is more than that. The other evening at dusk coming from Bryanston Square I am certain that Uhland himself followed me.

Walking towards the Park down a narrow and ill-lit street I heard that tap of his stick and the hesitation of his step with which I have been so long dreadfully familiar. For a while, I dared myself not to turn, but at length my curiosity was too strong for me and, looking around, I saw in the light of a lamp the thin figure of Uhland, his dark beaver hat, pale face, black clothes. He stood there, without moving, leaning on his stick. I hurried on through a street now absolutely silent. He seemed to follow me now incorporeally.

Pray do not laugh at me in this. Your sturdy mind cannot imagine what such fears and terrors may be. You remain undaunted by that other world so far more real than this one. Between the Haunted and the Unhaunted there is a gulf that can only be bridged by love, and I am not one who can love more than one or two. Why does he hate me so, Adam? What have I ever done to him? What is this strange Feud in our family that is for ever forcing its way in?

But, for a moment to be practical, pray discover for me if you can, while you are at Uldale, whether Uhland has been recently in London. It would relieve my mind greatly if it had not been he. Meanwhile this is the one only subject about which Elizabeth and I do not speak. There is a shadow here, the size of a man's hand ...

But to be cheerful and *daylighty* again, pray when you write tell me all the news of Uldale, of Aunt Judith, Roger, and in especial Margaret and yourself. When do you return to Town? You know that I do not think your *Charter* the cure for all our ills but times seem to become with every week more serious – the rick-burnings, riots and the rest – and I have little confidence in either Melbourne or Lord John. Your loving friend,

JOHN

Judith Paris to Sir William Herries, Bart

ULDALE,
January 10th, 1841

DEAR WILL – I write to congratulate you on your *Marriage* and, with that, to be as *honest* with you as I have always been. What do old people like you and me want with marriage? There is something *indecent* in it, do you not yourself think so? For you have always been the most *commonsensical* of all our Family and I cannot believe that, sitting in a corner, you do not laugh to yourself and wonder at your own action. You were lonely I must suppose. Well, so indeed are all of us. What do you say to an old woman of sixty-six sitting *all by herself* in a house under a *Mountain* miles from anywhere – or from *anyone* except your beastly Walter in his stone prison? Well, have it your own way – only I refuse to tell you that you have done a *fine* thing. If we cannot *laugh* at ourselves we are lost souls and although your sense of the *comic* has never been very strong in you, still you have a certain *dry* picture of yourself I know. I *trust* your widow will give you every *satisfaction*. Do not think me unkind nor unfriendly, dear Will. I am neither, and I have an especial *Gratitude* to you just now for what you have done for dear John and Elizabeth. That was especially noble of you seeing that your Walter hates them so (although *why* I cannot understand. Now that poor Christabel is gone he cannot *still* be thinking of that broken Fan). Moreover we were *Babies* together and that I can *never* forget although you were a dry and calculating child with a passion for *sums* (that I always detested) from the very start. Do you remember how you rode over to *Stone Ends* to fetch me back home and how I snapped my fingers at you? Yes, and would do it again if the same occasion rose. I am in marvellous health, thank God (although I doubt whether it is His doing). Dorothy comes with her babies to see me. She has now three *Girls* – one born this last November – Veronica, Amabel and Jane. Timothy is four – a fine child. Bellairs is in poor health – some disorder of the *Stomach.*

I must close. I am sending you a *Cumberland Ham* as a wedding present. You have everything in the world that you need, save only a Cumberland Ham – and there are no other Hams so good in the world anywhere. Your most affectionate

JUDITH

Margaret Paris to her father, Caesar Kraft
(This letter was never posted but was
found, many years later, by Adam Paris
among his wife's papers.)

ULDALE, CUMBERLAND,
April 6th, 1841

MY DEAR FATHER—It is very likely that this letter will never be
posted. I am writing it at two of the morning, sitting under a
candle in my dressing gown while Adam sleeps in the bed close
behind me, sleeps so soundly as he always does, sleeps as I alas
just now so seldom do!

For, Father dear, that is why in the morning I shall not post
this letter, because I shall be ashamed of my mood. I am unhappy
tonight, desperately unhappy, unhappy as I have never been in
my life before. Now listen, father. I know that Adam loves me, I
know that they all wish me well here, I know that Adam is as
proud and ambitious for our work as you and I. I am well in
health and so is he. We have money enough. Best of all I have
you, dearest, dearest father – and yet tonight my courage is all
gone. I have at the moment no resistance.

I think perhaps that my marriage has been the most dreadful
mistake. I love Adam more, far, far more than when I married
him and I am well assured that he loves me. I think his character
noble, strong and generous. I was not mistaken in thinking it so
when I married him. But, father, I think there is no woman in
England so lonely as I am at this moment.

They are all so strange. This wild rough country is so strange.
Adam's mother is so strange. Adam's mother! Perhaps that is
where all the trouble lies! On my first visit here with Adam she
was, as I told you, most friendly. She wanted to love me as a
daughter, she said, and that is I know what she intended. But
love does not come like that. She was resolved to feel no jealousy
of me and in that very resolve felt it. You know how quiet I am,
father. You have always understood that I feel more than I can
say and that I cannot force myself to any feeling if it is not there.
'Madame' (as they all call her here) is the opposite of this. I have
never said much about her to you. You have never seen her. You
cannot imagine her. She is unlike anyone else in the world, a little
tiny woman with snow-white hair, a pale brown complexion,
wearing the brightest colours, her eyes sparkling, carrying an
ivory cane, and alive in every inch of her! I cannot convey to you

how alive she is! I do not know her exact age but it is certainly
between sixty and seventy and yet she is more living than anyone
else in the neighbourhood. Everyone knows it. Everyone recog-
nizes it. She is a great figure here. She is compounded of two
opposites. Her mother was I believe a gipsy and thence she has
her gay colours, her restlessness, her laughter, her generosity, her
tempers, her childlike pleasure in little things. She will dance to a
music-box tune or pick up her skirts and run down the road, or
rate a tramp like Queen Elizabeth, or play Backgammon like a
baby, kiss and stroke the cheek and love you in a passion! And on
the other hand she has a good business head, runs the house and
property like a lawyer, disciplines the servants, has her finger in
every pie.

But her passion is for Adam. Adam is everything to her. She
would like to possess him, every bone and vein of him, and his
soul beyond. But she is wise enough to know that she cannot and
that she can only take from him what he voluntarily gives her.
That is a great deal. They have the strongest bond, the two –
almost without knowing it, without wishing it. It is not only a
bond of mother and son but a bond of family too. All the Herries
I have met, whether in London or here, have something in
common although they are all so different. What it is I cannot
say. It is as though, inside the family, they are all against one
another, but that against the outside world they are all united.
Even Adam has something of this, although he is for ever saying
that he is illegitimate and does not belong to them and disap-
proves of their worldliness and pride and materialism. For they
are material, grossly so *and* proud – proud with the worst kind of
English pride as though they were God's people. John Herries in
London is the only exception I have seen – yes, and *part* of
Madame. Part of *her* is non-Herries, hates that blood and would
like to escape from it.

In any case I am shut out, father, however kind they *wish* to
be, I am shut out. I am shut out by them all and by this hateful
hard, raining, hostile country. It is all sodden hills and grey
cloud and stone walls here. When the sun shines everything is
harder than ever. The stones have a hard face, the people look as
though they would like to kill you, the cattle lower their heads at
you. I know that it is only on visits that we are here and that
Adam will never leave his work in London, but I am afraid lest
one day his mother will win and bring him back here for ever. He
is so silent. He cannot express his feelings at all. When I lie in his

arms I know that he loves me, but he will never say so. He is so shy of expression and when others are there I sometimes think that he almost hates me. Of course he does not. He is true and loving and noble, but why cannot he say something to me once and again, only some little things to reassure me? Then he goes off – for a whole day, leaving me with his mother and without a word to any of us. He loves this country so passionately that I do not count for anything beside it. I was so happy with you, dearest father, living with you, working with you. I needed no one. And then he came and at the first sight I loved him with all my soul as I shall always love him. But here I seem to fight every stone wall, every little stream, every sulky cloud. If only he would speak to me, tell me once that he loves me, defend me against my fears ... Oh, father, why ...

Judith Paris to Adam Paris

ULDALE,
March 4th, 1842

MY DEAR SON – Dorothy and the children arrived last week. I cannot say I am sure how this *experiment* may turn out. I confess that I am not altogether easy in my mind. When Bellairs died two months back Dorothy certainly had no *idea* of it, nor had I. But she found the house more and more melancholy and longed every day more ardently for Uldale so she must have her way. We can but see and I admit that it is agreeable to have company again.

Dorothy has grown very *stout* but is kind and much *improved* I think. She was always *amiable* as you know, but had a strong conviction that she must *manage*. I have explained to her that the children are *her* business and the house *mine*. She was at first inclined somewhat to think me an *old lady*. She discovers that I am not so ancient as she supposed!

And now, Adam, I have had a great *adventure*. I have spent two nights in Watendlath! What do you say to that! I have stayed in the old house, eaten at the old table, walked the old ways. I have seen where Charlie Watson is buried and will confess to you that I shed a *tear* or two. I have seen again my Georges. Yes, standing by the Tarn, just as he used, smiling at me, because he had done something that he should not, and to-day was yesterday. I was a young girl again and all *life* was in front of me. Well, that is over, my son. As I looked across the water to the hills and down to Rosthwaite where your grand-father lived, I knew what I had *thrown away* when I remained at Uldale. I sold my *soul* perhaps that day but what does it matter? There are too many souls already in space for the loss of one little one to be of importance.

Alice Perry's son reigns and a fine fellow he is, with four fine *children*. His wife I thought a poor feckless creature and her *hodge-podge* a disgrace, but for once I kept my old tongue quiet and told her only *compliments*. For an hour I was *wild* again, old woman though I am. But the wildness passed. Here I am at my table adding accounts and the cows are going to milking beyond the window and Skiddaw is as mild and stout as Dorothy herself.

They all thought me *mad* to go. I have still a touch of madness, but it diminishes. Rackstraw has the *gout*, Mary – the new maid (from Cockermouth – a good girl) – the toothache, her face swollen twice its size. I shall never see Watendlath again.

I *long* to have you here. It seems to be the *only thing* I live for now, but I will not force you. You will come in your own good time. I passed Walter in the road last week. We did not speak. He is *immensely* fat and is not as careful in his dress as he was. There are awful doings at Ireby from all I hear, and many people refuse to go there any longer. I hear that he vows vengeance on us all because John and dear Elizabeth are happy in London – a poor sort of reason – but he cannot harm us. Give my love to Margaret. I am sending you some of my own *Preserves*, two *Hams* and a *wool-work ottoman* that I bought at old Mr Chancey's sale in Keswick as a present to Margaret. Your loving

MOTHER

Adam Paris to Judith Paris

7 FARRIMOND STREET, LONDON,
April 3rd, 1842

MY DEAREST MOTHER – This must be only the briefest of notes as I go this afternoon to a meeting in Manchester, but I thought you would like to know how we find our new rooms.

We think them exceedingly comfortable when we have time to consider them. I was never before as busy as now. People are still talking of Peel's Income-Tax and we Chartists will most cer-tainly not oppose it. It is a small step in our own direction but the state of the country is with every week worse and the conditions among the poor frightful.

We have seen none of our relations save John and Elizabeth. I am happy to say that Elizabeth and Margaret have become the greatest friends. I am most happy for that. Margaret has not been so well of late.

In great haste. Your loving son,

ADAM

Very many thanks for the Cheeses and Butter you so kindly sent. They are most welcome.

HOMECOMING IN WINTER

THE little town shivered under the breath of the helm-wind that, beating down from the icy caverns and hollows of Helvellyn, threw dark quivering shadows of cloud on the garden walls, set Main Street trembling with a half-worshipping, half-shuddering agitation, and caused Mrs Constantine, who had Mrs Trevelyan of Bournemouth as guest, to rub the tip of her nose with her muff a hundred times.

Fortunately at this moment of English history ladies were, by the dictates of fashion, more warmly clad than at any time before or after. So many petticoats, with solid padding, indeed did they wear that the crinoline must come in very shortly and assist them. Mrs Constantine was wearing four petticoats, and her poke-bonnet was lined with fur. Her peaked and animated face was for ever hiding itself in an enormous snowy muff. But it was right that it should be cold. Mrs Constantine, wife of one of the doctors in Keswick, told Mrs Trevelyan (whose heart, if the truth were known, was sick for Bournemouth) that it was right that it should be cold. She exulted in it, she revelled in it. It was but a week before Christmas and what was Christmas if not cold? The coach rattled down the street, old Tom Rawson blowing his horn with a fine Christmas flourish. The boys were just out of school and, wrapped up almost to the eyes in mufflers, rushed along the street screaming like sea-birds, playing 'shinny' as they went, the wooden ball lathe-turned, the 'shinny' sticks cut from the hedges. Keswick was its own quiet self in these winter months, lying peacefully beneath the purple wind-scarred hills. In the summer, as Mrs Constantine explained, it was now 'the rage', college youths from Cambridge, every house letting lodgings, the pencil-makers selling to every visitor enough black-lead

pencils to last a lifetime; spar-dealers, curiosity-mongers, boat-
men making a fortune; coaches tearing in and out, picnics everywhere, and until lately Mr Southey to be seen at any time, taking
his walk. Poor gentleman, nothing but tragedy now. So many
things to see! So *many* things to see! . . . But now all is quiet.
Soon sheep, their wool blown a little by the wind, move up the
street, the boys with their 'shinny' sticks racing in and out among
them, there is a sudden flash of sun from the wrack of cloud,
piercing like a sword drawn from its scabbard the cobbles, the
sheep, the boys, slashing into sudden colour the cold flanks of
Blencathra.

But Mrs Constantine was historical. History was her passion.
Oh, Keswick was full of history! There was Acorn Street where
the Royal Oak had been (oak – acorn – did Mrs Trevelyan see the
quaintness?) and the Friars Inn where Lord Derwentwater
quaffed a flagon of ale before riding to the '15, and Crosthwaite
Vicarage where the tithes – the wool, the pigs, the geese, the dairy
produce – were brought and a grand dinner with hodge-podge
followed. Here Mrs Trevelyan sneezed.

'You are not chill, my dear, I trust?'

'Oh no, not at all, not at all—'

And the old Moot Hall and the— Here she broke off to
murmur :

'My dear Eliza! This is most fortunate. Here coming towards
us is the most interesting person in Keswick.'

Mrs Trevelyan, blinded by the sharp wind and knowing that
she had caught a cold that would endure for weeks, stared a little
uncertainly.

But there was no doubt as to whom Mrs Constantine intended,
for, stepping out of a barouche, standing for a moment, resting
on a cane and looking about, then slowly walking up the street
towards them, was a most remarkable woman. She was small of
figure, but her step was astonishingly alert. She carried her head
as though she commanded the town. As she approached them
more nearly Mrs Trevelyan saw that her hair was snow-white
under her poke-bonnet, that was of a rich blue and decorated
with a feather. She wore a purple silk mantlet trimmed with a
shaded ribbon. She was distinguished, most dainty, most determined. Her hands were hidden in a purple muff. She tapped
with her cane, she looked about her eagerly, as though she were
sniffing the fragrant, frosty air. Some boys with their ball, racing
up the street, slowed down as they saw her. She smiled benignly

upon them. A gentleman, riding a splendid roan, touched his hat. She bowed like a queen. A bearded farmer, driving a cow, touched his hat and she bowed again. She arrived at the two ladies.

'Oh Mrs Constantine, how *do* you do?'

'Very well indeed, thank you, Madame Paris. Will you permit me to introduce to you my friend, Mrs Trevelyan, from Bournemouth.'

'With the greatest pleasure ... I hope you are well? You are paying a lengthy visit?'

Here Mrs Trevelyan unfortunately sneezed and was so deeply aggravated that instead of paying compliments, as she had intended, she could only stutter:

'The air in Bournemouth is more balmy—'

'It is indeed. But here, I fancy, it is more bracing. I am on my way to visit old Miss Pennyfeather. She has not been so well, you know. Pray, remember me to the Doctor, Mrs Constantine. If you would be so good . . .'

She moved on.

'A most remarkable woman,' said Mrs Constantine eagerly. 'They say her mother was a gipsy. She has a house at Uldale and is a relation of the Herries family. Her father was a Herries – long ago here in Keswick. She has had a most remarkable history—'

They passed on to the more sheltered side of the street, but not before Mrs Trevelyan, who felt her chill gaining upon her with every cut of the wind, had remarked: 'She appears to enjoy most excellent health. I never saw such spirits!'

No, indeed. She had not and she would not, for Judith was at the height of happiness. This evening, by the Lancaster Coach, Adam her son was arriving for the Christmas festivities. Adam was coming home. She had not seen him for nearly a year; he was bringing his wife with him and that was very pleasant, but for Judith no one and nothing mattered but Adam.

She was in splendid health. This wild wind, these steel-grey hills suited her. She was exalted, lifted up. Between a break in the wall, over a dry and wind-tossed garden, she could see the distant Lake, the small waves in feathered hurry racing before the tongue of the flicking air. Were her hands not so warmly in the purple muff she could have stretched them out and embraced it all – sky, hill, water, stone and tree. The freshness, the strength, the flashing scornful sun! Snow was in the air! Snow! And Adam was coming home, Adam was coming home. She saw Dr Constantine, very thin-waisted, in his high beaver hat, riding his cob. She bowed. He bowed. It was all she could do not to give a little hop, skip and jump for sheer joy of living! Adam was coming home! Even as she rapped Miss Pennyfeather's knocker she gathered him to her heart, felt herself lost in his embrace, knew once again that neither wife nor work could take him from her. He was yet in her womb!

Little Nancy, Miss Pennyfeather's treasure, opened the door to her and she was in the parlour. It remained unchanged through all these years just as the rooms at Uldale remained unchanged, although Dorothy was for ever talking of 'new furniture'. New furniture! Judith detested the great ugly, heavy, clumsy stuff such as you saw at the Osmastons' or the Applebys'. No, this delicacy was what she loved and her eye rested with gratitude on dear Miss Pennyfeather's blue Chinese wallpaper, the nodding mandarins on the mantelpiece, the delicate harpsichord with its painting of violets on the lid, and the pretty delicate chairs with their faded gilt. But she did not look for more than a moment, for there, dancing from foot to foot in front of Miss Pennyfeather, who was sunk deep in an armchair and all wrapped up in shawls, was the strangest figure!

He was an odd little man, scarcely five feet high, his head on one side as though he had a crick in his neck, his shoulders humped; he had (Judith saw at once and recognized from olden days) the most marvellous eyes, dark, luminous, living every life in their orbs, at one moment enraged, at another amazed, at a third delighted, at a fourth swimming in fun. He had long white locks, unbrushed, dishevelled, and they seemed to have a breath of their own as they moved. He was wearing a blue-lapelled swallow-tailed coat with brass buttons, two waistcoats, a black stock and a high white collar above it. As Judith came in upon him he was dancing round like a top, his white hair waving, and nursing in his arms two white kittens, while Miss Pennyfeather's spaniel, Bonaparte, barked at his heels. Yes, Judith knew at once who he was! Back, without a moment's interval, to that afternoon at Southey's when, her heart sore and indignant at Jennifer's unkindness, that boy with the flashing eyes had broken in ... and now ... this old man ... and she ... She had never seen him between then and now ...

She bent down and kissed Miss Pennyfeather. Then she held out her hand.

'Mr Hartley Coleridge! You will not remember me ... And, indeed, of course, you cannot. It is – oh, I fear to say how many years! I was a young woman, you a boy, tea at Mr Southey's ...'

He did not remember her in the least, but he put down the kittens and held her hand and looked into her eyes with his own lambent ones and pretended that he remembered her perfectly well. They stood together, hand in hand, much of a height.

'Remember you! Why, of course, dear lady, of course, of course. Hey-diddle-diddle, but that is a long time ago – sad things, many sad things since then. So many gone, so many failing of high hopes. But we won't be sad. We refuse to be sad. I can see that you are never sad. We are like these kittens, you and I. Here – the reel of cotton – I have lost it. Here, help me!' He was down on his knees searching under the harpsichord.

He looked up pleadingly at Miss Pennyfeather.

'Claribella, Isabella, Rosamunda – may I request a glass of beer?'

She looked at him sternly, then shook her head at him.

He sat back on the floor, his hand on a kitten's back.

'Well, a glass of water then.'

She pulled the bell-rope.

Then he was on his feet again. He danced about the room, talking all the time.

'Willie and Nannie Coates; you know, Lord and Lady Bacon because they kept so many pigs ... They used to say ... And Dinah Fleming – dear, dear Dinah – and you know the Mr Briggs and the Branckens and the Hustlers – at Tail End. Oh, you know them all, Claribella, and love them, and we'll go together! We'll pay calls together! We'll go round in a gig drawn by a goat all set up with lanterns. We'll stop on Dunmail and have goat's milk and I'll write a poem ...'

He caught up the kitten, held it in front of him murmuring,

Our birth and death alike are mysteries,
And thou, sweet babe, art a mysterious thing

'Jeanette,' he murmured. 'That was to Jeanette.'

He almost ran to the door. 'I must be away! Off! Gone! Vanished!'

He ran back and, with the utmost tenderness and delicacy, bent down and kissed the very old lady in the chair.

'Perhaps for the last time, Claribella, Rosamunda,' he said.

'Who knows but that beer may finish me one of these warm, spidery days?'

He stood in front of Judith and smiled so enchanting, engaging a smile that there were tears in her eyes.

'You saw me last,' he said, 'as a boy with everything in front of me. Now I can leap a brook and dance a hornpipe – not bad for an old man.'

He bent forward, kissed her hand, went to the door, bowed to both of them and was gone.

To Judith, his appearance, so unexpected, so brief, was the most extraordinary omen. He had been that to her on the only other occasion that she had met him. It had been then as though they had known one another always, sharing some secret life private to themselves. It had been so then. It was so now. All that he had lost, all that she had lost, rushed to her heart. She stared at the closed door as though it concealed a mystery. Then she recovered herself and was busy in cheering her old friend, who now was paralysed, whose doom was upon her, whose spirits were as brave and cheerful as those of the kittens that played with the ends of her shawl.

'Oh! He never had his glass of water!' Judith cried.

'Nancy will give it him. He is an old friend of Nancy's. He is with her in the kitchen now, chucking her under the chin. But she knows that she is never to give him beer – that I shall never forgive her if she does.'

Miss Pennyfeather lay back exhausted, her hands helpless, the yellow skin drawn sheath-like over the ridge of bones, only her eyes brave, defiant and amused. For an hour or more Judith made her happy.

'I enjoy seeing you so cheerful, my dear.'

'I enjoy it myself. But Adam is coming. I have not seen him this year.'

'And his wife?'

'Yes.'

'You should bring her to see me one day. I am curious. You don't care for her.'

'Oh, I do!' Judith shrugged her shoulders. 'Or I would. If she'd let me. She is a great calm, quiet woman. All the same I think she is a little afraid of me.'

Miss Pennyfeather said nothing.

'And you know that I am never my best with anyone who is afraid of me.'

'Now, Judith.' Miss Pennyfeather's eyes sought the other's very seriously. 'We have been the greatest friends for many years, have we not? Well, then, I can speak my mind. You must be good and generous to Adam's wife. Any other way lies catastrophe. Make her love you.'

'I have tried.'

'Yes – with reservations. "I will love you," you have said, "if you recognize that I come first with my son." ' Then suddenly, with an odd galvanic energy: 'Possessive love – I detest it.'

Judith bent over her friend.

'Very well, dearest . . . You are right. I will make Margaret love me.' She laid her warm white hand on the dead yellow one.

After a pause Miss Pennyfeather said:

'There is another thing, my dear. Gossip. They come in here and gossip although I tell them not to. Is it true that you are having John and Elizabeth for Christmas?'

'Yes. And Sylvia and Garth Herries also. They are coming down from Edinburgh.'

'Look out, then, for trouble from Mr Walter. I hear that he is enraged beyond all measure that you should have John and Elizabeth.'

'Why should I not have them?'

'After his casting Elizabeth off – and after John marrying Elizabeth. Oh, my dear, you are not as a rule so slow!'

'Yes . . . I see. Well, I am not afraid of him.'

'They say that young Osmaston and Fred Kelly and others are always at the Fortress – card-playing, drinking . . . Gossip. But no decent person goes to the Fortress any more.'

Judith smiled.

'I told Walter years ago that he could not do it. From the moment he laid the first stone of that building everything has gone wrong with him. Jennifer's ghost haunts him. And Uhland's ingratitude. And now his father's marriage . . . Do you know that old Will may be a father any day now?'

'Never!' cried Miss Pennyfeather.

'Yes, and he is seventy-two years old. Well, my father was the same. They are strong men, the Herries . . . Goodbye, my dear. I shall be in again very shortly and shall bring Adam's wife with me.'

When Judith was in the barouche again and turning towards home the afternoon was already gathering in. A pallid bar of shuttered light lay between heavy clouds above Skiddaw. The wind had died, but little sobbing breaths rose and fell among the bare trees. The hills were cold, clothed in an ashen shadow, and over the long, thin fields a chill, hard and remorseless, laid its hand. A few hesitating flakes of snow were already falling.

Halfway along Bassenthwaite they approached a horseman and, in the half-light, Judith saw that it was Walter. She would have had old Bennet drive past him, but Walter, at once recognizing her carriage, rode his horse in front and across it. Bennett pulled up the horses and Walter came close, laying his gloved hand on the back of Judith's seat. She had not spoken with him for over two years.

'Good evening, Judith,' he said.

His voice was thick and husky. Now that he was close to her she could see the gross double-chinned face, the purple veins in nose and cheeks, the little eyes half closed under the heavy lids. He was very large in his riding-coat. He towered above her. He looked rather pathetic, she thought, and she was not in the least afraid of him.

'Good evening, Walter.'

'I shall not detain you a moment,' he went on, turning to curse his horse that it did not keep still. 'I have only a question to ask.'

'And what is that? We shall have snow, I fancy.'

'Yes. My question is not about the weather.'

He leaned closer to her, and his breath was coarse and hot.

'Is it true, as I hear, that you are entertaining my daughter at Uldale this Christmas?'

'Perfectly true.'

'You are aware that she disobeyed me flagrantly and that by entertaining her you are insulting me before the whole countryside?'

His voice quivered and again she thought: 'Poor Walter!'

'Now, Walter, this is a cold, chilly moment to discuss such a matter. I shall invite whom I please to my house.'

His big hand quivered on the board.

'Then you must take the consequences,' he said very low.

'I can look after myself – and my guests.'

'Well – I have warned you.'

She rested her hand for a moment on his.

'Come, Walter. This is foolishness. Forgive Elizabeth. Pay us a visit. Let us slay this stupid feud that has lasted so long. Hatred never did any good.'

He shouted: 'By God, No! ... By God, No!' – dug spurs into his horse and charged away down the road.

Old Bennett drove on. His broad back (shoulders now bent and round) represented his proper emotions. He served Madame. If anyone did her a hurt, he would see to it. But words – words break no windows. That Herries of Ireby was crazed, and the way, so they said, that he carried on with women was shameful. Bennett, with all the virtue and fidelity of the unimaginative, scornfully flicked his horses' ears.

Judith was only for a moment perturbed. It had been strange, that dual recurrence of little Coleridge and of Walter – her past breaking in. But as she grew older she found that past, present and future began to merge. Time was becoming of less and less importance. There were these facts: her visit with Warren to Rosthwaite, the awful birth in Paris, Adam the baby teasing Walter on his white horse, Reuben as he fell mortally wounded in the lighted garden, Jennifer crying 'They've begun to build! They've begun to build!' or, long long ago, a beautiful naked woman and a young man on his knees, old Uncle Tom and Emma sitting by the fire at Stone Ends, David dropping, as though a stone had struck him, on the bright green grass, Georges throwing her out of bed at Watendlath, Georges falling, falling while the Old Man with the white beard ... She looked up through the trees to the dark sky. All these things had occurred together, at the same moment of time, and meant but this – that they had been signs to light Judith Paris the way to salvation – and she had not gone ... There was somewhere a Door ... and somewhere a Key ... and all History, whether of Nations or Families, was but this ... Have you found it? Are you in touch? Have you made the Connexion? ...

She sat back, drawing her mantlet more closely about her. No, they meant but this, all these shining moments, these figures woven into her tapestry – that she adored her son Adam, that he was coming home tonight, and her head would for a moment rest on his breast, that they would be together, together ...

Her heart began to beat so that she must lay her muff against it.

The house was alight with candles. They had not gas yet, although Dorothy was always urging it. Judith refused. Candles and lamps. This gas hurt the eyes. It was dangerous. And how pretty the candleshine against the Chinese wallpaper, or lighting you up the twisted stair.

'How modern you are!' she said, pinching Dorothy's fat cheek. Then added: 'I shall be gone soon. Then you may have gas.'

She was managing very well with Dorothy, who had grown in experience as well as in physical size. She was now a great woman with big breasts and wide beam and a face like a dairy-maid. Having children had taught her a deal; she managed them well. They obeyed her, indeed, better than they obeyed their Great-aunt Judith, as they were taught to call her. Timothy was a normal lively boy already like his father. The three little girls – Veronica, Amabel and Jane – were docile, happy-natured. Veronica was the pretty one. She had dimples and dark hair like her grandmother's. Yes, they were good children.

By eight o'clock the whole house quivered with excitement. For one thing, with the coming of Adam and Margaret the stir of the Christmas festivities might be said to commence. John and Elizabeth were arriving tomorrow, Sylvia and Garth Herries two days later. Christmas Night there was to be a dance. The children could scarcely contain themselves, and the little girls were busy, secretly, all day long, painting, sewing, cutting out, making their presents.

Adam and Margaret would take a post-chaise from Kendal, so one could not be sure when they would arrive. Judith walked all over the candlelit house, seeing that everything was right. She pushed open a window a moment and listened to the bell-ringers practising at the church a mile and a half away. She could hear the running water, and felt, with a thrill of contrasted warmth, the cold dark paths running up the mountain-sides, the gullies down whose flanks the wind was tearing. One cold flutter, then another, touched her cheeks. It was snowing.

She lingered especially in the room where Adam and Margaret would sleep. This had been Jennifer's. Here Francis had surprised Jennifer, here Jennifer had lain while John read to her and the reflection of the flames that the rioters had lighted danced on the walls. Yes, everything was well. The four-poster was ready, there were flowers (Christmas roses) on the davenport, the stamped fleur-de-lis wallpaper looked fine in the candlelight. Dorothy would like tall pier-glasses and grates of shining steel and heavy cornices. Not while Judith was in command! She came out and stood at the top of the stairs, holding a candle and listening. The house was very still, only the ticking of the clocks, a door opening and closing. Stillness, peace. A great wave of thankfulness flowed over her. She had not done so badly then. After all the turmoil of her life it had come to this – that, hale in health, honoured and trusted, in this old house that she loved, she stood there waiting for her son whom, by wise dealing, she had kept in her heart. She smiled to herself, thinking of the moment when, in that room close to her, he had defied her. He had climbed out of the window just as she had once done. Bone of her bone, flesh of her flesh . . .

The bell pealed through the house. The knocker shook the door. They were here, they were here!

She ran down the stairs, across the hall, flung open the door, was out on the paved path. Bennett and the boy had come from the stable with lanterns and all the dogs with them, barking, yelling, yelping. And there beyond the gates, like a visitant from another ghostly country, was the post-chaise. A moment later Judith was in her son's arms.

Half an hour later Margaret stood alone in the bedroom, hesitating to blow out the candles before she went down. Adam had already preceded her. She stood there beating down her fear. She saw herself in the glass, her image flickering uncertainly in the blown candlelight. Yes, she was tall, broad, plain; clear straight eyes, dark hair brushed carefully, cleanly, strong, but – dull! Oh, dull, dull, dull! And this little woman with all her oddity, liveliness, sharpness would find her with every visit more dull.

It was all she could do to keep the tears back from her eyes. The journey had been very long, the train stinking of oil from the ill-trimmed lamps, the last drive in the chaise chill and rough. She was terribly weary. Had she had her way she would have gone to bed, then and there, and slept for a night and day, but Madame would think that weak and foolish.

'What! A strong woman like Margaret! What a wife for my son!'

And Adam – why had he not *felt* her isolation, dread, loneliness? Her father would have known in an instant what she was feeling, but Adam seemed to have no intuition. Oh! he loved her, of course! But he never seemed to wish to tell her so. She scolded herself here as she had already done a thousand times. What was this need in her for reassurance? It had not been so before her marriage. She and her father had never spoken about their love. But Adam was so strange. Even now, after their years of marriage, she did not understand him. Perhaps no one understood him except his mother. He would escape from her – at any moment. At one time he was there, and then, in a second, he was gone! And it never occurred to him to suit himself to her mood, to ask what *she* was thinking! Maybe all Englishmen were like that! It was her German blood that made her ask for sentiment, sympathy, little loving words and actions. At night, in the dark, his heart beating against her heart, her arm around him as though he were her child – ah, then he was hers! But why with the first flash of daylight must he cease all demonstration as though he were afraid of the light? Oh, these Englishmen – but they were difficult as husbands!

He was downstairs now with his mother, and here was she trembling at the smell and feel of this hostile house, at the thought of the dark cold hills that closed it in, at the anticipation of that little woman with her sharp eyes, her way of suddenly looking at you as though she wondered that you *could* be such a fool!

Well, she must fight it. Adam was so happy to come home. She must make him think that she was happy too.

She came down and found them as she had expected, in the parlour seated on the sofa with the roses (Margaret *hated* that sofa), Madame's white sharp hand resting on Adam's broad knee with so proprietary an air!

Adam jumped up.

'Come here, my dear,' said Judith, patting the sofa. 'I am sure that you must be tired. Come and sit beside me.'

'Thank you,' said Margaret, feeling large and awkward and clumsy in all her limbs. 'I am not tired at all, thank you.'

She sat down beside her. There was a pause then, as though Margaret had interrupted a very intimate conversation. Then Judith continued again the excited narration of people and events that she had been pouring on to Adam before Margaret's entrance.

Then Dorothy came in, red-faced, smiling, her corsage of puckered taffeta too tight for her figure, her hair a trifle untidy. Margaret liked Dorothy. She was kind and unalarming – somehow rather German.

They went in to supper. How happy Adam was! Margaret's heart ached with love of him as she watched him across the table. He was like a small boy again, asking about everything, the dogs, the horses, the cows, the dairy, Dorothy's children, all the neighbours. He had forgotten, she saw, all his distress about the poor, the Corn Laws and the rest – the things that would make him so unhappy in London that he would walk the room, tossing his head, beating his hands against one another, crying out ...

She saw, too, Judith's happiness, how the small lady, sitting so straight at the head of the table, was almost breathless with happiness at having her son home again. How excitable she was at her age, what a child still in many ways! She would rap out an order to the parlour-maid like a general addressing a soldier, and then in a moment would forget it all and clap her hands at some joke, or throw to one of the four dogs – that sat with staring eager eyes near her chair – something from the table, or laugh at Rackstraw. And once she jumped up and walked, strutting with an affected gait to show them the absurdity of some old man in Keswick.

'Yes,' thought Margaret, 'what a poor creature I am to grudge them their happiness in being together! I will win her heart, make her love me.' But the words would not come. She could only answer in monosyllables. Some reserve stuck in her throat. 'Oh, what a fool and a spoil-sport they must think me!' she cried to herself.

After supper, the Waits came. First they could be heard behind the closed windows, faint shrill voices and the sudden plaintive squeak of a fiddle. They were summoned into the hall and stood there in a semi-circle – three boys, an old man with a white beard, a stout countryman in a smock, and a thin tall man with spectacles who was the fiddler. The servants came to listen. The dogs sat solemnly on their haunches in a group, yawning once and again.

The boys sang in piercing trebles while the old bearded man had one of the deepest voices, surely, in the world. They sang their carols without fear or hesitation, looking at no one but holding their heads up and staring into the ceiling with a kind of ecstatic frenzy. When it was over they were given money and hot drinks. They vanished into the night, and a flurry of snow blew in through the open door.

Afterwards they sat around the blazing fire in the parlour talking, listening to the wind that had sprung up and now was howling round the house.

When they all went up to bed Adam followed his mother into her room. When the door was closed she held him in her arms as though she would never let him go.

They sat down close together at the foot of the bed.

'It has been a long time, Adam.'

'Yes, Mother, I know. It is not easy. There is so much to do.'

'Are you happy?' She looked at him sharply.

'Happy? Who is happy?'

'Then you are not. Why not?'

He stared, under frowning brows, into the fire.

'The state of the country is dreadful. Never been so bad. No employment, trade fearful, no faith in Parliament, living conditions frightful – and everyone helpless. What is coming, Mother? Surely something disastrous.'

She put her arm around him, and he his around her.

'Yes,' she said. 'But I know something about life now. Nothing is so bad as you expect.'

'No. Perhaps.' He hesitated. 'I come in for a good deal of criticism, Mother. Many of them think me priggish, snobbish, out for my own hand. It was a shock the first time that I realized it. I had thought that I was so genuine, really moved by the love of my fellowmen, truly believing in them. And then when I heard myself called a self-seeker I was miserable for a while. I allowed no one to see it – not Margaret even – but I thought, "Well, perhaps I am this. I am deceived in myself." There's a little man, rather a power in London, he believes in nothing and in nobody. He says frankly that if you say that you love your fellowmen or trust your friends you are a hypocrite. He hates and despises me. I know the sort of picture he draws of me behind my back, amiable, filled with noble sentiments, but a snob because I am a Herries and making my own career under a cloak of caring for others. Yes, I was unhappy for a while – so long as I thought it might be true. But it is *not* true. There is something in me stronger and deeper than my intentions or my words or my acts. I *do* believe in my fellowmen, I *do* love them. I know that most of them intend the best. I know that Henry Cray is wrong with his bitterness and cynical mind. I have ceased to disturb myself. I am tranquil again.'

'Yes.' She drew his hand into hers.

'That is hard – the first time you really see yourself as your detractors see you. But it is grand too. At last you are seeing the whole picture. You are a spectator of yourself. That happened to me years ago in this very house, when Jennifer hated me. I could not *believe* that anyone could see me as that – mean, sly, intriguing. But only those who love you know you. There is good criticism, though, in the view of your detractors. You take yourself too seriously, Adam, I don't doubt. Pompous, sentimental! No, you are not, but you think perhaps too much of nobility and fine living. Life's a magpie's hoard – an occasional gold piece quite by accident among the broken glass and bits of coal. Take life lightly, my son. Believe in it, but laugh at it and at yourself.'

He kissed her. 'Later on. I'm too solemn, I know. I am always feeling it. But I live so much by myself, in my own thoughts . . .'

'And Margaret?' she asked him.

'I think I love Margaret more every day – but I don't grow closer to her. She wants something from me. I don't know what it is. Something I cannot give her. I have never been able to say in words what I feel. I'm tongue-tied. It seems to threaten my freedom if I speak too much. She is very quiet, too, of course. We are both too quiet together perhaps.'

'I am going to make Margaret love me this Christmas-time,' Judith said. 'She is lonely, Adam, and she loves you more than anyone else ever has – except myself.'

'You and she, Kraft, and John,' Adam said slowly, 'the four in my life who have loved me. But for the most part men cannot come close to me. I used to dream of helping to make a great Brotherhood in England. Now I know that I never shall. I am not the man.'

'No,' she answered. 'Maybe you are not. It is not for us to choose what we shall be. We have to accept and without protest.'

She kissed him most lovingly, and he went to his wife.

THE WILD GOOSE

THE wild goose, the same bird that Orlando was afterwards to see, flew over the house as the light was just breaking. The whirr of its wings stirred the perfect stillness of the crystal scene. The early sun was dim, but a pale glitter showed every tree and blade of grass sparkling with crystal. The whiteness of the snow, even in that thin light, dazzled the eye.

The sun rose higher – the wild goose was gone – the sheathed snow, stretching in a translucent glory to the line where Skiddaw cut the sky, now faintly blue, ran to the very foundations of the house and was marked only by the tiny feet of birds.

They were all going to church – Madame, Adam, Margaret, Elizabeth, John, Sylvia, Garth, Dorothy, Veronica, Amabel, Timothy, Jane, Rackstraw, Bennett, old Mrs Quinney, Martha Hodgson, Jack Turner, Alice, Clara, Wilson, Mrs Wilson.

Nearly two miles to the church. Some had walked ahead, some were driving, all the dogs had gone charging across the field, little clouds of shining iridescent powder rose up above the purple shadows that darkened the snow.

John and Elizabeth walked.

'Oh, I'm so happy!' said John. 'This is the loveliest Christmas!' But was he speaking truly, for over his head, frowning down upon him, was the Fortress? It looked sardonically threatening with its battlements and turrets; the walls met above the hill like a great hanging eyebrow; the stone was dull, heavy, squat, but snow fell in a sheet of dazzling light from its grey shoulders and it could not disown, however it might wish, the blue peerless sky that overlooked it. Light struck the walls and the preen of the two peacocks that Walter had bought. They stretched their tails on the miniature battlements.

'Is not Aunt Judith wonderful?' said John.

'I love her so much,' said Elizabeth.

She thought that it must be impossible to be happier than she was at that moment. And perhaps – who knows? – she would meet her father in the road, all would be forgiven, he would come to the Christmas party . . .

Was that, John thought, Uhland sitting his black horse under the yews? There! There! Cannot you see? His heart was chilled. No. There is no one there . . .

They were approaching the church, and the bells were ringing like mad. The quire were in a small gallery and were almost throttled with evergreens, holly and ivy and mistletoe. There was fiddler and a clarionet. The young ladies in delightful bonnets, some small boys shining with soap, the village postmaster, Mr Collins, Farmer Twistle, Farmer Donne, young Donne – they all played and sang with such a vigour that some of the holly fell with a rattle and clatter from the old beam. There was an anthem in which all the parts went wrong and nobody cared. Two of the dogs from the Hall – Satan and Mischief – strolled up the aisle and pushed with their noses at the door of Madame's high-walled pew. Then they lay down, their tongues hanging out, their eyes fixed in front of them. How everyone sang 'Oh, Come, all ye Faithful'! . . .

In the churchyard afterwards, old Mr Summers, the Vicar, stood and shook hands with everybody.

They all walked home, and it was passing through the second field that one of the important events of Adam's life occurred to

him. He was to remember afterwards, with a rich sense of gratitude, that shiny expanse of snowy field, and how in the sunlight
the snow turned to rills of sparkling water that glittered through
the grass, and how over the hedge Sam Longford's cottage that
he knew so well sent up a banner of purple smoke that fluttered
against the stainless sky.

For a thick-set, broad-shouldered man, touching his cap,
spoke to him.

'You won't remember me, sir?' he said. 'I've been working
Penrith way the last five years – Will Leathwaite.'

Adam stopped and smiled but looked bewildered.

'You will think me very uncivil,' he said.

'Why, sir,' said the man, smiling all over his rather simple
countenance. 'The Summer Fair of 'twenty-seven, when I
won t'race up to Druids' Circle. Why, sir, you rode with my poor
old fayther on his mare, Jessamy, and you was shouting for me
fit to burst your lungs. And I won, sir, I won! Bit too heavy now,
I reckon!'

Why, of course, Adam remembered! He saw the whole scene,
how their horse charged the village street, and how they must
pause on the road until the runners caught them up. He heard
his eager cry to the old farmer: 'Do you think Will will win, Mr
Leathwaite? Do you think Will will win?' And here was Will!
And Adam, looking at him, liked him.

They talked a little while. Will stood there, awkwardly, kicking
the snow with his boot. Then he looked up, his face red.

'Not wanting any kind of servant, sir, are you?'

'Why, no,' said Adam. 'I'm a poor man, Leathwaite, a poor
man.'

'I'd come to you,' said Leathwaite, looking Adam straight in
the eyes, 'just for my keep.'

'What! Aren't you married?'

'No – nor likely to be.'

Adam nodded his head and smiled.

'Well, if I ever do want one – I'll tell you.'

They shook hands and Adam moved on. The wild goose, flying
in from the sea, circled over Skiddaw, then swerved towards the
water of the Lake, already thinly crusted with silver, dark in the
shadow under the hills.

As the afternoon lengthened excitement grew. All life was
inside the house now. The dining room was filled with the long
extended table; it was a place of mystery. Behind closed doors the

preparations for the ceremony went on. On every fire all over the house the great logs blazed. Sylvia poked her head through the door of Judith's room.

'That's right, my dear. Come in.'

Sylvia came in.

'I must go and make myself grand.' She stood and looked at the old lady who sat toasting her toes at the fire. Sylvia considered her. She loved Judith, had done so from the first moment of their meeting. She would not have spent her Christmas in this outlandish place had it not been for Judith. Yes, and her curiosity. She had now, for so many years, intrigued, manipulated in her London world that she was intensely curious and inquisitive. She took it for granted that everyone intrigued, that no one was what he or she seemed, that all private lives trembled for ever on the edge of crises. And there was something – should she speak of it to Judith or no? Judith also loved her, but, considering her, now, found that she was not so lovely as she had once been. She had aged lines on her forehead, had something hard and even a little desperate about the corners of her mouth. So many Herries, she reflected, aged before their due time.

'Oh, Judith, I have never had a happier Christmas.'

'That's good. Sit down for five minutes. We have plenty of time.'

'It must make you happy to have Adam and Margaret.'

'It does,' said Judith, kicking a shoe against the fender.

'I do wish that we saw them more often in London. But with Adam's views . . .'

'Yes, I know.'

'*I* of course do not care in the least, but some of our friends think the Chartists would murder us all in our beds had they the chance—'

'Yes, dear. Absurd.'

Sylvia sighed. 'It is so restful here. I dote on the country. I hate my London life.'

'Then why do you lead it?'

'Oh, I don't know. What else should one do? Garth would be bored to death in the country.'

'I suppose he would.'

'You know that Will's wife may be brought to bed at any moment?'

'Yes, my dear.'

'Fancy – at his age! And how provoking for Walter!'

There was a pause and then Sylvia said:

'I suppose that Walter still keeps up this ridiculous feud?'

'Yes,' said Judith. 'He is furious, I believe, that I have John and Elizabeth here.'

Sylvia said:

'I saw him yesterday.'

Judith looked up sharply.

'Saw whom? Walter?'

Sylvia nodded.

'I was out walking. I had got on to the moor and was standing looking around me when he rode up behind me. You cannot imagine the start it gave me! You know – or maybe you do not know – in any case a few years back he was attracted to me. It began years ago when I stayed at Ireby for their opening Ball – the time when poor Jennifer died. I have seen him since once or twice – not for a considerable while though.'

Judith looked at her. How far had that gone? A strange shiver of repugnance – the consciousness of herself being in any close contact with Walter – for an instant held her. But Sylvia's beautiful face was quite unmoved. She was absolutely calm.

'How altered he is! Quite shocking! So gross – I must confess that I was uncomfortable. Dusk was falling and although the house was not far distant—' She broke off. 'Well, I can look after myself of course. However, he did not get down from his horse. We exchanged only a few words.'

'What did he say?' Judith asked.

'He inquired how I did, said it was long since we had met. Then he asked whether Elizabeth was staying at Uldale. I said she was.'

'Well?'

'He was very strange. Most odd. Judith, I think he may be coming here tonight.'

'Coming here?'

'Yes; he said something about it, something about a surprise visit. He said that it would make a fine bonfire if he burned this house down and everyone in it.'

Judith smiled grimly.

'We will manage him if he does come.'

Sylvia bent and kissed Judith, then went, but at the door she turned. 'The Herries men are so very peculiar,' she said. 'If they cannot have what they want they rush to destruction. Garth is just like that.'

In another room Elizabeth lay in John's arms. She murmured:

'Darling, I must dress.'

He stroked her hair, kissed her eyes, held her passionately close to him.

'Oh, Elizabeth,' he whispered, 'we must never be parted, never, never, never, never.'

'Nothing can part us,' she said.

'Nothing? No one? Never?'

'Nothing. No one. Never.'

'I could not believe that love could grow when it was from the beginning so intense. But when I look back to even a year ago it does not seem that *that* was love at all.'

They held one another in an embrace that, they thought, defied Death itself.

Before she went down to dinner Margaret looked into the nursery. Dorothy, when Margaret had asked her permission, had suddenly kissed her.

'I am fond of you, Margaret, I am indeed. We are more alike than anyone else in this house is like either of us.'

Perhaps they were. Two large, plain domestic women. Margaret had not thought that she was domestic. She had lived so long working happily with her father for a Cause. Now she was domestic. She wanted a child. It might be that all German women were so.

So she went into the nursery. When John and Dorothy had been children, there had been no nursery, but now, on the top floor, they had knocked down a wall and bludgeoned a passage. The room had sloping roofs, and wide windows stared out to Scotland. You could see the Firth stir under the sun like a slippery silver snake. When Margaret came in the four children were in bed, but of course not asleep; Timothy was five, Veronica four, Amabel three, Jane only two: Dorothy had been faithful to her duties, and then Bellairs, having planted his seed, had incontinently died.

Timothy was typical Bellairs, brave, stupid, kind and greedy. But the girls were all Herries, Veronica and Amabel of one kind and poor little Jane of the other. Veronica and Amabel were proud, sensible, determined and self-satisfied. Nice little girls, they already gave the impression that Herries little girls were much the best. But Jane, dear Jane, was the true descendant of the Rogue, of Francis, of all their cloudy ancestors before them. She dreamt dreams, she cried for no reason, brokenly she tried to explain that she saw things, a white horse, frozen water, a lady with red hair; she was a nervous, sensitive child, shy but most responsive to affection. It was to her cot that Margaret went. The children lay, their eyes staring, their cheeks hot, thinking of the marvellous day that it had been. In a heap near the window were the new toys. There was a rocking-horse, a doll's house, a 'shinny' stick and ball for Timothy.

They gave cries and shouts when they saw Margaret. They did not know who she might be, but today everyone was a friend. She talked to them, kissed them, but she knelt down beside Jane's cot. Jane, whose head was covered with yellow curls like a duckling's, smiled, stroked Margaret's cheek with a fat finger and fell asleep, and Margaret knelt there, her heart aching as though she were the loneliest woman in the world.

Down in the hall the boys from the village had arrived, Mumming, and it was a great pity that they had chosen so bad a time, for soon guests would be here and the ladies of the house were dressing.

However, Madame miraculously appeared to have time for everything, and there she was, sitting at the foot of the stairs, almost under the mistletoe, dressed in her best and beating her hands to the music. The boys, in the middle of their play, could not but look at her, she was so very fine. Her white hair gleamed, her naked shoulders shone (amazingly white for so old a lady). Her dress had three skirts – cream, silver, cream again – and was decorated with crimson roses. She wore silver shoes.

'Bravo! Bravo!' she cried, tapping with her stick. The boys were without coats and their white sleeves were tied with ribbons, their hats decorated with evergreen, and they carried thick staves.

There was a fiddle and a drum. Their dance was clever and most intricate, advancing, retreating, advancing again and striking their sticks the one against the other. They shouted Cumberland shouts and brought with them into the candlelit hall the rough tang of the mountain-stream running under grass, the windswept 'top' bare under the rushing cloud.

'Excellent! Most excellent!' Madame cried, thinking that they must go to the kitchen for beef and ale, and the kitchen in confused disorder because of the great Dinner.

One stout boy wore a fox's head and carried a fox's tail. Another boy wore a mask with a huge nose and bulbous cheeks.

'I know!' cried Madame. 'That's Willy Caine ... you can't

deceive me. How is your Aunt, Willie? She's up again, I hear.'

She drove them, hot, flushed and happy, off into the kitchen.

Then the guests began to arrive. The Reverend Mr Summers and his old, old wife, although they had the shortest way to come, were of course the first. There were the Osmastons, the Applebys, poor old Miss Keate from Keswick, a dry old maid, but she had nowhere to go for her Christmas dinner, the two Miss Blossoms all the way from Penrith (friends of Dorothy's), and Deborah's grandchildren, Fred and Anne Withering, from near Carlisle.

They would sit down twenty altogether – quite as many as the dining-room would hold – but Judith was bound to acknowledge that she was proud of her table when, seated at the head of it with stout Mr Osmaston on one side of her and old Mr Summers on the other, she looked around her. She had her dear Adam near to her and quite enough Herries to make her feel patriarchal. As you looked down the two sides of the table you could pick without any trouble the members of that family – Adam, Dorothy, John, Elizabeth, Garth, the two Witherings. Unlike though they might be, they were yet alike in these two things – in the high prominent bones, the tall erect heads and straight shoulders – and in their consciousness that they were dominating the rest of the company and came first wherever they might be.

The room is looking beautiful, she thought. The old dark green wallpaper was a fine setting to all the candlelight; the fruit, piled high between the silver candlesticks, had a hard brilliant edge of colour as though it were made of metal. Everyone smiled, laughed. There was not a care in the world.

Old Bennett, dressed up in a green coat with silver buttons, came in carrying a silver dish, and on it was a pig's head with a lemon in its mouth. Everyone stood up: there was a great clapping of hands; then, after an interval, attended by the stable-boy (also dressed in a green coat with silver buttons), who carried two lighted candles in silver candlesticks, old Bennett was back again bearing the Wassail Bowl. This was a magnificent china dish, crimson and gold, and the recipe of the drink had come all the way from old Pomfret of Westaways and he had it from the old Elizabethan Herries of the Mines. Roasted apples floated on its surface, and the aromatic scent of it was as the spices of Arabia.

Speeches were made, healths were drunk. Before the ladies left the table Madame gave the speech of the evening; proud, happy,

her eye passing once and again to Adam, she was said by them all
to resemble Queen Elizabeth – Queen Elizabeth in an amiable
mood, be it understood.

When at last the gentlemen joined the ladies the Wassail Bowl
was empty and the house was flaming with jollity. To Fred
Withering it seemed there were three staircases, and old Mr
Summers confided to Osmaston an affair of his in his Oxford
days that was anything but clerical. Only John seemed apart
from the others ('Oh, the most beautiful man I have *ever* set eyes
on!' Miss Keate confided to Sylvia), his eyes resting constantly
on Elizabeth with an adoration that had something poignant in
its heart as though he were well aware that all was illusory, vanishing at the touch, doomed to destruction.

'Cheer up, old boy,' cried Garth, who was completely drunk
but very charming.

John smiled and laughed; he was happier than he had ever
been in all his life.

While the dining-room was cleared for dancing they played
games – Cumberland games moreover. Instead of *Oranges and
Lemons* there was the Penrith *Down the Long Lonnins:*

> Down the long lonnins we go, we go,
> To gather some lilies, heigho, heigho!
> We open the gates so wide, so wide,
> To let King George and his men go by.

And then *Sandy O.*

Here Judith, Dorothy, John and Adam, who had been all
brought up on it, sang the words with all their youth in their
eyes:

> My delight's in Sandy O,
> My delight's in Brandy O,
> My delight's in the red, red rose,
> Come along, my Annie O.
> Heigho for Annie O,
> Bonny Annie O.
> All the world would I give
> For my bonny Annie O.

For this game there is a girl in the middle, and she chooses one
from the ring; the tune is *Hops and Peas.*

And another 'ring' game, *Hops and Peas and Barley-corn:*

> Hops and peas and barley-corn,
> Hops and peas and barley-corn,
> Hops and peas, hops and peas,
> Hops and peas and barley-corn.

> This is the way the farmer stands;
> This is the way he folds his arms,
> Stamps his feet, claps his hands,
> Turns around to view his land.

How they all stamped and clapped!

'Yes, well,' said Miss Keate, who was wearing, quite out of fashion, a turban, 'I never imagined for a moment—'

But best of all was *Green Gravel*.

> Round the green gravel the grass grows green,
> All the fair maidens are shame to be seen;
>   Wash them in milk,
>   And dry them in silk;
> Last down wedded—

At the word 'down' all slip to the ground, the last down is married. Then she stands in the middle, and they sing a song about her. Then she is asked which she likes best, butter or sugar. If she says 'sugar' it is her sweetheart she likes; if 'butter' it is some other.

After a while Margaret slipped from the room. It was very hot. She could not help it, but she felt isolated, alone. Everyone knew everyone so well. Adam had been placed some distance from her at the supper-table, and he was enjoying himself so greatly that he had thought of nothing but his enjoyment. Men were like that: children when they were happy. And she loved to see him so; that was the desire of her heart, but once she caught John's eyes as they rested on Elizabeth's young enchanting beauty and that glance stabbed her. Elizabeth was so beautiful, so young and virginal and good. Margaret seemed to herself old and soiled with all her hard life with her father, the shabby places in which she had lived, the poor desperate rebellious people who had been her companions. She had been proud of the new dress that she had been wearing, but now it seemed heavy and coarse. In the wild extravagance of her mood it appeared to her that she had lost Adam for ever . . .

She slipped upstairs and found her room. She threw herself on to her bed and burst into tears. This was, perhaps, the first time in her life that she had ever shed bitter tears; she had been always calm, controlled, and had wondered, often enough, that women should weep so readily and in front of those whom they loved. She was in years only twenty-two, but she seemed to herself to be so much older. She had felt often like a mother to Adam, to her father even, and now that she should, like a little child abandon herself to her grief! But she could not stop. Faintly she heard, coming up to her from below, the singing and laughter. Her curtains were not drawn, and she could see the snow falling in a thick tide beyond her window. How cold and desolate those hills, how bleak this North Country, how harsh the loneliness that lay like an icy hand on her heart!

The door opened and, turning on her bed, she saw that Adam had come in. He came in, happy and sweating. He was laughing, and his black hair lay damp on his forehead. His eyes shone in his brown face. His blue evening-coat with its dark velvet collar was waisted almost to effeminacy, as was the fashion of those years, and the tails of it stood out over his thick sturdy thighs. He looked always better in rather rough loosely fitting clothes. He came in laughing and humming the last notes of the *Green Gravel*; then he saw Margaret. He stopped dead, and the change in his face was almost ludicrous. Neither he nor anyone else had ever seen her cry before. No, not her father when her mother died.

'Margaret!'

It seemed to him in his astonishment that his heart turned over in his chest.

'Margaret! What is it?'

She sat up, found her handkerchief, wiped her eyes and, rather wanly, smiled.

'I suffered from a terrible headache. It was the heat.'

Clumsily, still bewildered, unable to realize what he saw, he sat down on the bed. He took her hand, which was trembling but suddenly lay quiet as it felt the tranquil reassurance and strong bones of his brown one.

'A headache? But why did you not say?'

'Why should I disturb anyone? You were all so happy.'

He looked at her more closely.

'That's not true. You would not weep for a headache.'

As he saw her, whom he loved so dearly, with her hair in disorder and her cheeks stained, his love that was so deeply secure in his heart that he never questioned it, began to be restless and uneasy.

They could neither of them lie to the other ever about anything, so she said quietly:

'No, it was not the headache.'

'Well, what then?'

'I was foolish. Nothing but foolishness.'

He put his arm around her and drew her to him, but they were not really together. He had been twenty-seven in September, so that he was not very old, and he had no experience of women at all. He began to be frightened as though something within him had whispered: 'Take care, you may lose her.'

'But what is it, Margaret?' he repeated. 'Have I done something.'

Then she said, dropping her voice, looking away from him:

'I thought you loved me no longer.'

His agitation increased. Loved her no longer, when he worshipped her? Loved her no longer when only last night? . . . But now his old trouble, that he could never find words to express himself, attacked him.

'Love you?' he stammered. 'But, Margaret, I – I . . . I could not love anyone more,' he ended, looking at her.

'No – I am sure. Of course. But perhaps it has been a great mistake. I am not handsome. I am not clever. This is your world and not mine . . .' Then she burst out with a sudden cry, a note in her voice that he had never heard before. 'Oh, Adam, I have been so lonely!'

The shock to him then was one of the worst of his life. He had taken everything for granted. He had gone quietly on, troubled about his work and his feeble achievement in it, troubled at the state of the world and the general unhappiness, but sure always of two things – his love for Margaret and his mother, and their love for him. These were so sure that he never dreamed that they needed expression. Like so many other Englishmen he lived in a man's world where expression of feeling was something too foreign to be decent.

The thought of his mother stirred, a recognized solid fact, in the middle of all his bewilderment.

'But my mother? Has she been unkind to you?'

'No. She has been very kind. It is not her fault that she cannot like me.'

'But she does like you. She said so last night.'

Ah, then they had been discussing her! The two of them together wrapped in their own intimacy! But Margaret had a

noble nature, above and beyond all smallness or mean jealousy.
She put her arm around Adam's neck.

'My love . . . Forget this. I have had so little experience of the
world, and all women are foolish sometimes. I have felt sometimes
that we could speak to one another more, say more what was in
our hearts – and tonight you were all together, you knew one
another so well. I was foolish . . . Forgive me, forgive me.'

Then, with her head against his breast, she cried again, not
wishing to stop her tears that, in their flow, seemed to release and
set free all her misery of the last weeks, release it so that it would
never return again. He held her in his arms as though at any
moment she might escape him. The shock and the surprise were
to him tremendous and the effect of this would remain with him
for the rest of his life. His heart was so tender, he hated so
passionately to wound or hurt anything alive (unless it were an
enemy, someone or something that he thought cruel and evil)
that the knowledge of hurting her was terrible to him.

'Margaret! Margaret! Don't cry. You shall never cry again.
What I have done, wrapped in myself, never seeing . . . But I
never can say what I feel. I don't deserve that you should love
me. I shall make it up to you now all my life long.'

He stroked her hair. They stayed, cheek against cheek, in
silence. At last he said:

'We shall understand one another now.'

She kissed him and, holding his head passionately against her
breast, looking out to the falling snow beyond the window, murmured: 'Now no one can separate us. I shall never be afraid
again.'

A little later, intensely happy, hand in hand they went downstairs and rejoined the company.

Now had it not been for an excellent journal known as *The
Cumberland Paquet* the astonishing events that made this evening for ever memorable (so that years later they were, in a much
exaggerated form, often recalled) would never have been known
to the outside world. But it happened that there intervened now a
short pause in the festivities – a pause between games and the
dancing, and Miss Keate, hot in the head with exercise (and some
of the Wassail Bowl), and young Mrs Appleby found a place on
the corner of the stairs where they might cool. From their position, it must be noted, they had a perfect view of the hall and the
hall door. Miss Keate had with her a copy of *The Cumberland
Paquet* of December 13th which she had discovered in a corner

of the parlour. She had secretly abstracted it that she might have 'a quiet read with it at home'. She was just such a lady, a kind of magpie, and, being of very slender fortune, picked up once and again 'things that she was sure no one else could want'. But now being with Mrs Appleby cooling on a corner of the stairs it was natural that they should look over it together. Had they not done so they would certainly have joined the company in the dining room and shared in the dancing.

The Cumberland Paquet was, however, of surpassing interest. There was a leader about the Emperor of China and the vast sum of money that he had paid to the British (most gratifying to British pride), something about India, and something about the very mild season so that a 'blackbird had been heard in the neighbourhood of Springfield making the neighbouring woods echo with his melodious strains'.

'Poor blackbird,' sighed Miss Keate, whose heart was most tender, 'he must be quite dead by now.'

There was a fascinating advertisement which both ladies, their heads close togeher, read with absorbed interest, that 'Mrs Taylor begs most respectively to inform the ladies of Ulverston and it vicinity that she has just received an assortment of SIMISTER's PATENT WOVE STAYS, which are now ready for inspection.

'To those Ladies who have made trial of the Patent Wove Stay comment is unnecessary, but to those Ladies who have not—'

'Have you, my dear?' asked Miss Keate.

'Well, no,' answered Mrs Appleby. 'You see ...' and then followed five minutes of delightful intimacy.

The real news, however, that kept them glued to the stairs and so made them witness of what followed was a thrilling account of the doings at the Whitehaven Theatre. It was headed: THE-ATRICAL FRACAS, and it began: 'We stated in the last number of the *Paquet* that Mrs Paumier, the wife of the Manager of our Theatre, would take her benefit on Friday evening, and expressed the hope that the play-going public of this town would, as they had done on a former occasion, give her a bumper.' Unfortunately the bumper was prevented because, just before the rise of the curtain, the rest of the company struck for higher wages, the audience grew restive at the delay, and 'some sharp words passed between Mrs Paumier and the performers'. Something very like a riot followed. There was in another part of the *Paquet* a public statement: 'indeed Mr and Mrs Paumier seemed in universal trouble'.

'Why, just listen!' murmured Miss Keate, and she read to her companion:

'It being currently reported that Mr Gilfillan has signified to all persons visiting his wife for beneficial purposes, that he has received from Mr Paumier little or nothing on account of his (Mr Gilfillan's) services at the Theatre, Mr Paumier deems it his duty to publish the following receipt bearing Mr Gilfillan's signature, in order that his (Mr Paumier's) character may in some measure be redeemed until a full and printed statement of his outlay shall be given.'

'Well, did you ever?' said Miss Keate. 'Actors and actresses! What a life they lead! Quite another world from ours! Living on the edge of a volcano. I dare say if the truth were known—'

Miss Keate always afterwards said that it was at this moment (she would remember the name of the Paumiers, she said, so long as she lived) that she had the strangest premonition that something dreadful was about to happen. There was certainly no reason for any premonition, for a more perfect Christmas scene could not be imagined. Everyone now was dancing and the screech of the violin could be heard through the closed doors. Both hall and parlour were deserted; the ladies had only the mistletoe and holly for cheerful company.

But Miss Keate would for ever swear that she had her premonition. She put up her head, caught Mrs Appleby's hand, dropping the *Paquet*, and listened. Immediately after there came a terrific banging at the house-door. You would have thought that everyone within a mile would have heard it, but the door of the dining-room was closed and inside the room the music, the laughter, the tramp of feet as the country dances went their way made it a world enclosed.

Miss Keate and Mrs Appleby sprang to their feet; after a short interval the knocking was repeated and now more violently than before. Soon a maid came to the door, hesitated and then, as the knocking was renewed a third time, opened it. It was then that the two ladies knew the sensation of their lives, for with the open door the wind, carrying with it a flurry of snow, blew into the hall, set the mistletoe rocking; with the wind came a man. The ladies did not, in the first moment, see who it was, for his riding-coat blew about his face, but a second after he looked up and about, stared at the ladies, and they instantly recognized him. It was Mr Walter Herries.

The door banged behind him, and he stood there, his bulk

filling the hall, his face red and angry. The little maid did not
know what to do, nor for the matter of that did the two ladies
either. Then he cried out in a voice like a bull's:

'I've come for my daughter!'

Miss Keate was very good, in after years, as she pictured the
scene. She had a sense of the dramatic. She described the holly
and mistletoe, the sound of music and dancing, the frightened
eyes of the maid, and then, about Mr Herries, she would say:

'Oh, you never saw a more enraged man! His face was crimson. You could conceive him bursting. You would have supposed
that he would pull the house down. Clara Appleby trembled all
over; I had to place my arm around her to steady her or she
would have fainted, I am sure.'

There is something absurd, of course, in a man roaring out
that he wanted his daughter, and Miss Keate, who had quite a
satiric turn when she liked, saw that clearly:

'He was standing right under the mistletoe. Too absurd when
you come to think of it!'

He said no more, but stood there waiting. The maidservant
went to the dining-room and returned, an instant later, with
Judith. *That* was a moment for the two ladies – a very great
moment indeed.

'Madame,' Miss Keate would afterwards relate, 'must have
known whom to expect. She came out to him like the Queen of
England and she said, in a voice as clear as a bell and as though it
were the most ordinary thing in the world, "Well, Walter? Good
evening. And what can I do for you?"

' "Do for me! You can fetch me my daughter and be damned
to the lot of you!"

' "Yes – we had better discuss it in here, I think." '

To the exquisite disappointment of the two ladies Judith and
Walter vanished into the parlour. Miss Keate always afterwards
said that from the very beginning Judith Paris appeared to have
some power over the man. The two ladies stood there staring, and
listening with all their ears. For some while there was little to
hear or see. A maid knocked on the parlour door. Then the
dining-room door opened, throwing into the hall a burst of
music and gaiety, and out came John and Elizabeth. They had
been given some message. They hesitated in the hall, then, hand
in hand, went into the parlour, closing the door behind them.
For a while again there was silence, and then—

But Miss Keate was never to know what exactly occurred
inside the parlour.

And what occurred was this:

'Sit down, Walter,' said Judith, when they were both inside. He stood just by the door, glowering at her, his head thrust a little forward. Judith saw that he had been drinking, that he had a smear of mud on his chin, and that he held, in one gloved hand, a riding-whip. The room was in complete confusion, the carpet turned up, a chair on its side, holly dripping over the mantelpiece, a lady's ribbon on the ground, a lace handkerchief.

'Sit down, Walter, pray,' said Judith. 'And tell me why—'

'You know why,' he answered, his eyes shifting up and down the room. She sat on the sofa and twirled a large white feather fan in her fingers. Her ivory cane (which she was not at all sure she might not have to make use of before the end of the interview) rested near her.

'Indeed I do not, Cousin Walter.'

He came nearer to her.

'I warned you. I told you that you could go too far. Too far! By God, you've always gone too far!'

He was, she supposed, about fifty years of age and he looked sixty with the heavy black pouches under his eyes, the purple veins in cheeks and nose. Oddly, the strain of liking that, in spite of all that he had done, she had always had for him, still, she discovered, survived. Poor Walter! What a mess he had made of everything!

'I have come for my daughter.'

'Elizabeth? Certainly you shall see her.'

'She returns with me to Ireby tonight.'

Judith looked at him impatiently.

'But, Walter, that is absurd. She is no longer a child. She is a married woman.'

'We can soon stop *that* marriage. It shall be dissolved. She was married by force.'

'Indeed she was not!' answered Judith indignantly. 'If ever anyone married freely she did. The marriage has been the greatest success.'

She was listening with all her ears. At any moment dancing revellers might break from the dining-room into the hall and the parlour. She had seen Miss Keate and Mrs Appleby on the stairs. She was determined to finish this scene as quickly as possible.

'It has, has it?' said Walter, coming yet closer to her.

She saw that he was in a confused drunken rage, uncertain as to what he would do or say but determined to assert his power.

'And I know who contrived that marriage. It was you, my fine lady. It has been a long battle between us. You think I forget, but I forget nothing. Do you remember how I whipped your naked little bastard up at Hawkshead years ago? Well, I'd whip him again—'

'It is Elizabeth that we are speaking about,' Judith answered quietly.

He paused to pull himself together. Word slipped from word, sentence from sentence. There was a fog in his brain.

'I demand to see my daughter,' he muttered.

'Certainly you shall,' she answered briskly, pulling the bell at her side.

He was swaying a little on his feet.

'Why don't you sit down, Cousin Walter?' she asked him again. 'You don't look at all well.'

'I am in perfect health,' he answered furiously. 'Never better.'

'And Uhland?' she asked politely.

But this politeness bewildered him. He shook his whip at her.

'Look here, Judith!' he said. 'You're damned clever. You always were. But you don't get round me this way. Do you hear? You can't abduct my daughter from under my nose and I have nothing to say. No, I'm damned if you can. And then marry her to that young swine . . . I always swore that I'd finish him, and by God I will. The whole lot of you. Rude to my mother, was she? I told her she'd repent it.'

He was referring now apparently to Jennifer, and a picture rose before Judith of that poor bewildered lady walking in her black dress across the fields.

The maid appeared.

'Please tell Mr John and Mrs Herries to come to me here immediately.'

She turned to Walter.

'Now, Walter, pray let us have no scenes. These are old, old quarrels that should have been long ago buried. Elizabeth is a sweet girl. She and John are devoted. What else is there left to build enmity upon? I am sure that you are not angry with me. You never were. And, although you have behaved badly once and again, I forgive you everything. Now let us be friends—'

John and Elizabeth entered the room. Inside the door they

released hands and Elizabeth came forward, her head up. She held out her hand.

'She was the loveliest creature,' Judith afterwards said, 'I ever saw. There were roses all over her silk skirt, roses in her cheeks. Her curls were untidy with her dancing and she had the face of an angel. Any father would have been moved by it.'

Walter, however, was not moved. He disregarded her hand and, swaying on his heavy feet, said: 'You are to come back with me.'

She looked round at John for a moment, then smiling said:

'But I am married, Father.'

She, who had been afraid of him all her life, had no fear at all.

Then he began to storm.

'You shall obey your father, do you hear? It was no marriage. You're not married to him. You disobedient . . . disobedient . . .' He began to choke and he put his hand to his throat. He continued to look past Elizabeth to John; all his great body was increasingly agitated. Judith rose from the sofa and went up to him, putting her hand on his arm.

'Walter, this is absurd. You must see that it is. John and Elizabeth are married and have been for a long while. And why not? They love one another, and John has a fine position in London. You don't know him. You've scarcely ever seen him. All your silly hatred is built up upon nothing. Now make the best of it. Shake hands with them . . .'

But he had not been listening to her at all and, suddenly, he rushed forward catching John by the shoulder with one hand, raising the whip with the other.

'You damned puppy! I'll teach you a lesson. I'll teach you a lesson. I'll kill you for stealing my daughter. Steal my daughter, will you? I'll teach you.'

He raised his arm and, clawing John's collar, slashed at him with the whip. No one but Elizabeth saw that in that moment John turned white as the mistletoe berries above them, or that, at Walter's touch, his body seemed to collapse as though his bones had melted. She saw that and, knowing John's courage, realized even at that moment of touch that there was some additional horror here, something old and inborn, quite beyond physical terms.

But it was Judith who had the centre of the stage. Walter's touch on John seemed to swing her into one of those old rages of hers that had for long now been disciplined, for she rushed and threw herself on Walter with so much vehemence that the surprise of it tumbled him forward. She caught his arm and, small though she was, swung him right round and then slapped his face as though she were tearing paper. The whip fell; Walter put up his hand to his cheek and stood there staring.

'You dare! You dirty bully! You come into *my* house again! You blackguard! I'll show you where you are in *my* house. Go! . . . There's the door! You show your face again! You dare! You . . .'

She stamped her foot; she raged like a fishwife, glaring into him as though she would tear his nose out of his face.

He turned, bent half down as though he would pick up the whip, but let it lie there.

'Pick it up! Pick it up!' she stormed. 'I won't have any of your filthy things in *my* house! Christmas Day too! Where are your feelings? Where's your decency? Never you dare to set your foot . . .'

He picked up the whip, stared at her still in a dazzled, confused fashion, muttered something, fumbled for the door.

As he opened it they were all suddenly aware of social conventions; they heard, with an immediate pressing clarity, the murmur of the music and the dancing feet. They all three followed him into the hall.

Judith herself opened the big door for him and stood there, with John just behind her, while the snow whirled in the wind that blew the light over the porch.

'Goodnight, Walter . . . Goodnight,' Judith said.

Miss Keate saw him go out, his head down. 'As though she'd whipped him,' she always ended her story.

Elizabeth went to John, putting her arm through his; the dining-room door opened and someone ran out.

'John! Elizabeth! You must come for "Sir Roger".'

'Don't mind, John. Don't mind,' Elizabeth whispered. She was beginning a new relation with him from that moment.

But he whispered back: 'There was Uhland there – standing in the porch under the light.'

She didn't hear. She pressed his arm with her hand. 'It's nothing,' she said again. 'I have finished with my father for ever.'

But John stared at the door. It was not Walter Herries but Uhland that he was seeing.

Part Three

Cumberland Chase

UHLAND'S JOURNAL

IREBY, *January 5th, 1843*

FINISHED tonight that stuff-and-nonsense book Carlyle's
Heroes. Wonder that I had the patience to read it on to the end,
but I fancy that I was always going further to see whether all his
tall words and German sentences would lead to anything. They
do not any more than does this damnably silly Journal of mine.
There is just this difference. Carlyle is a hypocrite and I am not.
He knows he is no hero but says he is one – I know that I can be a
hero as suitably as any of his Fredericks and Cromwells, but
prefer not to be one. And why do I prefer? Because the world is so
crammed with fools and conceited coxcombs that it is a finer
thing to sit by and watch – to watch, if you like, the decline and
fall of the house of Herries and myself with it. Bang – Bang –
Bang – Whiskers – Whiskers – Whiskers. This is nothing but the
sound a blind man makes seeing himself to bed with the light of a
thick stick and the smell of the candle-end. And it is also, if you
like, the noise that my beloved father and Sam Osmaston are
making just under this floor of my room, both as drunk as cock-
chafers in lamplight, on their knees most likely, searching for a
goose's feather.

But this Journal is supposed to say what I do. Well, what do I
do? Get up, you lamentable cripple, and look at yourself in the
glass, examine once again your ugly wry face, your ribs, like an
old mans' counting-board, and your white bit of twisted bone
politely called a leg. Good, good! That's the thing, my boy!
That's the way to bring your conceit down and sit on the floor to
talk about Heroes. But the soul's the thing, is it not? Does not old
Carlyle say so? The soul! The soul! Where may you be, soul?
Stuck in that leg of mine? Hiding like a rabbit behind a rib or
two? Well, come out for once! Let's have a look at you! Where
are you, green, crimson or mulberry; and your shape? Are you
tortoise-like with a shell like a snuff-box, or thin and spidery,
catching flies for your food, or just a pincushion with pink lace
and a blue silk bow?

What a week I've had too!

They've all been here. The Newmarks with all their brood,

Phyllis a female Alderman, Newmark the prize prig of the market, Horace as long in the leg as a pair of stilts and as wooden, *dear* little Emily and *dear* little Barnabas. All with the latest news of my good grandfather's new offspring. 'Oh, *what* a sweet infant! the dearest little boy!' until I thought my father would throttle the lot of them. Amery Herries too with eyes like gooseberries, the merriest drunken bachelor, and old Rodney from Polchester, sixty if he's a day, touring the Lakes and Scotland with one eye on his clerical dignity and the other on the destiny of every halfpenny! Lord, how I hate the lot of them and how they hate me! Didn't I make little Emily cry by blowing out the candle, and isn't old Rodney afraid of my humours? A family sinking to rot, my masters, cursed because, between too much money-bag on the one side and too much indecisive dreaming on the other, the way to Salvation is missed every time. Not that there *is* any Salvation, even though you search for it. Nothing but madness or death from over-eating whichever way you go.

But now when the house is silent and every stone in this building can be heard scraping its reproaches, I wonder at my indignation. Indignant? No, I have not blood enough for so bold a word. I sit here, sneezing, rubbing my knees the one against the other, healing Rob's ear in the basket, raising my perpetual theme of hatred of my dear John brother-in-law and do nothing, positively nothing. Neither lust urges me nor greed nor envy nor desire for knowledge: only if I had John's neck here I would twist it until his eyes were in his back, and even that is a fancy – nurtured lust, something bred of years of coddling. It *had* a reason once and now I've fed my brain with so many centuries of imagination that to see him tortured in my fancy is as good as the actual deed.

And yet it could have been otherwise. Only this stupid mutton-faced Journal shall know how otherwise it might have been! Another father, flat-faced Adam for a brother and a pair of legs like anyone's, and I had the power, the wish, the ambition. I could have written a book or two, I fancy, better than Bulwer at any rate, or played in a laboratory and made a discovery, or talked as wittily as any Disraeli or Palmerston of them all. I have more brains in my toenail (those on the withered foot have an especial brilliancy) than all my Herries cousins lumped together. But from the very first I was outcast. *That* at least is no imagination. I make no claim for it and I ask for no pity, but to be different from birth, to have the street children mock at you and the dogs bark, and visitors to the house look the other way – it is a kind of allowance for hatred. They say Carlyle has dyspepsia and yet he thinks himself a Hero. Well, am I not a Hero that I sit here and think, and think, and wish myself a villain? And my father still loves me. He thinks me a miracle of brilliance and perversity. All that is left to him, poor man, for his brain is fuddled with drink, the ladies won't call, his fine house is a stony desert, and they flourish at Uldale like the righteous!

Ah! there's the rub! Cousin Judith as lively as a flea, Cousin Dorothy and her children fat as good cattle, John and Elizabeth like sucking-doves. There! He is singing. I can hear him under the floor. And Sam Osmaston with him – a fine out-of-tune chorus . . .

IREBY, *November 13th, 1843*

Rob's ear has this canker again. It's his perversity, I well believe, for he knows truly that once his ear is well, out he'll go, to be stoned by the Keswick boys again, I suppose. And the odd thing is, I shan't care. He's been with me almost a year now. I enjoy his face like the parson's, with its side-whiskers and a slobbery white patch like spilt milk on his nose. He's fonder of me than any dog's ever been, but I hate that sycophancy. I'm near shooting him at times or hanging him from the beam with a rope – yes, even while I wash and clean his ear with the tenderness of a woman.

And now what do you think, O my Journal? What has our dear father done but buy a piece of the moor just above Uldale and build a small cottage on it and into that shove Peach and his dirty brood. There is just one patch, it seems, that great-grand-father David neglected to buy, a measly brown bit that even the sheep neglect. He has done it to vex Aunt Judith of course, and vex her it must to have the filthy little Peaches at her garden gate, and Peach at war with her drunken Rackstraw.

Since she scratched dear father's cheeks last Christmas-time he's been all bent on vexing her, although in my view he thinks her a damnably fine old woman. So she is! She and Adam – another brood from the rest of them.

November 22nd

I am just back from Rosthwaite where I have been limping about all day like an old woman looking for eggs. But something or someone (Algebraical formula? $x + y = xy^2 = $ God?) had put it into my mind of late to be interested in my old Great-great-grand-father, the Rogue. It seems that he spent half his life longing for a gipsy girl (Aunt Judith's mother by oddity) who, when he got her at last, incontinently died. I like the smell of that old man and have picked up a pack of curiosities about him, how he sold a stout mistress at Keswick Fair, was given a scar in a duel, fought for the Pretender outside Carlisle or some such thing, married his gipsy at Rosthwaite and cuffed and kicked the guests down his stairs, how she ran away and he roamed the hills for years look-ing for her; then, catching her at last, gave her Judith whom she died of. There is something deeply sympathetic to me here, for he was outcast as I am, a rebel as I, if I had the guts, would be, a hater too, I fancy, only he would not play Hamlet by the year as I have done.

His old house is a ruin, some tumbled barns swallowed in weed and swiftly vanishing. I sat on some broken mouldy stairs this afternoon and could have sworn to seeing the old fellow watch-ing me ironically. It's his irony I like the taste of. None of the Herries have irony save Aunt Judith. I would like a picture of him, but father says there is none; however, an old cottager well over ninety years with whom I talked today – a lively cursing old man with no teeth, so that he must hiss like a snake when he talks, but his hearing is mighty sharp – he remembers him, how he came striding over the little bridge by Rosthwaite, in a plum-coloured coat with a scar down his cheek, and how he and his gipsy lay both dead in the house together and an old man rode up on a horse and carried the new-born child (Judith, by all that's comic) away on his horse with him. The only man of our family with whom I have any touch, and he dead these seventy years! Grandfather Will must remember him. Next time in London I shall harry his wits over him . . .

I am planning a long London visit. This house is the devil. It is colder than any crypt, and the stone, cover it as you may, breaks through and snarls at you. Every wind in the country whips it and the trees moan like kitchen-maids with the toothache. Also I have the ambition to touch up Cousin John a trifle. I could look in at his window and give him a queasy stomach. What is this hatred? Contempt of his mealy-mouthed propriety? Rage at his impertinent marriage with my sister? Jeal-ousy of his strength and whole limbs? Something taught to me in my cradle by my father? Yes, and more than all this. I hate him

because I have always done so, because of what he is and because
he is happy and I am not. These are honest reasons, but behind
these there is the pleasure of the pursuit. As my old roguish
ancestor pursued his gipsy so I pursue my John. We freaks in the
Herries stock must have our revenge on the normal ones; there is
a warfare there that has necessity in it. And I have no other
emotions. I have never lusted after a woman in all my days, nor
cared for a human being save Adam. Is that my own fault? I
could have asked for quite another destiny, but I had no say in it.
So, to my only pleasure, to see him start at the sound of my step
and flinch under my hand. My leg aches in sympathy.

12 GRANGER STREET, LONDON
February 12th, 1844

Three weeks in London. What a folly! Dinner at Richmond or
Blackwall, the Cave of Harmony, the Coal Hole and such; the
inner sanctities of Meadows' and 'Seven's the main' of the caster,
and 'Gentlemen, make your game' of the groom-porter. Cards
everywhere and, even without the perils of lansquenet, with a
pony on the rubber, five pound points and betting on the odd
trick, you are caught before you are hooked. There is scarcely a
quiet respectable house in all London where they won't rook you
if you give them half a chance.

All the same there's a strange curtain of hypocritical respect-
ability over this town since my last visit. They say it is our good
little Queen and our handsome German Prince. No nonsense at
Court, they say. All heading now for the Virtues.

Last night a party at my grandfather's where, if you please, we
sat round in a circle and a woman with teeth like a grinning hag's
read us the poems of Mr Tennyson. Poor old grandfather would
have slumbered happily in his corner had not Mrs Will in a pink
dress with 'volants' almost up to her waist (and there must have
been at least eight rows of them) pinched him after every melancholy verse. She had time too for elegant flirtation with a fat
young man whose whiskers were as long as a horse's mane! I have
never disliked anyone more and her loathing of myself is badly
concealed by her extreme endearments. She was frightened of
me, I believe and hope. But I perceive that I throw a gloom on to
every party that I encounter. All the better. This London is a
meeting-place of all the snobs, hypocrites, sharps and idiots of
Christendom.

But I remain, for I have my own quiet amusements. One of these is the clearing of Cousin Garth's pockets, for such a juggins at cards deserves clearing.

Another is to listen to the bombast of old James or Carey who both have the fancy that *their* England (*theirs*, mark you) is the most Christian and at the same time the most commercial miracle that this weary planet has ever beheld! To hear them talk of old Pam or of Peel you would fancy that we had no Chartists nor starving populace whatever, and to listen to their contempt of *any* foreign country is to realize to the full *one* side of the beautiful Herries shield!

I listen and then with one remark blow their soap-bubbles to air – and don't they hate me for it too! It is worth the boredom of London to see old James flush his double-chin and stutter: 'But, my dear sir – my *dear* young friend . . .'

I have a deeper pleasure than these mild amusements, though. I have discovered Cousin John's hours: he leaves Bryanston Square five of an evening and for the good of his precious health walks across the Park. Thrice a week at least I see to it that he shall encounter me. We never speak; indeed one glimpse of me is enough to destroy his peace for the rest of the day. He would take a cab were it not that he fights his cowardice, and it has happened twice that when he has taken one I have followed him in another, coming from mine as he issues from his. This game gives me a wild and sensual pleasure. There are certain streets and houses that are marked with the colour of our meetings. Best of all I learnt from Sylvia Herries last week that he and Elizabeth would be at the theatre. They had a box and I in the pit enjoyed my evening to the full. At every meeting it seems to me that we come closer together even as my father grows closer to Uldale. I am contented to bide my time, for there is no pleasure for me in life like this chase. Is this madness? It may be that it is, for it seems to me that I am now two persons and when the one is not with him the other is. I sleep but little and walk the streets at night, hearing my own step in pursuit of myself, that same halting stumble that must, I know, haunt the bowels of Cousin John. I would swear that last night, dressing for grandfather's party, I saw two figures in the mirror and neither shadowy . . .

March 13th

I have had an encounter that has moved me oddly. Yesterday afternoon in the Strand I walked straight into Adam. He was brown and ruddy and sturdy, dressed roughly, books under his arm, his eyes serious and kindly as they ever were. May the Devil forgive me, but I was pleased to see him. Our talk was thus:

'Why, Adam!'

'Why, Uhland!'

'Are you well?'

'And you?'

His hand was on my arm and I felt, for a foolish minute, that I would have followed him anywhere. He is the only one in the world not to glance at my leg, to be perfectly at ease with me, to give me some glimpse of a normal world where men are honest and mean their words. Yet I doubt not he is a prig and thinks highly of his own virtues. Yet he was kind without hypocrisy. He asked me to visit them and he meant it, I think. But I turned away. I could have struck him for moving me as he did. I could have struck him, but I looked back after him as though I were letting my best chance go. He is still on my mind today. He has given me his address and I have half an impulse to visit him. But for what? I should but despise his amiability and suspect his seriousness. There is no place where we can move side by side and I do not know that I wish that there should be.

IREBY, *April 7th, 1845*

I am so much better that I can at last get to my Journal again. Not that I hunger for it, but it is at least a testimony to some energy. And today has been a day as warm as milk and so still that you can hear the cows munching. There was all morning a mist like thick honey with the light breathing behind it a glorious exultant spirit. The sun has been dim all day and Blencathra and Skiddaw have been like whales, unicorns, blankets of soft down, and this afternoon when the sun came fully out and the air was blue they rolled over in delight as puppies do when, deliciously expectant, they want their stomachs stroked. It is not like me to write of the weather, but I have been ill for so long and have smelt nothing but candle-ends, slops and the horsey grain of my blankets.

Last evening I had an odd talk with my father that needs recording. He came in wobbling a candle, in a bed-gown, his chest exposed, but in spite of this very sober. I have been dimly conscious of him the last months, coming in and out of my fantasies. And *what* fantasies! Myself hanging, bare save for a thin shift, from a beam, my toes turned in, and my second self

exuding like milk from an udder out of my left ear – and I was
Grandfather Will's infant, guzzling at a bottle and clutching a
money-bag, and the room was on fire and myself in the middle of
it frying like an acorn, or I hobbled on Stye Head, the mists
chasing me until I fell headlong into Eskdale, and once a white
horse, flashing up a frozen mountainside, caught me with its
teeth and flung me down into ice. In and out of this, then, has
come my good father, but only last evening did we have any
serious conversation.

He tells me that he has not had a drop of liquor for the last six
months, during my illness. And I can believe him. For once he
does not look more than his fifty odd years. His fat is dropped
from him – yes, and his spirits have gone too. He is a little
crazed, I think, as I am. This house has the seeds of craziness in
its bones. For he says that Aunt Judith has poisoned me, some
insane story about her bribing the cook to spoil my food! There's
real craziness as I told him, for whatever that old lady may be
about it will never be poisoning. He tells me, however, that Rackstraw whipped one of the Peach children within an inch of its
existence for stealing out of the Uldale kitchen window and that
one of the Uldale barns has been set on fire. He wants to have
Aunt Judith in jail, but I tell him that the countryside would
burn the jail down to get her out.

When all this loose talk of revenge and the rest had died away
he besought me not to leave him. He has a fear, it seems, that I
shall steal away just as Elizabeth did. He moved me for he loves
me with the strongest mingling of pride, fear and egotism. God
knows I don't want his love. I have no regard for him except that
it seems to me we are caught in the same trap. My illness has left
my head clear and empty. I am imprisoned and cannot be free
until some act frees me. Death, perhaps, of which I have no fear.
But death liberates only one of myself. The other remains imprisoned.

My father held my body in his arms. How lonely and isolated
an act! No one has ever held me close to their breast since I was
an infant, and my father is not a man of sentiment, but he sees
everything else going – health, reputation, wealth – save his love
for me and his hatred of the Uldale lot. I tell you we Herries are
lost men if we let our dreams go too far, be they good or bad, and
this old folly of hating one another is a dream like the rest, for
there is no satisfaction to be found in any egoistic desire. I can see
that we are intended to lose ourselves altogether in something

impersonal, and once Cousin John, the pretty, were gone I could be lost, I fancy, turning with what relief into the thick honeyed air like a child loosed from school . . . But what a couple the two of us, my gross father straining my bony wasted fretfulness against his bare chest, and our eyes refusing to meet! And myself, round the corner, peering and grinning at the idiocy of the scene from behind the wardrobe.

When he kissed me I shrank into my twitching leg and he felt me shrink and for once I hated my unkindness. He is a very simple man, my father. He meant this Fortress to be a great symbol of Herries power – just as Cousin James and Rodney and Grandfather and Amery are building up their fine Victorian England – but to lay stone upon stone is not enough. That is a thing that the building Herries have never understood. I do not believe in God but I do not think that you can build anything without Him.

My father wishes me to take my proper place here when I am recovered. He is reformed, he says – no more the rake. We will attend to farms and property. Yes, but no Herries has ever wanted to accumulate property. We do not care for it enough. We think too much of ourselves and will not yield our personal conceit to anything, not even to property.

And we must get Aunt Judith out of Uldale, he says. And we must make this house warm, he says. It is always so devilish cold. He does not know that there is a rat eating away the foundations. And, when all is said, he loves me like a dog, not knowing why, and I care for nothing and nobody, not I. It is something though to see the gold light again lying evenly over the hills and to hear the stream running down the hill. I have grown, during my illness, a pale forked beard. I look, in the glass, like a green radish.

LONDON, *January 14th, 1846*

Yesterday I had a half-hour of sanity that is worth recording. I spent it with Grandfather Will. He requested me to pay him a visit. Why? Even now I do not know. Some intention perhaps of compensation because he has thrown my father and myself aside for ever and young Ellis reigns in our stead. (Why Ellis? A dreary, dry-as-dust, left-over-from-yesterday pantry kind of name, but its mother has rich cousins thusly.) Nor do I blame him for that. We are not a pair to be proud of, I suppose. And so

I went. Appalling that house in Hill Street. No rain-washed air sweeping Blencathra here, but furniture spawning everywhere, masses of it, heavy and despondent, groaning between thick rep and treading down the thick Turkey. There are pallid sightless statues and old Herries gilt-edged on every wall. I was alone in a vast room with my grandfather, and we crept together for safety. 'Keepsakes' were our only company. But I am modern for my time. I am a hundred years hence. I am sickly with the odour of 1950. He is bent now, his hair white, his clothes fitting him, black and stiff, as though they were made in a Bank. But in his old age he is kind and eager. I should judge that this baby is the only human soul for whom he has ever cared, although he spoke of Elizabeth's beauty and seeing her alone in this room one day in the past 'like a vision'. He meant, I fancy, that it could not be true that she was my sister. He thinks me misshapen and dangerous and cannot understand that I should be descended from his loins. Something has gone wrong somewhere and he is bewildered because he has always done the sensible thing. But he intended to be kind, sat close to me although I made him creep, and by not looking at my twitching leg he only looked the more intently. He asked me how I did. He had heard that I had been ill. He feared that he would never see Cumberland again although in his youth he had seen eagles sailing over Glaramara. He has a trick of fingering his coat-buttons as though they were counting-house money. He wanted me to tell him something. But what? That things have not turned out as they should do, his brother Francis a suicide, his son a drunken fool, his grandson a deformity? Well, there is little Ellis, and I see as though under glass his heart beat up again and his old eyes, weary with gazing on figures, open out at the new hope. Then he is proud of England. It is as though he had made it, put a hump on Skiddaw here, added a tomb to Westminster, straightened the Strand, bidden the sea halt in Norfolk, and run the railway to Newcastle. He is tired, he explains to me, and then with great courage lays his hot bony hand on mine.

'For I am seventy-five,' he tells me, 'and have worked hard all my days.'

He hopes that we are all now reconciled, for there was once a silly quarrel. Something about a fan. His wife, 'your grandmother,' was concerned. But that is all so old, so very very long ago, and he hopes that now all is well. Do I see Judith Paris often? A remarkable woman with much spirit and character. And

I think of the little Peach children setting a match to Aunt Judith's parlour, and Aunt Judith slapping my father's face.

But he hopes that all is well. We must be friends, all of us. Our family must stand together. They mean something to England. He talks of Palmerston and Peel and the Corn Law crisis and says the 'rotten potatoes have done it,' and how angry the Duke is and that Melbourne told the Queen 'that it was a damned dishonest act,' and that John Russell has come out of it all 'damned poorly', but they are all dim figures to him now. Ellis aged three has swallowed up the firmament. He has a little rheumatism in his legs, he tells me, but otherwise he is well enough, and so he pulls himself up and slowly, slowly, very stiff and straight, stamps from the room. And I go down into the street to meet my waiting double . . .

IREBY, *October 9th, 1846*

I have seen the 'Barguest'. I am a haunted man. I was lost yesterday afternoon in the wilds between Blencathra and Skiddaw, Skiddaw Forest way. I do not know where exactly I was. I could not find the same place again. I had plunged upward, limping and running and limping again in my own ridiculous fashion, treading down the dried bracken that in certain lights has almost a glow of fire running through it. I had looked back and seen Ireby with its stone turrets, its frowning eyebrow, squat like a discontented image staring down at Uldale. I looked forward and the rocks closed me in. They have that fashion here. They move forward of their own will; you can see them almost scratching their craggy sides. A moment before there had been the long swinging slope of bracken, fields below marked off and smelling rain, the stone wall running straight up into air, a round tufted tree holding the light, cottages and farms – and now only this pressing crowding observant rock, the ridge of the hill black against the October sky save for some little white clouds that like spies crowded to the ridge and looked over down into the amphitheatre. I am noting it down thus minutely because of what then occurred.

I seemed to be able to move neither up nor down; my leg limits me and I felt as though the slope of rock on which I was standing would slide down with me – maliciously, while the rocks round me shook with laughter. And then I saw the Barguest. An old man shaped like a whale-bone. He came along towards me on his hands and knees, and once and again he would stop, stare at me, and bite his long fingernails. But I could see through him; he swayed like water-mist, was at one time so hazily defined that there were wisps of him like clouds about the rock, then so sharp that I could count every button. It was no imagination – or I am mad perhaps with want of sleep. I stayed transfixed, and he came right up to me. I could smell his breath, an odour of mushroom and sodden leaves. He touched me with his long yellow fingernail and then dispersed into vapour. I know this is so. It is no dream and, if I am crazy, which for some months now I have suspected, what is reality? But I am sure that I shall see this place again and at some fatal time. When the Barguest had vanished I climbed a stone and all the scenery was restored again, the fields green in the October sun, and rain-clouds gathering up above the sea.

WAX FLOWERS AND THE REVOLUTION

ADAM tried, with all the self-control that belonged to his training, to forget what the day after tomorrow meant to him, but, try as he would, again and again something repeated inside himself: 'The day after tomorrow ... The day after tomorrow. Everything hangs on Monday, my whole life ... everything I've worked for.'

Margaret, in a brown bonnet, hanging on his arm, caught sight of the magnificent Beadle, whiskered, gold-laced, standing superbly at the door of the Pantheon Bazaar.

'Oh, let us go into the Pantheon ... I can find something there for poor little Daisy Bain, whose foot was crushed by that wagon last week. It won't occupy us a minute. Do you mind, Adam?'

They were both making a sublime attempt at proving that nothing was toward. Today was like any other day. And yet, with how many thousands around them, they were, it might be, on the eve of a new era, a new world, a world of light, justice and brotherhood. All London was making preparation for Monday's great Chartist rising. All clerks and officials were ordered to be sworn garrisons. Every gentleman in London was become a constable. (What a very grand carriage outside the Princess Theatre and what a hideous befrilled Pug in the window!)

After all, what an incredible year! In the month of March

alone fearful street fighting in Berlin, flight of the Prince of
Prussia, riots in Vienna and Milan, Hungary in revolt, revolution in Austria, and, above all, France tumbling either into a
chaos of disaster or a triumph of a new grand order!

And on Monday – Monday, April 10th, 1848 – England too
might see the turning-point of all her history. But Margaret had
always a child-like desire for pleasure, and Adam was, nowadays,
a great deal more easily pleased than he had once been. They had
walked out into the mild spring air that they might quiet some of
their almost trembling agitation. How odd it was to see the bird-
stuffer's shop with the birds of paradise and parrots, crimson and
gold and violent green, a statuary shop, with Canova's Graces,
the staymaker's, the fitter's shop with the little cork ball bounding
up and down on the perpendicular jet of water, the provision
shop with the Durham mustard, the Abernethy biscuits, Iceland
moss, Narbonne honey, Bologna sausages – these and many many
more, and to think that in another two days all these splendours
might be at the mercy of the mob, that the poor might have their
wrongs righted, the just come to their own . . . It must be truth-
fully added that any stranger seeing Adam and Margaret as they
passed the bowing Beadle at the Pantheon door would have been
astonished indeed at such revolutionary sentiments, for never did
a pair look more respectable and kindly – Adam, set and solid,
with his dark side-whiskers, his handsome high hat and gentle-
manly cravat, and Margaret in her brown bonnet and overjacket
of white embroidered muslin. Revolutionaries? Surely not this
respectable pair!

In fact they did forget for ten minutes inside the Pantheon
that they *were* revolutionaries. Margaret was so happy to be alone
with Adam for a little that she forgot all else. Adam was changed
since that Christmas at Uldale, more thoughtful, more demonstrative, but he was constantly preoccupied with his work, and
their rooms were from morning to night crowded with other
people. She did not often have him to herself. She was so happy
that it had been *his* suggestion that they should take this walk!
He did not often suggest that they should go off somewhere
alone. She sometimes almost wished that there *was* no Charter,
that that flamboyant boastful Feargus O'Connor had never been
heard of, that she and Adam and her father need not so continually be considering the wrongs of other people! And the Pantheon, when they were inside it, was enchanting! First they went
up to the gallery where they might look down on that exciting

coloured maze of babbling children, beautiful ladies, attendant footmen and subservient shopmen. Behind them (and they glanced in for a moment) was that queer neglected little picture-gallery with the dusty twentieth-rate pictures and tragic Haydon's enormous spectre-like 'Lazarus' dominating with its fruitless ambition and almost emerging misconceived genius the atmosphere not only of the Pantheon but the street beyond it, the people, the carriages, the houses. Once this was a theatre; here were the Grand Staircase, the Rotunda, the green room, the con-servatories, dressing rooms. Here were *Ariadne in Naxos, Daphnis and Chloe, Bellerophon, The Cruelty of Nero.* Old Will, a stiff prosperous conceited young man of the City, must here have applauded and Christabel feebly clapped her gloved hands and old Carey have slumbered! Even the lovely radiant Jennifer, with her proud parents, must here have been the beauty of the evening. Judith's Georges must have looked in with a companion to observe the legs of the chorus; Guimard danced in a hoop that reached nearly to her ankles. Those were the pigtail days of Du-vernay and Ellsler and Taglioni! Here George III's eldest son met the lovely Perdita, and Charles Fox in a domino shouted a tipsy applause!

A church, a waxwork show, an opera, and then one night, in the middle of *Don Giovanni,* twelve demons bearing torches of resin rose to seize the guilty hero, and behold there were *thirteen* demons, one of them carrying *two* torches and disappearing in a flame of real fire while the audience fainted and the manager vanished into a madhouse!

But Margaret and Adam were not thinking of the past: the present and the future were *their* concern! They were very young – Adam young for his almost thirty-three years, Margaret only twenty-eight. Everything was in front of them.

Before they descended from the gallery Adam turned.

'Margaret, are you happy?'

'Very, Adam.'

'You know that you are everything to me now. Whatever happens on Monday, whatever way things go, nothing can alter that.'

'Yes, I know.'

He kissed her and they went down the stairs like a couple of children. To purchase something for little Daisy Bain was no easy task, for the variety of toys was extraordinary and the young ladies at the stalls so *very* polite and superior. Margaret was always easily dashed by patronage and had she been alone would have fled from those elegant young women in dismay, but Adam confronted them so calmly and with so agreeable a smile that they were ready to do anything for him. There was the monkey on a stick, the serpent made of elastic (a compound of glue and treacle), a centipede at the end of an indiarubber string, and many another; but best of all were the wax flowers. Oh! how lovely they were! Margaret clapped her hands when she saw a whole stall of them! She had no eyes then for the tortoiseshell card-cases, the pink scented invitation cards with 'on dansera' in the corner, the muslin slips, the volumes of polkas with chromo-lithographed frontispieces, the sandalwood fans, the mother-of-pearl paper-knives with coral spring handles – all these could be bought at the Pantheon, but she saw only that blazing bank of colour – crimson, orange, violet, silver – the flowers smiling from their stalks – carnations, pansies, roses, lilies-of-the-valley, peonies – their wax petals soft and iridescent, as fresh, as vernal as though but a moment ago they had opened their smiling faces to the sun!

'Oh, Adam, are they not marvellous!' she cried.

Something then touched his heart, as though he had never truly loved her before and as though he were warned that, without realizing his treasure, it might be, at a moment, lost to him. He would buy the whole store-load for her! Revolutions, tumbling thrones, the rights of the poor, these things fell down before the wax flowers like pasteboard castles!

She chose an assorted bunch – purple pansies, icily white lilies-of-the-valley, a crimson rose.

'They will live for ever!' she said, smiling into his eyes.

They were packed very carefully into a box, and lying on tissue paper looked, Margaret thought, worthy of the Queen.

'They should be kept under glass to preserve them from the dust,' she said.

The stately young woman who served her smiled with an exquisite dignity.

'That is generally considered wise, madam,' she remarked.

'Oh, Adam, how kind you are!' Margaret whispered as they walked away. 'I shall have these all my life long.' Then dropping her voice, looking at him shyly but with a deep intensity: 'I do love you so'.

They passed the refreshment counter and enjoyed, each, an arrowroot cake. Daisy Bain had been quite forgotten, so hurriedly a doll with flaxen hair was purchased for her. They enjoyed the conservatory with the fountain that contained the gold and silver fish, the exotic plants and gay flowers. But it was very hot in the conservatory, and the parrots and cockatoos made an intolerable screeching. One cockatoo, as Margaret could not help observing, strangely resembled Mr Feargus O'Connor and, for a moment, a dread caught at Margaret's heart. What would happen on Monday? Was this their last peaceful day? Would they ever be so happy again? She looked at the box that she carried in her hand and sighed. She held Adam's arm yet more closely as they passed out through the waiting-room where some grand ladies were waiting for their carriages, and so into the light and fresh air of Great Marlborough Street.

On their return home they found themselves in another world. Adam discovered suddenly, looking at the room's disorder, the bottles of beer, the smoke from pipes, books thrown on to the floor, that he wanted to be out of it all, that his enthusiasm was dead, that he did not care what happened on Monday, that there was no Cause any longer. As he saw Margaret moving quietly into the farther room, carrying the box that held her precious wax flowers as carefully as though it were glass, he discovered that with her departure all the light seemed to have gone out of his world. He had reached some new relation with her during that half-hour in the Bazaar. She was more precious to him than ever before.

So with that rather stumbling, halting movement that made him seem short-sighted, but that was only in reality because his thoughts were elsewhere, he turned and took in his company. He saw at once that Henry Lunt held the floor. He would of course in any place where he was. He was in no way different from the day when Adam had first met him, still shabby, black, fierce, denunciatory, self-confident. Adam knew that he was brave and honest, but he knew also that he was narrow-visioned, foolishly impetuous, and that his temper was so violent that it was extremely dangerous. He had been twice gaoled for his share in riots and disorders: this had not made him either wiser or more tolerant. He was more conceited than he had been, thought he knew everything and had all the gifts of leadership; tonight he seemed to Adam a noisy, tiresome demagogue. There were now too many of his sort in the movement, and, in fact, the whole impetus seemed to be slipping away from the Chartists. The Irish potato

famine, the Anti-Corn Law League, above all the exciting spec-
tacular troubles in Europe, made the Chartist movement a little
old-fashioned. Louis Philippe's fall in February still possessed
men's minds to the diminution of all else. After all, people said,
bad though things were, they were not as bad as in France. We
English are too sensible for Revolutions. We are not of that kind.
Adam agreed with them. The Chartists, especially men of Lunt's
type, appeared now something foreign and affected.

Undoubtedly everyone in the room this evening felt a little of
this. Lunt talked the louder because of it, and, sitting on the edge
of the table, swinging his stout legs, harangued Kraft, Pider, and
Ben Morris and a young Jew, Solomon, as though he were, with
wonderful magnanimity, screwing their courage to the striking-
point.

Pider, it seemed, had said something mildly deprecatory before
Adam came in, and Lunt was all on fire over it.

'Aye,' he was shouting, 'that's just what I was expecting to
hear, Pider. There are too many of your sort about, and that's the
truth. Here we are slaving for years back to bring this thing about
and at last the moment has arrived. The great, magnificent
moment, the climax of all our efforts, and what do you do
but—'

'Yes, but,' Pider broke in, 'suppose the moment hasn't arrived
after all? Suppose Monday's abortive and there's nothing done?
Look at O'Connell!'

'Yes, look at O'Connell!' cried Lunt fiercely, jumping from the
table and waving his short arms. 'He's dead, isn't he? And deserved to die. They may have given him a fine funeral in Dublin,
but we know what he was, a faint-heart whose courage failed him
just when it was needed. Feargus O'Connor's quite another sort
of man—'

'I don't know,' said Pider doubtfully. 'I've heard men say of
O'Connor—'

'And what have you heard men say of O'Connor?' Lunt
shouted. 'There are always men jealous of their leaders, but I tell
you that any man who says O'Connor will fail us is lying in his
throat, and so I'd tell him to his face. I know O'Connor. I've
eaten and slept with him, and a grander, finer leader of men the
world doesn't hold! Answer me that, Pider, and tell me that you
know O'Connor better than I do and I'll tell you it's a falsehood.'

Pider, who was not lacking in courage and was in no way

afraid of Lunt, started fiercely forward. Kraft came quietly in between them.

'Now, now,' he said, smiling. 'Where's the good of our arguing about what will happen on Monday? Who can say how things will turn? We've done the best we can and must leave the rest to God.'

'God! God!' Lunt shouted fiercely. 'It isn't God we're wanting, but confidence in ourselves. I tell you—'

But Kraft gave a sign to Adam and turned off into a little side-room that he used as a study. Adam followed him and closed the door behind him. He put his arm round Adam and drew him close.

'You look weary,' Adam said.

'Yes, I am weary. Their shouting makes me weary. There are times when I'm sick at heart of the whole thing, times when I wish that I'd never heard of the Cause at all, and had spent my days mending watches or keeping sheep in a field.'

'It's not like you,' Adam said, 'to be down.'

'No, maybe it's not. But tonight I have a kind of foreboding, a sinking of the heart.' He pressed Adam's shoulder. 'What is it, Adam, creeps into all Causes alike, a kind of worm that eats the heart out of them? It's a sort of egotism, I suppose. You grow to think of your own part in it all, to admire your own energy, your fine speeches, to be jealous of others who are praised, to want personal rewards. To be impersonal, to care nothing for yourself, it is the only lesson of life, and no one can learn it!'

'Yes. If there is a lesson!' Adam's dark eyes slowly clouded. 'When you watch the Churches fighting as they are, when you see Jews like Disraeli bringing off their clever fireworks, while you watch a sot like Walter Herries at home trying to frighten women ... It may be there's no lesson, no plan, no future, no God—'

Kraft shook his head.

'I feel my immortality,' he said. 'I cannot doubt it, but it is perhaps a poor kind of immortality. God *may* be a sort of flash Jew like Disraeli or a dandy like D'Orsay or a storyteller like Charles Dickens or a ranter like Lunt – it may be one long swindle – but it goes on, I *know* that it goes on.'

'Yes,' Adam continued, nodding his head, 'and emotions like my present love of Margaret. That's no present from a cheap Jew; or walking down by Sour Milk Ghyll on a summer evening when the water is whiter than snow and the hills clouds –

D'Orsay couldn't make *such* a gift to anyone. But this, Caesar, all this that we have been working for for years – I see no New Heaven and New Earth *this* way. Men don't change. Why do they not change, Caesar, that's what I want to know? Why do *I* not change with all the experience I get? I can remember when I was a tiny boy bathing one evening in a tarn above Hawkshead. My mother was there, and an old fat fellow, my uncle Reuben, a sort of itinerant preacher, who told me stories. He was a wonderful man as I remember – I daresay he was not in reality. He was killed after a riot when they tried to burn Uldale down, set on by Walter Herries. I owe Walter Herries something, you see. But what was I saying? Oh yes – that night. What was I? Four, five? I don't know. We lit a fire under the trees, there was a dog, and Uncle Reuben told me stories. All beauty, all loveliness is in that night as I look back. Not now. Not here. Not then as I knew it, I was happy, of course, but recognized nothing extraordinary. But looking back I see now that there was something divine in that wood that night. Why,' he burst out, laughing, 'there was something divine in Pantheon Bazaar this afternoon. My love for Margaret. Hers for me. Let me recognize it now and offer D'Orsay-Disraeli-Dickens-Jupiter my thanks for it.'

Kraft smiled.

'What has happened to you, Adam? You are usually so silent. Words are pouring from you.'

'I know. I'm living at an extra intensity tonight. As though there were only a thin strip of paper between myself and discovery – discovery of what? I don't know. D'Orsay's rouge-pots?'

'I know,' Kraft answered quietly. 'I am the same. It is our excitement about Monday, I suppose. A Scotsman would say I am "fey". I can see my shroud, Adam.'

Sunday night he slept so little and woke so early that while it was still dark he slipped from Margaret's side, dressed hurriedly, and went out. He walked through the quiet streets for some while without thinking of his direction, then found that he was in the City. Here it was as cool and silent as an oyster. The wall of the Custom House was a dead wall, the Coal Exchange was sleeping, but soon he was down on the wharfs where life was already active and earnest. Here were tubs smelling of oranges, shops – already opened – packed with salt fish, dried herrings, Yarmouth bloaters, mussels and periwinkles, dried sprats and cured pilchards. For he was in Billingsgate. Here the Billingsgate marketeers were drinking from massive blue and white earthenware mugs filled to the rough brims with coffee; here porters were busied clearing piles of baskets away, putting forms and stools in order, in eager preparation for the fish auction. The wharf is covered with fish, and the great clock of Billingsgate booms forth five o'clock. The stands are laden with salmon, shoals of fresh herring, baskets full of turbot, while the crowds are gathering thickly, and everyone is shouting and crying at once.

Adam watched with increasing pleasure. Close to him a fine fellow stood, a hat tall and shiny as though he were a habitué of Aldridge's Repository, his sporting neckcloth fastened with a horseshoe pin, while round his giant stomach was bound the conventional blue apron; he was wearing galligaskins and straight tight boots of sporting cut. Here were the eight auctioneers; here Bowler's, Bacon's and Simpson's, the noisiest taverns (at this hour) in the whole of London. Now was the excited selling of the 'doubles' and the 'dumbarees'. Fish, fish, fish! Plaice, soles, haddocks, skate, cod, ling ... Suddenly he recollected. My God, this very afternoon, and the gentleman in the galligaskins and blue apron might find all his occupation gone! By five of the evening of this very day, all the soles and cods and haddocks might swim peacefully in the sea for the attention paid to them! This very street, instead of its stream of fish-scales, bones and dirty water, might be running in blood! Instead of gaiety, laughter, money business, there might be death, ruin, a blaze of fire, smoking catastrophe!

There was a sick dismay at his heart. He had been working for years with an earnestness and eagerness that had possessed every energy he had. He had lost in these years much of the fantasy and humour that had been part of his childhood. At this stage he was grimly serious, taking nothing lightly. At that moment in the Billingsgate Market he saw himself as someone fantastically absurd, working like a labourer at piling brick upon brick, and as he laboured the bricks turned, before his eyes, to straw.

A joke, a farce, iridescent fish-scales floating down the teeming gutter. He hurried home.

This morning, Monday, April 10th, was a lovely day, the sun streaming down with that soft mild radiance that brings a spring scent of flowers into the London streets. The Chartist detachment to which Kraft and Adam belonged moved off very early to Kennington Common. There was no definite procession to the Common; the Procession, presenting the great Petition, was to march at least a hundred thousand strong, under the leadership of Feargus O'Connor, to the Houses of Parliament.

Here the Petition was to be presented, and what would follow after was the question on everybody's lips. Men like Lunt declared that what would follow would be the greatest Revolution in England since 1688. But how precisely that Revolution would take place, no one precisely knew. It was true that the Queen and her Consort were not supremely popular, but no one had anyone to propose in their place, and even the Lunts of the movement could not claim that the whole of England was at all ready as yet for a President or a Dictator.

The very troubles that the rest of Europe were battling with made many Englishmen proud of their own passivity.

Nevertheless, a Revolution there would be, some sort of a Revolution. What the average man, both Chartist and non-Chartist, feared was that, simply through ill-directed and undisciplined contact, there would be riot and bloodshed, meaning nothing, leading nowhere; men perceived, from the recent Paris example, that one small unexpected event could lead to vast and unexpected consequences. Let fifty thousand shouting Chartists reach Westminster ... Why, then, both sides being armed, some horrible catastrophe might take the whole civilized world by surprise. No one in London was happy on that lovely spring morning and, if the truth were known, most certainly not Mr Feargus O'Connor himself, who, in spite of his descent from Irish kings, had no wish to find himself in gaol before the evening.

Neither Adam nor Kraft was happy. They had one last word together before they set out.

'I have the oddest feeling,' Kraft said. 'I dreamt last night, of what I don't know, but I woke saying to myself, "Yes, that's the answer." Now, I know what it all means. I seemed, in that brief dream, to have passed through all experience and to have realized that envy, greed, jealousy, disappointment, lust, bodily sickness – it was not until I had known them all and tranquilly accepted them all, that I began to live. Tranquillity. I tell you, Adam, I am as tranquil this morning as a pond-weed. My anxiety is gone, but my desire too. I cannot imagine what it is that has agitated me so deeply all these years.'

Adam frowned.

'I am not tranquil. I am afraid of what a parcel of fools are likely to do before the day's out.'

It was still very early when the three of them reached the Common. On their way thither they had been impressed by the silence of the town, as of something strongly on its guard. There was little traffic in the streets, very few people about and many of the shops closed. Adam learnt afterwards that many of the important official buildings round Westminster were defended with guns and that Whitehall was in reality an armed camp.

When they arrived at the Common they saw that there was the crowd that had been confidently expected. There were many banners flaunting devices like 'The Charter, the whole Charter, and nothing but the Charter,' 'Justice for All Men and No Favour,' 'Up! Up for O'Connor!' and there were a number of brass bands.

Men, women and children sat and walked about, rather listlessly, dressed, some of them, in their Sunday clothes, while others seemed to boast their poverty. There were many pale, thin, with angry, restless eyes and hungry faces; others appeared to have come to enjoy the sights. There were some booths with food and drinks.

Everything was very quiet, there was a murmur of voices, a sense of expectant waiting as though at any moment a miracle might break out in the sky above their heads.

Soon after their arrival Lunt joined them.

'Not so many as were expected,' Adam said.

'Pooh,' Lunt answered. 'They'll turn up. It will take many of them time to get here. And this is nothing. You wait until the Procession starts for Parliament and see how many join us. You listen to O'Connor when he makes his speech and you'll hear something.'

Soon it happened that everybody began to press together towards the centre of the Common and the crush became uncomfortable; toes were stepped on, umbrellas and sticks poked into innocent faces, women lost their children, and children were crying, pockets were freely picked.

Adam saw that it was towards O'Connor and one or two gentlemen near him that the crowd was thronging, and soon, owing to Kraft's important position in the movement and the badge that he wore, he found that they were enclosed in the magic circle. He was so close to Feargus O'Connor that he could observe him well. A wild theatrical gentleman, he seemed both over-decorated and shabby, for he had on the breast of his blue coat a number of ribbons and medals, but his pantaloons were older than they ought to be and stained with mud. His hair fell in untidy ringlets from under his high hat, and he waved with a great deal of excited gesture the cane that he was carrying. In the other hand he had a stout roll of paper that was supposed by everyone to be the famous Petition. He was, it was clear, excellently conscious of the attention that he was receiving. Once and again he would put up his hand to his rather soiled cravat, the cane would drop to the ground and be obsequiously lifted by someone. He would dart his head up rather as a suspicious hen might do, stare with proud and melancholy indignation at some small boy who, open-mouthed, was gazing at him with all his eyes.

It appeared that he had some reason for indignation, for it seemed that his pocket had been picked. Had anyone ever heard the like? The leader of the country against tyranny and oppression, and his pocket had been picked! How much had there been in his purse? He could not be sure, but a very considerable sum; also a blue silk handkerchief to which he attached sentimental value.

But Adam quickly realized that Mr O'Connor was not at all at his ease. While he talked with an excited and incoherent fervour his eyes were for ever searching the horizon and searching it with a kind of terrified preoccupation as though he expected at any moment to see a large scaly dragon, vomiting fire, issue from the Kennington trees.

He greeted Kraft absent-mindedly and shook a finger with Adam (the rest of his hand clutching the sacred roll of paper) without seeing Adam at all.

He became with every moment more deeply agitated. Beside him was a long, thin, cadaverous man who looked like a Methodist clergyman, and a stout, rubicund fellow like a butcher. There was no sign, however, of any organization or leadership. From time to time someone broke through into the magic circle, whispered mysteriously to O'Connor and vanished again. He on his part would nod his head with great self-importance or shake it or look up to the heavens or wave his cane. He alluded again and again to the fact that his pocket had been picked, and once and again would burst into a fine frenzy, invoking the Deity: 'My God, have I been chosen to lead these people at this great hour? Have they come to me hungry and shall they not be fed?' Then, dropping his voice: 'What is it, Forster? Has Cummin not arrived? Where is Whitstable? Have they got the thief that has my purse? March to Westminster? But where are the others? This is not the half of them! And my toes trodden on and my pocket picked . . .'

The crowd waited with a most exemplary patience. They were, it seemed, ready to picnic on the Common for the day if necessary. Many of them, Adam was convinced, were not Chartists at all. Many were rogues and vagabonds who had come to gather what they might out of so large a crowd. He saw, as he looked about him, many incongruous figures, here a rather shabby young dandy in pea-green gloves and a shirt embroidered with dahlias and race-horses, then a stout serious-looking gentleman with peg-top trousers, chin-tuft and eye-glass, and close beside him a sturdy fellow who might have come straight from the Billingsgate of the morning, green apron and galligaskins all complete. It could not be said to be a very murderous crowd, and, as Adam looked, his fears of red revolution died away. There would be no revolution here. But for what then all these years had he been working? Not for revolution certainly, but also not for a contented humorous crowd like this. He drew Margaret's arm through his and waited for what might come.

What soon came was an excited stir through the crowd. It whispered like wind through corn. Someone had arrived. Something had occurred. Two men pushed through and spoke to O'Connor; at once his countenance turned red and then white again. He dropped his cane and no one picked it up. He stood, hesitating, his head turning first this way, then that.

The crowd was dividing; it was the Constable, Mr Mayne, followed by three of his inspectors. Mayne, a fine, resolute-looking man, took his stand a little way from Adam, and sent one of his inspectors forward to O'Connor. It was clear that O'Connor was in a terrible fright. 'Afraid of arrest,' whispered Kraft contemptuously to Adam. O'Connor, after a second's hesitation, clutched his cane and roll of paper and went to meet Mr Mayne. The two men made a striking contrast, and in that moment of seeing them together, it seemed to Adam that any alarms or hopes on the part of anyone that Revolution would ever again break out in England were finally dissolved.

'Mr O'Connor,' said Mayne, 'I am here to inform you that the meeting on this Common is permitted, but no procession to Westminster.'

O'Connor said something.

'No. No procession whatever.'

O'Connor spoke again.

'Certainly, Mr O'Connor, I am very pleased to hear it.'

O'Connor held out his hand; Mr Mayne shook it.

The Revolution was over.

Mayne, with his inspectors, disappeared, and O'Connor came forward to address the crowd. There were stands with flags and banners for him to appear on, and he did step up on to one of them, attended by some half a dozen gentlemen, but very little that he said could be heard. It appeared that he himself was going to the Home Office that he might present the famous Petition there; there would, however, be no procession; in fact, everything was over, or rather, the Meeting might continue as long as it pleased, but he, Mr O'Connor, would not appear in it.

He vanished, and there followed an extraordinary scene. Many of the more peaceful citizens, laughing and jeering, turned to leave the Common, but at the same time crowds of roughs and hooligans, urged on by the more violent Chartists, drove their way towards the stands with shouts and threats. Women were screaming, children crying, men shouting, no one seemed to be in command, someone tore down two of the banners.

'We had best be out of this,' Adam said, turning to Margaret. Then he saw Lunt. The man seemed to be in a frenzy and was orating, waving his hands, his hat off, his face congested with anger. In his hand he carried a short, thick club.

'Come,' said Kraft sadly. 'The curtain is down. The play is over.'

They turned together, but at the same moment Lunt caught sight of them. Like a madman he rushed at them, stopped in front of Kraft and shouted:

'Now where are you? You white, shaking coward! You and your friends! This is your work, with your psalm-singing, chicken-hearted caution! You have brought England to her knees, sold us like slaves!'

Kraft said quietly: 'Come, Henry. This is a farce.'

'Farce!' Lunt screamed. 'Yes! and who has turned it into a farce?'

'You and others like you,' Kraft answered sternly, his voice ringing out so that all heard him. 'I have warned you again and again, but you would not listen. With your violence you have frightened most decent men away. Aye, and lost most of our battles before they were even fought.'

Lunt's shouts had drawn a large crowd about them. Some excited men pressed forward, shouting incoherently, some laughed, some agreed with Kraft. But Lunt was beside himself; he moved in a whirlwind of passion in which he could distinguish nothing but his own disappointment, the failure of all that his egotism, yes, and his melodramatic self-sacrifice had for years been planning. He closed up to Kraft, who did not move.

'By heaven!' he shouted, 'I will show you who is a traitor! I'll teach your dirty cowardice!'

Kraft caught his arm.

'Be ashamed, man!' he cried. 'Go home to your wife and children!'

The touch infuriated Lunt, who thrust himself free, swung his club and brought it crashing on to Kraft's head. Kraft fell, his hand catching at Margaret's dress as he went down. Instantly there was silence. It was as though a hand caught the Common, the crowd, the sunlight, and, crushing it all into nothing, flung it away. There was emptiness and the sun shining on Kraft's white shirt and his twisted hand.

Adam was on his knees, his arm under Kraft's head that was crooked and veiled in blood. He looked up. 'A surgeon!' he said. 'For God's sake, someone, quickly, a surgeon.'

But he knew that Kraft was dead – the finest man in the world was gone. Tears blinded his sight as he bent again to the ground.

CHILDE ROLAND TO THE DARK TOWER

THIS was one of Judith's good days. This year, 1850, had not opened too well for her. For one thing in January she had had a splendid quarrel with Dorothy, had slapped Amabel (now a big stout girl of eleven) for riding one of the calves, had ordered Dorothy out of the house, had been told by Dorothy that she would not go, had discovered old Peach talking to one of her maids, had dismissed the maid and been of a mind to go up to the Fortress and tell Walter what she thought of him.

When this lively afternoon was over she had gone to bed, lain on her back and laughed aloud at her own bad temper. Dorothy had come in later to make the peace and discovered the old lady sitting up in bed, her lace cap a little askew on her snow-white hair, laughing and doing household accounts. They had embraced, as they always did after a quarrel, and Judith had settled down to the reading of Mr Thackeray's *Vanity Fair*. She had a passion now for novels, although she considered Thackeray too sentimental and something of a hypocrite. Becky, however, she could thoroughly enjoy and considered that there, but for the grace of God, went Judith Paris. Amelia and Dobbin she could not abide, but Rawdon had quite a deal in common with her dear Georges, who was as close to her still as he had been in 1790.

At the end of a chapter she had blown out the candle and lain down to sleep. She had slept for an hour or so and then woken suddenly to a sharp pain in the side. It was the first sharp pain she had ever known and she greeted it humorously as much as to say, 'Well, I knew you would come sometime. Now that you are here, behave as a gentleman.' The pain behaved badly at first and then, like a new acquaintance, having left his card, departed. But in the morning she felt very unwell indeed, tried to get up but could not, was finally in bed for a week. She was attended by Dr Fairchild from Keswick, a little wizened sarcastic man of middle age. They got on very well, were rude to one another, gossiped a good deal, and found that they had much in common.

He told her that she had the rheumatics and he put her on a diet. It was from this moment that she began to care about food. Food had never, all her life, been very important to her. She had always had a healthy appetite and took what came. But now that she was forbidden, she lusted. She liked to forbid herself, but hated that anyone else should forbid her anything. Moreover, Dr Fairchild, with a deliberate maliciousness, as it seemed to her, forbade her the very things for which she cared the most, and especially meat. She had encountered at odd times cranky persons who pretended to live entirely on vegetables. There was poor young Ivison, son of Mr Ivison the bookseller in Keswick, whose pale earnest countenance both amused and irritated her. It was said that he ate nothing but carrots and cabbage, and once, when she met the poor thin boy beside Mr Flintoft's Model of the Lake District, he had incontinently fainted there at her feet! So much for carrots and cabbages.

Nevertheless, she did on the whole as she was told, and now, at the beginning of March, was in fine vigour again. Her spirits were all the livelier, because just at this time John was given a holiday and came up with Elizabeth on a visit. It was a year and a half since they had been at Uldale. The house was very full and she adored it to be full. Dorothy's children were growing – Timothy was thirteen, Veronica twelve, Amabel eleven, and Jane (Judith's especial pet) was nine. Old Rackstraw taught Timothy Latin, and there was a governess, Miss Meredith. Miss Meredith Judith did not like at all, but she could not deny that she was an excellent governess. Miss Meredith, who was round and plump like a barrel, had all the present popular conventionalities. It was Judith's constant delight to shock her, for Judith could not in the least understand this great wave of propriety that had swept over the country. To allude to legs or bosoms or ardent young men or any of the processes of human creation seemed to Miss Meredith like death, and Judith perceived that not only Dorothy but the little girls themselves approved of these reticences.

'But, my dear Dorothy,' Judith would say, 'what is there shocking about being born? Why, I remember at Stone Ends when I was a girl—'

'When you were a girl, Aunt Judith,' Dorothy answered firmly, 'the world was a very different place. Not civilized at all.'

'I am sure,' Judith retorted, 'I can't say about being civilized, but babies are born in exactly the same way now as they were then. It would do Miss Meredith all the good in the world to be flung into a hedge by a tramp—'

But Dorothy was so greatly distressed that Judith desisted.

'*Please*, Aunt Judith,' Dorothy said. 'Do not offend Miss Meredith. She is the best governess in the world. Exactly right for the children. I don't know where we'd ever find such another.'

So Judith refrained, and only teased Miss Meredith when the temptation was quite irresistible.

She loved the house to be full, for she knew that she was a miracle for her age. Dorothy, with all her energy and obstinacy, had no say whatever in the running of the house. And Judith was not at all the conventional tyrannical old woman so common in works of fiction from the days of the Egyptians and maybe long before them. Everyone loved her. She was cared for now as she had never been in all her life before. How in the past she had longed to be liked! How it had hurt her when Will had disapproved and Will's mother hated her and Jennifer plotted against her! But now, when she had all the love that she could possibly desire, she did not greatly care for it. She hated sentiment and always preferred common sense.

Adam, of course, was a thing apart; she was deeply fond of John and Elizabeth, had an affection for Dorothy and the children, but, with the possible exception of little Jane, Adam was the only human being in the world whom she loved.

She certainly did not love herself, but she was proud of her age, her strength, her capability and, above all, her scorn for and successful battles over everyone at Ireby.

Of late Walter had been trying to irritate her in every way that he knew. Things were stolen, her house was spied upon, her servants were bribed, if there was any malicious story possible about anyone at Uldale it was spread in every direction. But Judith and Dorothy were exactly the women to fight a campaign like Walter's. They had much common sense and a strong feeling for the ludicrous. Dorothy was lacking in a sense of humour, but her sense of fun was so strong that to see a gentleman slip on the ice or a lady lose her bonnet in the wind made her stout sides ache with laughter.

So Walter seemed to her silly and Uhland unwholesome.

On this sunny day in March the weather was so warm that John and Elizabeth could walk comfortably up and down the lawn together. Judith, looking at them for a moment out of the parlour window, smiled with approval. John the night before had been most entertaining. If not of Parliament he was near it enough to have plenty of inside information. Both Judith and Dorothy were thrilled with interest as he told them of the hatred that the Queen and Prince Albert felt for Palmerston. Palmerston was John's hero, so he was a trifle malicious about the Queen and the Prince. Lord Clarendon, it seemed, had, a few weeks ago, dined at the Palace, and now it was all over the Town that the Queen in the drawing room after dinner had lost all control and spoken with so much vehement bitterness that Lord Clarendon had not known where to look; and when she had done the Prince had begun and, when Clarendon had visited him next day, had orated about Palmerston for two hours without stopping.

This gave the two ladies great pleasure to hear, not because they wished the Queen or Palmerston or anyone else any harm; simply that it brought the lawns and hedges of Uldale straight into the Palace.

So Judith looked out of the window at John and nodded her

approval. It was so fine a morning that she had put on a new
dress for the first time, a dress made especially for her by Miss
Sampson in Keswick. She wore more sombre colours now, although she still loved a touch of brightness here and there. As she
was wearing long drawers trimmed with lace, a flannel petticoat,
an under-petticoat, a white starched petticoat, and two muslin
petticoats under the dress, she had, for an old lady, a good deal to
carry. Very soon now the stiff bands of the crinoline were to
relieve ladies of their outrageous burden. Judith was wearing a
dress of grey taffeta with twelve flounces all of a dark shade of
green. Out of this 'like a lily-stem out of a flower-tub' rose her
dark-green bodice with pagoda sleeves and a very lovely white
lace collar (this last a present from Sylvia Herries the preceding
Christmas). Her only concession to her years was her white lace
cap. Her small, alert, vigorous body carried its cumbrous clothes
with grace and ease; her eyes sparkled like little fires. She had, as
she had always had, an air of crystalline spotlessness. The
muslins, the collar, the cap were new minted as though direct,
that minute, from some most perfect laundry. And so in fact they
were. Everything was laundered in the house and Mrs Kaplan
the housekeeper (Judith's slave) saw that all was perfection.

They were rich now at Uldale. Dorothy had money from Bellairs and her portion of Herries money. Judith's own investments,
shares in Liverpool concerns inherited from David Herries, land
and property round Uldale excellently supervised for many years
by Rackstraw, all mounted to an income well beyond their needs.
Judith had no desire for wealth, but she liked to have everything
handsome about her. Everything *was* handsome. On this lovely
March morning Uldale glistened like a jewel.

She went her rounds of the house, tapping with her stick and
humming a tune. She visited everything, the high-ceilinged
kitchen, pantry, servants' hall, housekeeper's room complete with
black cat, work-basket and flowered footstool. Then, perhaps
after the dairy the place that she loved best, the still-room. Here
were cakes, jams, preserves made; here was the china washed and
the dessert set out. Then the lamp-room, the store-room, the
meat-larder where were the weighing machine and the great
pickling jars. Then the wood and coal stores, the laundry, the
pump-room and the dairy. She stayed for an especial time this
morning in the kitchen, for its brick-floored spaciousness bathed
in sun was exceedingly pleasant. She stood there, smiling at the
maids, leaning on her stick, looking at the roasting-spits, the

Dutch oven, the chopping-block, the sugar-nippers, the coffee-grinder, the pot and pan racks, everything shining, gleaming, glittering as though active and happy with conscious, individual life.

All was good; all was well; still humming her tune she went out on to the sunlit lawn to find John and Elizabeth.

For a moment she looked back at the house – dear house to whose safety and comfort she had, through all her long life, returned again and again. There had been terrible hours here. She could see David Herries fallen, stricken on this very lawn, she could catch again Sarah Herries' distracted glance, could see Jennifer waiting for her lover, Francis' mad return and frantic exit, the rioters and poor Reuben's slaughter, her own tragic sur-render of Watendlath, the Christmas party and the fracas with Walter. There had been every kind of tragedy, farce, drama here; birth, death, ruin, love, humour, light easy days, pain and laugh-ter. She had come through it all, as one always did come through if one kept on patiently enough, did not take oneself too seriously, saw the sequence of event, of change, decay and birth in proper proportion. One came through to this sunlight, to this lovely landscape, this quiet English calm; then, turning, she saw that John was walking towards her and, with that quick intuition that she always had, wondered instantly whether after all the tale was told, whether there were not a number more of chapters to be added.

For John was alone and, she saw at once, in trouble. She had never quite understood John. She had loved Francis, his father, but had never understood him either. The alarms, fears, super-stitions, doubts of those two were foreign to her direct sensible nature. The part of her that had shared them she had deliberately killed.

John's slim, upright body, his pale hair, beautiful almost femi-nine features, had always marked him apart from other men. She thought, as she saw him approach her: 'John will never be out of trouble. He will never know what it is to rest.'

He came straight up to her and, his voice quivering a little, said:

'Aunt Judith. I have told Elizabeth I am going up to Ireby.'

She was astonished. A long grey shadow seemed to fall across the sunny lawn.

'Yes. Didn't you know? He has written her a letter: that scoun-drel Peach brought it half an hour ago.'

'A letter?'

'Yes. Here it is.'

He handed her a large sheet of paper scrawled over in Walter's big clumsy hand.

DEAR ELIZABETH – As a dutiful daughter you are to pay me a visit. If you don't come of yourself I shall fetch you. Your loving father,

WALTER HERRIES

'Loving father!' said Judith, her voice shaking with anger. 'What impertinence!'

'Yes. But of course Elizabeth mustn't go. She wished it, and I forbade her even to think of it. But *I* am going – and at once.'

As she looked at him he was again the small boy when the nurse had thrown the rabbit out of the window. He stood there, his head up, his nostrils quivering (exaggerated pictures of him, she thought, but spiritually true), like a high-bred horse, defiant but afraid of the whip because of the catastrophe that a contact might bring. She, too, was afraid of some disaster. She knew, as she looked at him, that she had always been afraid of it for him.

'No. Don't you go, John. I'll pay him a visit. I've been wishing to for weeks.'

'Nonsense,' John said roughly. Then, recovering himself, added: 'Pardon me, Aunt Judith. I didn't intend to be rude, but this is *my* affair. You must see that it is—'

She did not attempt to stop him after this, but only sighed to herself as she saw him mount his bay, wave his riding-whip to her, turning with that charming, rather weak, altogether lovable smile that was so like his father's that it always made her heart ache.

Where would this thing end, she thought, as she entered the house. When had it begun? – back, back, maybe to the days when her father had been a wild young man and sold his woman at the Fair, an old eternal quarrel between beauty and ugliness, normality and abnormality, sense and nonsense – a quarrel born, as all quarrels are in this world, of jealousy and fear. But she did not care for philosophy; she took things as they came, and what immediately came now when she entered the house was a quarrel with Dorothy, who wished to buy a sofa covered with wool-work and fringed with beads that she had seen in Carlisle. To buy this

monstrosity and place it in the parlour instead of the lovely old
one that had the red apples.

'But it's all the mode!' cried Dorothy. 'The Osmastons have
wool-work everywhere.'

'They may,' said Judith grimly, 'but so long as I'm up and
about that sofa remains in the parlour. Why, I was resting my
hand on it when I came to the most important decision of my
life.' Then she added as she tapped away on her stick: 'It's all
Prince Albert and his German taste. I detest the man.'

Meanwhile John rode down the road towards Ireby. It suited
his mood that the sky became overcast as he reached the bottom
of the Ireby hill. On his left a bubble of seething little white
clouds rose on the Skiddaw ridge, and other clouds rushed up to
the sun and, with gestures of sulky annoyance, swallowed it. He
hated himself for this fear that had seized all his bones like water.
The very thought of Uhland made him sick. But perhaps
Uhland would not be there. He did not mind Walter at all; he
was simply a gross, quarrelsome, bad-mannered fool. His
thoughts went back to that day in his childhood when, with
Adam, he had watched Walter on the moor. He had been afraid
then, but he saw now that it had been Uhland's shadow behind
Walter that had, like a prophecy, frightened him. He had been
afraid of Uhland before he was born.

He tried now, as he rode slowly up the hill, to formulate that
fear, to bring it into the open. But it would not come. That was
the awful thing about it. When he forced himself to think of
Uhland, or was compelled to do so, he saw him as a shapeless,
boneless animal emitting some sickening odour, as one sees a
creature in a dream, lurking in shadow in a dank cave or the
corner of a cellar, or behind a stone. The hide-and-seek that
Uhland had played with him now for so long had introduced
into his own soul and body some sickly element, so that, at times,
he believed that Uhland was some part of himself – that part we
all have, hidden, shameful, lurking. There was nothing shameful
in his life except this one cowardice. In everything else he was
brave, and so all the more did he feel this one exception to be
real.

He raised his head as he saw the grey stone house squatting, in
its trees, on the top of the hill. Today he would force this thing
into the open; it should skulk, just out of touch and feeling, no
longer.

He tied his horse to the wall outside the garden and walked up the flagged path to the door. Stone frowned at him everywhere.

The gardens were trim but dead. It was late March, and the daffodils were in full golden flood under the rosy Uldale walls. Here, too, beneath the dark trees beyond the flowerbeds they flamed in little cups of fire, but the garden itself was black and gritty. As John stood there banging the knocker of the door, the whole place leered down on him.

It was not that it was so large, but that it was so dead. The windows had no faces, the stone turrets were like clenched fists, and worst of all, there was no sound at all anywhere.

At Uldale there was always sound – laughter, singing, running water and the light chatter of birds. He wondered, above the beating of his heart, that there was not a bird singing in the Ireby gardens.

At last there was a creaking of bolts and the door slowly opened. An old bent man whom John had never seen before stood there; he had bow legs and was dressed in the style of thirty years earlier, black worsted stockings, black knee-breeches, a rather soiled neckerchief, and a dull brown tye-wig that cocked a little over one eye. He had a tooth missing, and his words whistled through his lips.

'Is Mr Walter Herries at home?' John asked.

'If you'll wait I'll see,' said the old man, looking out into the garden as though he expected to see a lion rooting up the bulbs. 'What name shall I say?'

'Mr John Herries.'

His mind seemed to be on other things as he ambled away, leaving John in the hall. The hall was stony and bare. There was a fireplace with grinning fire-dogs and a large stand hung with heavy coats and stacked with whips. There was no carpet on the stone that struck the feet icily. He stood there, wondering whether the old man would not forget him, when a green baize door to his left opened and a woman came out. She was not young but not old either, and very extravagantly dressed in a Russian short jacket of gold brocade figured with bunches of flowers in coloured silks. Her skirt had so many flounces that she appeared to be robed ten times over. She wore a bonnet lined with rosebuds, and her cheeks were rosebuds too, only extremely artificial, for John had never seen a lady more brightly painted. This brilliant person brushed past him as though he were not there, and she was swearing like a trooper. She turned towards the stairs and shouted:

'Hell take your meanness, Walter!'

She was so angry that she stared at John without seeing him.

As though from nowhere a very large stout man in a night-cap and a rich flowered dressing-gown appeared on the stairs. He was grinning, his nightshirt was open at the neck and he carried a very small brown hairy dog in one hand by the scruff of its neck. Very good-humouredly he called out, leaning with his free hand on the banister: 'Au revoir, my dearest,' and threw the dog to the lady. John started forward, but the lady was quicker, caught the dog with wonderful dexterity, and rushed from the house, banging the door behind her.

Walter wiped his large hands in a handkerchief that very deliberately he took from his dressing-gown. He was about to vanish when John called out:

'Cousin Walter.'

He peered forward down into the dark hall.

'Hullo. Who's there?' he asked.

'John Herries. I wish to have a word with you.'

Walter came slowly down the stairs, drawing his dressing-gown about him, his slippers tip-tapping. He came right up to John and bent forward, peering at him.

'Oh, it's you, is it?' he said at last. 'Where's my daughter?'

He was very clean-shaved, and his cheeks, round and rosy, shone like a baby's and smelt freshly of some scent. His face was fat, but his neck and exposed chest were white and firm. His mouth, eyes, and thin hair protruding from the night-cap gave him the look of age, for he was only fifteen years older than John in reality, but looked quite of another generation. His body was of great size and had a balloon-like appearance under the dressing-gown.

'May I speak to you?' asked John.

'You may,' said Walter quite amiably. 'Come upstairs.'

John mounted after him, and Walter led the way into a room that was as untidy and uncomfortable as a room could be. There was a spitting, smoky little fire in the grate; a carpet, red with a buff pattern and a large tear, in front of the fireplace; two pier-glasses; a wool-work ottoman and a large harp leaning against the wall. The room smelt of caraway-seed and was very close.

Walter, his legs stretched, stood in front of the fireplace and motioned John to a seat.

'If you're cold,' he said, 'I can't help it. Didn't know you were coming. Have a brandy.'

'No, thank you,' said John, turning his hat round and round in his hands.

'Well, what do you want now that you are here?'

'You wrote a letter to my wife. I am here to answer it.'

Walter scratched his head under his night-cap and grinned. Then he sat down in a large faded green leather chair and stretched out his thick hairy legs, kicking off one slipper and crinkling up his toes.

'Forgive my attire, Cousin John,' he said. 'That bitch of a woman put me out this morning – and now I've put *her* out.' He threw his head back and laughed. 'Have a brandy. Pray, have a brandy,' he said again.

'No, I thank you,' said John very ceremoniously.

'Well, I will.' He pulled an old red worsted bell-rope and so still was the house that the clang of the bell could be heard echoing, echoing into eternity. 'Now then,' he said, 'why isn't my daughter here?'

'She is not here, neither is she coming.'

'Well, that's straight enough. But she *is* coming if I want her.'

'You have no sort of right to her,' John answered hotly. He was glad if he was getting angry. That made him less conscious of the silent house, less aware of his own anticipation of Uhland's entrance.

'And why have I no right? I'm her father, aren't I?'

'You ill-treated her, and then when she ran away because she was so miserable you made no kind of inquiry as to her whereabouts. She might have died for all you cared.'

Walter yawned, scratched his breast, leaned forward, shaking a fist.

'Look you here, Cousin John. Let me tell you something. You are in danger, you are. It began with your mother, who was impertinent to my mother. I gave her a warning, but she wouldn't listen, and I frightened her into her grave. When she was gone I warned you that you'd better be after her – all of you. But you wouldn't take the warning, and, more than that, you have the damned impertinence to marry my daughter – 'gainst my wishes too. I don't bear you a grudge. I don't bear anyone in this world a grudge except my old father who goes cohabiting with a woman young enough to be his daughter and gets a child by her. Disgustin' – simply disgustin'. No, I don't wish you ill, but I've been telling the lot of you these years back to move out of

Uldale, and you will not listen. You are in danger, Cousin John, and if you won't drink a brandy like a gentleman you'd better be off. I've had an irritating time already this morning, and I don't want another.'

'You needn't think,' said John, getting up, 'that we are afraid of you. We know all the dirty little games you've been playing, putting Peach on to rob and spy, bribing the servants, but it doesn't affect us, not an atom.'

'Does it not?' said Walter cheerfully. 'No, because you've that old woman in the house. She's a hard-plucked one, she is. I've been fighting her for years, and upon my soul there is no one in the world I admire more. But it won't go on for ever, you know. Dear me, no. There'll be a nasty family crisis one of these days. You can tell the old lady so.'

The old bow-legged man with the brown wig arrived with a bottle and two glasses. Walter filled one tumbler half full and drank it off.

'That's better,' he said. 'And now you'd better be going.'

He got up and shuffled his great body across the room, yawning, scratching his back, his night-cap tilted over one ear.

'Dam' bitch,' he said. 'I wish I'd broken the bones of that dog.' He kicked the harp with the toe of his slipper. 'That was her doing,' he said, jerking his head. 'Thought she could play on it. Forced me to order the thing from Carlisle . . .' He swung round at the door.

'Uhland hates you, you know,' he said, grinning like a schoolboy. 'Hates you like a poison. Don't know why. Always has.'

John said nothing.

In the passage Walter said:

'Ever been over this house? Chilly place. Draughty as hell.' He threw open a double door. This was the salon where the fine opening Ball had been given. Here were the tapestries, and the decorations, hanging garlands and the dazzling stars of heaven. But the floor was filmed with dust, there was a large patch in the gilded ceiling, a corner of the tapestry flapped drearily against the wall, a chair was overturned, and there were bird-droppings on the long windowsill.

'Fine room,' said Walter. Then, closing the doors behind him, he said: 'There are rooms and rooms in this place. Too many rooms.'

Somewhere a dog was howling and a door banged, monotonously, like a protest.

'Goodbye, then,' said Walter, nodding. 'I am sure I don't know why you came.'

'I came in answer to your letter.'

'Ah, yes. Well, it's my daughter I wish to see. No one else.'

'I came to tell you that. That she will not come.'

'Yes.' He nodded. 'She will, though – if I want her. Damn that dog. There's no peace in this house.' He shuffled off, disappearing quite suddenly. And he was replaced, for John, hearing a sound, looked to the left, and there on the stone step of a little winding stair stood Uhland.

He said nothing. He was dressed in black, with a single flashing diamond in his stock. He said nothing, he turned back up the staircase, tapping with his stick. And John followed him. The silence of the house, broken only by the distant yapping of the dog, compelled him, and the film of dust that seemed to be floating everywhere in the house compelled him. But he went because he was ashamed not to go; the fear that so maliciously squeezed his heart would mock at him all his life long if he did not go. And he went because Uhland wanted him to go.

At the top of the little stone staircase the tapping stick led him through an open door into Uhland's room. This was furnished with a four-poster, a parrot in a cage, a sheepdog lying on the floor by the window, a grand view straight down the hillside to Uldale, a bookcase, a pair of foils and a bare shabby table and two old brown chairs.

Uhland stood in the middle of the room and looked at him.

'And pray what have you come for?' he asked him.

They faced one another for the first time, as it seemed, for many years, and even now John could not bring this face and body to any definite terms. It was indistinct, floating in dust, wavering into space. The room smelt of animals, the bed was unmade, the sheets tossed about. The sheepdog paid them no attention, but slowly licked a paw that was wrapped in very fresh white linen.

John was not indistinct to Uhland. He hated, as he looked, every particle of him; the high aristocratic carriage of his head, his gentle amiable eyes, his handsome clothes and, most of all, he both hated and loved his fear of himself. He drew lines with his stick on the worn dusty carpet.

'What have you come for?' he asked again.

John's words stuck in his throat; he could not help himself. It may have been the close air and animal smell. He forced himself, as though he were beating with his foot on the floor, to speak.

'I came to see your father about a private affair,' he said at last. 'But now I am here I should wish to know what the hell you mean by following me, spying on me in London and elsewhere during these last years?'

'Ah, you've noticed that, have you?' said Uhland.

They both knew that it would need only a gesture, a careless movement, for them to be at one another's throats. If Uhland had not been lame, John must have sprung forward, and oh! the relief that that would be, the clearing away, as one sweeps off cobwebs, of years of dreams, nightmares, shame and terror. But he could not touch a cripple, and, more than that, as Uhland drew lines with his stick on the floor, he seemed to place a barrier between them.

'Well,' Uhland said, 'it has amused me to make you uncomfortable. You are such a coward, so poor a creature, that anything can frighten you. And you had the impertinence to marry my sister.'

'If you were not lame,' said John, 'I would show you whether I am a coward or no.'

'Ah, don't allow that to stop you. Lame though I am, I can look after myself. You have always been a coward. Everyone knows it.'

'If you were not Elizabeth's brother—'

'Another excuse.'

John drew a deep breath. He could not help himself, but this thick close air made the room swing about him. Uhland's stick hypnotized him.

'I'll show you—' he began. 'If I am disturbed by you any more I shall forget your weakness and make you sorry you were ever born. I've warned you. I won't warn you again.'

He turned to go. He saw the dog raise its head, heard the parrot scratch the bars, then knew that the closeness of the room gripped his windpipe, darkened his eyes. The floor swirled up like a wave and struck him. He fainted, sinking limply back against the legs of the chair.

Uhland looked at him, hesitated, then went to the washing-basin, fetched the jug and bent down, his arm under John's body, splashing his forehead with the water.

He had John's body in his arms. He put his hand beneath his shirt and felt the smooth firm warm skin above the heart. He drew the body close to his own, and his long thin fingers passed over the face, the neck, the open shirt. His own heart was beating tumultuously. With one hand he very gently bathed the forehead just as he bathed one of his wounded animals, with the other he pressed his fingers on the mouth, felt the warm lips under his touch, stroked the strong throat, looking always into the eyes.

His hand pressed more intently on the mouth; then he shuddered through all his body. He saw that John's eyes were slowly, dazedly opening, so he drew away, letting the other collapse against the chair. He got up, threw a look about the room, and, very quietly, went out.

EXHIBITION

'I AM as excited as a child,' said Judith.

'You *are* a child,' answered Dorothy severely. 'Do wrap your shawl more closely or you will catch the most dreadful chill.'

'Chill – pooh!' said Judith, leaning over the edge of Will's most handsome carriage that she might see the better an extraordinary Frenchman in beard, felt hat and full pantaloons.

They had come to London to stay with Will for the opening of the Great Exhibition.

Long before their departure from Cumberland the Exhibition had penetrated their seclusion. For weeks and weeks no one in Keswick, Bassenthwaite, Cockermouth, Buttermere Valley, Penrith or anywhere else had had any other thought but of the Exhibition and the possibilities of a visit to London. Old Bennett, for example, had received from somewhere in London a plan of a monster lodging-house that would be designed to 'put up' at least a thousand souls from the country at one and the same time 'for one and three per night', and for this small sum each and every person was to be provided 'with bedstead, good wool mattress, sheets, blankets and coverlet; with soap, towels and every accommodation for ablution, a surgeon to attend at nine o'clock every morning and instantly remove all cases of infectious disease'; there was to be 'a smoking room, detached from the main building, where a band of music was to play every evening, gratis' and 'cold roast and boiled beef and mutton, and ditto ditto sausages and bacon, and pickles, salads and fruit pies (when to be procured) were to be furnished at fixed prices', all the dormitories were to be 'well lighted with gas'; to secure the complete privacy of the occupants they were 'to be watched over by efficient wardens and police constables', and finally, 'the proprietor pledged himself that every care should be taken to ensure the comfort, convenience and *strict discipline* of so large a body.'

What could be fairer than that? Everyone was going. On a certain morning almost the whole of Uldale and Ireby villages departed in carts and carriages for the 'Travellers' Train' at Cockermouth. Others journeyed to Carlisle and met the train for London there. For hundreds of persons round and about Judith's little world this was the first real journey of their lives.

And it was, in fact, oddly enough, Dorothy's first train journey too. She was never one to allow her emotions to get the better of her, but she did cry a little as she left Timothy, Veronica, Amabel and Jane to the rotund Miss Meredith. She had never before been absent from them for a single day, but Miss Meredith was 'the safest person in the world', nothing could have appeared more secure that morning than the Uldale lawns and rosy walls happy under the soft April sun. When, at the station, she beheld the porters in their green velveteen jackets, heard the engines fizzling, and the large bells announcing the coming of a train that soon arrived, bumping and groaning as though in fearful agony; when, safely in their carriage, they were entertained by a stout gentleman with the grandest whiskers who warned them in a voice, husky and urgent, about the perils of London – the cracks-men, the rampsmen, the snorzers and thimble-screwers, all these exciting varieties of pickpockets and murderers – when at last arriving in the Metropolis and waiting outside the station for their luggage to be brought to them, there occurred, 'under their very noses, just as though they were in a theatre', a 'school of acrobats', and an 'equilibrist' spun plates high in air, balanced burning paper-bags on his chin, and caught cannon-balls in a cup on the top of his head – why, then Dorothy forgot her children entirely and surrendered completely to her adventure.

She had thought that her main occupation in London would be to take care of Judith, but she very quickly discovered that Judith took care not only of her but of everyone else in her company.

During the first evening at the house in Hill Street, Judith put the second Lady Herries in her proper place in exactly five minutes. She laughed at her, pinched her chin and exhorted her thus: 'Now you mustn't mind me, my dear. I'm seventy-seven years of age and nothing ails me. Wonderful, isn't it? I need no looking-after. I came to London as a very young girl and was not at all alarmed by it, so it's most unlikely that I shall be alarmed by it now. I knew Will long before you were born – that is the prettiest cashmere, my dear; where *did* you discover it? – yes, and Will knows me too, do you not, Will? So you are not to disturb yourself about me. I shall have *everything* I want, I am certain. And now, may I not see little Ellis? I am dying for a sight of him.'

Dorothy perceived that no one in the large cold house had anything of Judith's fire and vitality, and that that same fire burnt only quietly at Uldale. She realized for the first time how much of her personality Judith subdued in the country, and how patient Judith had often been with herself and her children.

'Judith is a marvellous woman,' said Will that evening. 'More marvellous every time I see her.'

'Yes,' said Dorothy meekly.

That was Will's opinion of Judith; Judith's opinion of Will was that he was pathetic. Will was eighty-one years of age and could only go out for an airing, sitting in his carriage, wrapped up like a mummy and with someone at his side to blow his nose, see that his feet were warm and that his hat was on straight. This 'someone' was never Lady Herries, but rather his attendant, Robins, a thin, severe, black-haired man of very religious principles. Lady Herries paid no attention to her husband whatever. She made a sort of a show on the first night of Judith's visit, gave him his pills and wrapped a shawl around his shoulders, but after that the virtuous Robins did everything, cutting his meat for him, pouring him his wine and suddenly remarking sternly: 'No, Sir William. No potatoes. They are forbidden.'

However, Will did not seem greatly to care. Judith was astonished at his subservience. Was this the stern and austere Will who had commanded so implacably poor weak-jointed Christabel? 'Shall I be like that soon?' thought Judith. 'I prefer death.'

But Will did not care, because he had one constant, eager, unceasing preoccupation – 'little Ellis'. Little Ellis was now eight years of age and as small and wizened a boy as you would be likely to find. He was accounted exceedingly sharp, had a money-box into which he was constantly putting sixpences, and inquired the price of everything. Will thought him wonderful and quite frankly now spoke of Walter and Uhland as ungrateful wretches.

He saw Judith as Walter's principal aggravator and this made him admire her more than ever. He liked to dilate on the riches that he was leaving Ellis — Walter was not to have a penny, nor Uhland, 'that surly peevish cripple', anything either. John and Elizabeth, however, were to receive a good legacy. Elizabeth he now loved. He had her to the house whenever he was able, and she, better than anyone else, seemed to understand and comfort him.

Of his wife he never spoke, but his allusions to 'poor, good Christabel' gave Judith to understand that ghosts can, once and again, have their proper revenge.

Now that it was clear that Will would not live much longer, visits of members of the Herries family to Hill Street were frequent. It was not that they were greedy: they cared neither for money nor poverty. But Will was now the most important member of their family, and the death of an important Herries was, in their eyes, a world affair. Carey Rockage, James Herries (a most tiresome and pompous old bore of seventy-two), Stephen Newmark (who considered himself a Herries and then something), Amery, Fred Ormerod (cousin by marriage of Monty Cards and a gay, drinking bachelor), Bradley Cards (a nephew of Jennifer's), Tim Trenchard (a busybody cousin of Garth's and Amery's), all these men with wives, daughters and appendages drove up to Hill Street, left cards, came and sat in the long, dreary drawing-room and asked Lady Herries to receptions.

Of them all Judith liked best to see Sylvia. She had loved Sylvia from the moment of their first meeting and she loved her still, although the beautiful, bright, impertinent girl she had first known was now a weary, over-painted, discontented middle-aged woman. Sylvia had been fighting too long the battle of living above your means. Had it been her lot to have married a man of large and assured fortune she would have been a brilliant and successful leader of Society and, at the last, a contentedly reminiscent old lady. But Garth was a cheerful, corruptible vagabond. They had neither of them morals nor honesty. They had stolen, cheated, lied all their lives long, always without any desire to hurt or damage, but hurt and damage they had — first their friends and acquaintances, last of all themselves. Moreover, the London that now surrounded them was not their own; the raffish, speculating, bouncing world of the Thirties was succeeded now by the serious, earnest, virtuous and hypocritical world of the Fifties. To be fair to Sylvia and Garth, they did not know how to be hypocritical, nor did they think it good manners to be earnest. So they were shabby and left-behind and out at heels.

Sylvia wept on Judith's bosom; the paint ran down her cheeks, and before she left she accepted ten pounds from Judith with a readiness that showed that every day of her life she was accepting small sums from someone.

Elizabeth had one talk with Judith that disturbed her greatly. Elizabeth was now thirty-six but was as remotely lovely as she had ever been. That delicate bloom and fragrance belonged to her still. On the afternoon of this talk she was wearing a costume of the new 'crystallized' gauze so that she seemed the floating cloud to which ladies at that time were so fond of comparing themselves. She was quite unaware of her loveliness: Judith, watching her with sharp, practised eyes, thought that it was as though she lived under a glass bell with John, everything and everybody shut away from them. And she was very unhappy about him.

'He cannot sleep at night,' she said. 'He thinks that I am not awake and he talks to himself. He slips out of bed very quietly and goes into the other room and walks about. I am so frightened, Aunt Judith.'

Judith kissed her, held her hand, but there was always something stiffly independent about Elizabeth. She asked for help but refused to accept it. Also she loved John, Judith thought, too deeply for it to be healthy.

'Is he worrying about your father?'

'I suppose so – or rather it is Uhland. Uhland obsesses him, and since he went up to Ireby that day last year it has been worse.'

'Well, my dear child, I've been fighting your father for years and am none the worse. John should see this sensibly.'

'But it seems like something in his blood, something inside himself. As though he were pursued by Uhland. It is a fantasy, Aunt Judith – not real at all. After all, what can Uhland do?'

'His father had the same, and his great-grandfather; something that would never let them alone. Well,' Judith sighed impatiently, 'I cannot understand it. I never could. When there's a difficulty or a danger, face it. Don't run away from it.'

'John does face it,' Elizabeth answered indignantly. 'You must not think he is a coward, Aunt Judith. He's tremendously brave in everything – but this is like a sickness.'

Judith nodded her head; there were two worlds, she knew, and unless you found the connexion between them you never found peace. Once she had herself had to make a choice. She had made it and was now the old woman she was in consequence.

Then she found that it was a very fine thing to give cheap advice to others, but that she had her own trouble to face. Her trouble – one that she had never expected nor considered – was that she was plunged, willy-nilly, into a sea of jealousy about Adam. Willy-nilly because, cry out as she might, refuse to be, at her age, so mean and small and petty, there she was in it up to the neck.

Adam had of course been the great central fact of her visit to London. To see the Great Exhibition certainly, but to see it with Adam. To lean on Adam's strong arm everywhere, to have the delicious intimate little talks with him, simply the two of them alone in her room, that had been for many years now her greatest happiness in life, to feel, above all, that no one had the close relationship with him that she herself had. It was not that she wished to shut Margaret out. She was neither so selfish nor so stupid. Moreover, she had fought that battle before and had won a victory. But her later life had been built up on the absolute intimacy of herself and her son, an intimacy that no one and nothing could break. She was, however, becoming greedy, greedy of her vitality, her uniqueness. She was 'Madame', the most marvellous old lady in Cumberland and, if she wished, the most marvellous old lady in London. This was nothing in her as cheap and petty as conceit, but the sort of amused triumph we all feel when we are clever at a game. All this was on the surface, but her very soul was possessed by her love for Adam. No one knew how deep that went. She had only loved two people in all her life, her husband and her son, but she loved them like a tigress. At the same time she had human enough wisdom and tolerance enough to keep the tigress behind bars.

Never before had her relationship with Adam been threatened as it was now. She perceived at once that the reason of it was the sudden and violent death of Margaret's father. She had not known of the scene between Margaret and Adam that Christmas-time at Uldale. That would have informed her yet further had she been aware of it. But since Caesar Kraft's death she had seen very little of Adam and Margaret. They had paid only one brief visit to Uldale. She was quite unprepared for this change.

It was not that Adam was not as devoted as ever. He was there at Hill Street to meet her on the first evening. When they were alone in her room, he took her in his arms and hugged and kissed her as though he would never let her go.

'Why, how strong you are, Adam!' she cried, laughing and crying and happy as a queen. It was after this that she perceived that his thoughts were always on Margaret. *He* was of course as silent as ever, but her first sight of Margaret told her that there was here a new assurance and certainty. Margaret possessed Adam now and was quietly radiant because of it. They had three rooms in Pimlico. Adam wrote for the papers, knew Dickens and John Forster, Yates and Wilkie Collins. He was not of the writing world, stayed quietly outside it, made few friends, but made those few firmly. He wrote considerably about politics, reviewed books a little, and said cheerfully to his mother that the only things he really wanted to write were fairy stories.

'Fairy stories!' Judith cried, looking at Adam's stocky, thick-set frame and ugly unromantic countenance.

'Don't be afraid, Mother,' he said, laughing. 'I shall never write them. I must earn our bread and butter, but a good fairy story – there must be a handsome satisfaction in writing a good fairy story.'

This was nonsense of course, so she told him sharply, but it annoyed her that Margaret should think it quite a natural thing for him to do. 'Yes,' Margaret explained, 'he has found real life so very absurd.'

'Nonsense,' Judith answered. 'I never listened to such stuff. Fairy stories! A man like Adam! Why, he has a chest like a bull's!'

She soon discovered that her relations with her son and daughter-in-law were complicated by her advancing years. She was a wonderful old lady, but she could not do as she used to do. She took her breakfast in bed every morning and did not rise until midday. She was forced to confess that she returned to Hill Street exceedingly weary after her shopping expeditions. It was necessary, therefore, for Adam and Margaret to come to her rather than that she should go to them, and she thought that Margaret accompanied her husband too frequently.

Being direct and honest, she immediately said so.

'My dear boy, I am in London for a very brief visit. I have one foot in the grave. I love Margaret, of course, but I love you more.'

He said nothing (he never did say anything), but he came

alone. Then she fancied that he was thinking of Margaret and wishing that he were with her.

She would interrupt some Cumberland piece of gossip with a sharp: 'Now, Adam, you are not attending. You are thinking of Margaret.'

Jealousy began to mount in her as the tide swells a sea-pool. She slept now but badly, and before had not minded that, for she would lie and think of the old days, of Georges and Reuben and Charlie Watson and Warren, Adam's father, until the room seemed crowded with their figures; but now she could think of nothing but Adam, and, with the fantastic exaggeration that the night hours give, she would beat her thin little hands together and cry to herself that she had lost him for ever, that she was a miserable, deserted old woman, and that she might as well die. It was then that her poignant despair at the choice that so many years ago she had made for the sake of Jennifer, John and Dorothy, would strike her like a voice of doom.

'Ah! if I had but gone with Adam to Watendlath he would have been mine for ever!'

But in the daylight she was by far too sensible and blessed with too strong a sense of humour to tolerate such obvious melodrama. She laughed at herself, her fears, her selfishness. Nevertheless her jealousy mounted. She was as sweet as Tennyson's Miller's Daughter to Margaret, but Margaret was not deceived. The trouble with both Margaret and Adam was that they were so quiet. You could not tell what they were truly thinking!

Poor Judith! Jealousy is from the Devil. It was hard for her that she should have to fight her first real battle with him at so advanced an age!

The Great Day approached. The Great Day arrived!

But the whole of London was by this time an Exhibition. Foreigners were everywhere – Germans, Turks, Americans, French and even Chinamen. On every side amusements were springing up, M. Alexis Soyer opened his Restaurant of All the Nations, there was 'the Black Band of His Majesty of Tsjaddi with a hundred additional bones', the Musicians of Tongoose, the Troubadours of Far Vancouver, the Theban Brothers, and the most celebrated Band of Robbers from the Desert. Barnum provided a splendid entertainment, whereby for a rather costly ticket a guest was provided with 'a bed, a boudoir and a banquet, together with one hour's use per diem of a valet and a private chaplain, free admission to theatrical green-rooms, a seat in the House of Commons, and a cigar on the Bench of Judges'. Mr Catlin reopened his Indian Exhibition, and Mr Wyld would take you on the 'Grand Tour of Europe', or a visit to Australia or New Zealand for threepence a time.

But it was enough for Judith and Dorothy simply to view the crowds in the streets. The road to the Crystal Palace was an amazing scene. Trains of wagons lengthened far away, like an Eastern caravan, each waiting for its turn to be unloaded. Omnibuses, carriages, carts, barrows congested the road. The public houses, of which there were a great number, hung out gay and patriotic flags, and their doors were crowded with loafers, soldiers, beggars and women with shawls over their heads. Along the pavement were lined the hawkers shouting their wares, trays filled with bright silvery-seeming medals of the Exhibition, pictures of it printed in gold on 'gelatine cards', many barrows with ginger-beer, oranges and nuts.

Along Rotten Row troops of riders galloped noiselessly over the loose soft ground at the rear of the Crystal Palace, while in front of it an interminable line of carriages crawled slowly past. Close to the rails were mobs of spectators on tip-toe, their necks outstretched, seeking glimpses of progress. All along the building were ladders with painters perched high upon them and walking on the crystal covering which miraculously sustained them. At the end of the building were steam-engines puffing clouds of steam, and amid the wreckage of thousands of packing-cases were giant blocks of granite, huge lumps of coal, great anchors, the ruins of a prehistoric world. The noise, confusion, turmoil – who, asked Dorothy, could describe them? She was given to platitudes, and irritated Judith by insisting that 'such chaos is an emblem of man's energy working to a just end'. The Exhibition in fact turned her head a little spiritually, and made her so deeply proud of being a Herries that she seemed to walk like a goddess. All the Herries felt the same, that the Exhibition was their especial work and Queen Victoria the head of the family.

On the Great Day itself, the First of May, the heart of London beat with a pride and exaltation that was to affect the country for at least another fifty years.

Judith, Dorothy, Lady Herries, little Ellis, Adam, Margaret, John and Elizabeth had, all of them, thanks to old Will's power and position, splendid seats for the opening ceremony.

They started early, and that was wise, for the carriage was soon

involved in a long, wearisome procession of carriages from whose
windows every kind of bonnet and hat was poking and shrill
feminine voices exclaiming: 'But this is monstrous! We shall miss
the Queen! It is really too bad!'

John and Elizabeth were to join the others inside the building
and were already there when Lady Herries, dressed in a
magnificent purple bonnet and superb cashmere shawl, her head
very much up, led in her little procession. Judith came last,
leaning on Adam's arm.

They had excellent places, and the Sight, the Vision, the Glory
– this, as Dorothy remarked, 'exceeded all Expectations and
showed what Man could do when guided by the Divine Will'.
(Dorothy was not, in her normal Cumberland domesticity, in the
least like this. 'You are a little over-excited, my dear,' Judith had
told her that morning.)

Yes, it was superb! Their seats were in one of the galleries, the
galleries planted like flower-gardens with bonnets of pink,
yellow and white. The Great Central Glory was the Glass Fountain. Of this Archdeacon Rodney Herries' son, Captain William
Herries, RN, wrote in his *A Jolly Tar's Capers* (Weston and
Mary, 1895): 'This glorious fountain in the centre of the building, shining, as the sun's rays came slanting down upon it
through the crystal roof, as if it had been carved out of icicles, or
as if the water streaming from the fountain had been made suddenly solid and transfixed into beautiful forms. Although but a
rough, careless little Middy at the time, I can remember well that,
standing beside my father, at that time Archdeacon of Polchester
in Glebeshire, tears welled up into my youthful eyes and pride of
my country fired my ambition.

' "It is such families as ours in such a country as ours," I
remember my dear father remarking, "that, under God's Grace,
can create, for the benefit of the world, such wonders." '

It must be confessed that Judith saw it all less romantically.
Rodney Herries she had, incidentally, always detested. But
nevertheless she was carried away, forgetting years, jealousies,
aches and pains (for this morning she had a little rheumatism).
For one thing the noise was terrific. The waiting multitude was
quiet enough, but around them, throughout the building, all the
machinery had been set in motion – the MACHINERY, key-note
of the Exhibition, symbol, relentless, humourless, of the new
world that this day, May 1st, 1851, was introducing. There were
in the machine-room the 'self-acting mules', the Jacquard lace

machines, the envelope machines, the power looms, the model locomotives, centrifugal pumps, the vertical steam-engines, all of these working like mad, while the thousands near by, in their high hats and bonnets, sat patiently waiting, passive, unwitting that the Age of Man on this Planet was doomed.

Judith and Adam, John and Elizabeth, were most certainly unwitting. Judith's little hand was thrust through Adam's thick arm, while John and Elizabeth were holding hands under Elizabeth's shawl. Margaret was thinking of her father and wishing that he were here, Dorothy's mouth was wide open, and Lady Herries was studying a coarse-grained Chambéry gauze near to her and wondering whether she could obtain one like it. Yes, a superb scene! The canopy above the royal seat, adorned with golden cornice and fringe and a small plume of blue and white feathers at each angle, the floors clean and matted, at each corner of the central square stages for illustrious visitors, from the gallery tops magnificent carpets and tapestries hanging, here the Spitalfields Trophy with its gorgeous silks, and there, the supreme triumph for many, the wonderful plaster of Paris statues, so white, so gleaming, their nudity draped so decently with red cloth. A sob rose in many throats, too, at the sight of the splendid equestrian statues of the Prince and the Queen, so large and lifelike that you might imagine that at any moment the horses might start to charge down the central aisle. (This was Dorothy's fine whispered thought.) Here, to quote Captain William once again: 'Behind these was another Fountain' (it appears that he nourished a passion for fountains!) 'that made the stream as it rushed up from the centre and divided itself into a hundred drops, flashing in the sun as they fell, look like a shower of silver sparks – a kind of firework of water; and beside this rose the green plumage of the palm trees embedded in moss, while close at their feet was ranged a bed of flowers, whose tints seemed to have been dyed by the prismatic hues of the water-drops of the neighbouring fountain. Then appeared the old elm trees of the park, looking almost like the lions of the forest caught in a net of glass; and behind them again was a screen of iron tracery, so light and delicate that it seemed like a lace-work of bronze.'

A little later he continues: 'But it was when the retinue of the Court began to assemble that the scene became one – perhaps the most – gorgeous in colouring and ever beheld; for it was seen in the clear light of the transparent roof above. The gold-embroidered bosoms of the officers seemed to be almost alight with the glitter of their ornaments; there stood all the ministers of state in their glittering suits; the ambassadors of every country, some in light blues and silver, others in green and gold, others in white, with their bosoms' (incidentally a favourite word of the Captain's) 'studded with their many-coloured orders. There was the Chinese mandarin in his red cap, with peacock's feathers dangling behind, and his silken robes with quaint devices painted upon them in front and at the back. There was the turbaned Turk, and the red fez-capped Egyptian; and there were the chocolate-coloured Court suits, with their filigree steel buttons, and long, white embroidered silk waistcoats.

'There was the old DUKE too' (these are the Captain's capital letters) 'with his silver hair and crooked back showing most conspicuous amongst the whole. At the back and sides of the throne stood the gentlemen-at-arms, in their golden helmets, with the long plumes of white ribbon-like feathers drooping over them. Beside these were the portly-looking beefeaters, in their red suits and black velvet caps; and near them were the trumpeters, in their golden coats and close-fitting jockey-caps, with silver trumpets in their hands. Near these were the Aldermen, in their red gowns of office, and the Common-Councilmen in their blue silk gowns, and the Recorder in long powdered Judge's wig, the Archbishop in full lawn sleeves and close curly wig, the Musical Director in his white satin-damask robe and quaint-looking black cap, the heralds in their emblazoned robes, the Garter King-at-Arms in his gorgeous red velvet coat becrusted all over in gold – while round all these were ranged sappers and miners, in their red and yellow uniforms; and behind them were seen the dark-blue coats of the police.'

And the brave Captain complacently comments:

'It was a feast of colour and splendour to sit and gloat over – a congress of all the nations for the most hallowed and blessed of objects – one, perhaps, that made the two old soldiers, as they tottered backwards and forwards across the scene, the most noticeable, because in such a gathering for such an object, the mind could hardly help looking upon them as the last of the warriors to whom the nation would owe its future greatness. I could not but reflect,' the Captain adds, 'that my own family that has been proud to call England its mother for so many centuries had, under God's divine direction, helped sensibly by its honest devotion to duty and its consistent patriotism to bring this Great Country into its supreme world-dominating position.'

Then he continues after this little spurt of family pride: 'At a few minutes before the appointed hour the royal carriages with their bright liveries were seen to flash past the windows of the northern entrance; then darted by a troop of the Life Guards, with their steel helmets and breastplates glistening in the sunshine, and immediately after, the glass sides and roof of the Crystal Palace twanged with the flourish of trumpets that announced the arrival of the Queen. At this moment the gates were flung back, and within the crimson vestibule appeared a blaze of gold and bright colours.

'Then advanced the royal retinue, with the ushers and chamberlain in front, bowing as they moved backwards towards the throne; and after them the Prince leading the Princess Royal, and the Queen with the Prince of Wales, and followed by their Court.

'As the Queen moved onwards with her diamond tiara and little crown of brilliants scintillating in the light, the whole assembly rose and, waving their hats and fluttering their handkerchiefs, they shouted forth peal after peal of welcome.'

And here we may leave the excellent Captain in his happy state of obsequious reminiscence. His book is unquestionably of value, quite apart from its Herries interest, and is certainly worthy of a modern reprint. It attained six editions in the 'nineties.

Sad to say, Judith was not at all moved as was Rodney's son. For one thing the seat on which she was sitting was exceedingly hard, for another she was bothered by the noise of the machines, for another she was feeling odd in the head, a little as though she had been drinking. And for another she had never, in all her life, been impressed very greatly by domesticity: the Queen, the Prince, and their two children appeared to her so dreadfully domestic. That was on her father's side. On her proper Herries side she would have been undoubtedly more deeply impressed had she been quite at her ease. But she was distressed about John, about Adam, and a very little about herself. Most certainly she felt queer, as though there were a weight pressing on her heart, as though, unless she were careful, she would see double. She thought that, in all probability, this glittering and scintillating glass disturbed her. Absurd to build so large a place entirely of glass!

She could not resist, however, some beating of the heart when, as the Queen moved forward, wearing her diamond tiara and crown of brilliants, everyone rose and, waving hats, fluttering handkerchiefs, shouted their cries of welcome. Judith rose, fluttered her handkerchief, shouted with the rest. For a moment she was deeply stirred. The sturdy figure of Victoria appeared to divorce itself from all the world around it, as though it said: 'I am lonely. I am a Queen. I represent loneliness, austerity and power.'

She had that quality, was to have it all her life, of sudden dignified remoteness, so that she became a symbol, a promise, a prophecy. Judith, old enough to be that same Queen's grand-mother, felt that now. The white head and light-blue coat of the Master of the Queen's Music appeared on the rostrum, he raised his baton, and above what Captain Herries called 'the melodious thunder of the organ', the National Anthem – led by the choris-ters – filled the glass dome and was caught by the light and glitter and flung into the sunny heavens. The Archbishop asked for a blessing (the Machinery frantically responded), the Queen and Prince walked in procession, and then Her Majesty declared the Exhibition open. And to end once again with Captain Wil-liam: 'Immediately were heard the booming of the hundred guns without, telling the people of the Metropolis that the Great Exhi-bition of the Industry of All Nations had been formally inaugur-ated.'

Judith recovered herself and sat down. That reaction that inevitably follows all climaxes seized her. What, after all, was all this fuss about? It would only make the country and everyone in it exceedingly conceited. And how tiresome the Exhibition had already become! For months in advance of it no one had talked of anything else, and now for months after it no one would have any other topic. She looked down from the gallery, and the mere thought of all the plaster statues, the great organ, the fountain, the machinery, the furniture, the stalls covered with goods, the endless cups of tea, the ferns and plants and blossoming shrubs, the crying children, angry husbands and disappointed wives, all this wearied her beyond measure.

'I think that I will return to Hill Street,' she said to Adam.

'Very well, Mother dear, but first you must see just a few of the sights.'

She did not want to see any of the sights. She would like to be seated safely and privately in her armchair in her room at Hill Street.

Says Captain William Herries: 'Well might the nation be proud of its Crystal Palace. No other people in the world could have raised such a building . . .'

That is exactly what Judith thought, straining up her old eyes

to the glitter and the shine. 'All this glass,' she thought, 'so osten-
tatious', and her dislike of Prince Albert, assuaged for a moment
by the National Anthem, returned in full force.

Adam took her by the arm and she walked gaily along, with
Dorothy and Lady Herries very patriotic behind her, Margaret
on her other side, and John and Elizabeth not exchanging a
word.

'Why don't they speak?' she thought. 'Aren't they happy?' She
was wearing a soft grey bonnet and a mantilla of shaded grena-
dine. She walked as though she were twenty, with every once and
again a step that was rebellious, originating in some quite other
person. She still saw double on occasion, and there was a twinge
of pain in her right shoulder.

There were of course a great many things to see, and oh dear!
So many people! Bonnets and polkas, polkas and bonnets, green
and brown 'wide-awakes' and fluffy beaver hats – and then the
People, this time with a capital P! They will be *much* worse on
the shilling days, but there seem to be a great many of them, even
as it is, many with babies in their arms, many with baskets, many
with fat bursting cotton umbrellas.

'There are too many people,' Judith said to Adam. The pain in
her shoulder had spread to her armpit. 'Really,' she thought,
'Lady Herries is an *idiot*!'

Oh dear, there are a *great* many things to see! Here is a rail-
wayman, family following, his japan pouch by his side, hurrying
to see the locomotives; there a carpenter in a yellow fluffy flannel
jacket pointing out to two small boys the beauties of a huge top
formed of one section of a mahogany tree.

'Ridiculous!' Judith thought. 'No one in the world can wish
for a top as big as that!'

Here is a hatless and yellow-stockinged Bluecoat boy mounting the steps of one of the huge prismatic lighthouses to see the
way that it is made ... Look! There is a model of the Italian
Opera House, and behold! There is a minute and most extensive
model of Liverpool with a looking-glass sea and thousands of
cardboard vessels. This last Adam examined with the most
serious care. 'Remarkable! Very remarkable indeed!' he repeated
again and again.

Judith could not explain it, she was greatly ashamed but she
wanted to slap him. As with all mothers in the world there were
moments when she wondered whether these very prosaic results
were at all worth all the pains that she had taken.

'Did I bring him up for this?' she thought as she watched him so seriously count the cardboard ships. Then she caught Margaret's calm look of devotion and she hated Margaret. There was no doubt but that she was not at all well.

Of course they must see the machinery. For hours Judith had been dreading this moment. Pressed close against the stout limbs of a member of the National Guard— 'Really a *childish* costume,' she thought as she looked upwards to his conical hat with its little ball on top, and smelt the rough texture of his red worsted epaulettes and full-painted trousers – she was compelled to admire the power-looms, and then there was the steam brewery, then the model carriages moving along the new pneumatic railway, the hemispherical lamp-shades made out of a flat sheet of paper, the exceedingly noisy flax-crushing machine, the splashing centrifugal pump, the whirling of the cylindrical steam-press . . .

'Adam,' she whispered, drawing him a little closer to her, 'I am glad that I am an old woman. All these machines – what a very unpleasant world it is going to be!'

She whispered, because Dorothy and Lady Herries were in a state of fluttering ecstasy. 'Stupendous!' 'What an achievement!' 'Do observe those wonderful little wheels!' 'Man's triumph over Nature!' Dorothy was proving herself a true Herries. She saw Herries everywhere. If it had not been for the Herries family . . . Strange! Judith must certainly be unwell, for she wanted to slap both Dorothy and Lady Herries.

'Adam,' she whispered, 'I fear that I *must* sit down!'

There was no reply and, looking up, she saw that Adam was not there. Looking farther she discovered Adam and Margaret, a distance away, their backs turned to her, close together examining a piece of machinery. That was possibly the worst moment of her life. Absurd – so little a thing! And yet the horror of Georges' death, the tragedy of Francis' suicide, the awful evening of Adam's birth – none had touched the loneliness, the isolation of this neglect. Lady Herries was examining a miniature engine with a great assumption of technical knowledge, Elizabeth and John had disappeared.

Judith proudly, her bonnet up, walked away. As she reached the outer hall pain seized her, her heart was beating strangely. Her limbs trembled. Everyone around her seemed weary. On the steps of the red-cloth-covered pedestals weary women and children were seated, some of them munching thick slices of bread and meat. Around the fountains were gathered exhausted families drinking out of thick mugs. All over the floor were orange-skins, dirty pieces of paper; Judith sat down on one of the crimson steps, resting her head on her hands. Was she going to die in this ridiculous place with all these strangers around her? The noise of the machines rattled and quivered, piercing her very backbone. 'Am I going to die? Is this the end?'

A stout woman near to her, her legs spread, crooking a baby in one arm, was drinking out of a bottle. Strange, Judith thought, to allow such people in on the day of the Queen's first visit. But that was right. All were equal – all women together. She had read somewhere that after a certain hour the general public would be admitted. The sight of the woman strengthened and comforted her. She was herself a vagabond, born of vagabonds. No Herries, but daughter of a gipsy. Even though her son deserted her, even though all the pains in the world attacked her, even though this horrible machinery invaded the world, destroying peace and privacy, no one could touch her, she was independent.

She looked up, and there was John. He was standing quite near to her but did not see her. On his face was a look of pitiable distress. He held himself taut, his hands to his side, as if he were answering some charge. On every side of him the crowd pushed and thrust, but he was as alone as though no one else were in the world.

The sight of someone in trouble always caused her to forget herself. She rose, although her knees trembled, walked over to him and touched his arm. He started; her touch had drawn him from a dream.

'John, dear. Take me home. I am very tired.'

That charming kindly smile that she loved in him so much warmed her heart.

'Why, of course, Aunt Judith. We will find Elizabeth.'

She had her hand lightly on his arm. No one should know how ill she felt.

'Such a noise! So many people! I am realizing, my dear John, what a very old woman I am.'

'Nonsense, Aunt Judith,' he said, patting her hand. 'This would be too much for anyone.'

But as he looked at her with so kindly an expression, she realized that it was true: she was an old woman at last.

THE FUNERAL

THE last visit to London that she was ever to pay was early in 1854, and the occasion was Will's funeral.

They all said that it was defying Providence for her to go, for she was seventy-nine that Christmas, but she was determined: nothing and no one should stop her. In honest fact they all knew a fearful pride in her resolve. Seventy-nine and going to London! No one but a Herries could have done it, but the Herries always lived to a great age and died in their boots! Look at Will! Eighty-four and in the City three days before his death. It was true that he had been strapped up in his carriage like a mummy, and had held a sort of reception there in Threadneedle Street with clerks and people bowing to him on the steps of his offices: nevertheless, eighty-four and working in the City!

Judith was perfectly conscious of all the things that the different Herries, scattered about the country, would be thinking of her enterprise and, being half Herries herself, she was pleased that they should be pleased. Then of course she insisted that she must pay tribute to Will, for Will was part of her whole life, and now, when her youth was for ever present with her, intermingling with all the current events of her day so that it was often impossible to tell which was past and which was present, Will was perhaps nearer to her than he had ever been before. For as a girl she had never liked him; as a woman she had often despised him; but now, joined as they were in their old age together, she almost loved him.

She had, however, two principal motives for her departure. One was that she would see her beloved Adam, a motive sufficient to carry her *and* her coffin if necessary to the North Pole; and the other (although this she confessed to no one in the world) her desire to show Walter Herries that she was still alive and kicking.

Now, when she could not move about as she had once done, but must sit, either in the garden when it was sunny and warm, or in the parlour before the fire, or in her bed with her lace cap on her head and mittens on her fingers just like any other old lady (although she was not in the least like any other old lady!) events and persons were inclined, if you did not keep them in order, to acquire a gigantic significance.

On the one hand she was tranquil as she had never been in her life before. Old age certainly did that for you; and on the days when there was no pain to bother her (for pains of one sort and another paid her now quite constant visits), when she was neither wildly excited by some pleasure (like an unexpected dish for dinner or a sudden visit of a friend, or something entrancing that little Jane had been doing, or a piece of gossip) nor exasperated by some bit of foolishness or some alarm about Adam, why, then this tranquillity was marvellous! You just sat there, or lay there, and it lapped you round like a radiant sheet of golden light, light within you, above you, around you, while the trees burnt in gold steadily against the sky and the streams ran murmuring to your feet, and all this lovely world stood still for you. It was at such times (and they were many) that the past became the present and the present the future. Then there was no Time. She was a child again, watching them ride the horse up Tom Gauntry's staircase, and she was eating roast goose at the 'Elephant', she was walking beside dear Charlie Watson at Watendlath – all was alive again, nothing had died, she herself was immortal.

Nevertheless the things that disturbed, disturbed violently, and the thing that disturbed the worst was Walter. No climax had come as yet to their quarrel. That moment when she had turned to Jennifer and said (ah, how many years ago! Poor Jennifer!): 'Do not be distressed, my dear. I am going to remain,' that challenge had as yet reached no climax. But the climax would come. She knew it as though she were a prophetess and could see the future. Already enough unhappiness had been generated by that old, old quarrel. John's life, Elizabeth's life, Jennifer's life, Walter's life, Uhland's life – all these had been damaged by it, as hatred and jealousy and envy always damaged any lives that they touched. Her own life and Adam's had been changed by it, for she would have been in Watendlath long ago but for it, and still there was worse to come. She had stayed in Uldale and protected them all, but Walter was still there, the Fortress was still there, Peach's cottage (there was now a younger Peach in command) was just over her garden wall; Walter was a sot and Uhland a crazy misanthrope – but they were not gone, they still remained.

She had been told, only a week or two ago, that Walter had said of her: 'That old bed-ridden gipsy.' Bed-ridden, was she? She would show him! She would go to London if for no other reason!

· Nevertheless, it was Will that she was thinking of as she made her departure. Her heart was soft with tenderness.

Dorothy came with her and was full of matronly care and fuss. After the day of her visit to the Great Exhibition, Judith, to everyone's surprise and offering no reason, abandoned her gay colours and adopted a kind of uniform, black with white ruffles and white lace at the throat. With her hair that had the shining softness of snow and the deep white upon white of an evening cloud, with her small pale face, her exquisite neatness and cleanliness, carrying in her hand her cane, she had the air of some austere Mistress of Ceremonies. But then her whole body and nature laughed at austerity. As she grew older her sense of fun, enjoyment of little things and active consciousness of that enjoyment, her eagerness for news, her avidity for sharing in everything, these things constantly increased in her. Her heart – she was warned that she must be careful of her heart. 'My heart?' she laughed. 'It's as sound as one of Dorothy's muffins' (for Dorothy was a good housekeeper but a heavy-handed cook). Then there was the rheumatism, and sometimes she felt faint. Once indeed she fainted in her bedroom, but no one was there with her and no one was told of it. On many days she was as well and strong as Veronica and Amabel – both very healthy girls. One afternoon she slapped Veronica very heartily indeed because that child, aged now sixteen, told her that God disapproved of reading common books on a Sunday.

'You are a prig, the most dreadful animal in Creation,' Judith cried, and when Veronica, losing her temper, shouted, 'And you're a gipsy,' Judith slapped her. Veronica, who was not a bad child, was appalled at what she had done, and Judith walked all the way upstairs and brought her down a bag of peppermints. (Judith liked peppermints and always kept a store in her bedroom.) All this in one afternoon.

Moreover, with her favourite Jane, now a wisp of a child of thirteen, she would play games by the hour and never tire. They would play backgammon and Pope Joan, and then Jane would read to her – Macaulay's *History*, Ruskin's *Seven Lamps of Architecture*, *Pendennis*, *Hypatia*. Judith thought Ruskin 'a bit of a prig' but didn't say so, because Jane thought him so beautiful. After Adam, Judith loved most in the world this dreaming romantic child who was of the tribe of Francis and Reuben and John. 'I am afraid she will be unhappy,' Judith thought, 'but she will have some of the joys none of the others will know.'

When she set off with Dorothy for London it was Jane who came into her room alone, Jane she held to her heart with all that impetuous feeling that years could not dim, Jane who gave her a parcel of three little handkerchiefs that she had worked, Jane who stood in the road staring long after the carriage had disappeared. Timothy, now a big stout fellow of seventeen, who bore a strange resemblance to the portraits of his great-grandfather David Herries, teased her:

'She's a nice old lady, but whew! what a temper!' he remarked.

Jane gave him a queer look.

'All right,' he said uneasily, pinching her ear. 'I daresay I like her as much as you do, if all the truth were known.'

She was so weary when she, at last, reached Hill Street that she felt as though her whole body had been crushed under the wheels of the train that had conveyed her.

She saw Lady Herries for a moment, and her tenderness for poor Will enveloped the stout painted lady, whom she had never liked, who, however, looked better in her full black silk than she had ever looked in gay colours. She was sitting in the vast dismal drawing room and wearing a bonnet of velvet and crêpe. Everyone was wearing velvet just then.

'That's one thing,' said Judith to Dorothy as she began to undress. 'I shall never wear velvet, my dear. Never! I shall die first!' She added: 'I am dead now, I think. The smell of gas in that train was quite awful. Give me Mr Thorpe's *Northern Mythology*. It's at the top of my bag. It will send me to sleep if anything will.'

The maid who brought her her breakfast in the morning was full of information. There was nothing that Judith liked better than to have someone with whom she might chat while she was having her breakfast.

It seemed that Will had died quite suddenly of heart failure at three o'clock in the morning. He had not felt well and had gone to his wife's room and had fallen down there dead.

The maid did not know, Judith did not know, no one would ever know of the awful little conversation that had taken place on that last morning.

It was true: he had felt very unwell and had stumbled to Lady Herries' room. He walked with great difficulty, but she had woken to see him standing there, swaying on his feet, a candle in his hand.

'I think I am going to die,' he gasped, his hand at his heart. She had jumped out of bed, found the drops that were to be given to him if there were a heart-attack. He had sunk, blue in the face, into a chair. He recovered a little, looked up into her face, and saw in those pale-blue eyes a look of eagerness.

'You are glad that I am dying,' he said.

'Will! Will!' she cried, sinking on to her knees beside the chair. 'How can you be so cruel?'

'It is very natural,' he replied. 'I don't blame you. It is perfectly right. You never even pretended to love me. No one has ever loved me. Not even Ellis—'

She protested and tried to hold his hand. He waved her away with a gesture of great dignity. Then his face became purple.

'I have wanted the wrong things—' he murmured, and died.

The funeral was to be at twelve. A great many members of the family were expected. Soon Adam came in to see her. She held out her arms and he knelt by the bed, took her small white hand in his and laughed for sheer joy at being with her again. For, when you had said everything, there was something between these two, stronger than life, stronger than death, something that no one shared with them, something that if it could be caught and held, hard and shining in one's hand like a flaming crystal, would explain, quite sufficiently, what everything is about and why we are travelling at all. But of course it can't be caught.

'Isn't this room absurd?' Judith said, laughing. She could never grow accustomed to the fashions of the time. She belonged in taste to the end of the eighteenth century. Looking back, everything of that time seemed to her to have lightness, brilliance and form. Everything in 1854 was huge, heavy and static, wrapped, too, in a sort of damp fog.

In her room there was a sofa covered with red rep, a copper scuttle and scoop (quite gigantic), a huge fender of brass, fire-irons of set steel, a hearthrug of white sheepskin, two great Minton vases with a floral design on a turquoise ground, a picture made out of seaweed in a frame of Tunbridge ware, a work-box – also of Tunbridge ware – that had a lid with a bouquet in mosaic and sides with 'Berlin wool' mosaic, and a vast dressing-table and mirror, trimmed with glazed linen and muslin. All these things and many more jostled one another in the room that was chill with the chill of the grave. In their centre, very bare, very innocent, was a tin bath.

Among these things Adam knelt and held her hand. He was a broad square man now, brown of face. She didn't like his whiskers, although, of course, every man wore them. She loved his eyes, which were bright, shining and most kindly. He had great breadth of shoulders, looked as strong as an ox. He was absentminded, but not with her. He wrote for one of Dickens' papers, reviewed books. He was happily married. He was thirty-eight years of age. All these things were apparently true. But the only thing that was true for her was that he was a small child running up the path from the Tarn at Watendlath, calling out to her that he had seen a kingfisher.

These glorious moments came to her very seldom, but, after that awful hour at the Exhibition, she had beaten down her jealousy. Killed it? No, perhaps not, but she was nearly eighty years of age and must learn to accept facts. Was there anything else to learn of life?

She stroked his brown cheek, kissed him, chattered, laughed, then sent him away. She must get up and face the family.

It was a moment that they none of them afterwards forgot, her entrance into the big drawing-room where they were all gathered together. The blinds were drawn and the room was lit with gas which giggled like a silly schoolgirl. The gas was, however, the only jester. Everyone was immensely solemn. Lady Herries sat on the sofa, Ellis at her side. All around her were grouped the family. James Herries was the oldest – he was seventy-five. He stood beside the sofa, a vast, swollen, pompous effigy in black. There was Archdeacon Rodney, with his wife Rebecca, one of the Foxes of Ulverston, and their son the naval officer. There was Stephen Newmark, close to him Phyllis, now very stout, and four of their seven offspring, Horace, Mary, Katherine and Emily; there were, of course, Garth and Sylvia and Amery, that gay bachelor Fred Ormerod, Bradley Cards and his little wife who was like a pincushion in figure, Timothy Trenchard, his wife and two daughters, Carey Rockage, only a year younger than James and almost as stout, with his wife Cecily and their children Roger and Alice. John and Elizabeth stood quietly by themselves in a window. Walter, Will's eldest son, and the new baronet, was not present, nor was his son Uhland. Everyone thought this disgraceful.

When Judith entered, followed by Dorothy and Adam, a wave of emotion swept the whole assembly. Even Lady Herries, who disliked Judith and was eagerly jealous of her position as the centre of this day's ceremony, was moved. For this was what the

Herries above all else loved. Survival. Perpetuity. To last longer
than anyone else. To have life and vigour when all your contemporaries had failed to last. Even as once upon a time they had
made eager bets on the centenary of Great Aunt Maria, so now
their excitement and pride were kindled, for Judith Paris was
seventy-nine and yet walked with a firm step, her head up, her
eyes shining, the most commanding figure of them all.

But there was more than this. Judith had, in all these years,
won a great reputation among them for honesty, kindliness and
fair charity. They were not, on the whole, very charitable to one
another. No members of any family are very charitable to one
another. They know all the wrong things. But Judith, because
she had lived in the North, had been outside their squabbles,
rivalries and jealousies. They thought her a fine generous-hearted
woman. She herself, as she saw all those Herries, so solemn and
so black, felt a strange mixture of two quite opposite emotions.
She thought them absurd and she felt that she would like to
mother them all. They *were* absurd – old James so conscious of
his baronetcy, so stout, his black legs like pillows, his grizzled
whiskers like cauliflowers; Newmark, his head perched above a
high stock and collar so that he resembled a dignified but anxious
hen; dear Phyllis, so *fearfully* fat and her dress so voluminous
that all her brood could comfortably have nestled beneath it;
Sylvia, alas, no longer pretty, badly rouged, the black velvet on
her dress cut to resemble pansies; Rockage, with an odd resemblance to dear old Maria, long dead, but living again in her
son's untidiness and a kind of shabby good will (how well Judith
remembered that occasion when she had slapped his face at the
house in Wiltshire for his riding to hounds over the drawing-
room chairs!); Horace Newmark, now a plump pale-faced man
of thirty-five in large spectacles and resembling a little in his air
of high discontent Mr Thackeray – yes, they were absurd and
lovable too. How Will would be pleased did he see this great
gathering! How he would approve of the black and the dignity
and the solemnity! At the memory of him, to her own surprise, a
tear stole down her cheek. 'Old ladies cry easily!' she thought, as
she kissed the widow's plump cheek.

She walked about among them, and they were all very kind to
her. It was all crêpe and black broadcloth. Robins, followed by a
thin young footman with a cold, walked around offering sherry
and a biscuit.

She sat down in a chair near the darkened windows, and the

low-murmured conversation went on around her like a draught
creeping in through the walls and the floor. It was late February
and very damp. There was a discontented, peevish fire in the
huge fireplace, but as is so often the case with English fireplaces
the heat went up the chimney and left the room severely alone.
Nearly everyone seemed to have colds; the sneezing was pro-
digious. It was understood that a thin rain was falling outside.

Soon she had John and Elizabeth beside her chair. Elizabeth
looked lovely but not, Judith thought, very happy. When
Elizabeth moved away to talk to Margaret, Judith caught John's
hand in hers and said:

'Well, dear John, how are you?'

They were away from the others. She felt his hand clutch hers,
tightly, and had an impulse to put her arms around him and
hold him safe.

'Very well, Aunt Judith, thank you.'

'And the Secretaryship?'

'Oh, splendid! They are so very good to me.'

'And Elizabeth?'

'We are more in love than ever.'

She nodded her head.

'That's right!'

He was the handsomest man in the room by far. But as she
looked at him she caught the oddest resemblance in him to his
father Francis. Just that way had his father looked at Uldale that
night when he had implored her help. Her help against what?
Against nightmares, ghosts, his own frustration . . .

'It's odd, isn't it,' John said, 'Walter and Uhland not
coming?'

'Very wrong of them.'

'Yes, I suppose so. Have you . . . have you seen them at all?'

'No, my dear.' She smiled grimly. 'They poison our cows once
and again. Walter threatened to bring an action against Bennett's
boy for stealing his timber. Let him try, that's all!'

'Yes, Aunt Judith . . . You know, Elizabeth wrote a letter to
Walter the other day. She thought she ought to. She heard he
was ill.'

'Did she, my dear?'

'He never answered her, though.'

The time had arrived. St. Luke's Chelsea, a church that Will
had attended for many years because he liked its Gothic and the
length of its sermons, was their destination – a long journey at

the pace that their carriages would take them. The hearse had plumes, almost as large as palm trees. The array of carriages was magnificent. Judith accompanied Lady Herries and Ellis in the first carriage.

That is always a problem, the conversation on a funeral journey, but Lady Herries made it no problem at all. First she cried, looking out of the carriage window, pleased and satisfied with the attention that the procession was securing. Then she set about the task of convincing Judith that her life was now at an end, that she had only Ellis to live for, and that she alone, of all God's mortals, had understood Will and given him what he needed. Ellis, who was now eleven years of age, less shrivelled than he had been, but bony, horse-faced like all the Herries, with sharp eyes above a large bony nose, said nothing. Did he care at all, wondered Judith? Did he know that he had been the one comfort and pride of his father's old age? At any rate, he looked like a gentleman. It was extremely difficult for any Herries *not* to look like a gentleman, which was perhaps what was the matter with them. Judith noticed that once and again Ellis stole a sharp look at her. Of what was he thinking? Of her age, in all probability. How old she must seem to him! And yet he had been accustomed to old people! A sudden sympathy for the poor child caught her. She put out her hand and held his. The little hand, in its shiny black glove, was as cold as a seashell.

'Will altered,' Lady Herries was saying. 'Altered immensely in the last years. He depended upon me for everything. I say nothing against his first wife—' ('You'd better not,' thought Judith) '—but to pretend that she understood him was absurd. Poor Will! Everyone thought – even those nearest to him' (this with a glance at Judith) 'thought that his great interest was money. Erroneous – quite erroneous. If you had heard the way that he would talk late in the night—'

Judith began to be angry. But she saw her anger coming from a long way off. She had, through many years' practice, trained herself to meet it and turn it back before it reached her heart. Bad for old ladies to be angry, and in any case waste of time. But how she did hate this woman! False and greedy and sham! Poor Will! how lonely in those last years he must have been! Old pictures began to crowd up again – that familiar one when she and Will and Francis had watched the fireworks by the Lake and had prophesied about their lives. Soon she would begin to cry. She *must* not cry. She *would* not before this woman – all scent,

whale-bone and crêpe. She could not see her face for the heavy
black veil that covered it, but she knew how small and mean those
eyes were, how tight and hard the little mouth! Those were not
the thoughts for a funeral, poor dear Will's funeral, so she looked
out of window and saw a French poodle walking beside an old
lady; he had a peaked nose, woolly wig, leggings and tail-band,
and a horrible shaved, salmon-coloured body. The old lady was
younger in years than Judith but not half so vigorous. She
walked as though she were a hundred.

They were passing slowly through a mean, shabby street.
Groups gathered, children ran, men took off their caps – for this
moment the Herries dominated the scene. It did not make them
proud. It was their right, now and always – so much their right
that they gave it scarcely a thought. Here is a gin-palace, here a
seedy French *pension*, children in torn pinafores gazing at the
sweetshop window, here a rag shop with tobacco-pipes crossed in
the window and turpentine-infected bundles of firewood.
Through all this, drink, poverty, childhood, sweets and tobacco
and gin, Will is grandly riding for the last time!

'Without my care and affection I shudder to think what his
last years would have been—'

Judith clutched the top of her cane with her two little hands.
In all her seventy-nine years, with the single exception of Mrs
Ponder, she had never disliked anyone so much. She heard a
sniff, a strange little strangled sniff. Ellis was crying, tears were
trickling down his bony nose. She put out her arm and drew him
closer to her. He stayed against her as stiff as a whalebone. But
she was glad that he was crying. He *had* cared for his father then.
He *had* cared! She would do something for Ellis. Ask him to
Uldale, let him play with Dorothy's children . . . Then she found
that she too, under her veil, was crying, and suddenly she wanted
to lean forward and take Lady Herries' hand. Perhaps what the
woman said was true. She *had* cared for Will – in her own
peculiar undemonstrative way.

They have arrived at the church. Herries wing out of carriages
like crows from a nesting-tree. But silent. Immensely solemn.
How broad and deep the hat-bands on the black hats, how heavy
the whiskers, the stocks, the voluminous black skirts, the umbrellas, the thick black boots! A crowd has gathered about the
church door. The church has all its attendant offices and officers
– the stout, self-important beadle, the neatly grained high boxes,
the three-decker pulpit, the wizen-faced pew-openers (two of

them). The church is icily cold, and the hassock on which little
Ellis kneels is hard as iron. He is miserable and feels a sense of
aching loss, although loss of what he has really no idea.

Judith, sitting there, watching the big coffin draped in black,
wondering about the pew-opener in the black bonnet who had
already retired to a corner behind a pillar to count the pennies,
thought that the Herries must have multiplied themselves three-
fold since they entered the church. She thought – for her imagination was fantastic now with weariness and chill – that the
ghosts of departed Herries must have joined the living. Maybe if
she looked more closely she would see poor Warren there, gazing
at her as he used to do with that dog-like devotion, Francis,
Jennifer, even David and Sarah, and Deborah Sunwood whom
she had loved so dearly in her childhood, and Jennifer's father
and mother, and poor Christabel. When you reached her age the
dead and the living were all equally alive – no one was dead, no
one was living.

Yes, Adam was living! He sat beside her, and sometimes he
would look at her to see that all was well with her. Then quietly,
with that solid protection that she loved so in him, he put his
strong arm round her: and then, to her shame, to her great disgrace, she fell fast asleep!

She woke hurriedly to find that the coffin was leaving the
church and that she, with Lady Herries and Ellis, must immediately follow it. 'Oh, dear! How disgraceful!' she thought. 'I do
hope that nobody saw me!' But she walked down the church,
very firmly, all the Herries' eyes upon her. She did not care for
the family now. She was thinking only of Will – Will, whose
last grand ceremony was over, who would do sums on paper no
longer, would be denied potatoes by Robins never again; with the
exit of that body out of the church one long chapter of her life as
well as his was closed.

Later they were all in the long dining-room. The table was
covered with food: drink of every kind was on the vast sideboard
that looked as though it had once formed part of a great mahogany mountain and was still marked with the pick-axes of ardent
climbers. Judith, dizzy with an almost drunken weariness, sat in
a chair near the fireplace. All that she wanted was to go to bed;
meanwhile she must listen to the Family. Inhuman furniture and
human bodies, high mountains of ham and beef, chickens, pies,
great loaves of bread all circled round her together. There was a

marble group near the window – 'Sir William Herries, Bart, and
Lady Herries' – poor Christabel like an early Christian Martyr in
a long icy flowing robe. The fender was of painted mahogany.
There were six dessert-stands in ormolu with monkeys carrying
silver nuts. On the mantelpiece were some towering vases of
Copeland ware, gold on a cobalt blue ground.

'Everything is so large,' she thought, and once again had the
old, old wish that her own legs were longer. Soon, however, she
forgot both her weariness and the furniture in her interest in the
conversation that went on around her. They had forgotten her,
all save Adam and Margaret. But, more than that, they had
already forgotten Will. Gone were those hushed voices, vanished
that sad solemnity. As they crowded about the table, eating like
wolves and drinking like the damned, their voices rose ever
higher and higher, their excitement, with every moment,
keener.

For now, liberated from that momentary consciousness of
poor William, aware that he was safely underground and that
they could therefore move freely forward with the enterprise and
energy that belonged to their Herries blood, they were discussing
the War.

It was, she reflected, natural that they should do so, for only
yesterday, February 27th, England's ultimatum to Russia had
been despatched. She herself detested war, any war, every war.
She had been in Paris in 1815 and had borne Adam there, seen
his father die there, suffered agonies and terrors that had affected
her whole life. Why anyone should be *glad* about war she could
not imagine, but not only was everyone in the room *glad*, they
were *triumphant*.

She saw, too, with that detached observation that came from
her mother Mirabell (who had been quite certainly not at all a
Herries) that this was for them not an English war but a *Herries*
war. It was the Herries who were indignant at the Massacre of
Sinope, the Herries who applauded and supported every action
of Lord Stratford, the Herries who had advised Lord Palmerston
to resign, the Herries who thought Louis Napoleon a hero, the
Herries who mocked poor Mr Cobden and silly Mr Bright for
their support of the Peace Society.

As Judith listened she realized with every moment more fully
what it was that separated her from the Herries clan and all the
other clans in the world like them – what it was that had separated her father and Francis and Reuben, what it was that gave

John his terrors and made little Jane walk apart from her healthy
and energetic sisters. Here it was, this quality of the uneasy imagination, this desire for a beauty that was never to be caught,
this consciousness, pursuing, relentless, unceasing, of a world
behind the world. She could have got up from her chair and,
stamping her cane on the floor, have cried: 'You fools! You
fools! Will nothing teach you?' – but all she did was to smile a
little, refuse a plate of ham courteously offered her by the Archdeacon, and consider pensively the silver monkeys with their
silver nuts.

So, over Will's dead body, they sang their Song of Triumph.

Old James, whose chest was congested so that he wheezed like
a harmonium, coughing over his plate of chicken, cried to
anyone who might listen: 'I tell you, sir, these damned Russians
must be put down.' He caught the ear of Cecily Rockage, a thin
woman of sixty who greatly admired him (as she admired indeed
everyone, for she was a humble woman). 'I can tell you for your
private ear, my dear Cecily, that in the Club a day or two back
Clarendon himself told me that in his opinion Newcastle had
managed Palmerston exceedingly well, getting him to withdraw
his resignation without any conditions, you know. Of course, the
Radicals are disgusted, and so they may be. But in my
opinion—'

'That's just what Carey says,' Cecily Rockage murmured,
looking about her in her dim, peering way to see that her beloved
son Roger was having plenty to eat and was thoroughly happy.

'They are important,' Judith thought. 'They are beginning to
cover the country.'

In her Cumberland retreat she had not realized *how* important
the Herries had grown. Once upon a time there were but a few of
them, a gambler here, someone there riding a horse into a wilder-
ness, an old man and an old woman drinking over the fire, but
now the times had favoured them. They believed in England,
they believed – almost terribly – in themselves. Oh! how they
believed! What unquestioning confidence they had! Everything,
everything was right with England from her Government to her
furniture, and Judith realized, as she looked about her, as she
heard Ormerod's gay laugh, and the Archdeacon's benevolence,
and Stephen Newmark's solemn blessing, as she saw the women
billowing in happy pride about their men, Sylvia a little elated
with wine, Phyllis the proud mother, Rodney's Rebecca the eager
listener, that there was something fine and grand in their faith,

that these men and women *were* making England what she was, England the dominant Power of the world, the Queen of the Earth!

Only – was it worth the trouble: all this hard work, energy, faith? Queen of the Earth! *Was* that really important?

'I am really very tired, darling,' she whispered to Adam. 'I think I'll go up to bed if no one minds.'

No one minded. Earlier in the day, when William was still above ground, she was of importance. Now she was forgotten; England's Glory had taken her place.

Later Adam came to say goodnight to his mother. As he climbed the high stairs, leaving the boom and whisper of voices behind him, he felt a great longing to take his mother and Margaret, wrap them in shawls and whisk them off, with himself, to a desert island – a glorious island of burning sun, coral sand, heat and light and colour. The three of them alone, living for ever, always warm, always private, telling one another stories, and making necklaces of shells. He stopped on the landing opposite a dark engraving of Prince Albert and the Queen, and laughed. Two mice heard him laugh and, surprised out of their lives, whisked away.

He entered his mother's room carefully. There was a fire burning; the copper scuttle-scoop, the brass fender, the steel fire-irons shone resplendently. The old lady was lying, her pillows propped up behind her, apparently staring at a large oil painting entitled 'Little Black Sambo', which showed a small black child daintily covered with the leaf of a palm tree, sitting on the sea-shore sucking his thumb while two little white girls, clad immaculately in muslin and long pantaloons, stared at him with speculation. The firelight danced on the wall; the rain beat against the pane – it was not an uncheerful scene. She did not turn her head nor move when he entered. In spite of his heavy figure he trod very gently, sat down on a chair beside the bed and waited.

Then suddenly an awful fear seized him that she was going to die. Her face was always pale, but her small hands as they lay on the gay patchwork quilt had a marble pallor. And she lay so very still. She was, after all, of a great age. She should never have made the journey to London; this day must have been of a fearful exhaustion for her.

The thought that he might lose her at any moment now – that

she might go out like a candle carelessly blown by the wind –
made him catch his breath, constricted his heart. The only three
people in the world whom he loved, now that Caesar Kraft was
dead, were his mother and Margaret and John. His nature was
deeply modest, acutely sensitive. He could not believe that men
and women liked him, and it was true that, at present, very few
knew him because he was so silent about himself and thought
himself a useless, cumbering failure. He had had great ambitions
for the good of man and they had all failed. At that moment
when Kraft had fallen and died at his feet, all his hope of helping
his brother man had died. He had not the confidence nor the
power nor the will. He was so shy of thrusting himself forward,
so shy of display or self-advertisement, that men thought him
proud and arrogant. At the newspaper office, in the little Club to
which he belonged, even with a man like Charles Dickens, genial,
friendly, exuberant, he could not let himself go. But these two
women understood him, his mother and Margaret understood
him, and to lose one of them . . .

And there was one more thing. He was only half alive in
London. His soul ached for Cumberland, but Margaret did not
like it. She was unhappy there. Stones and clouds, clouds and
stones . . .

She turned her head and saw him. She put out her hand and
caught his.

'Dear me, how nice, Adam! I have been dreaming, I suppose.
But I don't know. I never know now whether I am dreaming or
not . . . I was very tired, I must say, but bed is most comforting.
There is no place like bed. I am sure that I never expected to feel
that. I used to be so very energetic. But it's my body that's tired,
not my spirit . . . How disgusting old James is, eating such a lot
at his age!'

They talked quietly and happily together.

'Mother,' Adam said. 'One thing I hadn't told you. Will
Leathwaite is coming to London to be my servant.'

That interested her. 'Is he indeed? What a good thing! I like
Will so very much.'

'Of course it's absurd that I should have a servant with the
little I make. But he wants to come. He says he doesn't care what
I pay him, and it will be a little piece of home.'

'A very big piece,' Judith remarked, chuckling. 'That's nice for
you, dear. Are they still guzzling and drinking down there?'

'I suppose so.'

'And what a deal they talk. Chatter, chatter, chatter. They are all delighted there's a war – why, I cannot imagine.' She closed her eyes and dreamt again. She talked as though out of a dream. 'I fancied just now that God was in the room. A God a little like Georges and a little like yourself, Adam. Perhaps that's what God will be – composed of the people we love most. He was so very kind and most reassuring. I have never been a religious woman, you know, Adam. Reuben Sunwood used to be greatly disappointed with me. He was so very certain. But I suppose an old woman may be allowed her fancies. I find that everyone is very certain about God in these days. Quite different from when I was a girl. It's as though they had made Him themselves.'

She sat up, climbing up out of her dream, full of energy again.

'I do hope you are happy, dear Adam,' she said.

'Yes,' he said. 'When I am with you and Margaret, Mother. But I'm terribly shy. It grows on me, I'm afraid.'

'Yes, your father was the same. But I shouldn't worry. We are different – you and I and poor John and little Jane. And the Herries family is an awkward family to be different in. All my life I have been fighting them. And now I am not fighting anyone any longer, even Walter. Too much trouble.'

She lay back again, closing her eyes.

'How lovely life is, all of it – having a baby, fighting Walter, pains and aches, food and riding up to Watendlath, poor Jennifer, the garden at Uldale, dear Adam, dear, dear Adam ...'

She had fallen asleep. He sat there for some while watching her, then bent down and kissed, very gently, her forehead, then stole from the room.

CLIMAX TO A LONG SEQUENCE

I

JUDITH AND WALTER

WILL LEATHWAITE had come to say farewell. He was going at last, after six months' delay, to London to be Adam's servant. Judith was able to sit on the lawn in the September sunshine, it was so warm. The sun had the shininess of a hot sea and the lawn was like misty waters; the colours seemed gently to roll in shades of pale citron, of silver-grey, from the floor of the little Gothic temple to the walls, faintly pink, of the beloved house. Across the road, beyond the old peach-stained stones, rose the shadowed forms of the mountains, stretching themselves like great luxurious cats in the sunshine. A flight of curlews broke the pale wash of the sky, and you could feel, even though you could not see, the rough grass of the brown moorland, the icy glitter under the warm sun of the running moorland streams. Those green slopes, as yet scarcely purpled with heather, heaped up like a wave above the house answering the plaintive windy cry of the curlews.

In the middle of this peace, listening as always for her delight to the rhythm of running water, water slipping happily under the sunlight, she said goodbye to Will Leathwaite. It was as though she were sending Adam a piece of the North. Will was nearly fifty now and towered above her as he stood, his cap in his hand, staring in front of him. His colouring was very fair and there was a bald patch on the very top of his round bullet-like head. His features were stamped with simplicity, obstinacy, strength and kindliness; his cheeks were russet with good health, and there were little wrinkles at the corners of his very blue eyes that spoke of extreme good-nature. His body was large, broad, clumsy, his shoulders a little bowed. It was plain that he saw only one thing at a time and that once he had an idea in his head, nothing – no earthquake, no thunderbolt – could loosen it. He stood up in the thin Northern sunlight as though he had been created by it.

'Well, Will, you will look after Mr Adam, will you not?'

'I will, ma'am.'

'Will you like town life, do you think? It is very different from anything you've been used to.'

'So long as Mr Adam is satisfied, I'm ready,' he answered.

'It will be a great thing for Mr Adam. He hasn't many friends, you know.'

'Yes. T'nature of him is slow like my own, ma'am.' Then he smiled, a delightful slow, considering smile. 'T'best way, I think, ma'am.'

The children, Amabel and Jane, ran across the lawn, laughing and shouting, with a ball. He turned and watched them with a quiet decorous pleasure.

'Write to me, Will, and tell me how you find everything.'

'Yes, ma'am. Thank you, ma'am.'

He touched his yellow forelock and stepped slowly, steadily away, moving his great body with the ease and dignity of a gentleman in his own right. She sighed happily. It would be nice for Adam to have so trustworthy a man at his side.

She was glad that she was feeling strong and vigorous and that the air was warm, because she had much to think about. Both Margaret and John were staying in the house. Adam had written to say that Margaret was tired with the London air and needed a holiday, so she had been at Uldale a week and, so far, the visit had been a great success.

John had suddenly appeared with only a telegram's warning. No one knew why he had come. Then Elizabeth had written to say that she had sent him because he could not sleep in London. The summer had been hot: his master was in Switzerland. She herself was going to stay with the Rockages at Grosset. It was better that she and John should be apart for a while. This was sufficiently alarming, but John had said nothing until suddenly last evening, wishing Judith goodnight, he had told her that Elizabeth was going to have a baby.

'It's all wrong, Aunt Judith,' he burst out. 'I should not have a child.' He was quivering and his face was strained with distress.

'What nonsense!' she said. 'I never heard greater nonsense. Why, it's splendid for dear Elizabeth to have a baby.'

'It will be a coward – as my father was, as I am.'

He left the room without another word.

After that she slept very badly. Dream followed dream, and every dream was filled with apprehension. Every part of her past life seemed, in her dreams, to be now connected and to point to some inevitable result. She was once again with Georges at Christabel's Ball, with Charlie Watson in Watendlath, with Warren in Paris, and someone cried in her ear: 'Had it not been thus this would never have come about.'

'But what?' she cried.

But she could not see the event. She struggled, her heart full of love and fear. Adam, approaching her, tried to speak to her but was prevented. John waved to her a despairing hand before he vanished from sight. But she could do nothing. She was held, as one is in dreams, impotent, with no power in her limbs to move. Suddenly the old cruel figure of Mrs Ponder, Jennifer's servant, appeared. She was on her knees searching Judith's private papers.

'*Now* you will have to leave the house!' she cried, raising her malignant face.

'But I will not!' Judith answered.

And she had not. That was one thing upon which she could look back with pleasure, that in spite of all the odiousness and spying, in spite of Jennifer's lazy treachery, she had faced Mrs Ponder to the end, seeing the hateful woman at last out of the house. But what had Mrs Ponder to do with John? Ah, she remembered the little scene when that vile woman had thrown John's rabbit out of window. Was that, too, one link in the chain? Had every event, however slight, its inevitable result? But she must do something about John. She must not allow him to slip into tragedy as his father, Francis, had done. She must do something about John, and then she looked up to see Margaret coming across the grass towards her. She was now thirty-four years of age and a fine strongly built woman with a broad carriage, a calm open countenance and great quietness and repose in all her movements.

'She has grown,' Judith thought, 'like Adam and Adam like her, as many married people do when they have lived much together and love one another.' As she thought this a spasm of the old jealousy bit her as it might be a little animal jumping from the grass, but she brushed it away with her hand.

Margaret was wearing a simple grey muslin with panniers of white taffeta *placed* at the edges. In the bosom of her dress she had a white rose. Her dark hair was brushed back on either side, parted in the middle. She was carrying her hat in her hand. She brought peace and assurance with her.

'I like this woman,' Judith thought, as though she were seeing her for the first time. 'I am friends with her at last.'

The children had tired of their game and had run into the house. The sun was very slowly sinking, and the golden glow moved, travelling from place to place, softening the mountains with a purple flush while the sky faded slowly from bright blue into a translucent amber. Soon there will be a world of grey and silver and the hill will be dark, chill and strong. But that is not yet. The two women have half an hour to talk, the running stream the only sound in the world save their voices.

'You will not be cold, Mother?' Margaret asked, laying her broad strong hand on Judith's black dress.

'Oh no, my dear. And see that the grass is not damp for you.'

Margaret laughed. 'I have so many petticoats,' she said, 'I could sit in a stream and not be wet.'

Her voluminous grey dress spread out on the green grass and the light transmuted it.

'Have you seen John?' Judith asked.

'No; he has been away all day,' Margaret answered, sighing. 'He seems dreadfully unhappy. He has been so for months. He would talk to Adam at one time, but lately he has avoided him too, and Adam loves him so much. Elizabeth says that he will not talk to her either.'

'Yes – he is as his father was.' Judith beat her small hands impatiently on her lap. 'I can catch hold of *nothing*.'

'Adam thinks,' Margaret began, 'that it all began from the day when someone near here told him about his father and mother. He had a shock then that has weakened him like water, and it is of no use to say that he *ought* not, that I would not be like that, that *I* would not let the past touch me. We are all different, and it seems to me that the Herries who *are* weak are weaker than any others, as though someone had said once: "If you are born a Herries and refuse to have common-sense you shall suffer as no one else suffers. Have common-sense or die." Adam has just enough common-sense to save him.'

'Well, he is only half a Herries, my dear,' Judith said briskly. 'His father was only half a Herries and I am only by nature quarter a one, for my father was a wanderer and a vagabond and so was my mother. And here I am as warm and comfortable as a cat, thank goodness. It's more than I have deserved.'

Margaret hesitated. She found words no more easily than Adam, but there was something that she had been wanting for a long while to say, and now was a good time.

'Mother,' she began at last, slowly, in her deep rich voice, looking down at the grass. 'You do not hate me any longer, do you?'

'Hate you? Why, no, my child, I love you.'

'You did hate me once.'

Judith shook her head. 'No, I never hated you, of course. How could I when Adam loved you? – and besides all my life I must confess that I have found it very difficult to hate anyone. John's mother for a while once, and a horrid servant she had. Walter, perhaps, at odd moments. No. But I was jealous of you, I must confess.'

'Yes, I knew it.' Margaret stroked the grass with her hand.

'And it made me terribly unhappy. But I have never been able to express myself. I am so very shy of feeling, and women are not supposed to have any feelings. It is not thought nice.'

'In my young day,' Judith said, nodding her head vigorously, 'women had plenty of feeling and showed it. I don't know what's come over the world. Women are not supposed to have legs any more, and children are found in gooseberry bushes. Stuff!'

'And you are not jealous any more?'

'No. All my fires have died down. I sit and look on. But I love you, my dear. I do indeed. Adam has been the passion of all my life since my husband died, but a time came when I saw that someone else must do the things for him that I had done – and more things than I could ever do. How fortunate I have been that it was a woman like you, not one of these coarse painted creatures or one of these niminy-piminies all affectation, or one of those good perfect creatures like the woman in Mr Dickens' *David Copperfield*. What was her name? Agnes. But, of course, Adam would have chosen well. He would have had a whipping from me if he had not.'

'I have wanted to tell you,' Margaret said slowly, 'how grateful I am to you, how dearly I love you. I cannot say things, but I thought that once I must tell you—'

She leant up and put her arms around Judith. The two women kissed, and Judith laid her hand for a moment on Margaret's broad forehead.

'God bless you and keep you in all His ways, dear daughter. And now,' she went on quite sharply, 'I must go in. The sun will soon be down. How nice! I shall read Mrs Gaskell's *Cranford* over the fire. They say it is all about old ladies who are frightened by cows – like Mrs Potter at Threlkeld. Give me your arm, my dear. My right foot has gone fast asleep.'

A little later she was sitting in front of the parlour fire, her feet propped up on a worsted stool, a thick woollen shawl round her shoulders, and large spectacles on the end of her small nose. Her trouble was that her nose was *too* small. The spectacles *would* slip off! It was only of late that her eyes had begun to fail her. She was reading *Cranford* with many chuckles.

'How true this is! We are just the same here round Uldale. "*In the first place, Cranford is in possession of the Amazons – all the holders of houses, above a certain rent, are women. If a married couple come to settle in the town, somehow the gentleman*

*disappears; he is either fairly frightened to death by being the
only man in the Cranford evening parties, or he is accounted for
by being with his regiment, his ship, or closely engaged in business all the week in the great neighbouring commercial town of
Drumble, distant only twenty miles on a railroad. In short, whatever does become of the gentlemen, they are not at Cranford; ...
but every man cannot be a surgeon. For keeping the trim gardens
full of choice flowers without a weed to speck them; for frightening away little boys who look wistfully at the said flowers
through the railings; for rushing out at the geese that occasionally venture into the gardens if the gates are left open; for de-
ciding all questions of literature and politics without troubling
themselves with unnecessary reasons or arguments; for obtaining
clear and correct knowledge of everybody's affairs in the parish;
for keeping their neat maidservants in admirable order; for kindness (somewhat dictatorial) to the poor, and real tender good
offices to each other whenever they are in distress – the ladies of
Cranford are quite sufficient." '*

Judith laid the book down on her lap and considered.

'How very excellent! That is exactly Miss Poole and Janet and
Mary Darlington and Mrs Withers and Mrs Spooner. We are a
world of women. Why? Why is Dorothy so important? She is not
very clever nor is she at all beautiful, but she has a kind of
kingdom. Now I *never* had a kingdom—'

The door opened. The little maid Eliza, her face twisted from
its rosy simplicity with surprise, horror, alarm, excitement and
general sense of drama, whispered something.

'What do you say, Eliza?' Judith asked, turning round and
pushing her spectacles back on to her nose.

'Sir Walter Herries, ma'am.'

Walter! Her book dropped to the floor. She stayed, for a
moment, listening as though she expected to hear some dreadful
sound, but all that came to her was the cheerful shrill voice of
someone singing in the kitchen. Then, sitting up very straight,
she said:

'Ask Sir Walter to come in.'

A moment later he was standing beside the sofa, very stiffly
bowing. He was dressed for riding and carried his hat in his
hand. His hair was grey now (he was sixty-two) and he was
clean-shaven, which was most unusual and gave him an odd
babyish appearance. His red face was purple-veined, but he was
not so stout as when Judith had last seen him. He was untidy, as

though he had no one to look after him. Judith, against her wish, felt sorry for him.

'Well, Walter, how are you? Won't you sit down? Been poisoning any of our cows lately? How are the little Peaches? Humphrey, the stableman, found one of them in our gooseberry bushes not long ago.'

Walter sat down. He spread his legs, looked gravely at her; she noticed that his mouth was not very steady and that his hands shook.

'You are looking well, Judith,' he said.

'I am very well, thank you.' She took off her spectacles. She did not intend that he should say that her sight was going. Then sharply, as though to convey to him that she had not all day to waste:

'Why am I honoured?'

'A damned pretty place you've got,' he said, looking about him. 'Everything very fresh and charming.'

'Well – well. That's not what you've come to say.'

'No, it isn't. Sharp as ever you were!'

'Nor have you come to pay me compliments. Do you mind that window? If so, pray close it.' (For the window was open. Judith, unlike her contemporaries, loved fresh air.)

'No matter, thank you.' He hummed and hawed, then began a long rambling statement.

She could not make out what he was after. He had a lot to say about the past. Was it not foolish that they had wasted so much of their lives in quarrelling? He had been a young hot-headed fool, had done many things that he now regretted. Looking back, his ill-temper seemed to him now to have been very aimless, motiveless. But it was his father who, from the time he was a baby, had persuaded him that his mother had been insulted, and then Jennifer and Francis – well, Judith would agree that their conduct ...

'I will agree to nothing,' Judith said.

But he did not appear to hear her. He went rambling on. He was afraid that he'd taught Uhland the same doctrine. He saw now what a mistake he had made. He saw now that he had been mistaken in many things.

'Well, I'm glad of that anyway,' said Judith. 'But there is no use to go back on the past. If you are asking me to forget and forgive, Walter, frankly I cannot. Too much harm has been done – Francis, Jennifer, Reuben, and Jennifer's children. My own life, too . . .' She coughed. She could not but be sorry for him a little. There were spots on his waistcoat, and his stock was badly tied. 'But what do you *want*, Walter? What have you come here for?'

He hesitated, looked at her as though he were begging her to help him. Then he said an extraordinary thing.

'Hatred, Judith, is a very rare quality in men. One seldom meets it.'

She did not know what to say.

'Very rare,' she answered drily.

'I have never hated you. My mother never hated anybody. Jennifer never hated anyone. You yourself have never hated.'

'Well?'

'What I intend to say is – I am clumsy at expressing myself – but out of all this past quarrelling, not very real, you understand, there has come much unhappiness.' He paused, rubbed his cheek with his hand. 'I myself am not a happy man. All my own fault, I admit it. I have lost my daughter quite through my own fault. There is something bad in our blood which, if it is indulged—'

He stared at her in quite a fuddled way as though he had been drinking, which it was likely that he had. But what was his meaning? What was his intention? For what had he come? She remembered the scene in this very room when she had slapped his face. He was not the kind of man either to condone or forget.

'Hatred, Judith, – real hatred – is a sort of madness.'

'Well?'

He went on again, finding words very difficult.

'You see . . . you know . . . you must understand . . . Upon my word, I am extremely clumsy – you must forgive me – but my boy – Uhland—'

'Yes – Uhland?' she said, more softly, because now, as always when he spoke of his son, there was a new and moving note in his voice.

'I had great hopes for Uhland. I may be a man who has made a mess of his life. When I am sober I am ready to make such an admission – but Uhland was to be different. He had a heavy handicap' (his voice was gathering ardour now that Uhland was his topic) 'his lameness – the sense that he was unlike the others. And then his mother was not strong, and I was not the wisest father. I was anxious to indulge him, too anxious perhaps, and he was unusual, unlike other boys—'

He paused again, and gently, looking at him almost as though she were his friend, Judith said:

'Yes, Walter, I understand. In that at least I have always understood you.'

Encouraged, he went on:

'I am another man when I am in my cups. I will be quite honest with you. I have spoiled many things by my follies, but Uhland I have always kept apart. I saw from the beginning that he was by himself, alone. He has never cared for anyone except your Adam. He has never, I fear, cared in the least for myself, and the knowledge that he did not made me wilder, wilder than perhaps I would otherwise have been. But what I would point out is that all our quarrels, yours and mine and our parents' before us – the events in the life of your own father so many years ago – have found a kind of resting-place in poor Uhland's nature. He was born with a grudge and all his instincts have been twisted. In a fashion he is a scapegoat for the errors of the rest of us.' He stopped once more, wiped his mouth with his hand.

She was, in spite of herself, deeply touched. This was a different Walter from any that she had ever seen. She felt behind his precise, artificial, clumsy speech almost an agony of apprehension, and her own apprehension that she had been so conscious of all day rose to meet his.

She almost cried out:

'Oh, Walter, what is it? What has happened?'

Enemies though they had been all their lives, they were now almost allies.

He went on, staring at her as though that assisted him.

'Uhland has grown ever more strange. Our house is not an agreeable place. I will not pretend that it is agreeable, but of late Uhland's conduct has frightened me greatly—'

'Uhland's conduct?'

'Yes.' He found now the greatest difficulty in choosing his words. 'He is, I fear, most unhappy, but he will speak to no one. He shuts himself in his room. He walks over the house. The servants are afraid to remain where he is. And for myself, I think he hates me.'

She said nothing. He went on more swiftly.

'But it is not of myself that I wanted to speak to you. I came ... I came because—' He said urgently, leaning towards her: 'You have John staying with you?'

'Yes,' she said.

'You know, of course, that from the time of his childhood Uhland has always especially hated John.'

'Yes,' she said.

'It has been a sort of madness in him. I fear, I greatly fear that I was myself originally responsible for that. It seemed to me in those days unfair – unfair that John should be so handsome while my son—'

'Yes, I know, I know,' Judith said quickly.

'Then I implore you, Judith – I beg of you – send John back to London immediately. Immediately. Uhland knows that he is here. He has, during the last week, been very odd in his behaviour. He talks – he was talking last night – as though that old grudge had reached some kind of climax. We are, all of us, responsible for the past, I more than any, and if anything were to happen—'

'But what could happen?'

'There have been many acts of violence in our family,' he went on. 'It is as though there were an element of violence in our blood ... No. This is perhaps foolish, unreal. We are, I suppose, the most sober and sensible family in England, and just because of that when we are not sensible—'

He got up and she could see that he was greatly agitated.

'Never mind our family,' he said. 'Damn the family! This is urgent, personal to ourselves. I implore you, send John back to London tomorrow.'

She nodded. She looked up and gave him her hand for the first time for many years.

'Yes, Walter. You are right. Thank you for coming. It could not have been easy. John shall return to London. In fact this is no new thing. I have been aware of it for many years. John has been under some kind of shadow all his life, as his father was before him. I will see that he goes tomorrow.'

Walter held her hand, looked at her, bowed, then said almost defiantly:

'I have not come here to confess my sins, Judith. I shall be tomorrow as I was yesterday. I shall find myself a fool, I don't doubt, for coming to visit you. But for an hour at least I see sense. Goodbye. I can find my own way out.'

Judith sat on, her hands folded in front of her, looking into the fire, wondering as to which would be the best way to persuade John. This, had she known it, was a waste of energy, for John had heard everything, standing among some flowerpots, his hands scratched unwittingly by the nails of rose-briars fastened to the wall. He had returned from his ride and had seen Walter's horse tied to the gate. A quarter of an hour before he had seen both Walter and Uhland riding down the road from Ireby. He had come round the wing of the house towards the front door when, very clearly through the open window, he had heard the words in Walter's thick ropy voice: 'You know, of course, that from the time of his childhood Uhland has always especially hated John.'

So he stayed there, his body pressed against the wall, his eyes staring out into a sky that swam in frosty September light with one blazing diamond star. He heard everything. He heard Walter say: 'If anything were to happen—', and Judith later: 'Yes, Walter. You are right ... John has been under some kind of shadow ...'

So it had come to this! 'Under some kind of shadow! Under some kind of shadow.' And they planned to smuggle him away to London lest anything should happen ... anything should happen.

He went back to the stable and got out his horse Barnabas. A small terrier, very devoted to him, Mumps by name, little more than a puppy, came rushing across the cobbles when he saw Barnabas let out again. He had thought that the fun was over for the day, but apparently it was not. John went quickly by the gate that bordered the orchard. This brought him straight into the village street and he knew that he would be now ahead of Walter. The sun was just sinking, and hills, fields, pasture and stream lay in a mirror of light; you could fancy that if you swung, lazily, god-like in the sky, you would look down and see your Olympian features reflected in this sea of gold. Almost at once, just out of the village, at the dip in the road before it turned left to Peterfield, he found Uhland, waiting for his father, while his horse cropped the grass.

He knew that he had very little time before Walter came up, and, guiding his horse quite close to Uhland's, he said softly:

'I think that we must end this. It has gone on long enough – and by ourselves where no one can disturb us.'

It was as though because of their connexion through so many years they had grown to understand one another like the closest and dearest friends, for Uhland did not appear startled, nor did he ask 'End what?' or 'What has been long enough?' He simply drew his horse a little away from John's and nodded his head.

'Well – if you wish it. As to ending it—' Then he said sharply in his cold rather thin voice: 'What is it you want?'

'That we should have it out, the two of us, once and for all – alone.'

They both heard the tap-tap of a horse on the road. It would be, likely, Walter.

'Yes, I agree.'

They were like two schoolboys arranging a rendezvous for a fight; from the beginning there had been something childlike and something eternal too in their relationship.

Uhland went on, as though to himself: 'Yes, I have had enough of this. I must get rid of this.' He said coldly: 'Well – what do you propose?'

'Tomorrow. I will meet you somewhere.'

Uhland paused. They could see Walter coming down the hill.

'Yes. What do you say to the house opposite Calva in Skiddaw Forest? Tomorrow afternoon at four.'

'Yes. I'll be there.'

John turned his horse and a moment later passed Walter without a word or any greeting.

CLIMAX TO A LONG SEQUENCE

II

SKIDDAW FOREST

ON the following day, Uhland, waking very early in his tower, lighted his candle and began to read in a brown stubby volume. It was a translation of Vasari's *Lives of the Italian Painters*. After a while he came to this: *'Whereupon having taken this buckler with him to Florence without telling Leonardo whose it was, Ser Piero asked him to paint something upon it. Leonardo having taken one day this buckler in his hands, and seeing it twisted, ill-made and clumsy, straightened it by the fire, and having given it to a turner, from the rough and clumsy thing that it was, caused it to be made smooth and equal; and afterwards, having covered it with* gesso *and having prepared it after his own method, he began to think of what he might paint on it, that should be able to terrify all who should come upon it, producing the same effect as once did the head of Medusa. Leonardo therefore, to this end, carried to a room into which no one entered save himself, slow-worms, lizards, field-crickets, snakes, moths, grasshoppers, bats and other kinds of such-like animals, out of the number of which, variously put together, he evolved a most horrible and terrifying creature, which poisoned the air with its breath, and turned it into flame; and he represented it coming out of a dark and jagged rock, belching poison from its open throat, and fire from its eyes, and smoke from its nostrils, in so strange a manner that it seemed altogether a monstrous and horrible thing; and such pains did he take in executing it, that although the smell of the dead animals in the room was very noisome, it was not perceived by Leonardo, so great was the passion that he bore towards his art . . .'*

'So great was the passion that he bore towards his art,' Uhland repeated to himself and closed the book and blew out his candle to let the moth-like colour of the early morning strengthen in the room. So it was to be a great artist, such would he have done had he had the opportunity and the power. He had neither, only the longing. He had done nothing with his life, which now was over. He was certain that it was over and that this was the last time that he would see the early light spread about the room. But today he would release something from within himself that had been there since he was conceived. If he could live after that was released – ah! then perhaps he would become an artist.

He always had a headache now when he woke in the morning, a pain that pressed on his forehead like iron, and his eyes for the first hour were misted so that he had read the Vasari with great difficulty, and his lame leg hurt him sorely. But this morning when later he bathed and dressed he felt a glow, a warmth, a deep and burning excitement. That miserable coward had at last faced up to him. He would see him standing in front of him. They would be alone, removed from all the world. He would strike him in the face and see what he would do. This was the moment for which all his life he had been longing, to revenge himself upon the whole world for making him twisted and a cripple, all those people who had watched him as he walked, all the kind Herries relations who had despised and pitied him. Today he would revenge himself upon all his family – the crowd of them, so

pleased with themselves and their strong bodies and the children
they had begotten, so scornful of anyone unlike themselves . . .
and the fellow had dared – had dared – to marry his sister!

All morning he limped about the house thinking of a thousand
absurd things – how his grandfather Will, now, Heaven be
praised, dust and ashes, had looked at him across the dining-
table in Hill Street as though he said: 'This poor misshapen
creature – how can he be *my* grandson?' How Amery had invited
him to ride with him, adding: 'You *can* ride, can't you?' How he
had slipped on the stair at the Fortress, and Archdeacon
Rodney's young son had muttered (but Uhland had heard him):
'Poor devil!' How Sylvia had looked at his leg and then blushed
when he caught her – all, all, all pitying him, despising him,
scorning him! Leonardo had filled his room with newts and
toads and lizards and from them had constructed a figure so
horrible . . . There was power! Ah! there was power indeed! And
today he would be revenged on them all. He would make that
figure, seen all his days as the type of all that he himself despised
and hated, cringe and shake and fall – a strange fire ran in his
veins so that he felt almost as though his limp were gone and he
as strong as any of them.

With the exception of his own place and the servants' quarters,
his father's room was the only one in all the Fortress now that
was cared for. The rest was tumbling to ruin. The walls were
strong, but dust lay everywhere, and all the other rooms were
damp-smelling and foetid. But he went everywhere as though he
were saying goodbye to it all, a happy, glad goodbye. They called
it the Fortress first in admiration, now in jest and mockery. So
with this damned country: they thought that they were building
a Fortress, eaten up with conceit they were, but one day it would
be like this house, rotten and a jest to all the world. Pity he
couldn't live to see that day . . .

Later, with his gun over his shoulder, he went in to say farewell to his father.

Sir Walter Herries, Bart, was playing backgammon with his
housekeeper, a thin painted woman called Mrs Throstle. Mrs
Throstle enjoyed bright colours and was expecting friends from
Keswick, so she was dressed in a worsted poplin of bright yellow
and wore the most elaborate sleeves in the prevailing fashion,
ruffed muslin with coloured ribbons at the wrist. She had coral
bracelets. Over all this her sharp face peered anxiously at the
board, for she was a mean woman, and they were playing for

high stakes. Or so they seemed to her. But she always came out
right in the end, because if she won she won, and if she lost she
went through Herries' pockets at night after he slept and took
what there was. But there was not much these days because
everything was going to rack and ruin.

She was discontented, too, because Herries would not drink at
present. He was sober and cross and peevish. He had struck her
last night for saying that Uhland was a lame duck. She hated
Uhland, as indeed did all the servants.

Walter, very soberly dressed, gave only half his attention to the
game. He had been worried for weeks about Uhland, and his visit
to Judith yesterday had done little to relieve him. Indeed, it had
added to his discontent, for the Uldale house had looked so
bright and shining. He had liked Judith too, that neat, capable,
strong old woman, and all the silly enmity over which he had
spent so much of his energy seemed to have blown into thin air.
But enmity, hatred and all uncharitableness are never wasted, as
he was to find out before many days were over.

He looked up at the door opening and hungered with love for
his son. He saw that he was dressed for going out and had a gun
over his shoulder; at once he was alarmed with a strange interior
fear, the room seemed to fill with smoke before his eyes; his hand
trembled, and he knocked the backgammon board off the table.

'There now!' said Mrs Throstle. 'And I was winning too!'

'Clear out!' said Uhland sharply. 'I want to speak to my
father.'

Mrs Throstle rose, trembling. She was terrified of Uhland; one
look at his contemptuous face and she shook all over. She gathered herself together, touched her coral bracelets indignantly,
tossed her head and went. The round backgammon counters lay
on the dirty carpet, but Walter stared at his son.

'Going out?' he asked.

'Yes, Father.'

'Shooting?'

'Maybe.'

Walter rose heavily, stretched his arms and yawned.

'I think I'll come too. Fresh air will do me good.'

'No, Father. I'm going alone today.'

Uhland looked at his father and felt, to his own surprise, a
certain tenderness. He could remember – he did at this moment
vividly remember – old, old days at Westaways when everything
had been so rich, many people about, the house shining with

colour, and his father bursting with health and self-satisfaction.
But his father had wasted himself on emptiness, had let everything dribble through his hands like grain falling idly through
the air. Grain falling – it lay now, in layers of dust, thick upon
the floor. They had done nothing with their lives, either of them,
and he saw for perhaps the first time that if he had returned some
of his father's love things might have been otherwise. His father
had had no return for either his love or his hate. A dry, wasted
man ...

He did what of his own free will he had never done before –
limped up and put his hand on his father's shoulder.

'Better I go alone,' he said. 'I'm in a sulky temper.'

Walter was so deeply moved by his son's gesture that he said
angrily: 'You are always in a sulky temper.' He leaned his big
heavy body towards his son's. He touched the gun.

'Going shooting?' he asked again.

'Maybe,' answered Uhland. 'Goodbye then.' He moved
towards the door.

'When are you returning?'

'Oh, any time. Don't count on it,' and he went out, his backward glance from the door showing him his father bending his
great stern towards the floor that he might pick up the backgammon counters.

He rode down the hill and then slowly along the ridge of the Fell
towards Peter's House. He had plenty of time to be at Skiddaw
House by four. It was a day in which everything seemed restrained, as though the sun were longing to break out but was
held back by a strong hand. He passed an orchard where the pear
trees were a bright yellow, and then in the distance he saw how
the yellow hills were already autumnal, the heather resting on
them in a rosy shadow from place to place. He had always been
alive to beauty, although he resented it often because he felt that
it, like the rest of the world, mocked at any cripple; now today
the shadowed sun, the bright yellow of the leaves, the distant
hills, were all part of his own purpose. They knew what would
happen, and it was strange to him that they should all be able to
see ahead of him, certain of the event before it had occurred.

'Everything is arranged then,' he thought. 'It is quite settled
what I shall do. Every past incident contributes to this. I am
what I have been made. And yet I could turn back if I wished. I
would cheat God if God there be. I am greater than God, because

now if I wished I could ride up Ireby Hill again and go in quietly and play backgammon with my father.' He stayed his horse for a moment, and had the fantastic thought that 'just to show them' he would ride back. But he could not; of course, he could not. Old 'Rogue' Herries; his father's words when he was very little: 'Don't you hate that conceited young cousin of yours, Uhland?'; Rodney's young son muttering 'Poor devil!' . . . no, fragment after fragment had with infinite patience been brought together, all that he might ride to Skiddaw House to meet John Herries. And once again at the thought of that meeting his blood was hot.

Jane Bellairs was the only one in the house to see John go. She had two great devotions in her life – one for her great-great-aunt Judith, the other for her uncle John. She eliminated, as did her brothers and sisters, the degrees of greatness from Judith, and called her quite simply (and very proudly) 'my aunt'.

'But, dear, she cannot be your aunt,' tiresome Mrs Munberry in Keswick had years ago said to her. 'She is far too elderly. You mean great-aunt.'

But Jane had simply thought Mrs Munberry a foolish old witch, with her grey hair and sharp eyebrows. For all the children Judith was ageless. She had lived, of course, for ever, and would live for ever. She was like God, only more easily loved. But Uncle John was Jane's especial property. When he was absent in London, Jane not only prayed for him night and morning but also talked to him when she was alone, asked him whether she could fetch him anything, and thought about him before she slept, because she was certain that he was lonely. This idea that he must be lonely had come to her at a very early age when, rocking her doll by the fire in the parlour, she had looked up and seen him staring out of window.

She had given him her doll to care for, and also, although he did not perhaps know it, herself at the same time. The others laughed at her for her devotion, especially Veronica, who was a good hearty girl with no nonsense about her. But Jane did not mind when they laughed. She had long grown accustomed to having her own private life, a life that no one understood but Aunt Judith. Her mother least of all, for Dorothy would perpetually be saying: 'Dreaming again, Jane. Where's your work, child?' and Jane would pick up her piece of worsted on which she was embroidering a red rose or a ship with sails and, with a small sigh that nobody heard, pricking her forefinger and biting her lip, would set about it. She was, however, as Dorothy frequently declared, the easiest of all the children, for when she lost her temper she was quiet, not noisy like the others, and could amuse herself quite happily all the day long. Although she was nearly fourteen years of age now she was very slight and small.

'That child will never grow,' Dorothy exclaimed, and Judith replied: 'My dear, don't be foolish. I'm eighty and have never grown an inch since I was eight.'

And now she was the only one of all the family to see John go. All morning she had been painting a picture. This was her favourite pursuit, and here too the others laughed at her because she did not paint easy things like cottages and cows and the sun, very red with rays like wires, setting on a mountain, but things much too difficult for her, like the Queen in her Palace, the whale swallowing Jonah, and Noah seeing dry land. Yesterday on her walk she had seen some horses drinking from a pond, and this morning she had been drawing a great white horse swimming. Beyond the pond there were mountains, and for some reason (she did not know why) it was winter and the pond was black with ice. She covered the pond with purple paint. This painting was to be for John and, before dinner, she looked for him everywhere to give it to him. She found him coming from the stable, leading his horse Barnabas, and the small dog Mumps was with him. He smiled when he saw the little girl in her pink bonnet. Her dress, with its double skirt and fan-shaped corsage, made her quaint while on the other children it seemed quite natural. It was as though she were in fancy-dress.

'Hullo, Janey!' he said.

'Are you going to ride?'

'Yes.' He put his arm around her and kissed her.

'I've been up to Auntie's room and she's sleeping yet.'

Judith had not been well that morning and when she was not well all the house was quieter. Jane considered him. Should she show him her painting? He was busy because he was going riding.

Yes, she would. She *must* show him.

'I've done a painting and it's for you.'

'Let's see.' He bent down, while Barnabas and Mumps stood patiently waiting. All he saw was that some kind of animal was sitting on a floor of purple paint. But he guessed that the animal was a horse.

'That's a grand horse,' he said, pinching her cheek.

'Yes, and it's swimming in a pond all frozen with ice, and then it will ride up the mountain.'

'What a splendid horse! Is that for me?'

'Yes.'

He kissed her and held her for a moment close to him. Then he put the painting very carefully in his riding-coat pocket.

'Goodbye, my darling.'

'Where are you riding to?'

'Oh, only a little way.'

'Will you be back before I go to bed?'

'Yes, sweetheart.'

'Will you read *Nicholas Nickleby*?'

'Yes, if there's time enough.'

She stood in the gateway waving to him until he was out of sight. At the corner before the houses of the village hid him he turned on his horse and waved back to her. She ran into the house and wondered what there would be for dinner.

When, beyond the village, he was riding by Langlands he noticed an orchard and how yellow the leaves of the pear trees were. That made his heart beat, and the thick grass under the trees, the spikes of some of the sharper grasses, were already brown at the tips. There had been frost every morning of late. Then, as he turned towards Over Water, he realized that Mumps was running most confidently at his side, his little black eyes sparkling, his mouth open, stopping for quick snatched moments to sniff at a smell, his whole person expressing extreme content and happiness.

He must not have Mumps with him on this ride, so he pulled Barnabas up and said sharply:

'Go home, Mumps! Go home!'

Mumps stopped and looked at him as though he had just received the surprise of his life, as though he could not, in fact, believe his ears.

'Go home, Mumps! I mean it.' And he flourished his whip. Barnabas also exchanged a look with Mumps, saying: 'Yes. This is genuine.'

Mumps ran forward, pretending that he had discovered so rich a smell that John must be pleased, and being pleased, would soften his heart. Then he stood, with one paw raised, intently listening. Then when that was of no avail he sat down and scratched his underparts. Then, that accomplished, he looked up at John pleadingly. All of no value. The stern order was repeated, so, after one more imploring stare, he surrendered and slunk down the road, his tail between his legs. Round the bend, he reconsidered the matter. He saw that his master was slowly riding on, so, slowly, he followed, maintaining a tactful distance.

When John had Over Water on his right and was approaching Orthwaite Hall, he heard a bell ringing, the kind of bell that rings from the belfry of a manor-house calling the servants to a meal. It came beautifully through the honey-misted air. 'It is as though,' he thought, 'some giant were holding back the sun.' Thin patches of sunlight lay on the fields, and on the hills the heather spread in clouds of rosy shadow. All was dim, and the little sheet of water was like a buckler on whose surface someone had been breathing, silver under cobweb, without bounds, raised in air above the soil.

'It's funny,' he thought. 'Aunt Judith has always said that she could see Over Water from the windows of the house. Of course she could not. She must have the neck of a giraffe.' And yet he himself had often thought that he saw Over Water from those windows – a mirage. But how friendly a little piece of water it was! All his life he had loved it – his whole life long.

Then, with a sharp stab of anticipation, he was aware of what he was about. Somewhere already in this misty countryside Uhland Herries was riding. They might meet on the way. He was somewhere near, shadow behind shadow – and the bell, still ringing, echoed in the air: 'This – Time – is – the – Last. This – Time – is – the – Last.' He was conscious of an awful temptation to turn back. Perspiration beaded his forehead. Why should he go on – to his death maybe? This lovely land that all his life he had adored; why should everything have been spoilt for him so long by one person to whom he had never done any harm? No. He must recognize that Uhland was only a symbol. Life would have been for him always a place of fears and terrors even though Uhland had never been born. What did the ordinary man – men like Garth and Uncle Will and old James – know about such a life, know how it was to wake in the night because you heard a sound, to turn in the street and look back over your shoulder, to watch a picture lest it should drop from the wall, to hear a mouse scratch in the wainscot so that your heart thumped, to expect with every post bad news, to fight, all your life long, shadows, shadows, shadows? ...

Oh, to be done with it, to throw fear out of your heart like a dirty rag, and then perhaps he would be like Adam, so quiet and sure, a little ironical about life but never afraid of it, with a heart so unalarmed that it could spend itself on love of others. He thought then that he heard a horse's hoofs knocking on the road behind him, and he turned sharply. But there was no one. The bell had ceased to ring. At last, today, it would be over. He would settle with Uhland for ever. *That* fear at least should be killed.

He rode on, past Peter's House, up on to the path across the Fell leading to the road that climbed under Dead Crag up steeply past Dash Waterfall. On his right were the Caldbeck Fells humped against the sky and stained now with every colour, the rose and purple of the heather, silver grey where the grass was thin, a bright and burning green of fields between walls, and down the side of one fell splashes of white quartz ran like spilt milk.

He looked about him to see whether anywhere there was another rider. He could see for a great distance now, to the right to the sweep of the Bassenthwaite Woods, to the left where the dark wine-stained sea of heather, grass and bare soil ran in a flood to the feet of the Caldbeck Fells, breaking, as it began to climb, into patches of field, a farm with a white wall, cows and sheep grazing. But no human being moved in all the landscape. Under Dead Crag, before he began to climb, he thought of the ravens for which the Crag was famous. He looked up to where the jagged edge cut the sky, and two birds, as though in answer to a call, floated out like black leaves, circled silently in the still air. The only sound was made by the Dash that tumbled with fierce gestures from the height above. It was full and strong, which was strange when there had been so little rain.

He was sorry that he had not been able to see Aunt Judith before he left, and yet it was perhaps as well. She had sent down word that she would like to see him in her room after her three o'clock dinner, and of course he knew what it was that she wanted – to persuade him at once to return to London. He wondered what reason she would have given: something about Elizabeth, he supposed, and at the thought of Elizabeth his heart seemed to stop its beat. If he did not return from this ride . . . if he did not return . . . Never to see her again . . . He climbed the steep road.

When Uhland reached Orthwaite Hall and looked across Over

Water the bell had ceased to ring. Then suddenly it began again, softly, steadily, persistently: 'Going – going – gone . . .'

Uhland looked at the Tarn, and then turning to the hills saw a thick tangle of mist like the ends of a woman's mantilla stray loosely over the tops. If the mists were coming down that would be serious. Many a man had been lost for hours between Calva and Skiddaw when the mist fell. The House would be hard to find, and, as though he had made a bet with some contestant, he was pledged to reach the place by four. The sun that had been shining so warmly when John half an hour before had been there, now was withdrawing. The light still lay in patches on the fields and the moor; down the Caldbeck Fells the shadow slipped, leaving the glow bare behind it as the skirts of a woman might fall.

But Uhland was aware now of a great impatience. Nothing should cheat him of this meeting. He longed to have John close to him, to see him flinch, above all to put to the final test all that those years and years of shadowing had anticipated. He urged on his horse, hearing the bell follow him as he rode up towards Dead Crag and the shining tumble of the Dash. He looked up at the steep road that ran up under the Crag and saw three birds circling like black leaves above the line of rock.

'Those must be ravens,' he thought, and remembered how, when he was a very small child, he had heard men tell of the ravens that haunted Dead Crag, and how, years ago, after the 'Forty-Five Rebellion', they had flown above the corpses of men, crying and calling in a vindictive triumph. He looked about him, down to the Bassenthwaite Woods that were now black like iron, then across to the sequence of fell-tops, but he could see no other rider.

'Is he behind me or before me?' he thought, and again that hot excitement as of wine pouring through his body exalted him. He felt a sort of grandeur that he had never known before. His lameness did not handicap him now. He was as good as anyone, and better, for he was on his way to dominate and conquer that supercilious, disdainful fool whom he would have down on his knees before the day was over.

But when he had almost reached the top of the road and the waters of the Dash were loud in his ears, he saw that the mist was beginning to pour like smoke from behind the hills. It came in eddies and whirls of movement although there was no wind. Greedily it ate up the farms, the fields, rose for a moment as

though beaten by the sun, then fell again. When he was actually
on the height he saw it advancing from every side. He pushed his
horse forward and a moment later felt its cold fingers on his
cheek. The whole world was blotted out.

The first thing that John heard when he started away from the
Dash was the eager, excited breathing of a dog. He looked back
and saw Mumps, his tongue out, happily racing towards him.
The dog knew that now there was nothing to be done. Too late
now to order him to go back. He felt a strange comfort as though
this were a sign from Fell House.

He was soon lost in the spaces of Skiddaw Forest. There was
no forest here; there had never perhaps been trees; the name was
used in the old Scottish hunting sense of a place for game. John
knew slightly General Sir Henry Wyndham whose land this was,
and his keeper Donald Grant, who lived at the House, his present
destination. The House was one of the loneliest dwelling-places
in all the British Isles, the only building from Threlkeld to Dash.
John knew also that, at this moment, Grant was in Scotland, his
family with him. He had heard only the week before that the
House was closed.

He could not anywhere in the whole world be more alone than
he now was. A chill, in contrast with the warm valley below, was
in the air, and the patches of heather, the sharp green of the grass
where the bilberries had been, the grey boulders, all had lost the
brilliance of their colour. He looked back once before he went on
and saw the Solway lit with a shaft of sunlight that glittered and
trembled under the line of Criffel and his companions. He was
leaving that shining world and with every step of his horse was
advancing into danger. On his right the flanks of Skiddaw began
to extend and he could see the cairn that marked its peak against
the sky. Calva was on his left. A moment later he saw the bounds
of his journey's end, on the right Lonskill Crag, and on the left,
extraordinarily black and angry, the sharp line of Foul Crag,
Blencathra's edge. Between them, far away, in sunlight like the
smile of another world, was the ridge of Helvellyn. Sunlight
behind him, sunlight before him, but his own country dark,
shadowed, without form, guarded by hostile crags. He knew that
under Lonskill was the House, and at the thought that he was
now so near to it a shudder that he could not control took him.
Soon he would come to the Caldew river, and, crossing that, he
would move into his fate, a fate that had been advancing upon

him since the day of his birth and before whose menace he had
been always helpless.

It was then that he noticed the mist. It came on the right from
Skiddaw, on the left from Calva. It tossed and rolled, crept
almost to his feet. Was Uhland in front of him or behind? And,
even as he asked himself, the whole world was blotted out.

CLIMAX TO A LONG SEQUENCE

III

In a Dark House

WHEN Uhland felt the wet mist close in he was conscious of
an almost desperate irritation. He was of so morbid and irritable
a temperament that he had always been unusually susceptible to
weather, to places, to trees and hills. He did not, as did John and
Adam, feel that this country was in any case beloved, that, whatever it chose to do, it was to be accepted and welcomed as an ally.
It had seemed to him all his life bent on his frustration, and, like
others of his kind, he discounted lovely days but recorded all the
disappointments and, as they seemed to him, the malignancies.

The fellow, he now contemptuously thought, would take this
mist as an excuse: 'I could not find the House. When the mist
came on I turned back' – and it seemed to Uhland that there
would never be an opportunity again. If he missed this he missed
his power over the man. He would hate him no longer but would
henceforth hate himself, and, more than that, be choked till he
died with this passion of which he could not rid himself.

He rode a little way and could not tell whether he were going
forward or back. He had been often in such mists before, but had
never been baffled and blinded as he now was, and, as always
when it was damp, his lame leg began to ache, as angry as he was
at this frustration.

He stopped to see whether he could hear the Caldew. It must
be somewhere near, but he had never in his life known such a
silence as had now fastened about him. The absence of any sound
or movement closed in upon his ears like the beat of a drum. He
moved on again, and as one often does in mist, thought that

someone was close behind him. It would be just like that fellow to stab or shoot him in the back, an easy way once and for all to rid himself of his enemy, and, although Uhland was not afraid, it would be the last fitting irony of the injustice that he had all his life suffered under to be stabbed in the dark and dropped into space like carrion. He listened. Behind him something moved, pebbles were displaced, or there was a soft crunching of the grass.

'Herries, are you there?' he cried, and his own voice, the voice that he had always despised and hated, came back clogged with wet mist. 'Herries, are you there?'

The scene was fantastic, for at his feet and just in front of him little fragments of ground were exposed, were closed, and were exposed again. The mist immediately surrounding him was so thick that it was like fog and so wetting that he was already soaked through and through his clothes. It cleared at the top of Calva, and the round shoulder of the hill sprang out like a live thing on his left. It was so clear that he could see the patches of bright green and bare boulders lit with a chill iridescence as though in moonlight. Calva frowned at him, then raced under mist again, leaving only a fragment like a bare arm lying nonchalantly in space.

His horse struck pebbles, and then he heared the slow stealthy murmur of the Caldew. Well, he was moving forward, for not far beyond was the rising hill on which the House stood. Behind the House was a wood, and if Wyndham's keeper should be at home they could finish this affair among the trees. No one would see them on such a day.

There should be a little wooden bridge over the Caldew. He pulled in his horse, jumped off and peered around him. Now, if John Herries was really behind him, would be the time for him to come at him, and perhaps they would struggle there where they stood and end it once and for all.

He spoke again: 'Now, Herries, I'm on foot . . . Are you there?' There was no answer. If Herries *were* there he was sitting motionless on his horse, and Uhland fancied that he could *see* a horse there in the mist, and on it a gigantic figure, motionless, waiting. He stumbled and almost fell over the rocks into the stream. With an oath he pulled himself back and began to find his way along the bank. Now he had lost the horse, for the mist was around him like a wall, but the horse whinnied, and at the same moment he discovered the wooden bridge. He went back and led

the horse safely across. Now he knew where he was, for at once
the ground began to rise. He came to a gate, opened it, leading the
horse through.

It was at this point that it was exactly as though someone stood
in his path. For a moment he *could* not move, and he felt as
though a great hand were pressed against his chest.

'Let me through, damn you,' he said, and stumbled and fell.
His lame leg often failed him, but now it was over a rock that he
had fallen. He had cut his hand, and his body pressed into the
wet soil, just as though someone were on his back holding him
down. The soil was filthy, soaking, deep in mire. His cheeks were
muddy and the knees of his breeches heavy with water. He
pushed backwards and was suddenly freed, as light as air, the
mist thinning so that, as he got on to his feet again, he saw the
House only a little way above him, swimming in air like a ship in
the sea. He moved forward, leading the horse, unlatched the gate,
passed through a small tangled garden of cabbages and currant
bushes. His feet grated on a gravel path, and he saw that in one of
the windows of the House a candle was shining.

Uhland's thought had not been far out. John, as the mist en-
folded him, had felt stir in him that weak boneless animal, so
long so hated a companion, who whimpered: 'Here is a way of
escape. You can say that you were lost, had to turn back.' He
stopped his horse and stayed there, listening and considering. At
once an odd memory came to him, odd because he had not
thought of it for years, and now it touched him as though there
were suddenly a warm, strong hand on his shoulder. He remembered how once, when they were little children, Aunt Judith had
told them a story of their grandfather, David Herries; how he
had run away with their grandmother, years, years ago when she
was a girl, and fleeing with her from Wasdale up Stye Head had
been pursued by an uncle or someone of the kind – and then by
the Tarn, in swirling mist, Grandfather David and the uncle had
fought while Grandmother Herries watched, and Grandfather
David had killed the other. It had sounded then a grand story,
like a story out of a book, unrelated in any way to the warm fires
and old armchairs of Uldale. Now it was real. The mist that at
this moment swirled about him had swirled about David Herries
then, and David Herries had won. It was almost as though someone rode beside him, smiling at him as they went. So then he rode
forward, but nevertheless the memory of an old story could not

kill the struggle within himself. 'Turn back! Turn back!' the
boneless creature said. 'You know that you are afraid. You know
that when you are face to face with him that old terror will be too
strong for you, and at the first word from that voice you'll
run.'

And the other companion at his side seemed to whisper: 'Go
on! You have nothing to fear. All your life you have been
fighting shadows, and today at last you will discover what
shadows they have been.'

Yes, that was true. It had begun in his very babyhood when in
his cot he had seen how the reflections from the fire had made
fearful shapes on the wall. Then his nurse, old Mrs Ponder, how
he had shivered as he heard her heavy step on the stair, and her
voice as she said, 'Now, Mr John. I dare you to move!' and he
had stood, his heart thumping, transfixed; then the day when she
had thrown his rabbit out of window. The day, too, when he had
first seen Uhland, Uhland limping down the Keswick street, and
that pale face had turned towards him and something in him had
bent down and hidden away. The evening, too, when with Adam
he had seen Walter sitting his horse, silently, on the hill. But
Walter Herries had never meant much to him; the dread of his
whole life had been concentrated in Uhland, and it was of no use
for others to say, 'But this is phantasmal. There is no reality
here.' For his father, too, had found the real world a prison, and,
year after year, had allowed his mother to be mistress . . .

He threw up his head. 'I am revenging my father,' he thought,
'and my son, when he is born, will be fine if I am brave now.' For
he felt, as many men with imagination have done, that with the
vision they are given they can see that no men are apart, that
History has no Time, and that all souls struggle for victory
together.

So, greatly strengthened and as though suddenly he were
seeing his destiny for the first time, he pushed through the mist
as someone in a cellar pushes through wet cobwebs.

He now heard the running of the Caldew, and at the same
moment thought that Uhland was just behind him. He stopped
Barnabas and was aware of a multitude of noises. There was the
murmur of the stream, the thin breathing of the little dog, and, it
seemed to him, a multitude of whispering voices. Also dimly
there sounded music in the air. Since he was a boy he had known
that hereabouts was the place in Cumberland for finding the
Musical Stones – certain stones and boulders which, when cut,

gave out musical notes when you struck them. At the Museum in Keswick there was a good set of these stones, and Mr Cunningham at Caldbeck had a set on which he and his sons played many tunes. They beat them with a leather-covered hammer. Often as children Adam and he had come up to these parts and searched for them, and he had once had a stone that gave out a great ringing sound like an organ note. He had heard that in ancient days the Romans here had used them in their houses for gongs. This memory came to him now and pleased him. There was certainly some kind of music in the air. He waited. Maybe Uhland was also there waiting, but it was hard to see in the mist. If so this would be a good place to end it.

At last he said out loud: 'Is anyone there?' and again, 'Who's there?' But there was no answer.

He dismounted from Barnabas to find the wooden bridge across the stream, and at once Mumps found it for him, going in front of him and looking back to see whether he were following. After that, it was easy to mount the rising ground, and soon, leading Barnabas, he passed through the gate, along the little garden, and up to the door of the House. The mist floated about the walls in smoking wreaths. He could see dimly the wood. He found, as he had expected, that the door was locked. There was no one there. He went to the window on the right of the door and to his surprise it was slightly open. Then he tied Barnabas to the garden wall, pushed up the lower pane and easily vaulted into the room. It was so dark that for a while he stood there accustoming his eyes to it, and the mist poured in through the open window as though all the outer world were on fire. After a time he stumbled about, knocking his knees against a chair and the edge of a table. He found the fireplace, and on the mantel his hand closed on a candle. He struck a match from a box in his inner pocket and lit it. He waited, listening. He opened the door and went into the passage.

'Is anyone in the house?' he called.

There was no answer. He heard some hens running. Then he went back into the room, and almost immediately after there were steps on the pebble path outside.

Standing back against the mantel he heard the steps go to the door, he heard the lock shaken, then back to the window, a pause, and Uhland had climbed into the room.

As they faced one another the room at once became of great importance, and when Uhland closed the window behind him the

candle, that had been blowing wildly, steadied itself and seemed
to watch thereafter with a piercing eye. There was very little in
the room. A deal table, and on it a bright green mat and some
pallid wax fruit under a dusty glass cover. On the mantelpiece
were two large china dogs with bright red spots like a rash on
their bodies, a clock that pointed to five minutes to four although
it was not going. In the corner there was a grandfather clock that
leaned forward drunkenly, on the walls a large highly-coloured
print of the opening of the Great Exhibition and an engraving of
the Duke of Wellington covered with yellow damp-spots. There
was a wheel-back armchair with a patchwork cushion and in the
corner a child's rocking-horse. In another corner there was a
spinning-wheel. The floor was of brick. In the window there was
a dead plant in a pot.

Uhland set his gun against the wall and sat down. His leg hurt
him confoundedly. He rested his arms on the table, and stared at
John. As he looked he was reassured. He had thought that
perhaps now when they met at last he would find that there was
nothing to be done, nothing to be said. All this chase and pursuit
for so long had been a chimera. He would not be rid of the mad
impatience and restlessness in his heart by any contact with this
poor fool. He would just look at him contemptuously and let him
go. But it was not so. The very sight of John started his rage.
John had taken off his riding-coat. He wore a narrow blue tie
over which his shirt collar was folded, and his shirt had an inset-
breast of the finest linen. He wore a waistcoat of dark blue pat-
terned with tiny dark red flowers. He was not a dandy, but
everything about him was exquisitely clean and well-fitting. His
features, pale, keen, sensitive, gave him an air of great aloofness
and high breeding without, however, any conceit or arrogance,
and he seemed, in some way, in spite of his years, still a boy – for
his figure was slim as a boy's and his air as delicate and un-
touched by life as a boy's of seventeen might be.

Uhland knew that he himself was muddied, wet, and that his
hand was stained with blood. There was mud on his cheek. Yes,
he would spoil some of that beauty and aloofness before he left
that house, and once again the blood began to beat, hot and
insistent, in his veins.

He tapped with his fingers on the bare table.

'I'm here,' he said. 'What do you want to say?'

'I want to say this.' John found to his disgust that his hands
were trembling. He held them tight against his sides. 'I want to

ask you a question. Why for years now have you followed me – in London, here in Cumberland – everywhere? I have never done you any harm that I know.'

'I fancy,' said Uhland, 'that I may go where I please. Who says that I have been following you?'

'You know that you have, and that you have done it because it offends me. It must cease from now on.'

Uhland paused. Then he repeated softly: 'It must cease ... But why?'

'Because I say that it must.'

'You talk like a schoolboy,' Uhland replied. 'We are grown men. Of course I go where I please and do what I please. You are a coward, you know. You are the son of a coward, you were born a coward, you will be a coward until you die. Otherwise you would have faced up to me years ago.'

'No,' said John. 'I could not because you are a cripple.'

At that word Uhland's fingers ceased to beat on the table. A little shiver ran through his body.

'That makes a good excuse for you,' he said at last quietly. 'Now listen to me for a moment. It is quite true that I have always hated you. Your family is a disgrace. Your father allowed your mother to be a man's mistress for many years. I daresay the fellow paid him to keep quiet. Then your father was challenged to a duel and ran away. Then, because there was nothing else for him to do, he shot himself in London. Well, it has not been nice for the rest of us to have such relations at our very gates. It was very painful for my father. From the very first you gave yourself airs, you mocked at my lameness, you spread scandal about my father's manner of life. You were always – although you did nothing but walk about Keswick in your grand clothes – a vain fool. The very sight of you was an irritation, but an irritation that pleased me because you were, and are, so miserable a coward that a very look from me made you quake. And then you had the damned impertinence to marry my sister.'

'We will leave her out of this,' John said.

'Oh no, we will not. That is a score that I have been waiting a long while to pay ... Why, look!' he suddenly cried, with a mocking laugh. 'You are shaking now!'

'Yes,' John said, and he drew a little kitchen chair to the table and sat down. 'I will sit down. I am trembling, as you say, but that is because you always affect me so. A sort of disgust that I cannot control.'

But, as he spoke, he knew that it was more than disgust, it was fear from the disgust. Now if ever was the moment to which all his life had led. If he failed now, everything would be lost – his father, Elizabeth, their child. And he did not know that it would not be lost, for something within him – the traitor to himself that had been born with him – was urging him to run. 'Run! Run! Climb out of that window and run for your life.' His limbs were moving with a power that was not his own at all. He had to hold his feet against the brick floor. The fight within himself was so arduous that he could scarcely think of, or even see, Uhland. It was something more than Uhland, and something worse.

'If I move I'm lost,' he thought. He fixed his eyes on the pallid, deathly wax fruit. He fixed his eyes but he could not fix his heart. Ah, if only he could rise and throw himself on Uhland, that would be an escape as well as the other, but the man was a cripple, a damned cripple—

'I see,' said Uhland. 'I fill you with disgust. But it's yourself you're disgusted with. Because I found you out years ago. You've cheated the others, who think you a mighty fine fellow. I've shown you to yourself. Every time that I've been near you you've felt what you are. You have at least the grace to be ashamed . . .'

Then an odd thing occurred. Uhland stretched one of his arms out along the table, and his hand lay there, almost under John's eyes. It was a lean white hand, the knuckles red, and on the back of it thin hairs faintly yellow. The nails were long and dead. The hand seemed to John to curve and twist on the table, like a thing in a nightmare, and, when it was close to him, he was suddenly strengthened. Was it that hand that he had always been fearing? Was this the ghost? Was this all? His eyes cleared. The room was formed and plain. The spinning-wheel was real, the Duke looked at him with grave, stern eyes. His legs were no longer trembling.

'Well,' he said in a clear strong voice that had no quaver, 'whatever the past has been, I am afraid of you no longer. You should have done more with your life than to spend it over one man, in especial if he's the poor creature you think me. I am afraid of you no more, so you can follow me no more. Nor shall you insult my father and mother again. You may be lame or not lame. After those insults your lameness is of no account, and before we leave this house you are down on your knees – on your knees. When you please. Choose your time. We can be here all night if you wish.'

Would his courage last? Was this a true lasting thing that he felt? For the first time he looked Uhland straight in the face.

Uhland withdrew his hand. He now was trembling, but with anger, the choking wild anger that so constantly came to him from the sense of his own ostracism. It was as though, at John's repeated 'lameness', all the world laughed, and a little crowd of sympathizers inside himself massed together and begged him to avenge them.

'You coward!' he cried in that odd shrill voice that should have been, if fate had been fair, rich, deep and generous. 'Why, you are afraid of your own shadow! You shall stay here – do you hear? – and you shall not move! Stay there without moving until I bid you, and then it is you who shall be on your knees, and beg and pray, and beg—' He half rose, leaning forward on his arms, his thin muddied face staring into John's.

And John could not move. He would have risen and he could not. Something within him was melting, loosening . . . in another moment it would be too late for ever.

It seemed that an hour passed. It was only a moment. Then, his head bent as though he were putting forth all his strength, at the instant when his power seemed gone, he pushed over the table.

It fell with a crash, the wax fruit with it, and the glass shattering on the brick floor.

His eyes shining, he stood back to the wall. He would not touch the man! He would not touch the man! But all fear was gone. He was strong with his whole strength—

'Come on, Uhland. Down!' he cried, laughing. 'I won't touch you. On your knees and then off with you. Back home—'

He saw Uhland stand. He marked every part of him, his hair thin on the top, the mud on his cheek, his damp stock, the round buttons of his coat. He saw Uhland take his gun from the wall. He thought, 'Elizabeth!' Uhland fired.

At the noise the little dog on the path outside began to bark. He barked running up and down outside the closed door. Then he began to whimper, again and again scratching at the door. The room was filled with smoke and mist. Slowly it cleared. Uhland stood for a long while with the gun in his hand, but at last he leant it carefully against the wall and went over to the empty fireplace. He bent down and looked at the body. John lay there, his face hidden in his arm. Very gently Uhland turned him over, unfastened his waistcoat, felt for his heart. John was dead.

'Well, that is the end,' he thought.

He felt no relief; only an increased grudge of injustice. He felt sick, too, with that accustomed nausea that had so often attacked him. He sat in the wheel-back chair, licking his dry lips with his tongue. The whole aim of his life was gone, and what it had been he had now no idea. He was sorry for no one but himself, and even about himself he felt now a bitter, savage irony. All those days and years for nothing. He had had a right to be in a rage, but how purposeless rage was! He was the victim of the grossest injustice, but what a poor, muddy, shabby victim! He felt an especial rage with his nausea. To be sick now would be the last indignity. But he would not be sick. At least he could prevent that. And this was all the long pursuit had come to . . . nothing . . . sickness . . . and his hand was bleeding again. He looked about the room. He knew what he wanted. A piece of paper. He got up and limped here and there, almost stumbling once over John's body. There was no paper anywhere, and why to God was that dog outside whimpering? He blundered against the clock, and it lurched as though it tapped him on the shoulder. No paper anywhere. He knelt down, with difficulty, because his knees were stiff. Then he got up again. No, he would try first the riding-coat. In the inside pocket he found a paper and drew it out. It was once folded. What the devil was this? a crude paint-ing, a sea of purple and some animal, a horse, a cow. But the reverse side was blank.

He sat down at the table and, taking a pencil from his pocket, wrote:

To all whom it may concern.

This is to say that John Herries of Fell House, Uldale, and I, Uhland Herries of High Ireby, met here at Skiddaw House by appointment. After a discussion we quarrelled, and I shot John Herries, he being undefended. After, I shot myself.

UHLAND HERRIES.

September 23rd, 1854

He laid the paper on the table, then unfastened his stock and laid that beside it.

He went to his gun, loaded it, placed the muzzle inside his mouth and fired.

Part Four

Mother and Son

BIRTH OF VANESSA

'Eighty-five! Is she, by God!' said Captain O'Brien, putting up his eyeglass.

'Yes,' said Veronica, smiling. 'But you mustn't swear. You swear dreadfully, Captain O'Brien, and I don't think it's at all nice.'

'Do I, by God?' said the Captain. 'I mean to say, Miss Veronica, I'd no idea ... 'pon my soul, I must get a hold on myself. Is it our turn? Damn the game! Always getting in the way ... What I mean to say—'

'Yes, I suppose it is our turn. What do you think, Captain O'Brien? Shall we have war with France? Louis Napoleon is *very* dangerous, isn't he? But of course we've got the Volunteers.'

'Ho! the Volunteers!' shouted the Captain in derision. 'The Volunteers! That's good. Damned useful they'll be. But I tell you what, Miss Veronica.' But it *was* his turn. Amabel, who was playing (most reluctantly) with the Reverend Mr Hall, a bony, black-bearded clergyman from Penrith, had missed her hoop.

The occasion was a garden-party given by 'Madame' to her friends and neighbours on an afternoon of the summer of '59. Most fortunately it was a lovely day – fortunate because in August you never could be sure, the most treacherous month of the year in these districts. But today was lovely indeed, as Mrs O'Brien said over and over to anyone who would listen to her. 'Most lovely! Most fortunate! Who would have supposed? And such a lovely garden!'

The old house was gentle and benign under the small ivory clouds that floated in shreds and patches on the summer sky. The lawn was a smooth stainless green. The part of it that spread under the cherry-coloured wall had been laid out for croquet. Near the Gothic temple a tent had been set up for tea; the servants were coming backwards and forwards from the house.

Chairs were arranged under the wing of the house near the croquet-lawn, and in the shade of the trees by the Temple there were more chairs, two or three, placed beside Madame's. To these, people were led up in turns to talk to her – 'Not for too long, you understand,' Dorothy explained. 'So as not to tire her, you know. But she enjoys everything. She was never better in her life. Yes, eighty-four last Christmas. Most extraordinary! But she has always enjoyed the best of health! She does delight in a talk! Everything interests her!'

'A very pretty scene!' Judith thought happily. Although she was in the shade, the sun warmed her through the trees. She was wearing the black dress with the white lace at her throat and wrists that had been for so many years now her costume, but around her shoulders was the beautiful Cashmere shawl that Adam had given to her last Christmas, a shawl light, soft and bright, embroidered in silk with a heavy knotted silk fringe at its edge. On her head she wore a cap of white lace and, every once and again, she held over her head a black parasol. Against her chair rested her famous cane. Her face now had the pallor of ivory, but the cheeks were stouter than they used to be. Her eyes shone with a startling brilliance. She missed nothing. On her breast she wore a locket that contained Adam's picture. 'A very pretty scene!' but nevertheless she thought the crinolines ridiculous. They were not, perhaps, quite so absurd for young girls like Veronica and Jane, but Dorothy now! Yes, Dorothy was monstrous. She was a woman of fifty-one and had grown very stout. Her crinoline was vast and very heavy. It was of Chinese gauze and had twelve flounces. Her sleeves also had many flounces, and they looked as though a number of horns had been stuck one within another. Her bertha had ruches, embroideries in profusion, and she wore on her shoulders a Scottish plaid which the Empress Eugénie had made the fashion after her visit to her maternal home. A graceful woman might do something with all this – but a woman of Dorothy's figure! And when she moved in the house all the furniture was in constant peril!

The girls were pretty; at any rate Veronica in white, with her bonnet far back on her head, showing her really beautiful dark hair almost to the crown; and darling Jane, so fair, so slender, although no one thought her pretty in comparison with Veronica, was, in Judith's eyes, bewitching.

As the figures moved across the lawn, in their wide swinging dresses, white, rose and blue, the sun shining down so benevolently, no sounds save the click of the mallets and the balls, the murmur of voices, the clink of the china as the servants (Lucy and Emily – *such* good girls) arranged the tea, Judith felt a deep, satisfying content. The only thing was that Margaret was not so well. Her child was due very soon now, but Doctor Bettany said not for a week, he thought. But she had not been well this morning. Adam was anxious. Strange to have, after all these years of marriage, their first child! And Margaret was not so young any longer.

Ah, here was that tiresome, silly Mrs Osmaston. Mrs Osmaston was thin, withered and weary. She had had so many children that nothing remained of her but a bone or two, a nervous cough and an interest in gossip. She was neither kind nor unkind, discreet nor indiscreet. The only two facts certain about her were – one, that she had been a mother many many times, and two, that she was exceedingly stupid. She was afraid of Judith, who, she was sure, mocked at her when her back was turned. No one in the world ought to be both so old and so vigorous. There she was, a magazine on her lap, and she had been reading without glasses.

'Oh, what is it you have been reading, dear Madame Paris?' Mrs Osmaston asked, seating herself with care in the garden chair. Her crinoline was of the latest fashion, that is, its steel hoops were lowered so that they did not begin immediately below the bodice but only at the knees, and in this way the dress fitted under the hips and only began to grow wider below the knees. This scarcely suited Mrs Osmaston's thin figure, but she was very proud of it and thought herself smarter than any other woman present. And *what* she thought of Dorothy Bellairs! Oh, but she would entertain the family circle when she arrived home this evening! (She could not see, fortunately, the Shade of her great-grandmother-in-law, who, a swearing, horsy, good-natured Ghost, looked out from the Gothic Temple, remembering how she once had drunk tea on this very lawn, and wondered, in her hearty indecent fashion, at this ridiculous Ghost of a descendant-in-law.)

'Yes, what is it you have been reading, dear Madame Paris?'

'Interesting,' said Judith, picking up the *Quarterly Review*. 'There are some comments on Mr Tennyson's *Idylls of the King*.' She read: '*The chastity and moral elevation of this volume, its essential and profound though not didactic Christianity, are such as perhaps cannot be matched throughout the circle of English literature in conjunction with an equal power.*' She paused and gave Mrs Osmaston a sharp look. Then she continued, a little lower down:

'*He has had to tread upon ground which must have been slippery for any foot but his. We are far from knowing that either*

Lancelot or Guinevere would have been safe even for mature readers, were it not for the instinctive purity of his mind and the high skill of his management . . .'

Judith looked Mrs Osmaston full in the face and casting the *Quarterly* upon the grass, repeated: 'Chastity and moral elevation! Stuff! Did you ever hear such humbug and hypocritical nonsense, Mrs Osmaston?'

Mrs Osmaston, who had just been preparing to say that she thought it one of the most beautiful critical utterances she had ever listened to, sent her Adam's apple up and down in so swift a necessity for reversal of judgement. She gasped like a fish suddenly raised from the water.

'Oh yes . . . indeed, yes . . . very absurd. I have not yet read Mr Tennyson's *Idylls.*

Judith wished that she had not been so impulsive. The last thing that she wished was to make Mrs Osmaston unhappy. The older she grew the greater need she saw in the world for general kindness and charity, and the harder she found it to suffer fools gladly. That was why life was always difficult, amusing and exciting.

She knew that now, simply because of this little incident, Mrs Osmaston would go away and talk, like a hen scratching in a backyard. Judith could hear her. 'Not softened in the least by that awful tragedy of five years ago. You would have thought that such a *terrible* thing . . .'

Not softened! Judith's heart and gaze left the garden and the figures moving across the lawn, and she was caught up again, as she so constantly was, into that dreadful afternoon and evening . . . Yes, five years ago . . . when, lying in bed, she had heard first that John had ridden out, no one knew whither, and how then, with a frightened pathetic foreboding, she had lain there listening to every sound, and at last she could bear it no longer but had got up and come downstairs. And she and Dorothy had sat there, waiting, listening. Then the opening of the gate, the rap on the door, the news that his body was outside . . .

And after that, old though she was, she had held everything together. There had been a wild, mad, hysterical letter from Walter; Elizabeth had come, a lovely fragile ghost, and in February of the next year had borne a boy, here at Fell House, whom she had named Benjamin. There had been Jane, too, who for a while had seemed to be mentally unsettled. The poor child had fancied that there was something that she might have done, might have held him there, prevented him from riding ...

The excitement in the neighbourhood had gone on and on and on ... It was only, they all said, what they might have expected. There had always been a strain of madness in the Herries. Didn't old Herries in the eighteenth century sell his mistress at a Fair, kill his first wife with unkindness, and marry a gipsy for his second? Hadn't Madame always been crazy, clever though she was? And all the sorry, stale business of Francis and Jennifer came up again, over and over, and then all the drunkenness and evil living at the Fortress, and Uhland of course was mad – everyone knew – but to shoot his cousin who was defenceless, there on Skiddaw, miles from anywhere – and the little dog had been whimpering like a human being when they found the bodies.

But somehow, by sheer strength of personality, Judith had dominated it all and beaten it down. Now at last the full value and force of her character was seen. For one thing so many of them liked her. She had done so many kindnesses, she was no respecter of persons, the same to one as to another, and yet she was dignified and commanding. She was the more commanding in that she no longer went about, and only visitors to the house saw her, and not many of *them*. But when they had visited her they always returned home with wonderful stories. Everyone obeyed her as though she were a General in an army, and yet everyone loved her. She thought of everyone and everything, and yet could rap you over the knuckles with a sharp word. She didn't care who it was that she rapped. The whole County was proud of her, admired her, talked of her without end, told every sort of tale about her. She was a legend.

And here was Adam coming towards them! She knew everything that was passing through his mind. She saw his quick glance at Mrs Osmaston, his loving look at herself. She smiled back, saying at the same time: 'Well, to my mind there's far too much nowadays of making small children feel that they're born in sin. Do not you think so, Mrs Osmaston?' She liked the beard that he had grown in the last year. It suited him; he looked well, solid and muscular, not stout as she had once feared that he would be. How dearly she loved the half-humorous half-cynical brightness of his eyes. He suffered fools no more gladly than she – in fact, she thought comfortably, they grew more like one another every day. But she could not persuade him to wear his party clothes. He would wear his sack coat and round hard hat, and the checks of his trousers were so *very* pronounced. All his clothes hung about him loosely, and there was Captain O'Brien with his great moustaches and tightly fitting fawn trousers so *extremely* elegant. She did hope that Veronica would not fall in love with him nor with young Mr Eustace, the curate, who with his fluffy hair and surprised gaze resembled a chicken just out of the egg!

'How do you do, Mr Paris?' said Mrs Osmaston a little stiffly; she was no more comfortable with the son than she was with the mother. And why did he wear such very ill-fitting clothes? He also wrote for the London magazines, which made him very dangerous, for you never knew that he might not put you into something!

Adam sat very close to his mother, his big square body protecting her tiny one. He exchanged, in a whisper, one quick word with her.

'I have just been in to see Margaret, Mother. She really is not so well. Do you think that I should send James for Bettany? He is over at Greystoke, you know.'

She nodded her head.

'Yes, dear, I should. Just as well.'

Adam bowed to Mrs Osmaston (sarcastically, she felt) and strode towards the house.

Ah, now, Judith thought, they are moving to the tent for tea. She had an impulse of impatience to run across the lawn that she might see that everything was right. But of course she could run no longer. But Lucy was a *good* girl and Dorothy had sense. And one good thing – she could now rid herself of Mrs Osmaston.

'Tea, Mrs Osmaston,' she said. 'I see they are going to the tent for tea. Mr Hattick,' she cried, her voice wonderfully sweet and clear, 'will you take Mrs Osmaston to tea?'

Mr Hattick was a stout red-faced manufacturer from Birmingham who had bought a place on Bassenthwaite Lake, a very common man. The County was still undecided whether to cut him or no, but he had been kind to Judith and presented Timothy with a fine bay, and if he was kind that was enough. And now it would be good for Mrs Osmaston that she should be taken into tea by Mr Hattick.

She was watching them moving across the lawn with much amusement when an awful thing occurred. Amabel suddenly appeared, and in her voice were the notes of excited surprise and exceeding pleasure.

'Oh, Aunt Judith — what do you think? Miss Martineau has come!'

Harriet Martineau! Of all appalling things! And now, when she was already a little tired and was thinking that she would go in presently and see how Margaret was . . .

Alas, Judith did not care for Miss Martineau, and had often congratulated herself that Ambleside was far distant from Uldale. She recognized that she was exceedingly wise, immensely learned, and possibly the greatest woman now alive in England, but Judith did not care for so much learning. She had never herself had much education, she was not a Positivist, she detested the thought of mesmerism, and she envied the way in which Miss Martineau milked her own cows and ploughed her own fields. Moreover, Miss Martineau never ceased to talk — about Comte, about America, about her marvellous Cure, about her weak heart, about her pigs and cows, about her novels (Judith thought *Deerbrook* a very silly book), about Mr Atkinson, about her *Guide to the Lakes*. Miss Martineau spoke always of the Lakes as though they were her own creation and would not have existed had it not been for her. She *patronized* the Lakes. In addition Harriet was all for women taking man's place; Judith did not see how they could possibly do so. They were very nice as they were: pretty Veronica twining Captain O'Brien around her little finger, and Margaret indoors about to present the world with a dear little baby. Harriet wanted women 'to rise up and take their proper place in the world'. As though, Judith thought indignantly, they had not their proper place already. And this was all very bad for Amabel, who said that she did not care for men and would like to be in Parliament. In Parliament! Women in Parliament! You might as well make doctors of them. Amabel adored Harriet Martineau, and was always hoping that she would be invited to stay at the Knoll.

But worst of all was Harriet's trumpet. Judith had, in spite of herself, a little scorn for deaf people because her own hearing was so extremely good. But a trumpet! . . . And Miss Martineau was so proud of it. Moreover, in a most irritating fashion, she would remove it in the middle of one of Judith's sentences. Malicious people said that she always did that if she thought that something was coming that she did not wish to hear. However, here she was — in no time at all she was striding towards them. 'Is it a woman or a man,' an old lady once said of her to William Howitt, 'or what sort of animal is it? said I to myself; there she came — stride,

stride, stride – great heavy shoes, stout leather leggings on, and a knapsack on her back – they say she mows her own grass, and digs her own cabbages and taturs!'

She was decently enough dressed today, with no ridiculous crinoline (that is in her favour, thought Judith), large boots certainly, and a thing like a Scotsman's bonnet on her head, and one of the fashionable Scottish plaids over her shoulders. In her right hand she held her trumpet; Amabel, listening to her every word, was beside her, and Adam, coming from the house, was not far behind.

'Well, well, well, Madame Paris, and how are you? I have been for the night in Caldbeck and am to be this evening in Keswick. I am giving an address on Domestic Economy as you have doubtless seen by the papers. And I have brought you my *Letters on the Laws of Man's Nature and Development*. It was published as far back as '51, you know, but Mrs Leeds told me that she was sure that you had not read it, and I thought that I would have your opinion. And here are some peaches straight from my garden. I said to myself, "Madame Paris shall have those peaches because she is a woman I admire. She should have been a man and represented us in Parliament." '

'Indeed I should not,' Judith answered indignantly, and then discovering that she was speaking into the air when she should have spoken into the trumpet, seized that instrument and shouted down into it: 'Indeed I would not have been a man for any money!'

'Would you not?' said Miss Martineau complacently and with a look of kindness at the old lady (for she liked those bright eyes and that independence, for she was as good-hearted and free of meanness as she was egoistic and free of sensitiveness). 'Well, I had no notion that you had a party.'

'Yes,' said Judith, catching the trumpet again. 'They are in the tent having tea. You had better go and have some.'

'Indeed I will not,' said Harriet, laughing. 'I have come to see *you* and I cannot stop more than a moment. My enlargement of the heart, you know, forbids me to stay long on a visit. Old Colonel Albany in Keswick insists on a talk. He says that he has several criticisms to make on my *Suggestions for the Future Government of India*. Criticism indeed! I shall like to hear what he has to say. All these old Colonels are the same. It has needed a woman to tell them the truth about their own affairs.' She kicked one leg in front of her and thrust her trumpet almost into Judith's eye.

'Now tell me what *you* think about India.'

'I, my dear?' Judith shook her head. 'Why, I have no thoughts about anything. I live in the past and not the sort of past that interests *you*, Miss Martineau. My past is all pin-cushions, lavender-water and parasols. I assure you there was never anyone with less opinions.'

'Don't you believe her, Miss Martineau,' said Adam, laughing. 'She is a mountain of opinions. There never was anyone with so many.'

But Miss Martineau had caught only the word 'mountain'.

'Mountain! That's what I said to Coleridge once—'

'Ah, you knew Coleridge,' Adam said eagerly. She caught that and it pleased her.

'Yes. I talked to him only once. Not that I can say that his career is anything but a warning. All that transcendental conversation, you know, was all nonsense. Nothing but nonsense—'

'Yes, but,' Adam shouted down the trumpet, 'what was he like? Tell us what he was like.'

'Oh, very fine – a perfect picture of an old poet. Neatly dressed in black as I remember, with perfectly white hair. And what I especially recollect was his underlip that quivered with a very touching expression of weakness – very touching indeed. The face was neither thin nor pale as I remember it, but the eyes! No, I must declare, although in my opinion his poetry will not be remembered and as to his philosophy – I cannot express the scorn I have for his philosophy – but I never *saw* such eyes. The *glitter*! The amazing *glitter*, and shining so that one was nearly afraid to look at them! All the same, the glitter was only opium, you know, nothing but opium.'

'The father of my little Hartley,' Judith thought, smiling to herself – and in some strange way now, at this moment, while the late afternoon sun threw long purple shadows over the grass, and, behind the temple, the trees, whose leaves were tenderly touched with orange, massed like a solid cloud against the line of faint and silver hills, the thick dreaming figure of the poet seemed to wander towards them across the lawn.

The girls, moving like dancers, came smiling from the tent. In the clear still air the rich unctuous voice of the Reverend Mr Hall could be heard saying: 'Ah, but, Miss Bellairs, you misunderstand me. It is against the rule of my cloth to have a bet with you, but nevertheless . . .'

'Mr Coleridge! Mr Coleridge!' Adam could have cried. 'Come

and sit with us and we will assure you that your poetry will never die!'

But Miss Martineau must be moving on. She was pleased that that sensible-looking child (Amabel) gazed at her with such evident devotion. Maybe she would invite her to stay at the Knoll. Her heart was warm and kind, and it was not *her* fault that she knew such a terrible deal about so many very different things. But, as she wished goodbye to Judith, she thought: 'I should like to become an old lady like that.' Then she stamped away to her carriage.

She was hardly gone when Will Leathwaite appeared and, standing solidly and quietly beside Adam, said: 'The doctor is come, Mr Adam.'

'I'll be with you,' said Judith.

He gave her his arm. Veronica came running towards them.

'Aunt Judith, can I help you?'

'No, my dear, thank you. It is growing chilly for me. You must be hostess, Veronica, my dear.'

They went into the house together, she leaning on Adam's arm, Will Leathwaite following them like a bodyguard. It was splendid to have Leathwaite: he was as obstinate as he was devoted, as scornful of what he did not understand as he was faithful to all that he loved. He loved Adam and all that Adam comprehended, but only *because* Adam comprehended.

'Will tolerates me,' Judith said to Adam, laughing.

'Will loves you.'

'Only because I'm your mother.'

'And what better reason could he have, pray?'

Stopping for a moment in the hall she said: 'Ah, there are Harriet's peaches and her book. I shall eat the peaches and not read the book. She's a kind soul, but I never wish to listen to what *she* wishes to tell me. Adam, I'm weary and shall go to bed.'

It was then that, looking up, they saw the doctor coming down the stairs towards them, and in that one glance the world was changed for both of them. Gone were Miss Martineau's book and peaches, crinolines swaying in the sunshine, pleasant lawns and rose-coloured garden walls. Adam jumped to the stairs and caught the doctor's arm.

'Bettany, what is it?'

'Labour has begun,' Bettany said gravely.

'Well, well?'

'It will be difficult. You can do nothing, Paris. Best stay down here.'

But Judith at once took charge.

'Yes, Adam. Wait in the parlour. All will be perfectly well. I am sure of it. Remember Margaret is a strong woman. There, there, Adam.' She leaned up to him and kissed his cheek. 'Don't be nervous. There is nothing that you can do. Women understand these things. Come with me, Doctor. Is there anything further you require?'

Then there came to all of them a sound from above, half-moan, half-cry. It seemed to break the silence, the indifference of the house as a rough hand tears tissue paper.

'Oh, my God!' Adam whispered.

But they were gone. He was alone. He summoned all his fortitude and turned with firm step to the parlour. Will Leathwaite was standing by the hall door.

'Is the mistress bad, sir?' he asked.

'Yes – no – I don't know, Will. But the labour pains have begun. Would you go into the garden and tell Mrs Bellairs quietly? Don't draw attention to it, you know. Ask her to come in to my mother.'

Leathwaite went. In the parlour Adam sat down on the old familiar sofa with the rosy apples. Nothing was changed, for Judith had forbidden any change. There was the spinet, there was the Chinese wallpaper, the silhouettes above the fireplace of David and Sarah Herries. Only Dorothy's needlework-box spoke something alien. Without knowing what he was doing he had it in his hands, and all his life after he was to remember it – with its polished walnut wood and satin-wood edge, the painted flowers on the top and sides, and inside it a tray painted pink, the wooden bobbins wound with coloured silks, the pin-cushion, the miniature hand mirror, the folding memorandum tablet in a morocco case, the needle-cushion of red and green wool with yellow beads, and a star-shaped piece of boxwood. The red and green needle-cushion he took between his hands and turned about and about a thousand times.

He had known nothing like this since Caesar Kraft had, on the day of the Chartist meeting, fallen dead at his feet. That had been one of the great crises of his life, because at that moment when Kraft had died in his arms he had resigned for ever all his life's hopes of Men's Brotherhood, of some movement that would catch the whole world up into some heavenly universal understanding and sympathy. Resigning those hopes, he had turned to his mother and to Margaret, the two persons in the world whom he supremely loved. His nature had developed a certain cynicism about the world in general. Men were not destined to understand one another and therefore, not understanding, also would not love. Love was to be found rather in the relationship with one or two individuals and in service to them. So he had lived for his mother and Margaret, and in a lesser degree for John and Elizabeth. John's death had once again set him back, for if so fearful a thing could happen so causelessly what was God about? He understood then that there was real evil in the world, that a battle was always in progress, and that one selfish, cruel act led to many more. One bad thought even had incalculable results. He understood from watching so small an entity as his own family that a battle between good and evil was even there always in progress. His was an age that believed quite definitely in good and evil, in God and the Devil, and in so far as Adam shared that belief, Adam was a man of his period.

With Margaret, after that scene in the bedroom here at Uldale one Christmas, his relation had grown ever richer and richer. He discovered that true love between two persons means a mutual interaction of beautiful, gay and noble discoveries. Both must be fine persons if love is to be full and progressive, and unless it is progressive it is not alive. He learnt that Margaret was far nobler that he, richer in unselfishness, in uncalculating generosity, in ever-growing charity, but as she rose higher she carried him with her. Love was this and only this: a companionship that was grander in trust, in humour, in understanding with every day.

He sat there, his broad legs widely spread, fingering the furniture of the needlework-box, the little wooden bobbins, the box-wood, the needle-cushion of red and green. He was maddened by his inaction. He walked about the room, sat down again. Once Dorothy looked in.

'How is she?' he said eagerly. 'Can I not go up?'

'Oh, well enough. The doctor is doing everything possible. No, better not go up just now, Adam. Margaret is wonderful. Her courage . . .'

Yes, Margaret was wonderful. But if she were to go now . . . A hundred scenes rushed in front of him – Margaret lying in bed, her hair spread about the pillow, waiting for him; Margaret singing some German song as she went about her work; Margaret sitting opposite him, sewing; Margaret listening as he read her some article or criticism or one of his fairy-stories that he loved to write and was so shy of showing to anybody. All quarrels and disputes were forgotten, or if remembered had an added colour and glow because of their intimacy. He crushed the needle-cushion out of shape, he jumped up and shook his fist at the ceiling, then creeping on tiptoe to the door like a child, he opened it and listened. There was not a sound in the house. Where were they all? Were all the guests gone? The hall was in a half-light, but Leathwaite stepped out of the dusk.

'It's warmer in the library,' said Will confidentially, and then relapsed for a moment into Cumberland. 'The spumkey fire's burning fine – and I've told Jeames to give the mare watter and a teate o' hay for he was driving her fast to t'doctor. But t'doctor was on t'road anyway. Lucky thing that!'

He drew near to Adam as though to protect him, and Adam put his hand on his shoulder. They whispered in the hall like two conspirators.

'Will – how is she, do you think? It's been a terrible long time.'

'It's a' reet, Mr Adam. It's a' reet. Dinna fash yersel' now.'

They stood close together, shoulder to shoulder.

'I don't know what I'd do without you, Will,' Adam said. 'If I were to lose her—'

The two men exchanged a handshake.

'It's not that she's pampered,' Will explained. 'Now some ither lass, delicate, but t'Mistress – she's strong as a horse.'

Adam went into the parlour again and it comforted him that Will was outside, as it were on guard. Will always fell into broad Cumberland when he was deeply agitated, but showed his agitation in no other fashion.

The minutes passed; the clock struck the half-hour. Adam's forehead now was damp with perspiration. It was like him to do as he was told. They would come for him when they wanted him, but his agony gripped his stomach as though he were taking part in *her* agony, as though he were inside her and she inside him. The room was dark now. He did not think to light the candles. He stood in the darkness, his hands pressed the one into the other, the nails digging into the flesh.

In the hall Lucy had lit the gas and saw Leathwaite drawn up stiffly outside the parlour door.

'Eh!' she cried and started. 'I didna see ye.' Then hummed, looking at him:

The lasses lap up 'hint their lads,
Some stridin' an' some sydeways;
An' some there were that wished their lot
Had been what Ann's, the bryde was,
          Ay, oft that day.

'Hist!' he whispered indignantly. 'Can't you be still?'

But she tossed her head, smiled back at him and walked slowly up the stairs, the taper in her hand.

Doctor Bettany almost knocked her over, hurrying his little fat body – all fobs and cravat – down to the hall.

As he passed Leathwaite he cried: 'It's a girl! A fine girl!'

'The Lord be praised!' said Leathwaite piously.

Bettany strode up to Adam and wrung his hand. 'A girl, Paris. A grand girl!'

'Yes – but my wife?'

'All's well. You may see her for a moment – only a moment, mind.'

As Adam tore up the staircase a slow smile lit up Leathwaite's eyes and mouth. Then, feeling in his pocket for his tobacco, he turned towards the kitchen, sharing with Adam the position of the happiest man in Cumberland.

SAYERS *VERSUS* HEENAN

ONE of the most remarkable scenes that the London Bridge terminus ever witnessed occurred in the very early morning of Tuesday, April 17th, 1860. The darkness of the early April day was illuminated only by some pallid and evil-smelling gas-lamps. The platform, the offices behind the platform, and the street outside the station were thronged with a pushing, swearing, laughing, spitting, drinking, smoking throng, all men, all happy, all strung to a key of an intense excitement. They had assembled that they might be carried by the special monster train to Farn-borough to behold in the fields near by the great fight between Tom Sayers, Champion of Great Britain, and John Heenan the American. Impossible to say who were there and who not in that thick semi-darkness smelling of damp hay and train-smoke and escaping gas, unwashen bodies and morning air. At any rate there were fish-porters from Billingsgate, butchers from Newgate Market, pugilists of course, poets and journalists of course, dandies as well, celebrated statesmen, and even, so it was afterwards said, some eminent divines.

Most striking at the first showing was the amazing variety of smell – decaying vegetables, mildewed umbrellas, fumes of vile tobacco and stale corduroy suits – but nobody minded, nobody cared, everyone was happy. Clothes are of an amazing variety; there are the friends of sport, quite naturally in the majority; there may be a white neckcloth and black broadcloth, but the cut is unmistakable; hard-featured men, spare-limbed, fond of burying their hands deep in their coat-pockets and never in their trousers. Some are in fine plush galligaskins, top-boots, fur caps, and have sticks with crutches and a thong at the end. There is the 'swell', with his long surtout, double-breasted waistcoat, accurately folded scarf, peg-top trousers, eyeglasses, umbrella and drooping moustache. And there is the dandy with lofty heels to his varnished boots, great moustache and whiskers, ponderous watchchain bearing coins and trinkets, starched choking all-round collar and wonderful breezy necktie, and, lastly, there is a certain number of quiet, severe, retiring gentlemen in tremendous top-hats, dignified black with one pearl or diamond in the black necktie, sucking as likely as not the heads of their heavy canes.

The small group of Herries gentlemen going down to enjoy together the great event had members, it appeared, in all these different classes, for Garth, now purple-faced and corpulent (although he was but fifty years of age), might because of his horsy appearance be making straight for Tattersall's. His brother Amery was something of a dandy and wore an eyeglass. Barnabas Newmark (Phyllis' youngest boy, now about thirty, and known to all his friends as Barney) was altogether the 'swell', with his double-breasted waistcoat of crimson and his trousers of the loudest checks (but, as was characteristic of the Newmark strain, he was, in spite of himself, a little behind the time, coloured waistcoats having just gone out). Lord Rockage (Roger, who had succeeded his father two years earlier) was stout, very fair in colour, with light blue eyes. He was dressed gravely as became his position and sucked reflectively the marble head of his cane. (But he was not reflecting. He was thinking of nothing at all.) The remaining Herries was young Ellis, Will's son. He was now a boy of seventeen and strikingly resembled his father, thin of body with the high Herries cheek-bones and prominent nose, serious, reserved and fully conscious of his duty to the world.

Garth, Amery and young Barney were taking sips of brandy from a silver flask and were as merry as merry could be. Garth was for ever recognizing friends and acquaintances.

'Hullo, Sawyer!' he cried to a stout red-faced gentleman in tremendous checks. 'What did I tell you? Didn't I say you'd have a bid for Satan before you'd been on him half an hour? I told you what to do. Just to keep jogging on him to qualify and you'd get all you wanted.'

'We tried him, Mr Herries,' Mr Sawyer said in a deep melancholy voice, 'yesterday morning against Polly-Anne and beat her by more than a length.'

'There! What did I tell you? . . . Well, how'll the fight be?'

'I've known Tom,' said Mr Sawyer, more gloomy than ever, 'since he was a lad high as my boot. Why, I knew him when he was a bricklayer at Brighton. Why, God Almighty can't beat him!'

'Heenan is five inch taller than Sayers,' said Garth, 'and three stone heavier.'

'Why, blast my soul,' said Mr Sawyer, 'he won't bloody well get near him. There's no one on this bleeding firmament as quick as Tom is.'

It was not more than a shed under whose shelter they were all crowding, and the noise was now terrific, the back-slapping tremendous, the drinking ferocious and the oaths Rabelaisian.

' 'Pon my soul,' said Rockage vacantly, 'there's a lot of fellers crowdin' about. And there'll not be a Fight perhaps after all. Wish I was in bed, 'pon my soul I do.'

Ellis looked at him with exactly that look of cold superiority that had been his father's in *his* youth. But he was not feeling superior. He was conscious of a deep and burning excitement and of pleasure in the scene. But he would not show it. He was by temperament intensely cautious and by training suspicious, and, mingled with these two strains, there was an odd element of personless, rather noble philanthropy. He was already persuading his guardians, his mother, Stephen Newmark and Amery Herries, that he would like to assist the Institute for Necessitous Orphans in Wigmore Street, and the Home for Irish Immigrants in Penelope Place. He liked to do good with his money on condition that he need not encounter those whom he benefited.

'Odd fish!' Amery had said to his sister-in-law Sylvia. 'Damn'

generous so long as he don't have to be personal. He'd give anything to a charity and quite a bit to an Italian organ-grinder, but
he seems to me to have no heart at all — no feeling for individuals, you know.'

'Wish I were an Italian organ-grinder,' Sylvia had said with a
sigh, for although they lived now in two poky little rooms near
Victoria Station, they were always quite hopelessly in debt.'

So Ellis now felt a cold distaste for all the humanity surging
about him, but had someone on the platform begged from him he
would have plunged his hand into his pocket and given him a
handful of silver on condition that he did not speak to him after.
He had come down from Eton last Christmas, although only
seventeen, and, after the summer, was to go into the City, in his
father's firm of Herries & Herries. He had all his father's genius
for turning one penny into two, but he was more deeply concerned than Will had been with the magnificent power of his
family. He was, indeed, even at this early age, family mad. The
Herries were the greatest family in England; even at Eton, where
he had encountered heirs of all the ages and heirs with quite as
genuine a belief in their inheritances as his own, he had never
wavered. Howards, Buckinghams, Beaminsters, Warwicks, Cecils
— they had all, in his own mind, bowed before the Herries. His
closest friend at Eton had been young Beaminster, whose mother,
then a woman of thirty-eight or so, was afterwards the famous
and hideous old Duchess of Wrexe. Beaminster said to him
once:

'Someone, Ellis, told me the other day that your great-grandfather was a sort of highwayman fellow who married a gipsy.'

'Quite,' said Ellis, stretching his long thin neck, 'and now see
what we are!'

So today he felt that this fight was arranged principally for the
benefit of the Herries: it was America *versus* Herries. He looked
upon the crowd: they were all off to Farnborough to see Herries
whack America. It was high time America learnt a lesson; it was
not the last time that a Herries would be conscious of such a
need.

The bell sounded and they all crowded into the railway carriage. There was no ceremony about places, and Rockage discovered to his disgust that a great 'labouring-man' as he termed
him, in galligaskins and a fur cap, already far away in liquor,
with a black bottle in one hand and a vast ham sandwich in the
other, was spreading all over him, and even before the train had

started had planted a large red hand on his own elegant stout knee.

'Here, my good fellow,' Rockage said, trying to move his leg away. But he was wedged remorselessly and, as was his fate constantly in life, no one heard what he said.

Garth Herries and Barney Newmark had secured places together by the window. Just before the train started Garth touched Barney's hand: 'By God, young Barney, look there!'

On the platform a great scramble for places was going on. Everyone was good-natured as, in England, everyone is unless it is felt that injustice is being done. There were shouts and cries, bodies were pushed forward through crowded doors by other bodies, there was laughter and singing. A tall broad-shouldered man with a high top-hat, a rather shabby stock, white hair longer than the fashion and straggling white moustaches, waited quietly apart from the struggle. He had a body that must once have been full and strong. It seemed now to have shrunken, under the black clothes. His shoulders were bowed. At the last moment he walked forward and, without any effort, entered a carriage.

'By heaven!' said Garth. 'I thought he was coming in here.'

'Why?' said Barney. 'Who was it?'

'Walter Herries!'

'What?' whispered Barney in a voice of awed interest. 'You don't say!' He peered out of window, but the train was already moving. He looked across to Ellis who was at the opposite end of the carriage. 'Imagine if he had come in here!' he excitedly whispered. 'What a family scene!'

'Yes, poor devil.'

'What did he look like? They say he was all cut up by his son's death. A pretty little murder that was. What do you think, Garth? Was Uhland Herries mad?'

'Mad as a hatter. Young Harry Trent was up North last year and he thought he'd call on Walter – out of curiosity, you know. Besides he was some sort of relation of Jennifer Herries – John's mother. His father was her cousin or something. Well, he *did* call, and he says he never had such an hour. Gloomy house on the top of a hill. I've stayed there in the old days. They call it the Fortress. But it's all gone to ruin, and there was Walter Herries in a dirty dressing-gown drinking with an old woman. Harry says he was very courteous, walked about and tried to do the honours. And then he took him up to Uhland's room. He'd kept it just as it was when Uhland was alive – cold windy place at the top of the tower they have there. And Harry says he began a long

wandering thing about Uhland, said it was all his own fault
because it was he taught Uhland to hate John Herries or some
such nonsense. Harry says he suggested Walter should get out a
bit, do some shooting or hunting or something, but Walter just
said that he hadn't the heart ... Poor devil! Hope we don't
stumble on him at Farnborough. Wonder what he's doing down
here!'

But the train was now in the country. It was yet dark, the land
shadowy about them, but with the running into air and space the
hissing spluttering gas in its grimy glass covering seemed at once
incongruous and even itself ashamed. They had not gone far
when Garth called out: 'Why, Collins! What are you doing
here?'

A large handsome fellow with a high, broad head, plenty of
brown hair, very gay in a brown velvet coat, white waistcoat and
brown pantaloons, was sitting next to Ellis. He jumped up, re-
gardless of Herries, showing himself a man of great size and
strength, and wrung Garth's hand.

'Herries, by God! So it is.'

Garth introduced him to the other members of the family. 'Mr
Mortimer Collins, a friend of mine. One of the most promising
poets in England; one of the most important editors in England
too.'

'Now stop your codding, Herries. How are you, sir? How do
you do, sir? Fine day we're going to have. I've come all the way
from Plymouth, gentlemen, to see this fight, and by God if the
"Blues" interfere I'll know the reason why.'

'He's a friend of Adam Paris,' Garth explained, 'and editor of
the *Plymouth Mail*. Christopher North said he was the best
young poet in England – did he not, Collins? All *I* know is that
he's wiser about dogs than anyone I've ever met and he can tell a
pretty girl when he sees one – can't you, Collins?'

All the carriage looked at Collins with great interest, but
Collins was not at all abashed, laughed and ran his hand through
his brown hair and began to talk at a tremendous rate.

How was Paris? Clever fellow although lazy. Always had his
mind elsewhere, and he'd been running off when he ought to be
working. Always talking of Cumberland, but Collins could
understand that. Collins thought Cumberland a grand place.
He'd paid a visit to the poet Wordsworth once – in '48, it was –
and Wordsworth had looked like 'an old Roman Senator dressed
as an English farmer'. First-rate the Lake Country! Everyone
lived to be a hundred there. But who cared about Cumberland

this morning? He'd have walked from John o' Groats to Land's
End to see this fight. Why, he'd known Tom Sayers since he was
a lad. He saw his first fight with Abe Crouch in '49, and although
Crouch was two stone the heavier, Sayers smashed his face to
pulp. And he'd seen him fight Jack Grant of Southwark for two
hours and a half and just beat him. That had been a *grand*
fight!

He was so jolly in his general enthusiasm and the way in which
he took the whole carriage into his confidence that they all felt
very friendly even though he *was* a poet. Barney Newmark was
especially taken with him because he had always had a notion
that he himself might be a bit of a writer. In fact those books
Miss Rich of Manchester and *Fox and Grapes* (which were declared at the time to be quite as good as Whyte-Melville) and, of
more importance still, the *Chapters from the Life of an English
Family* might never have been written had it not been for his
friendship, begun at this meeting, with Collins. Nor, in all probability, would some of the best passages in *Sweet Anne Page* have
been quite what they were had Collins never known Barney.

But now they were approaching Farnborough and excitement
ran mountains high. Two gentlemen were so thoroughly drunk
that it was little of the fight that they would see. (In fact they
never got farther that day than the Farnborough pub). The train
drew up and everyone swarmed out. Once outside, a frenzy
seemed to seize the world. Light was in the sky, the grass was
fresh to the feet, the trees in their first spring green, overhead
(Collins noticed it because he was a poet) larks were soaring and
singing. And he was the only one, maybe, in all those thousands
who did notice it, for, from every side, multitudes were pouring
(the crowd was afterwards estimated at three thousand persons),
men climbing the hedges, leaping the walls, running over the
grass, racing, laughing, shouting. The meadow that was to
witness the great scene had been cunningly chosen, surrounded
by ditches and double hedges that it might be difficult for the
authorities to take anyone by surprise. Already there had appeared in *The Times* a little notice:

THE FORTHCOMING PRIZE FIGHT

HERTFORD, *Saturday*

This afternoon Colonel Archibald Robertson, Chief Constable of the Herfordshire Police Force, made application to the

justices assembled in petty session at Hertford for a warrant to apprehend Thomas Sayers, the 'Champion of England', and John Heenan, the American pugilist, in order that they might be bound over to keep the peace . . .

It happened that Amery and Ellis were separated, as they approached the meadow, from the rest of their party. They could see just in front of them the broad gesticulating figure of Collins, Garth laughing and Rockage picking his way as carefully as a hen in a hothouse. Amery felt his arm tapped and turned to see Walter Herries at his side. He said afterwards it was one of the most awful moments of his life. It was not only that he had Ellis with him, that, so far as he knew, the two step-brothers had never met in their lives before, but something in Walter Herries' appearance caught at his heart. He was not an emotional fellow, Amery. He had all the caution of his kind of Herries, and then some more, but he had not set eyes on Walter for many years. When he had seen him last he had been stout, jolly, blustering, self-confident, ready to shout any man down, but now he stood beside him as though he were bewildered, lost, and as even Amery, with all his fear of exaggeration, put it, 'he had aged a century'.

'Why, Walter!' he said.

'How are you, Amery?' Walter said gravely. 'I trust you are well.'

'Very, thanks. I thought you were in Cumberland!'

'Cumberland? No. Business has brought me South, and I thought that by coming here I might recover something – might recover something—' He looked at Ellis without any recognition, and Ellis looked at him. There was nothing else for it.

'This is Ellis, Walter. I don't know whether—'

Walter held out his gloved hand to his brother.

'Indeed?' They shook hands. A strange emotion seized them all. For an instant they were so isolated that they alone might have inhabited the globe. Then Walter walked forward by himself as though he had already forgotten that the others existed. It was from that moment of meeting, Amery said afterwards, that young Ellis, he thought, got all his peculiar notions about the family – his sense above all that the family must not be 'queer'. No one knew, no one ever was to know, what Ellis had thought about the terrible Uhland-John scandal. He must have heard about it again and again, child though he was at the time, for all

the Herries in London were for ever discussing it. The papers
had had, of course, plenty about it, and every decent normal
Herries had felt it a dreadful slur on the family. Young Ellis had
been undoubtedly conscious of this, had, in all probability,
brooded on it. For he was simply the most normal Herries who
ever lived; all the Herries' dislike of queerness, poetry, public
immorality, all the Herries' distrust of the Arts, of anything un-
English, of odd clothes and eccentric talk, met its climax in Ellis.
The wandering ghost of the old Rogue and all his family found
at last their match in Will's younger son. If indeed there had
been for years growing in him a hatred of the unusual, of the
'sport', the 'misfit', how he must have hated the Uhland scandal!
But perhaps he did not realize this disgust of his fully until the
moment when he saw this figure of his own brother, dishevelled,
unhappy, alone, at a gathering so particularly normal, British
and Herries as this one. In any case this is certain – that after this
day he never mentioned poor John or Uhland or Walter if he
could help it. You could not offend him more than by any allusion to them.

All his later troubles and the troubles of Vanessa and Benjamin,
and of the other Herries connected with them, dated perhaps
from this meeting at Farnborough with his brother. It is not
fanciful to imagine so. And that meeting, it is also not altogether
fanciful to imagine, became inevitable when, nearly a hundred
and fifty years before, Francis Herries rode, with his children,
for the first time up Borrowdale.

Amery and Ellis soon joined Rockage, Garth, Barney and Collins
at the ringside. Garth, of course, had friends who were in the
inner circles of Pugilism, so he had seen to it that his little
company had fine places, and Mortimer Collins was with them
by the right of the Press. The arena was a twenty-four foot one.
Behind the ropes a great multitude was pressed, body against
body, and on every face was that mingled gaze of joy, expectation, anxiety and a sort of childish innocence as though no one
present were more than eight years old.

For Barney Newmark, compounded as he was of escape from
all the repressions of his early youth (his father, it may be said,
was deeply disappointed in his youngest son, who seemed to him
to have neither reverence for the things that mattered nor any
discipline of character), of imagination and sheer joy of living,
this scene with the early morning sun overhead, the turf at his

feet, the ardent eager crowd, the brilliant green of the prepared Ring, the excitement of the event, and above all his personal adoration of Tom Sayers, made up the supreme morning of his life. (And, perhaps, never again would he know anything so good.) He had never seen Sayers, but had read every scrap about him since he could remember. And he had never heard anything but good, because Sayers was a grand fellow – serious of mind, modest and unassuming, utterly fearless, generous and good-living. To do the Herries justice – men like Garth and Ormerod and Rodney – he was the kind of Englishman they *wanted* to create. They felt indeed that they had created him, and would not have been at all surprised had it been discovered that he had a drop of Herries in him somewhere. It might be that every man in that crowd felt that he had created him just as he had created this England that was beginning once again, after years of uncertainty, to dominate the whole world. Nelson, the Duke, Tom Sayers – they were all Herries men.

So Barney waited, his heart beating in his ears, his mouth a little open, and his hand resting on Collins' broad shoulder.

'That's the great Tom Oliver,' said Collins.

'Oh, where?' gasped Barney, and was pointed out an aged and grizzled gentleman superintending the last details, testing the ropes, looking up at the sky, consulting with other important gentlemen, inspecting anxiously his watch. For there was not a man in the crowd who was not aware that at any moment the authorities might arrive and the Fight be 'off'. And if that occurred this multitude of amiable citizens would be changed in one brief moment into a howling mob of savages!

It was seven-twenty by Barney's watch. A great sigh of excitement went into the air. Sayers had thrown his hat into the ring and a moment later followed it. So this was his hero! For a second of time Barney was disappointed. Sayers was no classical beauty. His face at first sight was ordinary, that of a quiet commonplace stable-man or agricultural labourer. He seemed slight in figure although he had great shoulders, but nothing, it seemed, of a chest. Nothing extraordinary, for a moment thought Barney. Heenan's hat followed, and a second later Heenan was inside. Then when he stripped a murmur of admiration followed, for this was surely the most magnificent human being God had ever made. Heenan was six feet two inches in height, Sayers but five feet eight, so that the American towered over his opponent. Moreover, Heenan was a beauty. The sun, growing ever more powerful, shone on his shoulders; his chest was superb, his face handsome and distinguished. Sayers looked an ordinary hard little middle-weight, which was what by weight he really was. Moreover, he was eight years older than Heenan.

So that when Sayers stripped Barney drew a deep breath of alarm. How could this stocky grave little fellow hope to approach that giant? The thing was absurd, and he heard comment all around him expressing the same fear. 'The match is a horse to a hen,' said a wrinkled dark man beside him. A big stout gentleman in a very high hat swore with many oaths that 'Heenan would knock Sayers into a cocked hat in ten minutes,' and someone else cried out: 'Tom may beat him, but may I be fried in hell if he can eat him.'

Collins seemed to understand Barney's alarm, for he turned to him and said: 'All right. Don't you worry. It's not that Tom's so quick – Charlie Buller was quicker and so were Langham and Ned Donally – but you wait till you see the force he uses – and his timing! There's never been such timing since the world began! It's the way he moves that saves him. You watch!'

And Barney did watch. He saw Sayers look at his man, then nod as much as to say 'I can manage that'. Then they tossed and a groan went round: 'Tom's lost the toss,' and a large crowd of Americans in Heenan's corner shouted with glee. Sayers now must take the lower ground, but Barney's hope rose again when he saw him stand in so perfect an attitude, tapping the ground with his left foot, his arms down, his head well back, and a smile on his face.

'Oh, God, make him win!' Barney whispered to himself. 'He must win! He *must* win!'

They shook hands and then, as they moved round, each man to his right in order to avoid the other's right hand, they laughed at each other, as cheery and friendly a laugh as you could see anywhere on a lovely spring morning.

They sparred, closed, and Sayers got down easily. Their seconds sponged them down, gave them water to rinse their mouths with, and they came up again. It was plain that Sayers was absolutely confident. He had beaten big men before – size was nothing to him. Heenan led and led again, but always missed; then he got one on his opponent's mouth, and Sayers reeled. Sayers returned but was banged on the forehead and went down in his own corner, whereupon the Americans whooped their delight.

And it was now that the great crowd became part of the fight. Wives, mistresses, children were forgotten. All the trades and all the labours, the small shop, the wide curve of the field as the horses ploughed it, the window at the Club, with the last private scandal, the hiss of the white wave at the boat's keel as it swept from the shore, the call on the bare windy 'top' as the sheepdog ran to his master's bidding, the gossip under lamplight at the village wall, the last climb into the dark wood before the lovers found their longed for security, all aches and pains and ills, triumph and failure, all bitterness and jealousy, all were lost and forgotten as though they had never been. Every man was drawn into that Ring and fought for a victory that seemed just then to be a whole life's aim. Garth forgot his last quarrel with Sylvia when for the thousandth time she had wept and he had sworn, Amery thought nothing of that 'pretty good thing' in Railway Shares that Ormerod had told him of, Rockage forgot his cows down in Wiltshire, Ellis forgot his dignity, and Collins thought nothing of his ambitions that he hoped would bring him from Plymouth and establish him in London as the finest writer of his time. Barney? Barney was part of Sayers' very soul. He had always *been* Sayers. Every blow that Sayers dealt was Barney's – every knock that Sayers got he felt on his own heart.

Only Walter – standing not far from his relations – remained in a world that would not set him free. He watched because something was going to happen. His loneliness would be terminated and he would return to a moving, breathing life from which, since that moment when they had told him that Uhland was dead, he had been always excluded. He bent forward, watching intently, but it was neither Sayers nor Heenan that he was seeing.

Four times Sayers was down, and every time that he fell all England fell with him. Once Heenan got in a severe right, once trying to avoid the sun he slipped, and once Heenan with a terrible left altogether floored him. Nevertheless, Tom's footwork was marvellous, in and out, in and out, avoiding that long arm and always on the retreat when a blow threatened him, so that the force of it was lessened.

Collins was in an ecstasy. 'Oh, look at his feet!' he cried. 'Look at his feet! Oh, the darling! There's beauty! There's movement!' He was beside himself with excitement, gripping Barney's arm, rolling his head to the rhythm of the fighting, stamping with his feet on the ground. Nevertheless, the sun was bothering Sayers (he tried continually to get Heenan to change his ground but always failed), he was now severely marked and had an awful cut over his eyebrow.

Would he last? Many voices, shaking with excitement, the words coming anyhow, could be heard saying that Tom was a beaten man. 'The American's too big for him.' 'He's taken a size too large for him!'

Barney caught Mortimer Collins' arm and in a piteous whisper said: 'He isn't beat, is he? Oh, he can't be! He can't be!'

'You must wait,' said Collins between his teeth. 'He hasn't begun.'

It was then that Walter Herries suddenly began to feel deep down in his loneliness that everything would be different for him henceforth if only Sayers won. Uhland could not return, but life would begin again. That strange cessation of time that for five years now he had endured would lapse. It was as though he waited for a door to open, and, even as, years before, Georges Paris had staked his future on the result of a wrestle on a hill-top in Cumberland, so now Walter Herries held his breath and waited.

'Now!' suddenly cried Collins. 'Do you see that?'

Heenan had sent out a smashing blow which Sayers had avoided, and then, jumping right back, Sayers had landed a terrific hit on the American's eye. It was one of those sliding upward hits, almost splitting Heenan's cheek.

And now Sayers was growing happy. You could see it in his quiet confident gaze, the hint of a smile that played about his bruised lips.

'I've got him now! I've got him now!' Barney whispered, his nails digging into the palms of his hands in his excitement. Indeed, it seemed that Sayers had. Stopping a hard lead with his forearm he dealt a harder one, then suddenly, as though inspired by the kindly heavens, launched out with such a thunderbolt that it seemed as though Heenan's nose must be crushed in. The tremendous fellow was all but lifted off his legs; the Americans in his corner gave a kind of 'Oh!' of wonder, and how the rest of the world shouted, Herries and all! Even Ellis cried: 'Bravo, Sayers! Bravo, my man!' just as though he had been an honest hardworking gardener in the Herries employ.

But for five foot eight to raise six foot two from the ground was no minor feat. Yes, Tom Sayers for all his quiet peace-loving friendly countenance could hit.

Again in the seventh round Sayers struck Heenan another fearful blow which sent the blood gushing from Heenan's nose; so weak and tottering was the American that he grabbed at Sayers' body and they hugged, although Sayers got in some nice body blows before they fell together.

And Barney, in his innocence, thought it all over. The American couldn't stand any more of that; another little tap and he'd be gone, put to sleep for the rest of his natural.

'Oh, he's got him! he's got him!' he cried, enchanted, dancing up and down on his two feet like a little boy, and even Walter, not far away, began to feel as though a great weight were lifting from him.

'I think Sayers is winning,' he said very gravely to a man with a broken nose, standing beside him.

'I wouldn't be so sure,' said the man with the broken nose. 'Why isn't Tom hitting more with his right?'

Barney, in fact, was increasingly aware now from the atmosphere around him that something was going wrong. What it was he couldn't tell. Everything *seemed* to be all right. To look at Sayers you wouldn't suppose that he had an anxiety in the world. His face, that would have been solemn as a churchwarden's had it not been for the twinkling crowsfeet about his eyes, was expressionless and innocent. He had the earnest and serious gaze of a student of Mr Darwin or Mr Huxley. But something was wrong.

'What is it?' Barney whispered to Collins.

'It's his arm, his right arm,' Collins whispered back. 'I think he's broken it.'

Barney always said afterwards that, of the three or four most dramatic crises in his life, that moment when Sayers broke his arm in his fight with Heenan (or a tendon as it turned out after – a happening quite as disastrous in the circumstances as a broken arm could be) was the most thrilling. Life seemed to stop: the world was held in a frozen mask, the air like ice, and no sound in the universe. Exaggerated it sounded later, but that's how it was just then.

And now it was that Barney Newmark loved Sayers, loved Sayers as he loved himself plus the love that he had just then for Miss Nellie Blossom of the Adelphi plus the love that he had for his mother, brother, and sisters, and his French bulldog Louis. All the different loves of his life were concentrated in that little stocky man when he saw him holding his right arm across his chest in the orthodox position as though nothing were the matter, relying now altogether on his feet for his defence and his left for attack, although it had always been his right that had won him his victories.

And then the beautiful thing happened, for Sayers grinned, grinned as though he were greeting an old crony, and Heenan, although his face was marked as though it had been slashed with sabre-cuts (for knuckles could cut into the flesh as gloves cannot do), grinned back. Indeed so completely was Sayers master of himself that, sending Heenan down with a horrible smasher, he used the twenty-five seconds that he might have had for resting in going over and peering into Heenan's face to see what it was like when they had wiped the blood off it. He might get some useful information that way.

Next there was a terrific round: one of the historic rounds in the history of British boxing, when they fought for a quarter of an hour and were, both of them, so badly exhausted at the end of it that they had to be carried to their corners by their respective seconds.

It was after this round that a new element entered into the fight. Heenan was now a fearful sight, for his face looked as though it were gashed with deep wounds. He was bleeding dreadfully, and one of his eyes was completely closed. The gathering of men, who felt as though they, too, had been fighting all this while, began, spiritually, to move in a new world, or rather in a very old primitive one. The tenseness was frightful. Men drew deep breaths and groaned in agony of spirit, stranger held stranger by the shoulder as though he would never let him go. Sweat was beaded thickly on Garth's forehead. Amery could not stand still but kept beating with his fist on another man's shoulder. The betting was now frantic. The Americans kept up a continual roar from their corner, and a strange rhythmical stir seemed to beat through all that multitude, the mass of human beings rising and falling with every movement of the two fighters.

They, indeed, seemed less seriously concerned than anyone else, for once Heenan picked Sayers off his legs and threw him, and then there they were both laughing at one another, and it was a strange sight to see that great American with one eye closed and his cheek in strips laughing as though this was good fun – although a trifle rough perhaps!

Indeed only once in all this time did Sayers show a sign of anger, and that was when he spat some blood and the American laughed. He was stung with that and rushed at Heenan, sent him reeling with a left, and then another and then another! When he hit him a fourth blow Heenan staggered; had Sayers had his right arm he might, indeed, have finished the whole thing with a knockout. Of one blow on Heenan's ribs *The Times* correspondent afterwards said: 'It sounded all over the meadow as if a box had been smashed in'. On the other hand, had Heenan been clever with his right the match might ere this have ended the American way!

It was now that a sort of madness seemed to swing down upon that meadow. Not an ingnoble madness either, for here were these two men, heroes if ever heroes were, laughing like boys at play, and one of them with his face a pulp, blinded, so that he struck his second in mistake for his opponent, and the other had been fighting for an hour with one arm useless, a mass of bruises and fearfully swollen. Nor was their Cause ignoble, for they were showing to all the world that their countries had strength and courage, restraint and control, fairness of mind and an honest cheerfulness, manifesting these qualities indeed a great deal more plainly than their countries often did!

And now all the Herries (save Walter only) were shouting like mad: even Ellis was crying 'Go on, sir! Well done, sir! Very fine indeed!' and with him were shouting many other Herries, the old Rogue with his saturnine humour, and stout David, his son – the best wrestler in Cumberland – and old Pomfret waving a bottle, and young Reuben in defence of the bear, young Francis rising slowly to face his invisible enemy, and poor John winning a victory in the loneliness of Skiddaw. They were fighting to be free, as every man in that crowd was fighting to be free – with every blow that Sayers struck, with every reply of the mighty blinded Heenan, three thousand men drove with them to freedom.

But the spirit of madness grew more powerful. Sayers was weakening, Heenan blinded. They had been fighting for over two hours, and in the rear of the crowd policemen – the hated 'Blues' – were trying to break their way. Once Heenan caught Sayers, closed, and hit him when on the ground. What a yell of 'Foul!' went up then, and the Americans roared back 'No foul!' and the umpire said that all was well because 'the blow was struck in the heat of fighting'. Would Sayers last? *Would* Sayers last? Barney himself now was weak at the knees, his mouth was dry, his eyes burning. He had been fighting, it seemed to him, week upon week. As for a moment he leaned forward, his head rested on Collins' shirt. It was soaked with the sweat of his body. And Walter, in his place, was shaking. He did not know it. He knew neither where he was nor how he had got there – only it seemed to him that Uhland was fighting there in the Ring, and that the moment would come when he would turn to him, crying out:

'Father, you must come and help me. I'm nearly beaten' – a cry that Walter had all his life waited for in vain.

Then, suddenly, came the climax. Heenan had Sayers' head under his left arm when in a corner. He was too weak to do anything but lean on the stake and hold on to Sayers as though trying to strangle him. He said after – and it was likely enough it was true – that he was too blind to know what he did.

Sayers did all he could to free his head, but could not; with his left he got in a blow or two. But Heenan twisted round so that Tom's neck was hard against the upper rope and then he leaned on it. Poor Tom was black in the face and it was plain that he could not breathe.

Then came pandemonium; men were fighting and yelling. 'Foul!' 'Foul!' 'Foul!' The umpire called out 'Cut the rope!' The ringside was broken and the crowd poured in, hemming the fighters round so that they could only stand up against one another. Each hit the other and they both fell down – there, prone, at the feet of their admirers.

The police stopped the fight.

They had fought for two hours and twenty minutes. The result was a draw. The last great contest of fisticuffs on English soil.

Walter moved in a dream. On a wall in front of him that seemed always to be receding, a great cock with a crimson crest was crowing. It crowed and crowed.

A little common man in a fur cap kept pace beside him.

'Well, Guv'nor, that wor' grand. I call that GRAND!'

'Thank you,' said Walter. 'I enjoyed it greatly' – and went back to the Fortress.

SHE VISITS THE FORTRESS FOR
THE LAST TIME

ELIZABETH, forty-seven but looking oddly like a young girl in distress, confused in fact by her inexperience, stood one very wet morning beside Judith's bed and stared at the old lady with, if the truth is known, a good deal of irritation. At her side, the cause of her worry, stood her son Benjamin, now aged seven.

'It isn't,' said Elizabeth, in a clear sweet voice, 'as though he didn't know he'd done wrong, Aunt Judith. He knows perfectly well. Besides, Timothy beat him when he found out the truth. But he doesn't care in the least.'

Judith in her lace cap, mittens on her little hands, her face smiling and serene, the article in *The Times* about Mr Lincoln and the North and what the Americans had better do next open on her lap, knew two things – one, that Elizabeth wished her to be very serious in order that Benjamin should be impressed, and the other, that she thought it high time that Elizabeth gave up her widow's cap and black silk dress. Poor John had been gone nearly eight years now, and gentle colours, silver grey, dove colour, rose, suited Elizabeth so very well. Moreover, Elizabeth would be all the happier if she married. Mr Morant of Brough was eager to marry her. She was wasted as a widow, and Benjamin was altogether too much for her. Judith was smiling because she was thinking of the other children who had been too much for their relations. She had been too much for David Herries. Adam had at one time been too much for herself. Barney Newmark had been too much for Phyllis and Stephen. But Benjamin was a little different, for in this present time children, whatever they thought in secret, had outwardly to conform. All over England children were conforming, saying 'Yes, Papa' and 'No, Mama', looking up to their parents as to God, believing (apparently) all that they were told about both the creation of the world and the creation of themselves (the first in six days exactly, the second in a gooseberry bush), above all observing Sunday with the ritual and solemnity of a Sacred Order.

All this was correct, Judith supposed, although it had not been so when she was young, but she was now a very old woman and must not expect the world to stand still. (The only question was:

was it perhaps going back? But how could one ask that when Britain was triumphant among the nations?)

It was Sunday that had been young Benjamin's trouble. He was quite unlike Adam as a child, for although Adam had been independent and gone his own way he had given no one any trouble except when he had disappeared for a whole day without warning. Moreover, he always listened to reason. But Benjamin would never listen to anyone, and this was the stranger when you considered that he was the son of John, who had always listened to everyone too much. It was perhaps because of John's tragedy that everyone had been over-indulgent to Benjamin in his baby-hood. Poor little infant, born only a few months after his father had been brutally murdered, murdered by the child's own uncle! Could anyone have a more pitiful start in life? Had Benjamin been a delicate, sensitive soul everyone would have approved and everyone would have been satisfied. But, so odd are the workings of nature, that that was the very last thing that Benjamin turned out to be! He was plump, healthy and merry. No one had ever known him to cry. He laughed all day. He did not of course know as yet of his father's tragedy, but it was feared that when he did know it would not affect him very greatly. It was not that he was cruel, nor that he was heartless, but he had none of the right and proper feelings. At Uldale, Veronica and Jane made much of him. Dorothy petted him, even Tim paid him attentions. They all thought him a sweet little child, for he was round and rosy and had large yellow curls on the top of his head. But he yielded to none of their blandishments. Jane was the only one who could do anything with him, and she not very much. It was not that he was hard or selfish. He was everybody's friend, would give every-thing that he possessed away to anybody (they had to stop him giving his toys, marbles, sweets to the village children); no, the awful thing was that he had no morals!

That seems a hard thing to say about a child who was only just seven, but what they meant by it was that he had no idea at all of the difference between right and wrong. The first occasion had been when he had stolen the piece of sandalwood out of Dor-othy's needlework-box. She had missed it; they had searched everywhere for it. Benjamin had been challenged, had denied that he had it, and then it had been found on his person. Timothy had whipped him, Elizabeth had explained to him what a dread-ful thing a lie was, but he had remained cheerful and unre-pentant through it all. But unrepentant was the wrong word. He was simply unaware that he should not tell a lie if to tell a lie was of benefit to him. He laughed like anything when Dorothy, in her vast crinoline, tried to instruct him.

Of course he was very young at the time, and Dorothy elaborately expounded to Elizabeth that very small children never knew the difference between right and wrong. They were born in sin and only later became the children of Grace. But whether Benjamin would ever be a child of Grace seemed to Elizabeth, who knew him better than the others, a sadly uncertain question.

He was for ever in hot water, and at last he committed his worst crime: he dropped a handsome silver riding-whip of Timothy's into a deep empty well at the back of the stables. On this occasion he at once confessed. He said that he wanted to see how far it would fall. He was whipped, sent to bed without supper, lectured. He minded nothing, would not say that he was sorry, and at last was brought up to Judith to see whether she could do anything with him. He looked at the old lady in the big bed and thought how small she was. His round and chubby figure smiled all over at the old lady, and the old lady smiled back at him. This, thought Elizabeth in despair, was not at all what she had wanted.

'It makes it so much worse, Aunt Judith,' she said, 'that it should be Sunday.'

'I don't know, my dear. Do you think that it does?' She drew off her mittens and then with her slender white fingers used a silver knife to peel a large rosy apple. She had always for breakfast a cup of coffee and an apple, a meal that everyone thought eccentric.

Benjamin watched the peeling of the apple with wide-eyed excitement. Would she be able to strip the whole apple without breaking the skin?

'You see, Elizabeth dear,' Judith went on in her very small voice that had a touch of tartness in it like a good preserve. 'I'm nearly ninety years of age, you know, and though I've got all my faculties, thank God, still I do live a great deal in the past. It's very hard for me to tell very often which *is* the past and which the present. You see, for one thing I've lived in this bedroom much of my life – always coming back to it. It was very much the same when I was a little girl as it is now. Of course the wallpaper's changed. It used to have blue Chinese pagodas on it. Very pretty it was. But that tallboy is the same, and this blue tester over my bed, and these charming acanthus leaves carved on the wood . . .

What was I saying? Oh yes, about Sunday. Well, you see, living so much in the past I don't understand this not allowing children to amuse themselves of a Sunday. Of course they get into mischief. There is nothing else for them to do.'

This was not at all what Elizabeth wanted. And the old lady was becoming very garrulous now. Moreover, Benjamin, fascinated by the apple, had drawn ever closer and closer to the bed and had completely forgotten that he had come there to be scolded. He was grinning with all his might and, unconsciously, his small chubby *and* grubby fist was stretched towards Judith.

'There! would you like a piece?' She cut off a section with the silver knife. 'Now what do you say?'

'Thank you, Aunt Judith.'

'They all call me Aunt Judith. Isn't it charming? And I'm ninety years old. Well, well ...' She put on her silver-rimmed spectacles. 'That's the only thing, Elizabeth, that's beginning to fail me. I can't see to read newspaper print as I did. Ah! there's another poem about the poor Prince Consort, although he's been dead six months. And as to Mr Lincoln – the *Times* man says that if he would only–' She was aware that Elizabeth wanted something of her. She stared at Benjamin severely over her spectacles.

'Your mother is very unhappy about you, Benjamin, because you will not say you are sorry to Timothy. You are seven now and quite old enough to know that you mustn't throw other people's things down wells.'

He smiled at her.

'I'll say I'm sorry,' he said.

'But are you sorry?'

'No.'

'But are you not sorry to make others unhappy? And do you not see that the whip belonged to Timothy? What would you say if Timothy took your soldiers and threw them in the road?'

'He can have all my soldiers,' said Benjamin.

'You see, Aunt Judith,' Elizabeth said in despair ('it is quite impossible to make him realize.'

A new tone came into Judith's voice, that same tone with which once she had spoken to Will at Stone Ends, once to Mrs Ponder, and more than once to Walter.

'Benjamin,' and he was suddenly grave, looking up into her face. 'Will you please go at once to Timothy and make your apologies? Without waiting another minute, please.'

'Yes, Aunt Judith,' he said, and instantly left the room.

'There, you see,' Judith said, greatly pleased. 'All that is needed is a little firmness.'

Elizabeth shook her head, smiled, shook her head again.

'I don't know. He's such a funny boy. He'll be going to school presently – that's, I suppose, what he needs. But I am so frightened for him. He seems to have no idea at all as to what is wrong. He plays with the servants just as though they were not servants at all. He is so restless. Jane tries to teach him, but he will never settle to his books.'

'There, my dear,' said Judith comfortably. 'Come and sit down for a little. Benjamin has his own idea of right and wrong just as I had when I was a little girl. He is generous and loving, is he not? And he is happy too.'

Elizabeth sat down beside the bed.

'Aunt Judith, I'm not tiring you?'

'Tiring me! Oh dear, no. Why, it is only the beginning of the day. I can do with so very little sleep now, or perhaps it is that I sleep most of the time—'

'There is another thing,' Elizabeth began.

'Yes, dear, tell me.'

'I am most unhappy about father. Oh, I know that it would be of no use to go and see him. He would not see me, I suppose, if I did go. We have talked of it before and decided that it would be of no use. But now I hear that he has a really dreadful woman there, a Mrs Pangloss – a terrible creature who bullies him and of whom he is afraid. Father afraid! Why, when I lived with him you would say that he would never be afraid . . . But it is terrible to sit here and know that he is shut up in that horrible house with that woman. I don't know what I should do, but it makes me so unhappy – thinking of it – being sorry for him.'

Judith stared in front of her. Then suddenly she clapped her hands.

'I know!' she cried. 'I'll go myself and see him!'

'Oh no, Aunt Judith! No, no! Why, it's a dreadful day! It's a deluge – and you haven't been farther than the garden for months.'

'That doesn't say that I couldn't if I wanted to. I'm lazy, that's all. It's an excellent idea. I have wanted to speak to Walter – poor Walter. Yes, it is all over, our quarrel – quite finished, and it has brought misery enough on everybody. Yes, I'll go and see Walter. An excellent idea!'

There was a knock on the door. Dorothy, Margaret, Adam and the three-year-old Vanessa all entered. Every member of the family paid a visit of a few minutes every morning. This had become a ceremony as almost everything to do with Judith had now something of the ceremonial about it. Not that she wanted it to be so. All that she wanted was that she should feel that she was in touch with everybody. She loved them all, man, woman and child – and she also wished to know exactly what they were all about.

Dorothy was dressed for going out. She was in the very newest fashion – a brown 'pork-pie' but with a dark red feather, a chignon, and her crinoline raised several inches from the ground, revealing that her stout feet were encased in miniature Hessian boots. This was the first time that Judith had seen these and at once she burst out laughing.

'Oh, Dorothy, my dear. What *have* you got on?'

She sat up in bed, leaning forward, settling her spectacles exactly on her nose that she might see the better.

Dorothy blushed, but she was as phlegmatic and good-natured as she was stout.

'Very handsome *I* call it. And I am wearing an American Cage for the first time. You've always complained that my crinolines are too large.'

'I don't know, I'm sure,' said Judith, 'why with your figure you should run such risks.' Then, to Vanessa: 'Come here, my darling, and see what I've got for you. Give me that little silver box from the table, Adam.'

Vanessa promised to be a very beautiful child. She had hair as dark as Jennifer's had once been, and large dark serious eyes. She had Margaret's broad calm forehead and something of Adam's humorous, almost sarcastic twinkle. When she had been a baby sitting quietly on her mother's lap she would unexpectedly look at you inviting you to agree that the world, although pleasant, was quite absurd. She already adored her father, and he worshipped her. She had a lovely little body, slim and straight. Baby though she was, she carried herself with a beautiful easy natural gesture, bearing her head high and looking all the world in the face.

As a child she was no trouble at all. Adam had insisted that she should be called Vanessa.

'There was once a Vanessa, a lovely lady. And there was an Irish Dean – and there were some letters . . .'

'Oh, you mean Swift!' said Dorothy, who was as literal as any Herries. 'All the same it's a very odd name.'

'My grandmother,' said Adam, 'was called Mirabell, and that was a man's name out of a play by Congreve.'

'Yes,' said Dorothy. 'But I don't see why because your grandmother was odd you should be.'

'Don't you?' said Adam gravely. 'I do.'

'I do wish, Adam,' said Judith as he brought her the little silver box, 'that you wouldn't wear that hideous sack coat. You are too stout for it.'

'Yes, Mother,' he said, smiling. 'But it's comfortable.'

(And, oh, how she loved him! When he approached the bed, bent down and kissed her, her whole body thrilled and it was all she could do not to put her arms around him and hold him tight to her. But not with all those women in the room. Oh dear, no!)

'There, darling.' She took two sugared almonds out of the box. This was a daily ritual.

'Thank you, Grandmother.' Adam lifted the little girl up, and for a moment the three of them, grandmother, son and grandchild, were caught together into a loving relationship that no one else in the whole world shared.

'And now,' said Judith comfortably, 'I am going to get up. Send Lucy to me, somebody, and tell James to bring the carriage round. You can go in the barouche to Keswick, Dorothy. I am going up to Ireby to see how poor Cousin Walter is doing.'

She knew that this would be a bombshell and she enjoyed greatly the effect of it.

'What!' Dorothy cried as though she had just heard that the end of the world had come. 'Going out! On a day like this! When you haven't been out for months! To the Fortress! Why, you're crazy, Aunt Judith!'

And even Margaret, who thought now that everything that Adam's mother did was wise, said: 'Oh, but, Mother — surely that is incautious! Listen to the rain!'

'Thank you, my dear. My mind is quite made up.'

Adam, who knew that the more his mother was opposed the more determined she was, said, 'Well, then, Mother, if you go up there, I go with you.'

'Certainly not. What should I want you for? It is quite time I had a little air. Now it is settled. Go along, all of you.'

'But, Aunt Judith—' Dorothy, who was in truth deeply distressed, broke in. 'You can't—'

'Nobody says can't to me!' Judith answered. 'No one ever has, and no one ever will.'

'But Doctor Bettany—'

'Doctor Bettany doesn't know everything. It will do me a great deal of good. And there is something I must say to Walter Herries.'

'But you know what that house is. And there is some horrible woman there now. She will be rude to you and—'

'No one is ever rude to me. At any rate after the first minute. My mind is quite made up, so it's of no use your talking, Dorothy. Now I want one word alone with Adam, if you don't mind.'

Elizabeth, who had been listening in great distress, stayed behind the other two.

'Aunt Judith, *please*. If it is for my sake, I beg you not to go. I would never have said anything if I had thought you would have such an idea—'

'That is quite all right, my dear,' Judith said, smiling at her. 'Your father cannot eat me. I am too old an old lady for anyone to be rude to me. The drive will do me good. Now, go and see that Benjamin isn't getting into mischief. Jane will be teaching him his lesson.'

She was left alone with Adam.

'Mother, is it wise? Walter is very odd, they say, and the house in terrible disorder. At least let me go with you. I can remain outside in the carriage.'

He sat on the edge of the bed. She laid her hand in his large brown one.

'Is it not strange?' she said. 'Do you remember, Adam? In this very room I undressed you and bathed you and you asked all kinds of ridiculous questions. And now see what you are! You are still untidy as you were then, and you have that same brown gipsy colour. And you are not as stout as I feared you would be—'

He sighed. Then he looked at her whimsically. 'Aye, I'm brown and heavy but not fat, and I'm not a dandy – and what I am as well is a failure!'

'Oh no, Adam! Oh no!'

'Now come, Mother. You had great hopes of me, hadn't you? And I've disappointed all of them.'

'Of course not,' she said fiercely. 'All that I hoped for you when you were a baby was that you would be a farmer and live in Watendlath. That, I suppose, was the mistake of my life – that I did not go to Watendlath. But it doesn't matter now. That is the best of being old – nothing matters very much. It is very pleasant to sit outside and watch.'

He laughed '*You* watch! Why, you are in the middle of everything! No one does a thing in this house but you know it—' He paused, then added slowly: 'We are rather a multitude here. Let me see, not mentioning the servants there are – you, Dorothy, Veronica, Tim, Amabel, Jane, Elizabeth, Benjamin, Margaret, Vanessa and myself. Eleven of us.'

'And not one too many!' she said sharply. 'Now, Adam, I know what you are going to say. You are not to mention buying that land you were speaking of. We have plenty of money. The house is large. There is room for everybody.'

He looked at her with that deprecating shy glance that he had always used with her, since he was a baby, when he had something to confess.

'I have bought it, Mother. The thing was settled yesterday.'

She took her hand from his. All that old anger that rose in her when she was circumvented, all that old distress and alarm that she always felt whenever he was going away, seized her. She began to tremble all over. She glared at him through her spectacles. She pushed *The Times* away from her so violently that it fell on to the floor.

'Now listen, Mother,' he began, speaking quickly. 'I am forty-seven years of age. I have tried everything and failed at everything. Once I tried to do something for my fellow men and *that* failed. Then I tried to write, and although that did not exactly fail it has never come to anything at all. Mortimer Collins was right when he abused me one night and said that I failed at everything because I could not *stick* at anything. As soon as I was settled anywhere I wanted to run away. I have *that* from you, Mother. You know that I have. Only I haven't the character that you have, nor am I so unselfish. You would have been a wanderer all your days had you not thought so much of others. But I – except for you and Margaret, Kraft and John – I've loved no one but myself! But John's death shocked me. Kraft's death shocked me once and John's completed it. I must settle. If I do not now, I never shall – and there is only one place where I *can* settle. On my own piece of ground in this country. Then I fancy that I still can do something. They all say that I can write – Dickens said so, and Yates and Collins. I shall never write anything that matters *much*, but it will be something. It is not that I shall be far away. The piece of ground above Manesty that I have bought is no distance. I shall come here constantly. But I must have my own place, and Vanessa must have *her* home to grow up in. There are too many women in this house, nor is it fair for Margaret.'

'I am sure dear Margaret is very happy,' Judith broke in.

'Yes, she is happy, but not so happy as she would be in her own home. You *must* see it, Mother. You who are so wise and so sensible . . .'

She saw it. She had always had the capacity to see other people's point of view. But this was the end – the *End*.

She had only a few more years to live. Adam was all that she had in the world. If Adam left her . . . All that she said was:

'Pick up *The Times* for me, will you, dear? I think that it is *most* ridiculous that Germany should wish to have a Navy. I saw a very funny picture in *Punch* last week—'

He bent down and kissed her, and when he felt her body tremble, he put his arms round her. But he said no more. He knew that she would realize this was best for himself and Margaret, and that when she had realized that she would never say another word on the matter.

Nor did she. All the while that Lucy was dressing her she scarcely spoke. When the dressing was finished she sat down in a chair.

'Lucy, did I not hear that you are engaged to be married?'

'Yes, Madame.'

'I hope he is a good man.'

'Very good, Madame. He helps Mr Boulter, the butcher, in Keswick.'

'Oh yes . . . I hope he is sober.'

'He never touches a drop, Madame.'

'Well, I trust that you will be very happy. We shall be sorry to lose you.'

'Thank you, Madame.'

Veronica came in and helped her downstairs.

'Thank you, my dear. How pretty you are looking today!'

'It's terrible weather. Do you think you ought to go out, Aunt Judith?'

'I don't think – I know,' she answered. 'Now you can tell James that I am ready.'

James Bennett, son of Bennett Senior (now with God), a stout sturdy fellow and practically speechless, arrived with a very large

umbrella to shelter her over the garden-path. She was settled in
the carriage with rugs and a foot-warmer. She waved out of the
window to Veronica and Jane in the doorway, and Margaret,
Benjamin and Vanessa in an upper window.

But, so soon as the carriage had started, she fell into a fit of
melancholy – indeed saw herself, a poor little aged worn-out not-
wanted creature, lying at the very bottom of the sort of damp
dark insect-ridden well into which Benjamin had thrown Timothy's whip. Such a mood was very rare with her. Now for a
quarter of an hour she thoroughly indulged herself.

In the first place the weather helped, for it was one of the worst
days of rain and storm that the year had yet seen. From the
eastern sky the rain swung in a solid sheet – you could see it,
slanting, as though in the folds of some thin grey stuff blown by
the wind against the horses' heads. It hissed through the air and
all the ground was running with water; you could see through
the window rivulets of rain bubbling on the grass, and the rain
leaping on the roadway; the wind drove it across the land from
Solway in gusts of lines and spirals and curves.

'Dear, dear,' Judith thought. 'What a day to choose to come
out in after months indoors.' She wondered what impulse had
decided her on this visit; she was so very comfortable indoors,
and this announcement of Adam's had swallowed Walter completely as though he never had been.

It was as though her whole life through she had been trying to
catch Adam and he had always eluded her. Of course he loved
her, but not as she loved him, for she must share him with Margaret and Vanessa. Margaret was an excellent woman and Vanessa a sweet baby, but after all they were not his mother. Here to
her own surprise and disgust she felt a tear trickle down her
cheek. She took her handkerchief and wiped it indignantly away.
It was years since she had shed tears; not indeed since John's
death, and then only when she was alone. But when you were
old your body was feeble, boast as you might to others. You
could not be sure of commanding it.

This decision of Adam's was dreadful. He said that he would
see her often, but he would not. Once he was away there on the
hills above Derwentwater his visits to her would be fewer and
fewer. She cared of course for the others – for dear Jane especially – but they were not inside her heart as Adam was. And
she was not – although she would not admit it – at home in this
new world that was growing up around her, a world of material

riches and prosperity, a world in which the men seemed to be divided from the women so that an elaborate sort of hypocrisy sprang up between them when they met. Dorothy was shocked — or thought it proper to be shocked — if you talked of cows calving or sheep lambing. Jane and Amabel were quite resigned to being old maids, it seemed. The countryside was covered with old maids, and yet, on the other hand, all the girls in the County thought of nothing but marriage, only they must not say so and indeed must pretend that they had no notion of the barbarous practices that marriage involved. It had been very different in Judith's youth, and she had a sudden picture of herself and Georges and Emma Furze in London and the things that they would discuss and that other people would do!

'If it goes on much longer like this,' Judith had said to Dorothy the other day, 'there will be no more babies, for parents will be ashamed of creating them!'

She disliked too a kind of religion that was beginning to be prevalent, a religion that Dorothy took an interest in and that even the beautiful Veronica pretended to admire. It came, she believed, from Oxford, and Mr Hall and Mr Eustace were its local prophets. It consisted, so far as Judith could discover, in talking in a high affected voice, bowing and scraping in church and professing the saintly life. She believed that Mr Hall *was* perhaps a Saint — she knew that he gave everything away and lived entirely on potatoes — but Mr Eustace with his shrill voice and ogling eyes revolted her. She had been given to read a novel that, so she was told, portrayed the ideal saintly character of this religious movement — *The Heir of Redclyffe* by Miss Charlotte Mary Yonge — but she had found it mawkish and unreal and had wanted to throw it into the fire. In all this she was of course very ignorant; she knew nothing at all about the Oxford Movement, but it all helped to make her feel, when she was depressed, that she had lived far too long and had wandered into a world that was not hers.

However, she was not often depressed and she did not intend to be long depressed now. She dried her eyes, blew her nose and tried to pretend that she was as independent of Adam as she was of everyone else in the world. If he *wished* to go and live on a patch of ground above Derwentwater, why, let him go! How absurd of her, when she should be thinking of her approaching End, to be disturbed by what *anyone* wished to do! Nevertheless the pretence was not very successful. The very thought of Adam, smiling, untidy in his sack coat, so ludicrously absentminded, so clever (as she thought him), so well-read and wise and learned but so exceedingly modest about it ... she had only to think of him to bring him right into the carriage beside her! And so, after all, it might be when he was living on Cat Bells! He could not *really* be very far away from her!

The carriage was now driving through the storm up the hill to Ireby. She must prepare herself for the encounter with Walter. This meeting with him was in fact no new idea. She had had it in mind ever since the awful catastrophe of John's death. She must tell him, before she died, that their quarrel was ended, that she forgave him everything – yes, even the deaths of Francis and Reuben – and she must try to console him a little and try if he would not perhaps see Elizabeth and his grandson.

As Bennett, down whose cape the water was now pouring in a vicious stream, whipped the poor horses up the hill, the carriage met the full force of the storm. The wind tugged at the windows, the rain lashed them, and she rose to the vigour of it. 'This is the way I like it,' she thought. Something in her bones, that had crept into them when old Squire Tom carried her the first day of her life through the snowstorm, excited her now. She pushed her nose against the window to see whether she had arrived, but could realize nothing because the wet blur of the rain was so thick. Then the carriage stopped; Bennett got down from his seat. With difficulty he opened the carriage door and then had to push his chest right inside to avoid the wind. His rough red cheek, fresh with rain, was close against Judith.

'Well, are we there, James?'

'Yes, Madame.'

'What do we do now?'

'Well, Madame ... best for me t'pull t'bell while you stay inside t'carriage.'

'Pull it then.'

She could see dimly through the window now and thought how desolate the Fortress had become. The building was dark, naked and repellent. The stone seemed to have blackened under rain as though it had been smoked. The wood behind the house moaned and wailed. A pile of earth stood near the flagged path in the garden as though in preparation for a grave, and all the plants were beaten down with the wind. A tree somewhere rocked and screamed. She could see so dimly that she could not be sure what she saw. She could fancy that figures moved in and out through the rain, and especially her fancy, the growing faintness of the sight of her old age, made her imagine that the shape of a woman in black cloak or shawl moved out from the trees and stood motionless, staring at the carriage.

Suddenly she disliked so greatly staying in the carriage alone that she picked herself up, found her cane, adjusted her bonnet and climbed down into the rain, then walked with great assurance up the flagged path and joined Bennett.

She heard the bell pealing through the house as though the place were empty and deserted. She could smell the wet stale smell of laurels and elder bushes. Then the door opened and a slatternly girl poked her head through. Just then there was a gust of wind so violent that Judith, slight as she was, was blown into the house.

She stood in the hall and the girl gaped at her.

'You'd better close the door,' Judith said gently. 'It is terrible weather, isn't it?'

The girl's hair had been blown across her cheek, and she stared at Judith as though she were an apparition.

'I think I'll sit down,' Judith said, and so she did on a hard straight-backed oak chair with arms that she remembered well from the old Westaways house. A cat came into the hall, mewing . . .

'Who might you be wanting?' asked the girl.

'Would you tell Sir Walter Herries that Madame Paris from Uldale would like to see him for a moment?'

The cat came over to her and rubbed against her leg. She bent down and stroked it, then with her two gloved hands resting on her cane leaned forward and waited.

She did not have to wait long, for a door swung back and there stood before her a great fat woman in a mob cap. 'This,' she thought, 'must be the Mrs Pangloss of whom I have heard,' and noticed with great dislike her face red as a ham, her thick bare neck, her big uncontrolled bosom, her long peering nose and other more unagreeable features. Her personal, almost passionate, love of cleanliness made a woman such as this very unpleasing to her.

The hall was dark and the woman stared about her.

'Well?' she said, glaring at the girl. 'What are you standing there for? Haven't I told you—?'

'There's someone—' said the girl.

The woman turned to Judith.

'Yes?' she said. 'What can I do for you?'

'I was wondering,' said Judith, 'whether I might see Sir Walter Herries for a moment. Pray forgive my sitting down, but I am not so young as I once was.' She smiled.

The woman at once recognized her. She said: 'Oh yes? Indeed! Well, I fear that Sir Walter is not very well today and is unable to see anyone.'

'I am sorry to hear that. Perhaps if I were to see him for a moment only—'

'Impossible, I'm afraid.'

The woman stood staring as the maid had done. Judith was so famous a figure that this visit was astonishing. The woman's slow brain doubtless was moving through a maze of questions. What did old 'Madame' want? Did this threaten her own power here? Was there some plot hostile to herself?

'Would you at least,' said Judith patiently, 'tell Sir Walter that I am here?'

'Mustn't disturb him.'

'It is of importance that I should see him – great importance.'

'Excuse me,' said the woman more insolently, as though she had made up her mind that Judith was not to be feared. 'Another day perhaps, but today. Sir Walter is not to be disturbed. I'm in charge here. I'll tell him that you inquired.'

The door to the left of the staircase opened and Walter appeared. He was in slippers and a faded snuff-coloured dressing-gown. At first he could not see who was there. Then, almost knocking against the chair, he stumbled back.

'Why, Judith!' he cried.

She held out her hand.

'I am delighted to see you, Walter. Your housekeeper said that you were indisposed, but I shall not keep you long. Can you give me five minutes with you alone?'

He plainly did not know what to do, and she was so sorry for him and felt so strong an impulse to carry him off there and then from under the sharp nose of Mrs Pangloss that any old enmity there might ever have been fell, dead, once and for all.

The woman did not move.

'Why, certainly,' Walter said. 'I have not been well. Mrs Pangloss was correct. This is Mrs Pangloss, my housekeeper.'

Judith gave a little bow.

The woman said angrily: 'Now you know what the doctor said – that you wasn't to see anyone, no matter who it was, and you'll

catch your death away from the fire, you know you will. Sorry,
ma'am, it's the doctor's orders, and another day when he's more
himself it won't matter, I'm sure – but I have to see to his health.
If I don't, nobody does.'

Here, however, Walter plucked up courage; it must have
shamed him that Judith of all people should have seen him
thus.

'Very well, Mrs Pangloss. You are acting for the best, I am
sure, but now that Madame Paris has come all this way on such a
day . . . Pray ask Alice to light a fire in the library. That will save
you the stairs, Judith. Allow me to give you an arm.'

Mrs Pangloss stood there, looking at them. She never moved
and, after they had gone, stood staring at the spot where they had
been.

The room into which Walter led Judith had already a fire
burning in the grate and a rich brooding odour of spirits about it.
A decanter and two tumblers, one half filled with something that
was, Judith thought, gin and water, stood on a table. This, she
realized at once, had been Mrs Pangloss' sanctum that morning.
Otherwise it was desolate enough. A picture of a hunting scene
hung crooked on a nail and there was a screen with pictures of
boxing scenes pasted on to it. Very little else. Walter settled
Judith in an armchair whose grey and disordered stuffing protruded from the seat. A window looked out on to the soaked and
neglected garden. The wind whistled behind the wallpaper.
Walter sat down on a hard chair near Judith. She was greatly
distressed at the change in him. She had last seen him three years
before, riding in Keswick, and on horseback, wrapped in a high
riding-coat, he had had something of his old carriage and even,
she thought, arrogance. Now he had a rugged grey beard, his
cheeks had fallen, and as he sat with his old dressing-gown hud-
dled about him he looked more than his seventy years.

'If that woman was rude to you,' he said abruptly, 'I shall
dismiss her.'

'Not at all,' said Judith cheerfully. 'She said you were not well
and should see nobody.'

'She's a good creature in her way,' he went on. 'She means well
by me – the only one who does.'

'Now, Walter, that's nonsense. We all mean well by you if you
will let us.'

'Fine words, Judith, fine words.' He drew the dressing-gown
closer about him. 'I'm always cold now. This house is damp. You

wouldn't think so when I built it, but the damp's come in just as everything else has gone out. What have you come for?' he asked bluntly. 'We've been meeting like this all our lives, but our meetings never come to anything.' Then as though he had said nothing: 'How old are you now?'

'I? I'm nearly eighty-eight.'

'Eighty-eight! Wonderful! And still able to get about.'

'Well, I don't get about much now, you know. There is plenty to do in the house.'

'Yes; got your fingers on everything, I suppose, just as you used to. What have you come to see *me* for?' he asked again.

'I have come for two reasons, Walter. First, I want you to know that our old feud is over. At least on my side. You must not think that I am angry or feel any enmity. The past is dead. At any rate our quarrel is dead.'

He rubbed his finger against his stubbly cheek. 'The past is never dead,' he said. 'You know that as well as I do. When you come to our age we live in the past. It is all I do live in. Back – back – to when my son was alive, when he could walk into this room just as anyone did and say "Good morning". Not that he cared for me, of course – he never did that – but he was there. He was in this house. I could hear him moving over stairs. You could tell his walk, you know, because he limped. Uhland was lame from birth, you know, Judith, and that is what made him bitter – that and my telling him when he was a baby that he had an injustice, being lame. And so he had an injustice, poor boy, and cleverer than anyone in the County. That is why he thought poorly of me. He could see I had no brains, never had any. But it's too late now. The harm's been done, done years and years ago, before we were born.'

He would have continued to talk forever. Indeed he had forgotten her, but she was so deeply touched that she rose a little in her chair, leaned over and took his hand. Even as she did so, she thought: 'Twenty years ago! If you had told me that I would ever feel so tenderly! But what does it matter now? We are both so old!'

He let her hand hold his, which was hot and dry to the touch.

'Listen, Walter!' she said. 'That is what I have come to say. You must not think that you are alone in regretting the past. That old quarrel has done us all much harm, but I feel that – that – that catastrophe eight years ago – it was terrible, tragic – but

John and Uhland by dying rid us all of an enmity, something bad in the blood, that must not come back again. John left a son, you know – a grandson whom you have never seen – and it would be wicked, *wicked*, if his life was spoilt by it. It seems to me now when I am old that we cannot do anything without affecting someone else, and one bad, selfish cruel thing can spread and spread into the lives of people we never see . . . I want you now to be friends with us all, to see Elizabeth and your grandchild . . . to help us all so that his life at least shall suffer no effects from all that past trouble. Let Elizabeth come . . .

She had not been sure that he had heard anything that she had said, but at the repetition of Elizabeth's name his body trembled and shook, he caught his hand from hers and sprang to his feet.

'No, no!' he cried, swaying on his feet and gesticulating with his hands as though he were beating someone away from him. 'She's no daughter of mine and you shan't come round me with all your talk. She left me, and good riddance. She married my boy's murderer. Oh yes, she did! Don't you tell me now! Do you suppose that he didn't taunt him with his lameness, and she too? Uhland knew. Uhland heard what they said, the two of them. Now you can go, and pretty quick too, and don't let me catch you here again . . . And put some coal on the fire before you go,' he said, his voice suddenly dropping. 'This room's as cold as hell. Hell's cold – not warm as they say. This is *my* house, and no enemy of my boy is going to sit in it.'

He stood looking at her, shaking, his legs wavering.

'Well, you are an old woman,' he said, sitting down again. 'You can stay if you like, but don't talk such nonsense. You ought to know better at your age.'

'Very well,' she said quietly. 'I'll stay, Walter, but not if you're rude and violent. We do no good by shouting at one another.'

'No, I suppose we do not,' he said, nodding his head. 'I tell you what it is, Judith. I'm not used to company. A while ago I went to London. You didn't know that, did you? And I saw a Fight – a fine Fight it was too, but the man I wanted to win didn't win, and so I came home to be by myself. I said, "Now if you win, everything will be all right. Uhland will come back." But he didn't win, and so what was the use in seeing anybody any more? So I came home, and I'm not very good company. You must forgive me.'

She saw that there was nothing more to be said just then about Elizabeth. Nevertheless something had been achieved by her visit.

They sat close together now like two old cronies.

'You see, Walter, I'm very old – very old indeed. I may die at any time. Not that I mind dying, but I wouldn't wish to leave any bad feeling behind me when I go. When you are as old as I am, bad feeling seems so very stupid – and I hope it won't continue into another generation. Your grandfather, David, used to tell me many stories about your father. Fancy! He has been dead now almost a hundred years! But David Herries used to say that he thought all the trouble in our branch of the family started when my father as a young man sold his mistress at a Fair in a temper. You've heard the old story. It's a legend, they say now, but it was all true enough, I believe. My father was a good man but he had a hot temper. That is perhaps what Uhland had too – but now those stories are all so old and so long ago and there is a new generation growing up. Dear little Vanessa, my granddaughter, such a pretty child. And Benjamin, your grandson – a very lively high-spirited boy. I don't want them to be in any family quarrel when they grow up. The world is more sensible now than when I was a girl – too sensible, I sometimes think, with people like Mr Gladstone and so much church on Sundays. Of course I think young people ought to go to church, but not as a duty. I'm rambling on, but what I really mean is that I want Vanessa and Benjamin to grow up without any hatred. Hatred is silly – waste of time and temper.'

She had talked on, but it seemed that he had listened to none of it. He only sat there staring in front of him, scratching his cheek. She was trying to reconcile him with the stout, cheerful, bullying man she had once known. How could Jennifer and the others have feared him as they did? He had never had any brains, only some instincts, and so he had collapsed under the pressure of events. You must have either intelligence or spiritual faith to stand up against life. When you had both you could be a conqueror. Jennifer had never had any brains, so she had gone the same way.

'Well, I must go now. Will you help me to my carriage?'

She rose a little unsteadily. When she stood beside him her little body was at his height, he sitting.

She kissed him.

Then, to her distress, she saw slow unmeaning tears trickle down his cheek. He did not try to stop them. He did not perhaps know that he was crying. Gently she stroked his rough unbrushed hair, speaking to him as though he were a child.

'There, there, Walter ... Things are not so bad, my dear. I will come again and see you. I am glad that we are friends at last. If you want anything, you have only to send to Uldale. There, there, Walter. Remember that we are all your friends. You are not alone any more. Uldale is no distance, you know.'

He rose slowly, looked about him in a bewildered fashion, then very courteously offered her his arm and conducted her to her carriage.

ON CAT BELLS: ESCAPE FROM ECSTASY

ADAM, turning on his side, caught the light from the window. The morning clouds, fiery with gold, were piling up above Walla Crag. *His* field – the field of all his life with its five little trees and its arch of sloping green – rolled into the glow; then, as though with a sigh of satisfaction, held the light; the little trees stood up and stretched their morning limbs. He looked at the field, thought that it was late (but they had not returned from Ambleside until one this morning), looked over his shoulder and saw that Margaret was yet deeply sleeping, then stretched out his brown hand to the bedside table and found Barney Newmark's letter.

There was light enough now to read by. Barney described Thackeray's funeral:

'... You would have been moved, Adam, although you thought the man proud and sensitive. So perhaps he was, but he had reason to be. Maybe he was the loneliest man I have ever met. One of the kindliest too. I could not but remember the first time I ever went to his house – his table covered, not with books and papers as you might think, but with compasses and pencils, bits of chalk and India ink, and little square blocks of box-wood. He was drawing, not writing. There were no signs of the author in the room, only the appliances of the draughtsman, and when we chatted he would rather talk about drawings than about books. And in what a kind, generous way, putting his hand on my arm, he said: "Well: and how can I be of any service to you?"

'And then there I was at Harlesden and a labourer going to his work said, quite casually: "You must make haste if you want to see him buried." It was a bright December day, everything shining and glittering, a dense black crowd waiting by the grave, and then the hearse – quite a common one, one of those plain, dull, black-painted boxes upon wheels without feathers or any ornament, drawn by only two horses: two or three carriages following, and then the straggling mourners – Dickens looking defiant as though he would like to knock someone down, Cruikshank, Millais, Louis Blanc, and the *Punch* people – you know, Mark Lemon, Leech and Tenniel – a lot more. The eight men could scarcely carry the coffin – he was a giant, wasn't he? Then the short ceremony – thank heaven it *is* so short! – and the mourners elbowing their way through the crowd to take a last look. And wasn't this an irony? There was a heavy prosaic policeman by the grave and as we filed past he said to the man in front of me: "Now don't be in a hurry; follow each other to the right, and you will all see comfortably." Would not Thackeray himself have liked that. The younger men of course are saying that he is already old-fashioned, but I myself think . . .'

Adam did not just then discover what it was that Barney thought. He put down the letter and lay for a while looking out across the Lake to Walla Crag. Thackeray was dead and he himself was forty-eight, and his mother, amazing woman, was eighty-nine; the Americans were fighting one another, and Bismarck was bullying the Danes; he must widen the vegetable-patch beyond the trees to the right of the house, and today he would start his fairy story – the one that had been in his head for more than a year now – and young Benjamin was riding over for the day and night from Uldale. It was the last week of his holiday before he returned to school – and here he was, he, Adam Paris, who had done nothing with his life as yet at all, but was happy, happy, happy . . . here in this January of 1864, in his own cottage that he had helped to build with his own hands under the brow of the hill, and Margaret his wife lying beside him, and their child cradled in her arm (for in the night, when they had returned, she had wakened, climbed out of her cot and demanded to come to them). Well, well . . . and Thackeray was dead, dead and buried.

He stretched out his hand again, this time for a volume of a novel. The novel was called *The Ordeal of Richard Feverel*; it was written by a young man, George Meredith. Although it had been published some four years or so, he had only now heard of it. An unusual book! Fantastically written but new – new in thought, in style and in audacity. And Thackeray was old-fashioned. Thackeray was dead. He rolled over and laid his arm

very lightly but protectively over Margaret. They had sailed all
the perilous seas now and were in harbour, through passion (but
Margaret had never been very passionate), through that strange
period of isolation the one from the other, when they knew one
another too well and yet not nearly well enough. (That had been
ended by the scene at Uldale that Christmas-time.) Then through
the wonderful stage of renewed passion and a heightened glorious
intimacy. (This stage had included Caesar Kraft's death and the
end of Adam's 'Brotherhood' ambitions.) Then, back in Cumberland, out of passion and into this, the real glory of every
marriage that can attain it, a confidence, a trust, an intimacy so
great and deep and calm that it was like Derwentwater there
beyond the window.

She would never *quite* understand him. There was a vein of
cynicism running through his nature that was quite foreign to
her. Nor would she ever understand his restlessness. Once she had
his love and the love of their child, and *knew* that she had them,
nothing could ever disturb her again – except, of course, losing
either himself or Vanessa. Always when he left her, even for an
hour or two, a little wrinkle lined her calm brow. She was not
really happy again until he had returned. But she was no longer
possessive as she had once been. That was because she was sure of
him now.

At that thought he moved a little restlessly. Did he want her to
be sure of him? Did any man want his wife to be sure of him, and
was not every wife unhappy unless she *was* sure? That was
perhaps one of the eternal misunderstandings in marriage. And
in this his mother completely understood him. In every way his
mother understood him, shared his restlessness, his longings, his
disappointments in himself, knew him as no one else did. He and
she were wanderers constrained by the circumstances of life to be
stay-at-homes. Had he not married Margaret what a useless,
worthless wanderer he would have been! Like his old legendary
grandfather! Yes, he had been lucky to marry a woman like
Margaret, so good and loyal, faithful and true. Once he would
have been wearied and irritated by too much goodness and
fidelity.

He got out of bed very quietly and went down to the yard
behind the house for Will to sluice him down.

Although it was early January and mortal cold, he did
not shrink from the sluicing. The yard was hidden from
the world save for the little wood on the rise of the ground.

No windows looked on it, and it was sheltered from the winds. Will was already there, cleaning the boots and hissing away at them like a hostler. He straightened himself when he saw Adam and stood up, grinning, his yellow forelock straggling over his forehead, his eyes as blue, direct and unflinching as those of an honest and fearless child, his body balanced easily on its strong legs.

'I'm late this morning, Will.'

'Aye. You was late last night.'

'Lovely day.'

Will looked up. The sky was blue and laced everywhere with little clouds that still had tints of amber and rose.

'Cold this morning,' Adam said.

He looked at Will with great affection. The whole day started wrongly if he did not have a brief talk alone with Will at the beginning of it, for his relation with Will was that of man to man, rid of all the uncertainties, sudden crises, sudden darknesses that haunt like ghosts the relation of the sexes. In a way Will understood him better than did either his mother or Margaret. In a way Will loved him better than did either of the women, for it was a love completely unselfish, that asked nothing in return, that was disturbed by no moods or reticences. When Adam was in a temper or caught into some creative distance far from all human agency or had a cold or a headache or felt his liver, Margaret was disturbed as though she were in danger of losing something (although she had learnt to conceal this disturbance, Adam knew that it was there and it irritated him), but Will was unchanged. Let Adam have what mood he wished, Will loved him just the same. He could be jealous, and was often confoundedly obstinate and pig-headed, but his loyalty, devotion, trustworthiness never varied a hair's breadth.

Two wooden buckets filled with cold water stood side by side. Adam threw off his shirt and breeches, then shivered as the cold air struck his bare flesh.

'Quick, Will. Quick, you devil!'

Will took up one bucket in his two arms and with a heave threw the water over Adam. Then the other. Then quickly he caught a rough towel that was hanging on the back of the kitchen door, seized Adam and rubbed him with great violence, hissing furiously.

Adam ran into the kitchen and stood naked in front of the roaring fire. Now he was glorious. He was in fine condition. Drops

of water clung to his beard and his hairy chest. His flesh was firm
and strong. His heart beat like a good steady hammer. He took
deep breaths. Will watched the operation with high satisfaction.

'You know, Will,' Adam said, stretching out his bare arms, 'my
mother has told me that her father used to have his man swill
him down at Rosthwaite where he lived, in just this way. He was
a queer character, he was. My mother has a heap of tales about
him from his son, her stepbrother. He was years older than she
was – David Herries, I mean. And now she's nearing ninety.
Takes you back a long time, doesn't it?'

'Aye,' said Will. 'It does that. We're born and we're wed and
we're dead before we know. 'Tis odd when you think of it, Mr
Adam, that folk make the fuss they do when they're dead so
quick. About little things, I mean. Now there was that man
from Seathwaite last evening. Was in here with a long tale about
a cow he'd lost. I told him not to fret and he was furious, as
though I'd stolen the damned cow myself. Mary will be in
likely. I can hear her coming.' This was the old woman from the
farm halfway to Grange. She came every day as help.

Adam pulled on his shirt and breeches and went upstairs.

Later he was sitting in his room waiting to begin his fairy story.
This room – not very large – was square, papered a dull rather
shabby red, and the two windows looked full on to the Lake and
Walla Crag. The wall opposite the windows was lined with
shelves, and there were his books, not a great collection, some
four or five hundred in all.

They were, moreover, a mixed lot, in no sort of order. A faded
row of little blue volumes of the *Iliad* and *Odyssey* had for companions *Pickwick* in its shilling parts (the covers of some of the
numbers disgracefully torn), Rogers' *Italy* with the handsome
illustrations, Arthur Young's *Travels in France* and Leigh
Hunt's *Story of Rimini*. There were thirty volumes of the 'English Poets', ten of Chaucer, *Sir Charles Grandison* and *Tristram
Shandy*. On the table at his side were two volumes of *Richard
Feverel*, Huxley's *Man's Place in Nature,* and *The Woman in
White*. By itself on the other side of him was a fresh brilliant
copy in green and gold of Barney Newmark's first novel*
– *Dandy Grimmett* – in three volumes.

* *Dandy Grimmett*, by Barnabas Newmark: 3 vols, Suller & Thorne
1863.

'They have bound young Barney very handsomely,' he thought. (He still looked on Barney as an infant although he was now nearly thirty-four years of age.) He felt a pang of envy, regret, sadness. There was young Barney, of whom no one had thought very much, publishing his first novel and some of it not bad either, especially the racing scenes, the fight (plainly taken from Sayers and Heenan), and the last chapter when old Dandy, dying, is brought back to his rooms in London and hears the carriages rolling to the theatres, the cries of the newsboys, and the thick heavy ticking of the clock on the marble mantelpiece. He's been influenced by Thackeray, of course – not doing anything new like this young man Meredith. But is it important to be new? Nothing is new but superficials. He can paint a scene that is real. He knows his world . . . Damned clever sketch of his father, old Stephen. He'd deny it, of course . . .'

His mind went floating away to the lake that lay in the morning sun like a snake's skin, grey and rippled, convulsed, it seemed, with little shudders. The sunlight hung above it on the flanks of the hill as though afraid to descend. He pushed open the window and looked out, heard the stream running at the back of the house, smelt the dead bracken, the gritty flakiness of the dead earth, and saw a snowdrop, solitary and beautiful, bend its stem in the breeze.

He heard Vanessa calling. His heart warmed. It was all he could do not to go out to her, but he knew that once he had left that room incident after incident would occur to prevent his return to it, as though a malicious Fate were determined for ever to hold him back from doing anything. With a sigh he closed the window and went back to the table. He picked up a number of *London Society* that had just arrived and read from the serial story:

' "*Nor need you wish to do so, Miss Fleming,*" *said Jane quickly. "Nor, if you were thrown on the world, would you ever be what Milly and I are now. We have had unusual advantages from our cradles, and with great natural aptitude, have improved them to the uttermost.*" '

He sighed again. 'Great natural aptitude . . .' 'Impoved them to the uttermost.' No, people did not talk like that. Why were novels so silly?

But this seemed to encourage him. *He* was going to write a fairy story. He sat down resolutely, drew the paper in front of him and wrote in his firm strong hand:

THE DWARF WITH THE PURPLE COMB*

He sat, looking out of window, biting the feather of his quill. Then he was off and away!

Once upon a time there was a King who had five lovely daughters. The names of the five Princesses were Hazel, Rosamond, Amaryllis, Mellicent and Mary. Mary was the youngest and she was not given so grand a name as the others because the King, her father, had wanted to have a son and was so grievously disappointed when the Doctor told him that the baby was a girl that he shut himself into his bedroom for four and a half days and refused to see anybody, even the Queen. He lived all that time on bread and water. So at least it was said. But Fortunatus, the son of the Woodcutter in the Forest near by, saw the Palace gardener climb on a ladder and hand through the King's bedroom window a gold tray that had on it a gingerbread cake, a roast goose, a Christmas pudding and a dish with oranges, plums and apricots.

Fortunatus told his father, the Woodcutter, what he had observed, and his father said that he must never mention it to anyone or he would lose his head. Mary, who was the loveliest child ever seen – she had hair as dark as the ravens and a smile so sweet that everyone at the Court loved her – was always punished when her sisters did anything wrong. For example, one fine morning Princess Rosamond was given a beautiful dress by her Fairy Godmother (it was her birthday). The dress was made of tissue and silver and it had buttons of green jade, a collar of emeralds, and the sleeves were decorated with the feathers of the Bird of Paradise. When Princess Mellicent saw this beautiful dress she was so angry because *her* Fairy Godmother had given her on *her* birthday only a needlework-case. So she took the gold scissors from her needlework-case and when Princess Rosamond was practising the piano in the Green Drawing-room she went into her sister's bedroom and cut the beautiful dress into shreds.

Now when this was discovered and Mellicent had confessed to what she had done, Mary was put to stand in the corner of the Audience Chamber with her face to the wall so that everyone who passed by could see her.

* *The Dwarf with the Purple Comb, And other Stories;* by Adam Paris, Harris & Sons, 1865.

It happened then one fine morning that Fortunatus, the Woodcutter's son, was sent by his father to the Palace with a wheelbarrow full of logs for the Royal fireplaces, and, peeping in (for he was a very inquisitive boy) at the door of the Audience Chamber, he saw the lovely little Princess standing with her face to the wall . . .

Little Vanessa ran down the path and up the road. It was time for Benjamin to be coming, and from the corner where the stream ran from the tops straight like a silver arrow into the Lake you could watch the higher bend of the road. She danced about, clapping her hands because it was cold.

She was wearing a dress of green and black checked taffeta, which was the new material. She was immensely proud of it and had begged to be allowed to wear it because Benjamin was coming. She was already tall for her age, carried herself to her full height, and now, when she was dancing, every movement was natural in its grace as the silver pattern of the stream, the dull amber of the dead bracken and the bare wood whose trees were flushed in the distance like an evening sky against the grey Lake filmed with ice. Skiddaw and Blencathra were powdered with snow, and hard round clouds like snowballs hung above their lines. Vanessa's mind was intently fixed on Benjamin. Although he was over four years older she thought that he was a perfect companion. She was even then an excellent listener; her curiosity was acute, and she could never be told enough about anything if someone wanted to tell her. Benjamin told her the most extraordinary things. Everything that happened at Uldale was of absorbing interest to her, and she spent so much of her time with grown-up people – her mother and father, Will, and Mary from the farm – that although she was entirely a child and in many things still a baby, she understood the *lives* of grown-up people, knew why they did things and could *imagine* their world. Her grandmother – the old lady who was as smart as a pin, all white and black (and the very *whitest* of white!) with her cap, her ivory cane, her shoes with the silver buckles, who was so kind, amusing, understanding, but could, all in a moment, be so sharp and commanding (very like the Queen of England) – was to Vanessa simply the most miraculous person in the world, composed of magic, fire, ice, diamonds. There she was in her room, older than anyone had ever been, but more acquainted with all that Vanessa was thinking than anyone save her mother. Then

there was Aunt Jane, the nicest of all the Aunts. Aunt Veronica
who was beautiful, Aunt Amabel who could throw a ball like a
boy, Uncle Timothy who was so big that he could take the whole
of you in his hand if he wished, Aunt Dorothy who was always
busy, James the coachman, Daniel the stableman, Martha the
cook – and so on, so on – a whole *world* was in Uldale. One could
never have enough of it.

And Benjamin was her Uldale storyteller. She would like him
to go on for hours telling her things, but he could never be still,
never stay in one place more than five minutes. And Vanessa
thought this unusual, because his mother, Aunt Elizabeth, was so
quiet. She would sit all evening in the same corner of the sofa
reading a book – only often, as Vanessa had noticed, she was not
reading, but would put down her book and sit staring in front of
her. Benjamin had no father, which, Vanessa thought, was terribly sad for him.

Ah! there Benjamin was! He came trotting round the corner
on Albert, his pony (named after the Prince Consort, who had
died the very month that Uncle Timothy gave it him). Mumps
the dog was running at the side. Mumps loved Benjamin, and
even now, when he was ten years old or more, would never leave
Benjamin's side he could help it. The boy saw Vanessa and
waved his riding-whip. When he came up to her he burst out
laughing. His round, plump face was crimson with the cold air
and the exercise, and his funny small nose needed wiping.

'You're wearing a new dress!' he shouted.

'Yes,' she said, still dancing. 'And there's ice on the Lake. It
will be frozen perhaps tomorrow – enough to skate on.'

They went up the path to the cottage, and as soon as Benjamin
was off the pony he felt in his coat-pocket and produced a large,
very sticky chunk of toffee.

'Have some!' he said, trying to break it.

'Did Uncle Timothy give it you?'

'No. I stole it from the kitchen. Mother said I wasn't to have
any because I was sick last time from eating so much, so I had to
get it from the kitchen, and Martha nearly caught me.'

Benjamin always puzzled Vanessa in this way, because he was
for ever doing things that he was told not to do. When he was
caught he never lied nor did he seem in the least to mind pun-
ishment, but it appeared that you had only to make a rule for him
to want to break it.

However, she took some of the toffee and, with their mouths

full, they went round to the back to put the pony up and see Will. When they were in the back-yard Benjamin turned a somersault. He had just learned to do it. 'There's a boy at school called Turnip,' he explained. 'And he can do it and he said I couldn't, so now I can.'

'What a funny name to have!' she remarked.

'They call him that because his *real* name is Turner – see?' Benjamin said, turning head over heels again.

In the living-room of the cottage Adam had few books, but he had been given two things out of the parlour at Uldale and these he prized over all his other possessions – one was the old spinet with roses painted on its lid, the other the music-box with the Queen in her green dress and the King in his amber coat. When Judith, growing too old to argue violently with Dorothy, saw that big heavy new furniture was coming into the parlour do what she would, she insisted that Adam should have the spinet for his cottage. She would have given him the sofa with the red apples also had she not felt a superstition. Her hand had rested on that when she had made her great decision . . .

Adam's living-room had not much furniture. There were the wax flowers that he had bought Margaret at the Pantheon. The square carpet had eight groups of flowers on a light pink ground. There were three carved mahogany chairs with needlework seats and backs. There was a chiffonnier bookcase, brown and gold with marquetry panels. These things had been presents from various members of the family. Carey Rockage's wife had given him two cornucopias, Will Herries the bookcase. On the walls against some very variegated wallpaper was a watercolour called 'The Lady of the House', an engraving of Watendlath, and a Baxter print, 'Dippers and Nest'. In one corner of the room was Vanessa's joy, a Peepshow of the Central Hall at the Great Exhibition. Over the mantelpiece was hung a Sand Picture, 'Saddle Horse', by James Zobel. Barney Newmark had given him this one Christmas. So the room was an odd jumble, and he didn't care for anything in it save the music-box and the spinet. But it was in this room and among these things that he experienced a little scene with young Benjamin. He had reached a point in his fairy story where the Dwarf had tapped on the Princess Mary's window. The Palace Garden was flooded with moonlight. She came to the window, and, standing on top of the ladder, he whispered to her that, if she would come with him, he would take her to the orchard and there, hidden in the ground at the roots of an old apple tree, he would find for her the Purple Comb . . .

At that point everything had ceased. He could see no more the Princess, the Dwarf, young Fortunatus. All had vanished, the Lake rippled under its silver shading of ice, and Blencathra had the bloom of a plum. Soon it would be time for the meal. He was hungry, so, rubbing his hands, he went into the living-room. A moment later Benjamin came in.

'Uncle Adam,' he asked, 'can you wrestle?'

'No,' he said.

'Try,' said Benjamin, and without a moment's warning he pushed himself on to Adam. He butted his stomach with his round head, tried to bring his arms together around Adam's broad thighs, twisted his small legs round Adam's thick ones. He put a ferocious energy into this, blowing and grunting, straining every muscle in his body. For a moment he made Adam rock. Adam could feel the muscles of the boy's leg strung to their utmost against his calf. The two small hands tore at his waistcoat. A button flew off. The hands groped inside his shirt, pinched his flesh.

'Hi!' he called out. 'That's enough! You're hurting!'

'I'll do it! I'll do it!' Benjamin gasped. 'I'll bring you down!'

Adam, laughing, put out his arms, caught the boy to him with a bear's hug, then swung him into the air and held him there.

'Now what will you do?'

Benjamin kicked. Then he was rolled on to the floor, lay there for a moment panting.

'Things look funny from here,' he observed. He got up. 'I haven't it right yet. There's a trick you do with your left leg. Next time I shall manage it.' His hair was dishevelled, his cheeks crimson, his shirt open. He grinned.

'You have torn one of my buttons off,' Adam said.

'Oh, that's all right. Aunt Margaret will sew it on for you.'

He came close to Adam, leaned against him, looked up at him, smiling, but with a strange mature glance.

Adam said: 'Are you liking school? I hear that you were in all kinds of trouble the last term. Why was that?'

Benjamin nodded.

'I can't help it, Uncle Adam. If anyone tells me to do anything I don't want to do it.'

'Why's that?'

'I don't know. I expect it's because my uncle killed my father.

There isn't another boy in the whole school whose uncle killed his father.'

The words came out quite easily, with no sense of self-consciousness, no unhappiness – a clear statement of simple fact. To Adam those words were like thunder in his ears. The floor seemed to rock. He didn't know that the boy had any notion of the way that his father had died. They had, all of them, for years been in a conspiracy to prevent any allusion to it before the boy, and although at first it had seemed a vain hope that he should not hear, as the years passed they all thought that they had succeeded, for when Benjamin spoke of his father it was quite naturally. He seemed to believe that he had died of some illness just like any other man.

Benjamin nodded.

'You thought I didn't know. I have known for years and years and years. First a farmer at Peter's House told me. I know just what they did. They rode through the mist to Skiddaw House. They had arranged it all, and my uncle shot my father and then shot himself. And my father hadn't a gun. So you see I'm different from all the other boys, and I'll be different all my life.'

Adam did not know what to say. He moved off and looked out of window. Then he turned round.

'Your father,' he said, 'was a very fine man and I loved him. He always did the right thing and so must you.'

Benjamin answered quickly, as though he were speaking in someone's defence.

'I love my father more than anyone, and if I had been there with him I would have taken the gun from my uncle and shot him, and all my life I'll kill men like my uncle who are beasts and cowards. I don't care. I'm not afraid of anyone, and I'll never do something just because someone tells me . . .' His voice suddenly was the voice of a small boy. 'I'll be like Robin Hood. He was an outlaw and I'll be an outlaw. I have a band of outlaws under me at school and we're not afraid of anybody.'

To Adam there came a quick picture of a wood, a pool, a man on a white horse and himself dancing in defiance of that rider's whip . . .

He came across the floor to Benjamin and put his arm around him.

'I was like that myself once and now I'm an old gentleman who writes fairy stories. The great thing,' he went on, holding the boy close to him, 'is not to be bitter against life because of what happened to your father. Don't allow things that have happened in the past, Benjamin, to spoil your life. The past is past. They are ghosts, all those dead men.'

'My father is not a ghost,' Benjamin said. 'I have his picture and a riding-whip he had and his hairbrushes. I took the hairbrushes out of Mama's room and I've hidden them. No one knows where they are but me. And one day I shall meet someone like my uncle and I will shoot him just as he shot my father, except that he shall have a gun, so that it's fair.'

Adam shook his head. 'That's no good,' he said. 'Because a wrong was done once, to do another wrong doesn't make things better.'

'Look here, Uncle,' Benjamin said. 'I can make a somersault. I *think* I can make two now. Here! Look!' and he turned two somersaults, one after the other, in the space between the chairs and the table. He tumbled straight into old Mary who was helping Margaret to bring in the meal.

Had Benjamin affected him? When they were sitting after the meal quietly watching the sunlight stain the flowers of the carpet, the gilt of the bookcase, and strike, as though maliciously, the simpering self-importance of 'The Lady of the House', he felt a curious and abnormal ecstasy of perception. It seemed to him that his senses were all tingling with an extra activity.

Margaret, opposite him, was making a basket cover in old silk patchwork. On a ground of dark green she was forming a kaleidoscope pattern of glittering scraps – flakes of crimson, sea-green, primrose, hyacinth blue, the rose of apple orchards, the gold of corn. On the grey stuff of the lap of her dress the fragments of silk lay scattered, her look so serenely safe and happy that it caught at his heart. Once and again she would glance up at him and smile. Vanessa and Benjamin were stretched on the floor, their heads together, looking at a book of Japanese drawings. From where he sat he could see the brilliant figures of birds and men in blue and crimson carrying burdens over bridges and the wide expanse of purple seas. Everything was colour and everything was peace. Tiny details seemed to wear a heightened significance, the buttons on Vanessa's dress, freckles on Benjamin's snub nose, the needlework pattern on the chairs.

He was filled with a kind of immortal ecstasy. This he had achieved. Through all the disappointments and failures of his

life he had caught this and held it – love, fatherhood, security.
The patch of ground upon which his feet were set was his, this
hill, the silver birch gleaming in the sun beyond the window, the
stream of music he could hear, this Cumberland that all his life
long he had worshipped, and beyond it England, the hills running to the sea, the valleys running to the South, all this land
that, now that he had his home, flowed to the North, South, East
and West. Running from his door to all the seas, his for ever and
ever, although his realization of it lasted only for a moment.

His happiness caught him at the throat. His eyes were blinded.
He moved in his chair, and Margaret looked across at him and
smiled.

Then Benjamin glanced up at them and sprang to his feet.

'I want to go out! Come along, Vanessa! I'll race you!'

They opened the doors and ran out into the garden.

It was as though he had himself spoken. He felt suddenly that
his security was dangerous. He did not want it. He was bound, a
prisoner. Somewhere, a small child, he was running, running,
escaping, shouting, and his mother was with him. Panting, they
raced up the hill to see the sun rise. The woods fell below them,
the Tarn was dark, and he could hear the sheep rustling past him
up the dark path. His mother was a gipsy and he was her gipsy
son. He could see the lights from the painted carts – a horse
neighed . . . waving his arms and shouting he breasted the
hill . . .

He woke as though he had been sleeping, and saw Margaret
choosing the colours from the fragments of silk, holding a scrap
of rose against the light to see how it would do . . .

'I'll be back, Meg,' he said.

He went to the door and almost ran from the house. He began
to climb through the dead bracken above his stone wall. As he
mounted he heard the voices of the children from the garden, a
cart was creaking down the road that was already a white ribbon.
The Lake rose and he saw that the sun had veined it with patterns of light, here there were pools of grey and ashen pallor and
there deep shadows of saffron – all confined by the hills, Skiddaw, Saddleback, Walla Crag. As he climbed, the Lake and the
hills climbed with him. The air was cold like a whip, but so fresh
that it struck his cheeks as the water had done when Will sluiced
him that morning.

Then he began to run, he called aloud, he shouted. He

stumbled and fell over the stones and thought how old Rackstraw
had told him once: 'Clouds and stones! Stones and clouds!
That's what this country is!'

His breathing hurt him like a knife, for he was no child now
but a stout middle-aged man with a beard and middle-aged
habits of comfort and laziness. But he liked the catch at his
lungs, the bruise on his knee where the stone had hit him. He
climbed, stumbling, waving his arms, turning to catch the Lake
and the hills with him and draw them up. He did not know that
he was climbing like a madman, climbing as he had never
climbed that hill before, because he was part of the hill, the wind,
the sun. He hurled himself over the last boulders and flung himself on the strong, resilient turf, lying there at full length, his
arms spread out, his chest heaving. Why should he ever return?
Something wild and authentic in his blood beat in his brain.
Margaret, Vanessa, his mother, they were nothing to him because
he was not himself, Adam Paris, but something beyond himself,
beyond time, the past, the present and all that was to come.

He lay on the turf, the soil was in his beard, his hands dug into
the short sweet grass, the grit of the land, chilled, hardened with
a frost that had outlived the midday sun. He stood up. Below
him was Derwentwater to the east, Newlands to the west veiled
now in the shadow of the lengthening day. He saw Catchedicam
to the left of Helvellyn top, and southwards was Langdale Pike o'
Stickle. Why should he ever return? He started to run again on a
surface so buoyant that it seemed to run with him. Up the easy
slope of Maiden Moor, Scafell and Gable coming to meet him
between Eel Crag and Dale Head. Why should he ever return?
Borrowdale and Grange were below and now the Pillar was in
view between Dale Head and Hindscarth. He might race on for
ever – Hindscarth and Robinson, then down to Buttermere
across to Ennerdale, over to Waswater, to Eskdale and the sea!

He was a wandering man, a lost man, a man at last his own
master!

He shouted. 'Oh, hoi! Oh, hoi!' All the hills echoed him as it
seemed to him, and the waters of a thousand streams roared
about his ears.

He flung out his arms and embraced the world . . .

Folly! He sat down, hugging his knees. He brushed the soil from
his beard. He pulled up his trousers to see whether his knee were
bleeding. It was not. He could barely see the scratch. Two sheep

came wandering towards him and stood a little way off him, watching. Then, reassured, began to graze again. The sun was gone; it fell swiftly behind the hills on these January days. Helvellyn burned in a haze of rosy smoke, and all the air was frosty as though the ice had suddenly thickened on the Lake below and the hills around him. Maiden Moor, Robinson were breathing in gusts of cold thickened air. The sky paled to become the white field of one solitary star that glittered, a spark of frosted fire. Dusk and a great silence enwrapped the world.

He started home. The thought of home was comforting. Margaret sitting by the fire, and he would tell Benjamin and Vanessa a story . . .

He started down the slope, singing as he went.

A DAY IN THE LIFE OF A VERY OLD
LADY

SHE rose and then sank again, sank and rose, on a great billowy cloud of softest down. The movement was so exquisite, and she was herself so lazy, that she abandoned herself completely, although there were, she knew, a thousand things that she ought to be doing. Everything, far and near, was of a dazzling white save only Adam's nose that was purple and dripping with cold. Had she the energy she would tell him that he must blow it. There was the cloud available and it would irritate her, did she allow herself to be irritated, that he did not make use of so convenient a remedy. But she would not permit herself to be irritated. She was altogether too happy. As she rocked she sang softly to herself a song that Emma Furze had taught her, but she would not sing loudly lest she should wake Georges who was snoring on a cloud near by. How well she knew that snore – it was part of her whole life – and although she did not care for snores in general, Georges' snore was her own property and he must sleep long, here in Watendlath, for yesterday had been the clipping and he would be weary.

Moreover, just round the corner was the whole family – Dorothy, Tim, Veronica, Amabel and dear Jane. They were busy at some game. She could not quite see them, but she knew what they were about. Practising at archery, as indeed they must, for in a week's time there was the contest in Keswick and Veronica had a chance of a prize. It was winter, but in visions such as this all seasons were confused. How lovely she looked, Veronica, her body stretched, her bow held straight from her arms, her beautiful head thrown back! But Jane would be clumsy. If she were not careful they would laugh and then Jane would blush, pretending not to mind, but hurt at her clumsiness ... and she would call from her cloud, as so often she had done before, 'Jane! Jane! I want you!' simply to save her.

Things began to press in upon her consciousness. A great white bird, the sunlight glittering in silver on its sweeping wings, flew slowly above her head, and the white blossom fell, at a touch of the warm breeze, there across the lawn in the orchard, the petals hovering, wavering ... hovering, wavering! The sheep, their fleece stained with red, were pressing up the road at Watendlath, and Charlie Watson, motionless on his horse, watched them go. There was something that she must say to Charlie Watson, and so, raising herself from her cloud, she called softly 'Charlie! Charlie!'

The sky was blinded with a white radiance. The great bird, shaking showers of brilliance from its wings, beat upwards towards the sun. The radiance was so bright that she put her hand before her eyes, crying out with joy at so much loveliness, then heard – close beside here – Jane's eager laughing voice.

'Wake up, Aunt Judith! Look at the snow! It has fallen in the night! There never was such a beautiful day!'

She turned her head, rubbed her eyes, then reached for her spectacles. Putting them on she caught, in one sweep, the whole of the real world, for Jane had drawn back the blinds and, from her bed, she could see the flanks of Skiddaw glistening in crystal snow, and snow heaped on the windowsill. Above it all, there was a burning blue sky and the sun blazed over all the room. Jane stood there with the basin of water, the sponge, the soap, the towel, the silver brushes, the ivory comb, and, on a table not far away, breakfast was waiting.

'Well, my dear,' she said with a little sigh of happiness. 'I've had a very good night, thank you. I woke once and heard it strike three and that was the only time. Dear me, what a splendid sunshine! And how are you, Jane dear? I hope you slept well. I dreamt you were practising archery with Veronica.'

'I have had a very good night, thank you,' said Jane, and at once she began, with a dexterity and neatness that Judith adored (she would allow no one but Jane to perform these offices), to hold the basin, to see that the sponge was not too full, and then, when the washing was concluded, to bring the round mirror with the green wood and the gilt doves, so that Judith might see clearly to brush her silver hair.

'Mary will be in shortly to set the fire. There are plenty of logs, I told James yesterday.'

'What is there for breakfast?'

The tray was brought to the bed and carefully arranged.

'I chose those two brown eggs myself. And there is the damson preserve.'

'Dear me, how pleasant!'

'Adam is coming over today, you know.'

'As though I could forget, my dear.'

'He is bringing Vanessa.'

'Of course, of course,' Judith said, quite crossly. They would treat her – even dear Jane did this – as though she found it difficult to remember things. She remembered everything – *everything*. It was true that it seemed to her as though Georges and Charlie Watson were still in the room. Past and Present were one and the same. Jane herself would discover that one day. But because she, Judith, was ninety-five years of age (she had had her birthday a week or two ago) was no reason why they should think her helpless. It was true that she could not, any longer, walk very much, but for the rest she was as active and alive as any of them. She took off the top of one of her eggs and said:

'How is everybody? How is Timothy's cold?'

'Bad. But he doesn't mind. He has ridden off to Orpen Farm to see about the Hunt tomorrow. With the snow like this it will be difficult, but it will thaw this afternoon, I dare say. It never lies long here.'

Judith enjoyed her breakfast. Every morning as she drank her tea and ate her toast and preserve, she considered her state. She was no hypochondriac, but from a kind of outside consideration she summoned her forces. Had she a headache? Did her eyes smart? How was her throat which, a day or two ago, had been a little sore? How was that sharp pain in the right elbow? And the soreness just above the left knee? Was her stomach (which Dorothy thought it most indelicate ever to mention) preparing to upset her or was it lazy and good-natured today? (She saw her stomach as a kind of cat, sometimes full of warm milk and purring, sometimes in the worst of tempers, always selfish.)

But how was the Captain of her Ragged Army, her Heart? Everything depended on her Heart. While she felt that her stomach was definitely hostile, didn't care a rap about her, her Heart, she considered, was on her side, disliked extremely to distress her, would not miss a beat and then beat twice in a hurry if he could help it. Her Heart was a Gentleman who was making the best of it in very difficult circumstances.

Although she held this review every morning she never spoke to anyone about it. She could indeed carry on a perfect domestic conversation with Jane at the very moment when she was saying inside herself: 'Well, Knee, are you wishing to be tiresome today? You are very quiet just now, but I dare say you've got something up your sleeve for later on.'

And, behind all this, was her terrific pride at reaching her present age. Every morning when she woke to find herself alive she made another triumphant notch on the slate of her mind. It soon might be – it might be indeed at any moment – that she would slip into a stage of semi-consciousness when living would be nothing but a dreaming preparation for Death. When that came she would not be able to reckon her triumph, so now she would make the most of it. On November 28th last, her ninety-fifth birthday, she had had messages, letters, gifts, from Herries all over the country – from Ellis and his mother, Janet and Roger at Grosset, Stephen Newmark, Phyllis, Barnabas, Katherine (who had married Colonel Winch of Forrest Hatch, Salisbury), Emily, from Garth and Amery and Sylvia, from the Ormerods at Harrogate and the Cards at Bournemouth, from all the Witherings near Carlisle – yes, from Herries and Herries all the country over. They had all been kind and generous, but she knew what it was that they had all been thinking. She must reach her Hundredth Birthday! At all costs SHE MUST LIVE TO BE A HUNDRED!

Not for many, many years – not in fact since old Maria Herries who had been born on the day of the Battle of Naseby – had any Herries come so near to a Hundred. Great-Aunt Maria had missed it, and they were all disappointed even now, after all this time, that she had done so.

But Judith was their pride and their hope. True that she had not always been their pride, true that her father had been a disgrace, that she herself had married a rascal of a Frenchman who had died shamefully in a drunken scramble, that she had lived like a farmer's wife in the country, that she had had an illegitimate son, but that was all long ago. She had become a famous person, a legend. All over the country Herries said: 'Oh yes, we are a strong stock, live to a great age. There's old Madame now, ninety something, and commands a houseful of women up in Cumberland as though she were twenty. Wonderful old lady! She'll reach her Century, you may be sure. Nothing can stop her.'

Judith knew that they were saying this and she was proud of it. Of course it was foolish, but then the Herries *were* foolish – foolish and rather charming, in their childishness. When she felt well, as on a morning like this present one, she thought that she could live until two hundred. Why not? What was to stop her? There *were* days when she was infinitely weary and longed for it all to be over. But as soon as the bad days passed she forgot them.

Today her mind was as clear as a crystal. She remembered everything. Timothy's cold, the calf that had been born two nights before, the new maid Hannah from Seathwaite, the proposal that Captain Forster of Runner Hall, near Penrith, had made to Veronica a week ago (would she not accept him? She was thirty-one years of age and had she not been so beautiful would have been long thought an old maid), a chair that Dorothy had bought for her in Carlisle (it was of hand-carved walnut and its seat was covered in maroon plush; Judith had thought it hideous but did not wish to hurt Dorothy's feelings), Adam's visit, a present of a miniature set in Bristol jet ware (teapot, sugar-box and cream-jug) that she had for Vanessa. Jane had found it in Keswick and it was exactly what Vanessa loved ... all these things she had in mind while Jane talked and the snow glittered, the sun flooded the room, and the damson preserve tasted most excellent ...

Afterwards she had her bath, warm and delicious, while the logs blazed and the large tortoiseshell cat purred on the rug; then Jane helped her to dress and at last she was seated in her armchair near the fire ready for the Visits.

'I think, Jane dear, I'll be able to go downstairs a little this afternoon!'

What a picture she made, Jane thought, in her black silk with her snow-white cap, the lace at her throat and wrists, the thin long gold chain that hung almost to her waist, her black shoes with the glittering buckles!

'Yes, dear, I think you can on such a lovely day.'

It was at this moment when she was not so well, just before the Visits, that she had to pull herself together, to drag herself up out of that other world, the Watendlath world where Georges and Charlie laughed and rode, where Christabel and Jennifer quarrelled before a fantasy of masked figures, where an old man with a long white beard stroked his nose . . . On her bad days that past was more real than any present. But not today. She was all alert, and when Dorothy, followed by Amabel, entered with their 'Isn't it a beautful day, Aunt Judith?' and Dorothy began at once, as was her custom, with a cheerful 'tit-tat-tat-tit' of conversation (her manner with very old people) Judith was all alive.

Dorothy was wearing a new dress, the upper skirt caught up almost to the hips and the back of the skirt descending in a straight sloping line from the waist to the ground. The upper skirt was of brown silk and the lower of bright blue taffeta. This suited her stoutness better than the old exaggerated crinoline. Judith knew at once what the new dress meant.

'You are going into Keswick, my dear?'

'Yes. Veronica is coming with me. *What* do you think? Veronica intends to accept Captain Forster!'

Here was news indeed! One less of the great virginal army! And Captain Forster was not so bad. On the stout side and not very clever, but devoted, with a charming place, money enough, a kind heart. Veronica should have been in London. She might then have married *anybody*. But she was lazy. There was something of Jennifer in her blood. She had told Judith once that the only man she had ever really loved had been a farmer from Buttermere way. That had been only her fun. Of course Veronica would never think of such a thing! But why not? Had not Charlie Watson been a farmer?

Never mind. Here was Captain Forster – plump, clean, adoring.

'Are you certain?'

'Well, she hasn't confessed it in so many words. But he is to be at the Osmastons'. I am *sure* that she means to accept him.'

Amabel, who was always dressed severely and thought men contemptible, tossed her head.

'What she can see in that fat man!'

'Well, dear,' said Dorothy complacently, 'it is she that is going to marry him, not you.'

'Yes, thank heaven.'

They talked for a little, then Dorothy said:

'We will leave you now because I think Elizabeth wants a word. She is unhappy about Benjamin.'

'What has he been doing?'

Dorothy sighed.

'What hasn't he been doing? He had a fight in the village last evening with Marston's boy, and his report from Rugby has come. It is terrible, really terrible. You must speak to him, Aunt Judith. You are the only one who can do anything with him.'

They went and Elizabeth came in.

Elizabeth was fifty-four and as beautiful now as she had been at twenty. She wore a grey dress, her fair hair flat on the top and gathered into a large bun at the back of her head, a golden glory even in that so hideous fashion. She had the air of remoteness that had been hers ever since John's death. She was not priggish nor superior in this. She joined in everything that went on, laughed, sang, played games, hunted (she was still a splendid horsewoman), but nothing could bring her into the real current of life that the others shared. She loved her son, she loved Judith, she loved Jane, but even they, even Benjamin, were shades compared with John. When he was killed she received a blow that was mortal, and Judith, seeing her, knew that the Herries battle was not yet over, and that the consequences of old long-ago histories had still their own history to make.

But because of her own story she understood Elizabeth as did none of the others. Her own Georges had suffered sudden death, as had John, and for ten years after it she, too, had been herself a dead woman. She had had the fears for Adam that Elizabeth now had for Benjamin, but she had been spared because fate had chosen John for its mark instead of Adam. All the more reason that she should help Elizabeth now.

Elizabeth, sitting close beside her, began at once.

'Aunt Judith, we have had Benjamin's report, and it is dreadful.'

'What does it say, my dear?'

'It says that we must take him away if he does not improve. They acknowledge that he is clever but he will not work, he obeys nobody. He is always fighting.'

'Well, my dear, he is a healthy boy and has to let himself go, I suppose.'

Elizabeth shook her head.

'Yes, but he will obey nobody and he does not care. When I

speak to him he only smiles. He is not cruel nor selfish. In fact, as you know, there never was a more generous boy. It is not that he is absent-minded. He throws himself altogether into anything that he is doing. But there is something *wild* in him. He says he wants to be a gipsy!'

'A gipsy!'

'Yes. He wants to go away in a caravan and eat roasted hedge-hogs. Then ... there is another thing ...' She hesitated. 'Two afternoons ago I saw him kissing Hannah; in the passage under the backstairs. Of course it was nothing. He is only a child – he is not yet fourteen and he is tremendously honest. He conceals nothing. He says that he bet her a shilling that he would kiss her ... I am in despair. He is so merry, always laughing and doing things for others – but he will listen to nobody!'

'He kissed Hannah, did he?' said Judith, thinking how different he was from his father John. And from her own Adam too.

'Yes,' went on Elizabeth. 'I am sure, too, that it is my fault. Aunt Judith, I have been wrong not to *force* my way into Ireby. But I hated it so that time I went ...'

(Two years before Elizabeth had gone to the Fortress, had asked for her father, had suffered a fearful scene with Mrs Pan-gloss who had refused her entry.)

'You know that I have written again and again and he has never answered. But if I had gone and refused to be beaten by that horrible woman and stayed with father whatever she did, I feel that Benjamin would respect me more. He never speaks either of his father or of his grandfather. I don't know even now whether he knows ... whether he knows ...'

She broke down, hid her head in her hands, then suddenly knelt at Judith's feet, burying her head in Judith's lap. The old lady gently stroked her hair. Even on her very alert days she had moments of slipping off into a dream. Now with her hand on Elizabeth's hair she saw the room filled with sparkling snow: whorls of dancing crystal filled the air, which was shot with splinters of golden sun. The windows had faded and a great sea of virgin snow, upon whose breast waves of iridescence quietly formed, broke and formed again, spread from the hills' horizon there to her very feet. She was herself as light as a snowflake, and it seemed to her that she had to exert especial power not to float away on the current of that white loveliness and never be seen again ... Was this Death – and if it was so, why did men fear it? So sweet, so friendly, so just ...

'. . . You see, Aunt Judith,' Elizabeth's voice came like a soft key closing a door, and the room swam back, the bed with the hangings, the ugly chair that Dorothy had given her (oh, why had she forgotten to thank her just now?), the sparkling buckles on her own shoes. 'I seem to have no will-power any longer. I do things with everyone else, but my real self is not here. It is away with John. It is as though he were always whispering to me things that I ought to do – be more firm with Benjie, live with father and make him more comfortable. I had will-power once, but John's death did something to me. Grief doesn't break your heart as the novels say, but it takes your character away. I don't *grieve* for John. I am sure that he is happier now than he ever was here. But I am not alive. When you lost your husband did you feel at all the same?'

'Yes, dear, I did. Just as you describe. For nearly ten years I lived with the Rockages in Wiltshire and I had no real life at all; but it comes back in the end. Nothing can kill you. Nothing.'

Elizabeth rose from her knees and stood before the fire, her long slim body irradiated by the leaping light, her soft grey dress like a cloud against the sparkling logs.

'Aunt Judith,' she said. 'Do you believe in God?'

'I don't know.'

'You are not certain?'

'My dear, I have been a pagan all my life long. I know now that everyone is very religious, and if you don't go to church on Sunday it's very wrong, but in my young days it wasn't so. Going to church is just a fashion, I think. At one time it's the thing and at another it's not. My husband thought it foolish to believe in anything you couldn't see, but a great friend of mine, Reuben Sunwood, was as sure of God as I am of this room. For myself, now I am so very old, there *seems* to be another world – but that may be my old age and my body failing. On some days, you know, my hearing is bad and I cannot see very well. Then I seem to be in another world. But I don't know. When one loves someone very much one seems to go beyond bodily things. When one's in a bad temper or loses one's spectacles or the servants are tiresome it's different.' She rapped her fingers impatiently on her spectacle-case.

'Dear Elizabeth, you must pull yourself together a little more. It is quite right what you say. Benjamin needs more discipline. Send him to me, my dear. This morning. In the afternoon I'm often sleepy.'

Elizabeth bent down and kissed the dry, withered cheek. How

very old Aunt Judith was! It was wrong to trouble her, but then she liked to be troubled.

'If I can find him I'll send him to you now.'

When she was alone in the room again she gave a little sigh of satisfaction. She liked to be alone, and she liked also to be in the centre of things. She was happy this morning because neither her heart nor her stomach troubled her, because it was a beautiful day and because, old though she was, they still wished to consult her. The world was whirring around her! Veronica would marry Captain Forster, Benjamin was naughty, Adam would soon be here . . . She arranged her spectacles on her nose, picked up from the table at her side a number of the *Spectator* and read its opinion of Mr Longfellow's *Hiawatha*, an old poem now but still criticized with reverence: '*Mr Longfellow's* Hiawatha *is one of the really permanent contributions to modern literature, and no other genius known to us would have been in any way equal to the work. It is not the grasp of imagination, so much as the grace and sweep of a peculiarly majestic* fancy *– a fancy like the impulsive fancy of children . . . How bright and playful is the picture of the lower animals with the little Indian prophet . . . But it is not only in the details, it is in the whole spirit of the poem – the fanciful joy and beauty, the equally fanciful weirdness and gloom – that we enjoy the touch of a master hand.*'

Well, that was very nice for Mr Longfellow. But she was not sure. The writer used the word 'fanciful' a great many times. That was perhaps a warning. In any case she could not read for very long in these days – Jane read to her every afternoon – a lengthy poem, read aloud . . . No, she thought she would not bother with *Hiawatha*.

There was a knock on the door, and Benjamin came in. He was shooting up; he was no longer the small chubby child. He would not be a handsome man, although he had fine clear eyes, a splendid colour, and a strong stocky body. As usual he seemed to be enjoying a joke of some kind. She could see that he knew that he had come to be scolded and was endeavouring to be grave.

'Is that you, Benjie? Come over here where I can see you.'

He came and stood beside the chair in the attitude of straitened attention that children must observe before their elders. His cheeks were flushed with the cold and his hair was in disorder. He tried to arrange it with his hand. He looked her in the face, giving her all his mind, not as Adam had so often done when he was small, thinking of something else.

'Now, Benjie, I have sent for you because they tell me that your report has come from Rugby and it is shocking. They say that you will be sent away if you do not behave better. Your mother is very unhappy. What have you to say?'

What had he to say? How very, *very* old Aunt Judith was! And so small and so tidy. There came from her a pleasant scent of exquisite cleanliness and the smell of some flower, a carnation perhaps. But what must it be like to be as old as that? Why, her father had been born at the very beginning of the eighteenth century! There wasn't a boy at Rugby who had a relation as old as this! Something to be proud of. He pulled himself together and tried to attend. He always attended to the thing in hand, and the thing in hand at the moment was that Aunt Judith was going to scold him about his report. He didn't mind. He liked her. He liked everybody.

'I am very sorry, Aunt Judith.'

She kicked one shoe impatiently.

'Yes, but that is not enough. You must do something about it. You are a big boy now and threaten to be a disgrace to us all.'

She looked at him and her heart melted within her. She worshipped small boys, and although Benjie was very different from her own Adam, he had Adam's independence. She adored independence.

'Why are you so naughty?'

'There are so many rules and they teach you such silly things.'

It was the tradition in England that all children obeyed absolutely their parents, did nothing that their parents didn't wish them to do, were preparing, one and all, to be the heroes and heroines of the future. But Benjie seemed unaware of the tradition.

'You know you belong to a very fine family,' she began, 'and, when you grow up, everyone will expect you to make your family proud of you.'

'I know. They are always talking about the family, but I don't see why I should think about the family. I'm myself, aren't I?'

'Yes, but—'

'When you were a little girl you ran away. Your father was always against the family. My grandfather shot himself in London and my father was killed, when he couldn't defend himself, by my uncle. I'm not like the rest of the family. I'm different and I'll always be different. Mother and Aunt Veronica and Aunt

Amabel and Ellis and Cousin Amery – *they* are the family. But I'm different. I'm by myself.'

Her heart began to beat furiously. Her eyes dimmed. She could have caught the boy to her and kissed him. And with that odd exaltation (so bad for her heart) was fear also. Would this battle *never* be ended? She seemed for an instant to behold her father, whom she had never seen, standing, erect, triumphant, against the snow . . .

She beat down her emotion and in a voice that trembled a little said: 'Yes, but, Benjie, you must understand that being different is *not* amusing – not amusing at all. It seems to you, I daresay, very splendid to stand up now and say "I'm different", but I'm a very old woman and have had great experience and I can tell you that the world does not like people to be different, and especially our family does not. You can't know yet how powerful the world is and how *right* the world is too, because if everyone was independent and refused to suit themselves to the world's rules, nothing would ever be done. My father learnt that, I have learnt it, your grandfather learnt it. You *have* to do as you are told unless you want to fight all your life long.'

'I do like to fight,' he broke in eagerly. 'You see, Aunt Judith, I think it's stupid to do things just because other people do them.'

'Yes, but do you never think of others? You must see how selfish it is always to have your own way. You can see how unhappy you make your mother—'

'But I don't *want* to make her unhappy. I don't want to make anyone sorry for what I do. They needn't be, only half the time they are glad they are sorry.'

She had nothing to say. She was on his side, so terribly on his side, and yet it would never do if he were disgraced at Rugby . . .

'Well, then,' she said as though some silent comprehending confidence had passed between them. 'You must promise me to do your best for the sake of those who love you – for your mother's sake and mine. Will you promise?'

He smiled, staring straight into her eyes. She really was a *dear* old lady and he was proud of her because she had lived to so great an age. He nodded.

'All right, Aunt Judith. I'll try.'

'And you won't fight?'

'Well, I don't know . . . I can't promise if another boy goes for me—'

'You won't be the first in any case?'

'It's so hard often to tell who *is* the first. You see—' But this was too technical.

'Kiss me then. And I shall expect a good report next term.'

He kissed her. How dry her cheek was! Towards the door he turned.

'There's one thing,' he said. 'Why do I never see my grandfather?'

'Your grandfather?'

'Yes. Up at the Fortress.'

'He is very ill and sees nobody. He was very unkind to your mother once, you know.'

'Yes, but that was years ago. You can't go on remembering things for ever, can you? I shall go one day and see him.'

Then he came back to her chair and, grinning, said: 'Aunt Judith, would you like to see my ferret?'

'A ferret? Oh, I don't like ferrets.'

'You would this one. It's grand. James gave it me.'

'Very well. You can bring it one day.'

He nodded and went humming out.

The talk had affected her deeply. She took off her spectacles, wiped her eyes, put them on again. Her heart was beating oddly. It was not good for her to be agitated, but what was she to do when all the old questions, so long answered and dismissed, came surging up again?

When Jane brought her her dinner she found her greatly excited. She had her favourite dinner – fried sole, apple-pudding – but now she did not care. The talk with Benjamin had, although it was so short, exhausted her: old terrors and alarms would surround her and hem her in, did she allow them.

'I don't think I'll come down this afternoon after all, Jane dear. I'm a trifle tired.'

'You have seen too many people, that's what it is,' Jane said firmly. She had the air a little, as she arranged the silver dish containing the apple-pudding in front of Judith, of a witch or a fairy, someone from another and slightly inhuman world. She was growing into that especial product of the British Isles, the queer old maid, someone enterprising, eccentric, kindly, and very much alone. Jane would be eccentric, she would suddenly snap her fingers, dress quaintly (she was wearing now a funny old black velvet jacket), roll her bread at a mealtime into little pellets, talk to herself, but she had a heart as rich and warm as any fairy godmother. She loved Judith with a passion that was almost unholy. Although she was religious, virtuous and indeed prudish, she would have committed any crime for Judith, married anyone, killed anyone, stolen from anyone. So now she realized that Judith was weary and had added in a moment, as old people do, twenty years to her age. An hour ago she had been seventy, now she was ninety, soon, if one were not careful, she would be a hundred and ten.

'Yes, I don't think I'll go down . . . Jane, what do *you* think of Benjamin?'

'He is a fine boy. I love him!'

'Yes, yes, of course!' She knocked her silver spoon against the plate. 'We all love him, but I am afraid that he is a very naughty boy.'

'Oh, he has fights, but so do all proper boys.'

'Jane, why don't you marry someone?'

Jane blushed. She said almost in a whisper: 'I don't like men – not in that way.'

'Dear, dear!' said Judith. (She was beginning to recover.) 'It was a very nice way. Everyone is so prudish now that they are ashamed to talk of going to bed with a man. It's perfectly natural. Nothing to be ashamed of. But although they won't speak of it they think of nothing else. It's all the same whoever it is – Mrs Osmaston, Helen Withering, Mrs James Anstruther. How shall we marry our daughters? We must put our girls to bed with a man the first possible opportunity, do everything we can, dress them so as to accentuate their figures, throw them at every man we see, everything to marry them – but speak of what happens when they *are* married – oh, dear me, no!'

Jane disliked it when Judith talked like this. She did wish that she wouldn't.

'Now, there's Dorothy! In *such* a flutter this morning because Veronica is going to marry. She'd marry Amabel to *anybody* if only somebody would have her, but a pestle and mortar is the only thing Amabel will ever marry. Yes – well, that pudding was very good. I think I'll have my nap now so as to be ready for Adam.'

When Adam came she was quite ready for him. Her nap had refreshed her. The afternoon sun shone into the room like the reflection from a pale cloud of gold. The eaves were dropping with the heat of the sun and, when her spectacles were on, she could see blue shadows on Skiddaw. There was a strange mountain lightness over everything, and the logs in the fireplace were crimson with heat, and crackled like mad. As soon as Adam came in, sat beside her, took her hand, they were enclosed as though there were no one else in the world.

She wanted to talk about the Trades Unions. She had had a letter from Horace Newmark, who was in business in Manchester. 'He is as proud of all the chimneys as though they were bluebells,' she said. 'He says Manchester is nothing but smoke and dirt and it's grand. It's making England what it is, the mistress of the world. Stuff! Who wants to be mistress of the world? So like a Herries!'

Two years before, a man called Broadhead in Sheffield had, it was proved, paid for men who had rebelled against his Union to be murdered, and had paid out of the funds of the Union of which he was secretary. The tyranny of 'rattening' whereby noxious workers' tools were destroyed, women were blinded, men were shot at, was prevalent, and in Manchester, among the brickmakers, the clay which offending brick-makers were to use was sometimes stuffed with thousands of needles in order to maim the hands of those who worked on it. But the investigations into these crimes had proved, too, that many of the conditions of work were iniquitous and had remained unaltered since the days of Elizabeth.

Judith was greatly interested. 'What do you think, Adam? What about these Trades Unions?'

'I think they are necessary. The more England becomes an industrial country – and she *is* now the first industrial country in the world – the greater the power of the working-man. He will rule England one day, mark my words, and I hope he'll be wise enough to know what to do with the power when he has it. That was the trouble with the Chartists. They weren't wise enough nor clever enough. But in fifty years' time there'll be few big families left. Everything will be shared – and quite right too.'

'I don't know,' Judith said. 'England was very nice once when there were no railways and no chimneys. Isn't it strange? I've been in a sedan-chair and saw a boy hung in the streets of London. Yes, and bears were baited, and I've danced at Vauxhall. I feel sleepy. It's the fire. Where is Vanessa?'

'Vanessa is downstairs with Benjamin.'

'And how is Cat Bells?'

'Cat Bells is covered with snow.'

'And how is dear Margaret?'

'Margaret sent her love and is coming soon to see you. She is baking today and Will is helping her.'

'It all sounds very pleasant. And how are you yourself?'

'I am very well.'

'And the book?'

'Nearly finished.'

'It's not a fairy story this time.'

'No, it's about two boys at the North Pole.'

'What do you know about the North Pole? You've never been there.'

'No. That's why I know so much about it.'

'But how can you write about what you've never seen?'

'There are two sorts of writers, Mother, just as there are two sorts of Herries. One sort believes in facts, the other sort believes in things behind the facts.'

'The books I like best,' she answered, 'are those that have both sorts in them.'

'For instance?'

'Jane is reading me a very amusing story called *Under Two Flags*. It's silly, of course – not like real life at all – but most enjoyable. And then there's *Alice in Wonderland*. And then there's Mr Huxley's *Man's Place in Nature*.'

Adam laughed. 'Mother, what a ridiculous mixture!'

'They all come to the same thing in the end.'

'What thing?'

'The world is made up both of fancy and reality, I suppose. Oh dear, I don't know ... Adam, now that I cannot move from this house I can see how *nice* England is.'

He smiled.

'Yes. I know you say "Foolish old woman at her age to love anything with a passion." But I am not senile. The moment I'm senile, Adam, you shall drop a pill into my chicken-broth and finish me off. No, I am very wide awake, and I can see that all my life I've loved England. Why do you not write a book about England?'

'How would *you* do it, Mother?'

'Oh, I would put in everything – men sowing the fields, the horses ploughing, old ladies selling sweets in the village shop, Mr Disraeli with his oily hair and Mr Gladstone with his collar, Horace's Manchester chimneys, all the Herries thinking *they've* made England, my father riding up Borrowdale, the snow on Skiddaw, the apple-pudding I had at dinner, sheep on a hill, the man lighting the lamps in Hill Street – and you, Adam, running by Charlie's horse in Watendlath, at Chartist meetings in London, writing stories at Cat Bells . . .' She broke off, her finger to her lip. 'That gives me an idea – I have an idea!'

'What idea?'

'No matter. I shall tell you when it has got further on. Dear me, I've talked such a deal today. One day I talk; another day not a word. Sometimes I sleep all day. I'm ninety-five, you know.'

'Yes, I know. You're always telling me.'

She took his arm and, quickly, shyly caught his hand and kissed it.

'My whole life has been you and Georges.'

'You said it was England.'

'You *are* both England to me. We are sunk in the country, you and I, up to our necks. That's why I am so strong. Do you know, Adam, I have never had a day's illness in my life? Even when I was bearing you I was only ill for an hour or two – ugh! – that was horrid. There was an elephant . . .'

He drew his chair closer, bent over her and put his arm round her.

'Are you sure you are not tired?'

'No, indeed . . . I was a little but I had a nap. I can go to sleep whenever I wish. Oh yes, I remember! Benjamin! Adam, what do you think of Benjamin?'

'A grand boy – brave, generous. He will do fine things.'

'I am not so sure. He has had a dreadful report from Rugby.'

'All the best boys have.'

'Yes, but he was in here this morning and I scolded him, and he said that he didn't care because he was different from other boys, different because of his father and his grandfather.'

Adam nodded. 'Yes, he told me that once too. But that's all right. It's only that he feels wild sometimes. Why, I feel wild myself at times, Mother. A year or two ago I went mad and ran up Cat Bells – thought I would never come back.'

She smiled. 'I am delighted that you are wild still sometimes. I thought you were so contented that you'd never be wild again. If I had the strength I'd climb out of the window now just as I did when I was a child. Is Vanessa wild?' she asked.

He sighed. 'Vanessa is an angel. But I am sometimes troubled. She is so generous, so trusting, and believes in everyone.'

'Well, there is no harm in that as a beginning.'

'No, but she must suffer ... Oh well, we all suffer. She adores Benjie. He is her God at present.'

'Can I see her?'

'Yes. I will go and fetch her.'

He went quickly from the room. She thought – Benjamin, Vanessa, the new generation, and I shall be gone ... soon I shall be gone. How strange and how familiar that thought that this room, her old companion, would continue with Skiddaw beyond the window, the snow falling, and she not here to see it, to move the chairs, dust the china, put a log on the fire ... She looked at the table where was the parcel of the miniature teaset. She'll like that, she thought. She had always adored giving presents. Adam came in, bringing Vanessa with him. Vanessa was ten and tall for her age. She was wearing a dress of red taffeta, and her little skirt stood out stiffly. She had beautiful legs and arms, and her head with its black hair was carried with a wonderful dignity for so young a child. She came and made a curtsy, then she kissed the old lady, then waited patiently, smiling.

'I have a present for you, my dear.'

Vanessa's whole body was transformed with joy. You could see that her heart was beating with excitement; she compressed her lips so that she should not burst out into indecorous cries.

'Yes ... Bring me that parcel, darling.'

She brought it very carefully. It was unwrapped. She knelt down on the floor so that she could see the wonder. She picked up each tiny piece, the teapot, the cups, the saucers, and held them, one by one, against the light.

'Oh!' she said slowly. 'It is the loveliest ... Oh, Aunt Judith! ... I never thought ... I never expected ...' Then she reached out for her father's hand. He pulled her to her feet. Even now, with all her joy, she controlled herself. She remembered how old Aunt Judith was, she kissed her tenderly and with great care. Then she stared at the precious things as though she would never take her eyes away.

'Do you like them?'

'*Like* them!' She curtsied again, then turned to the window as though her feelings were so great that she must hide them. Once again the three of them had the sense that they were enclosed, away from all the world, rapt into a private communion of happiness.

'I must show them to Benjie,' she said.

Judith nodded. 'Yes, show them to Benjie. And come again and say goodnight before you go.'

'I will be off too,' Adam added. 'I will help her to carry the tea-things.'

'Yes,' said his mother, her sharp eyes staring with some secret excitement. 'And send Jane to me if you can find her. My idea! My idea! I must go on with my idea!'

She tapped impatiently on the silk of her dress.

'Tell Jane I want her at once. *At once* – whatever she may be at!'

Jane arrived, quite breathless. She had been washing Dorothy's bitch Maria, an old and sulky spaniel who was washed every Thursday, come what might: and today was Thursday, Dorothy was in Keswick, and there was no one else . . .

'I've left Hannah to finish her!'

'Now sit down and get your breath.'

'What is it, Aunt Judith? Adam says you have an idea.'

'Yes, I have . . . Look in that wardrobe near the window, and among those bundles of letters you will find a manuscript book in a dark-green leather cover. Yes – that fat one . . . Now you have it? There's not a word in it, is there? No, I thought not. Francis gave it to me years ago on a birthday. He thought the dark-green leather handsome. Now bring the little writing bureau closer. That's it. Near the fire so that you will be warm and will hear what I say. Excellent. Have you a pen that suits you? Now listen, my dear. I was talking to Adam about England. You know old ladies talk and talk until they are quite exhausted. I have often noticed it – the older you are the more you talk. Dear Penny-feather at Keswick was like that. Her last years you could *not* stop her . . . a constant flow. Well, now I intend to talk to some purpose. Adam and I said we love England and so we do. Then I had an idea. You know I never saw either my father or my mother, but my half-brother David – he was old enough to be my father, you know – would often, before he died, poor man, tell me stories of them. He liked to take me for a walk, or we would ride to Bassenthwaite or Caldbeck or to the Dash, and all the way there and back he would tell me about the old days and my father.

'Now I think that I should write it down – or rather that *you* should, Jane dear. I may die at any moment. Oh yes, I may – of course I may – and what a pity! All this lost for ever. No one knows it but I. And that was a very odd life my father lived in Borrowdale. David told me that he remembered exactly the night they first arrived in Keswick. No, but wait. You shall write it down. Do not you think it a good idea, Jane?'

The old lady was so eager and excited that it would have been cruelty to prevent her. But Jane did not wish to prevent her. She was herself greatly interested in that world and in that very strange man, her great-great-grandfather. How very curious that the *father* of Aunt Judith sitting there so comfortably before the fire should be her own great-great-grandfather! It was like stepping on to a magic carpet and swinging back into another fairyworld. So she took her pen and began to write in the dark-green leather book.

'Now tell me, dear, if I go too fast. Well, you'd better begin in this way. "I, Judith Paris, was born at Rosthwaite in the valley of Borrowdale, Cumberland, on November 28th, in the Year of Our Lord 1774 ..." There! Have you got that? That's a good solid beginning, I think, rather like Macaulay's *History*. Now to continue. "I never knew my dear father and mother because they both died on the day I was born, and had I not been found and rescued from the cold by Squire Gauntry of Stone Ends, who happened to be riding past that day and heard me crying, I should undoubtedly have perished."

'Have you got that, Jane?' She peered over her spectacles on the very edge of her nose. 'Let me see, my dear. Yes, you write very nicely. Am I going too fast for you?'

'Not at all, Aunt Judith. How very interesting this will be!'

'I hope so. I certainly think it may. Well, to continue. "It is not, however, my own history about which I write, but rather about some of the early days that my father spent in the valley of Borrowdale. My father himself lived to a good age, and I myself am now a very old woman, so that I am a link with the long-ago past. I have heard very much of what happened in those longago times from my half-brother David Herries. David Herries was my father's son by his first wife, and he was fifty-five when I was born, so that I could have been his granddaughter. He was very famous as a young man as a boxer and wrestler and runner. He had great strength as a younger man, but when I knew him he had grown stout and was living very happily with his family at Uldale, where I also was living. He would take me for walks and rides, and it was then that he would tell me these stories.

' "He told me that he remembered exactly the night that he first arrived in Keswick. He could remember every detail, and so do I, even at this distance of time. How he was in the inn at Keswick in a big canopied bed with his sisters Mary and Deborah. The canopy that ran round the top of the bed was a faded green and had a gold thread in it. There were fire-dogs by the fire with mouths like grinning dragons. And he remembered that a woman was sitting warming herself in front of the fire, a woman he hated. Then his father came in and thought he was sleeping. He remembered that his father was wearing a beautiful coat of a claret colour and a chestnut wig, and there were red roses on his grey silk waistcoat. He remembered, too, that his father said something to the woman by the fire that made her very angry, and she began to talk in a loud, heated voice." '

Jane went on, and in that clear little voice like a bell Judith refashioned this old world to her, describing the inn and the servants running hither and thither with candles, some relations who had a meal with them, and how David's uncle wanted to make him drink wine and he would not. Then the dark mysterious night-ride to Borrowdale, and how he sat on the horse in front of his father and how proud he was, and his father asked him whether he were frightened, and he answered bravely that he was never frightened where his father was. How then they came to a house on a little hill and David ran forward and was in the house first, and there were two shining suits of armour in the hallway.

'There,' said Judith suddenly. 'I am tired. That will be enough for today. I think you shall help me to bed.'

'Oh, Aunt Judith,' said Jane. 'That *is* interesting!'

But Aunt Judith was weary. She had suddenly collapsed, her head nodded, she yawned and yawned and was almost helpless in Jane's hands as she undressed her. It was dark now beyond the window; a faint powdery blue framed the silent masses of snow; some stars, lonely in that cold sky, were like sparks blown up from a fire. Jane drew the cherry-coloured curtains. She saw that Judith was propped up with pillows and two candles lit by her side (how tiny and soft her body had been – like a child's), then she left the room to return with some tea, a small sponge-cake and some raspberry jam in a blue glass saucer. Then, most unfortunately, Aunt Judith lost her temper. It had been a tiring day, there had been something too exciting about that dropping back into the past – the past that was not only the past, but the present and future as well.

So she lost her temper over the sponge cake. It was a plum cake that she had wanted. Dorothy only yesterday had promised her a plum cake.

'But, Aunt Judith, it is not good for you. Doctor Bettany said that plum cake was too rich—'

'Doctor Bettany never said anything of the kind.'

'But indeed he did!'

'So I am a liar! Thank you, dear Jane. I am glad I know.'

'No, of course not. But you know that last time you were upset—'

'I was not upset!' She was trembling, her eyes were filled with hot tears of anger. She was in a rage, so that for tuppence she would have taken the teatray and thrown it and its contents all over the room. How dare Jane say that she was a liar! And she hated this soft soppy sponge cake! They thought they could do what they liked with her! She was so good to them all, and yet they tried to starve her! After listening all day to their troubles they could so ill-treat her!

She took the sponge cake and with a shaking hand threw it into the middle of the floor.

At the same moment Adam and Vanessa came in to say good-bye, and with them were Dorothy and Veronica back from their party. But Judith did not care. She was not ashamed. They should see whether they could bully her.

'You promised me plum cake!' she cried to Dorothy.

'Oh, I am so sorry! . . . Aunt Judith, Veronica is engaged to be married! Captain Forster—'

'I don't care! You think you can do what you like with me, all of you, just because I am an old woman—'

But the sight of Veronica's beautiful happy face was too much for her.

'Oh, well . . . Come here, my dear, and give me a kiss! There! That's right! Don't spill the tea-things! What did he say to you? Did he go down on his knees? Were you very gracious? . . .'

A long while after as it seemed to her, the room dark save for the flicker from the fire, she lay there, very happy, on the edge of sleep. It had been a wonderful day. She had never left that room, but all the world had come into it. The elderly Dorothy, Adam, Elizabeth, with all their personal histories hot about them, and the young, Veronica engaged to be married, dear Jane so sweet and good, and the children, Vanessa and Benjamin. All the generations! They had come to her for advice and help and to tell her what they were doing. They had wanted to know what she thought. They could not get on without her.

She herself had welcomed the sun, eaten delightful food, read a little, given a present, discussed serious matters like God and the Trades Unions with Adam and Elizabeth, sunk back into the

past, thought of Georges and Warren and Adam as a baby, and
then gone behind that again to her own childhood and dear
David, and then back beyond that to a hundred and forty years
ago when her father had been a young man and worn a claret-
coloured coat – all this without leaving her room, all within a
day. And she was ninety-five. All the Herries all over England
were waiting to see her grow to a hundred.

Well, she would. Nothing was going to stop her! How could
she possibly disappoint such a great number of kind relations?

So, in that happy thought, she slipped away and once again
was rocking on that billowing cloud of softest down. She rose
and then sank again, sank and rose . . . Georges was sleeping near
to her. He was snoring with that snore so familiar to her that it
was also hers. All about them the world was of a dazzling white,
shining with a million crystals.

She rose and then sank again, sank and rose . . .

AT VICTORINE'S

In London, a boy aged fifteen stood on an October afternoon
pressing his nose to the window of a house in Hill Street. This
boy was young Benjamin Herries.

This was the day, the evening, the night of his life, for on this
day, October 14th, 1870, he was to become a man.

It had all happened in the most surprising manner, and the
cause of it had been the death, one evening while he was drinking
his tea, of old Stephen Newmark. Everyone had been expecting
him to die for years, but with that priggish obstinacy characteristic of him he had refused to go, degenerating into a tiresome
silent old gentleman with a female nurse of whom, in the opinion
of the family, he was much too fond.

Poor Phyllis had predeceased him by some years; as he was not
a Herries no one had very much interest in his attaining a great
age. He died in the act of pronouncing one of his almost hourly
anathemas on Mr Disraeli.

Most unexpectedly it was decided that young Benjamin must
be present at his funeral. It seemed that Stephen had a great
regard for Elizabeth and had declared that 'he would do something for her boy one day'. So Benjamin had been sent for from
Rugby (where he still survived, much to his own astonishment);

Lady Herries had invited him to stay in Hill Street for the funeral, and here he was.

The funeral, two days before, had been great fun. Everything was great fun for Benjamin, and he could not be expected to feel much grief for Stephen Newmark, whom he had rarely seen. Moreover, he noticed that Stephen's children were not greatly downcast, and his own close friend Barney made no pretence of sorrow.

'The Governor never liked me,' he confided to Benjamin on the way to the funeral. 'He disapproved of me altogether and never even looked at my novels. I don't blame him for that, but I'm not going to be a crocodile about it. I leave that to sister Emily.'

Lady Herries, who was now a rather ancient and (in Benjamin's opinion) a very silly lady, did the honours with much satisfaction, and Ellis Herries, already a man of importance in the world of affairs, was dignified and solemn. Benjamin had got considerable pleasure out of his days in town. He had never really stayed in London before.

He had had a number of projects. Why should he return to Rugby? He thought of being a stowaway in some vessel chartered for the West Indies or (his old cherished dream) joining some gipsies somewhere. He took a liking to an Italian organ-grinder, with whom he talked in Berkeley Square, and fancied that he might buy a barrel-organ. But his principal notion was that, if he could get money enough, he would escape to France and, in some way, slip into Paris and enjoy a bit of the Siege. He had followed, with eager excitement, the Franco-Prussian War from its commencement. He had cut out from the illustrated papers pictures of the Emperor, Bismarck, MacMahon, Palikao, Bazaine, Frossard, the young Prince Imperial, and many of the Empress. He was in love with the Empress; he would be delighted to die for her. He wanted nothing but to run on some mission for her, be shot in the discharge of it and fall dying at her feet. He could not understand why his companions at Rugby were on the whole so indifferent.

Then, with the catastrophe at Sedan, his whole soul was on fire. He learnt every detail of the battle by heart. He knew the exact positions of Bazeilles and Balan, of the Donchery bridge, where were the Villa Beurmann, Illy, and the fatal spot where the Prussian Guards crossed the Givonne. He was sure that, had he been in command, he would not have fallen into so complete a

trap, and the moment when the Emperor, old and sick, cried out
'The firing must be stopped at all costs!' was, for him, a real
agonizing piece of personal experience.

He hated and detested the Prussians; he adored the French,
and Barney, listening to him, was amazed that so young and jolly
a boy could feel so intensely. When he read how the Empress,
escaping from Paris, hailed a cab and was recognized by a street
urchin, he drew a deep breath as though he himself had only just
missed a great peril.

And now that Paris was invested it was for him as though he
himself shared the siege. When he heard how, on October 7th,
Gambetta escaped from Paris in a balloon he shouted 'Hurray!'
and gave all his pocket-money towards a dormitory feast in its
celebration. However, here he was now in London, and his own
immediate affairs demanded a lot of attention. Tomorrow he was
to return to Rugby, and he had a sad feeling that he *would* return
instead of making use of this magnificent opportunity of adventure. Indeed, had it not been for his mother and Aunt Judith, he
would have certainly tried the stowaway adventure. But they
would grieve, although why they should he could not understand. But women were queer and these two women he did not
wish to hurt. Moreover, Aunt Judith was so *very* old. He had
better wait until she was gone.

Then, this very morning, after breakfast, Barney had arrived
at Hill Street and, pulling Benjamin aside, had whispered to him
that he intended that evening to take Ellis and himself out to
dinner. 'Not a word to a soul,' he confided. 'Emily and the others
would make a terrible row if they knew. But we must do something. These last days have been too gloomy for anything.'

So Benjamin stood at the window, all ready dressed, waiting
for Barney to arrive.

It was the bewitching hour when the lamp-lighter has gone his
way and the lamps star the streets like nectarines. A faint wisp of
fog – having in it to Benjie's excited nostrils a slight sniff of
gunpowder (he was thinking possibly of Paris); from beyond the
window came magical sounds of London, the clop-clop of a
horse, the rattle of wheels, feet mysteriously echoing, the distant
plaintive murmur of a barrel-organ. On the top of area steps
belonging to the house opposite a housemaid was entertaining,
for a moment, a policeman. A brougham was waiting a few doors
away and down the steps came a stout, pompous, old gentleman,
pilloried in starch, a red shaven face and a white waistcoat and

white gloves that seemed to Benjie too big for him. The fog increased a little, the lamps spread into a hazy iridescence, some old man in a large and battered high hat came slowly down, ringing a bell and calling out something in a melancholy voice, a carriage rolled by with two footmen in cocked hats standing up at the back of it – and always that soft rumble of sound as of a fat, comfortable nurse singing lullaby to her children.

His excitement was intense; it was all that he could do not to jump about the room, turn his favourite somersault. But Lady Herries or Emily Newmark might come in at any moment. He thought them safe and secure in the great cold draughty drawing room upstairs. But you never could be sure. Grown-up people were always creeping about and opening doors unexpectedly, like that old beast 'Turker' Evans, head of his House at Rugby. His thoughts were oddly jumbled. It was a pity that Ellis was coming; it would be very much pleasanter without him. Not that he disliked Ellis, or he would not did he not patronize him. Of course Ellis was *years* older, a grown-up man who did business every day in the City. And he was very kind. He had given Benjie ten shillings only yesterday, but, for some dim obscure reason, Benjie would rather not have taken it. Ellis did not really like him – not *really*, as Barney and Adam Paris and Thornton Minor and James at Uldale liked him. And then again, looking out at the lamps and the misty street, suppose there was no God as Barney said. Barney had sprung this astonishing piece of news upon him at the funeral.

'Of course there's no God,' he had said, as though he were sure of it.

'Well, what is there then?' Benjamin asked.

'Nothing at all,' Barney had answered gaily. 'We're nothing but monkeys, old boy. You are old enough now to read Darwin. He'll tell you.'

What an astonishing idea! Then all this going to church and saying your prayers, that had been going on for hundreds of years, meant nothing at all. There was no gigantic old man with a white beard sitting on a cloud and listening! His mother and Aunt Jane and the others were all taken in! A stupendous thought! But he had only Barney's word for it, and you could never be sure whether Barney meant what he said!

Oh! there was the organ-grinder coming round the corner! He could just see him in the dim light, and there, joy of joys, from the opposite side was the muffin-man approaching! There *must* be a God, or why should there be muffin-men and organ-grinders? Would the organ-grinder have a monkey? The door opened and Lady Herries entered. She was a little, faded, old woman now, and Benjamin was certain that she painted her cheeks. He thought she looked ridiculous, her dress bunched up behind and her rather scanty hair dressed in a cascade of curls at the back of her head. She was, of course, in the deepest black and she walked with small mincing steps.

'Why, Benjamin! Dear me! Why has William not lit the gas! All alone! Emily was asking for you! Come and tell me what you have been doing. Ellis tells me that you and he are going to have dinner at some quiet place with Barnabas.'

'Yes,' said Benjamin. 'Won't it be fun?'

'I don't think this is quite the time to talk of fun, Benjamin dear. It has all been very distressing. However, you are too young yet to realize what death means.'

The front door banged. That must be Barney. They went into the hall, and there, praise be, Barney was, looking very smart in his evening dress and high black hat. He was growing stout, and looked like a very amiable clown, Benjie always thought. Chalk his face white and give him a red nose and he would be a perfect clown!

They all went upstairs to the drawing room, which was as cold as a mausoleum. They stood in a group beside the sulky peevish fire and talked in low grave voices.

Emily Newmark, a heavy stout woman in tremendous black, joined them. It is a temptation for every generation to deride any world that was fifty years its predecessor: Judith, Veronica, Elizabeth, Jane – these were, in their own kind and character, women to be proud of. They were generous, humorous, courageous and idealistic without priggishness. No period that was their background could conceivably be a period to be mocked. But Emily Newmark was frankly a pity, and was one, among others, responsible for providing our satirists with a living. She believed that Politics and the Services were the only polite careers, and the Land and the Funds the only springs of wealth that could be called decent. She was a snob and a toady. If a gentleman smoked in front of a lady he was insulting that lady's morals. She was always ready to be insulted. She looked absurd in her gathered flounces, draped skirts, and hair-plaits at the back of her head, but thought she was magnificent. She approved of the Queen in retirement and was preparing to be shocked by the Prince of Wales. (She *wanted* to be shocked.) She considered *all* foreigners (including – very much including – Americans) false, obscene, dangerous and unwashed. (Her own ablutions were neither so constant nor thorough as you would suppose.)

She approved of archery, croquet and painting in water-colours for young girls, but thought that that was enough excitement for them. She was an exceeding prude with a passionate private curiosity in sexual matters. She believed in good works, Missions to the Heathen, and patronizing visits to the slums. She was, in fact, *all* wrong, being hypocritical, snobbish, unkind to servants, a worshipper of wealth and a devout believer in a god whom she had created entirely after her own image. She was not a typical woman of her period – only typical of the section of it that was the easiest for after-generations to caricature.

She disapproved, of course, entirely of her brother Barney; she thought his novels 'horrid' with their racing, gambling, and loose women. Sometimes he brought men like Mortimer Collins to the Newmark home, and they smoked and drank together in Barney's sanctum. Now that both Phyllis and Stephen were gone, that Horace lived in Manchester, that Mary was dead, and Katherine married, Emily took charge of the Newmark remnants, Phyllis (named after her mother) who was a weak character, Barney who was not, and Stephen who was a lazy ne'er-do-well. She thought that she dominated all three, but Phyllis agreed with her in order that she might get what she wanted – new hats, novels from the library and a succession of silly young men; Stephen stole money from her, and Barney laughed at her. But Emily, in her blind self-satisfaction, arrogant patriotism and hypocritical prudery, learnt nothing. She had, however, her effect on others . . .

She had her effect on this particular and very important evening, for had she not entered the Hill Street drawing room just when she did she might not have exasperated Barney to his point of later recklessness.

'What's this I hear, Barney?' she cried. 'You are surely staying indoors this evening?'

'I am not,' said Barney.

'Well, of course,' and her voice was of a sepulchral gloom, 'it is not for me to say, but father has only been buried two days—'

'Father won't mind,' Barney said. 'He has other things to think of.'

Emily had but just sat down on the sofa. She rose.

'I will not hear such blasphemy. Nor shall this poor child. Benjamin, come with me.'

'Benjie is my guest tonight,' Barney remarked. 'He is to share my humble chop in some decent quiet place where we can think reverently of the past and pray hopefully for the future.'

Emily was aghast. She was truly and honestly aghast. This seemed to her a horrible thing. She broke into a flood of oratory in which their poor father, their poor mother, their poor sister Mary, all looked down from heaven in an agony of distress, in which childhood and vice, innocence and nasty men of the world, insults to herself and Lady Herries, all confusedly figured.

'Ellis will at least support me in this.'

'Ellis is coming with us,' said Barney.

She burst into tears.

'Oh, dammit, I can't stand this!' Barney cried. 'Come along, Benjie.' And Benjie rather sheepishly followed him out.

Down in the hall they found Ellis.

Ellis, waiting, looking up to the staircase, down which they were descending, had then the oddest hallucination. He was not an imaginative man, but, staring in the rather dim gaslight, he saw this: Barney had vanished. Benjamin, not a boy but a man of mature years, had halted on the stairs. Behind him stood a very beautiful lady in a white evening cloak with a high white collar. There was a Chinese clock at the turn of the stairs, a tall, thin clock brilliant in gilded lacquer. He noticed the time on its round face. It was twelve-thirty exactly. He was conscious of a violent, suffocating rage, and he heard his own voice, high, shrill, convulsed: 'Get out, both of you! Get out! Get out!'

As quickly as it came, it was gone.

There was no clock. Benjie jumped the last two steps.

'Hullo, Ellis!' he cried.

This only meant that Ellis was tired and had a headache. When one had a headache one did not know what one was seeing or what one was hearing. These last few days had been trying, with so many members of the family in and out of the house. But he always felt a little queer with Benjamin, never quite at his ease. He was not perhaps comfortable with small boys, and you could never be sure whether they were not laughing at you. But it was more than that. Ever since that day, ten years back, of the Heenan and Sayers fight, he had had an almost nauseating impression of Walter Herries. He could see him now, wandering,

lost, drunk, you might have said, a disgusting old man, and also
his own half-brother. He hated to think that he had any link with
him. And here was the man's grandson. They said that Walter's
life in Cumberland was a disgrace. That horrid man's son had
murdered this boy's father. Everything that was abnormal, fantastic, revolting – cruelty and illicit passion and madness – were
in the strain of that branch of the family. And he was himself
mixed in it, he who loved everything to be proper and sane and
wholesome and virtuous. He had a passion for virtue! But old
Walter and he had the same father. He would have cut all that off
as he would have cut off a diseased arm, and so he would have
been able to do were it not for this boy. The boy seemed normal
and decent enough. But he was young yet. You could not tell
what the future would be. And just as something in that branch
disgusted him, so something attracted him. He had insisted that
the boy should be invited to Hill Street. He tried to be friendly
with the boy, but he was not clever at friendliness, poor Ellis. He
wanted to be so many things that nature prevented him from
being.

'All right,' said Barney. 'Shall we go?'

They found a cab in Berkeley Square and, on the way, Barney
enlarged to Benjamin on the delights of London life.

'You shall have a night out, young 'un. We'll have dinner at
Duke's. No, be quiet, Ellis. It's my evening. What are you, Benjie?
Fifteen? Dammit, you look seventeen anyway.' He'd like to give
the boy a week. He'd take him to the Café Riche, Sally Suther-
land's, Kate Hamilton's, Rose Young's, Mott's. Cafés were open
all night. Pity he hadn't been with Barney at the fight between
King and Heenan, driving across London Bridge three in the
morning with a pork pie in your pocket. Mott's, too, where old
Freer kept guard. None of your tradesmen let in there – not that
Barney minded tradesmen. 'You're in the City, Ellis, yourself,
aren't you, my boy?' But still a gentleman was a gentleman when
it came to eating together. It was at Mott's you could have seen
'Skittles', famous for her ponies, or lovely Nelly Fowler. And
Kate Hamilton's – well, Benjie was still at school so he'd say no
more. But you should have seen a raid at Kate's – carpets turned
up, boards – under which bottles and glasses were hidden –
raised, all in the twinkling of an eye.

Or the 'Pie', where you were positively bound to have a row
before the night was up and where you tipped the Kangaroo so
that he shouldn't knock you down.

Barney wasn't a bad fellow; he was warm-hearted, generous, a famous friend, but tonight three things drove him on – the thought of his sister Emily, Ellis' air of wanting 'to be a sport' and wanting, too, to go home to his comfortable bed, and Benjie's excitement. He really loved the boy that night as he sat there, a proper little gentleman, his high hat tilted a trifle, his lips parted with his eagerness, his fresh colour, his sparkling eyes, his laugh, his readiness to trust anyone, his impulse to throw himself into whatever adventure was forward. 'I'll look after him,' he thought. 'I'll see that he comes to no harm.'

Duke's, near St Alban's Place, was half-hotel, half-hostelry. In the bedrooms the beds were cleanly enough, and most of the residents slept in them all day because they were out and about all night. A number of the residents may be said to have never been sober.

Excellent joints could be had for dinner, and the best of eggs and bacon any time of day or night, but the establishment *did* exist mainly for drinking – no one pretended other. Brandy-and-soda, rum and milk all day, sherry and bitters before breakfast, and a glass of brandy for tea.

A later generation might have thought Duke's eating room a little on the stuffy side. Everything was a trifle close, smelly, thick with tobacco and brandy fumes, linen and under-linen not quite clean, a strange air of rooms littered with feathers from an old bed, warm with the odour of unwashed bodies, cats furtively picking at fish-bones on a sanded floor, and the Chairman banging with his hammer on the table in the smoke-thickened distance. Stuffy! That was the word for the night-life of the London of the 'sixties.

But for Benjamin, Duke's room was Paradise. He gazed with eyes of wonder and admiration at old Charles, the presiding deity, who shuffled about in a tiny snuff-coloured tail suit and slippers, who – Barney told him – was never known to sleep, for at any moment of day or night he was ready to assist a drunken gentleman from a cab, or part two combatants. There were two chuckers-out, Jerry and Tom – men, it seemed, of almost legendary strength. It was nothing, Barney said, to see a long wooden coffin come down the stairs into the middle of the diners. One of the gentlemen had died upstairs, of delirium tremens. No one thought anything of it at all.

Dinner went well enough. Ellis was quiet. He seemed even to be enjoying himself and watched a young swell with an eyeglass and long moustaches drink one brandy and soda after another. 'Marvellous, isn't it?' he said in his precise careful voice. 'Can't think how he does it!'

But it was here and now that Benjamin had the first brandy and soda of his life. He had tried gin up in Cumberland, but had not liked it. Cherry-brandy had been an adventure at Rugby. But this brandy and soda was different. It may be said, in a way, to have changed his whole life. He was ready for it. In many ways he was old, very old; in others he was a baby. But the recklessness, the urge to do something simply because it was forbidden, the bravado that led him again and again to challenge anybody at anything, the absence in him, not of a sense of good and bad, but altogether of a sense of right and wrong, all these were pledged by him that night in that glass of brandy and soda. As he drank it down he may be said to have whispered to his familiar spirit the words that were to be his Creed all his days: "I'll do what I want. I'll see all that I can see. I'll love and enjoy with all my heart. I'll do no one harm but nothing shall stop my adventure.'

To be fair to Barney it was true that Benjie *looked* seventeen. There was something in his hard blue eye, in his confident carriage and his air of assurance that made him seem, even then, mature. But he was not; in one meaning of the word, he would never be. After that brandy and soda he was ready for anything and he thought that it would be amusing to tease Ellis.

Ellis was twelve years older. He was staying in Ellis' house, and Ellis had been kind to him. For all these reasons he should have been polite to Ellis. But he was happy, he was reckless, he liked old Ellis even though he *was* a bit of a woman and even though Ellis didn't like him. So, on their way to the 'Paragon', he broke out:

'I say, Ellis – what relation are you to me really? Ought I to call you Uncle?'

'No, of course not. What an idea!'

'But *what* are you? My grandfather is your brother, ain't he?'

'My half-brother,' Ellis answered stiffly.

'Oh, so you're my half-great-uncle! What a funny thing to be to anybody!'

'All right,' said Ellis, yet more stiffly. 'We'll forget it!'

'Oh, I shan't forget it! I say, Barney, isn't that funny? To be someone's half-great-uncle?'

He hadn't a notion that Ellis was minding. All life was rosy and golden. Never, never had he been so happy before. He loved Barney and would do anything in the world for him. The streets were a glory of light and splendour. Wouldn't it be fine to be going to the Opera in the Haymarket – and then, all in a moment, they are out of Piccadilly and walking down a street where the gas is flaring over coarse scraps of meat, where linen-drapers are still, at this hour, invaded by poorly dressed women wanting pennyworths of needles or farthingsworths of thread, where there are little open dens, reeking with the odour of fried fish and sausages, where a lady in a mob-cap is instructing a sailor in the mysteries of the famous dance 'Dusty Bob and Black Sal', where a huge Negro, his teeth gleaming white under the gaslight and his brown chest bare, is turning somersaults for pennies!

Then, as suddenly, they were in broad lighted streets again and passing through the wide painted doors of the 'Paragon'.

'We'll walk about,' said Barney. 'We can see just as well from here.'

Benjie had never been to a real theatre before. It was a while before he could take all the dazzling brilliance into his system. First the stage with its blaze of light held him. A group of young women in low green bodices and wide skirts were dancing while two gentlemen in evening dress, one at each corner of the stage, waved flags. A large box, protruding over the stage, contained a crowd of gentlemen, very elegant and noisy, smoking cigars and leaning over to shout encouragement to the girls. At the back of the theatre everyone was walking about, talking and laughing. There were little tables at which ladies and gentlemen were drinking. Men stood up in the pit and shouted at one another.

'Hullo, Connie!' Barney said. 'Never thought I'd see you here.'

'Oh, didn't you? Well, where were you last Friday night? I was waiting an hour and a half and wouldn't have had no supper at all if a gentleman hadn't taken pity on me. Nice treatment, I call it!'

Benjie thought that, save for his mother and Veronica, he had never seen anyone so beautiful. She was fair with bright blue eyes, ringlets and a dress the colour of primroses, gathered into great festoons at the back. She was angry, anyone could see, but Barney was not at all discomforted, only more like a clown than ever, his hat on one side of his head, grinned and stared over his shoulder to see who else might be there. Benjamin feared that she was about to do something desperate, she looked so angry, but her eyes fell on himself. She smiled, a lovely, entrancing smile.

'Hullo, baby,' she said. 'Where's your mother?'

He smiled back, and murmured something with proper bashfulness.

'Isn't he a pet? What's your name, dear?'

But Barney was, in an instant, the guardian. He put his hand on Benjie's shoulder.

'Now then, Connie, enough of that.'

Her voice was soft. She stared at Benjie as though she could eat him.

'All right,' she said quietly, 'I shan't hurt him.'

There were two chairs near to them. She sat down in one and motioned Benjie to the other.

'There! Now we are at a proper distance. Is he your guardian or something?'

'No,' said Benjie.

'What's your name then?'

'Benjamin Herries.'

'Well I never! Do you often come here?'

'It's the first time,' said Benjie.

'But not your last, I'll be sworn. Here! you want a flower in your buttonhole. Take this.'

She had two small white roses at her waist. She took out one and gave it him. Very proudly he stuck it in his buttonhole.

'You're the prettiest boy I've *ever* seen!' She drew her chair a little closer. 'Like to come and see me one day?'

'I should very much,' said Benjie. 'Only you see—' He was about to say that tomorrow he would return to school, but that seemed to him childish, so he altered it to 'I don't live in London.'

'Where do you live then?'

'In Cumberland.'

'Where's that?'

'Up in the North.'

'Oh, never mind where you live. Here, see, I'll give you my card and then—'

But it seemed that Ellis, who had been standing awkwardly by himself, was now remonstrating, in great excitement, with Barney, for Barney broke out:

'Come on, young Benjamin. We'll go and visit the Captain. Ta-ta, Connie. See you again.'

Benjamin had to go. He had just not courage enough to demand that he should stay, but as Ellis and Barney turned ahead of him, the lovely Connie, coming so close to him that his nose was suffocated in some scent that seemed to contain a whole garden of flowers, caught his neck in her fair hand and kissed him.

He ran after the others, his heart hammering, his cheeks flaming, and his mouth tasting of some sweet powder. Who had ever dreamt that life could be like this?

They went behind the stage to a large room in which ladies (performers evidently) were drinking with bearded and high-hatted gentlemen, while a funny little man in a very light waistcoat and bushy side-whiskers claimed Barney as his most intimate friend, bowed gravely to Ellis, and asked them all to have a drink.

But Benjie saw and heard nothing. He sat in a dream of happiness. Oh! what a lovely lady! How kind, how generous, how amusing! It was always his first thought when he met anyone whom he liked that he wanted to make his new friend a present. What could he give her in return for his rose? He had the ten shillings that Ellis had bestowed on him – or, at least, he had some of it. He could buy her flowers or fruit. Barney would tell him where she lived. He would go to visit her . . . Into the middle of these charming dreams Ellis gruesomely plunged.

'Benjamin, we are going home, you and I.'

'Going home?' he gasped.

'Yes. You must not be up late. You are returning to Rugby tomorrow. I myself am tired.'

'But of course I am not going home!'

He hated Ellis, who had the sad long face of a horse pining for its stable.

'This is no proper place for you,' he said.

'Why not?'

'Well – it's plain – you are only a boy— Places like this—'

To do Ellis justice, this was one of the most difficult things that he had ever had to do. He did not wish to preach, to improve others; on the contrary, his desire was that he should be a jolly companion, a merry wit, a Prince of Good Fellows. But nature is too strong for us. Good fellows are not made, they are born. His capacity for finding life shocking was abnormally large. It was not his fault that it was so. It was simply his destiny. He did not want to spoil Benjamin's fun; he only thought it dreadful that

Benjamin should be finding this fun at all.

'You are to come with me,' he said, his voice trembling. He looked out of place, absurd, in that room.

Benjie saw it and, unhappily, Benjie laughed.

'You don't know how funny you look, Ellis!'

Then Ellis hated him. One thing he could not forgive – mockery that seemed to him unjust. It was his misfortune that all mockery of which he was the victim seemed to him unjust.

He caught Barney's arm.

'Benjamin and I are going home.'

Most regrettably Barney was by now drunk enough to find seriousness a farce and gloomy faces a pantomime. He roared with laughter.

'I say – don't be so sad, Ellis, old buck. Why, dammit – oh lor! look at your face—'

'We are going home,' Ellis, pale, tortured, terrified of a public scene, repeated.

'Well, *I'm* not,' Benjamin cried. 'I'm not, am I, Barney?'

'No, of course you're not. Here, Captain, this is my young friend, *very* young friend. Never been to a Green Room before, never seen a pretty girl.'

'Shame! Shame!' Ellis cried in the best transpontine manner. He caught Benjie's arm.

'You are coming with me!'

'I'm not,' said Benjie, struggling to be free.

Two girls laughed. A gentleman with enormous side-whiskers, holding a glass of champagne rather uncertainly, came forward.

'What's the matter?' he said.

'Let me go!' Benjie said indignantly, wrenching himself from Ellis' hold.

Ellis let him go, and in that moment hated his half-great-nephew with all the hatred that a shy, self-conscious, awkward man feels for anyone who makes him the centre of a scene. Lowering his head, picking up his hat, he slipped away.

Benjamin was invited to sit at a table. Several ladies talked to him. Somebody said: 'You can have four monkeys to one if you like.'

'Put it down,' said someone else.

'By Gad,' some voice cried, 'if you can put me on to a good thing, Gordon, I'll be eternally grateful.'

He drank some champagne. He felt a little sleepy. The ladies were kind to him, but they were nothing, nothing at all because

Connie had kissed him. Then he heard the Captain, the gentleman with the flowing whiskers and very light waistcoat, say:

'What about Victorine's, Barney, old boy?'

'I'm agreeable,' said Barney.

'What about the boy?'

'I'll look after him. We shan't be long.'

Benjamin found himself accompanying the Captain, who
confided to him as they went into the street:

'I've got a boy just your age. What are you? Seventeen?'

'Yes,' said Benjie, lying proudly. 'And a half.'

He felt about forty, or what he supposed that forty would feel.
Nothing excited him like something new – something he had
never done before, the company of someone whom he had never
seen before, a new place, a new trick, a new risk, a new danger.
Now, feeling like a knight of old, he strode through the streets,
trying to keep pace with his two friends so that they should not
discover how short his steps were. He did a little trot, then a long
step, then a little trot again. Where were they going? Would
Connie be there? Victorine's! That sounded exciting. They came
at length to a barren waste surrounded with railings. In the
centre of the waste was an equestrian statue. Here were oyster
rooms, public-houses, night-houses. Here was Jerry Fry's
Coffee House and there a small theatre with a large lady in black
tights painted on a crimson ground over the doorway. A four-
wheeler, lonely and disconsolate, wandered from darkness into
darkness.

They turned into a narrow, intensely dark street, found their
way cautiously down a kind of tunnel.

'Here we are,' said Barney.

Behind the door, through a little window, two janitors were
watching. They recognized both Barney and the Captain; the
door swung back. As they passed in, the barren waste of Leicester
Square seemed to follow them, bringing with it the 'Shades', one
of the wildest eating-houses in London, where the spoons and
forks were marked 'Stolen from the Shades' as a delicate hint to
its patrons, and the 'Tableaux Vivants', a festive hall almost next
door to Victorine's, where, for a shilling, you could listen to more
filth within half an hour than in any other place in London.

'Victorine's', however, seemed as respectable as a church-ser-
vice. Barney, Benjie and the Captain seated themselves in a
corner and brandy and sodas were ordered from a benevolent-
looking old man with a hare-lip and snow-white hair. It was not

a very big room. In the far corner was a billiard-table at which several gentlemen were playing. The centre of the room was cleared for dancing and there was a shabby piano decorated with two dusty ferns in pots wrapped in green paper; at the piano a large ringleted lady in a crimson dress was playing. Two staircases vanished into upper regions. Several ladies were drinking at little tables with several gentlemen. But the great glory of the place was Victorine herself, a huge woman weighing over twenty stone, who sat at a raised desk near the piano. It was said that she drank champagne all day and all night. Her countenance was hideous, for her nose was flat, she had a scar across her upper lip and a number of chins. Her little eyes were wrapped in fat.

Benjie gazed at her with excited fascination. Her bodice was cut very low and her enormous bosom shook with every movement. He had never seen anyone so ugly and he felt that he would like to talk to her. The gentlemen at the tables embraced the ladies, and one stout female balanced herself precariously on a stout gentleman's knee. Benjie was always a great observer; he missed very little, and was capable of a detached non-moral attitude that permitted him to see life steadily and, unless his own emotions were aroused, with great fairness.

His emotions were not aroused now except that he was greatly enjoying himself – for had not Connie kissed him and given him a white rose? He was still, in the back of his mind, considering what sort of a present he should give her. He had better wait, perhaps. Christmas-time he would be in funds.

Then Victorine noticed them and beckoned Barney over to her. After a while he returned and said to Benjamin:

'Ma wants to speak to you. She won't eat you. Come along.'

Benjamin went over to her, feeling rather self-conscious as he crossed the floor, but he was ready for any adventure. He stood on the raised platform beside her, laughing. She spoke in a deep husky voice. She held out a large dirty hand.

'How are you?' she asked.

'Very well, thank you, ma'am,' said Benjie.

'How do you like my place?'

'I think it's very nice,' said Benjie.

'First time you've been here, isn't it?' she asked him, suddenly bending towards him, and he thought that he had never known anything so terrifying as that great round soiled, misshapen face with its little eyes, its flat nose, its grotesque mouth coming so close to his own.

'Yes, it's the first time.'

'You can see for yourself how quiet it is.' Her little eyes stared into his. 'There isn't a quieter house in London. It's these — — — who come with their — — — interference who make all the trouble. Take my word for it.'

It was astonishing to him, the quiet friendly manner in which she used words of a terrifying impropriety. They were not, it is sad to say, new to him, because boys at Rugby, or anywhere else, understand many words that would frighten Billingsgate. Not that they had ever done Benjie any harm, these words. They were simply counters in a normal day's play.

'You see,' Madame Victorine continued, her voice lower than ever, her manner extremely confidential, 'I am a mother to all the boys and girls who come here. You wouldn't believe all that I do for them. Saved their lives again and again. Mother I am and Mother they call me. I'm a widow, you know,' she added unexpectedly. 'My late husband was a Captain in the Army and he died in the West Indies of a yellow fever.'

'I am sorry,' Benjie said. He could think of nothing else to say.

'Yes. It was a tragedy.' There was a tear in her eye. Her vast bosom heaved. He thought that she was going to cry, but instead, to his great surprise, she banged with her fist on the desk and yelled in a voice of thunder, 'Here, you dirty —. Get out of here! Didn't I tell you last Thursday not to show your — face in my place again? Here, Cormey, put him out! Knock his — face in if there's an argument!'

Benjie turned to see a very mild-looking little man, bearded, in a dirty sack-coat and pepper-and-salt trousers talking with a big man in his shirtsleeves. The little man gave one glance round the room and vanished through the door. At the same moment Barney came and rescued Benjie, bringing him back to their table.

Barney was never so drunk that he did not know what he was doing. Now he preached Benjie a little sermon. 'You see, my boy, I've brought you here to show you life a bit. But never do anything you'd be ashamed of your mother knowing. You're young yet, but how are you to know what to avoid if you don't look round a bit?'

'I say, Barney,' said Benjamin. 'I want to give that lady a present. I'm going back to Rugby tomorrow so there isn't much time. Do you think you could give her something from me? I'll pay you back when I get my pocket-money. I've got a bit now that Ellis gave me, and with two weeks' pocket-money—'

'Here you are, my boy,' said Barney, diving confusedly into his pocket.

He produced two golden sovereigns.

'I don't know what you are talking about, but if it's money you're wanting—'

Two sovereigns!

'Oh, I say! But, Barney, I shan't have two pounds for months!'

'Oh, never mind! Keep them.'

'No. If I give her something, you see, I want it to be with my own money—'

He kept a sovereign. With luck he could pay that back by Christmas. A sovereign! He could buy her something fine – a scarf, a pin, a brooch ... And it was then that the fun began. Over the silver image of his divine Connie he saw, rising as it were from the floor, a thick-set squat fellow, very hairy, very unkempt, very drunk. He wandered, as though he were describing with his feet a geometric figure, towards one of the little tables, raised a glass of champagne stationed there in front of a gentleman and drank from it. At the same time, grinning amiably, he knocked off the hat of the gentleman. Then, turning, he began to orate to the room:

'In the name of our Queen, of Mr Disraeli and little Lottie Heever, down with the French! Down, I say, with the French! Are they eating dogs in Paris? Poodle dogs? And is elephant their one luxury? Right and right again! To hell with the French!'

But he proceeded no further, for the two strong men, who had been watching the billiards, were across the room, had the man by the legs and were trundling him towards the door. At the same time the gentleman whose drink had been abstracted – stout, plethoric, with a beard of the colour of jet – cried something in a kind of frenzy and rushed towards one of the staircases. Benjie, looking in that direction, saw that two young ladies, most scantily dressed, were peering over the stair-rail. One of them, seeing the bearded gentleman, vanished with a scream, the gentleman after her.

Then everything happened together. The victim of the strong men wriggled from his captors and, his trousers tumbling towards his knees (for the strong men had burst his buttons), lurched towards the piano; there were shouts and cries from the upper floor which drew Madame Victorine, panting, upwards; some gentlemen ran in from the billiard table; the lady at the piano stayed with her back to it, cursing at the height of a shrill soprano; a large tortoiseshell cat crept from nowhere and began to feed eagerly upon a sandwich that had dropped; a table fell, glasses and bottles crashing with it; and the Captain, who had been dancing very solemnly with a stout lady in green, left her where she was and reeled (for he was very drunk) towards Barney.

'Here,' said Barney. 'We must be out of this.'

And then a fantastic thing occurred. At the end of the room there was a long mirror hung with yellow and green papers. Reflected in the centre of this mirror was the old waiter with the white hair and the hare-lip. He seemed to Benjie to swell and lengthen. As he grew in size, another figure, long and thin, spread out behind him, caught him from the back, in the neck, and began to twist his head round. The mirror grew ever more unusual, for now it was swinging, slowly swinging on its nail, and the two men reflected in it increased to three, to four, to five. They all struggled together, and behind them and around them the room swayed with them, tables and chairs, Madame's desk, the coloured portraits of the Queen and the Prince Consort, the piano, overturned tables, all swaying, swinging, swaying again.

Someone threw one of the flowerpots and it struck the mirror in its centre: a great crack like a spider's web struck the bodies, faces, furniture . . . Someone turned out the gas.

It was then, in that strange darkness, smelling of spirits, dust and tobacco, filled with cries and shouts, that Benjie felt a great exultation and a wild spirit of enterprise.

'Here! Benjie! Where are you?' he heard Barney crying.

But nothing could stop him. He plunged forward into the darkness, tumbled over a recumbent body, was up again, had found the piano, was enveloped by large female arms. Some woman held him to her. She was crying, sobbing.

'Oh dear, oh dear! . . . And I had a nice supper at home waiting . . .' And then, in a whisper over Benjie's head, 'Mr Archer, are you there? Are you there, Mr Archer! Oh dear, and if it hadn't been for the five shillings he promised me—'

'It's all right,' Benjie said, feeling real wet warm tears dropping on his cheek and, in sympathy, patting with his hand what was, he imagined, a huge naked arm. 'Only a moment and they'll have the lights—'

But the lady murmured, sobbing as she spoke, 'Don't you move, Charlie, my darling. You'll be killed for certain if you move a step—'

She planted a wet kiss on his cheek. She began to croon in a drunken kind of lullaby, her vast arms now tight about him, and then surprisingly, in the middle of her crooning, in a sharp businesslike voice as though she were giving an order at a shop: 'Where are you, Mr Archer? I'm here, Mr Archer, by the piano.'

He ducked his head, slipped to his knees and had escaped. Everything was wild now. Fighting was on all sides. He could hear blows struck, bodies thudding to the floor. Women were screaming, it seemed, from earth and air. Someone again embraced him. This time it was a man – someone fat, paunchy and smelling dreadfully of brandy. They were entangled, intermingled, dragging along the ground together. The man said no word but breathed desperately. He had Benjie by the slack of his breeches, and Benjie had his fist in a handful of beard. The mirror must have fallen, for there was a great crash of shattering glass. Benjie, laughing, shouting he knew not what, tore at the beard, was released like a shot from a catapult, and half flew, half fell through a door, clutched at a wall to save himself and was caught by some hand. He looked up and saw that it was Barney, Barney hatless, his neckerchief torn, but Barney quite sober.

'Thank God!' He held Benjie as though he'd never let him go. 'Here's a piece of luck. Come on, my lad. It's the lock-up for us if we are not speedy.'

A moment later they were in the deserted street, surveyed by an orange-tinted moon and two gas-lamps. Dead silence. Dead, dead silence. A little breeze rose from the pavement and fluttered on their faces. Victorine's was gone. Everything in and around Victorine's was gone. Ahead of them was the desolate waste of Leicester Square with the equestrian statue.

'Walk! Walk!' said Barney. 'Can you walk all right? Have you got your legs?'

'Oh, I'm all right,' said Benjie grandly. 'Are you all right, Barney?'

'Hush!' said Barney, who now that he had found Benjie was, all in a moment, drunk again. 'Hush! We'll wake Emily.'

Benjie's head ached, he thought that he had lost a tooth, his right leg hurt a trifle. But he felt at his buttonhole. Miraculous! The white rose was still there! How had it escaped? Was that not of itself a triumph? He was dizzy with happiness, adventure, maturity, first love, the wine of battle, the ether of recklessness, the full, complete, uncensored actuality of life.

'Barney, I've still got my rose!'

But Barney was striding on ahead. Benjie did a long step, a trot or two, a step again.

With a sudden alarm he felt in his pocket. Yes, the sovereign was there. What would he buy for her? A scarf, a chain, a pin, a brooch? . . .

He did a long step, a trot or two, a step again.

BATTLE WITH PANGLOSS

ELIZABETH, walking through the dusky afternoon up the hill to Fell House, was stopped by a little man like a ferret riding a large bay mare. She knew at once who it was – Glose, the handy-man at the Fortress, her father's handy-man and, as always when anyone or anything connected with Ireby confronted her, she shivered with apprehension. Glose, who had sharp beady eyes and was always a trifle drunk, thought, as he looked at her: 'That's a pretty piece, although she *has* got grey hair.'

It was generally acknowledged up at the Fortress that Walter Herries' daughter, even though she was nearly sixty, was the most beautiful lady in the County. They liked to tell old Ma Pangloss so, when they dared.

'She'll be back one of these days and send you packing, Mrs Pangloss, *Madam*,' said a lively carroty-haired girl from Braithwaite who had just received her notice, 'and then we'll have a lady who *is* a lady'.

Elizabeth had a dark crimson coat with a silver-grey fur collar turned up above her slender neck, and she wore on her grey hair a feather toque with flame-coloured feathers. She was protected from the chill October wind by a thin veil. The twists and bands in which her hair was arranged at the back under the little feathered hat held lovely lights and shadows, so Glose thought. He was something of a poet where women were concerned, and afterwards in the kitchen at Ireby he declared:

'She had on a little hat all flaming feathers, and her hair was silver, you understand, and she has the figure of a girl of twenty, old as she is. Very pretty with the dusk coming on and the leaves blowing down, all the colour of her little hat.'

He was an Irishman, vagrant and worthless. He was in gaol for trying to knife a man in Keswick three months later.

But he had a letter for Mrs Herries. He was riding up to Fell House. He touched his cap, leaned down and gave her the letter.

Her hand trembled as she read it by the pale light of the saffron sky above the hill. It was written in a hand so shaky that it was difficult to decipher.

DEAR ELIZABETH – I am ill and would like to see you. – Your affectionate father,

WALTER HERRIES

That was all.

'Thank you,' she said to Glose. 'I will see to it.' She walked quickly up the hill. She was in a turmoil of emotion, but once in the house she told no one anything. She had always been quiet, reserved, by herself; her mother, who had learnt, through suffering, restraint, had taught her.

She peeped in to say goodnight to Judith, but the old lady was sleeping. Had she been awake Elizabeth might have said something, for although Judith was now ninety-eight and was being preserved as though constructed of egg-shell china, every noise, shock, sudden news kept from her, yet, inside this elegant glass case, she lived, Elizabeth fancied, an exceedingly alive and conscious existence. Judith knew more about Walter than anyone else at Uldale. It was she who had seen him last, who had known him longest. To her, Elizabeth might have spoken. But to Dorothy, who was now as fat as a tub and as contented as a pork pie, Elizabeth said not a word. Otherwise there was only Jane, for Veronica had been Mrs Forster now for two years, and Amabel had, of all mad things, gone to be a student at the Ladies' College at Hitchin. She had been there two years and was now at Cambridge, whither the College had just removed under the name of Girton. Ridiculous of Amabel, who was now between thirty and forty! She said, of all things, that she intended to study medicine!

So there were, besides Dorothy, Judith and Elizabeth, only Timothy (who showed no signs of marrying: he was fat, red-faced, cheerful – a proper Squire) and Jane. Elizabeth might have said something to Jane. She did not. Jane was such a dear old spinster, already ringleted and shawled, her face sweet and anxious and kind under her pale-gold hair, her small body *intensely* virginal. No, she would be of little use.

Of course Elizabeth must go to Ireby, and this time she would remain. From the moment that she received the note and read it in the gathering shadow of the autumn dusk she knew that there was only one thing that she must do. But oh! how she didn't want to! Her quiet, reserved, cloistered life, saturated with the memory and actual presence of John, devoted to Benjamin and Aunt Judith, was exactly right at Uldale. She was young no longer. She was nearing sixty. She shrank in every vein and pulse of her body from the roughness, violence, hateful rudeness that going to Ireby meant.

So she fortified herself with Adam and Margaret. On the morning after receiving her father's letter she told Dorothy quietly that she was going to stay at Cat Bells for a night or two.

'Are you sure that they want you, Elizabeth dear?' said Dorothy. 'Adam is just finishing his book, I believe.'

'I don't think that they will mind,' Elizabeth said. And they did not.

On that first evening, sitting by the fire after Vanessa had gone to bed, hearing Will softly singing as he occupied himself with something in the kitchen close by, Adam tranquilly smoking his pipe, they talked it all over.

The two women had a great regard for one another. Margaret had broadened into a maternal and seemingly placid woman, more German now perhaps in type than English. Her love for Adam was so strong that she could not sit with him five minutes without snatching a private glance at him to see that all was well. She knew that he loved her but she knew also, as nine out of every ten wives come to know, that she had not captured all of him; a certain wildness in him had escaped her. He was her friend and she was his, but she knew also that soon he would get up, knock his pipe against the stone of the fireplace, mutter something and slip off to Will – and that then for an hour at least those two deep voices would rumble on beyond the wall, and that they would both be happy together with a kind of happiness that neither of them could find with a woman. So she was glad to have Elizabeth then. They were two quiet, elderly women, sitting together by the fire; they were like hundreds of thousands of other elderly women sitting beside the fire that evening all over England – and the lives of those women contained sufficient courage, unselfishness and loving devotion to fill a Calendar of Saints.

Margaret, beneath her reserve, was frightened. There were many things in the Herries family that she did not understand, and what she understood least of all was that some of them were so very different from others! That you should have Garth and Amery, the Archdeacon of Polchester, Will and Ellis, Judith and Adam, poor John, crazy Uhland and his father, all of the same stock and closely related, seemed to her sober German imagination extravagantly improbable. Yet it was so, and she had long ago realized that the mad strain in the Herries family was not for her. She shrank from it with all her quiet strength because it was that element in her husband – although Adam of course was not crazy! – that prevented him from being entirely hers, and it had been that same element in his mother that had given her all her young married sorrows.

Now she was set, with all the determination of which she was capable, to keep the wildness from Vanessa! Vanessa as yet was as good and obedient and loving as a child could possibly be, but she was impulsive, fantastically generous, and – most perilous of all! – worshipped, increasingly with every year of her growth, Benjamin Herries. Now Margaret was Elizabeth's friend, but in her heart she was afraid of Elizabeth's son. Young Benjamin was wild; they said that he did wild things in London. He was eighteen years of age, and in another term he would be leaving Rugby. Then, Margaret supposed, he would come to live at Ireby and would be terribly close to Cat Bells. Margaret had to confess that when she was in the boy's company she could not but like him. He looked you straight in the face with his clear blue eye, he was merry, honest, open-handed, the friend of all the world. But he was wild. Margaret was sure that he had no principles, and although Adam sometimes laughed at principles yet he respected them as a good man should. Margaret was no narrow condemner of her fellow but she had acquired the prejudices of her time. She believed in righteousness, and for her own beloved daughter she would fight like a fish-wife if need be.

Vanessa would be beautiful – of that there was no question – and she must be guarded against Benjamin, but how she was to be guarded poor Margaret had no idea. Adam only laughed when she spoke to him of it.

And now Elizabeth was going back to that horrible place at Ireby with that drunken old wretch her father and the loose women he had with him. She was going back into all that craziness and wildness and bad living, and she intended to remain there. That quiet, frail woman, with her gentle face, shy, retiring way, so perfect and refined an English lady, thought Margaret, would live in a world that must revolt and disgust her at every turn. And, if she did remain, Benjamin would of course come to her there; he was heir, Margaret supposed, to that place, and any money the old man might have if, indeed, his dissipations had left him any. And Benjamin at Ireby meant Benjamin very near to Vanessa. At the thought of her child so peacefully sleeping in the upper room her whole protective fighting maternity was at arms. She felt inclined to cry out to Elizabeth, although she loved and admired her:

'Go away! Please, please go away and let neither your son nor yourself ever return.'

But they sat talking calmly; only once Margaret said:

'Do you think, Elizabeth dear, that it is *worth* going? Can you do anything for him? Is his life not too settled? Can it ever be your life?'

And Elizabeth answered, looking at Margaret:

'I know it's my duty, Margaret.'

Margaret shivered with some quick sense of chill and discomfort. Her German blood gave her an unusual sensitiveness to intangible influences. Many past events touched her moment's consciousness, and future events, linked to these, hung like clouds about her vision. It was as though the cheerful fire-lit room were, at that instant, fogged with smoke.

Elizabeth slept little that night and in the morning she shrank from what she was going to do as she had never shrunk from anything in her life before. After all, she was returning to the house where, it seemed to her excited fancy, Uhland's footstep must have left everywhere an imprint of blood. That was not a melodramatic exaggeration. John's death had been bloody, and, although his murderer had been her own brother, that did not make his ghost more stainless. In every room, at every turn, there would be memories, agonizing thoughts, vain, wretched recriminations. But nevertheless, she had no hesitation as to what her duty was.

Two things made the journey easier for her. One was the luxuriant splendour of the day. In October this country is often a fantastic dream, and on this especial morning the fragment of this world contained by the sky, the hills, the water, was a glory. Last night there had been the first frost and the lawn glittered in a dancing firefly extravagance under a pale autumnal mist. She stood in the doorway of the cottage and looked out to the Lake and Walla Crag. Near her was a mulberry tree; there were roses, chrysanthemums, currant bushes; someone was drawing water, and the smoke from the cottage chimney went up in a gay, fluttering pennon of thin colour. A squirrel watched her from a branch. She could see into the living room with the bright-blue cups on the white cloth, rough pottery with a pattern of flowers. All this world at her hand was clear and distinct with a hard edge to it. Then, in the space of the lawn, of a leaping jump, terrestial existence was cut off and mirage began.

The blue cold sky ranged like a sea infinitely high and remote from change: the tops of the larch and birch and fir suddenly, if they were high enough, struck a hard stainless light and were edged like cut paper, but so soon as the feathering vapours of mist rolled curtain-like across the scene colour so rich and varied began that the sky seemed to belong to another infinitely remote existence, unactual and a planet away.

The mist was neither ascending nor descending in clouds; it was not thick enough for form, it only caught the sunlight and transmuted it, and that sunlight, joyfully enclosed, glowed within, an imprisoned fire.

It is the quality of this country that with a structure of rock, naked fell and dark grim water, it has the power of breaking into an opulence of light and colour. So the Lake that could be cold as driving snow, harsh like shadowed steel, fierce with white foam as a bird's feathers are blown angrily by storm, now was streaked and veined with shadows of the grape that trembled, as though a hand gently stroked its surface. This trembling was not cold nor wind-swept, but burned with the sun-filled mist. Above these purple shadows the hillsides were orange clouds, orange in their brighter spaces, but like smouldering, glowing embers where vapour enshrouded them. An isolated field, a blazing tree, a strip of bracken against the dark plum-coloured islands, shone out like the gilt of missals, damascened, exotic, flaming to the eye where all else was mystery, but the mist above the gold was as dim as the white ash of burnt wood.

Because the sky was decisive with its virgin chastity of eggshell blue, the misted land in contrast took all the colours of purple, topaz, orange, and laid them under washes of pale gold. And yet, with all this dimness the hills were strong, striking deep into the Lake and, where they topped the mist, hard-ridged against the chill sky. And on Skiddaw there was a sudden flame-shaped crest.

Nothing but words of colour could describe this colour, but its final delight for Elizabeth was that it was friendly. The Lake, the cottage, the chrysanthemums, the sparkling lawn, wished her well. She could feel the warm quiver in the air, could think without extravagance that the sun laughed with pleasure as it struck again and again through the mist to touch with the point of its shaking lance the purple shadowy waters, the flaming autumn trees, the sharp dark ridge of Blencathra. She drew in a deep breath of the frosted air as she saw Walla Crag riding into the orange vapour like the bow of a Viking ship. The breath was as though she had leant her forehead against the pure cold of a newly riven stone . . .

And the second thing was that Will Leathwaite drove her to Ireby.

She could not have had a more perfect defence in perilous country. But before she went she had a moment with Vanessa. Vanessa came dancing on to the lawn, flinging her long arms out, running across the frosty grass, breathing in the air that stung the throat like peppermint. Her dark hair was in ringlets, her white strong neck bare. 'She will have big strong breasts,' thought Elizabeth, 'she will be very tall. I never saw a child carry her head with such majesty, and yet she is dancing about the lawn like a little pony.' She was going down with Will to Grange to fetch the carriage. They had to keep it in Grange. As she came nearer to Elizabeth the curve of her face from cheek to chin, still the face of a child innocent, open-eyed, fearless, gave promise of an almost startling beauty. You looked again to see whether that curve could be as perfect in shadowed line, in proportion and purity as you had at first supposed. And it was. Her eyes, lit now with happiness, were direct, unequivocal, so honest that they put you on your guard. What base part of myself am I going to betray here? you must ask yourself.

But Elizabeth knew that Vanessa was no perfect paragon. Her impulsiveness was always taking her into trouble; she had a temper. She was irritated often by stupid people; like her father and grandmother, she did not suffer fools gladly. Her mother was always checking her for answering back her elders (which no child was allowed to do), but, as Vanessa said, it was her father's fault because he encouraged her.

She was compassionate and generous, but not at all sentimental. At a time when both young men and young women 'gushed' and the world was on the whole more insincere than usual, Vanessa laughed. She laughed, it is to be feared, at Dorothy Bellairs, and Captain Forster who had married Veronica, and Mrs Ponsonby and a good many more. In fact Vanessa was not perfect at all. Margaret often shook her head over her.

'I am going down to Grange with Will. We'll be back in a twinkle!'

'Vanessa!' said Margaret.

'Well, but, Mama, twinkle is quite a proper word!'

'And as soon as you are back, Vanessa, you sit down to the German.'

'Oh, bother the German on this lovely day! I'm sorry, Mama; isn't it a pity that I don't like the German language better?'

She came to Elizabeth and said goodbye.

'Please, how is Benjamin?'

'Very well. He plays in the football team this term, and you know Rugby is very famous for football.'

'Yes. I am so glad.'

'Now, Vanessa, Will's waiting.'

'When you write to him will you tell him, please, that I asked?'

'Of course I will.'

'Now, Vanessa.'

Elizabeth thought it rather strange that Adam and Margaret should allow their girl when she was only fourteen to go off alone with Will – but then all the family at Uldale, except Judith, thought that Adam treated Will with far too great a familiarity. Servants were servants, and however good and valuable Will might be (certainly he was a *most* trustworthy man), still it was intended that a member of one Class should not be too intimate with a member of another Class. Emily Newmark, when she heard of it in London, tossed her head. 'Oh, well, we are none of us surprised. Adam Paris was a Chartist for years and would have burnt us all in our beds had he had the chance. Of course he *would* make friends with a common working-man.'

However, when Elizabeth was seated beside Will in the little carriage and they were driving towards Bassenthwaite she could not feel that he *was* 'a common working-man'. He was simply Will Leathwaite, and like most Cumbrian and Westmorland men, sons of Statesmen who have owned their own land for hundreds of years and been servants to none, he held his head high, said nought, and feared no man. But the great thing that Will Leathwaite was was comforting. He was a man of tremendous prejudices, prejudices often based on nothing at all, and he disliked more people that he liked, but if he *did* take you under his wings, then he would see that you were protected. There was nothing he wouldn't do for you, no danger, no strife of tongues (a thing that he greatly disliked) that he wouldn't face. His loyalty was absolute. He had long regarded Elizabeth Herries with a tender protective affection because of John Herries' death. Further than that, she was a member of the Herries clan. He did not think much of several Herries whom he had met, but his friend and master Adam was a Herries and that was enough for him. So Elizabeth was under his wing. As he sat there, staring in front of him, saying 'Gee-up', cracking his whip, his brow wrinkled a little above his very clear blue eyes, his rebellious lock of hair tumbling out across his forehead from under his old high hat, he said very little – but she *knew* that he was protecting her.

In actual fact he was wondering what he would do when they reached Ireby. He did not want to leave the elderly, delicate lady all alone there. There was every kind of bad story about the Fortress, and that Mrs Pangloss was a holy terror. *He* could deal with her – he would like to see any old fat whale of a woman get the better of him – but a lady like Mrs John Herries, so quiet and soft-spoken, what chance would *she* have?

At last when they were driving along the far end of Bassenthwaite Lake, he said: 'See here now, Mrs Herries. I don't like leaving you all alone, by yourself as it were, at the Fortress. Please pardon me, Mrs Herries, if I am saying what I shouldn't.'

By now, poor lady, she was dreadfully frightened, and her hands were trembling inside her muff, but Will must not know that.

'No, Will. You can say anything you like, of course. But I shan't need anyone. Sir Walter is my father, you know.'

This made it very difficult for Will, who considered that to warn a daughter against her own father was not at all man's work. Nevertheless, something had to be done. So he thought, looking straight in front of him between the ears of old Bartholomew the horse.

'Yes, Mrs Herries,' he said at last. 'I do hope you'll forgive me,

ma'am, meaning nothing but good intentions and doing as Mr
Adam would wish me to do, seeing that you are one of the family,
ma'am.' He cleared his throat, gave a crack with his whip, set
back his broad shoulders. 'You see, Mrs Herries, your father isn't
so young as he once was, and there's a woman — Pangloss, they
call her — who's no good whatever if the half they say is true. And
a lady like you and a woman like her . . . I thought if I was to
wait half an hour or so and you wave a handkerchief or some
such article out of the window to say that she hadn't done you no
kind of harm—'

'She won't harm me, thank you, Will,' Elizabeth said. 'It's very
kind of you, and I've met Mrs Pangloss. I know that she isn't a
very nice woman. But I'm not afraid, you know. My father himself has written to me to come and see him, so there is nothing to
fear.'

'Yes, Mrs Herries, I quite understand, ma'am,' said Will.
Nevertheless, he made a private resolve that he would not drive
away until he was well assured that all was safe for the poor dear
lady.

When they had driven slowly up Ireby Hill and the Fortress
came at last into view, Elizabeth drew a deep breath of astonishment. She had seen the chimneys and the two towers, of course,
every day from Uldale, but she had never, since her rebuff six
years ago, been up that hill. She could not believe what she saw.
How could someone as strong, as commanding, as powerful as
her father had been, have allowed what had once been his pride
to drop into this decay? She had seen the degradation begin in
him long before her flight, but the house itself, ugly and for-
bidding as it was, had been proud, well cared for, the gardens
kept, every kind of life and bustle about the place. And now!

She made Will stop the carriage round the bend of the trees so
that they could not be seen from the house. In this part the veils
of mist were thicker than above Derwentwater, and both Uldale
and Skiddaw were invisible. The sun burnt strongly enough for
the clouds of vapour to be faintly stained with rose, and here, as
on the islands of the Lake, the upper mist was grey above the rose
like the ashes of dying fires. But the top of the hill, the trees, the
house, were chill and clear, crowning the shrouded valley; their
detail was lined with sharpness against the cold bare sky.
Elizabeth could see everything, how the trees had grown until
they seemed to be throttling one another, how the garden was
overgrown with weeds, grass had sprung up between the stones

of the garden path, a shutter had swung off a hinge before one of the lower windows, there was an empty pane in the top window of the right-hand tower, stones had tumbled from the wall. There was something especially deserted today in the house outlined against so pale and bare a sky. As she looked it seemed to her that the house moved, its walls bulging outwards then sagging in again – an illusion of light.

She caught Will's arm.

'Is there not someone moving in the garden?'

'I don't see no one,' said Will.

'There – moving into the trees – a woman in black. No, it is my imagination. There is no one – not a soul . . .'

She put up her hand to her throat; this was so pitiful, this home of her youth where there had been so much life, now picked bare like a bone, or, to see it the other way, strangled with climbing triumphing vegetation.

'Leave the carriage here,' she said. 'I'll walk to the door. Bring my bag.'

She pulled her coat more closely about her, for it was cold up here, arranged her veil and walked quickly up the road through the gate, up the garden path.

She did not dare to hesitate for a moment lest she should lose all her courage, but it was a reassurance to hear Will's heavy certain tread behind her. Then she rang the bell and it pealed in the air as bells peal through empty houses. She looked around.

'No one has tended this garden. Look at those poor chrysanthemums. I feel as though someone were watching us.'

'Maybe it's the Pangloss woman from behind the window.'

She rang again and while the bell was still echoing the door opened. To her surprise a little girl, very ragged and tattered, wearing a woman's bonnet, was standing there. Elizabeth had thought out her plan of campaign and, taking her bag from Will, she walked into the hall and on into the small room beyond, which, in the old days, had been the gun-room. She knew it very well of course. But now it was quite different: the walls bare save for an old hunting-scene picture; there was a screen with boxing pictures pasted on it, and she remembered that this had been once an ornament of one of the spare bedrooms. There were the ashes of a fire in the grate and a stuffy stale smell of spirits in the air. She put her bag down and stood in front of the fireplace.

She saw that the child, who had large goggly eyes, was in the doorway staring at her.

'What's your will?' the child asked.

It was plain that she had not seen for a long time so grand a lady, for her gaze was rapt by the little dark green bonnet, the green coat with the velvet collar that Elizabeth was wearing.

'Will you please tell Sir Walter Herries that his daughter, Mrs John Herries, is here and would like to see him?'

The child said nothing but only gaped.

Elizabeth came over to her. She took her mottled red hand in her glove.

'Poor little thing . . . You are shivering with cold. Listen, my dear. Will you find Sir Walter for me and then say that his daughter has come to see him?'

The child vanished; the house was still. A mouse scratched behind the wainscot. She was glad that Will was waiting in the road outside. The door flung open and there stood a fat blowzy woman with a red round face, wearing a faded blue calico dress.

'I beg your pardon, madam,' she said, speaking very quickly. 'The girl shouldn't have shown you in here. This is private.'

All Elizabeth's fear had vanished at the sight of this woman, and she was so deeply filled with pity for her father that she could think of nothing else.

'It is not private to me,' she answered smiling. 'I am Mrs John Herries, Sir Walter's daughter, and I lived in this house for several years. So you see I know it well. We have met before.'

'Yes, and Sir Walter is not well enough to see anyone.'

'I know that my father is not well because he wrote to me, telling me so and asking me to come and see him.'

'Oh, did he? Excuse me for doubting your word, but he's not able to write to anyone.'

Elizabeth found the note and handed it to her. This brought them nearer to one another.

Mrs Pangloss read it very slowly, word by word.

'Silly old fool!' Elizabeth heard her mutter. Her great bosom heaved with indignation, but the letter had its effect.

'Well, I'm sorry, Mrs Herries, I'm very sorry, I'm sure. You're his daughter, as you say, and have a right – although for all the trouble his relations have taken all these years he might have been dead and buried, poor old man, for all they cared. What he *would* have done if it hadn't been for strangers taking care of him it's pitiful to think. However, perhaps you'll call another day, Mrs Herries, if it isn't a trouble. He isn't quite himself today – he's past eighty, you know, Mrs Herries – and it's the doctor's orders that he isn't to be disturbed by no one – not his nearest and dearest.'

Elizabeth walked back to the fireplace.

'I'm sorry,' she said, 'but I'm afraid, Mrs Pangloss, I can't do that. You see, I've come to stay. I have brought my bag. I intend to remain here.'

Mrs Pangloss gasped. Colour slowly mounted into her cheeks and changed them from red into a faintly streaked purple.

'Remain?' she brought out at last in a husky whisper.

'Yes. I have been far too long away. I should have come back years ago and would have done so, had I thought that my father wished for me. Now it is plain from this letter that he does. So will you take me to him, please?'

They stared at one another. This very slender elderly lady was, it seemed, nothing to be afraid of, for Mrs Pangloss changed her tone.

'No, Mrs Herries, I'm afraid I can't. Very sorry, but there it is. Doctor's orders, you see, *is* doctor's orders, and those were the doctor's very words. "I trust you to see, Mrs Pangloss, that nobody disturbs him, not on any account *whatever* – no account *whatever*. I wouldn't like to be answerable for consequences," he said. Those were the doctor's very words.'

'When was the doctor here last?' Elizabeth asked.

'Well, I'm sure, Mrs Herries, I don't see that it's any business of yours, but if you *want* to know – well, yesterday afternoon.'

'What doctor did you call in?'

'Now really and truly, Mrs Herries, you are going too far! Here you are, his only child, the only one left to him, poor old gentleman, and you living for years as you might say right at his very door and never so much as asking—'

Elizabeth's delicate face flushed and her eyes flashed – really flashed so that a light, indignant, proud, struck the thick heavy features of Mrs Pangloss. So, many, many years before, a young Buck in Islington had also been struck!

'I wrote several times,' she said, 'but received no answer. I understand now why I did not. I came once myself – perhaps you have forgotten, Mrs Pangloss? I did not wish to remind you because you were exceedingly rude and vulgar on that occasion. I admit that after seeing the kind of woman into whose hands my father had fallen I ought to have left it there, but I was anxious not to drive myself in upon him ... I was always hoping for a letter—'

'Oh yes,' Mrs Pangloss broke in. 'I can have you up for libel for that, Mrs Herries! I can indeed – "kind of woman" indeed – "kind of woman!" – and I the only one all these years who's been good to him. And *that* settles it! I'm a trifle wearied of having all his relations coming round poking their noses in, and it's got to stop! A year or two ago it was that old French Madame who should have been in her grave years back if she'd had any proper decency – and her mother nothing better than a road-gipsy if all they say is true. And now *you* coming worrying! Well, you've no right here, Mrs Herries – no right at all – and I'll thank you to be off!'

She had worked herself into a splendid temper and, shaking with an anger that had been plainly fortified with both gin and brandy, she advanced several paces into the room.

That was the very thing that Elizabeth desired. It was not very dignified perhaps, but dignity, on such an occasion, must be forgotten. She walked swiftly to the door and then, once outside, ran up the wide staircase, along a passage, up another stair, and through the door into the room that had always been her father's bedroom.

Thank God, it still was! Yes, and there was the same big four-poster with the yellow saffron hangings that, as a tiny child at Westaways, she had looked at with awe and terror, the picture of a hunt with gentlemen in red coats, over the stone mantelpiece, the two old chairs covered in green silk that she so well recollected, a walnut ring-stand, the mahogany cheval glass, the white sheepskin hearthrug, a mahogany washstand with marble top and two rosewood pole-screens – all articles that seemed to be part of her very life.

And he, her father, was in the four-poster. From the door she could see only the peaked nightcap but, at the first step forward, he roused himself.

'Who's that!' he called out. 'Alice, you bitch, I told you to bring me a drink. Hours back I told you.'

She came up to the bed. And this was her father whom she had last seen, on the evening before her flight, corpulent, rosy, covered with clothes even too strikingly elegant, master – as he thought – of his world. Now under the nightcap there was untidy grey hair, drawn cheeks with a week's grey stubble; his open nightshirt showed the bones of his throat as sharp and pointed as those of a plucked bird. For him, too, it must have been a striking vision – this very elegant lady with her grey hair, her little green bonnet and her long green coat fitting perfectly her tall slender body. He did not recognize her. He raised himself on his elbow.

'Why, what the devil—?' he said.

She stood close to the bed, smiling.

'Father, don't you know me? You wrote to me and I've come. Elizabeth. I should have come years ago.'

'Elizabeth!' he sat up, and at the same time, with trembling hands, pushed his nightcap straight on his head and pulled his nightshirt about his skinny neck. 'Are you Elizabeth? Dear me! Yes, I wrote that I was ill. But I should not receive you here. Go into another room a moment, my dear, while I dress—'

'No, Father; I've come to stay. You must—'

But she said no more, for Mrs Pangloss, bursting in, had interrupted her.

'If this isn't *shameful*!' she cried. 'I can have the Courts on you for this, madam. There he was just in his first sleep of the morning and me keeping all the house quiet so that it shouldn't be broken—'

But Walter, sitting up and grinning, said:

'Alice, you old washerwoman, this is my daughter. She has come to pay me a visit.'

'Yes,' cried Mrs Pangloss with a ripe round oath, for she was now too angry to care what she said (and had also, in the brief interval between the scene downstairs and this, fortified herself with more brandy). 'As she's come so she'll go. I'm mistress here, and the sooner she knows it the better. Forcing herself into a gentleman's bedroom, even if he is her own father!'

Elizabeth had crossed to the window which looked on the road and, glancing down, saw the thick solid body of Will Leathwaite stationed patiently by the gate. He looked up, saw her; she waved her hand.

Turning into the room again, she said:

'Now, Mrs Pangloss, have this perfectly clear. It is not of the slightest use for you to rant and swear. I am Sir Walter's daughter, he has asked for me – here I am and here I stay – and you leave within the hour.'

At the audacity of this Mrs Pangloss for a moment could not reply at all. She gasped and stuttered. Then, in jerks, the words came.

'Me! ... within the hour! You to order me ... You!' She strode to the door, flung it wide and called: 'Harry! Harry!

Where are you? Come here a moment! I want you!'

Walter, meanwhile, found it extremely amusing. He sat there, propped up by pillows, his eyes moving from the one to the other, grinning with his bare gums (his teeth were in a glass by the bed) and mumbling: '*That's* done it! *That's* a pretty thing! Now for a tumble!'

A moment later there arrived a heavy slouching man in corduroys, black rough hair over his eyes. He looked exceedingly sheepish, as well he might. Here was his master in bed in his nightcap, and Pangloss in one of her tantrums, and there, near the window, a beautiful lady in green. He was further embarrassed by the fact that the little girl (the child of himself and Mrs Pangloss) had crept after him (for although he beat her when drunk, she adored him as truly as she hated her mother) and, sucking her thumb, her old woman's bonnet on the back of her head, looked in.

Throughout the scene he kept muttering: 'Get away, Lucy . . . 'Tisn't no place for you . . . Go on or I'll larrup yer,' but the child paid no heed, and he, Harry Borden, restlessly shifted from heel to heel.

Mrs Pangloss turned to him. 'Now, Harry, you listen to me. This lady has been asked to go. Master has asked her. I've asked her. If she won't go, well – *you* shall ask her!'

Elizabeth went back to the window. She could see from there all the soft sprawling shoulders of Blencathra above the tops of the golden trees. The whole world swam in light this lovely morning. Inside the room the sun fell in coins and saucers of gold upon the faded ragged carpet. She felt the autumn sun, knew that Will was in the road below, and was conscious of a cheerfulness and high spirits that had not been here for many a day. She thought: 'Benjamin would enjoy this.'

'Well, Mrs Herries, ma'am, will you have the decency to go? You came uninvited – the sooner you go the better for all parties.'

'I did not come uninvited,' Elizabeth answered quietly. 'And I am certainly remaining.'

'You are not! You are not!' Mrs Pangloss found a glory of liquor at her heart and the fury of a righteous woman monstrously wronged in her head. 'If you won't go out you shall be put out! I'm in charge here, and so you shall know. Harry, if this lady won't go, you'll please *lead* her—'

But the ludicrous little scene was interrupted from the bed.

'Alice! Do you know to whom you are speaking? And who told

you to bring Harry Borden into my bedroom? And I want my drink – I'm sure it's well past eleven – and *The Times* newspaper of yesterday. You'll fetch me my drink, Alice, and give a poke to the fire before you go.'

But Mrs Pangloss, all control lost, strode to the bed, stood over the old man and screamed at him. Words poured from her. She flooded the room with her life story, her virtues as a child, her nobility as a young woman, the criminal errors of Husband One, the positive loathsomeness of Husband Two, her patience in bearing great suffering, a struggle with Husband Two that had nearly lost her an eye, her self-sacrifice in coming to the Fortress, her devotion, generosity in guarding and caring for a gentleman ... But, most unexpectedly, Walter rose to the occasion.

'Clear out, Alice. Clear out. I'm sick to death of you. I've been sick of you for years. There's been nothing but mess and filth here, and I'm too old to put up with you any longer. An old man wants his comforts, and you've always thought of yourself, you nasty old woman. And what are you thinking of, talking like that in front of my daughter? I asked my daughter to come and I'm glad she's here. So you be off this afternoon. Mrs Herries will pay you what is due to you. Harry can drive you in the cart. And tell the old hag downstairs to send up my drink. I'm parched.'

The poor woman was amazed. She was stuffed after all only with sawdust, and perhaps, Elizabeth, watching from the window, thought, she had a real affection for him. The look in her face of dismay and chagrin was not only brought there by drink and ill-temper. She stared through her stupid tear-filled eyes. She put out her hand as though she would appeal. 'You don't want me any more? ... After all I've done for you?'

'I'm sick to death of you, I tell you. I'm sick enough anyway, but I'll spend my remaining days in peace. There, there! ... I can't bear women to cry. Mrs Herries shall pay you what's due and Harry shall drive you in the cart ...'

The catastrophe had been so sudden that she could only look about her, turning her head now this way, now that, large fat tears coursing down her cheeks.

She must care for him or she would not so abruptly surrender, Elizabeth thought. She felt an impulse of pity.

But the woman turned to her, her words almost lost between anger and tears:

'It's you that have done this, Mrs Herries, and I shan't forget it either.'

Then, blowing her nose and wiping her eyes with a large check handkerchief, she went to the door.

'Come, Harry,' she said. 'They shall suffer for this.'

'Don't forget the drink,' Walter called after her.

When she was gone Elizabeth opened for a brief moment the window, and leaned out.

'Thank you, Will,' she called, waving her hand. 'There is no need to wait. Please tell Mr Paris that I am remaining.'

Will nodded and started down the road to the carriage.

She closed the window and came to the bed. She took off her bonnet and folded her veil.

'There are a number of things will need doing in this house,' she said.

He looked at her rather piteously.

'You'll be kind to me, won't you? I'm a very old man.'

THE HUNDREDTH BIRTHDAY

As the great day of November 28th, 1874, approached ever more nearly it may be said without very much exaggeration that all the Herries all over England held their breath. Would she do it? Could she last the course? Were they once more in their history to touch the Hundred? Or would she perhaps fail them just before reaching the post? A little chill, a window left carelessly open, a hot-water bottle neglected, the wrong food, a sudden shock . . .

Barney Newmark, who had been staying in Cumberland recently with Adam, declared: 'Pooh! She is as tough as an old hen! Not that I speak disrespectfully, for a nicer, jollier old lady you never saw. I had half an hour with her and her brain's as clear as a bell. She's got eyes like a child's. Of course, she's *old*. What do you expect at ninety-nine? She looks frail. She was always a pocket-edition but, dammit, she's sporting! *And* got a temper! But sweet-natured, you know, wants everyone to be happy. They all worship her and I don't wonder!'

In August she caught a cold and the news went right through England. Lady Herries in Hill Street (she detested Judith) gave a sniff and said the vain old woman had lived quite long enough, and for once Ellis became quite heated and said she had no right

to speak so. She was an honour to all of them and it would be
splendid did she live to her Hundred. Garth and Sylvia, pigging
it in a little alley off Victoria Street, were genuinely concerned
when they heard of the cold. 'Oh, she *must* live to a Hundred.
She *must*,' Sylvia cried passionately.

'Perhaps she'll leave us something,' Garth said gloomily. Then
added: 'I say, old girl, I lost on that damned horse yesterday.
You'll have to pawn that ring again.'

Emily Newmark remarked virtuously that the Lord knoweth
His Own Time. What He Giveth He taketh away; but Barney
said:

'By gad, Emily, you'd weary a saint.'

All over the country it was the same. In Wiltshire, Carey,
coming in from riding, was told by his mother and cried: 'Oh
lor! I hope she isn't beat at the post! A cold, do you say? Damn'
dangerous at ninety-nine.' Down at Bournemouth, where Jennifer's brother Robert had founded a little family (Robert himself
was dead and his son Bradley reigned in his stead), they were
greatly concerned, and Ruth, a pretty girl of twenty-two, thought
of writing to Dorothy with a cure for colds that a Bournemouth
doctor had given her. The Ormerods in London *did* write to
Dorothy, and Horace Newmark, now extremely wealthy in Manchester, thought of running up to see the old lady.

However, all was well. Judith quickly recovered.

'Nothing the matter with her whatever,' Dorothy wrote to
Sylvia. 'Of course it's very touching that everyone should be so
deeply concerned, but Jane and I are *quite* capable of looking
after her. And *what* do you think? Timothy is engaged at last, to
a Miss Greenacre of Taunton Hall, near Grasmere. She seems a
nice girl – quite a beauty but manners a little haughty. Timothy
says she'll make a good mother. I trust he won't be disappointed.'

The truth was that the Herries were very ready for a public
demonstration of their position. A century or so back they had
been nothing at all – and now look at them! A Peerage in Wiltshire (Carey intended to stand for Parliament at the next elec-
tion); Ellis, young though he was, one of the richest and most
important men in the City; Barney Newmark, a famous Novelist
(famous *enough* anyway); Adam Paris, a well-known writer (well
known at least to all the *real* readers of literature); Horace Newmark, one of the richest men in the North of England; Rodney,
Archdeacon of Polchester, and his son, a most oncoming Captain

in the Navy; Lady Herries in Hill Street, a leader of fashion; the Witherings, and the Bellairs at Uldale, among the first County families of the North; and Judith Paris herself, *really* famous so that all kinds of people asked after her. Mr Disraeli had known her, Dickens and Thackeray in their day had heard of her, the Bishop of Polchester often asked Rodney about her, and as to the North itself – why, everyone knew her and everyone was proud of her!

So they were determined to make this Birthday of hers a Herries demonstration, just to show the world what a Herries could do were he or she so minded! No other family in England, so far as was known, contained so famous an old lady.

Many of them intended to be present at Uldale for the event. As the day drew near, Dorothy, Timothy and Jane, who were the managers and presenters of the Ceremony, had great difficulty in arranging for what Timothy called the 'horse-boxes'. Where were all the Herries to be put? Fell House itself would have to entertain for the night – Veronica, Captain Forster, Amabel, Lady Herries, Adam, Margaret, Ellis and Vanessa. Quite a problem! Jane and Amabel must share, Margaret and Vanessa; Forster, Ellis and Adam would have to take one of the big attic rooms. The Witherings, who would drive over, could put up Garth, Sylvia and Amery, old friends of theirs. Horace and Barney could manage in the village. Will Herries, the naval son of Rodney, his wife and sister Dora were found rooms in the Peter's House Farm. There were two distant cousins – Rose Ormerod and Sophia Fanchard – who were to stay in Bassenthwaite, and, lastly, Ruth and Richard, the grandchildren of Robert, Jennifer's brother, were young enough and lively enough not to care where they were. The two little rooms over the stables would do for them. How fortunate that Elizabeth and Benjamin were now settled at the Fortress! That left more room for everyone.

When this was all settled there arose the question of the Orders of the Day. It was decided that the procession to Judith's room with the gifts and the little speeches should take place in the morning: that would be less tiring for her. Then there should be a grand dinner at two o'clock. In the afternoon everyone should go their own sweet way, and in the evening there was to be a Ball to which everyone of any importance in the neighbourhood was to be invited.

This all settled, two great questions remained – one, the state of the weather, and two, the state of Judith's health. Were it to pour all day – to come down a regular 'posh' as so easily it might – why, then we must all put up with it, smile, and say that we liked rain rather than not. Nevertheless, it would be provoking. All the afternoon the house would be unpleasantly crowded, for these Southerners were not accustomed to Cumberland rain and had not acquired the good Cumberland habit of going out in all weathers. Tempers would be strained and it would be annoying to overhear, as one undoubtedly would: 'Of course in the Lakes it always rains.' ... 'My dear, what do you suppose you came for? Here it never *stops* raining.'

The other question – of Judith's health – was the most serious of all. Of late she had had her bad days: how at her age could you not expect it? She was often dreamy, far away, lost in some other world. Sometimes she was cross and peevish when her digestion worried her. Sometimes she was very deaf and could hear nothing, although Dorothy always declared that she could hear perfectly and affected this deafness simply to give herself a rest. But her heart was her real trouble: any excitement was bad for her, but how could she enjoy her Hundredth Birthday *without* excitement?

And to make everything worse, she insisted upon taking the greatest personal interest in everything. She wanted to know exactly who was coming, *where* everyone was staying, what everyone would do. Her brain was often of an astonishing clarity. 'My dear, don't be a fool,' she would say to Dorothy. 'Of course, the Herries woman must have a room to herself.' Or 'Dora? That's Rodney's girl. I remember. Her brother was at the opening of the Exhibition. In the Navy. A prig.'

It was a delight to her that Adam, Margaret and Vanessa were to sleep at Fell House. It was a long time since they had done so. It became clear, as the day approached, that almost all her anticipation was centred round Adam. It was *his* coming, that *he* should be present at her Hundredth Birthday, that gave her the keenest pleasure. Had she had the strength she would have gone herself to see the attic where they were putting Adam and Forster.

'Is the wardrobe large enough? Adam is very untidy, you know, Jane. He throws his clothes all about. Is there a nice cheval glass?'

But of course she could not move farther than to the armchair by the fire. If she had one of her bad days she must not leave her bed and they must make their speeches as quickly as possible.

But on the great morning of the Twenty-Eighth all was well. It was neither a good day nor a bad day as to weather, but at least it was not raining. Clouds shaped like ram's horns twisted above the hills, whiter than other grey clouds behind them. It might be that they held snow, for it was cold enough. The larch trees were pale gold – like gold beaten very thin – against a background of rolling hills, grey and thick like flannel, and from this vast sprawling bed a point on Blencathra, palely lit, stuck up like an old man's nose. Nevertheless it was not a bad day.

By nine o'clock of the morning they thronged the downstairs and passages. The Ceremony was to be at ten. All the women were in their loveliest dresses, and there was no question but that Veronica outshone them all. Matrimony had improved her. She knew – and dear Robert, her husband, knew – that she was to have a child; as yet there was no sign of this, but the knowledge of it (for now she loved her Robert dearly) gave her an added colour and excitement. Her dress, too, admirably suited her, with its corsage like a cavalryman's tunic, the draped back, the in- numerable narrow flounces. At the back of her head her dark hair was piled in masses of curls, and she wore a little hat, very small indeed, pushed forward over her forehead. The colour of her dress was rose. She wore broad ribbons of rose on her hat. So she was the queen of the party, and Robert Forster was intensely proud of her. No one else was beautiful (Elizabeth had not yet arrived from the Fortress). Lady Herries was painted and affected, Sylvia's dress had too many flounces to suit her age, Dorothy, was too stout, Amabel too masculine, Jane was just a dear old maid, Rose Ormerod was a pretty little thing, Ruth Cards – grand-niece of Jennifer – was by far the most charming of the younger ones. She had a slight slender figure like a boy's, and the skirts of her jacket, projecting over her bustle, made her look like a boy in fancy dress. She and her brother Richard were rather new events in the life of the Herries. No one had seen them before. They won approval.

Of the men it may be said that Timothy was the most impress- ive, for he was host; he was large, stout and jolly, and he was but recently engaged to that stiff, haughty-looking girl in a purple dress, Violet Greenacre. He was of the type that the Herries admired, for he looked as though he would stand no nonsense and would live for ever. Barney was in splendid form, laughing with everyone. The Herries liked him because, although he *was* an author, he did not, thank God, look like one! Ellis was grave, dignified and, as usual, alone. They thought him haughty, stuck-up, and did not know that he, in his heart, was longing to be jolly, genial, generous as Timothy was, but didn't in the least know how.

And what of Judith upstairs?

She did not know, she told Jane, whether she had had a good night or no. She *thought* that she had slept well, but she could not in fact be certain because it was hard to tell when she was sleeping or when she wasn't.

She was, however, very cheerful, drank her tea and enjoyed her egg. *Of course* she would get up! She had, it soon appeared, thought out everything. The armchair was to be just here, near the fire but not too near, the small table at her side for her silver spectacle-case, her needle-case, a spare handkerchief and a silver-topped bottle of smelling-salts. She knew the Ceremony was to be at ten o'clock and she was glad that it would be early, because then 'she could have a nice time after talking to one and another'. Dressed, in her chair, she seemed, thought Jane, very small and very beautiful. Judith had never been beautiful, but it may be true to say that she approached more nearly to beauty on this her Hundredth Birthday than ever she had done before.

Her white lace cap had the brilliance of a jewel, the soft folds of her black silk dress shone in the firelight, her cane was at her hand, and on her black shoes were the diamond buckles that she wore only on very great occasions. The white lace at her wrists emphasized the fragility of her hands. Her only ring was the plain gold one that Georges had given her. Around her neck was the long thin gold chain that ended with a small gold watch in a pocket at her waist.

But it was her snow-white hair (once so brilliantly flaming) and the small face crowned by it that caught any observer's atten-tion. That small face was wrinkled across the forehead and at the corners of the eyes and was pale ivory in colour – yet its outlines were as firm as ever they had been. The mouth had not the weak indecision of the mouths of so many old people. The lips were firm, now parting in a smile, now ironic, now commanding and sometimes bitter, for all old ladies are bitter sometimes. The eyes, though, were never bitter. Their light was astonishingly bright for so long a history, shining, penetrating, merry, questioning and, above all, loving: never weak nor sentimental unless she suffered unexpectedly some childish disappointment, when she could look like a little girl not out of the nursery.

It would be idle to pretend that she was not feeling the fullest satisfaction in this her great day. What is more, she felt that she deserved every bit of it. Very few people lived to be a Hundred and it needed a lot of doing! She was proud of herself and proud of England. She had been thinking a great deal about England during this last year, not with any weak sentiment nor any boastful patriotism. She thought, it is true, of the Queen because she was another woman like herself and had suffered a bereavement just as she once had, but she did not otherwise think of any special events or persons – neither of Mr Gladstone nor of Mr Disraeli, nor of Oxford undergraduates breaking stones in the road for Mr Ruskin, nor of Cardinal Manning advising the Irish working-man to be temperate, nor of the Monday Pops, nor of the famous new Ladies' Golf Club at Westward Ho, nor of the great bicycling race from Bath to London. Even in the mornings now when Jane read her the newspaper she did not listen very much and often fell asleep.

The England that preoccupied her now was her own personal England which seemed, when she looked at it, to spread all about her, a bright, coloured, lovely country, infinitely gentle and infinitely kind. The England of the wild life at Stone Ends, of Uncle Tom Gauntry and Emma Furze, of the fireworks at the Lake's edge, of that moment in the hall at Stone Ends when Georges had proposed to her, of mornings and evenings and nights at Watendlath with the Tarn black under the hill, the fresh smell of the new bracken, the early-morning calling of the cows, the sight of Georges coming up the path with the crimson bird in the cage, Braund Fell and Armboth, Rosthwaite and Stockley Bridge. The England of London, of the cobbles and the sedan chairs, the Ball at poor Christabel's, Mrs Ponder and the Southey's and Jennifer, the hour at Rosthwaite with Warren. The England (her happiest England of all) of Watendlath and young Adam and Charlie (dying so foolishly after of a little silly chill), of Adam above Hawkshead laughing at Walter, running up the hill with her to see the sun rise . . .

And later than that England did not seem to go. After that many things had happened to England, she supposed, and Adam had grown, married, and had a child; the hills, her beloved hills, had darkened and been lit again by the sun, had taken on every colour and been blinded by the rain – but in this later England movement had ceased. Someone called Judith had lived there, but the real Judith by then had slipped away. And yet the real Judith was still here and Adam was here. He was coming this very morning to see her have her Hundredth Birthday. She had every reason to be happy.

She smiled at Jane, who was seeing that everything in the room was right.

'I think England is very nice, dear,' Judith said.

'What, darling?' said Jane, who thought that she had not heard aright, but that Judith had been talking about her breakfast.

But Judith did not bother to repeat. However, she said something else.

'Will Walter be coming?' she asked.

Jane was startled. 'Oh no, dear. Poor Walter is much too feeble. But Elizabeth and Benjie are coming, of course.'

'Walter!' thought Jane; 'what an idea!' He was now quite a foolish, brainless old man, and although Elizabeth had done wonders so that the Fortress was now clean and alive and wholesome again, the thought of Walter coming into the middle of this happy Birthday was most distressing.

'That's a pity,' said Judith.

'What, dear?' asked Jane, who was busy all over the room, as she loved to be, dealing with trifles.

'I said "That's a pity,"' said Judith. 'You are growing a little deaf, Jane dear. I've noticed it before.'

Jane said nothing.

'It's a pity, because Walter and I once had a quarrel and I should like to tell him that it's ended.'

'He knows that,' said Jane. 'The last time you ever went out you drove up to the Fortress and made it up. Don't you remember?'

'Of course I remember. But today would be a nice day to end it all up – a very nice day. Is Adam come yet?'

She had asked that already fifty times. Jane went to the window.

'Why, yes. There he is now. Driving up.'

Judith smiled.

'Very good. I'm very glad.'

Meanwhile downstairs, Adam, Margaret and Vanessa had arrived and mingled with the family. Vanessa's beauty startled everyone. Many of them had never seen her, and for others she had been still a child. Now, although she was only fifteen, her slender height, her rich colouring, her black ringleted hair behind her little dark blue hat, her girl's dress with the white flounces, the bustle only just pronounced enough to give her waist its perfect shape, her modesty and quietness mingled with the evidence, almost impossible to control, of tremendous happiness and high spirits, created a great impression.

'That's a stunning girl!' said Captain Will to his sister Dora. 'She's Madame's grand-daughter, you know. Yes, her mother's a German. Her father married a German. That's him – that brown-faced bearded fellow over there. Writes fairy stories, books for boys – that sort of thing.'

Adam and Barney were delighted to see one another.

'I say!' cried Barney, 'that girl of yours is growing into a Beauty. 'Pon my word, she is! Regular Beauty!'

Adam laughed, pleased and proud.

'She's as good as she's beautiful, my boy.'

'Not *too* good, I hope,' said Barney. 'Don't like 'em too good, you know.'

But it was Ellis who was stricken as though by lightning. Standing by himself, near the staircase, hating it all, wishing it over, wishing that his mother would not make a fool of herself, intensely proud at the same time, saying to himself: 'You couldn't find such a set of people in the whole of England,' proud of his relations and despising them, longing to be friends with them all, hating it if any of them came up to speak to him; it was Ellis who, seeing Vanessa for the first time in his life, as she waited a little shyly behind her father, just out of the crowd, received a blow at the heart from which all his life he was never to recover. It was not that he fell in love with her at first sight; it was, more simply, that he had never known what life was before, that he moved, at the instant, into a new world of colour, light, sound. He stood there, staring. He gazed and gazed. He did not know who she might be. He turned and found Garth, already a little gay with morning brandy, at his side.

'Tell me, Garth, who is that?'

'Who is what, my boy?' said Garth, who had already borrowed a considerable amount of money from Ellis and intended to borrow a lot more.

'Why, there – over there! That young girl with the black hair – in the blue hat.'

Garth followed his directing hand.

'Oh, that! Why, she's Adam Paris' daughter, the old lady's grand-daughter ... Damn' pretty child, if you ask me.'

Ellis said no more. He stood back against the wall, gazing.

There then occurred the great sensation of the day. The clocks pointed to twenty minutes to ten, and the party from the Fortress had not yet arrived.

Dorothy was distressed, anxious. She moved about like a great green whale, saying to everyone: 'Very strange! Elizabeth is so punctual! I hope that nothing has occurred. Very strange indeed! I hope that Walter has not died, this morning of all times!'

There was a stir by the door. They *had* arrived. All was well. Dorothy hurried forward. The door opened and Elizabeth, bringing the cold November air in a gust with her, came in. Leaning on her arm, looking about him in an interested but rather aimless fashion, was her father, Walter Herries.

Walter Herries! The news went round the company in a flash. Walter Herries, who was, they all supposed, a doddering old idiot whom Elizabeth had splendidly rescued from destruction and was now nobly devoting her remaining years to succouring! Walter Herries, once the villain of the Herries piece, now a harmless old imbecile – actually he had come to Judith's Birthday!

It was a real sensation that gave way presently to a grave and general satisfaction. This was well. This was indeed most fitting! The Feud that had distressed for so long all the Herries, that had had its climax in a terrible tragedy, was now, on this splendid occasion, to be finally closed. This was Elizabeth's doing, Elizabeth who had suffered more deeply from that Feud than any other. Could anything be more proper? Soon everyone was delighted. A chair was found for Walter in the parlour and down on it he sat, looking kindly about him, smiling, seeming quite happy, yet plainly without any idea as to where he was.

'Elizabeth's smartened him up!' said Lady Herries to Amery. He looked indeed quite elegant with his snow-white beard, a handsome blue frock-coat and a dark blue neckerchief.

And that brown-faced, healthy-looking young man with the bright blue eyes was Benjamin, Elizabeth's boy. Yes, the son of poor John ... A bit of a rascal ... He had left Rugby now and was looking after his grandfather's land, or *should* be ... But they said he couldn't stick to anything, was a great anxiety to his mother. Yes, he was eighteen or nineteen, just kicking his heels ...

Benjamin himself heard none of these whispers nor would he have cared if he *had* heard. He was enjoying himself outrageously as he always did enjoy everything. Where was Vanessa? His first thought was for Vanessa. What a rum lot of old codgers these relations were! How ridiculous old Lady Herries in her paint and powder! Garth he could see had already been at the bottle. By Jove, was not Veronica a picture? *There* was a woman! Beautiful figure and what a pair of eyes! What fun bringing Grandfather into the middle of all this! It had been the old man's own idea. In a lucid interval he had grasped that Judith was having a grand birthday. He had hunted round and found a brooch that had belonged to his wife, a pretty little gold thing with three pearls and a ruby. He would give her that and he would present it himself. He explained to Elizabeth that he and Judith had not been the best of friends – but that was all over now, quite finished. Much too sensible a woman to cherish a grudge. And his excitement had been tremendous. He had got out of bed himself at about four that morning to find a box to put the pearls in. He sat in the parlour now, clutching the box in his hand, patiently waiting until he should offer it. Rum old boy, thought Benjamin, rejoicing in his own youth and strength; but he rather liked him. He was just like a child, and Benjie played draughts with him most evenings. Not that the old boy could play. He just moved the counters about, but it gave him pleasure. And there the old man sat, clutching his parcel.

However, Benjie had not come there to look at his grandfather. He moved about looking for Vanessa. And then, of course, he knocked against Ellis, the last man in the world he wanted to see.

He had encountered Ellis only briefly since that rowdy night in London four years ago. He was aware, without any question, that that evening had made a breach between himself and Ellis. Not that they were ever the kind to get on well together, Ellis so solemn and proper, and himself – well, *not* so solemn and proper! But he could not know with what profound distaste Ellis now regarded him nor the deep shudder of disapproval with which Ellis had seen Walter's entrance. What did they want to bring that old man for? He had a wild fantastic notion that it had been done in some way to insult himself. As with all egoists and men unsure of themselves, like all men sensitive to an unpopularity that they would give their lives to alter, most things in life seemed to Ellis to be directed against himself. This dodder-

ing, wandering old man was his brother! Did they not know
that? Well, then . . .

It would be, he suddenly thought, just like young Benjamin to
have arranged this – maliciously, simply to distress him. Ever
since that night at the 'Paragon', Ellis had thought of Benjamin
as wild, malicious, reckless – all the things that he hated!

'Hullo, Ellis!' said Benjamin.

They made a strange contrast, Ellis, long-nosed, pale-faced,
grave, in his official dark clothes; Benjie, snub-nosed, brown-
faced, in a long brown sack-coat and a dark red tie caught with a
gold ring.

'How do you do, Benjamin?' said Ellis, offering his hand.

'Have a good journey up?'

'So-so. Cold, you know.'

'Yes, I suppose. Well, we'll be moving up to the old lady
shortly. Quite a gathering of the clans, ain't it?'

'Quite,' said Ellis.

Benjie moved off. He had no intention of wasting his
precious life over Ellis!

Where was Vanessa? He tumbled into Adam. Dear old Adam,
the man he liked best in the world and Vanessa's father!

'Why, Adam! Isn't this grand? I say, where's Vanessa?'

'Somewhere,' said Adam, who was rejoicing in every minute of
this great day that was to do his mother honour. 'How are you,
young Benjie?'

'So-so,' said Benjie, dropping his voice and grasping Adam's
arm. 'I say, this sort of thing makes a fellow restless. Ever feel
restless?'

'Sometimes,' said Adam.

'Well, *I* feel restless up at the Fortress. If it weren't for mother
I wouldn't stay.'

'Why, where would you go to?'

'I don't know. The sea perhaps. Or America.'

'Take my advice,' said Adam, 'and stay at home. There's no
place like home.'

'You didn't always think so?'

'No.'

'Nor do I. When I'm your age, Adam, I'll settle, but as it
is—'

He went off, laughing, poking Barney in the ribs, bowing ceremoniously to Lady Herries whom he detested, seeing little Ruth
Cards for the first time in his life and thinking. 'That's a pretty

girl. I wonder if she'd mind being kissed.' He did in fact kiss someone a moment later, for he wandered through the green-baize door at the back of the hall and there, in the passage leading to the kitchens, was Hannah, carrying a tray.

'Why, Hannah!' he cried.

'Master Benjie!' She smiled. They all adored him.

'Here, give me a kiss! No, there isn't a moment to lose! Here, I'll hold the tray!'

'No, Master Benjie, you're not to!'

But he put his arms round her, held her close to him, kissed her full on the lips. Then, laughing, ran off.

But where, oh, where was Vanessa?'

All the clocks struck ten. Everyone began to move upstairs. There had been a change in the arrangements. A very handsome volume in blue leather and gold had been provided, and in it every member of the Herries family who could be found had signed his or her name, agreeing that they from the bottom of their hearts congratulated Judith on her Hundredth Birthday and wished her health and prosperity.

It had been Barney's idea, a very pretty one. It had been intended that Adam should present this, but after Walter's unexpected arrival it had been thought that it would be excellent if Walter, the senior of them all, should make the Presentation. At first there had been some difficulty. He wanted to give his *own* present. He had come all that way to give his *own* present . . .

'But so you shall, dear,' Elizabeth whispered. 'You shall give them both. Only this is from all of us and the other is your special one . . .'

But he wanted to give his *own* present! However, at last he had consented to hold the blue leather book in one hand and his own precious little box in the other. Elizabeth guiding him, they headed the Procession up the stairs.

And up the stairs they all crowded, laughing, joking, excited, feeling that this was really a *great* Herries occasion, that, as it were, the eyes of all England were upon them.

On the way up Barney said one thing to Amery in a chuckling whisper:

'Very fitting, you know, old Walter making the Presentation. Closes the Feud. He and Judith were enemies for years. That's the end of *that*!'

At the same moment Benjie caught sight of Vanessa just ahead

of him. He brushed forward, almost, in his haste, knocking
someone over. He did not know (nor would he have cared if he
had known) that that someone was Ellis.

'I say! Vanessa! Vanessa! Where *have* you been?'

She turned. She was a stair or two higher. Her face was lit
with delight as she turned her head and saw him.

'Oh, Benjie! I've been looking for you everywhere!'

Ellis stared at her. The staircase seemed to rock beneath him.

'Hush!' Timothy said. 'We go in now, three at a time. Sir
Walter, you're first. Thank you. Elizabeth, if you wouldn't
mind!'

Judith sat looking at the door, Jane standing beside the chair.
She was quite calm, very dignified, extremely proud and
happy.

The door opened and Walter entered, led forward by
Elizabeth.

Jane gasped.

'Oh, Aunt Judith – it's Walter Herries!'

But to Judith it seemed perfectly natural.

'There, Jane, I said he would come. How extremely attentive
of him!'

Walter had no idea of anything save that it was Judith's birthday and he was giving her a present. But he realized, as he wandered, gazing about him, across the floor, that that was Judith
sitting in the chair. He knew Judith well enough. He had known
her all his life. But why was he in a bedroom? He stopped,
midway, and looked at the bed.

'Walter,' said Judith, smiling. 'How are you?'

That brought him to himself. This was, in any case, Judith,
and this was her birthday. He found himself by the chair.
Elizabeth was beside him.

'Well, Judith,' he said, his eyes still roving about the room.
'They tell me it's your birthday, so I've come and I've brought
you a present.'

He pushed the little parcel into her lap and dropped the blue
book. Elizabeth picked it up and put it into his hand again.

'Father, dear. You know what you are to say. You are to give
Aunt Judith this. It's from all of us, and you are to say that all
our names are here and that we all wish her a lovely birthday and
many more birthdays.'

'A lovely birthday and many more birthdays,' said Walter,

dropping the volume into her lap. Then, quite of his own accord, he bent forward and kissed her. Elizabeth had to steady him because his knees were very shaky.

Judith was delighted and greatly touched. She took her handkerchief from the table and wiped her eyes.

'Thank you indeed, Walter. Thank you, thank you. I am very glad you have come, because once we were not friends, were we? And now we are. I want to be friends with everyone today. And most especially with you, Walter.'

Walter began eagerly: 'And you must open *my* present, Judith.'

With very firm fingers Judith undid the parcel.

'Oh, isn't that pretty? *Isn't* that pretty? Do you see it, Jane? A lovely brooch! Walter, how *very* good of you—'

'Yes,' he said, immensely satisfied. 'It's a very pretty thing. I've had it a long time . . .' His eyes began to wander. 'Uhland would have come today, only – only – I don't know why – but—'

Elizabeth gently took his arm.

'Now, Father, you must make way for the others.' She led him to the window.

And Judith, now with her eyes bright and eager, was staring at the door. The great moment of her life had come. Adam would be next. Surely, surely Adam *must* be next!

She saw that they had all crowded to the door, and, all their faces smiling, were staring in.

A figure detached itself from the crowd. Grinning all over his face, moving his heavy body in his own rambling, comfortable way, Adam came forward.

At the sight of her son Judith's eyes and mouth broke into the loveliest smile that any member of the Herries family, here present, had ever seen.

Now her Hundredth Birthday was indeed a Triumph!

Christmas Eve, 1930
November 1, 1931